Previous novels by D. M. Samson

Silent Violence

In 1984 Dawn Marie travelled with her husband to Saudi Arabia. He had secured a job replacing the outgoing foreman of a secluded farm near Riyadh. Almost two years later she would return home. Alone. Broken.

In *Silent Violence* she tells us of her journey: a long downward spiral. From the first inklings of things not being right, a pet killer in the expatriate compound, clandestine excursions by the farm crew, through to the rising hysteria within the expatriate community, then the killings at the farm, the ensuing imprisonment, moral deterioration, government procrastination and eventual deliverance.

Without question her story is harrowing. Yet it contains a great deal of humour too. For humour was the life jacket that kept the displaced person buoyant in a strange culture.

After years of psychiatric treatment she was persuaded to write her story. The road to publication is a story in itself. Ultimately the book was suppressed in the interests of international relations.

Silent Violence should be a warning to prospective expatriates. Its portrayal of Arab mentality could help policy makers too.

Nails

There is little one can say about the plot. Succinctly put, it is the story of one day in the life of a car mechanic. Admittedly, not much in itself. But it's hard, raw, violent, sexy, sensitive, funny, poetic and philosophical to boot. It's a page-turner that grabs you by the short and curlies.

Bottle

In *Nails* Kevin was a prisoner of frustration, middling, but waiting for who knows what. In *Bottle* he's liberated with the proverbial "kick up the arse" he needs.

This book has got everything. Even the kitchen sink! It's teeming with life and death, tears and laughter, sex and violence, parents and children, brutality and tenderness, anger and contentment... But why should I go on? Look up further antonyms yourself. Or save yourself the trouble and simply read the book.

Although *Bottle* is the sequel to *Nails* it can be read in its own right.

About the author

David M. Samson, born in Wallasey (near Liverpool) in 1957, lives with his wife and two daughters in Germany.

Deutschisch

First published in 2011 by David M. Samson, 20 Arundel Road, Bath, Avon BA1 6EF.

Printed and bound by Lulu.com.
Lulu Enterprises Inc.
860 Aviation Parkway
Suite 300
Morrisville, NC 27560
United States of America

ISBN 978-0-9556796-3-6

British Library Cataloguing in Publication Data.
A catalogue record for this book is available from the British Library.

Cover design by David M. Samson.

www.davidmsamson.com

This book is dedicated to you, dear reader.

Thanks for taking the time.

Enjoy.

D.M. Samson
(October 2010)

June
Sunday
18:23

By the time *Hauptkommissar* Hofmann reached the second floor he was out of breath.

Rising after dipping under the tape outside had given him a moment of dizziness. He didn't show his infirmity to the media behind him and soldiered on. On such occasions he was grateful for his no-nonsense mask. His face was an ancient motorway pile-up, more crumpled than wrinkled, his skin rusting, almost flaking, brittle metal. It suited his fixed bulldog demeanour. More than the media he relished his ironclad authority over the uniforms. The lad with the clipboard on door duty almost cowered as he signed in. And the offer of paper overshoes and latex gloves could best be described as meek.

Hofmann would have liked to use the metal banister to pull himself up the concrete steps, but at least one technician was strategically dusting it for prints. A numbered plastic card on one of the steps marked a drop of blood.

On the second floor he had no option but to take a pause. Bent over, his hands upon his thighs, he coughed and rattled. In this position he noticed the small puddle of water and remainder of drops on the spacious landing. The flat door was open and he felt the others watching him, hearing their unspoken thoughts about soiling the crime scene.

His spirits lifted somewhat as he remembered an old joke about a student doctor who smoked. His dormitory friends continually said: "One of these days you're going to cough your guts up." He ignored their jibes and as a gag some of them got together and laid out all manner of internal organs on his chest whilst he slept.

In the morning he was pale when he came down to breakfast and they asked him what was wrong. "Guys, you were right," he gasped. "Last night I coughed my guts up."

"That's awful," said one.

"Yeah, but not half as bad as putting them back in again."

Hofmann regained himself. His breathing was down to a laboured wheeze.

Thiel, his partner, was at his side. "*Alles klar* (everything okay), boss?"

"Yeah, I don't normally put my guts in on a Sunday." He ignored Thiel's querulous look. "What have we got?"

"A double," said Thiel, leading the way to the flat. "A Turk and what looks like a national. It's hard to tell. His face is pulped."

Before entering the flat Hofmann stopped. Thiel had stepped over the small puddle. "What's with the water?"

"Don't know," said Thiel. "The first officer said it was already there when he arrived."

"Was it dirty?" Parts of it were blackened.

"I asked the same question," said Thiel, proudly.

"And?" said Hofmann, letting his lack of breath underpin his impatience. He knew Thiel was in awe of him. This was how a detective should be: thick skinned, larger than life and exceedingly bitter. Poor Thiel, to give his voice the right timbre he would have to increase his tobacco consumption five-fold and maintain it for at least a decade.

Many years ago Hofmann had tried to give up. The days counted as some of the worst of his life. He had felt sick and depressed.

"He thought not. You can talk to him."

"I will," he said gruffly. The water could have been dirtied by any number of people: the uniform first on the scene, a witness, emergency personnel, the killer or one of the victims.

"Identities?" he asked stepping into the flat.

"Unconfirmed," said Thiel. "But I think they were the occupants." He fell silent and Hofmann purposefully avoided inspecting at the bodies. Lorenz, the *Rechtsmediziner* (forensic medical expert), was crouched over the male victim and Hofmann could see neither of their faces. The girl looked asleep. Instead the *Hauptkommissar* surveyed the lounge and dining room. This was his way. Doors further in led to a kitchen, which appeared undisturbed, the bathroom that was in the throes of being tiled and the bedroom. Here the cupboards and drawers were all open as if someone had been searching for something. Was robbery the motive?

Thiel followed him about the flat like an obedient dog.

Hofmann returned to the lounge and turned his attention to the bodies. Lorenz was now standing looking down at the victims. The girl was in casual attire and the lad in an overall. Contrasting the peacefulness of the female victim, the boy had taken a severe battering.

"He took a pasting," said Thiel, unnecessarily.

"First impressions?" He knew better than to ask Lorenz for the cause of death.

Without looking up Lorenz said: "I thought we were about to have a third body at the door of the flat." For a moment Hofmann didn't know what he was talking about. Then he realised he was referring to his coughing fit. Hofmann gave a huff. "Rigor hasn't begun, so we're talking of a tee-oh-dee of two maximum three hours ago." This time of death margin concurred with the initial call to the police. "The girl's neck is broken. She died instantly. You can see the bruising to her jaw. It's ante mortem and probably knocked her out. The lad is another story altogether." His head glistened with blood, his mouth and lips were split, the jaw looked smashed. "He took a pummelling. The back of his head is cracked open too. That could be a result of trying to lift himself off the floor and being bashed down again. Or the person straddled him and lifted and banged his head a number of times and then laid into him. I can't see the marks of any weapon. But you can see from his neck that the cause of death may be strangulation. I'll know–"

"– more when you get him back to your lair," Hofmann said. Yes, he thought. The beating meant passion. Hatred. And he hoped that made it a *zwölf* (twelve).

Unlike other police forces that used code numbers to relate incidents the Hamburg police force communicated clearly. However, ever since a woman had killed her husband, stabbing him with a carving knife, because he hadn't cleaned the bath after taking a shower, the number *zwölf* had become synonymous with a domestic. During her confession she admitted that the trigger for her rage that led to the killing had been counting twelve of her husband's hairs in the bath.

The likelihood of this double being a *zwölf* raised Hofmann's hopes of clearing it. It would be nice to retire on a closed case. "What I–"

"Sir," said a technician behind them. Whether he was addressing Brauer, the chief technician who stood nearby or Hofmann was unclear. "You might want to see this."

He was pointing a torch under the sofa. Like all the technicians he too was clad in a hooded white overall.

"Anna," called Brauer, to the technician with the camcorder. "Have you done there?" He nodded at the sofa.

"Yes," she said.

"Then we may need some stills of what's underneath."

"Simon?" He was talking to the technician with the torch.

"There's nothing to dust. But I haven't done trace."

"Let's leave it in position and tip it on its back," Hofmann suggested.

Thiel went to one end, Simon to the other and tipped the sofa to reveal the floor underneath.

They all found themselves staring at a single dining fork. The prongs were stained red.

Book One

July
Tuesday 20:45
(25 months later)

Pride and fear sat uneasily on the hotel manager's face. Like an ill fitting photo-fit the top of his expression didn't match the bottom. Dannaks could see it in his smile and his eyes. The smile was fixed and nervous and prolonged well beyond sincerity. It was the sickly grimace of a schoolboy caught red-handed: a liar's smile. And the mania glistening in his eyes said that even he knew he was deceiving no one.

Anyone would think heads of state were visiting. Then, in a way, this was something of a state visit. Hadn't they just arrived in a mini motorcade?

"Someone will come tomorrow," said the young officer, who had not introduced himself and couldn't be more than twenty years old. A boy dressed like a soldier, fresh-faced and aghast with the burden of responsibility.

"When?" asked Dannaks's colleague, Reupke.

The hotel manager, following the conversation intently, seemed strangely unaware of what was being said; his face a set grinning mask.

As far as Dannaks could tell there were no women present. He was part of the loose inner circle of five men. Beyond them, distance diminishing their importance, was a cluster of ranking officers. Further still were a line of hotel staff and two waiters at the display table of colourful cocktails. Finally there were the uniforms standing like sentries at the entrances.

The boy officer spoke to his superior, a much older man in the full parade regalia of the Turkish National police with colours and medals, highlighting the lack of adornment on the younger man's uniform.

The superior's answer, like all his answers since meeting, was measured and clipped.

"Ten o'clock," the boy translated.

Reupke nodded and the hotel manager did too. But Dannaks stopped the officers leaving. "To show us the body and photographs."

11

Being shown the body was the reason for picking them up tomorrow. In the car on the way to the hotel Reupke had asked about seeing the crime scene photographs. The young officer had said he was not authorised to answer such a question. His superior had ridden in the limousine in front of them.

Irritation flashed across the youth's face before he spoke to his brass superior. For that is how he appeared to Dannaks. He was too old to be called bronzed. He was tanned and hard. The orange tinge to his skin, remnants of freckles, the gold bracelet of his expensive looking timepiece, the fair close-cropped hair and his overall stockiness reminded him of Gert Fröbe, the actor who had played the villain *Goldfinger* in the James Bond film of the same name. Dannaks watched him. His expression remained impassive, but this time his reply was not immediately forthcoming.

Even the hotel manager had suppressed his fake smile in favour of mimicking Goldfinger's expression.

Dannaks didn't need his smattering of Turkish to register the annoyance in the man's words. When Goldfinger finished speaking the young man said: "Yes." He then chose his words carefully. "Deputy Director General Özüdogru wants me to repeat that you are here as our guests." The tone implicitly conveyed that they were not here as investigators.

Goldfinger smiled. It was the first show of feeling since introductions at Antalya airport. But it wasn't a pleasant smile; it was a triumphant smile, a predator's smile.

Oh, he'd smiled for the photographers at the airport and in front of the hotel. But those formal smiles had been for the camera. Emotion hadn't been part of them.

Now there were no cameras. Security had kept all but the hotel photographer out of the building and even he'd been ordered away.

Hands were shaken. The Turks exchanged farewells. One of the half a dozen ranking officers behind Goldfinger issued a command and the uniforms left their positions at the entrances. Then *Oberkommissars* Reupke and Dannaks were left standing in the lobby with the hotel manager Erdal Tasköprü and a deputy of sorts. There was also a bellboy, loading their bags onto a trolley and an older man behind the front desk. The deputy's little golden name-shield pinned to the left lapel of his sombre jacket shone and Dannaks couldn't read it. Whoever he was, he was suffering in his suit. The sheen of sweat made him glow. And the strands of hair that spanned his glistening bald head clumped together like liquorice strings.

"Welcome to our hotel," said the manager, who was contrastingly comfortable in his suit. Even under pressure he had not appeared to sweat. His earlier nervousness along with his inane grin had vanished.

Of course he had already welcomed them. Yes, in the presence of the officials it had been a formal welcome. Even the refreshments had done little to ease the atmosphere.

The detectives could only nod and smile weakly.

With the departure of Turkish police the lobby took on a semblance of life. But apart from one person there were no guests. The staff went about their mundane business, still hushed by some vestiges of the formality that had forced them into hiding. Two waiters wheeled in a trolley and began removing the welcome drinks.

Dannaks had expected to meet a tourist representative or someone from guest relations. The German consulate minion had made his excuses on behalf of his office at the airport. Only the Turkish authorities had put on a show of importance. Even then, there were no government officials, only members of the national police and gendarmerie.

A frail old lady was sitting alone at one of the many sofa and easy chair arrangements around glass-topped coffee tables on the carpeted area. If it were not for the fact that all the furniture was the same the area could have been mistaken for a furniture showroom.

Dannaks assumed the area had been closed off to guests, but for some reason she had been given special dispensation.

"But of course you are weary after your journey." Jaded would have been a better word. Behind them was a three and a half hour flight from Hamburg to Antalya and a 40-minute journey to Side (pronounced See-dah).

Dannaks suspected the manager was eager to get rid of them. His day undoubtedly finished at five o'clock.

"Actually I could do with a bite to eat." They'd eaten nothing since the in-flight meal. And because Germany was an hour behind Turkey it was only eight o'clock for them.

Tasköprü was momentarily taken aback. He recovered quickly. "But of course, of course." He glanced at his gold watch.

"The kitchen is closed, but I am sure we can get sandwiches, okay?" Then as an afterthought: "And fruit."

"Great," said Reupke.

Dannaks nodded. He was wondering whether Tasköprü thought every German sentence began with the word but.

The manager said something to the man behind the front desk. "But you will eat in your room, okay?"

"Fine," said Reupke.

Dannaks nodded.

Despite the fact that the man behind the front desk was talking on the phone the manager spoke to him. He turned to the detectives again. "But first we have some formalities," he said ushering them to the reception desk. Then he seemed to notice his colleague. "But of course I will now leave you in the capable hands of our front office manager, Mr. Turgut. Okay?"

He looked to each of them and when no questions came he again welcomed them to the hotel. When he was gone Turgut took off his jacket and laid it on the counter. His wine coloured waistcoat – part of the hotel uniform – remained buttoned over his white shirt like a straitjacket.

"Please, you do not mind."

"Not at all," said Reupke, loosening his tie and opening the top button of his shirt. Dannaks followed suit. His neck was sore. He wasn't used to collared shirts and certainly not ties, of which he possessed only two. Reupke had donned his tie just before landing; Dannaks had made the mistake of wearing it throughout the journey.

A casually dressed man – a guest – wandered in from somewhere. He sat on an easy chair not far from the old woman, placed the drink he carried on the coffee table and opened a paperback he'd also been carrying.

Turgut leant over the counter to look at the monitor the man behind the desk was operating. They spoke and the man sitting behind the counter – his name-shield fastened to his waistcoat was beyond reading distance – called out. The bellboy, who'd been standing by the loaded trolley, stiffened. He then pushed the trolley out the front entrance.

Although the bellboy was probably called a porter, his spotty youth made Dannaks feel the label bellboy more appropriate.

Dannaks watched him until he was gone. He was a little disconcerted. His holdall was all he had. Reupke had turned up with hand luggage and a small hard turquoise case. The colour suggested it belonged to a woman. His wife's? Was he married? He didn't wear a ring.

Turgut took a form from the man in the waistcoat and placed it on the counter in front of them. He plucked a pen from his shirt pocket and placed it on the form. "Only one needs to fill it out. It is for the room."

"Room?" said Reupke looking at him and then at Dannaks.

"Yes, we have only one room. We are fully booked. All the hotels here are fully booked. This is the high-season."

"Twin beds, I hope," said Dannaks, jokingly.

Turgut looked at him severely. Reupke's face dropped. Dannaks blanched.

"Naturally," said Turgut, relishing the relief on the detectives' faces. He said something to Waistcoat behind the counter. Waistcoat smiled and shook his head.

Reupke laughed nervously. Dannaks smiled. He realised that apart from Reupke Turgut was the first person they had met since arriving who wasn't nervous or profoundly bored.

"I'll do this," said Reupke picking up the pen. "Do we get a safe?"

"Naturally." Turgut spoke to Waistcoat again who put another form on the counter. Since Reupke was occupied Turgut spoke to Dannaks. "You will have to sign for the safe. Three nights?"

"We leave on Friday," said Dannaks. "Yes, three nights."

Turgut wrote on the form and showed Dannaks where to sign. He then handed Dannaks something akin to a fountain pen refill but solid and made of a heavy metal. Dannaks dropped it in his trouser pocket hoping Reupke knew what to do with it.

"Passport," said Reupke. Dannaks handed his to him, noting that the procedure meant that all guests were traceable.

Turgut then held a strip of green plastic to him. Dannaks lifted his left arm. Seeing his watch he switched to his right arm. Turgut clipped it about his wrist, pressing it home with the end of a pair of scissors and using them to snip off an extraneous piece. Dannaks looked at him questioningly, but Turgut didn't answer until he was clipping one about Reupke's wrist. "This allows you access to all the facilities in the resort. All-inclusive, you know?"

"When it begins to pinch, you're over-eating," said Reupke to the form he was completing, then pushing away Dannaks's passport.

Dannaks retrieved it.

He got the impression that Reupke was treating the trip as a kind of holiday. Neither outranked the other, and Dannaks was dismayed that neither of them had been appointed to lead. It was an oversight.

Was it only yesterday afternoon that they were shaking hands with the police president in his fifth floor office? Dannaks had never met him personally. Oh, he'd seen him on numerous occasions, holding speeches in the large conference room. They were either for award ceremonies or they were pep talks to emphasise the importance of a crime before the case officer took over. Here the word importance was synonymous with media and therefore public interest.

Even when Dannaks had worked in the building he had never been to the upper floor. They housed the big birds. Like many establishments the air was rarefied, the tone old school.

The office of Hamburg's police president was not presidential. But by comparison it was plush, only because it was bereft of clutter. The carpeting was hardwearing and functional. The furniture was equally utilitarian, if not better kept than that in the rest of the building. This was a man who wanted to be on the same level as his officers. His office window offered a breathtaking view over the city park. Dannaks could picture him spending time pondering some strategy whilst staring at the view. His predecessor had been a train lover and had chosen an office on the other side of the building overlooking the U-Bahn station Alsterdorf.

When Dannaks and Reupke were ushered in, Wischnewski, or Iceman as he was known outside the office, the police president was not sitting behind this desk or looking out of the window. He was sitting with two officers at the small conference table near the door. He was the first to rise. Although he didn't introduce himself, he did his companions. They were the officers from *Zeugenschutz* (witness protection) who had liaised with the Turkish authorities until now.

Iceman's close-cropped shock of white hair seemed whiter than Dannaks remembered. And his ice-grey eyes were more piercing than ever. Although he had a suety complexion, his features were cast in mottled stone, as if the muscles of his face were set in such.

Many of the ranking officers had nicknames and the police president was no exception. For a while he had been known as "New skis" or just "the skis". If you were to meet him you were going skiing. And if he was dishing you a tough or bad assignment, then he was sending you down the piste. The story went that one of the computer whizzes had been working on their website and sent the text through an automatic translator for the English version of the page. Wischnewski's name had been translated into "wiping new ski".

Eventually he became Iceman because of his white hair, his renowned glacial silences and cold laser stare. So that when you were summoned he was either going to hand you an ice cream or send you out into the cold.

When Iceman re-seated himself in the chair at the head of the table, he regarded the two newcomers for a moment before speaking. Dannaks wondered if he was assessing their competence by the way they were dressed. Reupke was in blue designer jeans, but he wore a dark blue shirt with a blue and yellow tie. Whereas Dannaks himself could only offer his black jeans that had lost some of their blackness and his best sweatshirt with the Japanese water-like emblem of the band *The Waterboys*. Iceman and the two liaison officers were in pressed slacks, shirts and ties and it looked as if they shopped at the same outlet.

"Gentlemen, I don't want to keep you from your briefing, so I'll come straight to the point." He paused for a moment. His cold eyes that were at once piercing and vacant, as if he was disinterested or everything was bagatelle and didn't deserve his full attention. "I have to say that I would have liked to have sent at least one of our Turkish officers." As far as Dannaks knew there were only six of them in the entire police force and five were *Schupos* (of the *Schutzpolizei* – the uniforms that mainly did the soldiering). The detectives were *Kripos* (of the *Kriminalpolizei*). "I believe you speak some Turkish." He directed his terrible gaze at Dannaks, who thought a nod was appropriate. He would have liked to say that his knowledge was weak, but he sensed the man didn't approve of what he saw and didn't want to aggravate him. He obviously wasn't a *Waterboys* fan. "Firstly, your job is to collect the body. You are not there to investigate. If you're asked to assist, then fine. From what's happened so far I think that's unlikely." He glanced at the more senior of the two liaison officers, before returning to the detectives. "However, by all means gather as much information as you can. Asking to view the available evidence won't hurt, just don't push it. And there is no reason why they shouldn't let you see the body." He then leaned forward. "Now, I want you to bear one thing in mind when you're down there. Because I don't care what Matthias Kerner did. To me – and by default you – I care about who he was. And understand me correctly, I don't mean who he was on an individual level. I mean that he was a German citizen. That's all. So I want both of you–" he took a moment to stare at each of them "to know, that when you are there, that you are not only representing the Hamburg police force, you are also representing Germany. You are to all intents and purposes our ambassadors visiting their country." Ambassadors. Dannaks almost snorted and struggled to neutralise his expression.

Later Dannaks realised that Iceman was depending upon them more than was healthy. By snatching the task from under their noses Iceman had pulled something of a coup over the BKA (*Bundeskriminalamt* – equivalent to America's Federal Bureau of Investigation). Perhaps he was settling an old score. Or maybe he was calling in an owed favour. Whatever, he had left the BKA to head the Hamburg force. It wasn't a step upwards. At best it was a sideways career move. There had been much speculation about the move, not least by the media. There was talk of internal wrangling within the BKA and gossip about his health. Then, there was talk of his wife's job having an influence over their location. In any case the spotlight was on him and his men. And, as he would say: "by default", on Dannaks and Reupke.

And that was basically it.

The two liaison officers took the two ambassadors into the adjoining conference room. There they huddled at one end of the long table with sixteen vacant chairs extending away from them.

21:04

He heard the jingle of the trolley long before the bellboy arrived.

The hiss of the air brakes of a coach pulling up outside alerted them to the fact that more guests had arrived.

"Perfect timing," Turgut said, as Reupke pushed the completed form his way. He spoke in Turkish to Waistcoat or the bellboy or both. The bellboy came to them and Turgut handed

18

Reupke some hotel paraphernalia: numerous glossy flyers, a map and two cards with the hotel logo and the English words: towel card. "He will take you to your room."

The man behind the counter handed him a numbered tab with a key attached.

"Well, goodnight," said Turgut. They shook hands and then followed the bellboy through the main entrance.

A serious-looking man wearing a tracksuit top with the hotel logo and the word security on the back was standing near the wall watching proceedings and speaking into a slick-looking walkie-talkie.

The new arrivals were heaving cases out of the coach. An elderly porter with a gammy leg was standing next to a golf buggy with trailer. Another, a huge burly chap, was hauling cases onto the trailer. One of the male guests was complaining to one of the staff. "We were stuck in that coach for almost an hour, waiting for this palaver to end." Dannaks, who had recognised some of the other guests from their flight, caught his glare.

"We are sorry," said the girl, protectively hugging a clipboard like a shield or well-loved pillow. "Have a cocktail."

Dannaks and Reupke followed the bellboy off to the right. The path they took was bordered by bushes and trees and lit by waist high lamps, the bulbs behind milky glass under hats like upturned plates. There was a lot of space between these lamps, but the crazy paving style path made with huge slabs of stone was wide enough for the detectives to walk side by side, and just when darkness threatened to engulf their way, there was another lamp. The occasional steps told them they were climbing a slope. The further they went from the main building the more their surroundings resembled a forest.

The pines about them quickly absorbed the sound of distant revelry, a vague thump of music. They could have been in some alpine setting, far from civilisation, for it wasn't just quiet out here; it was hushed. Yet, only if the harsh incessant whisper of crickets was ignored or accepted as something of a sedative.

Dannaks remarked on the inadequate lighting. And Reupke commented on the lack of people.

But the detectives were too weary for proper conversation and quickly fell silent.

They passed a clump of a building. It was two storeys with a wooden balcony at each corner of the upper level. Underneath them, at ground level, were fenced terraces that could be climbed.

Then they were traversing a labyrinth of such buildings. All of them looked the same.

They took turns to the left and to the right until Dannaks was totally disorientated.

The bellboy rounded a building and stopped at a ground floor door. There was a token front garden little wider than a good step from the door. Dannaks was alarmed to see that their luggage lined the small wall to the left of the door. A wiry plant to the right forced the three of them into single file.

The bellboy unlocked the door, reached in, dropped the rectangular tab on the key ring into a slot of plastic attached to the wall and switched on the hall light. A little outside lantern by the door illuminated the room number.

"Stop," said Dannaks, grabbing the bellboy's shoulder as he reached down for Reupke's case.

"What is it?" said Reupke, behind Dannaks and furthest from the door.

"Look at the room number." He watched the recognition creep across his colleague's face as he scanned the numbers 1574.

The bellboy straightened and Dannaks released him. "Correct, correct," he repeated in German.

"Yes," said Dannaks, "but it's wrong." He knew he was not making sense.

"Number." The bellboy pulled the key and the lights went out. He held the tab to up to Dannaks. "Same. Same." In the relative darkness the number was barely discernible.

"Yes, but it's Matthias's – I mean P– the dead boy's room." Having stumbled over the name Dannaks could only repeat what he meant. "It's the dead boy's room." The bellboy's expression was one of incomprehension. Perversely Dannaks's own German deteriorated to match the pigeon of the bellboy. "Crime." He looked for a name shield, but couldn't find one. The boy was evidently a persona non grata. "Look, you get manager. Manager. Go." Dannaks gestured for him to leave.

The bellboy shook his head and made an attempt to explain again, but then gave up and left.

Dannaks had considered it a real coup being given accommodation in the same hotel/resort as the killing. But to be housed in the same room sprung his wildest expectations.

Reupke moved closer and peered past Dannaks into the room. "It may have been a crime scene a few days ago, but it's not any more." It was too dark to see anything. "Can't you smell that disinfectant? I think we can go in."

"Not without the key. He took it with him and it runs the electricity."

Reupke sighed and stepped away. After a while he plucked a handy (German for mobile phone) from the top pocket of his denim jacket. "See if I can get a net here. I promised my girlfriend I'd phone when we arrived." Dannaks nodded. So he wasn't married. Dannaks didn't know him well. Reupke was from the *Mordkommission* (Homicide). They'd only worked together once, last year on the Hangman case.

On the flight over conversation between them had been sporadic. Being sandwiched in tourist class they had not been able to talk freely about the case. However, Reupke had touched on it.

"I hope they don't want our assistance. Then all we have to do is bring back the body. Which means three days holiday."

Appalled Dannaks had said: "I'm going to keep my eyes and ears open."

Reupke had regarded him with a sour expression, his lips twisted with the taste of lemon. "I didn't mean I'd just laze around. We've got to be seen going through the motions." He then extracted a paperback he'd wedged in the seat pocket in front of him.

Dannaks wasn't impressed. He wasn't going to be seen going through the motions. Bearing in mind that they had been repeatedly told that they were only to assist if requested, he was going to be as active as possible.

From then on further conversation between them was severely hampered and never transcended the banal.

Reupke moved away from the building staring at his handy, looking up at the sky between the trees.

"Ah, got a net," he exclaimed triumphantly. But before he could dial they heard footsteps and he pocketed his handy.

A man in white appeared carrying a tray of sandwiches and a dark bottle at his shoulder. He was surprised to see the two of them standing outside in the dark.

"Sandwiches," he smiled, approaching Dannaks and bringing the tray to waist level. He wanted to take them into the room but Dannaks blocked his way. "Sandwiches?"

Dannaks looked past him to Reupke who simply smiled.

"Yes, we are waiting for the manager."

The man smiled and waited for Dannaks to continue. When he didn't the man grew embarrassed. "I, er, I will take them in." He nodded towards the open door.

Dannaks's expression became almost a plea. "No. We must wait."

Reupke laughed and the man turned. Was it all a joke?

Dannaks became irritated. "Give it to me." He reached out and the man gladly gave up the tray. He shook his head. And Dannaks could hear the words "crazy foreigners" going through his head.

The man wheeled round and hurried away, the night quickly swallowing the sound of his footsteps.

Reupke moved to Dannaks. "What's on offer?" Dannaks holding the tray with both hands was incapacitated and could only watch as Reupke lifted the plate to peel back the clingfilm from the decent heap of triangular sandwiches. He took a large bite out of one. Dannaks watched him with a lopsided smile. He had his back to the door and the wall to his right was too uneven for the tray. His only option, other than turning around and going in, was placing it on the ground. "Chicken," said Reupke. He pushed the rest of the sandwich into a second mouthful and then picked up the bottle. He turned the label to the meagre light the night had to offer. "Turkish bubbly. You feel like celebrating?"

Again footsteps alerted them. Turgut appeared followed by the bellboy. He was no longer in jacket and tie and his shirtsleeves were rolled up as if he was about to wash the dishes.

"Is there a problem?"

Reupke said nothing. He merely placed the bottle on the tray.

"This is the victim's room." Dannaks had decided it was easier not to address him by name.

"Yes. Did no one tell you?" Receiving no reply Turgut continued. "We are full. We have no space. All the rooms are taken." Dannaks nodded that he'd got the message. "The police gave the room back to us two days ago. I assure you, it was thoroughly cleaned." He allowed them a moment to speak. "Is there a problem?"

Reupke looked at Dannaks, who now felt stupid. "No, I guess there's no problem. I was just surprised."

Turgut said something to the bellboy as he went past to the door. The bellboy relieved Dannaks of the tray and followed Turgut. Dannaks snatched his holdall and went after them.

Turgut switched the light on in the room and turned to them spreading his arms. "You see. Clean."

Dannaks nodded surveying the room. It was indeed clean. Under a spotless mirror there was a small shelf with a splay of leaflets and pamphlets. A chair stood against one wall, a padded stool near the portable television on the waist-high shelf at the end of the wardrobe unit. Two bedside cabinets, one with a telephone, ashtray, pencil and notepaper, occupied the bed head corners. The twin beds were perfectly made; a matron had pulled the bed sheets so taut Dannaks feared he would cut himself on the corners. A folded blanket lay on top. The pillows were brilliant white, the walls looked patchy and worn, but had no doubt been scrubbed with disinfectant. A repainting was necessary. The only thing to break the monotony of the beige walls was a rather amateurish cubist work that hung above the headboards.

In a film there would be flashes of a struggle, frustrated violence and an obligatory spurt of blood splashing up a wall or across a surface. But there was nothing, just them standing in a bland room that probably looked like any other in the resort.

"Great," said Reupke, dropping his case as his handy began to ring. The press of his thumb silenced it.

"Good," said Turgut clapping his hands once. The bellboy looked stricken as he left with Turgut.

"Let's get some air in here," said Reupke, looking at his handy and opening the terrace doors. "It's a bloody SMS inviting us to an all-night party." He tapped some buttons before looking up at Dannaks. "I'll phone my girlfriend." Before he stepped through to the terrace he nodded at the tray of sandwiches. "Save some for me. I could be a while."

Dannaks pulled off his tie and thought about the bellboy's stricken expression. He picked up a sandwich and ate it slowly. After a while he heard Reupke talking softly. "This is the first opportunity I've had..." He picked up the bottle of sparkling wine, wondering whether *Altin Köpük* was a good one. Whatever, it was the last thing he felt like drinking. Of course a red wine would be a different matter.

Then he realised that the bellboy would have been hoping for a tip.

He replaced the bottle and strode to the short hallway that led to the entrance door. There he opened the door to the left of the entrance, reached in and patted the wall for the light switch before seeing it on the outside wall. He flicked it on. Pristine white tiles shone in the light. There was a sink and a bath with shower attachment and curtain and a further door. He went in and checked that it was indeed the toilet. At the sink was a small basket with miniature bottles of shampoo and shower gel bedded on a piece of fawn coloured flannel. The white plastic flip top bin that stood under the sink was so small it was almost useless.

He returned to the room and as if he was searching for something he opened all the available drawers and the main three-door wardrobe that lined the wall all the way to the terrace doors. The double doors of the wardrobe opened on to a rail with a sorry helping of assorted coat hangers. Behind the third door were three deep shelves. A sturdy gunmetal safe sat in the corner of the floor shelf. On top of the wardrobe were further half-doors. To open them he had to take the hard-backed chair and place it at the wardrobe. The double half-doors were empty. They could easily take a couple of large cases. The neighbouring single half-door housed spare blankets and pillows.

As he stepped down he noticed a dent in one of the doors. He inspected it with his finger. There were other wear and tear marks on the doors, but none had broken the surface like this one. However, there was no way of knowing the age of the dent.

Reupke was still cooing outside.

Dannaks took another sandwich. He looked at the dent again. Then he stepped back to take in the entire wardrobe. Eating his sandwich he wandered about methodically inspecting the furnishings. He looked at the brown plastic a/c unit above the opening to the short hallway to the front door. He pushed the switch on the small plastic box at eye-level on the wall just inside the room from off to fan. Nothing happened. He turned the temperature dial, but the unit remained silent, its blinds closed. He looked away and examined the line where the wall met the floor.

The cleaner was an expert. With the half-eaten sandwich in his hand he went down on his knees to look under the beds.

"I think Mecca's the other way."

Dannaks sat up.

Reupke was at the sandwiches. "Drop something?"

"No. Just looking."

"Find anything?"

"No. It's too dark." He got up. "And the cleaners were thorough." Despite his remark he brushed off his trousers at the knees.

"Even if they weren't, do you think you'd find something Homicide missed?"

Dannaks ignored the question. "Are you fussy about which bed you have?"

"No."

Dannaks sat on the bed nearest him and finished his sandwich.

"I hope you don't snore," said Reupke.

"Ditto."

They were quiet for a time. Reupke finished his sandwich and hauled his case onto his bed.

Dannaks got up and took another sandwich. "What have you got in there?" He saw nicely folded clothes and training shoes in a plastic bag. This reinforced his suspicion that his colleague was treating the trip as more of a holiday than an assignment.

"Everything you didn't bring."

He fished out a pen torch and flashed it once before tossing it onto Dannaks's bed. "Use that."

Dannaks picked it up and smiled. He no longer wanted to look under the bed. Reupke took off the pouch belted at his waist. He carried his ticket and passport in it. Dannaks, who carried everything in his inside jacket pocket, took the opportunity to speak about the safe. "The safe is in that cupboard." He held out the metal refill. "This is something to do with it."

Reupke took it. "You don't travel much, do you?"

"Denmark, North sea, Baltic," Dannaks said, as Reupke opened the cupboard and bent down to the safe.

"I thought so," said Reupke. Dannaks couldn't see what he was doing, but heard the whirr of a bolt and then electronic peeps. "Pass me my pouch. You want to put your valuables in?"

Dannaks hesitated. He was irked by the insinuation that he was naive because he hadn't travelled afar. Only because he wanted to be casual and worldly did he give up his passport and ticket. He would have preferred carrying them on his person. It occurred to him to put his colleague to the test. "I couldn't get the a/c to work."

"Close the terrace doors." Dannaks did so. The a/c took a moment to react then the unit shuddered into life and the brown slats slowly rotated open and the sound of air rushed.

He felt stupid as he put his holdall on the bed. Reupke was at his case, taking T-shirts and trousers to the cupboard and wardrobe. Dannaks was dismayed to see that his colleague had not only packed sports shoes, but also sports shorts and socks. And he appeared to have brought at least three pairs of swimming trunks. Dannaks had grabbed one only as a last minute thought. Indeed, he only possessed one. "One-five-seven-four-zero-zero."

"What?" said Dannaks.

"The combination. It had to be six digits, so it's the room number plus two zeros."

"Okay." Dannaks had brought three T-shirts, three pairs of socks, three underpants, one pair of shorts which he hadn't worn for a number of years, a pair of trousers, two bottles of sun cream, a full toiletry bag and a pair of cheap sunglasses he'd bought at Patel's. By comparison he had about a sixth of what Reupke had brought. So despite the fact that Reupke had started before him, he had his holdall empty and its contents in the cupboard long before Reupke had finished unpacking.

He grabbed another sandwich, picked up the torch and stretched out on the bed sitting up at the headboard. The lighting was poor in the room and he switched on the torch to follow the top of the wardrobe.

Reupke glanced at him. After a moment he spoke. "Don't waste the batteries. We might need them."

Dannaks switched it off. It was then that he noticed the underside of the slats of the a/c. He stopped chewing and squinted. He sprang up. He pointed the torch at the slats and chewed down what was in his mouth. Reupke saw him jump up from the bed, but left the room with his toiletry bag.

"Look at this," he said as Reupke returned from the bathroom.

On the underside of the two lower slats were brown splashes. Some were tadpoles others were sperm. "I'd say that's blood," said Dannaks, moving the torch along the slats, but always returning to the bigger marks. Many appeared to be going the wrong way: away from the wall. But of course the a/c would have been blowing and this would have distorted them.

His colleague nodded, but didn't say anything. He left the room again and returned with a cotton bud stick and a tiny plastic bottle that could have contained eye drops. He rubbed the end of the cotton bud on the largest tadpole. Then he unscrewed the top of the bottle and doused the same end with the liquid. "Funny what the *SpuSi* leaves lying around." (*SpuSi* was shorthand for *Spurensicherer* – a scene of crime technician who collected evidence.) The bud end turned pink.

Dannaks knew he'd just witnessed a peroxidase test.

"Of course it may not be human," said Reupke.

"Oh, come on," said Dannaks. Reupke wasn't being facetious, but he wasn't serious either. He was just being correct. "Do you think they took a sample? From here I mean."

"I don't know. It doesn't look like it. I should think they had plenty of samples to choose from." They understood the murder to have been particularly bloody. The victim had been beaten with a blunt instrument and then attacked with a knife. Leaving nothing to chance the killer had cut the victim's throat. The presence of blood on the a/c unit so high supported their understanding.

"Yes, but what if this is not the victim's blood?"

"Why are you calling him the victim all of a sudden?"

Reupke's pernicketiness irked Dannaks. Why couldn't he just answer the question? "Because until coming here I've called him Matthias. But here he was known as Peter."

"While we're here let's opt for Peter."

"Okay. So, what if this blood's not Peter's"

"It's possible. It could also have nothing to do with the crime. I'm not trying to annoy you. But it could be from some past incident. I know it's unlikely, but it's possible."

"Just as it could be the killer's blood."

Reupke looked at him. He screwed the top on his little bottle. "We'll mention it tomorrow." He took his bottle and cotton bud to the bathroom and Dannaks switched off the torch.

"If it makes you happy I'll bag the cotton bud."

Dannaks was aware of a problem growing between them. Hamburg should have made it clear which of them would be in charge out here. Instead they were to be a team. They had been chosen for their fields of expertise. Reupke's skills were obvious. Dannaks from *Soko* REX. He brought his knowledge of Germany's right-wing movement. His *Sonderkommission* (special unit) or *Soko* dealt with racism and extremism. Yet, despite their qualifications, their brief was to assist if requested, view the available evidence, but essentially just collect the body. They were here as undertakers.

On the plane Reupke had expressed his surprise at the continued existence of *Soko* REX. LKA 7 (*Landeskriminalamt für Staatsschutz* – State office of criminal investigate for State security) was responsible for monitoring the extreme Left and extreme Right. REX had been born to alleviate the workload due to increased activity in these scenes and also the addition of Islamist extremists and terrorism. Hamburg was still regarded as a centre for terrorists. Of course there was a hidden agenda. One theory was that the LKA 7 budget was getting too big and a *Soko* was a temporary arrangement. The other theory was that the *Soko* offered a pool of bodies that could be called upon by other departments. Whatever, Reupke's surprise, and his added remark that REX was a sleepy backwater, had jarred. The implication wasn't only that REX wasn't a proper department; it was also that no other department would have the members of the team. Unfortunately there was an element of truth in this latter insinuation. By comparison they were neglected: sharing a tired police station, in dire need of decoration, old furniture, shared PCs and shared telephones.

He looked at his watch. The murder had occurred about this time on Monday last week. True, it was quiet outside, but the killer would have been covered, if not drenched, in blood. How could he – or she – have left the club without being seen? The club complex was fenced. There was hotel security. A uniformed man sat in a concrete box at the main gate. The barrier had been up as they'd driven by. The security man had been talking to some tourists. Perhaps he'd been checking their armbands? The alternative was what the Turkish police thought: the killer had not left the complex. At least not immediately. And that the killer was a woman.

21:54

Although weary, Dannaks didn't feel like retiring. The sandwiches sat heavily in his stomach. And the strangeness of the environment unsettled him.

Reupke apparently felt the same.

They agreed to go out for a nightcap.

Reupke locked up and Dannaks carried the tray and empty plate. They didn't know the way and agreed that the best thing to do was to head downwards. Sooner or later they'd hit the road or reception.

The path they took was as convoluted as their ascent. At one point they heard some voices: whining children and admonishing parents. But they didn't see anyone.

Distant music and the jovial voice of a DJ reached them now and again, but their sources were indiscernible like echoes.

Dannaks noticed that signposts stood at some of the junctions, but they carried ranges of apartment numbers. Only when the path levelled out and they could see a building did he spot a sign pointing the way to the reception.

One thing was obvious to him: a blood-soaked killer, especially if seeking evasion, could have got this far undetected. But how could he have left the fenced complex? There was no way he could have got past the front gate security. Were there other points of access? Was there a tradesman entrance? The beach seemed the most likely possibility, but there would be security there too, wouldn't there? And if he wasn't a guest or one of the staff, how did he get into the place?

The bellboy was standing like a sentry just inside the building. Dannaks felt a pang of guilt about the boy's tip. He didn't have any money on him. His wallet, with the rest of his valuables, was locked in the apartment safe.

On the non-carpeted area of the lobby opposite the reception counter was the entrance to the bar either side of which were desks for booking golf lessons, trips and one was labelled guest relations.

A middle-aged couple sat with their luggage on one of the sofas in the carpeted area. The frail old lady was sitting in the same place, still like a fixture.

Reupke went straight to Waistcoat behind the reception desk. Dannaks followed and put the tray on the counter.

Reupke showed Waistcoat the apartment key and asked whether they could have a duplicate. The man looked dumbfounded and Reupke repeated the request. Did he speak German? Reupke began in English but Waistcoat interrupted him.

"We don't give out a second key."

"Why not?"

"It is hotel policy."

Dannaks cut in. "So nobody leaves a key in their apartment to keep the a/c running." He realised this as soon as the man said: "hotel policy."

"Exactly," smiled Waistcoat.

Dannaks was chuffed. It made him appear more travelled. But the apparent stab in the back annoyed Reupke.

When Reupke began to insist on a second key, claiming special circumstances, that they were independent people shoved together, Dannaks wandered off. He walked over to a row of photographs mounted on a rectangular board, itself fixed at eye-level on the wall. The board carried the words: "At your service: the Azure Skies staff" in English.

After Iceman's pep talk the liaison officers, Sturm and Leidner, told them all they had been given by the Turkish police. If either of the men from *Zeugenschutz* had been interested in making the journey they didn't show it. In answer to the question why the German police had not been brought in earlier, if not from the start, Sturm said that their help was not wanted. Dannaks said that national pride could also be at play. Added to this they agreed that diplomatic wheels turned slowly. The officers hadn't been given much. The Turkish police were interviewing one of the hotel staff. In typical police-speak he was said to be helping them with their enquiries. He, like the victim, was a member of the animation (entertainment) team. His name was Rafael. Leidner had heard that very morning that Rafael was no longer in custody but was having time off work to recuperate. Such was the ordeal of the interview. The Turkish police also wanted to find a girl, Meryem, also from the animation team, who had disappeared on the night. She was regarded as a key witness, if not the killer. Her blood type was found at the crime scene. The officers were under the impression that she and the victim had been intimate. Reupke asked whether they thought the Turkish police were being coy. Leidner answered that he thought they had nothing.

So there were two people of interest to Dannaks: Meryem and Rafael.

Of course the killer could be an outsider or a guest. The former was possible and the latter was unlikely, but not out of the question. A guest could have recognised Peter or even been contracted to kill him. Something as bland as an argument that had escalated could be the reason. But a member of staff was probable. And the hot candidate, as far as the Turkish police were concerned, was Meryem.

The first photograph starting from the left was a head and shoulders one of Tasköprü, the manager. The second showed four men and one woman standing in front of the hotel. Dannaks recognised Turgut. They were all dressed in wine-coloured suits, white shirts and black ties and looked like an airline crew without caps.

He was about to move on when he was interrupted by a voice behind him. "Excuse me."

She was a woman in her fifties. She'd filled out but had not begun to sag. Behind her was a man Dannaks took to be her husband. He divided his attention between them and the luggage clustered about the sofa they'd left.

"Yes."

"Are you one of the Hamburg detectives?"

"Yes."

"We're leaving, so we can't tell anyone else. Can you tell me whether they've found the girl?"

"I don't believe so."

She weighed up the truthfulness of his response before pressing on. "It was a terrible thing. Of course we wouldn't let it spoil our holiday. But tell me, did she attack him with an axe? You see, we've been told very little. So there're rumours going around. The staff won't tell us anything. Or they don't know. And you can't talk to the police when they're here." Dannaks dared to glance away to her husband, who suddenly chose to check that nobody had whisked away one of the cases at his feet. Dannaks's distraction did not go unnoticed. "I know I sound nosy, but I thought I'd ask someone responsible. And you do look responsible." Dannaks thought he was going to laugh. His shirt was dirty about the collar and his trousers were a tight fit.

"I'm afraid we've only just arrived."

"But surely you know whether it was an axe or not?" she insisted. "The papers said it was a knife. But how often do they get it wrong?"

"We've only received second hand information too." He saw that she still hadn't given up. "And as you no doubt know, from television and film, this is an ongoing case and I'm not at liberty to talk about it."

Her expression soured and she turned away. "I can't believe it was her."

"Oh?" Now Dannaks was interested. But she stepped away and Dannaks was forced to follow her. "Why not?"

"Bartells," called a man carrying a clipboard at the hotel entrance.

"That's us," said the woman's husband. She knew her own surname, and the unnecessary statement was an expression of his relief and his lack of support for his wife's interrogation.

Mrs. Bartells glanced at her husband who had now jumped into action. The bellboy moved to help him with the bags, but he waved him away.

"Why couldn't it have been her?"

"Oh, you only have to look at her," she said, somewhat abstractedly. Then she came to herself and moved down the wall of pictures. Dannaks followed. "Here." She pointed to the photograph in front of her. "That's her, in the front row. Far left."

"Gertrude," Mr. Bartells called. The man with the clipboard was helping him with the cases.

There was a group photograph of a dozen or so smiling faces all wearing deep blue animation T-shirts sporting the hotel logo, the lads in white shorts and the girls in almost as short white skirts. They were all in their twenties. Further along were portraits with name tags underneath. Peter's picture had been removed. And under the one of Meryem was a small note in German, English, Russian and Turkish. If you see this woman please report it to the police or one of the hotel staff.

"Do you think she did it?"

This time Dannaks couldn't tell whether she was prying or asking for his personal opinion after seeing what she looked like.

Dannaks shook his head, more in uncertainty than answer. Gertrude seemed satisfied.

"You can never tell with them, though, can you? Of course, when we discovered what *he* was, we didn't feel so sympathetic. Oh, please understand, murder is a terrible thing. But it could have been self-defence. He was a brute of a man. That's him at the back. He sticks out, doesn't he?"

Dannaks merely smiled. She'd said more than the words she'd spoken. Was he a brute? His murder had no doubt demonised him.

"We've got to go." It was her husband standing alone and empty-handed at the entrance. He smiled apologetically at Dannaks.

Gertrude regarded Dannaks for a moment. She looked as if he'd cheated her. "What I can't understand is why he came here. His sorts hate Turks, don't they?"

Dannaks shrugged. He produced a visiting card and rattled off his standard statement. "If you think of anything relevant to the case, please don't hesitate to call. If I'm not available one of my colleagues can take a message."

She took the card and examined it as if it could be a fake. But she seemed pleased. "We're not going back, yet. We're going to Istanbul."

When she left Dannaks saw that Reupke was no longer at the reception desk. "He wouldn't give me a second key." He started. Reupke was behind him. "We'll have to talk to Turgut." He nodded towards the entrance. "Did she have anything interesting to say?"

"Not really." He then pointed out the girl in the photograph.

Although she was smiling for the camera, her smile was tight-lipped and unwholesome. There was resignation in her face. Her eyes were melancholic. Dannaks was familiar with the look. It was the Muslim blues known as *Hüzün*. And Dannaks had a theory. Because in their worldview everything was written, the diminished sense of freewill bore a resignation that tended towards this melancholy.

What bothered Dannaks was that this slip of a girl could have been so brutal. It seemed inconceivable that she could have carried out the final act of slitting of Peter's throat.

"Rafael," said Reupke nodding to a photograph. He wore a paisley bandanna and a smile displaying a fine set of teeth. In contrast to the dour Meryem this youth was full of life.

"The guy at reception was on duty the night of the murder."

"Oh?"

"He didn't see anything. He just talked about the commotion and then the complaints and questions from the guests." He stopped as if he'd forgotten what he wanted to say. "Everyone is at the show. Let's take a look and get that drink."

"Excuse me." The detectives looked over in the direction of the feeble voice. The frail old lady was beckoning them with a weak wave of a limp-wristed hand.

She was a small woman and they felt awkward towering above her. When she rasped that she had something to tell them, they felt compelled to sit. Because she only took up half of one of the cushions on the oversized two-seater sofa, there was ample room for Reupke to sit next to her without appearing antagonistic. A black leather-bound bible lay between them. Dannaks took the chair, which was also generous in proportion, adjacent to her. She chose to speak to him.

Dannaks sensed that there was something not quite right with her. Her crinkly skin was like crepe paper and in places even this had become tracing paper, so that he could see the blue and red of veins and nerves. But this was not what bothered him. Only when he leaned forward to prompt her did he see that her feet weren't touching the carpet. She was sitting so far back in the sofa that her knees didn't reach the edge of the cushion and her legs dipped only slightly and stuck out like a child's.

"You saw that Rafael?"

"Yes."

"He's the killer."

Dannaks kept his attention on the woman. He avoided glancing at Reupke. Her hair was grey wire, cut short, over the ears like a boy. Her brown eyes were rheumy with age or tiredness or both.

"Why do you say that?"

"I hear they have released him."

"Yes."

"Well, I don't think much of the police out here."

"I'm sure they had their reasons."

"You'll sort it out, won't you?" And she looked at Reupke too, acknowledging his presence for the first time.

Reupke nodded and when she returned her gaze to Dannaks his partner rolled his eyes to the ceiling. Dannaks ignored him.

"Why do you think it was him?"

"Because, if he took that cloth off his head you'd see that he is a skinhead."

She smiled triumphantly and Dannaks smiled back.

"Oh, he's as friendly as the rest of them," she continued, "but they're all entertainers, aren't they?"

She was implying that they were actors.

She looked him in the eyes. "I know what you're thinking. He's South American. But listen," she paused, "he could have been indoctrinated by an old Nazi." She couldn't help her chuffed expression.

"We'll certainly look into it. Thank you."

She nodded. It was obvious she had said all she was going to say.

Dannaks got up at the same time as Reupke.

"Goodnight," she said.

"Yes, goodnight."

Reupke spoke when they were beyond earshot.

"Well, that covers the two prime suspects." Apart from the victim Meryem and Rafael were the only names they had in connection with the killing.

"What do you think?"

"I think she's been reading too much Agatha Christie."

Reupke seemed to know the way. They headed away from reception. A flight of stairs took them down to a lower level offering the entrance to a Hammam and wellness area and a corridor to conference rooms.

Dannaks thought about what Gertrude Bartells had said. He could hear the indignation behind her words. What a hotel. Fancy employing a man with his leanings. Surely they vet their employees?

Matthias had been a neo-Nazi. He'd turned on his so-called comrades and became Peter under the witness protection programme.

Dannaks could pick out another undertone in the woman's words. I can't believe it was that girl. She was such a sweet thing. So good with the kids. But you never can tell with these people, can you?

If there was a hush in the woods and a relative sleepiness in the reception area behind them, then here was sudden and growing cacophony before them. Dannaks couldn't tell when he started to hear it. It had no doubt been gradual. But its force was so formidable that it seemed sudden. How could they have not heard it?

In front of them the area opened up to a plaza of sparsely occupied tables and chairs beyond which was a long hut that was the bar. To their left was a building that was a short row of shops. To the right was a large swimming pool illuminated by sunken lights. But the detectives were drawn to the irresistible boom of the show-master to their left, beyond the shops. The stage, upon which he energetically paced, diffused with coloured lights from spots overhead, was at the bottom of a semicircular amphitheatre. A path at plaza level separated the amphitheatre into an upper half and a lower half. At the top of the amphitheatre, way above ground level, spotlights upon small towers flung shadows and sharpened the edges of buildings.

There were easily five hundred people watching the show. The tiers of the amphitheatre were concrete steps and the spectators sat on small red cushions.

On stage some kind of comedy sketch was being played out. The audience was collectively expressing their amusement, but Dannaks couldn't grasp what it was about.

He followed Reupke between the tables to the bar. He saw a guest take an upturned wineglass from the bar and hold it under a small wooden barrel or polished cask perched on a wooden frame. He was pleased to see the glass fill with red liquid. Reupke ordered a beer and Dannaks helped himself to a glass from the cask. He had always thought that the trick with these all-inclusive offers was that you spent most of your time queuing.

With their drinks in hand they moved a few paces from the bar to watch the show and still allow access to the bar. All the best seated-viewing away from the amphitheatre, whether on the high-stools at the bar or at the circular tables, were taken. But the two detectives were content to stand for the moment.

Dannaks sipped his wine and winced. He'd tasted better.

The nonsense on stage continued unabated. He couldn't catch what was going on. The show appeared to be a series of sketches. Dannaks assumed the performers were the animation team. He didn't recognise any of them from the photograph.

"How's your wine?" shouted Reupke.

"Vinegar."

"The beer's drinkable." Dannaks nodded. He didn't drink beer.

The noise rendered conversation barely possible and they fell silent.

Most of the people at the tables were middle-aged. The chairs were no doubt more comfortable than cushions on concrete. Conspicuously, three girls in their early twenties were seated here too. One was blonde and brash in a white jump suit. She was animated and laughing. A friend was smiling. The third girl was smiling too, but she appeared distant.

Bizarrely, two chess players were at a table, beers at their elbows, engrossed in their game, oblivious to the noise.

Suddenly the blonde girl looked over and Dannaks snapped his head away. He took a good gulp of his wine. This time he didn't wince. The burn parched the back of his throat and he coughed. Reupke didn't notice; he was watching the show or the crowd.

Dannaks's gaze wandered to the box at the top of the amphitheatre. He could make out the silhouette of a youth, his face partially visible from below, no doubt illuminated by a desk lamp or the instruments themselves. Peter had been the soundman. He would have worked in the box. Well out of the spotlight.

He returned to the stage. Five women and five men were performing a dance routine. It all looked good but not perfect, better than amateur but not quite professional.

Meryem had probably danced on stage too.

The detectives moved to allow a family of four to pass. "But we're not tired," whined one of the children. Then a couple moved away from a corner of the bar and Reupke and Dannaks took up the position. Occupied high tables and bar stools obscured their view of the show. They were also shielded them from the full blast of noise and they could talk.

"My parents used to bring us to these kind of places," said Reupke, staring at the audience. "They haven't changed."

Dannaks couldn't think of anything to say. He followed his colleague's gaze to the woman sitting in the amphitheatre at their end of a row. She sat upright, her slender arms resting in her lap, a calf of one of her crossed legs showing in the split in the side of her dress shooting like a flame. Her dark hair was silken. It covered her back and complemented her flowing midnight-blue evening dress that looked as if it was made of velvet. A slip shoulder protruded from under her hair and the light that played on the profile of her face highlighted fine features. She looked ridiculously out of place in the raucous vulgarity. And yet –

"Are you the Hamburg detectives?"

Dannaks turned. As he did he saw a severe-looking man behind a short concrete parapet of the amphitheatre looking directly at him.

The speaker was the blonde girl who'd caught Dannaks staring. She was carrying a drink. Behind her was her friend. She had a beaker in each hand. The quiet one was obviously saving their seats.

"Yes," Dannaks answered, but she stole a glance at Reupke. Her jump-suit top was zipped open and revealed a white T-shirt with the words OFF LIMITS in bold block capitals.

"Have they caught that crazy girl, yet?"

Dannaks could see she wanted to draw Reupke into conversation, but he'd calibrated his sights higher.

"I don't think so, but–"

"I'll catch you later," said Reupke. He barely acknowledged the girl and walked away.

"See you around," she said to Dannaks.

Then he was alone. He raised his eyebrows and sipped his vinegar.

The severe-looking man was gone too.

Reupke was sitting next to the woman in the midnight-blue evening dress. He was leaning her way now and then to take advantage of the relative lulls and speak.

Off-limits was again sitting with her friends. She looked snubbed, but then she laughed and so did her friends. Dannaks had wanted to ask her why she had called Meryem crazy. There was something definite in the way she had said it. He wasn't sure whether he was reading too much into her words. But was she merely referring to her being a murderess? And then, he didn't want to approach the table alone. Although he was old enough to be her father, she could get the wrong impression.

He was beginning to feel stupid standing alone when he was surprised to see that he'd finished his drink. So he was grateful for something to do.

22:23

There was no one at the cask and in a moment he had filled his glass. He sipped off the top and his taste buds initially reacted as if they were tasting it for the first time. By the time he'd swallowed the familiarity had returned. He moved aside to allow a woman in her fifties to fill two glasses.

"You get used to it," he said.

"Do you?"

He laughed. She smiled.

The entertainment team was still larking about on stage, but he had the impression the show was coming to an end.

The woman nodded to him before walking off with her glasses.

Dannaks looked over at the pool and then beyond. The bushes and palms united by darkness presented a forbidding jungle. He strolled towards them. He had to cross a small bridge that connected this large pool to a smaller one behind the bar. The plastic loungers that surrounded the pool had been pushed into blocks of twos, threes and sometimes fours. They sandwiched large collapsed umbrellas. When he reached the end of the pool some thirty metres from the bar he was quite alone. The stage mayhem, the clustered crowd, frenetic lights and even the sound dissipated in the vastness of the night. Out here the sky was black and glitter. There was a path through the foliage, but he chose to circle the pool.

He heard them before he saw them. They were huddled on a lounger pillow-talking. His approach had been slow and silent. The girl sat up and threw back her hair. She saw him and started. The youth under her looked up.

"Sorry," said Dannaks, briskly walking on.

They had been clothed, but he wasn't sure. He heard them talking, but didn't look back. His stroll had taken on purpose. The show was going on and he headed for the shops on the other side of the square.

Only the watches in the jeweller's shop window held his attention.

"I wouldn't bother with them." He looked up. It was Off-Limits walking by. "They won't last longer than the socks." She was gone before he could ask what she meant.

The next shop was also closed. The window offered T-shirts, swimwear, hooded sweatshirts, etc., all with the hotel emblem. A carousel of paperbacks stood immediately behind the door. Inside he could see snacks: biscuits, crisps and the like. The next shop was open. But it wasn't really a shop and little more than a kiosk. It was a photographer's studio. At the end of the room behind the counter, a door-high curtain had been drawn back and Dannaks recognised the hotel photographer he had seen earlier sitting on a couch against the wall. Behind the counter sat a bored girl filing her nails. The kiosk was like a corridor. On the walls were framed photographs. On each side of the room were pairs of high-tech columns like lecterns topped with touch screens continually offering new photographs.

Reupke was still sitting beside Midnight Blue. They were clapping.

The next shop was the last one before the stage. This too was open. This one was selling clothes. T-shirts, sweatshirts, skimpy dresses and belly-dancing outfits hung above and at the sides of the windows. Packed behind the windows were jeans, leather jackets, shirts, stylish summer dresses and sportswear. A tall carousel of sunglasses stood outside. And a rack of leather belts hanging from their buckles stood alongside a display shelf of socks.

An elderly woman was examining the different buckles.

Attracted by the low price tag he picked up a packet of socks.

He couldn't remember when he'd last bought socks or underwear. The material of many of his boxer shorts had worn thin with wear. He had accidentally ripped two in the last weeks simply by catching his toe whilst climbing into them. They were that worn. He'd been careful to pack socks without holes. Only when the holes got to toe-size did he throw them away. And when things got desperate he sometimes folded the end of his sock over the hole and under his toes before slipping his foot into his shoes.

Suddenly Off-limits came out from between the amphitheatre and the shop.

"Excuse me," he said, swinging his glass towards her and nearly dousing her with the remnants of his red wine. She stood arrested and he replaced the socks.

"They'll be worn out in a week," she said loudly. The proximity of the speakers made talking nigh on impossible.

He nodded, immediately understanding the inferred lifetime of the watches. But he had something else on his mind. "I wanted to know what you meant by *crazy* girl."

"She committed murder, didn't she?" she shouted and he nodded. He watched her think about going on. "But she was crazy before that."

"What do you mean?"

"See these toilets," she pointed behind her between the amphitheatre and shop, her silver thumb-ring glinting. He couldn't see. But a continual stream of people were coming and going.

She looked irritated when he gestured for her to follow him.

He took her round the corner. At the end of the short gap was a concrete block with two entrances. Here it was tinge easier to talk.

"We caught her coming out of there. And when we went in all the toilets were stuffed with wet toilet rolls."

"Who do you mean by: we?"

She nodded towards her table. "Those two and me."

"When was this?"

"I don't know. About a week ago. Before the killing."

"Did you tell anyone?"

"Of course. We went to reception."

"And?"

"That's it. They said they'd take care of it."

"It may not have been her."

She hesitated. Dannaks knew she wanted to get back to her friends.

"There's more," she said reluctantly. "But Nadine knows about that." He was about to speak. "She's at the table. You want to talk to her?"

He nodded. The crowd roared and applauded and the music was turned up as if to drown their revelry. There was whooping and yelling. The clapping became synchronised and a chant of "*Zugabe*" (encore) began.

By the time Dannaks had found and carried a chair to their table, the crowd had fallen silent and only the stage lights lit the stage. Although nothing was happening on stage the girls were suddenly attentive spectators and Dannaks was made to feel like an intruder. Nadine was the quiet one of the three. Whilst she spoke the other two watched the stage.

"She tells me you know something about the missing girl," said Dannaks, grateful for the lull. He felt something feather-like tickling his legs.

41

"No." She was genuinely puzzled as if it was an accusation.

Dannaks brushed his legs with a hand.

"He wants to know about the loo," said Off-limits. The other girl glanced their way. Then both of them looked back to the stage. A spotlight had started to search the stage area.

Dannaks waited for Nadine to find her words. Her hair was highlighted and cut in a trendy slope. But there was something about the way she held her lips. They were nervous. On another girl the way she dipped her head when she spoke could have been coy, but with her only shyness and lack of confidence came across. Then in the vicinity of the brilliance of Off-limits everyone probably wilted.

"She told you about the toilet rolls? The day before I went to the toilets in the main building, the ones near reception, and someone had smeared shit all over the walls."

"All over?" The tickling at his legs had grown irritating, but he didn't want to shift his position and disturb the conversation.

"The wall next to the drier, by the sinks."

A jolly white-haired man on the next table laughed and jiggled the little girl on his knee. All three generations were represented. "Gallop," called the girl, bouncing on his knee. The girl's mother told the girl to calm down.

"Was it just smears or–" music forced him to raise his voice "– could it have been writing?"

The irritation at his legs had become itchy.

She was surprised by the question. "I, er, suppose it could have been words. But not German. Maybe Arabic or Turkish."

Dannaks gave her another moment, before shouting. "What did reception say?" The performers were repeating their earlier dance routine.

The itchiness was intolerable and he pushed his chair without distancing himself so that he could sit sideways with his legs no longer under the table. He rubbed his calves. His ankles were burning too. He was being eaten alive.

"I didn't tell them." She dropped her eyes. "About an hour later it was picobello again."

Dannaks nodded and sipped his wine. She grabbed the opportunity to watch the show.

He looked under the table and saw some kind of coil lit at one end wedged in the metal framework. He couldn't see any mosquitoes, but he knew they were there. The coil was some kind of incense, but the only effect it seemed to have was to incense the insects into a feasting frenzy. His calves and ankles were on fire.

He gave her a couple of minutes before leaning forward and tapping her on the shoulder. "When was this?"

"About a week ago."

"I mean what time of the day."

"Afternoon."

"Did you see anyone?"

"What?"

"Did you see anyone in or around the toilets?"

"No."

"Not even Meryem?"

"No."

"But you saw her at the time of the toilet roll incident?"

"Yes."

"Could she have seen the toilets and have been on her way to reception to report it?"

"I suppose so."

Dannaks nodded and sat back. He finished his wine as the encore came to an end. The show master began talking over the applause. He wanted to see everyone at the Silver Star disco in a few minutes, but first there was the club dance. Many of the guests were already on their feet, milling around or leaving.

The Turkish music became appallingly loud. On stage the performers led the dance routine. Children of all ages had joined them, parents fussed after them. Row upon row of the audience stood and followed the lead. Even at the tables some of the people were on their feet. The three girls were also up and into the routine, shuffling this way and that, turning and clapping. Dannaks stood by limply. He couldn't see Reupke or Midnight Blue.

And then it was all over. The music was suddenly softer and the show master again said that he was looking forward to seeing them in the Silver Star. People began leaving in droves. There was a bottleneck at the box where the cushions were stacked. The girls nodded to him and left. Dannaks looked at his empty glass on the table. The bar was packed three-deep with people and there was a queue at the cask. Nevertheless he picked up his glass.

A woman was calling a name. "Astrid!" He turned back and looked down to the front rows and focussed his hearing on the woman. "Have you seen Astrid?" She asked a couple with a little girl. Dannaks didn't catch their reply but they too stopped to look about. "Astrid," the woman called again. She was becoming frantic. "Has anybody seen an eight-year-old girl?" Somebody asked her something. "She's got brown hair. She's wearing a green sweatshirt with a brown pony on it." Others hesitated but edged away. Then a woman appeared from the side of the stage with the missing girl. The woman rushed to them; she thanked the woman and scolded the child who began to cry. "Didn't you hear me calling?"

"I was hiding," whined the girl. "I said peep."

The mother then hugged her daughter. "It's okay, it's okay. Stop crying now. But I told you not to run off without talking to me." Then hugging her child to her she spoke to the other woman. "I'm not normally so, er, so on edge. But that girl's still on the loose."

22:46

Scratching one leg Dannaks walked over to where Reupke had sat. The amphitheatre was all but deserted. Some children were running about re-enacting part of the show, hyperactive with excitement and lack of sleep. A barman, carrying a tray, was systematically going up and down the rows picking up glasses. A little girl of about three was crying on the arm of her mother near the stage. Further up a man suddenly stood and holding up what looked like a cloth duck called out that he'd found it. There were at least three people in the sound box.

Dannaks looked back to the bar. His colleague wasn't there either. He sighed.

"Excuse me, do you know where the disco is?" he asked a lad walking by.

"Yeah," he pointed past the bar. "Straight on, turn left."

He didn't feel like going to a disco. With the end of the show and the shrivelling of the crowd to a small congregation at the bar, he at once felt weary. Even if he could find their apartment alone, without a key he was not getting to bed. Where could Reupke have gone?

He scrutinised the crowd at the bar as he walked by. The urge to scratch his legs was overwhelming. The disco was situated directly behind the amphitheatre. In fact it was built underneath the tiered seating of the upper circle. The entrance was through heavy double black doors, one of which was open. The closed door had half a silver star upon which the letters "heque" went up in a slant. He went in and descended the few steps. The walls were maroon, the ceiling black, criss-crossed with black pipes and peppered with small silver stars. Coloured fishes reflecting off the obligatory mirror ball revolved over the empty dance floor, but all of the plush walled-seating in the surrounding alcoves was occupied. He could see the bar but not the DJ.

Scanning the alcoves he came upon Off-limits, Nadine and their friend. They were huddled together, low, giggling behind their drinks. Reupke and Midnight Blue were not there.

He turned to leave. His anger so consumed him that he almost bumped into two women entering the disco.

"Sorry," he muttered.

When he was outside he registered the smiles from the women. He stood still and looked into his empty glass. The eye contact had been fleeting, so he was uncertain. There could have been genuine interest from one of them. Or was he kidding himself? Maybe they were just curious. Like Bartells in the foyer. By now everyone probably knew they were detectives.

He walked back to the bar area. His legs were burning, but he ignored them and resisted the urge to scratch them.

He was too tired to return to the disco. The thought that he was using his tiredness as an excuse not to act goaded him. Was he passing up an opportunity? Did Reupke have the right attitude? If nothing else he envied his colleague's decisiveness.

He'd passed the side of the bar when a glimpse of blue caught his eye. He stopped and looked into the crowd. There was a fine looking woman sitting at the bar. He couldn't quite see her dress, but her hair looked right. Then Reupke leaned forward from behind an obstructing head.

Dannaks wormed his way towards them.

"Hi," said Reupke, picking up his beer. "My colleague, Dannaks. This is Dagmar." She extended a slender-fingered hand. Dannaks wasn't sure whether he was meant to kiss it.

"Pleasant," he said, awkwardly shaking her fingers. Her smile appeared as a suppressed laugh.

He was silent for too long and Reupke spoke. "We were just having one for the road. What are you doing?"

There was no offer to join them. "I was just getting another." He held up his wine glass.

"How can you drink that stuff?"

"Practice."

"We'll be finished in ten or fifteen minutes," said Reupke. "You want the key?"

"No, no, that's okay." He smiled sickly and moved away slower than he wanted.

Why hadn't he taken the key?

There was nobody at the cask. He filled his glass and turned from the bar to the tables. Many were unoccupied. Those taken were mostly by couples or foursomes. There were three women sitting together looking his way.

Of course he didn't need a chat-up line. He didn't know any. But he could go over as a detective. He had the perfect excuse to speak to them. Had Reupke approached Dagmar on the pretext of conducting an informal interview? No, Reupke would have a catalogue of chat-up lines.

Suddenly the three women got up. One met his eyes, but he didn't know what to do. They were leaving. He watched them head for the main building.

Reupke was engrossed in conversation.

Dannaks didn't fancy walking past them so he wandered off in the direction of the pool. Before reaching it he turned left round the bar and found himself heading towards the disco. The door was still open and he peered in. The two women he'd almost bumped into were dancing together. There was a couple on the dance-floor too. Off-limits and company were huddled together disinterested in the favours of the two young bloods sitting with them. The entertainment team were at the bar with other guests.

He sipped his drink. The show master looked his way. Dannaks left before he could get coaxed in.

He took the path away from the bar and the buildings. He felt peculiar; knew he was peculiar. Why couldn't he let go? Reupke had the right idea. But he wasn't Reupke.

To his right was the smaller pool that connected with the adult one. This one had a number of slides, including twisting tubular ones. There was a further much smaller shallow round pool for toddlers and babies. Further on was a big field and to his left high fencing. Tennis courts, perhaps. Ahead a row of foliage and buildings met the sky. As he drew closer the rushing inhalation and exhalation of the sea soothed him.

A low-fenced playground met the field and separated it from a building. The whitewashed block was covered in bright murals. He stopped at the door to read the words and noticed someone behind him stop. The person kept his distance and was too far away to be recognised.

Over the door there were four words, but he could only make out two: Children's Club. He then noticed two surveillance cameras on the roof. These were dipped and pointed outwards towards the beach.

The fence came to an end and behind the row of bushes was sand. The concrete path stopped too. He was at a crossroads of sorts. Wooden slats stretched towards the black glittering sea. They went left and right too. In front of them were four rows of evenly spaced poles supporting roofs that resembled outsized straw hats. Clustered in groups of four under these umbrellas were the ubiquitous loungers.

He walked straight on staying on the wooden slats that undulated into the darkness. In fact it was so dark he saw the red flare of a cigarette before he saw the man. Although he was standing only a few paces away he'd been lost to the shadows.

"Evening," said Dannaks.

The man came over. "Yees."

He obviously hadn't heard Dannaks over the rush of the sea. "Security?" There was an emblem on the top of the arm of his tracksuit top.

"Yees." He held his cigarette away and leaned into Dannaks. He was young: not thirty. His eyes were dulled by the job.

"Everything okay?"

"Yees." He now held his cigarette turned into the cup of his hand pinched between his forefinger and thumb.

Dannaks could tell he didn't really understand, but he felt compelled to speak. The man was under the impression he'd called him over.

"Have you been here long?"

"Long? Yees, long." He was either pleased to have some company or pleased to be using his German.

Dannaks looked back along the path to the children's club. The person who had been following him wasn't coming.

"Were you here last week?"

"Yees, yees," he nodded with childlike enthusiasm.

"Were you here at the time of the killing?"

"Oh," he looked at his watch, tilting his wrist to the moonlight. "Nearly eleven o'clock."

"Thank you."

They were quiet for a while. The man took a drag on his cigarette.

Dannaks contemplated rephrasing his question. The man had obviously latched onto the word time. He opted for silence.

A couple strolled along the shoreline.

Distant lights flickered on the horizon. Like the sea and sky, the beach seemed endless. The rows of umbrellas ended in a no-man's land only to resume with umbrellas of another style; but it was too dark to see. They obviously belonged to the next hotel.

An electric cackle scratched the tranquillity. The man took a hefty drag on his cigarette before stepping to the lounger where he'd been sitting. He picked up a large walkie-talkie. It wasn't quite the war movie brick, but it was clumsy nevertheless. His words were lost to the static and the sea. And when the man spoke, he spoke secretively, cupping a hand over the mouthpiece.

He looked over at Dannaks who took the opportunity to give him a parting nod. The man returned a short wave with his cupped hand.

Dannaks made his way back. He passed the disco and resisted looking in. Reupke was sitting alone at the bar. There were half a dozen others at the bar and two tables nearby were taken. Otherwise the bellboy and an elderly porter were stacking chairs and shoving the tables to open a space on the plaza.

"What happen to Dagmar?"

"She went to bed." He seemed neither disappointed nor snubbed. Dannaks leant over to place his glass on the bar. "Shall we go?"

Neither of them spoke until they were the other side of reception. There was another man in the security outfit. He had a slim walkie-talkie clipped to his belt.

"She was here last week," said Reupke. He meant Dagmar was in the hotel at the time of the murder. "She said it was terrible." Reupke went on to say that for the first few days they were under siege. No one knew anything. Nobody could get hold of a paper or leave the hotel. Everyone was summoned to a conference room. They all had to fill out forms giving arrival, departure and their whereabouts at the time of the killing. And also whether they knew the missing girl or the victim. It quickly got round that a yes here meant an interview. They were all individually questioned, anyway. Their rooms were searched too. On the beach the media hounded people who wandered away from the hotel.

As he spoke Dannaks thought that maybe it wasn't all chat up after all. There again, he had been with her for a good hour.

Dannaks followed queue. "There are some security cameras covering the beach area. They may have caught something. I also bumped into a security guy on the beach. He didn't tell me anything, but I got the impression he was an undercover cop. They're easy to spot." He waited a moment. "They carry bulky walkie-talkies."

"Sounds like the Turkish police have as much money and resources as we do."

Dannaks didn't mention that the secretive way the man hid the tip of his cigarette was a sign of undercover work. Finally, a prerequisite for working here was surely passable German. The bellboy was undoubtedly borderline, but certainly not as bad as the man on the beach. He couldn't be one of the staff.

Dannaks then told him what the girls had said about the toilets.

"Sounds like kids," said Reupke.

"I'd agree except for the shit-smearing. Do you know where we are?" They'd left the reception building in the general direction of their building. Just as when they'd arrived there was not a soul to be seen.

"No, I thought I knew. I was following you. All these buildings look the same, especially in the dark."

"I think we're too far right."

They wandered for ten full minutes without seeing anyone. Just as they decided to take a descending route to reception, they came upon their room.

Wednesday
02:43

"We have to kill it," said Reupke thickly.

"I'll switch on the light." They winced at the sudden brightness.

Dannaks picked out a newspaper from the bin. It was one they'd received at Hamburg airport. He handed a section to Reupke. They rolled them and slapped their hands to check the sturdiness.

The two naked detectives then began scrutinising every surface. The walls and ceiling came first.

"I got one," said Reupke, nodding to the wall above the entrance. The shadow of the pesky speck on the white wall gave it body. Otherwise Dannaks would have missed it.

Was it responsible for the threatening whine at his ear? Frantic waving in the dark and pulling the sheet over his head had been futile: merely postponing an inevitable attack.

Dannaks didn't feel fit. His head was muggy. His throat was parched, the nausea of the wine dried upon it. The cool of a/c was harsh but welcome after the stickiness of the bed sheet.

He was still searching when the slap cut the air. "Get it?"

"Yeah," said Reupke.

They'd had a killing spree before going to bed, but it hadn't been enough. Dannaks had said that they should have closed the window. The high vent above the terrace door had been left open when they went to the show.

"If we had, the stink would have compounded your headache," Reupke had answered.

"I haven't got a headache," he said irritably. And he scratched his calf.

"Not yet."

Dannaks spotted one on the frame of the mirror of the dressing table shelf. "There's one here." He lined up, slapped the side of the mirror and missed.

04:14

The clap was a rude awakening.

"Mosquito," said Reupke. His irritation was noticeable in that one word. "I got it. Go back to sleep."

Dannaks's weary brain didn't question how Reupke could get the insect in the dark.

08:32

Dannaks woke before Reupke. His thirst had become unbearable and the plastic bottle on the bedside table was empty. His eyes didn't want to open. His throat protested. Then a buzz between his eyebrows forced him to squeeze the bridge of his nose.

The relief was instant but short-lived. The buzz simply moved to his temples.

The skin of his legs felt as if someone had gone over it with a blowtorch.

He opened his eyes. Daylight was already blazing at the edge of the curtains.

He got up sluggishly and fetched another bottle of water from the mini-bar. He opened it straight away and stood drinking it down. It was painfully icy.

"How are you feeling?" said Reupke.

"Like my head's a beehive."

"Told you." Yes, but he'd had worse.

Dannaks would have liked have gone back to bed after visiting the toilet, but Reupke was up. Twenty-five minutes later they were outside.

As they made their way down to reception, noting the route, they spoke of the sunshine and heat. Despite the hour it was in the early twenties.

Dannaks scanned the path and foliage too. But there was no trace of blood, nothing to suggest the violence done in the apartment they'd left.

The roof of the main building came into view.

"We'll get more if we split up," said Dannaks.

"Are you trying to avoid having breakfast with me?"

Dannaks smiled. "I was trying to be subtle. Okay, let's have breakfast together and then separate. It would have been nice to put up a billboard or make an announcement. Do some proper interviewing."

"The hotel wouldn't want it."

"Or the police."

"Or the guests."

"No, not after what you said Dagmar said. But some are interested. Most of them want to get on with their holiday. It wouldn't hurt to let it be known that we're detectives."

"I think everyone knows."

"Yes, but now we're disguised as tourists." The shirts and ties had been given up for short sleeves and shorts. Reupke was hatless in a white tennis shirt and Bermudas. Dannaks wore a baseball cap and was in shoes and socks, khaki shorts, the pocket bulging with his notepad, and a beige T-shirt with a row of spindly

Masai warriors, their elongated bodies and spears making up the word Kenya. He had felt embarrassed putting it on. But Reupke had not passed comment. Of course, he'd never been to Kenya. After he'd left home his parents had grown ever more adventurous with their holidays. And the T-shirts were like postcards of their travels. He was a walking testament to where they had been. "We'll meet at reception at a quarter to ten." The police were to pick them up and take them to see the body.

"Five to," said Reupke.

"You don't want to get changed first?"

"No."

Dannaks was mortified. Yet, part of him wanted to shed the shackles of formality. Was the holiday spirit affecting him?

"T-shirts and jackets. Miami Vice, then," he said, although he would have liked to hide the terrible state of his legs.

They went through reception. A cleaner in a headscarf – a reminder that this was a Muslim country – was vacuuming the carpet. They descended the two flights of steps and walked on to the plaza and bar. Towels had reserved many loungers, but only a barman and a man dragging the pool were about. Everything was closed, but in the foliage beyond the amphitheatre they could hear the buzz of people and the tinkle of utensils upon crockery.

Dannaks took up the lead along the path between the tables of the guests seated and milling. There was a building ahead of them. Inside were manned bars and laden tables offering a sumptuous hot and cold buffet. There was an old grey cart covered in small bowls of pudding. Leading off from the food area large rooms offered indoor eating. A few tables were taken.

They wandered about for a while before grabbing plates and splitting up. Dannaks was waiting for his omelette when Reupke appeared alongside him. Reupke's plate was sparsely laden with fruit, a croissant and a small pot of jam. Dannaks's plate carried a small mountain. He was using his fork to make room for the omelette.

"You want some help carrying your plate?"

Dannaks ignored the remark and collected his omelette. Reupke then led the way outside to the corner of a large table. A middle-aged couple sitting at the opposite corner nodded them a welcome.

They ate in silence.

Small sparrow-like birds, darting and swooping, more cautious than the flies, sought opportunities to scavenge.

Dannaks inadvertently caught the eye of the woman at their table. He could see her questions. So he was surprised when her husband addressed them.

"You're the Hamburg detectives, aren't you?" he said, leaning back and throwing a crumpled serviette on his plate.

"Yes," said Reupke. He too had almost finished eating. Dannaks was still making inroads into his mountain.

"You–" He was interrupted by a waiter collecting his plate. He smiled as the waiter took his wife's and then Reupke's plates.

Dannaks tried to eat faster. It was after nine and they wanted to check the victim's belongings before being picked up at ten. Out of the crowd he noticed the bellboy heading towards them.

"Please, you must come," said the bellboy. He saw that Dannaks was still eating and addressed Reupke. "You, please."

Reupke rose. "Sorry," he said to the man. He exchanged a nod with Dannaks and left with the bellboy. Had they made a mistake? Was the pick-up at nine instead of ten? He tried to eat even faster until he noticed the horrified look on the woman's face. He stopped, wiped his mouth and picked up his mug of coffee.

The man began suddenly. "Have they caught her? The girl I mean?"

Dannaks shook his head.

The woman took over. "We don't hear anything, you know."

"Yes," said the man. "We only heard what the boy was, on Saturday. Saturday. And we're staying here."

"The Friday papers were like gold," said the woman. "Even now they're hard to get. Have you got any?"

He thought about their paper coshes. "Thrown away. Sorry."

"What was he doing out here? I mean, a Nazi amongst these people. Can you explain it?"

Dannaks raised his eyebrows wearily. "He was an *Aussteiger*. Can you think of a better place to hide? And think of the Nazis. Their ideology didn't fit with South America."

The man nodded and Dannaks went back to his meal.

"Did she do it?" asked the woman

"I don't know." Even if she didn't kill Peter, she was an important witness. Unidentified blood had been found at the scene. The hotel records showed that it was her blood type. So it was either hers or the killers.

He nodded to the decrepit old lady being pushed past in a wheelchair.

"It's hard to believe. She was always smiling and very friendly. And quite striking on stage. I heard she was good with the kids too."

"It is hard to believe," Dannaks agreed.

"The frustrating thing is," the man said, "is that the man on the street in Germany probably knows more than we do."

The woman took up the thread. "When it was out, the media was banned from the hotel, but they still swarmed here. Camped at the main gate and pestered you on the beach. Then the hotel stopped all excursions. We weren't even allowed out to go shopping–"

"House arrest," said the man. "We may lodge a complaint."

A waiter pushed a trolley between the tables. It was stacked with dirty plates and cups and a plastic bucket for dregs. A large bin-liner hung from it too.

"There were police and security people everywhere. It's almost ruined our holiday. Of course it's not the hotel's fault. But we were like prisoners. And this killer was on the loose. There were rumours of this and that. We heard about it in the papers before they got us all to congregate in one of their halls. And like the media they wanted to know what we knew. "

Again the man interjected. "What we'd heard and seen. Whether we knew the boy or the girl. And–"

"My point was that they didn't tell us any more than what we'd already heard."

"Less."

Dannaks nodded sympathetically as he placed his knife and fork on his empty plate. Only after he'd wiped his mouth and picked up his coffee did he realise they'd fallen silent. He knew what they wanted but couldn't hide the weariness from his voice. "I'm afraid I can't tell you anything. We're not really here to assist in the investigation. So we know precious little." They didn't believe him. And he didn't believe it himself. If asked, they would gladly help. He hoped they'd be asked to check over interviews, looking over statements for anything that may have been lost in translation. Again, all this was only if they were asked. "We only arrived last night. We have an appointment with the investigating officers at ten." Although they were quiet, they seemed to be satisfied.

He noticed a moustached man, sitting alone on the corner of one of the large tables. He recognised him, but couldn't think why. Had he been part of the welcoming entourage?

"I did hear something about the night of the murder," the woman began.

Dannaks nodded for her to proceed.

"I heard it from another woman–'

"You mean about the–"

"Yes," she cut off her husband.

"But that–"

"I'm sure the detective can decide whether it's important or not."

Dannaks supported her statement with a look that silenced the man.

They were silent for a moment. "I heard from a woman that another woman saw a waiter outside on the night of the murder. It was about 4:00 am."

"What do you mean outside?"

"I mean around the guest accommodation."

"He could have been making a delivery," said the husband.

"At four in the morning," she protested. "Breakfast in bed or what?"

"I don't think room service runs all night," said Dannaks.

"Maybe it was an errand?" said the man.

His wife was about to speak, but Dannaks jumped in. "It could be nothing. But it's a lead that must be followed. It probably already has. Is the woman still here?"

"The woman who told me?"

"For starters."

"Well, I haven't seen her for a couple of days." She began looking about.

"Do you know her name?"

Continuing to look around she shook her head.

"Her room number, perhaps?"

This time she looked at Dannaks. There was a smile on her face. "No," she said. "But I can do better than that." Her smile broadened. "She's over there. See the woman in the green T-shirt with that baby. That's her."

"Excellent. But it looks like they're leaving." He began to rise. "Do you mind?"

"Of course not," she said.

"I'll be back for my coffee."

The woman was in her early thirties with sunglasses pushed into her wayward red hair. She wore beige knickerbockers and a white blouse. But it was her eyes that took Dannaks aback. They were the most amazing green. They bewitched him. Even her sprinkling of freckles became interesting.

"Excuse me," said Dannaks as she looked back at the table before pushing the pram away. It was a good habit. Dannaks had seen his brother find some item of his kids many a time under or on a restaurant table. This woman appeared to be on holiday alone.

"Yes," she returned, the blood draining from her face. He'd caught her off guard.

"I'm a detective from Hamburg." He stopped himself pulling out his brass tab or identity card. It was unnecessary, but ingrained. Anyway, he didn't have them with him. "They told me about the waiter Friday two weeks ago. I mean Saturday morning." She looked past him. He watched her smile at them before returning to him. She was visibly more relaxed.

"Yes. They told you it was what I heard."

"But you heard it first hand?"

"Yes."

"Is the woman still here?"

"No. She left, er, Monday. Yes, Monday, the day before yesterday."

"Do you know her name?"

"She gave me her address in Munich. I don't have it here."

"Could you copy it for me?"

"Of course."

"Leave it for Dannaks at reception." He pulled out his notebook and wrote his room number on a page, which he tore out.

She looked at it. But evidently didn't recognise the room number. She pocketed it and then turned to her child. Despite the noise the baby was asleep.

"Boy or girl?"

"Girl?"

"How old?"

"Four months."

He bit back asking about the father and could think of nothing else to say. "Could you tell me what the woman saw?"

"Now?"

"If it's not a problem."

"We could walk and talk. I could give you her address back at my room."

"I have to wait for my partner."

She sighed. "Let's sit down then." She returned to her seat and Dannaks sat next to her. "There's not really that much to tell. She told me that her son was sick in the night. She and her husband had to change the sheets. She washed them in the bath and when she was hanging them on the balcony she saw the waiter."

"What time was this?"

"After four in the morning."

"How did she know he was a waiter?"

"I suppose he looked like one." All the waiters wore white shirts, black trousers and black waistcoats.

"He could have been on an errand."

"No. She said he moved furtively. Yes, that was the word she used. You know, as if he didn't want to be seen."

"Was he carrying anything?"

"No. I don't think so."

Nonetheless Dannaks made a mental note to ask Turgut about reports of theft.

"Why do you ask?"

"Did she recognise him?"

"No. He was too far away."

"Have you—"

"Knock, knock." Dannaks looked up. He hadn't seen Reupke coming.

"You're back."

"Apparently," Reupke smiled. The woman smiled too. In that short exchange Dannaks felt her focus of attention slip to his younger colleague.

"I'd introduce you, if I could."

"Susanne, Susanne Voss."

"Olaf Reupke."

Despite having offered her first name, Dannaks remained formal.

"*Frau* Voss was telling me about an incident a few days before the killing."

"Actually I'd finished. You were asking me questions."

"True." He couldn't remember what he wanted to ask before Reupke's arrival. "I think we were about finished."

"I could tell it again," she offered. In that instant Dannaks knew that she was here alone. She was making a pitch for Reupke.

"That's okay," said Reupke. "I'm sure he's taken up too much of your time already."

She was crestfallen, but his colleague didn't see it or if he did he chose to ignore it.

"Besides," Reupke continued, "we've - unfortunately – got things to do. If you'll excuse us?"

She stood and Dannaks rose too. He thanked her and when she was far enough away Reupke spoke. "When the cat's away..."

"What do you mean?" said Dannaks. His irritation bemused Reupke, but effectively capped further comment.

"Never mind. There was some errand boy in a uniform at reception. He said that his *Supi* (short for supervisor) would see us after eleven."

Dannaks looked at his watch. It was nine twenty. "Great." At least the errand boy's superior had seen fit to get a message to them.

Reupke took advantage of the pause. "What do you want to do till then? Animation starts at ten. We could join in some of the activities and talk to more of the guests."

"Good idea. Before that we could have a look at Peter's belongings."

"Another good idea," Reupke said, somehow unconvincingly. "If there are any." Quite likely the police had it all.

They passed their breakfast table. The couple had gone and a family with four children had claimed it.

"Did they say why they couldn't make ten?" Dannaks asked when they were clear of the area.

"No."

Dannaks told him about the waiter on the night of the murder. At reception Reupke stopped at the events board and let Dannaks go to the front desk.

The girl behind the desk didn't know anything about Peter's belongings and disappeared into the back room. She returned with Turgut. "Ah, detective Dannaks, good morning, I trust you slept well. You wish to see the – er, his belongings, I believe?"

"Yes."

A guest started talking to the girl. He was asking something about changing towels.

"One moment." Turgut took a key from under the counter and returned to the back room. He emerged from a side door. "We've not much, you understand." Reupke joined them. "Most of it was taken as, er, ah yes, evidence." They followed him to a door near the entrance. The words 'luggage room' were printed on the door. "We had nowhere else."

Strip lighting illuminated the room, which was rectangular in shape. At the far end was a small frosted glass window that looked as if it had never been opened. Racks of heavy-duty metal shelving lined the two walls between the door and window shrivelling the room to a corridor the width of two people. There was a group of cases on the floor shelf nearest the door. On the waist level shelf to the right of the window were two cardboard boxes and a large Adidas sports bag. Turgut pointed to these. He was about to speak when another staff girl interrupted him. She spoke quietly and urgently and Dannaks didn't catch what she said. "I'm sorry gentlemen, I have to go. Please lock up afterward and hand the key in." He gave Dannaks the key and closed the door behind himself.

Reupke looked at his watch. "It's musty in here. I'll see if I can get that window open."

Whilst his colleague struggled with the window Dannaks slid the Adidas bag to a shelf of its own. Except for a slip of paper and a squashed packet of chewing gum, the side pockets were empty. There was something written on the paper in blue ink but it was so faded with age, the sun or both, that it was indiscernible. He put it aside.

Reupke gave up shoving the window frame with the heel of his hand. He sighed and pulled a box on to the floor. "This is probably a waste of time. If we hurry we could make the ten o'clock activities."

Dannaks zipped open the bag and recoiled at the smell.

"I drew the short straw here."

The clothing was overripe and in dire need of washing. He pulled out socks and daintily extracted used underwear between a finger and thumb. He took out a pair of training shoes and checked them for blood. He found pens, a curled paperback, toiletries and a Braun electric shaver. Evidently these were the loose items from his room.

Reupke had started on a second box.

Dannaks turned the almost empty bag to the light and tipped it letting the contents tumble and slide from one end to the other. He even put his hand in and lifted the plastic covered card flap that reinforced the floor of the bag. He found more bric-a-brac, but nothing that he considered significant. There was nothing belonging to a female, no hair clip or the like. There were no keys, no enigmatic keepsakes, no secrets.

As Dannaks locked the door Reupke said: "If I hurry I'll make the gym class."

So this was why he'd repeatedly talked of catching the ten o'clock activities.

Reupke, dressed in pristine white like a tennis player, was ready to go. All that was missing was the white V-neck pullover slung over his shoulders

"When does it finish?"

"Eleven." Dannaks raised his eyebrows, but Reupke had an answer. "They won't be on time. And they said after eleven. They can't complain if we're just mingling. There are plenty of clubs to check. Why don't you take the singles' club? I'm not being funny. Otherwise there's the children's club." The missing girl, Meryem, had worked there.

"I think I'll walk to the front gate whilst I'm here," said Dannaks.

"Okay. Pick me up from sport when it's finished." He was backing away.

"Where?"

"I don't know," he shouted back and was gone, leaving Dannaks to hand the key to reception.

09:43

Dannaks could see the gate-man's concrete hut when he heard his name being called. He turned. One of the girls from reception was running towards him. Behind her, at the entrance, he saw the moustached man from breakfast, the one he'd recognised but couldn't place. And now he had him in the shadow of the building he knew where he had seen him. He was the stranger in the amphitheatre: the one watching them rather than the show. He'd watched them at breakfast and now here he was following Dannaks. "Telephone," said the girl. "From Germany." They hurried back and the man stooped to tie his shoelace. Inside she pointed to a phone that had been lifted onto the counter.

"Dannaks," he said.

"That was quick." It was Reinhart. "I thought they'd be scouring the beach for you."

"Come on Reinhart. You know me." He ladled on the weariness.

"You sound terrible. Too much Raki last night?"

He'd overdone the weariness and immediately perked up. "No. The mosquitoes kept us up."

"Us?"

"Never mind. Think of the taxpayers' money."

There was a pause.

"Okay, I've got two things for you. The first is somebody else under *Zeugenschutz* was killed. Apparently it was an accident, but they're going to look at it again."

"*This* wasn't made to look like an accident."

"No. The gist of the story is that she was a junkie, her boyfriend a pusher. When they had a baby he lost interest and turned nasty. She lost custody of the child and tumbled him and his supplier. Things escalated and some real big fish were netted. Under the programme she went clean and got her baby back. Either the change was too much for her and she slipped into old habits and oh-deed or–"

"Somebody got to her."

"Right." Reinhart took a deep breath. "I mean this is after seven years in the programme. You'd think by then she'd have got her act together. Seven years is significant. It's the end of the support period by our boys. You know, baby-sitting and body guarding. Hand-holding."

"It could be the catalyst. You know, she suddenly felt alone or abandoned."

"Could be. As I said, they're taking another hard look at it."

"Is there any connection to our victim?"

"Other than that they were both on the programme, no."

The moustached man was looking at a leaflet on the golf desk.

Dannaks ended the short pause. "You said you had two things?"

"Yeah. The second thing is just as interesting." He took a breath. "Volker Herbst has a holiday apartment in Side. It's about twenty minutes from where you are."

"Now that is interesting," said Dannaks. Volker Herbst was a prominent figure in Hamburg's political scene. He represented the far right and was a strong campaigner for the "*Ausländer raus*" movement. Ironic that he should have a place in Turkey because the majority of foreigners in Germany were Turkish. More importantly he also had affiliations with the National Socialist Offensive (NSO), the organisation from which Peter fled and subsequently wrecked. "Until now that must be one of the world's best kept secrets." Had Peter known, he certainly would not have chosen to work here. Then again, Peter must have known that Side was popular holiday destination for the Germans: not exactly a wise decision for someone on the witness protection programme.

"I checked. Of course Herbst wasn't there at the time of the killing."

"You didn't expect anything else, did you?"

"No. But maybe someone else was."

Dannaks checked the time. It was almost ten. "Fax me the address," he said. The thought of somehow squeezing in a little detour to Herbst's place shot through his mind. Manavgat was the nearest city of speak-able size. Side itself had a small police station with just enough bodies to handle the traffic and drunken tourists. Most likely Peter would have been taken to Manavgat, where the autopsy would have been carried out. A homicide team would be based there too. So it was more than probable that the pick up at eleven today would mean a trip to Manavgat. He couldn't envisage getting to Herbst's beforehand, but afterwards was possible.

"You want to give me your room number?"

"One five seven four."

"Isn't that—"

"Yes. It's *the* room. I'll tell you about it, but not now. I've got to go."

"What? Has the cocktail bar opened?"

Dannaks obligingly laughed and then hung up. He decided to give the front gate a miss. Instead he'd check out the singles' club. The idea enticed him. And then he would move on to the children's club. He knew the former were meeting at the plaza bar, but he checked the events board nonetheless.

He went down the steps, turned a corner, stopped and waited a moment before seeing the board next to the wellness centre door. From here he could see anyone coming down the steps. He had no idea what wellness meant, but looking down the list of activities the centre leant more to beauty than wellness. On offer were manicures and pedicures with and without varnish, eyebrow and eyelash colouring, eye-lifts, wrinkle removing creams and treatments, hair-removal, peeling, anti-aging treatments, vitalising treatments, anti-stress treatments, relaxation therapy, beauty and make-up consultation and treatments, various massages.

The moustached man didn't come down the steps. After two minutes Dannaks returned to reception. Half way up the stairs he stopped. He could see the man was at the counter using the very telephone he had just used. Dannaks backed down the stairs until he was out of sight, then he turned and hurried to the plaza.

On the way he wondered about the tail. Then he thought about what Reinhart had said. Being in the right-wing scene Peter should have known about Herbst's place. There again, it was a well-kept secret. Maybe Herbst had bought the place after Peter's defection.

Well before he reached the plaza he heard the thud of what he took to be techno music interrupted by a voice explaining the events of the day.

Despite the DJ's enthusiasm there was surprisingly little going on.

The majority of people were in an after-breakfast slump on the loungers that surrounded the pool.

Adults with children of all ages had gathered on stage.

Nearest him a woman was brusquely tending to a boy's grazed knee with paper serviettes. Another boy stood limply nearby. The woman was admonishing both of them. "If you want to run, run on the grass. Or the beach. But not on the walls or those steps. How many times have I told you? You could have broken your leg. You don't want to spend the rest of your holiday in plaster, do you? No. Or stuck in a Turkish hospital? You never learn, do you?"

The DJ fell silent, a kids' club song began, and the children and adults on stage began a dance routine, led by three girls from animation that involved more handwork than footwork.

A man was heading for the toilets between the shops and side of the theatre. A couple emerged, followed by a woman in a large floppy white hat.

Dannaks wondered how someone could have found the opportunity to smear shit. As far as he could tell, these toilets served not only the plaza and bar, but the entire pool area too. Undoubtedly there would be lulls. But the area was nonetheless a hub.

At another table sat three women. A further two and a man stood. A younger man in a blue T-shirt with the word, CREW, in large white lettering on the back – a little like FBI – was explaining something to them. He was holding one of the black rods that were heaped on the table.

"Find yourself a pair," he said. "R for right, L for left." He and the three women began checking the Velcro wrist attachments. "Here." He handed two sticks to one of the women standing next to him.

The man looked up.

"Another single?" he enthused.

"Er, yes." Dannaks was overwhelmed.

"Well, you're at the right place." The man was brimming with enthusiasm. "Have you ever done Nordic walking before?"

"No."

"We're going to the beach. It'll be about forty minutes." His nameplate said that he was Fabio.

Dannaks looked at his watch. How could anyone be so full of beans about going for a walk? "Okay."

The seated women had their sticks and were rising. "Aren't you one of the detectives?" asked one. She was wearing rimless spectacles and a bright baseball cap, a tail of auburn sticking out the back.

"Yes."

Fabio's enthusiasm burst like a bubble. "Oh, I didn't know. You don't have to come."

"No. I'd like to. I may not do the full forty minutes…"

Was he stricken because he'd been over-enthusiastic despite the circumstances? Or did he know something and was now more wary than subdued?

His change of demeanour did not go unnoticed by the group. And Dannaks felt like the bringer of bad tidings.

"So, like I said," began Fabio, "twist and extend your sticks and set them to sixty-six percent of your height. What? No calculator?" He laughed. "Okay, so that your arm is bent like this." He then gathered up the remaining sticks. "I'll just put these away." Cradling the extra sticks he walked off to the radio shack.

The children's club song came to an end and the children and parents dispersed. Many of them headed towards the beach, but some went to the loungers.

"We arrived yesterday," said another seated woman. A red and white headband was stretched across her forehead and disappeared under her blonde hair.

"So we can't tell you anything," said Spectacles.

"But what have you found out?" asked Headband.

Dannaks was still setting his sticks and before he could speak the third woman of their group piped up.

"He can't tell you anything? It's an ongoing case, right?" She paused for Dannaks to nod. "Haven't you seen enough Tatorts, Maren?"

"Actually, I'm not here to investigate," he said.

"Then why–" began Maren.

"To pick up the body, silly," said the third woman.

Fabio was returning.

"That shouldn't take long," said Spectacles. She turned to Dannaks. "Then – no offence intended – we can get on with our holiday."

Maybe no offence was intended, but these three women were clearly suffering under the spotlight of investigation.

"Nordic walking was this morning at nine," said Maren the Headband. "This *is* the single's club."

Either she was having one last go at ditching him, or she was fishing.

"Then, I'm in the right place." Her expression said that she wasn't fishing.

Dannaks caught the sympathetic eyes of one of the women who had been standing.

"Ready to rock?" asked Fabio, who'd apparently recharged his enthusiasm batteries at the radio shack.

He led the way to the beach in clockwork fashion and they followed. Far off to the right at an open shelter, beyond the field and near the beach, Dannaks saw Reupke swinging his arms with others. He wasn't sure, but maybe Dagmar was there too.

Fabio led, followed by the three witches. The man and two women followed, separately. Dannaks was happy to trail.

Two gardeners in complete green overalls and ancient straw hats were hosing the hapless tufts of grass of the expanse to their right. The playground was busy too. And the atrocious din of children in the children's club emanated from the open windows.

Contrasting the sleepy plaza area the beach was a hive of activity. Of course loungers had been manoeuvred in to sun-worshipping or umbrella-shaded positions. Hotel towels were prominent, but there was the occasional individual one. Babies and very young children played in the sand. Some were at the sea with their parents. But there was a marked absence of older children. A continual stream of beach walkers, single or in couples moved along the water's edge. Hawkers laden with silk scarves, carrying plants, adorned with colourful beads, carrying plastic or cuddly toys or lugging a cool-box, wary of the security men, were constantly on the move, sometimes latching onto a walker or two to engage their interest. Guests were pulling on wetsuits for windsurfing or fussing about the lines of Hobiecat catamarans with the casual help of staff members.

Two things hit him when they reached the sand. The first was that he had intended to visit the security man at the main gate and the second was that he wasn't wearing suitable footwear. The sand they were on hadn't been smoothed by the tide. That was further out. This had been churned up by thousands of feet. Dannaks found it tough on his ankles and started using the sticks almost for support like a hiker or even a mountaineer.

They were reaching the limits of the hotel beach, signified by the bric-a-brac left in a no-man's land before the next hotel. Dannaks was thinking of giving up when Fabio turned to them. Walking backwards he slowed a mite and they bunched up.

"We'll stop now for some stretching and then we'll pep it up a bit." He ordered them into a curving line in front of him.

Dannaks found himself standing next to the woman wearing thick-rimmed glasses. Her eyes were sympathetic. Her blonde hair was clipped back. She was no spring chicken, but she was no older than him. Standing so close to her he could only get an impression of her: things about her that struck him immediately.

He caught her looking at his shoes. Her eyes sparkled and she smiled. Sympathetically.

He returned the smile, hoping it said something along the lines of he had no choice, rather than it's the best I can do.

They all followed Fabio as he swung his arms, opened his chest, rolled his shoulders, lifted his knees, balanced and rotated his ankles.

"Everyone warm?" he asked.

The others nodded and Dannaks made to speak but Fabio was faster. "Then let's pep it up. Are you ready to rock?" And he stared at each of them. "I can't hear you."

This brought on a spate of affirmative mutterings.

"No, no. Come on, people. You've got to say: 'Yes. Let's rock, Fabio.'" He checked that each of them had understood. "So are you ready to rock?"

"Yes. Let's rock, Fabio."

Fabio nodded his approval and Dannaks jumped in the lull. "I think I'll drop out here."

"Oh? Are you sure? We're just getting started."

"I haven't got the right shoes." They all regarded his shoes. The witches didn't mask their disdain. Dannaks avoided glancing at Sympathy. She stood right next to him.

"Okay. Hand the sticks in at the radio shack." Dannaks turned and met Sympathy's eyes. Was there something more there? "Let's hit it. I want to see nice big strides and swinging arms."

They set off at a cracking pace.

10:22

Dannaks watched them cross the no-man's-land. They moved on to the strip of beach between the sea and the loungers and umbrellas of the neighbouring hotel. There were other walkers and strollers and apart from the children daring to build castles with moats or dams this was a corridor for pedestrian traffic.

He regretted abandoning Nordic walking, not least because of Sympathy. Like last night at the discotheque he felt he was passing up an opportunity.

The hotel before him was similar to Azure Skies. The building was architecturally different, the hotel motif and colours too, but the guests were the same motley crew. Their armbands were yellow as opposed to his green. But the straps of his stick effectively covered his one. He undid his left hand stick and carried both sticks with his right hand.

His group of walkers was amazingly far away now. He could no longer make out Sympathy in the group. Dannaks followed their tracks through the untended area. He passed a circle of stones surrounding ashes and charred lumps of wood. Then he turned to the hotel. He was self-conscious as he trudged through the sand between the loungers. His armband wasn't completely hidden. Nobody looked at him directly, many were reading or in conversation, but he felt conspicuous. Pungent whiffs of sun cream, coconut or otherwise, assaulted his nostrils.

There was a big man coming towards him. His beer belly preceded him, broadly smiling from bottom of the stretched hem of his T-shirt. By comparison his arms seemed short and stubby. And Dannaks was reminded of a Tyrannosaurus Rex. Except for the fact that he was fleshy and his skin was pink and mottled. He didn't so much walk as waddle. This was a man who could only wear slip-on shoes and he had to guess where they were to put them on. The exertion of the stroll to the beach could be heard in his puffing. Not only was the man doing his skin no favours in this heat he wasn't thinking about his blood pressure.

A hut of a beach bar stood next to the path to the hotel. He exchanged glances with the handsome barman.

As he stepped onto the paved area fronting the beach bar he avoided looking at the security man.

This hotel didn't appear to have surveillance cameras.

Dannaks strode into the hotel. For most of the time he was ignored and he reached reception without trouble. Once there he wondered what to do. A girl behind the countered looked up. He smiled and glanced about as if he was waiting for someone.

The layout of this lobby was at first sight quite different to that of Azure Skies and yet the blueprint was the same. Reception, plush-seated waiting area, bar, etc., were present. Dannaks realised that only the structure and decor was unfamiliar.

Like Azure Skies this hotel hosted a row of placards highlighting the organisation and staff of the hotel. The exception was that they also had a board titled: 'Today's Activities'. Dannaks noted the full timetable, again not unlike Azure Skies. He was looking at the various groups, organised by age when someone stopped behind him.

"You're too late."

Dannaks swung round.

"Sorry, what?"

"Nordic walking was at 9:30." The lad was in staff pale yellow shirt. The word "Animation" was written in blue italics under this hotel's logo.

"Oh, that's okay. I'm waiting for someone."

The man nodded. "New here?"

"Umm." Dannaks turned back to the board and gestured to the groupings. "You've got an eighteen to thirty group here. Nothing for older people, then?"

"Singles? Not really. Our activity emphasis is on younger people. Kids, young parents and single. The oldies might go walking, but they usually hang about in the bars or beaches. A lot of them are into tennis and golf, though. But then they don't normally come as singles. You've chosen the wrong hotel, I'm afraid. Azure Skies, next door, is big on singles." He smiled broadly. "Especially the women. But hey, don't get down; I'll look around for you. What's your name?

"Dannaks."

"We're on first name terms here."

"It's still Dannaks."

The man regarded him queerly and then smiled broadly again before breaking into a hearty laugh. "Dannaks. Okay." He raised a hand and Dannaks obliged him with a high-five, low five.

Then he was gone.

Dannaks waited less than a minute and then left.

At the beach he saw the man who had tailed him earlier. He was standing away from the crowd close to the sea conversing with this hotel's security guard.

Dannaks chose to make his way back to the hotel between the loungers out of their sight.

Out in no man's area he was exposed and could easily be spotted, but he didn't look back.

The no man's area told him that one could reach the beach between the hotels. And he'd just proven that it was relatively easy to gain access to the buildings. You just had to look like a tourist. Only the armbands marked you.

Dannaks continued along the beach a little beyond the path to the children's club and entrance to the hotel grounds.

Next to the nautical club, a darkened room full of hanging neoprene suits like oversized bats, and a corner gathering of yellow scuba tanks, was a weathered concrete hut with the Azure Skies logo and the words: 'Coconut Bar'. At one end of the bar sat a small pyramid of coconuts. A bunch of kids was watching the barman doing a two-handed shake of a carton of coconut milk. The bar actually offered all kinds of cocktails, but the smell of coconut prevailed.

He left the beach.

Reupke was still at the aerobics area. He was now lying on a towel on mat a leg in the air. Dannaks didn't bother going closer. He found a bench and by turns removed his shoes, dusted them and his socks off. Then he went to the radio shack, traversing the small area between the toddlers' pool and the kids' pool with the twisting slides. The adults occupying the loungers here had one eye on a paperback, magazine or conversation, the other on the shrill mayhem in the pool.

The door to the discotheque was open and inside he saw stacks of plaza tables and chairs.

He handed in his sticks at the shack.

Hotel towels had claimed nearly all the loungers about main pool. A few were occupied. Two brightly coloured towels were not from the hotel. One was a striking print of a tiger's face.

Dannaks stopped at the bar at the plaza and ordered a black coffee. Two elderly couples were playing darts next to the bar. A few of the tables were taken.

The shops were open and some people were browsing the wares. The shopkeepers appeared happy to sit on chairs outside and drink tea out of small glasses.

Dannaks seated himself with his back to the amphitheatre, so that he had the shops to his right, the bar to his left and the plaza and pool beyond in front of him. Two lads in animation T-shirts were filling balloons with water from a hose.

He felt happy. The moment alone was something to savour. And he was content to listen to the snatches of conversation from those that passed his way.

"Well, think," implored the mother to her nine-year-old son. "Where did you last have them?"

"I don't know. Maybe at the, er, children's club."

"Then let's go there. Come on. Honestly, you'd lose your head if it wasn't attached to your neck."

The woman strode off and the boy had trouble keeping up.

"... I think that's one of them," said the youth to his companion. The two were silent until they were beyond him.

"I tell you it should be a walkover for Schalke." The two older men greeted Dannaks with nods.

Dannaks acknowledged them and sipped his coffee. Like the wine, he'd had better and he'd had worse.

He closed his eyes and turned his face to the sun.

"We'll get nothing at the pool-side now," grumbled a man's voice.

"Then we'll go to the beach," said a woman. "Really, you shouldn't drink so much. You're terrible in the morning."

"So, this is where you have been hiding?"

Dannaks snapped his eyes open. Reupke was standing in front of him, a hotel beach towel over one shoulder, his sports shoes laced together over the other. He looked flushed with exertion. The bellboy, persona non grata, stood awkwardly a couple of paces away.

"They're here," he said.

He sat up and checked his watch. It was not quite eleven. "Right," he said and stood. Reupke and the bellboy watched him hastily down the remains of his coffee.

Dannaks put his cup down and gave them a what-are-we-waiting-for expression.

"Your arms are looking a bit red."

Dannaks looked at his arms and Reupke turned away. The bellboy led them back to reception.

"Are you getting changed?" he asked as they walked along the path.

"Let's see what's happening."

Dannaks was reluctant to be seen outside the club in his Kenya T-shirt and shorts. Although he was doubtful, they could be meeting official hob-knobs again. Worse than this, there could be a photographer prowling about.

"I could do with a shower," said Reupke.

"How was the sport?"

"Tough. I thought I was going to start spitting blood."

10:58

"What did the front gate say?"

"Wh–" said Dannaks. He had been on his way to question front gate security when Reinhart's call had come. "I got side-tracked."

Reupke smiled. "I could see that."

Dannaks saw his smile but decided to leave telling him about the call until later.

They were at reception.

A man in uniform was leaning against the counter talking to the girl behind it. She was looking up to him, all smiles. He did look smart in his crisp uniform. When he saw the bellboy he straightened.

His demeanour hardened as he greeted the two of them.

Dannaks didn't catch his name.

After introductions – it was obvious he spoke no German – he turned to the main entrance and said something.

Another man in uniform, standing like a doorman, promptly handed a cardboard file to his superior.

The superior looked at the receptionist.

"He has photos of the crime scene for you," she said.

"He's not taking us to see the body?" said Reupke.

"No." She had been prepared for the question.

"Why not?"

"It's not ready."

"Not ready?"

"Available," she offered. Then after consulting the superior officer she revised her answer. "Not released."

Reupke and Dannaks exchanged looks.

"I won't bother getting changed," Dannaks muttered.

"Neither will I."

Reupke held out his hand for the file, but the officer just smiled. Then he gestured for them to follow him. The receptionist appeared at a side door and ushered them into a corridor. She led them to an office somewhere behind reception.

The desk had been tidied, but a computer screen and keyboard, a lamp, a three-tiered tower of trays, a stapler, a hole-punch, a pad of yellow post-its and an inverted tin-lid full of paper-

72

clips and drawing-pins, a metal cylinder sprouting pens, pencils, a short ruler and a letter opener reduced the surface area. Behind the desk was a high-backed swivel chair, in front of it a straight-legged chair with ornate curved armrests. They matched neither the style of the desk nor each other. Cabinets and shelves lined the walls, broken only by two small desks, one supporting a fax machine and packets of paper and the other a coffee machine, filter papers, metal tin of coffee, a white mug the inside of which was stained brown, a box of sugar cubes torn open at a corner, a tea spoon and a wad of tissues. Blinds covered the large window that looked out onto a patch of green, beyond which was a similar office window. The window was panoramic; the view was not. Despite the blinds the office, was bright with natural light.

This was a small single-person office: functional and impersonal.

The receptionist gestured them in.

Reupke grabbed the chair and hoisted it over the desk. Dannaks was happy to take the swivel chair.

The two Turkish uniforms followed and the receptionist edged her way out of the crowded room. Four people were a crowd.

Dannaks had noticed that the superior officer had difficulty discerning which of the two of them was in command and it was probably because Reupke was easier to reach that he handed him the file. But then because Dannaks had taken the comfortable chair the officer looked at him uncertainly.

Dannaks gave him a sagely expression, which he appeared to accept. He then nodded and left the room. The other uniform stood by the door. Did he think they were going to do a runner with the file?

Reupke opened it in front of them.

"It's not much," he said quietly.

The file contained about half a dozen large colour photographs. There was nothing else: no paperwork, reports, or whatever. Nothing.

"Let's lay them out," said Dannaks.

There were eight A4-size photographs in all, which they laid awkwardly in two rows of four. They were shots from inside the main room. There were none from outside, the short passageway or the bathroom/toilet. The other thing they had in common was that they all featured the body.

Eight measly photographs. Dannaks had expected ten times as many. Whoever had chosen them had decided that they would only be interested in the body.

They were some kind of preliminary photographs too. For there were no reference cards: crime scene numbered cards or graduated L-cards for scale or the like. And the photographer must have been some kind of contortionist to have tiptoed through the mess. He or she must have climbed onto the terrace from outside to take shots from the other side of the room.

The room itself was, of course, familiar. The furniture appeared to be the same too.

As Dannaks expected there was a lot of blood. He could almost smell the indescribable cloying stench of it. The body lay in a lake of it. It shot up the walls. There were streaks and patches on the bedding. On the cupboards was a series of brown blobs in a wavy line as if fired from an automatic paint gun. Each blob carried a tail sometimes two that edged a crooked path down the doors. The shapes were so similar the whole looked like a series of photographs tracing the movement of a jellyfish. The undulating motion inherent in the line reinforced this image. Peter's skin was drenched in it. Slips of untouched skin were rare. Even the smoky blue of his modified tattoos were awash. A hideously large smear covered one of the bed's covers.

This was a bloodstain expert's dream. Every type of blood pattern Dannaks knew was here. All the textbook stuff: sprays, drops, splashes, spurts, pools and smears.

Although the body was virtually central in every photograph and therefore the main subject, there was little to be gathered. Peter lay on his back. He was wearing only blue jeans. His feet and torso were bare. Because of the blood and lack of close-ups it was hard to spot the wounds. One side of his head was bashed and consistent with a blow from a heavy object. He'd been stabbed too. And of course, the cut across the throat was gaping and glistening darkly.

He still had a physically fine figure: lean and muscular. If the circumstances had been otherwise he could have walked straight off the set of a designer jeans advertisement.

He'd tried to disguise himself by dying his blond hair black and letting it grow long. But it was his tattoos that gave him away.

Dannaks didn't need to fetch the photographs Sturm and Leidner had given them. The *Parteiadler* (Nazi-party eagle) at the top of his right arm was visible. The horizontal-winged eagle originally sat upon a swastika-adorned orb. The swastika had been removed and the orb painted like the world. Dannaks knew that he would argue that it was a soldier's tattoo acquired during his stint of national service in the *Bundeswehr*. On his chest over his heart, discernible despite the cluster of wounds, was a solid black iron cross. This too had been adorned to appear an abstract motif.

"Not very helpful," said Reupke.

Dannaks didn't answer. He was absorbed more by the room than the body. He'd got the overall picture.

Now he wanted to look at each photograph closely. "Let's look at them individually."

"Okay," said Reupke.

Dannaks picked the top left one up. With their backs to the window their shadows darkened the photographs. He lifted it to the daylight, tilting it this way and that to shift the sheen.

Rather than pick up a photograph, Reupke opened a drawer. Under his side of the desk was a small three-drawer cabinet. Dannaks had the computer tower at his left leg. Essentially there was only legroom for one under the desk.

The uniform craned to see over the computer screen to what Reupke was doing.

Dannaks too was distracted.

"I'm looking for a magnifying glass."

"I doubt you'll find one."

"I know." Reupke shuffled the stuff in the next drawer down. After the third drawer he gave up and picked up a photograph too.

The two detectives began methodically working their way through the photographs. After about thirty minutes the door opened and the Turkish officer came in. He looked over at the detectives before talking quietly to the uniform at the door.

"I think we need a magnifying glass," said Dannaks to Reupke.

"Good luck," said Reupke.

"Er, hallo," he called.

The two uniforms looked over uncertainly.

Amazingly Dannaks didn't have to play charades. He simply looked through the circle he made of his finger and thumb and moved his hand back and forth over a photograph. "Magnifying glass," he said.

The uniforms looked at one another, agreed on something and then the superior left. He returned a moment later with a good-sized magnifying glass.

"Perfect," said Dannaks.

The superior waited a moment; then after exchanging looks with his colleague he again left the room.

Dannaks worked with the magnifying glass first, making notes in his notepad. Then Reupke took it and he too made notes using a page torn from Dannaks's notepad.

He spotted the dent in the cupboard. But it didn't tell him anything other than it had appeared before or during the crime.

The bed had been unprofessionally made. The quilt covered it, but the bed sheet showing at the side of the mattress was not tucked in.

Two unopened litre bottles of water had miraculously survived the violence and stood together next to the television. A small green rucksack was dumped at the leg of the nearby chair.

The chair stood askew against the wall adjacent to the terrace doors and the stool lay on its side, its legs protruding from under those of the chair. Beyond the chair, at the wall nearing the bedside cabinet, off this photograph was the tip of something brown. Unfortunately, even with the aid of the magnifying glass, Dannaks couldn't identify it. Although the lower ends of the beds were apart the heads were together.

The German media had gleaned little of the killing. They hadn't been able to penetrate the Turkish clampdown. But by accosting returning holidaymakers, including those from neighbouring hotels, they had bolstered their "Death in paradise" story. Dannaks remembered reading a report from a guest about hearing the screech of furniture upon the tiles, as if a cleaner was shifting furniture.

"Ready to talk?" Dannaks asked when Reupke replaced the last photograph and sat back.

"Yeah," he said, snatching up his piece of paper. "Whoever did this certainly saw red."

Dannaks smiled at his gallows humour. But his remark also conveyed the manifest rage.

"The cleaners must have used a high-pressure hose."

"First of all," Reupke began, picking up the photograph taken from the terrace. "What do you think that is?"

He was pointing to the brown object at the top edge of the photograph. "I was going to ask you the same thing. A piece of metal?"

Reupke shrugged. He was quiet for a moment before moving on.

"The beds pushed together like that imply he was having an affair."

"I agree," said Dannaks.

"Was his lover male or female?"

"There's nothing to suggest that he was gay. On the contrary a gay incident was the catalyst to him leaving the NSO."

Again they gave one another silence for additional comment.

"I'm no profiler," Reupke began, "but there is no disfigurement or covering of the face, so it wasn't necessarily personal."

"Yes, but look at the cluster of wounds on the tattoo on his chest. That looks passionate."

"Hateful. Like a Nazi hater."

"Or betrayal: a Nazi wanting to obliterate it, because Peter didn't deserve to carry it."

"Meryem could have seen his tattoos and flipped."

"The possibilities are endless," said Dannaks. He glanced at his notepad and then picked up another photograph. This one had been taken looking into the room from the terrace. The lower half of the blood-spattered a/c was visible, but Dannaks was interested in the shelf underneath it. "You saw this?"

"Yes. What do you think it was?" The shelf, like the mirror behind it was splattered with blood. But there was an abrupt gap in the spatters on the shelf, reappearing just as abruptly further on. Under the magnifying glass the smaller drops, misted at one corner, helped confirm the shape of the missing object. "A book? Folded newspaper?"

"Anything like that. Whatever it was, it was rectangular. It wasn't tall either."

"The splashes on the mirror," Reupke agreed.

"You think the police took it?"

"They shouldn't have moved anything before taking pictures." He meant the shots with numbered crime cards.

Dannaks nodded and then picked up another photograph. "What about this partial shoe print?"

The floor was a mess of shoe and bare footprints, all in blood.

"Training shoe, I'd say," said Reupke.

"Without a scale it's hard to tell the size."

"I doubt that they're Meryem's." Dannaks glanced at him. "They're bigger than Peter's feet. Look there." He pointed to the blood print of the side of a foot from heel to little toe. "Unless she's got big feet, of course."

Dannaks smiled before saying: "Rafael or someone else."

Reupke nodded.

There was a moment's silence in which Dannaks thought it strange that traces of her soles didn't appear in the scuffle. He was about to say so when his colleague spoke.

"Did you see those spots?" He had picked up a photograph showing the short corridor leading to the bathroom and main entrance. Both doors were slightly ajar.

"Yes," said Dannaks. Small isolated, under the magnifying glass, crenulated drops appeared amongst the sparse smears of what could be training shoe tread. Because of the relative regularity of the drops, some of which were smeared, it was easy to see that the struggle had not reached the main door or bathroom. "Somebody was wounded."

"And leaving or going to the bathroom."

"Without more photos it's—"

Somebody rapped on the door and the uniform almost jumped. He opened it and Dannaks spied Turgut. They spoke. Then the superior disturbed them. He came in and closed the door on Turgut. At the desk he mumbled something and gathered up the photographs. When he had them in the file he said something to the uniform, who opened the door to allow Turgut in.

Turgut smiled. "You have to finish now."

"Do we have a choice?" said Dannaks.

"They have to go."

"What happens next?" asked Reupke.

Dannaks wondered whether Turgut thought they were a double-act.

Turgut spoke to the superior uniform.

"He says you will be contacted this afternoon."

"When?" asked Reupke.

"He doesn't know."

"Can you ask him a question for us?" said Dannaks.

Turgut looked at him. Yes, he thought they were a double-act. He nodded and smiled.

"Something was rectangular on the dressing table. It has been removed. What was it?"

They waited as Turgut spoke to the superior. He didn't answer for a while. He was weighing up whether to say anything. Then from the way he spoke he had weighed up his phrasing too.

Turgut translated. "They think it was a book. That was how the room was found. Maybe the girl took it."

"Have they any idea what kind of book?"

Turgut spoke with the uniform, who again wondered whether he was overstepping the mark by giving them too much information.

"The victim's diary."

"His what?" exclaimed Reupke.

"They have heard that he was writing a book of some kind. A diary or memoir. It's missing. I–" The uniform interrupted Turgut. "He has to leave." The detectives nodded and the two uniforms left.

"I wanted to ask whether it could have been a laptop," said Reupke.

"I don't think he had one. You can ask one of the animation team. We have an Internet café. I'm sure he used that."

"How tall was Meryem?" asked Dannaks.

Turgut held his hand up to just above his own chest.

"About one-sixty, then," said Dannaks.

"What's the hotel policy on the staff, er, having affairs?" asked Reupke.

Turgut hadn't expected the question. "It is not frowned upon. The hotel does, however, expect discretion. There can be no flaunting or even holding hands in public."

"Because Turkey's a Muslim country," said Reupke.

"No," said Turgut, looking at Reupke for a moment. "It is hotel policy. The guests are free to do as they wish."

12:17

"At twelve thirty it's lunch," said Reupke. They'd left Turgut looking in a filing cabinet in the office and were standing in the reception area, which apart from them was virtually deserted. "I wouldn't mind dumping this stuff." His shoulders were laden with towel and tethered sports shoes.

"Let's go back then."

"Shall we tell reception what we're trying to do?" asked Reupke.

"What do you mean?"

"Trying to find our room," he smiled. "If we're not heard from within three days they should send out a search party."

Dannaks smiled. "Come on." An outsider would have been astounded that they could be so light-hearted after what they'd just seen. It wasn't that they felt no compassion. It was that they had analysed the photographs as a scene of the crime. Emotion had no place in analysis. The body had been another object in the photographs. Dannaks's initial nausea of the sickening stench of blood had disappeared with time.

"You know," Dannaks began. "I can't help feeling we missed something back there."

"What do you mean?"

"I don't know. I just get the feeling there was something more in one of those pictures. I would have liked to have looked at them longer."

"You're always going to feel like that."

There had been a semblance of easiness between them, perhaps down to the common experience of viewing the crime photographs together. But Reupke's remark seemed dismissive, almost a snub.

The two detectives made their way back to their room. Off the path, in the encroaching foliage, they noticed low-level stakes supporting wooden arrows sporting ranges of room numbers. Nevertheless, following the signs took them a roundabout route.

On the way Dannaks told Reupke of Reinhart's call and Herbst's flat.

"That must be one of the world's best kept secrets," said Reupke.

"Yeah, Peter couldn't have known."

They agreed that even if the right wing had got wind of a book, Peter had already done enough damage to give them a motive for killing him. That was the *Verfassungsschutz* (Counter-intelligence: equivalent to Britain's MI5) standpoint. Even so, the Right could be worried that he could give them further pain. They speculated whether Meryem or Rafael could have taken it, but found no motive.

A cleaner was backing out of a room wiping up her tracks with large swishes of her mop. The door was wide open, held back by a bucket of grimy water.

"We should check Herbst's flat," said Reupke. "To see if it's been used recently."

"Yeah, but we'll have to wait for the Turks to call first."

Reupke nodded.

"We, er, can't really ask the Turks for a ride out there," Dannaks began. They were not meant to be investigating. "And I'm not sure I can justify the taxi ride."

Reupke shook his head. "If this was our murder then the taxi would be a bagatelle expense that I wouldn't have to ask for. But it's not. I'll fax my boss."

Then Dannaks told him about the singles' club and Nordic walking. His point being that after leaving them he had no trouble entering the neighbouring hotel. So much for tightened security.

Apart from some lonely cleaners, the buildings were deserted. Everyone was enjoying the day. Like last night there was a hush amongst the trees. In the shade it was dull and cool, but in the sun the heat could be felt coming off the baked stone.

"I had a couple of minutes before gym started," said Reupke. "I spoke to the girl taking it, Fehime. She said Meryem was innocent, no matter what they said. According to her, Meryem was not capable of murder."

"What do you think?"

"I was inclined to believe her." He pondered before continuing. "He must have been lying down when his throat was cut. Such brutality in a woman is not unknown, but it's rare."

They found their room. As Reupke unlocked the door Dannaks spoke.

"The blow to the head was debilitating."

The room had been cleaned, the curtains were drawn, and

two bath towels had been twisted into swans on the made beds. This latter display was a thank you for the euro Reupke had left on his pillow. It was agreed that Dannaks would leave tomorrow's tip.

"Or cut," said Reupke, pulling back the curtains. Dannaks raised his eyebrows. "From the blood spurts I'd say she hit a main artery. Only the autopsy can tell us."

"You saw the drops heading for the door?"

"Yes."

"You think she was wounded?"

Reupke threw his sports shoes in the cupboard and draped the towel over the chair.

"Possibly. Or the drips came from the knife."

Dannaks went to the toilet. When he came out Reupke went in.

He looked about the room and then closed his eyes. The stains he'd seen fluoresced in his mind as if the walls and furniture had been sprayed with Luminol.

"Shall we re-enact?" asked Dannaks. He was standing at the open terrace doors.

Reupke considered for a moment. Was he weighing up whether Dannaks would lose his temper if he said no? "Okay. Close those doors. The main one was open, but it could have been closed and only opened when she left. What do you think?"

Dannaks closed the doors and went to the wall alongside the nearest bed; Reupke went the other side of the other bed. They pushed them together. "Let's leave it open."

Reupke opened the front door.

"I'll play Peter," said Dannaks. "Here, you can use my comb as a knife."

They stood in front of each other.

"To be Meryem you'll have to crouch a little," said Dannaks.

"You want to stand on tiptoe. Peter was taller than you."

Reupke crouched and although Dannaks didn't totter on his toes he straightened to increase his height.

"It doesn't matter whether they were facing each other or not. I think we can assume she dazed him with the blow to the head. Then her first cut would have had to be arterial." Reupke raised his comb. "Either it was lucky or she knew what she was doing."

"Whichever. She would have had to take him by surprise.

And even if she hit an artery he wouldn't have just stood there. He would have fought back."

"The chair was knocked over and one bed was slightly askew," said Reupke.

Although the beds had been pushed together they diverged slightly.

Dannaks nodded. "How long would he have had before collapsing?"

"About thirty seconds to a minute. Certainly under a minute."

"Even allowing for shock he had time enough to fight back. I can't believe she could inflict so much damage."

"She could have cut him some more when he was down. There was clustering at the tattoo, but otherwise the cuts were all over the place."

"Consistent with a struggle. And even if she had a knife, she was no match for him."

"Unless she was trained," said Reupke.

Dannaks nodded slowly. He pushed the chair to the wall and lay the stool on its side underneath it. Then he lay down on the floor on his back. "There's not much room here." To one side of him were the ends of the beds to the other the wardrobe and shelf for the portable television.

Reupke agreed. "Unless I'm over there." He pointed beyond Dannaks's head near the terrace. "But I think she must have straddled him." He stepped forward placing his feet either side of Dannaks's hips. Then he bent and cut the comb through the air near Dannaks's neck. He looked dissatisfied.

"What's wrong?"

"The cut was deep. Bent over like this, it's difficult to get the necessary pressure."

"Then she sat on him."

"Right."

As Reupke dropped down, they heard someone throat clearing. Dannaks craned and Reupke turned, lost his balance and landed heavily. Dannaks groaned.

The bellboy was at the door. He stood awkwardly. He tried to mask his embarrassment by proffering the sheet of paper he carried.

Reupke shot up and Dannaks used the end of the bed to

struggle to his feet. The bellboy came into the room holding the sheet out like a baton in a relay race. Dannaks dusted himself off. Reupke took the sheet. Both detectives saw the bellboy glance at the beds pushed together.

Nobody spoke. Only when the boy was outside did Reupke call out thanks.

Reupke and Dannaks looked at each other with a mixture of horror and embarrassment. But they didn't say anything. Instead they concentrated on the sheet of paper. Although there was little to concentrate on. It was a fax from Reinhart with Volker Herbst's Side address. They looked at it for too long.

"Maybe we can go this afternoon," said Reupke, trying to hide his sudden lack of enthusiasm.

"We'll have to wait for the call."

Reupke nodded. Then he looked at his watch. "Lunch?"

"Yeah."

Dannaks waited as Reupke changed his shirt.

When they left the room Dannaks spoke.

"I can't believe it was her."

"I think you've almost ruled her out. Looking at her photo I'd agree."

"Whoever it was would have been drenched in blood. They must have used the bathroom. There's no way they could have got away."

12:50

The restaurant was a hive of activity. Unlike breakfast people were awake and animated. Some kids were pushing their parents to the limit, testing the boundaries of their patience. But most of the children were elsewhere. Dannaks knew that there were other rooms, even other outside areas to the restaurant. One of the rooms was designated to families. But everyone had to collect their food from the various stations, some of which were unmanned like the salad bar or the dessert area. Others had cooks behind hotplates and grills cooking before your very eyes.

The sparrow-like birds appeared more frenetic and daring. Flies were also present, droning and edging across tables towards unguarded plates or landing on plates to be waved away.

The detectives had passed through reception without seeing the bellboy. It had flashed through Dannaks's mind to say something to him. But even if he could make him understand, it wouldn't necessarily make him change what he thought.

Dannaks found himself obsessively checking everybody's footwear. The staff, including security, wore proper shoes. The crew and many guests favoured training shoes. But a lot of the guests wore sandals, pumps and flip-flops. And of course, they would change their footwear for the evening. It was a fruitless exercise.

He was still filling his dinner plate when Reupke came up with a tea-plate of salad.

"It all looks so good," said Dannaks noticing Reupke's plate. "I saw the fish and thought: yes. Then I saw the spicy chicken and–"

"Don't worry, this is just my starter. Where shall we sit? Outside?"

"Yeah, but in the shade." They estimated the temperature to be about thirty degrees.

Reupke led the way out of the building.

A woman entering as they were leaving smiled at Dannaks. In reflex he returned the smile. When he was outside he remembered her as Sympathy from the morning's Nordic walking.

"Are these free?" he asked, referring to two unoccupied seats. An elderly couple and four people wearing blue crew T-shirts were sitting at the table.

"Please," said one of the crew. The others nodded and the elderly man interrupted his meal to prod in the direction of the seats. As the detectives sat, the speaker added: "We're almost finished anyway." He looked at his companions as if he'd given an order.

In contrast to the elderly couple the crew ate hastily.

"*Jawohl*," snapped Fabio, who smiled at Dannaks, who couldn't think of anything to say about the Nordic walking.

A girl spoke to Reupke. Her nameplate said that she was Fehime. "Have you recovered?"

Reupke smiled. "I can eat again." Then to Dannaks: "She's the one who made us sweat blood this morning."

Dannaks watched Fehime shove two bananas and an orange in her rucksack. She saw him. "It's easy to gorge yourself," she said. "Especially here. I like to eat bits throughout the day."

Dannaks, aware of his plate, smiled sickly.

"This is her new eating philosophy," said Fabio.

"I've got to get back," said Fehime, getting up. She seemed annoyed at Fabio. Picking up her rucksack she said to no one in particular: "See you in a minute."

The initial speaker nodded. His name was Habip.

"Still she doesn't look too bad for it," said Fabio, whilst she was still in earshot.

"Get back to where?" asked Dannaks, reaching over for the red wine bottle on the table and pouring himself a glass.

Fabio shrugged. "Her room?"

Reupke shook his head when Dannaks silently offered to pour him a glass.

"Who heads the crew?" asked Reupke.

"I do," said Habip.

"Any chance of speaking to you all?"

"Come to the theatre after rehearsals. We'll be finished around a quarter to two."

Dannaks immediately regretted taking the wine. His colleague was on the ball. And Dannaks felt outmanoeuvred. Wasn't Reupke the one with the carefree let-the-locals-solve-it attitude? And he the conscientious one? Nobody had told him that they'd switched roles.

The three youths had finished eating. They rose and picked up small rucksacks or shoulder bags.

"Has Rafael returned?" asked Dannaks.

Habip seemed surprised. "Yes he has. He should be at rehearsals."

"Good."

Habip expected a follow-up question. When none was forthcoming he simply said: "Enjoy" to the elderly couple and the detectives.

The departure of the crewmembers created something of a vacuum. The old man filled it, by speaking to a forkful of buttered carrots.

"They're all nice people. But they're all *wired*." His last word was in English.

"What do you mean?" asked Reupke.

The old man didn't look at them and continued to speak to his meal. Dannaks caught the woman's enquiring look.

"They entertain all day and are at the disco into the early hours too." He paused to chew on some meat. Still he didn't look up. "Hardly ever sleep. They run on pure adrenalin." He concentrated on cutting a new piece of meat. "After a season of this they're burnt out. They need the winter months to recuperate."

"Yes, but what do you mean by *wired*?" asked Reupke, using the English word too.

The old man looked up as if he'd been rudely interrupted in a Shakespearean soliloquy. Dannaks was glad he was not a recipient of the glare. This was a man who'd held a position of authority when he had worked.

"I was coming to that."

"Sorry," said Reupke. But Dannaks wasn't sure of his companion's tone. Was he trying to undermine the man's severity with a hint of levity?

The woman averted her eyes. She ate delicately with her elbows held tight against herself. Each morsel her mouth received was an event.

Suddenly a waiter was at their table gathering the used crockery and utensils. When he'd gone the old man resumed.

"I remember when I was a student," he began and Dannaks wondered where he was going. "We used to take caffeine tablets during the exam days." He was inspecting a carrot on the end of his fork. "Just to keep going." Satisfied it was okay he popped it in his mouth. "But nowadays it's all drugs." Now he stared at Reupke. "So, it wouldn't surprise me if some of them are on drugs. How else can they keep going?" Before anyone could answer he added: "Especially the girl." It was true; Fehime had looked on edge.

"Maybe they take caffeine tablets too?" Dannaks offered.

Now it was his turn to be on the receiving end of the scolding look.

Reupke piped up. This was to be a two-man assault. "With drugs there is usually a loss of appetite. That wasn't in evidence here—"

"You can't deny that they're all *strung out*." These last two words were also in English, but this time with a distinct American twang.

"Hooked up and buzzing," said Reupke, also in English.

Dannaks wasn't sure whether he was being patronising.

Whatever, the man remained undeterred. "This killing doesn't surprise me," he said to a piece of meat.

The detectives were suddenly attentive, but the man merely

ate in silence.

Dannaks wanted to know whether there was more. "You're not surprised because of their adrenaline high?"

"Yes," he said.

There was no more apart from this man's disparaging view of youth. But Dannaks had begun thinking about the group dynamics. Working so intensely together undoubtedly bonded. And repelled. Emotions could run high. High enough to kill?

"Are these seats free?" A slip of a boy of about nine was standing next to the table behind a plate supporting a small mountain of chips and a large blob of ketchup.

Reupke nodded.

"Mum," he called, placing his plate upon the table. "Over here."

His mother was somewhere behind the detectives and they only heard her.

"Your father's over there."

"He should come here."

"There's more shade where he is. Come on."

Begrudgingly the boy picked up his plate and shuffled off.

"I wonder where he puts it," said Reupke.

It took a moment for Dannaks to realise that he was talking about the kid and his plate of chips.

"That won't have an effect on him now," said a reedy voice.

Dannaks stared at the old woman. Had she spoken? She had finished eating and was placing her knife and fork neatly on her empty plate.

She looked up and continued speaking easily as if she'd been contributing all along. "When you're a kid – his age – you can eat what you want. It doesn't matter." Her mouth was small, almost a pout, her cheeks hollowed and her large eyes were a mite too close together. To Dannaks she really was bird-like. "But hit say, fourteen and you're still eating badly it starts to show. Unfortunately, it's difficult to break free of your upbringing. Bad habits and all that. Eating is a cultural thing. And food awareness is very important. You're never too old to learn." Although she looked at Reupke also, Dannaks felt that she was addressing him. "I'm not talking about dieting. I'm saying you should indulge your food. Eat slowly, taste every mouthful. Kids wolf stuff down. It's a sad fact a lot of adults do too."

"Look at Elvis," said the man. "He couldn't get away from his upbringing. They say all those burgers burst him."

But the woman continued talking evenly as if he'd not spoken.

"It's important to experience what you're eating. Take your time. You'll eat less too, because you're not throwing it all down at speed so that you get that awful over-stretched feeling in your stomach." Dannaks had exactly that feeling now, but there was still food on his plate and he wanted to eat it.

"You sound like you know what you're talking about," said Reupke.

"I'm a nutritionist."

"I don't want you to tell me about the quality of the food here," said Reupke. "We're not on holiday and we're trying to make the best of it."

Dannaks thought the food was fine.

"Oh, the restaurant is not bad for this kind of place."

"What do you mean: this kind of place?" asked Dannaks.

"Cooking for large numbers. They do use a lot of fresh stuff. But you do know that processed foods play havoc with your insulin production."

Although it was refreshing talking about something other than the killing, the subject didn't sit easily with him.

"But you're talking about the way you eat," said Reupke.

"Yes. It's not just the food. You've got to adopt the right attitude. And everyone is different."

Dannaks wasn't sure what she was talking about, but Reupke had an idea. "Positive thinking."

"Yes." She brightened.

The old man had almost finished eating. It was obvious that he'd heard it all before and even his Elvis remark was well worn.

"I don't know whether it's that easy to deny your background and change the way you're thinking," said Dannaks.

She smiled. "You're capable of anything. It's all up here." She tapped her temple with a spindly finger tipped by a long red nail. "According to aerodynamics, physics and whatnot the bumblebee shouldn't be able to fly. Somebody should tell it." She picked up her glass of wine, but paused before putting it to her lips. She smiled knowingly. "You know smiling, like yawning, is infectious." Dannaks nodded, smiling too. "Try this, it'll lift your mood," she said. "Look in the mirror and smile at your reflection."

13:41

There were still some people eating, but many of the tables had been abandoned, and a lot were bereft of adornment, wiped clean, and everything down to the condiments had been removed. Lunch was only until two. A latecomer would have to join an ever-diminishing number of available tables.

The old man and woman headed for the beach and the detectives proceeded to the amphitheatre.

The abandonment had seeped beyond the dining area. The morning activity had slumped into a few sleeping die-hards. Many of the loungers carried crumpled towels, armbands, blow-up toys, bags, glasses, cups, plates, straws, paperbacks, plastic tubes and bottles of sun cream. A large toy dolphin rocked at the corner of the pool. The water lapped and slopped into the bordering plastic grill. Nobody was swimming. Bright light danced on the surface, shooting laser-like flashes into Dannaks's eyes.

"Siesta," said Reupke, summing up the lull in one word.

Dannaks nodded. He'd only drunk one glass of red wine. But he felt fazed. The meal sat heavy in his stomach and that, with the heat beating down on him, made him feel clammy and sluggish. The only respite was the pleasant breeze.

An occasional guest came from, or went to, the central toilet. Again Dannaks wondered at the daring of the deed. Even during a slump like now it hardly seemed possible to vandalise it.

There was nobody behind the bar and the chess players had disappeared too.

Two boys were sitting in the front row, but they seemed more interested in the Gameboy they were hunched over, than the meagre activity on the stage. Most of the crew were standing about. They'd just finished some dance routine and a girl Dannaks had not seen was instructing them. Six children of various ages were leaving the stage.

But Dannaks was more interested in the lad wearing the faded paisley bandanna.

The detectives collected cushions and seated themselves some ten rows up, not far from the cushion box.

"How do you want to do this?" asked Reupke.

"Let's say it wasn't her," said Dannaks, "but that she was in the room."

"Okay"

"Then she knows the killer and he's still on the loose."

Reupke was silent.

The crew had left the stage, but voices came from behind the curtain.

"Maybe she's scared to come out – if the killer's here."

"With all theses cops?"

"Most are undercover. But let's just say she's afraid." Reupke nodded. "If she's still here, then who better to hide her than one of her friends?"

"Dannaks, there are a lot of ifs here and you're even assuming her friend is one of the entertainment team. It could be a cook or a waiter."

"Yes, but the intensity of working so close together..."

"That's a lot of supposition. But okay. What's your strategy?"

By the time they'd decided upon their approach they noticed that the stage area was silent. The two boys were still poring over the Gameboy.

Reupke and Dannaks looked at one another. And Dannaks thought Reupke was about to curse when someone appeared from behind the curtain. He looked up at them, a hand shielding his eyes. It was Fabio. "We're ready to talk, if you want."

The detectives put their cushions back in the box and descended the stone steps. There was no hurrying here. The slope wasn't steep, but the steps were a mite too long. A fall could mean a broken ankle or the knocking out of front teeth.

Reupke led the way, clambering up the wooden steps at the side of the stage. He pushed the end of the heavy burgundy curtain aside and slipped behind it. Dannaks followed.

There was as much stage here as in front of the curtain. Props and sets had been pushed to the sides, clusters of standing coloured spots tilted at different angles stood in a tangle in a corner. An aluminium ladder leaned against a wall. High up the matt-black rafts and beams were barnacled with spots and metal brackets.

The crew were indeed ready. They were sitting on wooden chairs arranged in a loose row. Some of the chairs were black with round seats and looked straight from a French café or some sexy stage act. The rest were squared affairs: cast-offs from a school classroom. Most of those seated had turned the chair, so that they straddled them, their forearms folded or leaning on the back rests.

Two empty schoolroom chairs faced the ensemble. Although Dannaks followed he turned his chair and seated himself, straddling it like many of them. He wasn't comfortable with the position, but knew it was necessary. Arguably he was mirroring them and seeking rapport. On the other hand the backrest acted as a shield and projected a defensive – even confrontational – stance. He took out his notepad and, resting it on the back of the chair, flipped to a new page.

Reupke stood behind his chair smiling for a moment; then he carried it forward to be closer to them. In doing so he created a group therapy feel rather than a speaker and audience one. But he didn't sit down. He stood beside his chair, a hand remaining on the backrest.

Typically for many interviews they had decided upon a speaker and observer.

"Thanks for your time," he began, leaving his chair and open-handedly addressing no one in particular. "We won't keep you."

This then was their agreed variation on the good cop, bad routine. Dannaks, being the older of the two, had agreed to play stern authority.

Rafael looked down at his shoes when he saw Dannaks watching him. He was wearing new training shoes without socks. His three-quarter length trousers revealed enough leg to show the tattoo of a dragon or some such fantastic creature climbing the side of his right calf.

Most of the crew were looking at Reupke. But some looked elsewhere. None of them had completely come to rest and they all looked profoundly bored.

Dannaks recognised some of them from the photograph at reception.

At the moment there was too much movement. He'd mentally targeted Rafael, but he wanted to watch them all. They were undoubtedly irritated that their precious free time was being eaten away.

Their postures said that they were closed. Those sitting behind chair-backs were being especially defensive.

Habip was an exception. He was perched on a long wooden box. The word 'bar' was written on the side in sparkling silver lettering with glittering red borders. He alone displayed the characteristics of someone at ease. With his arms at his side, palms resting easily on the surface of the box and his legs uncrossed he appeared to be open and relaxed.

Rafael stood to his left leaning his back against the bar. His arms were folded and legs crossed at the ankles. His training shoes were noticeably pristine. They looked new: the white on them was painfully brilliant. He looked fit, as did most of them. Apart from a silver ring on his left thumb he sported no jewellery. The worn bandanna on his head didn't completely hide his brown locks. Dannaks thought of the frail old lady's suggestion. A South American skinhead was bizarre enough, but that he'd stitched those locks of hair into the bandanna was too outlandish to contemplate. He smiled at the idea.

"For those of you who don't know us, my name is Reupke. You can call me Olaf. I'm from the *Mordkommission*. My colleague here is Dannaks. He's from a specialist team."

He gave them a moment to absorb this information. The group had become quite still. Dannaks could almost see them wondering about him. Reupke had purposefully left his role a mystery to add an element of opaque authority.

"Perhaps we could quickly go through your names and what you do," said Reupke. He'd dressed it up as a suggestion.

No one spoke.

Dannaks scanned them. One of the seated lads was shaking his leg left leg, pumping it up and down.

Then Habip broke the growing tension. "Come on people, let's get on with this."

Reupke looked at the Turkish girl to their far left. "Let's start with you." He strode over to her, his hand extended.

"Hülya, children's club, aerobics and gymnastics."

"Nice to meet you," he said shaking her hand. "Look, erm, Hülya, my spelling is atrocious. Can you write your name in here?" He gave her his notepad and pen.

Reupke took the notepad from her with a smile and a "thank you" when she had finished. A glance at the next person was all that was needed. He adhered to the same routine: shaking their hand, repeating their name and getting them to write it down.

Dannaks scrutinised them as they spoke. He too wrote. But he appended the name with a bracketed letter or symbol that represented first impressions. These weren't physical appearance to help remember their names. They all wore nameplates. These were mental first impressions. He would write "(v)" for *Verdächtig* (suspicious), "(z)" *Zu* (closed), "(?)" nothing and "(n)" for *Nervös* (nervous). He also added LH or RH for *Linkshänder* or *Rechtshänder* (left-handed or right-handed).

"Tanya," said the next girl. She was the only one who appeared to be struggling with her weight. "Head of the children's club."

"Hartmut, tennis instructor."

"Cemil, sound." He would be Peter's replacement.

"Patricia, choreography." She looked the part too: a waif, suitably emaciated, her gossamer outfit hanging from her as if her body had stopped developing when she was eleven or twelve years old. She was the only girl in a dress.

"Fabio, sport, volley ball, Nordic walking, entertainment."

"Necla, children's club." She wilted under the attention and looked down.

"Habip, entertainment manager."

"Rafael, aerobics, volleyball, gymnastics, entertainment. Like Fabio."

"Ercan, golf instructor." This was the lad who had been shaking his leg. He stood to shake Reupke's hand.

"Fehime, sport."

"I know," said Reupke, smiling.

"Yunus, lighting," said the last lad.

"Now, I know you've gone through this with the Turkish police, but we'd like to hear it from you."

"Look," began Rafael, "we *have* been through this. I was with them for two days. I'm sick of it. I got back this morning and I was hoping to get back to normal."

Dannaks wanted to speak, but held his tongue. His thighs had begun to ache with the discomfort of sitting with the chair back to front.

"I'm sorry," said Reupke. "Rafael? Right?"

Rafael nodded, but Reupke had only being buying time.

"Then the sooner we get through this, the sooner you can get back to whatever you want to do."

Rafael sighed, but accepted. He broke his crossed arms. One forearm remained across his waist, the hand cradling the elbow of the other arm, the hand of which hand come up to stroke the stubble of his chin.

"He's right," said Habip. "We are all quite fed up with this."

He had leaned forward, but hadn't changed his posture. He was being the leader; speaking for them all.

"Okay, I think we've got the message." He glanced at Dannaks, but nothing was exchanged.

The wilting Necla raised her hand uncertainly. "I'm, er, new here." She grew red at the sound of her own voice. "I arrived after the, er–" She was in danger of spontaneously combusting.

"After the killing," said Reupke. 'Necla, right?" She nodded confirming that she was Meryem's replacement. "So you don't know Meryem, either."

She shook her head.

"Well, you can go if you want, but it won't hurt to stick around, will it?"

Even though it didn't seem possible she shrivelled some more and only managed a timid shake of the head.

"Did any of you know about Peter's background?"

The question was met with blank stares. There was little movement, but some twitching.

Dannaks was reminded of his schooldays. The teacher would throw a question into the room that would mark the beginning of an expanding silence.

"Surely you saw his tattoos?"

"We were beginning to suspect." It was Habip. "We didn't really see his tattoos–"

"He always wore these black T-shirts," said Rafael.

Dannaks read two things in Rafael's interruption. The first was that he saw himself as the leader's right hand man. The second was more intriguing. He hadn't been able to completely conceal the element of scorn in his delivery. He hadn't liked Peter.

"Put your hands up if you suspected."

"Suspected what?" asked Fabio. He didn't wait for an answer. "That he was a Nazi? I think we all began to suspect that he had something to hide. But that was about it."

"Okay," Reupke said. "Put your hands up if you thought Peter was hiding something."

Some hands went up straight away, others straggled, but eventually all but two had a hand wearily in the air. One of the two was Necla.

Reupke nodded and they lowered their arms. Again he looked at Dannaks as if to check that he was paying attention. Dannaks glanced from him to the other one who had not raised a hand. It was the leg shaker.

Reupke consulted his notepad, before staring at the man who'd not raised his hand.

"You were the only one who knew him and didn't suspect anything."

He was stocky and with age he would no doubt become portly.

"Er, no." He blushed, a hand shooting to his lower lip.

"Why not?"

"I hardly knew him." His hand dropped to his lap.

"And you are – erm?"

"Ercan. Golf instructor."

Reupke nodded and jotted something in his notepad.

Rafael sighed and exchanged a tired glance with someone Dannaks didn't know. Again he caught Dannaks watching him and he looked at Habip, whose expression scolded him.

Fehime bit her lip and looked off at one of the props.

Reupke made a show of jabbing his pen onto his pad. A full stop had been made.

"Did any of you know that he was writing his memoirs or a book?"

The accentuated making of the full stop had been as much to grab their attention as a cue for Dannaks to watch carefully. It had been as good as suddenly raising his voice. Indeed Reupke had spoken a tick louder than before, almost theatrically.

Of course, it would have been so much better to carry out the interviews on an individual basis. But the detectives simply didn't have the time or the authority.

The silence was tremendous and no one dared move.

Habip, again feeling the pressure of leadership, spoke for them.

"No." Habip looked about for confirmation and Dannaks followed his gaze about the team.

Fehime shook her head, glancing furtively away, then at Reupke and finally Dannaks. But Dannaks continued to follow Habip.

Rafael also shook his head, but his hand had moved up to completely cover his mouth, his forefinger fingering the tip of his nose. He saw Dannaks watching him and dropped his hand to his side. But Dannaks stayed with Habip. The last two shook their heads too, but more for the detectives than for Habip.

"We'd like to find this book," said Reupke.

"Have you more questions?" said Rafael. He appeared about to explode.

Then his eyes quivered with water. His defiance had given way. "I just want everything back to normal."

"Yes," said Fehime. "Have you more questions?"

The rest of them, sympathising with Rafael, came to his rescue.

"Just three."

"Come on, then." It was Yunus. The group was ganging up, encouraged by some collective bravado.

Rafael's eyes had cleared, his jaw set; the defiance, bolstered by his friends, was returning.

"Was Peter having an affair with Meryem?"

"Yes," snapped Fehime, aggressively.

Reupke stared at her. "Okay," he said, drawing out the word, before looking at the others.

"Next question," said Habip eventually.

"Yes," said Reupke, but he wasn't ready to ask it. "Bear with me for a moment." He referred to his notepad. This time there would be no theatrics. That had been done. When he began, he spoke measuredly, almost quietly to achieve the required stillness. "The Turkish police believe that Meryem killed Peter." Dannaks wasn't sure this was true. "My colleague and I have spoken to a lot of people who all claim that she could never have done such a thing." Reupke didn't wait for anyone to speak. "The question is: why has she disappeared?" If the previous silence was gaping, then this one was awesome. No one had an answer. Even Habip was stumped. "If she didn't do it, why doesn't she come forward?" Fehime was looking at the floor. Rafael was a picture of hostility. The others seemed self-absorbed. Some were looking at Reupke, most looked elsewhere. "With so many police about, now is the time to come forward." He waited a moment. When he spoke he looked directly at Rafael. "The sooner that happens the sooner we may get back to normal here."

"How do you know she's not dead?" asked Fabio.

Reupke was surprised by the question, but recovered quickly. "I think the police would have found her by now." Nobody said anything. But Reupke was still considering the question. "I can't believe the killer kidnapped her. How would he get her out of the hotel?"

"He could have bundled her into a car," said Yunus.

"Possible, but I think front gate security would have seen something."

"Maybe she went willingly?" said Habip.

"Why?"

Habip shrugged.

"I haven't got time for this," said Fehime, looking to the others.

"Yes, you've had your last question," agreed Habip.

"No, I haven't." He left them no time to protest. "Did any of you know of Peter's past?"

They shook their heads.

"I meant did any of you suspect?"

Again negativity was displayed in gesture.

"You must have seen his tattoos?"

Habip looked at his troupe to confirm the consensus. "I think you've got your answer. But ... I did see his tattoos once. I didn't make anything of it."

"Me too," Fabio admitted.

No one else spoke.

"That it?" asked Habip.

Reupke smiled wearily and looked at Dannaks who nodded. "Okay," said Reupke, snapping his notepad closed.

Habip jumped down and his movement mobilised everybody.

Reupke and Dannaks got up and stood as if they were about to confer notes. Fehime approached them. "Sorry, but it's getting late and I need to get back to my room. I've got Salsa aerobic at three, if you're interested."

"Sorry, that's not my thing," said Reupke.

Dannaks simply looked horrified.

"What do you think?" asked Reupke.

They were sitting on stools at the bar. Other than the barman there was no one in the vicinity. But the Siesta was coming to an end. People were wearily returning to their lounges. The morning sun had taken it out of them and rendered movement laborious or they were in an after lunch slump or dopey after a short nap. Even the children were subdued.

Dannaks's thighs ached. He'd had trouble getting off the chair when they left the stage. His buttocks were sore too. But of course it was his calves and ankles that were visibly scratched and raw.

Their drinks were too hot. Reupke had chosen green tea and Dannaks a cappuccino.

Two waiters were erecting a long trellis table at the end of the plaza nearest the amphitheatre. A third was wheeling a trolley of rattling tea plates, cups, saucers, cutlery and packets of paper serviettes.

"They didn't verbally give us anything."

True, on the surface the detectives had received nothing.

"It was good that they were tired," Dannaks continued. "They were on guard, but lacked the energy."

Dannaks and Reupke had agreed that one of them should ask the questions and take notes. Note taking would give the speaker time. The other was to watch and take notes. Because Dannaks had recently done the body language and interview technique workshop they had agreed that he observe.

"I think you'll agree that Rafael was pretty edgy," said Reupke, impatient to get down to business.

"Yes. But maybe you could put that down to his experience in custody. Maybe he wasn't so much interviewed as interrogated."

Reupke nodded.

A large white tablecloth was draped over the table. The contents of the trolley were being placed at one end of the table.

"He was the first on the scene," said Dannaks. "And when you asked about Peter's book I got the impression he was holding something back." He waited a moment. "But I found Fehime more interesting."

"Oh yeah."

"Professionally," said Dannaks, forcing away the smile Reupke had induced. "I'm old enough to be her father."

"Go on."

"She just seemed closed off."

"Hiding in the group?"

"Yes."

"Anyone else?"

"I wasn't sure about Ercan–"

"The golf man?"

"Yeah. All the signals that he was lying were there, but that could just be him." The workshop instructor had reiterated more than once that body language was not an exact science. You had to take the signs in context and cross-reference them with others. The expressions and postures had to be taken in clusters. And then the person could be self conscious about a blemish and habitually hide the spot. They could have an itch to scratch, a headache or anything that could influence their posture or facial expression.

"What about Habip?"

Dannaks raised his eyebrows. "Well, if he was hiding something he's a pretty cool character."

Reupke again nodded.

"You think he was?" asked Dannaks unable to keep the surprise out of his voice.

"I don't know. It's always best to keep an open mind." He picked up his cup of tea and blew across the surface. He sipped and winced. "Anyone else?"

"Not really."

They were silent for a moment.

"I don't think they knew about the book," said Dannaks. "I think what I mean is: I don't think the Turkish police mentioned it."

"I'd have thought they'd have asked Rafael. They had him for two days."

"Maybe."

"The killer probably took it."

They fell silent.

"I thought you did well," said Dannaks.

"Thanks."

Yes, the points they'd agreed needed addressing had been covered. Most importantly two messages had gone out. The first was that they, the detectives, knew of the existence of Peter's book and they were looking for it. The second was that if Meryem could be reached then she should be made to realise that now was the safest time to turn herself in.

"I suppose if it wasn't Meryem it could have been any one of the staff," said Dannaks.

"Or all of them," Reupke smiled.

"Now who's been reading too much Agatha Christie?"

In answer Reupke raised his eyebrows.

"It'd be great if we could interview Rafael," said Dannaks.

"I don't think that's going to happen."

"There's no harm in asking."

Reupke and Dannaks drank.

At ten to three sedate announcements were made over the speakers. They were told that coffee and cake would be available. The girls would be waiting for the children at the children's club; Fabio was waiting for them at the beach for volleyball, down at the aerobic area Fehime would be taking salsa aerobic (pronounced eye-robe-ic). Here at the poolside would be a game with a prize to win. And at four there would be water polo with Rafael.

Crewmembers were going round the loungers gathering people for the poolside game. The game was played in two lines of pairs. By turns each couple had to throw and catch a water-filled balloon. After each round everyone took one step backwards. You were out if the balloon burst. The detectives were also asked, but they declined.

"I'll go to the main gate and talk to security. You may not make it," Reupke quipped. "I'll check out the kidnapping idea. I know it's unlikely, but we'd better get it crossed off."

"Have a look at the service entrance too."

"It was on my list."

"I'll wander over to the children's club."

Reupke looked at his watch. "We'll meet back here at four thirty."

Dannaks agreed checking his own watch. He had just over an hour.

Reupke downed the remains of his tea and sprung from his stool. Dannaks, who had finished his cappuccino some time ago, stepped down.

Three children were splashing and yelling in the water. Two were balancing on the dolphin, the third was either trying to push them or knock them off. Dannaks wasn't sure.

Reupke marched off but Dannaks waited a moment to watch the children. The third child was pushing, but the two riders were still trying to rectify their precarious positions and in seconds they were in the water.

Dannaks smiled. He turned on a heel and walked across the plaza in the direction of the toilets.

15:22

At the toilets he avoided a boy coming out of the men's. "Sorry, emergency," said the woman with him, nodding to the women's entrance. In front of it was a yellow plastic sign, hinged at the top and standing like an inverted V. Bold black lettering declared in English, German and Turkish: "Stop. Cleaning in progress. Apologies for any inconvenience." The boy had his head tipped back and the woman, presumably his mother, was walking with him holding a small wad of scarlet-sodden toilet paper at his nose. He had a mop of wild hair like straw and Dannaks thought that Peter might have looked like him as a boy. His parents had brought him to such a place on the so-called Turkish Riviera. Had happy memories made him choose to return? The guests were right: it was a strange choice for an ex-neo-Nazi. And yet, Volker Herbst, a bastion of right-wing ideals, had a holiday home here.

A man was at a basin washing his hands. By the time Dannaks had finished his toilet the man was gone.

After washing and drying his hands, he caught his image in the mirror. He stopped and looked himself full in the face and then smiled. He held the smile until melancholy clouded his eyes. Just before his smile grew diabolical, like the hotel manager's when they arrived, he turned away.

So much for positive thinking.

He left the toilet and headed past the plaza bar towards the beach.

The small pool was relatively quiet. The redhead with the gorgeous bewitching eyes was bathing her baby. The larger pool behind it with the slides was more popular.

Only one tennis court was occupied. Dannaks surmised that heat stopped play. Running across the grassy area to his left was a feral child gang, painted and stripped to the waist, brandishing sticks, straight from the pages of Lord of the Flies.

The small sandy playground, with the waist high wooden fence defining its perimeter, behind the children's club was also empty. Apart from the hardwearing canopy stretched over the sandpit the apparatus was exposed to the blaze of the sun. He could imagine the swings, slide, climbing frame that was a rope tepee and some weathered wooden horses on springs burnt to the touch.

Further to the right the thud of music from the salsa session couldn't compete with the lulling regularity of the sound of the sea. An occasional yelp or shout of a child reach his ears, only to rapidly sink under the relentless crash.

He couldn't taste salt but the air seemed heavy with it.

The children's club was a proper concrete house with a ground and first floor. The lower half of the beige walls was covered in a bright mural done by children: apart from the typical beach scene there were horses, cars, planes, butterflies, dinosaurs, people and houses. Above the door was a huge rainbow upon which sat a galleon made out of a bowl of fruit. Above this were the words: 'Captain Fruit's Children's Club'. Strange that the words should be in English when the clientele was predominantly German. Oh, he'd heard some French spoken, even some English, but the place was ninety-eight percent German.

Dannaks opened the door situated at the side of the building with respect to the sea. It was surprisingly heavy and he struggled. No small kid was going to escape the building unassisted. The door, dampened by a high elbowed hinge, closed with a majesty that didn't befit its plainness. Contrasting the languid pulse of activity at the beach and the brashness of the building's outer artwork, inside was like a mausoleum.

He had expected mayhem and stood for a moment in the empty corridor. He heard nothing other than the sounds outside. To his right was the outer wall of the building. At the far end was a door, doubtlessly opening out onto the playground. To his left was a door with a large glass panel. The wall continued and was broken by a similar door before reaching an opening for the stairway to the upper floor. Both walls of this corridor from waist level to the ceiling were plastered with children's pictures.

There was a cork pin board on the wall nearest him opposite the door. Part of it carried the same photographs of the crew he had seen at reception. He recognised Necla, Hülya, Tanya and Meryem. He saw two extra faces that had not been present at the after-rehearsal chat and made a note to ask about them. Captain Fruit presented his list of golden rules of behaviour. But sharing most of the board with photographs were three weekly timetables, one for each age group, broken down into daily events. Under the umbrella of Captain Fruit the three groups were cherries for children aged two to seven, oranges for the eight to twelve year olds and bananas for the thirteen to seventeens. Each group had a motif. The red cherry resembled a heart with a short stem and the orange was orange with a green dot. Only the banana gave Dannaks cause to wonder whether some Andy Warhol or Velvet Underground copyright had been infringed.

He looked through the door's glass panel into the room. He saw small wooden chairs lining long clean-swept bench-like tables. The shelves were bursting with tattered boxes of games and puzzles, picture books in various states of disrepair, stacks of plain and coloured paper, newspapers, pots, brushes and paints.

He tried the door. It was locked. He then turned and began walking towards the opening for the stairs. The second room was also empty with a similar interior: grouped chaos. He didn't try the door.

Before he reached the stairs a picture caught his eye and he stopped to look at it.

Whereas a lot of the crude paintings and drawings depicted beach scenes with lots of suns, rainbows, hearts, boats, pirates, etc. this one was of a solitary figure. With its irregular head, outsized and as big as the squarish body, twig arms and legs, big eyes and rather perfunctory lines for nose and mouth, it looked like a man. This was not what made it stand out. What had caught Dannaks eye was the red wax crayon. The man was scarlet. The body had been scribbled full and the slanted strokes suggested motion. This was probably unintentional. But Dannaks was reminded of his childhood and seeing pictures of DC comics' The Flash.

He scanned the other pictures, turning to check the opposite wall too. Like this one they all carried the child's name, age and the date, sometimes written by an adult. There was nothing like this picture. This was the only fiery red man.

Timi, 4 ½. And the date was the day after the killing.

15:31

He heard the noise before he was half way up the stairs. It was the excited babble of children. Like the ground floor this level offered two rooms. The first was empty, but the second was full of activity. A picture of an orange was pinned above the glass panel of the door.

Two goblins saw him through the glass and Necla looked over. She was directing the dozen or so nine to thirteen year olds in some kind of play. They were all in costume.

Dannaks was obliged to open the door. He stepped in and Necla strode over after giving the children an order.

She seemed totally on top of the situation.

"Hallo," she said. "Can I help?"

"Actually I was just passing through," he said. It was a ridiculous statement and he lowered his voice. "I wanted to see Meryem's workplace."

She nodded.

"Stop it, Bernd," she said to a boy who was getting over-enthusiastic with his swashbuckling. An unarmed boy was barely dodging the prods of his sword.

Necla wasn't the wilting novice of rehearsals. Her persona had taken a one hundred and eighty degree turn.

"I saw the crew photographs downstairs. I didn't recognise two of them."

"Oh, they come next week, when the number of children increases."

He smiled.

"One more question before I give you back to the wolves."

"They're not so bad. Cherries are harder to handle. We take them on in pairs."

He needed a moment to realise that she was talking about the two to seven year olds.

"There's a picture of a red man in the corridor downstairs. Have you seen it?"

"Yes."

"Do you know anything about it?"

"No. It was before my time. They stay up for about a month. I don't know how old that one is."

"It's over a week old from Timi, aged four and a half. So he'd be a cherry, right?"

"Yes, Tanya's group–"

"Necla–" It was a young girl dressed as a fairy. Her wand was held threateningly. "Are you going to be much longer?"

Necla looked at Dannaks.

"I'd better go before she turns me into a frog," he said.

"Tanya's on the beach collecting sand and shells with her lot."

"Thanks."

"But as I understand it you should be talking to Fehime. She was Meryem's best friend.

Dannaks nodded.

Before closing the door behind him the noise increased, becoming dreadful, before he heard Necla's raised voice dampen them.

He went back and took another look at Timi's picture.

Deciding to look for Tanya he looked at his watch as he left the building. He had only partly looked up as he turned towards the beach when a young teenager, perhaps fourteen, with attitude and dyed black hair with purple streaks, almost bumped into him. Whereas he had no time to apologise, she apparently had no intention of doing so. His smile did not affect her indifferent scowl.

The young punk marched off towards the hotel and Dannaks shook his head in dismay.

"That could have been a colourful carambolage," said a woman the girl passed.

Although he recognised her, he couldn't place her.

"Nordic walking," she said.

"Yes." It was Sympathy. "Yes, of course, sorry."

She nodded to the receding figure behind her. "Now, I wonder why she's not out with the bananas?"

She was being facetious, but Dannaks could only smile.

"Maybe if they were called the lemons she'd join," she continued. "Her sour expression would be an instant hit."

He knew he had to contribute or he would be finished.

"They're probably called bananas because that's how they go at that age."

Her laugh was delicious and he forced a chuckle.

"On your way to the beach?" she asked.

"Er, yes. Yes, I was."

They turned and walked towards the sea together.

"A walk at this time of day is wonderful," she said. "The sun isn't as fierce. It also keeps me away from the afternoon coffee and cakes: a terrible German custom."

"It doesn't look as though you have a problem."

"You're very kind."

"No, really," he blurted.

She blushed and he felt foolish.

"Sorry, I'm not very good at this." They were near the showers removing their sandals before stepping onto the sand. "Name's Dannaks."

He knew she would think him dour for not offering his first name and glancing at her he quickly explained. "I prefer the use of my surname."

"Is your first name that bad?"

"No. And it's not Adolf."

She waited a tick for him to continue. When he didn't she offered her hand.

"Katja."

Dannaks shook her hand, careful not to exert any more pressure than her. As he did he looked her full in the face. She reciprocated.

"But I don't think I can call you Dannaks. I think I shall have to call you Dee," she said.

"Then I'll call you Kay."

Her approval was in her smile.

To Dannaks she was beautiful. Her thick-framed glasses seemed to emphasise the fullness of her lips. Her eyes weren't noticeably magnified by the lenses. Oh, the hairlines at the edges of her mouth and those about her eyes belied her age. But the skin at her cheeks was taut. And in her overwhelming smile there was youthfulness, optimism, which vanquished his melancholy. He couldn't help himself and found himself brightening.

The little jewellery that she wore was practical. Her blonde hair was pinned up in a kind of controlled storm. Two wisps fell before her exposed ears. Small triangular silver earrings hugged her lobes. For a moment the boy in him considered whether they were isosceles or equilateral triangles. Added to this were her heart-shaped face, slightly angular cheekbones, almond almost catlike eyes and straight, hard-looking nose. He was drawn to the delicious blemish in the overall symmetry of her appearance. Just below her left eye was a brown mole the size of a nail head, which he would call a beauty spot.

She was wearing a bikini top under a see-through white shirt knotted above the navel. Her skirt was pastel blue and when the light shone through he could see the silhouette of her legs up to what was presumably her bikini bottom.

Strangely enough, he couldn't tell whether her eyes were brown or green.

Before the connection became embarrassing they disengaged and looked to the sea. Then they began walking again, heading in the same direction they'd taken that morning.

He hadn't seen Tanya along the beach behind them. That didn't mean she wasn't there. In addition to the multitude of people there were pedal boats, catamarans and, further away, an anchored yellow and white paragliding chute bulged and rocked in the breeze. He couldn't see Tanya in front of them either. There was too much activity.

Two volleyball games were in progress to their left.

Katja swelled as she took a deep breath. "Don't you just love travelling?"

"I could get used to it."

"But you've been to Africa."

For a split-second he wondered why she would think such a thing; then he remembered his Kenya T-shirt. He wouldn't be able to contribute much to a conversation about travelling. So at the risk of alienating himself he decided to be truthful.

"The shirt's a present from my parents."

"Oh."

"I'm a late starter, I'm afraid." Then he had the perfect answer. "I don't go on holiday much because I don't like travelling alone." There, he had told her he was available. What a coup! He was pleased with himself. But then, she could think him a stuffy hermit. That wouldn't do. "Not that I don't like my own company." Was this true?

"It's no big deal travelling alone," she said. "At these kinds of places you meet lots of people." Yet, as far as he could tell, she wasn't with anybody. Maybe behind the facade there sat a lonely person?

"I've never tried," he admitted. "I tend to work a lot."

"A workaholic, eh?"

"Guilty."

"Are you working now?"

"If you have something to say about last week, then yes."

She smiled. "I'm afraid I don't know anything."

"Good."

He was surprised by her lack of inquisitiveness. Then, as if she could read his thoughts, she said: "I'm sure I can't add anything to what you already know." As an afterthought she added: "Things have tightened up. The hawkers have disappeared. They were always going up and down here with silks and jewellery and fruit and drinks. It's been hard to relax. I know it's almost spoilt a lot of people's holidays."

They were now parallel to the neighbouring hotel. The loungers were four rows deep and all of them were taken. Nearly everyone was lying down. A man was sitting on one whilst two small giggling girls buried his feet.

There were other walkers some of whom walked at the edge of the sea, allowing the water to rush over their feet. Two boys and a naked – except for a knotted white handkerchief on her head – much younger girl were vainly trying to hold up a wall of sand against the reach of the sea. The boys gave frantic orders as the wall was breached and the girl screamed with excitement. About five people had braved the water. Their heads and sometimes shoulders riding the rise and fall.

A small boy struggling with the weight of a plastic bucket of slopping water cut across their path and they were forced to stop. They watched him reach an older boy who was digging a hole.

"Nothing like a relaxing beach walk," she said ironically.

A Frisbee flew by and although it was not near Dannaks made to duck. "No," he agreed. "Absolutely nothing like a relaxing beach walk. More of an assault course."

She laughed. And his laugh was easier and no longer forced.

A jogger in shorts, T-shirt, headphones and baseball cap was coming towards them.

"How did you enjoy the Nordic walk?" she asked.

"I didn't get very far. And to be honest I'm not really the sporty type."

"Hey, it's holiday. I try to do something once a day. You can overdo it."

It was on his tongue to rattle off: "*Sport ist Mord.* (Sport is murder.)" But he'd risked alienating her admitting his lack of travel. There was a fine line between being honest and appearing downright perverse. Also in the light of why he was there, jesting about murder could hint at callousness. A real faux pas.

A group of holidaymakers in life jackets was tugging a banana boat towards the water. A Turk was wading out to the attached speedboat that rocked on the sea.

A mother crossed their path, hurrying to a crying child sitting in the sand rubbing its eyes. A small guilty-looking boy stood nearby braced for a good telling off.

"Have you children?" Katja asked. She wore a simple gold wedding band on her right ring finger. (Germans wore their wedding rings on their right hand.) Was she not really single? Did it mean she still held a candle to her husband and harboured hopes of getting back together? Or was it for protection to warn off unwanted suitors? Had she seen him looking?

"Er, no. No."

"I have two: a boy and a girl. They're grown up now. And both have moved out. Eighteen and twenty." Pause. "I'm divorced," she added. At their age singles were either widowed, divorced, separated or, like him none of these and a little odd.

"You know the reason for so many divorces?" he asked.

"No."

"Marriage."

This time her laughter was uncertain. In one way this was positive. She was relaxed enough with him to be herself. Nonetheless he wondered whether he'd gone too far.

Dannaks saw Tanya closer to the sea coming towards them. Half a dozen small children surrounded her. There were other children nearby. Yunus, from lighting or sound, Dannaks couldn't remember, also had a small following. Two mothers and a father appeared to be helping out. In all there were at least fifteen children.

"Sorry, I have to speak to someone. I won't be a minute."

"Never off duty, eh?"

He smiled wearily.

"I'm surprised you haven't asked me what I know about the, er,–"

"Incident?" She nodded. "Do you know anything?"

"No," she grinned. "Now you're going to have to ask me where I was at the time of the incident."

He mockingly took out his notepad and pen. "And where were you?"

"At at the show with about ninety-nine point nine percent of the hotel."

He pretended to write. "Okay Kay. I don't want you to leave this beach." He then smiled and marched off towards the group. She turned to look at the sea.

Tanya looked up as he approached. "You're too late to help." She was carrying a plastic bag of sand and shells. Some of the children held on to their favourite shells, comparing them with each other, extolling their beauty or trying to show them to Tanya. "We're on our way back." She looked down at a tiny wisp of a girl. "Yes, it's beautiful Laura."

"I wanted to ask you about a picture at the children's club," he said, raising and lowering his voice with the rhythm of the sea.

"Yes."

"Tanya, Tanya, look at this one."

"Yes, it's very beautiful Tomas. We've got enough now. And we have to get back." She clapped her hands and raised her voice. "Children, children, listen to me." She looked about, catching Yunus's and the accompanying parents' eyes. "It's after four. We won't have time for the pictures if we don't get back soon. So that's enough collecting." To Dannaks: "You were saying?"

"There's a picture of a red man in the corridor. Do you know it?"

"Of course. It's Timi's." Dannaks nodded for her to go on. He left last week.

"It's an unusual picture. Did he say anything about it?"

"He called him Beelzebub."

"The devil?"

"Who's the devil?" asked Tomas.

"I'll tell you later," said Tanya.

"Anything else?" asked Dannaks, looking back to check Katja's position, for they had passed her. She was still waiting for him.

"He said he saw him when he was hiding in a game of hide and seek. I spoke to his parents and they said he fantasised a lot."

"Where was he hiding?"

"I don't know."

"Did you tell the police?"

Tanya stopped as if she had suddenly realised that this wasn't idle talk and that there could be consequences.

"No. His parents forbade it. They wanted the picture down, but Timi yelled and screamed."

"Why did the parents stop you talking?"

"They didn't want to get involved, I suppose."

Dannaks nodded, his posture keeping her from walking on.

"Do you remember their surname?"

"No, sorry."

A girl was poking the plastic bag with her finger. "I want that one."

"No, that's mine."

"You've got yours in your hand."

"That's another one."

"Stop it." She looked at Dannaks. "I have to get back." She made to move away.

"Yes. I can see you've got your hands full."

"Normally we have double this lot. A lot of the parents are keeping their children with them. The numbers are slowly creeping up again." Then as an afterthought she said: "I might be able to find Timi's surname."

"That would be great."

The little girl, awkwardly keeping pace with Tanya, was trying to locate her shell in the swaying bag.

"We have registration sheets for the children left in our care. The parents have to sign and give us their room number."

"I can get the rest from reception."

"I'll look for you."

"Thanks."

Dannaks exchanged nods with Yunus before backing away.

He looked at his watch as he approached Katja. It was almost a quarter past four.

"I've just noticed your legs," she said when he was in front of her. He looked down. The red blotches on his calves were ravaged with scratch marks. He'd probably done more damage than the mosquitoes.

"I have a cream you can use."

"That's okay."

"No. Really. It's very soothing and it's a repellent too."

"Okay. Thanks." He smiled, but he felt awkward. "Look, I'm, er, sorry." He watched her face. "I've made you wait. But I've only just seen what time it is – time flies when you're enjoying yourself – and I arranged to meet my partner in fifteen minutes." Partner may not be the best description. Could she think he was with a woman? "He's, er, maybe waiting already."

"If I didn't know better I could think you don't like walking. This morning you didn't get very far and now you're barely passed the neighbouring hotel."

"No, I do like walking," he insisted. "I didn't know I–"

"Perhaps you don't like my company?"

Her smile gave her away. "You're teasing me."

Raised eyes added to her smile.

Dannaks shook his head. He knew he had to take the initiative. "You can give me the cream at dinner."

She smiled and nodded.

He was bordering on an unaccustomed state of rapture and could hardly think, let alone speak. "When?" he asked.

"Seven?"

"Great. Er, at the restaurant?"

"They open at seven and it's always such a free for all. I prefer to eat a little later. What about the pool bar?"

"Yes, yes. Good idea."

He wanted to kiss her. She was unsure about the parting too and held out her hand which he limply shook.

"See you later, then. Dee."

"I'm looking forward to it. Kay."

16:19

Dannaks stood and looked out to sea for a while. Somebody was paragliding. Then he followed the laden banana boat. The few at the tail end were continually lifted from their seats. Their screams came as regularly as the crash of the sea. A man was following its progress through a pair of binoculars.

When Dannaks looked for Katja he was amazed how far away she was and only picked her out from the others by her clothes. He suppressed an urge to ask to borrow the man's binoculars and started walking.

"Come on; let's wash you in the sea." A mother had her reluctant son by the arm and was marching him towards the water. He was covered up to the neck in sand.

"But it's cold, mum."

"You don't have to go right in."

As he neared the hotel he noticed a girl staring at him. She was expecting to be recognised and after a moment he did recognised her. It was Off-Limits in a bikini. Without her T-shirt he hardly recognised her. He smiled and she made her way towards the rows of sunbathers. He projected her direction and spotted her two friends, one of whom he remembered was called Nadine, lying on loungers. They were topless, anonymised by sunglasses and headphones and with their arms at their sides looked completely lifeless: dead to the world.

He stopped near the showers, where the paved area of the hotel began and sat on a small wall to dust off his feet and put on his sandals.

Off-limits had removed her bikini top and joined her friends.

A father and daughter were sitting on the sand. Using a plastic shovel they were taking turns at cutting away an ever-precarious tower of sand made from an upturned bucket. There was a twig like a flag stuck in the top. They cut downwards, the little girl ever so careful now, slicing wafers. The father was more daring. He took chunks as close to the twig as he could. Then, probably on purpose, he overdid it and a good portion of the tower broke away, the twig sliding on a stream of sand. The girl yelped with delight. "Winner. Winner."

Dannaks smiled and got to his feet.

16:27

When he arrived at the plaza Reupke was nowhere to be seen. There were a lot of people sitting at the tables. An elderly woman was at the long table covered in a white linen tablecloth. In addition to the cutlery and crockery including a collection of small tea pots, the table was now laden with oversized plates of cakes and biscuits, two bowls of whipped cream, a large copper tea urn and a battery of coffee flasks.

The two chess players had taken up position. Two bright-yellow half-drunk glasses of beer stood next to the board. Dannaks wondered whether they'd positioned themselves for the show some five hours away. Then again, if yesterday was anything to go by, they wouldn't watch the show.

Some children were playing darts with one of the crew.

Rafael was standing at the side of the pool, a whistle in his mouth, refereeing a polo match. There was much splashing and shouting. But the energy was confined to the pool. For the shadows were growing longer and here at the plaza there was a strange calm: a real feeling of sedate afternoon tea and biscuits. An exhausting day lying about was coming to a merciful end. It was time to wind down.

Dannaks wasn't really hungry. Coffee and cake was something in which he, as a bachelor living alone, rarely participated. His parents made a ritual of bringing the family together some Sunday afternoons. As far as he knew, now, even though they lived alone, they still had coffee and cake on Sunday afternoons. In fact he thought that, having retired, they'd extended the tradition to almost every day. Or maybe every day was a Sunday.

But Dannaks didn't want to stand around and occupying one of the few empty tables empty handed didn't appeal.

So he made a beeline for the table and poured himself a coffee. The cakes were covered, either under see-through plastic lids or cellophane. Numerous flies and three or four wasps hovered and foraged for crumbs.

He had a look at everything before taking two Turkish biscuits. They were labelled as fig-biscuits. The cakes, coconut, apple, quark, chocolate and some gaudy Turkish creations looked inviting but rather heavy.

He went to an unoccupied table, nodding a greeting to the two elderly couples at a neighbouring one. He only momentarily wondered about Reupke's whereabouts for his thoughts were on Katja. He felt comfortable, yes, maybe happy, and he savoured the moment.

His dark self rose to goad him. What if Katja wasn't truly interested in him? What if she was only interested in details of the murder? But he was too buoyant for such musings and he laughed it off. So what? He would enjoy the acquaintance. If nothing came of it, then he would have lost nothing.

A Turkish-looking man sat alone at a table. The bulky folded newspaper on his table next to his espresso coffee cup attracted Dannaks.

He nodded to Habip and Fabio who were sitting at a table talking to a couple. He hoped they wouldn't come over. He was quite content to be alone.

He was almost finished when he noticed Fehime at the laden table. On her back was her rucksack; a towel hanging from the back of her neck was draped over her shoulders like a loose scarf. She held a plate and a litre bottle of water. She had to find space on the table to put the plate down to place a piece of cake on it. Then she had difficulty with the cellophane and had to place the bottle on the table too.

Dannaks looked at his watch. It was ten to five. Where was Reupke? Maybe he was gallivanting with Dagmar?

Fehime had finished collecting cake and was walking off. He had hoped she would sit down. He wanted to talk to her. But she was leaving. He looked about. Reupke was nowhere to be seen.

Dannaks got up and went after her. He saw her nod to a guest and was relieved when she didn't stop. He wanted their meeting to appear like a coincidence and he couldn't stall by dropping down to tie his shoelaces.

He kept his distance as they passed through reception. Again she greeted guests and staff, but didn't stop. Only when she was making her way up the path towards the accommodation did he increase his pace. When he was close enough he called out to her.

"Fehime." She turned on a step. "Hallo."

"Hallo." She smiled, but she was not pleased. She glanced beyond him and he turned to see the man with the bulky newspaper stop to light a cigarette.

"Going back to your apartment?" he asked when he was almost alongside her.

"Yes."

"I'm going that way too. I'm in Peter's old apartment." He couldn't tell her he didn't have a key. "Let me give you a hand."

"I'm doing fine."

"We're going the same way and I've got nothing." Her hands were full. Other than her training shoes he couldn't think what she had in her bulky rucksack. Whatever it was left no room for the bottle of water.

She kept the plate of cakes and handed him the bottle of water.

"You've got an appetite," he said. The plate carried three slices of cake: apple, quark and coconut.

"I burn so many calories I have to put some back."

Dannaks nodded and they walked in silence for a few steps. Two gardeners, a grizzled older man and a young lad were crouched in the ground off the path and tending the edges of the big plants. They were in full one-piece green overalls. In this heat these had to be described as boiler suits.

"Sometimes I want privacy," she said. "I like to eat in my room."

"I can understand that. You don't share, then?"

"No."

He waited a moment before speaking. "Actually, if you don't mind I'd like to ask you something."

He waited but she didn't answer and he glanced at her for a gesture.

"You were Meryem's best friend, I believe."

"Who told you that?"

Dannaks didn't answer.

"Rafael was right. I spoke to Turgut and he said that you were not here to investigate."

"I'm not investigating," said Dannaks. Rafael was understandably fed up with being asked questions. And undoubtedly they'd all been questioned. But Fehime shouldn't be that bothered. Either she had something to hide or she harboured a connection to Rafael that was stronger than sympathy. "I can understand you're fed up, but if you've got nothing to hide you—"

"Of course I've got nothing to hide. None of us have. We were all on stage in front of hundreds of guests when it happened."

"How do you know when it happened?"

"The police asked about our whereabouts between nine and midnight."

"Was anybody other than Meryem and Peter not at the theatre?"

"The police know all this."

"I'm afraid we've not been told. Sorry."

"Yes," she said. "Ercan. He wasn't feeling well."

The golf instructor was also on Dannaks's list of people to question again.

"This is your place," she said, nodding to the building on their left. "I can take it from here."

"A few extra steps won't kill me."

"It's not far. I can–"

"This is the only sport I get."

She looked at him. He saw a flash of frustration. Then she gave up with a smile. She had aimed for a comically quizzical smile, but her frustration had put her sights askew and she missed the mark. She knew this and before Dannaks's smile became questioning she snapped her head away and continued up the path.

He stood for a moment before stepping after her. When he was alongside her she attempted levity.

"I love this time of day. Sport is over and it's kind of peaceful. Especially up here. I love the smell of pine."

Dannaks nodded, although he couldn't smell anything.

"I – I'm sorry if you thought I was rude just now. This whole thing has got us strung out. Even without it on a good day I only get six hours sleep." Dannaks recalled the old boy's remark about them all being *wired*.

At a crossroads they turned right.

"I thought you'd all be housed together."

"No. We're quite spread out."

"Do all of you live on site?"

"All of the animation team have rooms." He felt that she now wanted to be helpful. "A few cooks and management people live here too. But most commute." Every room allocated to a member of staff was an obvious loss in revenue.

She made for the second house on the left.

They stopped. She put the plate carefully on the uneven parapet. Then she swung off her rucksack dropping it at the foot of the door with a thump. Dannaks stood behind her. She cleared her throat as she crouched and unzipped a side-pocket. Retrieving her keys, but still bent over her rucksack, she raised her voice slightly and said: "I can manage now."

She stood and gazed at him. "I can't invite you in. The place is a mess. You can put the bottle there." She waved to the plate of cakes. Dannaks nodded and carefully balanced the bottle on the uneven stonework.

Fehime turned to the door but dropped her keys. They jingled loudly and she cursed in Turkish.

"See you later, then," said Dannaks backing away.

"Yes, thanks." She had her keys and was picking out the right one.

Dannaks turned and walked away slowly. When he heard her door open he glanced back. She'd only opened it a crack and was bent over picking up her rucksack. As she rose he knew she would turn to pick up the plate from the wall and he whipped his gaze away.

Through the slight gap of the open door he'd seen past her into the room. Hers was identical to Peter's. He couldn't tell whether it was untidy. All he'd really seen was the chair at the cupboard, looking into the room.

As he walked on, he raked his mind for an excuse to return and knock on her door. But he couldn't think of anything.

When he reached their building he went to their door and knocked. There was a chance Reupke would be in. He knocked a second time, but heard nothing.

Deep in thought he walked back down to reception. On his way through he stopped at the unmanned golf desk. On it were a leather blotter, some leaflets, a standing photograph of Ercan and a ball-point pen attached to a clipboard with a sheet of paper divided into columns for names and times. At the wall behind the desk was a locked glass cabinet full of golfing attire and equipment sporting the logo of Azure Skies.

17:19

On his way to the plaza a woman smiled at him on the steps. Again, because she was out of context and in unaccustomed attire, he didn't immediately recognise her. She was dark-haired and very attractive. In complete contrast to Katja's taut skin hers was soft as if covering a layer of puppy fat.

"Hallo," she said.

"Hallo," he replied.

"He's waiting for you at the pool bar."

"Thanks," he answered. And just to show that he remembered her name he said: "Dagmar."

Reupke was perched on a stool at the bar upon which was a litre bottle of water like the one he had carried for Fehime. Reupke was not drinking. The long table had been stripped down to its tablecloth. Coffee and cake time ran only till five.

Dannaks was distracted by the commotion at the crew's shack. Habip, Fabio, Yunus and a fourth man were being boisterous and loud. This fourth man, also in a crewmember's shirt, was vigorously drying his hair with a towel. Their larking contrasted the relative calm of the area.

Except for two children in the far corner the pool was empty. Sole sunbathers, still too exhausted to move or with their head buried in a book, or clumps of two or three people, now in T-shirts, sitting huddled and quietly conversing, were separated by the many vacated loungers.

Reupke jumped down from his stool before Dannaks reached him. "Where have you been?"

"Ditto."

"I got held up."

"Yes, I just saw Dagmar."

"Ha, ha. I wasn't with her. After talking to security at the main gate, I went round to the service entrance and then on to the kitchens. That's where I got held up. What happened to you?"

"I waited until just before five and then helped Fehime carry some stuff to her room."

"Fehime again, eh?" Reupke nodded and smiled cunningly.

Dannaks opened his mouth to protest, but in the light of his acquaintance with Katja, he held himself back.

"Dagmar's a real catch. You're lucky."

"Changing the subject, eh? Well, there is no such thing as luck," he said quickly. "And if there is, you make it yourself." He gave Dannaks a moment to react. "You want a drink?"

"Not really."

"Let's go back to the room, then. I could do with a lie down and a long bath."

"I'd like to show you something first. It's–"

The noise of approaching voices, speaking excitedly like children, interrupted them.

Dannaks saw that the fourth member of the crew was Rafael. His hair hung down to his shoulders. But it was receding and thinning on top.

"Have you spoken to Rafael?" Reupke asked quickly.

"No."

When the four men were close enough and during the exchanging of nods and smiles Reupke singled Rafael out.

"Could we have a talk with you?"

He stopped. The others hesitated before moving on. "What do you mean: talk? Interview?"

"Yes."

He grew annoyed. "Look, I've spoken to my lawyer and he says I don't have to talk to you."

"Now, why did you speak to your lawyer?" Reupke feigned annoyance.

Dannaks was again drawn to the tattoo on his calf and then to the pristine condition of his training shoes. They were new. And Dannaks realised why.

"I'm sick of it, okay? I've said all I want to say. I thought I could get back to normal here. Now I'm not sure. Even some of the guests are looking at me strangely." His paranoia was most likely well founded. Quite a few of the guests held him in suspicion. Just because the Turkish police had cleared him, didn't mean he was innocent. The only consolation was that most guests were on a two week holiday and those around at the time of the killing had already left or would be gone within the next three or four days. "If you want to know anything, talk to the police."

Reupke held up his hands in a surrendering gesture. He opened his hands as if carrying a tray.

"You went into the room," said Dannaks. "And you took Peter's book, didn't you?"

Rafael glared at him before walking on.

After a moment Reupke said: "What made you ask that?"

"He was the first on the scene and he must have gone in. Haven't you seen his shoes? They're new. The police have his old ones."

Reupke considered this before nodding. "Come on, what do you want to show me?"

"How did he get wet? When I left here he was refereeing."

"Someone got hurt and Habip said he would referee. So, Rafael jumped in."

"This way," said Dannaks, leading him away from the bar. "I can see why he wears that rag."

"I can't. He should shave it all off instead."

Whatever, it put paid to the frail old lady's theory that he was a skinhead.

Tennis was continuing on at least two courts to their left. Five children were playing football on the expanse of harsh green to their right. Others were on the path, but walking towards them. The detectives appeared to be the only ones heading for the beach.

Reupke told him that he'd got held up talking to security and the kitchen. He said that the cooks started at 5:30 and the waiters shortly before 6:00. Breakfast tables were set after the previous evening's dinner. A skeleton staff manned the kitchens from about 4:00. One of these cooks had been in his room during the killing. Unfortunately he'd been wearing headphones and had neither seen nor heard anything. Very few of the staff lived on camp. Only some cooks, management, security and all of the animation team. Another cook said that he'd heard about all the taps running in the toilet. He found it spooky. Nothing of the sort had occurred since the killing.

The talk with main-gate security yielded little too. Guests were allowed on camp as guests of guests or, with special permission, staff. At the entrance he'd pondered a possible kidnapping: bundling Meryem into the boot of a car, for instance. Although not impossible the busyness made it extremely unlikely.

He had asked about the surveillance cameras, but the police had given the staff strict orders not to give such information away.

Dannaks tried the door of the Children's Club. It was locked.

"Damn," he said. Shielding his eyes with a hand pressed against the glass panel of the door he tried to locate the picture. He found it, but shadow all but suppressed its stark redness.

He turned to Reupke.

"You can just about see it, but it's not clear."

"What?" said Reupke, a hint of irritation in his voice.

"It's a picture of a red man done the day after the killing."

"Yeah," he said unimpressed.

"You have to see it. It's so different from the rest. It really stands out. A four and a half year old called Timi did it." Reupke's expression was turning from irritation to mockery. "I spoke to Tanya—"

"Dannaks. Is this all you've got? Maybe the kid couldn't get hold of any other colours and that's why his picture's red."

"No, Tanya said that he was playing hide and seek and saw the man on the night of the murder. He called him Beelzebub."

Reupke sighed. "He could have seen someone with terrible sunburn."

Dannaks was stunned. "It's possible, I suppose," he said deflated. "It might be worth tracing the family, though. They've left."

Reupke didn't disagree. But he didn't agree either. "Anything else while we're here?"

"No."

"Then let's get back."

17:51

There was a true sense of the lull before a storm. Two boys in the pool were being told to get out by their mother. At the bar the barman was alone drinking tea. Even the shopkeepers were outside sitting together at one of the plaza tables drinking, smoking, reading the paper, chatting. The chess players had disappeared.

At reception they nodded to the old lady who was sitting with a man of her age; the wheelchair was parked alongside their sofa. On the path between the accommodation buildings the two detectives were relatively alone. But from the buildings they heard televisions, showers and children. People were sitting on balconies and terraces, enjoying a semblance of solitude or, if luckily positioned, the last weakening rays of the sun.

The return to the room was uneventful and they found it without trouble.

All the way Dannaks thought of how he could break the news of Katja. His colleague would be a third wheel at the table. Naturally, the restaurant offered no chance of something like a romantic candle-lit dinner. There were no tables for two. And if breakfast and lunch were anything to go by it was – as Katja put it – a free for all. People were ravenous and queued impatiently. Having an aperitif and turning up later for dinner could thin the numbers and take the teeth out of that aggression.

He did hope they could sit together away from anyone they knew.

Under the door was a sheet of hotel paper. Reupke read it. "It's a fax. *Mordkommission* have approved the expenses."

"Good. We'll have to wait until we hear something from the police before going. Or do you think we can risk it."

"Herbst's place is twenty minutes away. Twenty minutes there, twenty minutes back, twenty minutes looking over the place, we'd be gone an hour. I think we could risk it. Squeeze it in somewhere."

"We could get up early."

Reupke nodded, but he didn't appear enthusiastic.

"I'm going to phone my girlfriend. You can use the bathroom first, if you like. I'd like to have a good soak."

Under the shower Dannaks heard the room telephone ring and then Reupke's voice.

After drying himself he stood in front of the mirror and smiled. This time his smile was genuine. More of his eyes were in it. Yes, he didn't look too bad or too old. Distinguished was the word. "You old goat," he said quietly to himself.

"All yours," he said entering the room in his underpants.

Reupke got up from lying on the bed. He looked pensive, almost worried.

"Who phoned?" Dannaks asked, opening the cupboard.

"Reception. They said the police would pick us up at eleven tomorrow to take us to the body."

"We'll just have to make sure we're back from Herbst's in time."

He looked at his choice of two T-shirts. He thought he could wear the shirt he had travelled in, but the collar wasn't up to it. He had two other collared shirts, both of which he wanted to wear on official occasions: one tomorrow when inspecting the body and the other for the return trip. So he was left with two T-shirts. He could take Hong Kong in bamboo sticks or Las Vegas in brightly coloured roulette chips. Neither inspired. He decided upon Hong Kong. It wasn't as loud.

"I fancy a glass of wine," said Dannaks going to the mini bar. He'd tell Reupke of Katja after a drink. "You want one?"

"That's a damned good idea. I'll have beer, though. It'll go well with my soak."

Dannaks smiled. "It's a tough life." He opened the mini-bar, ignored the bottle of bubbly and picked out a can of beer and a small bottle of white wine.

Reupke took the can from him.

"Look, er, Dannaks," Reupke began, stopping under the ventilator. "This is a bit awkward. I've arranged to have dinner with Dagmar and three might – Why are you smiling?"

"Because I'm meeting somebody too–"

"What? When?" Reupke was flabbergasted.

"Seven at the pool bar."

"I'm meeting Dagmar there too."

"At seven?"

"Yes. Who're you meeting?" Reupke sat on the end of the bed, placing the can on the floor between his feet.

"Katja. I met her at the beach."

"Wow," he said. "I'm speechless. I had you pegged as one of those miserable types."

"Dead wood, you mean?"

"Yes. But you're just a dark horse. So, where's she from?"

"I don't know."

Reupke nodded. "Well, if you have someone back in Hamburg you could be in trouble." He stood up. "Dagmar is from Stuttgart." Then he picked up his can and went to the bathroom.

Dannaks prayed that Katja was from Hamburg.

The terrace doors were open, but because he didn't want to pull on his trousers and he didn't want to sit outside in T-shirt and underpants, he took his wine to his bedside cabinet and lay on the bed. He wasn't a white wine fan and the liquid was very sweet and tasted like the juice of tinned fruit. Its texture was slick like a preservative and he wondered how long it had been standing in the refrigerator.

He stared at the air conditioner unit. The slats were closed: the stains hidden. Then he searched for and found the dent in the cupboard door.

Dannaks heard the birds chattering outside. And he felt good. And then for the first time he thought that he could do nothing. It was the Turkish police's case. They weren't giving anything away. They were keeping it to themselves. So, let them solve it.

Katja sprung to mind again.

He hadn't expected to meet anyone. His T-shirts were testament to that fact. But did he possess anything more suitable? Yes, he could think of three or four items of clothing he could wear on a date. They were all back in Hamburg.

Nothing like this had ever happened to him. It all seemed so quick. And then it had been easy and natural.

Another thing about her was that she hadn't asked him about the case. Yes, that was refreshing, like a breath of fresh air.

If their acquaintance carried on at this pace then, well – he suddenly realised that he didn't have any protection. There was a condom machine in the plaza toilets. Did it take euros? Maybe it was empty? Or broken? It would be just his luck. Reupke would have some. Dare he ask? Maybe Katja had some? He told himself to calm down. Of course this wasn't only about the condom. Anxiety was taking over. It had been a long time. He'd probably be rubbish.

Nevertheless he went over to the safe and fetched some coins from his wallet. He returned to the bed and put the coins on the bedside table.

He felt like an excited kid on a first date. Then, hey – for him it had been such a long time it could be a first date. Not only did he have to calm down, he needed to focus. He needed to get back on track.

The cynical part of him united with the detective in him and the thought that she could have killed Peter flashed through his mind. He dismissed it as absurd. And yet, the killer could have been a guest. The motive could be crime of passion. It wouldn't be the first time a guest had an affair with a member of staff.

The buzzing of a mosquito intruded and he searched for it. He got up and closed the terrace doors. The air conditioner unit shuddered into life and the slats rolled open. Dannaks picked up one of his shoes and sought the tiny beast. Finding it on the wall next to the headboard he hit it first time. A small red fleck, barely the stoke of a felt-tipped pen, marked its end.

Dropping his shoe he returned to the bed and contemplated the bloodstained underside of the slats.

He picked up his preservative, which, now that it had reached room temperature, tasted worse, like pickle water. After finishing it he jumped up and fetched a sheet of hotel writing paper and his notepad. Returning to the bed with a large brochure to lean upon he grabbed the pencil from the small pad next to the telephone.

18:37

By the time Reupke came out of the bathroom Dannaks had long finished his list. In fact he'd even dozed off for a quarter of an hour. The sound of the hairdryer in the bathroom had roused him.

"Leave in ten?" said Reupke.

"Yeah." But Dannaks didn't get up to put his trousers on. Instead he reached over to his bedside cabinet and picked up his list. "Olaf," he said, the name strange in his voice.

Reupke froze and looked over.

Using his name added a weight Dannaks had not intended, so he went on breezily. "I thought we might have a quick recap of what we've got."

His colleague relaxed and turned to the cupboard.

"I was worried there for a moment." Reupke then began shaking his head.

"What?"

"I thought you were loosening up."

It was true. Dannaks was slowly being seduced by the place and was desperately trying to hold on to their purpose.

"Come on. Fire away," Reupke said, taking out a pair of black socks bundled into one another in a clump. He sat on the edge of his bed and crossed an ankle onto a knee. He untangled his socks and pulled them apart.

"I'll read it as I've listed it. I started with the murder." He took a breath. "The victim was murdered in his apartment. He received a blow to the head and possibly elsewhere. He was stabbed and his throat was cut. There was a clustering of knife wounds at his chest tattoo, which suggests hatred—"

"You're suggesting it wasn't a Nazi attack? A Turk?"

"No. Not intentionally. Er, let's strike hatred and make that passion."

"I'll go with that."

"Okay." Dannaks checked the next point on his list. "There was a lot of blood and a training shoe print." He waited for comment, when none was forthcoming he continued. "Meryem was probably present."

"You still don't want to pin this on her, do you?"

"She could be the murderess. I've written a list of suspects."

"You got that all on one page?"

"Hardly. I wrote Meryem, Rafael, a waiter, Ercan, Fehime and then guests, staff and outsiders."

"The world and their dog."

"Basically."

"I assume outsiders include neo-Nazis."

"Yes, I, er, wrote madman too."

"Not leaving anything to chance, then?"

Dannaks ignored him. "There was that shit on the walls thing. And the toilet rolls. And you said something about all the taps running."

"Go on."

"We have Peter's missing diary or book." He hesitated at the next point, because he had bracketed it. "A kid playing hide and seek saw a red man on the night of the murder. That's it."

"Not much, is it?" said Reupke after a while.

"I saw a mother tell her son to wash himself off in the sea today."

"So this is how your killer got away?"

"If he didn't wash himself in Peter's bathroom, then yes."

"It's all conjecture."

Of course it was all speculation. What else did they have? Dannaks grew angry, but calmed himself.

Maybe Reupke noticed for he made an obvious effort to contribute.

"I'm sure all those on the staff who have camp accommodation would have been given special scrutiny. So let's go with the outsider. Like you said he could have entered via the beach. Front gate security is not lax, but they may take a bribe."

But Dannaks sensed that the conversation wasn't going anywhere. "I just hope we get some info when we see the body."

"If we ever see the body," said Reupke. "Come on. We should get there before the women."

Dannaks swung his legs and virtually jumped to a standing position.

Reupke raised his eyebrows at his sudden dynamism.

Dannaks fetched socks and a pair of beige coloured trousers he'd bought from Patel's.

"Going on safari?" said Reupke.

"Yeah, I'm after big game."

Reupke gave him a whimsical look. "Is there something you haven't told me about this woman?"

18:55

The plaza bar was surprisingly busy, but the detectives managed to collect drinks and secure a table before the women arrived. They turned up within minutes of each other. Dagmar arrived first, seating herself, whilst Reupke fetched a Bacardi-cola for her.

She looked sleek and demure. And Dannaks thought that evening dresses were made for this woman.

"So Dannaks," Dagmar began, 'I have one taboo subject for this evening."

"I can guess."

"Good. That's settled. So, how was your day?"

"Fine."

Tonight Dagmar's midnight blue evening dress had been given up to a similar cut but in deep purple.

"Did you get to relax at all?"

"A little."

"It's important."

Reupke returned with Dagmar's drink, but before he could sit Dannaks stood. He hadn't recognised her and had been attracted by the fact that she had stood and searched the area. Katja was transformed. She was wearing an oriental-looking green dress that just covered her knees. Not only was she made up with her hair down, but the glasses were gone too. Strangely without the glasses and more of her face visible the mole below her left eye wasn't as noticeable.

The length of the front of her silken dress had an impossible number of black knots of cloth through loops. Most had to be ornamental; otherwise she'd spend an hour doing them up and the same undoing them. The latter thought tantalised him.

When she reached their table Katja greeted Dannaks first and then the other two.

"Katja, this is Dagmar and my colleague Olaf."

Limp handshakes were made with utterances of nice to make your acquaintance.

Dannaks remained standing as she seated herself. "What would you like to drink?"

"Campari and orange with ice, please."

"Right." He looked at Reupke. "Olaf?"

"I'm fine."

He took his own glass to the bar and waited. People were ordering and someone was standing behind the person at the vinegar cask. He watched Reupke and the girls talking. The lack of animation told him it was small talk. Maybe the taboo subject had been announced. Reupke looked like charm incorporated. His smile and sparkling eyes said that he liked the looks of Katja, even if she was some five to ten years his senior.

Dannaks ordered her drink when it was his turn and moved to the person at the cask.

Just as the person moved away, and he held his glass under the faucet, a voice arrested him. "Ah, Mr. Dannaks."

Turgut was standing beside him. Despite the heat he was wearing a tie. At least the jacket was gone. There was a man holding two empty wine glasses behind him. Dannaks recognised him, but couldn't place him. The cold look he received said that the man had recognised him too. Yet, he felt sure he had never spoken to him.

"Hallo," he said, acknowledging Turgut, pausing, before turning back to fill his glass.

"Stop," said Turgut. "I see you have company. You don't want to drink that with the two ladies. Come here."

Turgut led him to the end of the bar. The man with the two glasses moved to the cask, and a glance said that he was watching them.

"The children are hungry," said the woman to a man perched at the bar.

"Give me a minute," he said, showing her the remaining half of his beer.

Although she was not pleased she turned and walked away. Dannaks glanced beyond her to a table of three scowling kids, arms crossed, brows knitted. Apart from them there was a noticeable absence of children.

The man returned to his beer and discussion with the fellow next to him.

Turgut called in Turkish and one of the two barmen, left a beer tap running to step over. The man nodded and returned to finish filling the beer glass. Placing it on the counter to a grateful guest, he turned, pulled out a bottle of wine lying in a rack and placed it and four glasses on a small round tray.

"This is much better," Turgut was saying. "I drink it myself. The guests have to pay if they want it. But this one is on the house."

"Thank you very much," said Dannaks.

The man at the cask heard their conversation. He appeared about to explode with anger. And it was this expression that placed the memory squarely in Dannaks's mind. He was the guest who had complained about waiting at the gate yesterday.

"We were stuck in that coach for almost an hour, waiting for this palaver to end."

"We are sorry," the girl with the clipboard had said. "Have a cocktail."

Dannaks would have liked to ask Turgut about the shit-smearing. If anybody, he would certainly know of similar incidents. But the moment was inopportune. He should have asked when they spoke to him after seeing the photographs, but he'd had other things on his mind.

"He will bring it to your table," said Turgut.

Dannaks nodded and made to turn, but Turgut held his forearm.

"I have heard that you have been interviewing people," Turgut continued as he made to protest. "The animation team. And your colleague was in the kitchens today. I am sorry, but I thought you understood." His grip subsided and his hand merely rested on his forearm. "I have now been ordered to tell you that the hotel wants to get back to normal." His hand patted Dannaks's forearm, before breaking contact.

"With all these undercover guys, how can you?"

"There aren't so many now." A plea entered Turgut's expression. "Everyone was interviewed. There was a threat of closure. But it is peak season and other hotels could not accommodate all the guests and the expense of cancelling... Well, you can understand that this has all been very traumatic for everyone. And you are upsetting people."

The barman had come round and was standing next to Dannaks, the tray at his shoulder.

"People are upset," said Dannaks. "Most of them have come to us. And you can understand our interest. Anyway, we're talking not interviewing. Listen; if it's any consolation, the two women we are with have made it a taboo subject."

Turgut acquiesced with a nod and Dannaks returned to the table, the waiter in tow.

"What's this?" asked Reupke, when he returned to the table with the waiter.

"Compliments of the hotel."

The women nodded to one another.

"Perks of the job," remarked Dagmar.

Dannaks smiled. He thought better of divulging the real reason: that it was more akin to a bribe.

"I wasn't sure whether you wanted the wine," he said, placing the Campari and orange in front of Katja and taking his seat.

The waiter handed Dannaks the cork, which he inspected before smelling it.

"We're not going to let you drink it on your own," said Reupke. He was animated and jolly with a "we're going to have some fun this evening" attitude. Dannaks shrivelled and worried that his colleague might show him up.

Dannaks smelt the splash the waiter poured in a glass. Then he sipped it as if it could be hot. After letting it roll about in his mouth he swallowed. The wine wasn't as full-bodied as he liked it. It was Chianti-thin. Perhaps the airing would swell it. The throat-burn was present, but milder than the stuff from the cask. He nodded his approval.

The waiter returned the nod, filled the four glasses, acknowledged the thanks and left.

"Katja was telling us she was from Poppenbüttel," said Reupke, letting Dannaks register the ghost of delight in his expression. She lived in Hamburg. Dannaks found it easy to ignore his colleague's relish, because he was pleased.

"Nice area," said Dannaks. "I live in St. Georg."

"Oh," said Katja. "I haven't been there in ages. I hear it's become very chic."

"Yes," he enthused. "There's a lot of street-life. You've still got the pushers, pimps and prostitutes..."

The alcohol on empty stomachs lubricated the conversation. At one point Dannaks noticed that the continual stream of people heading for the restaurant, which had turned to a trickle by seven thirty, had now dried up.

Because he savoured the atmosphere he bit back his hunger. He was in danger of filling himself with drink and sought distraction when he wasn't part of the conversation.

He couldn't help himself, but at one point he began checking footwear again. Naturally most of the guests had changed their footwear. Many were in proper shoes, although there were still quite a few trainers and open-toed sandals.

Shaking himself he turned and raised his glass to the two Turkish men drinking water a couple of tables away. They stared back at him blankly.

Turning back the girls wanted an explanation. Reupke shook his head and gave him a "you're on your own" look. Dannaks muttered that they were being followed.

"How exciting," said Katja. "Just like in the movies."

"Yeah," said Reupke. "Real subtle. With holes in their newspapers."

"Have they?" asked Dagmar.

They conversed as a group for most of the time, but occasionally they broke off into couples.

On one such occasion Katja showed him the tube of mosquito repellent. He said 'later' and because he couldn't carry it, she popped it back into her bag.

"Another postcard from your parents?" she said, referring to his Hong Kong T-shirt.

Reupke caught the remark and smiled. Dagmar insisted on being let in on the joke and, after explaining, Dannaks tried to hide his embarrassment behind flippancy.

"I'll have to get myself a T-shirt from somewhere I've actually been." He brightened. "An 'Azure Skies' one."

Later Katja would apologise for embarrassing him.

Running excited gangs of children appeared before eight. Some claimed front row amphitheatre seats by leaving cushions and jackets. Like flies they were all over the place, vanishing and reappearing, running up and down the stonework, playacting on stage, swerving between the plaza tables, walking around the edge of the pool. Their mischief disturbed the earlier tranquillity. A boy was crying, a girl's lone sandal drifted across the pool, two boys pointed laser pens on the stage curtains and the eyes of children upon the stage.

On stage a billboard proclaimed the evening show in bright 1950s matinee style. Dominating the oddly stagnant drawings of balloons, champagne glasses and a sweeping ballroom dancing couple were splashed the words: 'Mr. and Mrs. Azure Skies.' Ignoring the words, the party feel was peculiarly reminiscent of a fated New Year's celebration.

Away from the general mayhem, but attracting bunches of kids periodically, were a young man and woman, who'd set up camp near the animation team's shack. Portraits stood against the shed wall, most serious, some comical, two or three famous. He sat behind an easel, a pouch of pencils and what looked like a cast iron pot of tea; a powerful lamp stood behind him. Sharing the lamp, she had her own pair of chairs and small glass pots of paint, a ring binder of motifs, but no easel. Her function wasn't clear to Dannaks.

Adults were returning too. Many were probably parents of the horde. Although there was still space the bar was getting lined. A couple with a baby in a pushchair appeared. The chess players returned to their table, each carrying two glasses of beer.

By now the bottle of wine was finished and Dannaks was resisting the urge to go to the cask. Katja hadn't drunk her wine and Dagmar had taken a sip saying that she was a white-wine person. So he had drunk their glasses. He didn't feel light-headed, but he felt fuzzy. And he had to concentrate on holding his composure and fighting the dangerous detachment.

He asked Katja about her glasses and she said vanity compelled her to wear contacts lenses. During the day the heat tended to dry them out. Then there was the wind and sand and the fear of losing them. So beauty gave out to practicality.

"You look good in glasses too," he said.

She laughed and he felt clumsy.

"Sorry," he said addressing all three of them, "but if I go on like this, I'll be under the table. Maybe we should eat."

"Good idea," said Katja.

"First a small detour," said Dagmar.

"Me too," said Reupke, finishing his glass of wine. Wine on beer, you'll be queer, thought Dannaks.

The four went to the toilet.

Although the shops were open nobody seemed to be about. Dannaks hadn't seen the shopkeepers languishing at any plaza table.

He finished first and was drying his hands, choosing paper towels over the blow-drier, when Reupke approached the washbowls.

"Katja is a catch," he said.

Dannaks didn't know what to say. "Yeah, I like her."

"That's a bit of luck, because I think she's interested."

"Actually, I haven't got anybody back in Hamburg." The minute he said it, he regretted it. As if in admitting it, he had given some kind of trump card away. For in showing his hand he exposed himself to embarrassment should it all come to nothing. And he simply didn't know Reupke well enough.

"I thought so." Reupke was looking at himself whilst drying his hands. "You haven't phoned anybody since you've been here. And you didn't say anything when I suggested you check out the singles' club this morning."

Dannaks wanted to ask him about his girlfriend, but thought better of it. Instead he surreptitiously looked at the condom machine. It took euros and appeared to be in working order, but he didn't want to try it in front of Reupke.

"I think I know how the shit-smearer did the women's toilets," he said, when they were outside waiting for the women.

"Go on," said Reupke. It may have been on his tongue to remind Dannaks that such talk was taboo this evening, but Dannaks was ready to reply that the pact was only with the women. In any case, Reupke was obviously intrigued enough to ignore the agreement.

"There is a plastic stand..." He couldn't see it. "... saying 'cleaning in progress'. All the person had to do was put it in front of the door when the place was empty and then she'd have had all the time she needed."

"It's risky. But okay. You think it's a woman simply because only the women's toilets have been hit."

"Yes. I... Oh–"

The women emerged from the toilets together.

On the way to the restaurant they met Tanya and Ercan. Tanya stopped Dannaks and Ercan looked away. Gauging that this was a momentary interruption, the others stopped too. She handed him a piece of paper and merely said: "Timi's surname."

"Thanks," said Dannaks, but he hesitated. "This is going to sound like a strange question, but do you have a cleaner for your own rooms?"

"No," she said. Seeing Dannaks's surprise she added: "The cleaner comes once a week. Why do you ask?"

"Oh, it's nothing," he said. Nods were exchanged and they moved on.

Reupke frowned, but Dannaks brushed him off with a smile.

Dinner was a relaxed affair. They chose to sit in one of the three air-conditioned halls that converged on the buffet area. The restaurant was busy, but not hectic.

There were bottles of water, red and white wine. Dannaks poured, asking the waiter for another bottle of water when he came off short.

When they first sat together at the plaza, they were a group of individuals, their postures reflecting their individuality. Even Dagmar and Reupke only leaned into each other on occasion. At dinner, reassured by the table, cocooned by the presence of the other diners, warmed by alcohol, barriers fell away and there was much laughter and mirroring.

For the benefit of the other two, Katja said that she was divorced and had a son and daughter. Dannaks learnt that since the children had grown up she worked full time in the personnel department of a shipping company.

Dannaks felt good. He hadn't felt like this in years.

He was doing the buffet rounds together with Katja when he saw the trio from Nordic walking standing at the pair of cast iron soup pots.

"They weren't very nice to you this morning," said Katja.

"Did you hear what they were saying?" he asked conspiratorially.

"No. What?"

Relishing the intimate proximity of her, he said: "I think they were dropping something into the soup. I heard them saying: eye of toad, wing of bat..."

Katja laughed so loudly the three women looked over.

"Macbeth," she managed.

Dannaks was pleased. He could do no wrong.

However, the attitude of the three women did intrigue him. Why had they been so hostile? Yes, they wanted to get on with their holiday. But Dannaks couldn't help feeling that there was more. There appeared to be no real reason for it. Then, it could just be his imagination.

He had been worried that Reupke would show him up. That he would somehow undermine him. Perhaps with a disparaging remark about his lack of travel. Or indirectly with subtle boasts against which Dannaks could not compete. But he was pleasantly surprised. They came across as partners. Circumstance bonded.

Dannaks shocked himself into drinking more water than wine when he picked up a knife to eat his ice cream. Luckily no one appeared to see his mistake.

21:15

They would have gladly remained in the restaurant, but felt obliged to leave when, from about nine, the waiters began clearing everything away and setting the tables for breakfast.

Reupke and Dannaks waited outside whilst the women visited the conveniences.

"I'm going to have to slow down." said Dannaks.

"Me too," said Reupke. "But you're only young once."

Dannaks didn't know what he meant but couldn't be bothered pursuing it.

Instead he smiled and said: "You're all right."

Reupke nodded.

Dannaks thought he saw a wry smile on his face, which he sought to dispel. "You've got the right attitude."

"You're okay once you let go," Reupke conceded. "You should do it more often."

On the way back to the pandemonium that the plaza had become Katja casually linked her arm through his. Dannaks didn't care whether she chose to do this because Dagmar and Reupke were linked. He was pleased and that was all that mattered. He felt comfortably fuzzy. Oh he did worry that he was maybe too drunk should he be called upon to perform. He could do his duty, but he was afraid he would be rubbish. It had been a long time.

He touched his trousers pocket to reassure himself of the presence of his coins.

Half of the amphitheatre was filled. Nearly all the space in the front portion was gone. The music was some loud children's jingle about a choo-choo train.

From the stage to half way round the plaza adults had formed a long tunnel by clasping each other's hands above their heads. They swayed with the music, sometimes bringing their arms down to capture a child in the train that flowed through the tunnel.

Dannaks marvelled. It was about this time yesterday that they had arrived. It seemed aeons ago. How could they have not heard this tremendous noise?

All the plaza tables appeared taken and the bar was lined two deep despite the frantic efforts of the three barmen. But they managed to find a table, which, although neither close to the bar nor the amphitheatre, offered an oblique view of the stage.

The men saw the women seated and then went to the bar.

A young girl, not part of the train, which was now clambering back on stage, crossed Dannaks's path. She stopped in front of a table blocking his way. Reupke hadn't noticed and went on towards the bar.

"Look mum," she said to a seated woman.

She turned, saw Dannaks, but glanced at her daughter's leg nonetheless. Near her ankle was a faux tattoo of a rearing horse.

"Oh yes," said the mother, looking at Dannaks and touching the girl's forearm. "Come out of the way, dear."

The girl saw him and promptly moved into a space between the mother and the table.

Dannaks thanked her and moved on looking over in the direction of the shack. The standing lamp enveloped the group in a bubble of light. A portrait was underway with one sitter and a spectator and there appeared to be a queue for the tattooist.

The area was teeming with activity. Naturally he'd seen such a wealth of people yesterday. But only now, as he followed Reupke to the bar, did he realise the futility of what he'd been trying to do. There were all these impermanent guests, eight hundred or more, and then the staff: those behind the reception desk, the higher management, the cooks, the porters, bellboys, maintenance men, gardeners, cleaners, the massage and wellness people, shopkeepers, animation team, security people, scuba, sailing, parasailing, essentially watersports people. Then there were the tourist agents, artists, guest players, the people responsible for deliveries, shuttle, car hire and trips. And this was aside from the fact that the killer could be someone not linked to the hotel. Discovering the culprit without substantial intelligence was an impossible task.

He should be like Reupke: enjoy the time and collect the body. He was surprised, but as he had said to Katja, he could quite get used to the holiday life.

It *was* the Turkish police's case. They weren't giving anything away. Let them solve it.

Only two of the three barmen were frantically taking orders and serving. The third man was doing the rounds, collecting empties. Dannaks stood behind Reupke and was about to ask for a water when he noticed that the cask was free. It was too good an opportunity to miss. Surely one glass for the rest of the evening couldn't do any harm?

"You've slowed right down, then," said Reupke, turning from the bar and handing him Katja's Bacardi cola.

"Just keeping everyone company."

"Yeah," said Reupke, "and you mean not just our table."

Yes, it was probably true that he had drunk more than them. Before dinner he polished off three glasses of Turgut's red. And there was the minibar white in the room. Over dinner, although he drank no more than them, he didn't drink any less either. However, he knew that if he kept to the same poison he could handle himself.

At the table the four of them raised their glasses to holidays and Dannaks did a poor job of disguising his wince at the taste of the wine.

"No good?" asked Dagmar.

"Vinegar."

Although it wasn't particularly funny they all laughed. The joke was prolonged when Dagmar tried it and pulled a disgusted face.

"It's awful. How can you drink it?"

"You get used to it."

"You probably just numb your taste buds," said Katja.

"Into submission," Reupke added.

Katja brought out her tube of mosquito repellent and Dannaks thanked her and creamed his calves and ankles.

Floodlights went out and two spots came on. The discs of light wandered and flowed over the stage curtain. The children with their laser pens tried to catch these saucers. Dannaks found something extraterrestrial in the chase and he looked up into the sky, marvelling at numerous pinpricks of light.

A taped announcement in a firm crystal-clear voice in high class English bulldozed the noise of the crowd.

"Ladies and Gentlemen, please put your hands together. It's show time."

Obediently a monotonous clapping started up. There followed a short medley of party songs.

All the guests in the amphitheatre clapped, but those at the bar and furthest from the stage didn't bother. The two chess players seemed oblivious to it all.

The curtains were drawn back to reveal Habip in a shiny silver shirt, a large white bow tie with black spots, shiny black trousers with various-sized silver stars and a matching jacket and top hat.

Fehime, Necla and Hülya were standing behind him in outfits that resembled that of Playboy bunny girls. Minus the ears and tail puff they were little more than black off-the-shoulder swimsuits, complemented with fishnet stockings and stilettos.

Somebody gave a gutsy ear-splitting whistle, the kind done with forefinger and thumb extending the lips. Somebody else made a loud comment but Dannaks and the others didn't catch it. Whatever it was caused a collective laugh. Even Habip laughed, bringing the microphone to his stomach, covering it with a hand and half turning to the girls. Fehime's false beam became genuine and she lost her pose – one arm in the air, the other directing the attention to the show master. Hülya raised her eyebrows but remained poised. Necla seemed rigid with embarrassment. Fehime regained her position and toothpaste advertisement grin. Habip turned back to the audience and cleared his throat.

He spoke into his microphone above the raucousness of the crowd first in Turkish and then in German and English. Persevering he managed to drown them out until they quietened.

Habip explained that they were here to choose Mr. and Mrs. Azure Skies and for this they needed a jury. He wanted three men and three women. Sorry, no children. He started pointing directly at women in the audience. A spotlight swamped the area he was interested in. The girls left the stage to *help* people make up their minds. One woman got up and he demanded applause. Another shook her head. A second woman was cajoled onto the stage. Then Habip himself left the stage and began wandering up one side of the amphitheatre. He quickly found his third woman. But he began running out of wit by the time he was looking for his third man. He was reduced to threatening. If you weren't on the jury then there was a chance you would be competing for the Mr. and Mrs. Azure Skies title. The third man was plucked from a plaza table, much to the whooping glee of the rest of his table.

Dannaks recognised him as the complainer. He was the one that had given him the unsavoury expression earlier at the bar, the same man who had complained about being held up on the bus when they arrived.

Habip bounded across the stage and spoke with such haste one could almost believe he was on speed. He interviewed each jury member asking them for their name and where they were from. Any attempt at humour on their part fell flat under his barrage of wit. Dannaks was impressed by his showmanship. It was obvious why he was the leader. And yet, he wondered whether nervousness drove him.

The Complainer was Hartmut from Saarland.

Habip raced on, always in Turkish and then German and English. "And now for the contestants. We need six couples. And you don't have to be married... So do we have any volunteers?" Habip pointed and a spot found a young couple edging along a row of seated people.

Dannaks was distracted by the burst of shrieks and giggling from a group of pretty young things at a plaza table.

Habip was distracted too. "Have we candidates there? Yes, come on down. Come on."

A youth who could be a Turkish boy stood and held out his hand to his reluctant partner. She got up to the joy of the table. Dannaks recognised her immediately. It was Off-limits. He couldn't see her T-shirt. He checked the table and recognised her two friends. Three boys sat with them.

"Four more," said Habip. "Don't be shy. You're on holiday."

"You know," Katja began and they all looked at her. "My husband forbade me from doing anything like this. He didn't want to see me making a spectacle of myself. For a while I had aspirations of teaching aerobics. He didn't approve and I never got round to it."

"Well, now's your opportunity," said Dagmar. "If you want to, go for it."

"I couldn't."

"Why not?"

"If you always wanted to do it," said Reupke, "then there's no better opportunity. Nobody knows you here."

"I'm not a show-off," said Katja, with regret in her face, "but I've always wanted to really let go. When the kids were young I had an excuse. But my husband was always telling me to act my age. I'm too old now."

"Don't be silly," said Dagmar.

"It's only humiliation," said Dannaks.

"Jeez, Dannaks," said Reupke, not disguising his annoyance.

"No," said Katja. "He's right."

"Don't take any notice of him," said Dagmar. "Go for it girl."

Katja shook her head with uncertain determination.

Reupke was shaking his head too. His movement was with disappointment and it was directed at Dannaks.

"Come on," said Habip, "just two more couples and then we can get on with the show."

"I'll tell you what," said Dagmar. "If you go, Olaf and I will too."

Reupke's disappointed look instantaneously switched to horror and he stared at Dagmar, then at Katja.

"That means me," said Dannaks.

Katja nodded and smiled slyly. Dannaks was about to protest but she was standing, a hand in the air.

"Come on," said Dagmar to Reupke, "show some spunk."

"I–"

Habip had spotted them and their table lit up.

Katja turned her hand to Dannaks, much as the boy had to Off-limits. Reupke's expression was a challenge: maybe he really was dead wood. Dannaks blanched, but when he stood he was scarlet.

Dagmar was about to get up when the spot slid from them to an older couple ascending the steps of the stage.

Habip was blabbering but Dannaks didn't catch any of it as he walked towards the stage. He didn't know what to think. He was terrified. And he felt flattered to be holding Katja's hand. Alcohol gave the whole thing a surreal feel. As if it wasn't him descending the stone steps of the amphitheatre, someone else climbing up the steps at the side of the stage.

Necla directed them to the end of the line of contestants.

Hundreds of faces were watching them.

Dannaks struggled to calm down. He wanted to run away. Then he found the strength he needed when he looked at Katja and she smiled.

Habip had interviewed three of the six couples by the time Dannaks began to relax.

Under the bright lights he felt like a goldfish in a bowl. But the lights helped him turn the crowd into an anonymous dark mass. And he stared straight ahead, flicking his gaze as soon as he saw an individual. This was the only way he could cope. He had to annihilate them all.

Then Habip was interviewing Katja.

Dannaks noticed the flash of cameras. He then saw the hotel photographer on the ground his elbows on the lip of the stage the lens pointed at them.

"And finally, you are?"

"Dannaks."

"Very formal. You don't want to give us your first name?"

"No."

Habip recoiled at the firmness of the reply. Did the audience laugh?

"Okay. Mr. Dannaks, where are you from?"

"Hamburg."

"And what do you do?"

"I'm a detective of the Hamburg police."

He thought he heard some of the crowd make an ooh gasping sound.

Then some boy shouted: "Schimanski." A ripple of laughter flowed through the crowd. Schimanski was a household name of a German television detective played by Götz Georg. Dannaks didn't remotely resemble the actor.

Habip moved to the front of the stage and paced it like Mick Jagger. What he was saying didn't quite register with Dannaks. He looked over in the direction of the plaza, but couldn't see Dagmar or Reupke.

"... so ladies first," said Habip in English, backing away from the crowd to the first couple.

Hülya was pushing a trolley of see-through beakers. Some contained water, others beer.

"So, here we go," he said, passing a beaker of water to the first woman. "Quiet please."

The woman began gargling and Dannaks leaned over to Katja and quietly asked what she was doing.

"Gargling 'alle meine Entchen'."

"Shit."

"Don't worry; it's only for the women."

143

After each contestant there was applause. Off-limits took too much water and for a moment appeared to be drowning rather than gargling and spat out across the stage, falling to her knees with laughter. Dannaks saw that tonight her black T-shirt sported in white block capitals the words: Out of bounds. Maybe she'd bought her T-shirts in a batch.

The boy with her was doubled over, roaring in gulps that reminded Dannaks of a seal. He stumbled about, flicking his wrist as if trying to click his fingers. His tight blue jeans, black sleeveless muscle shirt and jet-black gelled up hair said that he aspired to being cool with a capital C. At this moment his composure was in tatters and he was far from it.

Eventually it was Katja's turn. She too stopped, but swallowed rather than spewed. She took another gulp and was off for the allotted thirty seconds.

Then Habip was at the jury. They were seated behind a long table, a cocktail of their choice before them. They'd been given numbered cards and were asked to judge each contestant. Katja received sixes and sevens from all but one of the jury. Hartmut the Complainer gave her a three. Out-of-Bounds came out with the least number of points.

"Okay, let's see how the men do," boomed Habip. He walked over to the trolley and raised a beaker of beer. "Now, this is what real men drink. I have six beers here and we're going to have a race. But..." he waited a beat "... no ordinary race, ladies and gentlemen."

The thought of beer repulsed Dannaks.

"We're going to see how fast they can drink these through..." and he picked up a cellophane packet "... straws."

Fehime took the packet and plucking individual straws darted them into the disappearing foam of each beer.

"It's as simple as that. But the men are not allowed to hold the glass or the straw. The women will hold it for them on the flat of one hand, like this." He held up a palm. "Now, because this is a race, the jury can take time out. The winner takes ten points, the next eight points, the next six, right down to the last with – yes; you've guessed it – zero points."

The three assistants began handing out the drinks.

"And, by the way, if you spill any it's zero points."

"This is going to finish me off," Dannaks said to Katja.

"No, it won't. And I didn't say we had to win."

Before Dannaks had time to take up position Habip said: "go." He had to bend to reach the straw. The beer was no longer cold, but it was refreshing under the glare of the lights and the crowd. Inevitably the taste did become nauseating. Katja spurred him on with words like "over half way", "you're doing well", "keep going" and "don't stop, my hand's aching". The "keep going" came when somebody dropped a beaker, beer exploding across the stage. One of the girls mopped it up.

Applause came before Dannaks had finished. Somebody else was faster. When he stood up, his shoulders hurt and he saw spots before his eyes. He felt hideously bloated and in desperate need of a burp.

"Are you okay?" Katja asked.

He didn't answer. He was afraid he was going to throw up.

Everyone had finished and Habip allocated points before announcing the next round. It was the women's turn and they had thirty seconds to draw an elephant. A flip chart was carried on stage and the first woman stepped up and did her best with the thick marker pen, much to the mirth of the audience, especially the kids. None of the others on stage could see her work. Habip tore off the sheet and after rolling it up gave it to the woman, telling her not to let the others see it. Necla took the woman back to the line of contestants, whilst Habip fetched woman number two. And so it went on. The remaining contestants and jury could only feed off the crowd's amusement.

When Katja drew there was some applause.

Dannaks felt sick, but in control.

Habip herded the women with their artwork to one side so that the jury could see. The men were clumped together. Points were awarded. Katja's was far superior to the other efforts and when Hartmut awarded her eight points, below the nines and tens of the other jury members, and one point above what he awarded the previous woman's work, he was booed. Even Habip passed a comment and asked him to think again. After a moments hesitation he lifted his number nine card.

Katja's elephant put them in a respectable third position.

"And now something for the men," said Habip. A black, French cafe style chair was placed centre stage and the stage-lights were dimmed. A spot focused attention on the chair. Patricia, the choreographer, also dressed as a bunny girl, moved a slender leg into the light. Then she slowly began to walk around it, lightly touching the rounded backrest. She touched it as if it were the shoulders of a man. Then she firmly placed a stiletto on it and threw her head back. She spun the chair round and spread her legs to crouch over it. Then she swivelled her buttocks on to the seat and shot a leg high into the air, her hands making a long slow stroke from the ankles as if putting on stockings. And so the sexually charged self-adoration continued, all to the accompaniment of "*El Tango de Roxanne*".

Dannaks was close enough to see the padding strategically stitched into her costume to fill out her girl's figure with womanly curves.

There were wolf whistles and other savoury noises. In total the exhibition lasted less than two minutes. The lights came up to clapping, whistling and shouts of "more". Patricia curtsied and rushed off the stage with small steps like a ballerina.

"You want more?" Habip asked. "Then more you shall have." He marched over to Katja and Dannaks while his three assistants lined up more chairs. Habip looked at Katja before abruptly turning to Dannaks. "You have one minute to be sexy with the chair." Dannaks cursed. "Excuse me?" said Habip pushing the microphone under Dannaks's nose.

"Great," he said, but his breath like a loud exhalation distorted the word over the speakers.

Habip backed away announcing that all the men were to come forward and be sexy. He was a good actor and yet Dannaks noticed that he was sweating as much as the contestants.

"Come on," said Habip ushering them towards the six chairs as the music started. However, their musical accompaniment wasn't as sensual; they were treated to the sound of "*The Stripper*".

Only Mr. Cool thought to remove his shoes so that he could later point his toes. He did by far the best job at copying Patricia. Dannaks rapidly exhausted his repertoire of moves and a sideways glance told him that apart from Mr. Cool the others had done equally appallingly. All of them were awkward and clumsy, their movements comparatively stilted. At a loss as to what to do, Dannaks, in a moment of inspiration, became camp. A palm affixed itself to a hip and the wrist of the other arm went limp. He resembled a teapot as he minced about the chair, regarding it with interest, pouting, pushing his hair behind his ears.

Habip made a running commentary that was suitably facetious and derogatory. There was laughter and a lot of cameras were flashing.

The same boy who had called out Schimanski, now shouted: "Schimi!" So Dannaks knew he was being watched.

Mercifully Habip called time up and the men stood around looking at their partners and one another forlornly.

The jury was called to evaluate the person Habip chose. He stood next to the contestants at random, choosing someone in the middle first. But his choice was with design. Mr. Cool came second to last and averaged nine points. Dannaks was last and all but one gave eights and nines. Hartmut offered six and when asked said that Dannaks had been gay rather than sexy. Habip nodded acceptance despite some protests from the crowd.

Habip then summed up. Out-of-Bounds and Mr. Cool were in second place, two points behind the leading couple. Katja and Dannaks followed closely. There was a large gap in the points between them and the remaining couples.

"We're coming to the end of the contest," Habip said and Dannaks gave a sigh of relief. "And for this round I want to call Ercan on stage." Ercan appeared immediately. He'd been waiting in the wings. Habip and his assistants clapped and the audience followed suit. When the applause died Habip asked if anybody knew what Ercan did. The question was almost rhetorical, because Ercan carried golf balls in each hand. Somebody shouted that he juggled. Habip laughed. Ercan smiled uneasily. He wasn't one for the bright lights and glitz. The contrast between the two men couldn't have been more pronounced than at this moment. And Dannaks realised that what he had taken as suspicious behaviour was actually natural nervousness. Somebody cried that he was the golf instructor.

"Correct. Ercan, what have you brought me?"

"Six golf balls," he said holding up his arms and trying to show the balls in his bunched fists.

Habip moved back to the line of contestants and choosing a middle couple explained what he wanted done. Hülya took a golf ball and crouched in front of the man. Habip explained. "The women have to take the golf ball up the left leg and down the right leg as fast as possible. The winner gets ten points, the next eight – you know how it works.

Katja's smile was slanted and Dannaks looked on dully.

"Oh," said Habip suddenly, "because we don't want it to be boring for the men, they have to blow up a balloon until it bursts." The girls handed out the balloons and balls. "Only then is the race over. Okay?"

There were no questions. Humiliation pure, Dannaks thought.

Just as Dannaks began stretching the neck of the balloon circus music started and Habip said: "Go." Katja was at his ankle, fingering the ball through his trousers up his left calf. He took a deep breath and blew. The balloon inflated but resisted. He saw spots again. Katja was at his thigh and he became distracted. He stretched the balloon again and blew into it again. Katja was nearing his crotch. From the corner of his eye he saw that one man had inflated his balloon. The golf ball was at his testicles and Katja was daintily trying to manoeuvre it to his other leg. His leg twitched spasmodically. The balloon went elastic and began to grow.

"I've lost it," Katja said, grasping the top of his thigh.

"It's gone round the back," Dannaks said as he paused for another breath.

"Got it," she said, having shifted herself to his right leg. The spots appeared again as he blew. And he saw the poster. The silhouetted dancers didn't look so sweeping or glamorous close up and the drawings of ticker-tape streamers and balloons looked like amateurish watercolours. Yet that fated feel remained. There was a foreboding to the celebration: a sense of enjoy today for tomorrow we may die. But then the danger was more real than that and they were laughing in the face of imminent disaster.

A yelp interrupted him and Katja. A wayward balloon farted a fly's route through the air, landing somewhere off-stage. Habip looked as if he was going to wet himself with laughter. Necla gave the man another balloon. Mr. Cool's balloon was the first to burst. Katja had the golf ball in her hand when the first couple's balloon burst. Then Dannaks's balloon exploded with a bang. A child was crying in the audience.

Everyone except Out-of-Bounds finished. She had reached Mr. Cool's thigh and got stuck. His jeans were too tight. Habip wiped the tears from his eyes and told her that the game was over and she should get the ball. But it was wedged and would not move in either direction. Habip could barely contain himself. Mr. Cool turned his back on everyone and opened his jeans. Even then he had difficulty retrieving the ball and had to peel his jeans to show off his black thongs. Whistling, catcalls and shouts for more abated when he pulled out the ball.

Habip awarded the points and Dannaks realised for the first time that they were in with a good chance of winning. As it turned out they had the same number of points as another winning couple. "It's a tie," said Habip. "But we can't have two winners. Let's sort out the runners up, first." Habip whispered something to Fehime, who left the stage for the sound box. Necla went to the wings, returning with a handful of baseball caps sporting the hotel logo and colours. They handed them out to the four couples. "Let's have some applause. They were all good sports. And the jury." The girls handed the jury caps too. "Right, are we ready for the tie-breaker?" He squinted as he looked up at the sound box. "Jury, listen carefully." He then turned to the two couples, before pointing to the sound box. "And you too."

There was some crackling and popping before the Tarzan call split the air. "Okay? No, let's have it one more time."

The call rang out again. Dannaks wondered how he had got himself into this situation.

"Okay men. You've got one shot. Has anyone got a coin?" Dannaks remembered his change and fished out an euro. "Good. You call." Dannaks chose correctly and opted to go last. "Quiet then," Habip said before holding the microphone under the other man's chin. The man cleared his throat. The call that he issued didn't resemble the taped one. It sounded like a cross between an opera singer tuning up and a long exclamation preceding an accident. "Oh dear," said Habip.

Dannaks looked at Katja before his turn. Her look said: you can do it. A part of him said: don't try. But he had no time to think of anything different, like when he went gay instead of being sexy.

Habip pushed the microphone in his face and two boys, one after the other, called out "Schimi!" But there was no laughter. Dannaks inhaled and let rip. His call was louder and broke in the middle giving it that extra oomph.

There was a hooray from the crowd and it appeared a hands-down win. The jury went through the motions and Hartmut, not daring to give Dannaks low points, gave him the same as the other male contestant.

The other couple were handed a cap each. Dannaks and Katja were ushered forward. "A round of applause for Mr. and Mrs. Azure Skies." They too received caps, but also T-shirts, wellness vouchers, good for a massage or beauty treatment and a bottle of bubbly. Hastily made up thrones were wheeled onto stage. They were seated and two of the girls perched golden paper crowns on their heads. The hotel photographer flashed off a number of photographs.

22:47

Dannaks wanted to leave, but they were forced to do the club dance, which, of course, he didn't know. But then he no longer cared. People were on the move. Then Habip was swiftly announcing tomorrow's show Lion King and that it was Gala night, for which black and white dress was a must, after which he said that he wanted to see everyone in the disco.

At the first opportunity Dannaks led Katja off towards their table. His relief was palpable. Reupke rose and clapped when they arrived. "Well done." Dagmar clapped too and congratulated Katja especially. Dannaks placed the bottle on the table and threw his cap and T-shirt on his chair.

"You got your T-shirt," said Katja.

"I'll get some glasses," said Reupke.

The thought of alcohol made Dannaks's head spin. "I'll be back in a minute."

He swung round and headed straight for the toilet. The amphitheatre was all but deserted. There was a press of people at the bar and the entrance to the disco.

The toilet was also busy; men and boys smiled and nodded. A cubicle became free and he went in and sat down. His trousers and underpants about his ankles he put his hands to his head and touched something. He found himself staring at a golden paper crown. Putting it on a knee he rested his head in hands, his elbows upon his thighs. He was surprised by the wetness of his hair. He sat for a long time; long after business was done. He took long deep breaths. The pungent fragrance of disinfectant was nauseous. Here in the cubicle he bordered on collapsing. It was as if until this moment some tension or sheer excitement had kept his drunkenness at bay. The spotlight and Katja's presence had done it.

Now, alone, he could give himself up to how he felt. He would rest and then pull himself together. Although he couldn't face leaving the cubicle he knew he would have to get back to the table.

Eventually he began listening for movement outside the cubicle for it had gone quiet. Convinced no one was about he cleaned himself and flushed. When he opened the door he was disappointed to see a man standing at the pans.

Dannaks walked as best he could to the washbowls. There he washed his hands and avoided looking at himself. But something caught his eye. He was wearing the paper crown, which he didn't remember putting back on. The urge to tear it off and throw it in the bin was strong. But he resisted. He took his time and the man washed and left. He turned to the condom machine. He wasn't sure he was up to anything. He felt wasted and quite drunk. Digging into his pocket he pulled out his coins and concentrated on focusing on them to finger out what he needed for the machine. His palms were wet and he felt a hot flush. The thought of the beer through the straw clenched his stomach and he swung to the bowl and turned on the cold tap. With his free hand he scooped up water and doused his face. He steadied himself on the bowl with his coin holding fist. The cold water felt good. He was too far-gone to say it felt refreshing, for he still felt hot. He wiped his face with his free hand, letting drops fleck his shirt and moved to the machine again. Opening his fist he wobbled for a moment and before he could close his hand he'd dropped his coins. They made a shattering sound and he went down on all fours to pick them up.

"Need some help champ?"

It was Reupke.

"Chump, more like it," he returned. His voice was slurred.

"We're waiting to make a toast. There's a glass of champagne going flat out there."

Dannaks grunted. "I'm flat in here."

Reupke helped him to his feet and nodded at the machine. "Feeling lucky, were we?"

"I was. Now I'm not so sure."

The sound of a toilet flushing was followed by someone coming out of one of the cubicles.

Dannaks groaned.

Mercifully Reupke turned to the mirror and Dannaks took to washing his face with cold water again.

The man gave them a queer look but essentially ignored them as he washed his hands and checked himself in the mirror.

When the man was gone Reupke spoke. "Do you want to get a packet?"

Dannaks nodded.

Reupke pushed the coins in and Dannaks said: "I probably won't get to use them."

"Knobbly, coloured, plain? They got ones with a sensual ring here too."

Dannaks looked at him dully.

Reupke smiled. He was enjoying himself. He turned the knob and a packet dropped down. "Well," he said, "that is a surprise. It worked."

Dannaks pocketed the small box and the remainder of his coins.

"Come on champ."

Dannaks wanted to tell him to stop calling him that, but he felt in his debt and meekly followed him.

The night was cool and there were few people about. There were no children. Half a dozen tables were occupied. There were three people perched at the bar, behind which stood a lone barman. A tangible sense of deflation in the aftermath pervaded. No one was at the cask, but merely the sight of it twisted Dannaks's stomach. He took as many controlled and deep breaths as he could between the toilet and the table.

"We were beginning to get worried," said Dagmar.

"We thought you'd fallen in," said Katja.

Dannaks took off his crown and flattened it upon Katja's, which lay upon the table. "Needed five."

"More like twenty-five," said Reupke.

They sat and Dagmar picked up her glass of bubbly by the stem. "Come on, then."

Dannaks reached over and raised his glass. He saw Katja observing him and produced what he hoped was a smile to reassure her. She smiled uncertainly.

"To Mr. and Mrs. Azure Skies," said Reupke.

Dannaks merely kissed the liquid.

"We were saying," began Dagmar, "that it was your gay impression that swung it."

"No," said Dannaks, not entirely comfortable with having to contribute. "Katja's elephant did the trick."

"Where did you get that gay stuff from?" Reupke asked.

"Yes," said Katja. "You were very good."

"Convincing," said Reupke. "I was beginning to worry who I was sharing a room with."

"I've seen enough Christopher street day parades." He hoped that would suffice, but then felt obliged to elaborate. "They're at St.Georg's Lange Reihe."

"Olaf and I are going to the disco after this," said Dagmar. "Are you coming?"

Dannaks cringed but silently looked at Katja.

Thankfully she said that she wasn't one for discos.

"Too much excitement for one day, eh?" said Reupke. He was either coming to Dannaks's rescue or he was pleased with the result. Probably both.

Dannaks nodded. He was flagging again.

"Come on then girl," Reupke said to Dagmar. "Get that down your neck."

Dannaks realised that both Reupke and Dagmar were tipsy at the very least. They were simply doing a far superior job of hiding it.

Reupke downed his bubbly in one and stood. "You two can bask in your glory and finish off the bottle."

Dagmar drank some more from her glass, but didn't finish it. She too stood.

"Oh," said Reupke. "Here's the key. Leave the door unlocked." Reupke placed the key and tab on the table. Dannaks stared at it, doziness clouding him. "Take care of him," he said to Katja. Then to Dagmar: "Come on, girl." And they were gone.

The sudden silence irked Dannaks and he hastened to fill it. "I'm sorry. Did you want to go too?"

"No. It really is not my thing."

"We can go if you want. I'm, er, just not up to dancing."

She hesitated before speaking. "I don't think you're up to anything other than a good night's sleep."

He smiled and then chuckled. Of course he was relieved. Was she just as relieved?

"You're right." He felt relaxed and was able to perk up. "It's been a long day and I didn't sleep well last night."

"Yes," she smiled. She looked delicious in this half-light. Perversely the urge to seduce her, to take her to bed, rose up in him. But the urge peaked within seconds and dissipated. "Oh, let's not forget the cream."

"Dannaks. I just want to say thank you for doing that."

"What? No. No, it was nothing."

"You're very sweet." She touched his hand. "But I know it's not your thing."

"Is it yours?"

"No," she laughed. He relished her joy. "But I'm glad I did it."

"Me too," he lied.

Three or so tables away he spotted the two men watching them. A flame of anger took him. He wasn't allowed any privacy.

"Shall we go?" he asked.

"Yes."

He walked Katja back to her apartment, which was on the other side of the camp from his place. Hers was not uphill and nearer the sea. When they came to part outside her door they hugged and he turned his head to peck her on the cheek. They pulled back but remained embraced. She held her key with tab in one hand, he the tube of mosquito repellent. After looking into each other's eyes they kissed. Dannaks didn't want the kiss to end and again part of his body was roused.

They parted.

"I'll see you tomorrow, then," she said. "At breakfast."

He felt deflated and glad. "Yes. Tomorrow."

She turned and he watched her open her door.

"Goodnight," he said.

"Goodnight."

Thursday 04.14
(Gala night)

He woke with a start. The sheets clung to him and he felt both hot and cold. He wasn't sure whether it was the cream on his legs that caused the sheets to stick to him or his overall clamminess. For a moment he wondered where he was. Then he fumbled for the bottle of water on his bedside cabinet. He found the light switch instead and decided to switch it on. He drank all the water and contemplated going to the fridge for another bottle.

Reupke was not in his bed.

Fragments of a disturbing dream surfaced. He was on an ocean liner dancing with Katja. His Hamburg colleague Reinhart and his wife were there. Volker Herbst was on stage crooning in a tuxedo. The ship rolled and they all ended up tangled at one wall of the ship. He managed to disentangle himself, but then he was holding on to one of Katja's arms, hanging from the edge of some airship balcony, the patchwork landscape peeking between the clouds below them. And he was falling away from her. She watched him indifferently before turning back into the throng of an ongoing party. That was probably when he woke.

He swung wearily into a sitting position. His head hurt. Somebody had pushed knitting needles between his eyeballs and was slicing his brain in swishing movements. Fragments of the evening surfaced like pieces of a dream. Habip's laughing shiny face loomed out of nowhere. Was he performing this crude lobotomy?

Dannaks groaned as he got to his feet and shuffled to the fridge.

He didn't want to be in this ailing body.

08:12

"Wakey, wakey! Rise and shine."

Dannaks groaned and pulled the sheet over his head as Reupke pulled back the curtains.

"Come on champ, we've got work to do."

"Don't call me that." Even he didn't recognise the cracked and splintered timbre of his own voice.

"What?"

"Champ."

"Yeah, sorry. Chump, wasn't it?"

Dannaks mind began to start. He peeked out at his clock.

"Have you just come back?"

Receiving no reply he pushed back the sheet. Reupke had gone to the bathroom.

Dannaks sat up and drank some more water.

His colleague returned, a toothbrush in his mouth. "You say something?"

"Yes. Have you just got back?"

"Turn down the Dolby and I might understand what you're saying."

"Have you just got back?"

155

Reupke smiled and nodded and brushed his teeth, white foam creeping out between his lips.

Dannaks nodded and Reupke returned to the bathroom.

When he came back into the room, Dannaks hadn't moved.

"Come on. We have to be back before ten. That means out by nine."

He then remembered that they planned to go to Herbst's place. Dannaks suspected that Reupke wanted to go to sport again. Whatever, they had to be back as soon as possible in case the Turkish police arrived. They'd surely be taken to see the body today. Huh, he'd almost completely lost sight of why he was here.

He exhaled loudly before getting to his feet.

"And, er, Dannaks, listen. Erm, you locked the door, right?"

"What do you mean?"

"I couldn't get in last night."

"I left it unlocked."

"No, you didn't."

"I did. Otherwise how did you get in just now?"

"Do I have to spell it out?"

Dannaks overcame his shock. He nodded his head and then shook it. "Okay."

"Good man."

Dannaks wasn't happy about being involved in such complicity, but he had no choice.

He went to the bathroom, where he didn't even attempt to smile at his reflection.

He laboriously went through his morning motions.

Reupke called that he should have a shower later. There wasn't time now.

He could only agree with his colleague. Although a shower would have done some good.

He noticed Reupke had again placed an euro on his pillow and Dannaks promised to leave the tip for the cleaner tomorrow. Then they left.

Dannaks was grateful for the cool air, but not the brightness that glinted between gaps in the canopy of green and branches and promised another scorching day. He felt wretched and wished there had been time for a shower. His breath wasn't up to much either. Brushing his teeth had disguised rather than dispelled the taste in his mouth.

"Did you sleep?" he asked.

"A little," said Reupke, unable to suppress his smirk.

After a few more steps Reupke turned round and looked up. The movement caught Dannaks unawares and he almost stumbled.

"What is it?"

"We need to know who our tail is."

Dannaks couldn't see anybody.

"Did you see anyone?"

"No, but I think someone is standing behind that bush."

"Shall we go up?"

"No. We just need to know what they look like."

"Why?"

"You are in a state, aren't you?"

Dannaks looked at him dully.

"So we can give them the slip."

Dannaks nodded. "Oh yeah. Sorry."

Reupke explained how to get to the service entrance through the kitchens.

The restaurant was quite busy and Dannaks shrank from the multitude of wayward kids and struggling babies. But the atmosphere was respectfully subdued. Seeing a boy slicing the yoke of a fried egg and scooping it up, dripping orange goo, forced him to look away. The incessant tinkle of cutlery upon crockery was a maddening cacophony that he consciously pushed into the background lest he scream.

He nodded to the frail old woman with crepe paper skin in a wheelchair.

"We sit out here, okay?" The tables furthest from the restaurant entrance were quiet.

Dannaks merely nodded. He wasn't sure he could eat.

They entered the building, which was a hive of activity.

Someone he recognised greeted him with a nod. He was grateful that this was the extent of the exchange because he couldn't place the man.

Reupke pointed out the kitchen ingoing and outgoing doors and then left him.

A boy spoke excitedly to another in the queue for eggs. "That's Schimi." Dannaks cringed and walked on to the container of scrambled egg.

He exchanged pleasantries with the nutritionist at the juices and realised that the man he hadn't recognised was her husband. He did his best, but he really didn't have the energy to brighten.

With merely a bread roll, some scrambled egg no bigger than half a tennis ball and an orange juice, he went outside. He couldn't see Reupke, so he chose an unoccupied table and sat looking in the direction of the entrance.

He lifted the flask of coffee and poured some into a cup. He then sipped his juice that was sharp and unpleasant to his throat.

Dannaks looked at his egg and picked up his fork. He wasn't sure he could eat it.

"Is here free?"

He looked up. A well-kept woman in an impeccably white jump suit was standing at the table. Her coiffure of ash blonde hair was how he imagined Marie Antoinette. Her skin was taut and alabaster white. She had softened her features with immaculate make-up. Her cream lipstick matched the colour of the nail polish on her slender fingers. She was a sculptor's realisation of classical beauty: a goddess. This was a woman not only with money, but also with the time to spend it. And her paleness made her look incredibly cool. Yet Dannaks sensed something masculine in the geometry of her chiselled features, something constructed and insincere. Her very aura daunted him. And he knew he was condemning her with some deep-rooted suspicion in his own make-up.

There were neighbouring unoccupied tables, so either she wanted a semblance of company, conversation or she knew he was a detective and wanted information.

"Yes, there're just two of us." The thought of half a dozen kids following her flashed through his mind.

"I'm on my own." Her accent told him that she didn't belong to the majority of guests. Most were Germans. He'd heard some Turkish, French and even American English, but this woman was Russian or Ukrainian.

Dannaks nodded. Another single woman. The place was full of them.

He forked up some egg.

"You're the detective?" she said.

Dannaks nodded. His mouth was full and he wasn't ready to swallow. The way he felt he wasn't sure he'd ever be ready to swallow.

She had a bowl of muesli and full plate of food: a bread roll, egg, bacon, sausage, tomato, and even some sautéed potatoes. For someone so thin he wondered where she put it all. And how she remained so pale out here was an additional wonder.

Reupke arrived.

"Morning," he said to the woman as he sat on the corner next to Dannaks.

He poured himself a coffee and said quietly: "It's the two guys under the big palm behind me on the right." Dannaks casually looked over. One of the two men, their stern expressions giving them away, was wearing a loud jungle patterned shirt: all huge palms and brightly coloured parakeets.

"Hawaii shirt?"

"Yes."

"It's got to be a joke."

"He thinks he's undercover. I think someone should tell him."

Pause.

"You're both detectives?" Her question was directed at Reupke who nodded. She looked at Dannaks. "You were on stage last night."

"Guilty."

"My husband thought your gay impression very good."

"Thanks."

"He had me worried," said Reupke.

She smiled although she had apparently not understood Reupke's remark.

"Your German is very good," said Dannaks. "Where are you from?"

"St. Petersburg." She was quiet for a moment. "My husband does a lot of business with Germany."

"Oh," said Reupke. Dannaks could hear his colleague's thoughts ticking over. Gangster, smuggler ... There was of course no reason why he shouldn't be a respectable businessman. That was the trouble with their line of business. They were naturally suspicious. "What does he do?"

"Buys and sells."

"He's having the lie-in I need," said Dannaks.

"No, he's playing tennis."

"This early?" said Reupke. There were few activities that started before ten. Some kind of greet the day Tai Chi happened at eight on the beach and general Nordic walking at nine, but that appeared to be all. Fabio had said that the singles' club ten o'clock Nordic walking had become a fixture by popular demand.

"Private tuition."

They ate quietly. Dannaks, who had finished most of his scrambled egg but had only taken a couple of bites out of his bread roll, poured himself a second coffee.

"You're not a big eater," she said.

"I'm feeling under the weather."

"Even so, breakfast is the most important meal of the day."

Oh no, he thought, even if she wasn't a nutritionist, he heard another consumption lecture coming. First accused of eating too much, he felt himself about to be frowned upon for eating too little.

"It's a crime not to take advantage of all this lovely food. When I was young we were very poor. Meat was a luxury and we ate a lot of bread. When we did get a slice of meat each, it was always smaller than the bread we put it on." Her gaze became distant as she reminisced. "So we used to move it on the bread so that we smelt it with every bite." She returned from her past to smile at them. "Only when the slice covered the last piece of bread did we eat it. Heaven."

If she was a gangster's moll, then she was a cool one to talk to the police so easily and readily.

"You were at gym yesterday," she said to Reupke. "Are you going today?"

"I'm not sure," he said, obviously not wanting to give anything away. "I need to. Every muscle in my body has seized up. I'm as stiff as hardboard from yesterday's session." Pause. "It was sweltering down there yesterday. You'd think the sea breeze would help, but the place is suntrap. That, plus Fehime's workout, had me soaked."

"She is good, isn't she?"

Dannaks made a show of looking at his watch. Reupke nodded. It had just gone nine.

"Actually, she has been campaigning to have the workouts away from the beach. She was hoping to get the stage. But it's not because of the heat or the ogling men, it's the sun cream."

"Sun cream?" repeated Reupke.

"Yes, that and the beach bar. When the wind is right the smell of coconut is quite overpowering. Fehime can't stand it. She says she's grown an aversion to it."

Dannaks had an odd feeling. But he couldn't pinpoint its source. "I love the smell of pine up here," Fahime had said. Coconut. Fahime had an aversion to the smell of coconut. Coconut. That was it. That was what was bothering him.

"Dannaks," said Reupke. "Didn't you hear me?"

His colleague and the Russian were looking at him strangely.

"No, sorry, what did you say?"

"I said we'd better get going."

Dannaks nodded distantly.

"Are you okay?"

"Yes, I, er–" He saw Fehime... Alone. "I'll be back in a minute."

"Dannaks!" Reupke exclaimed.

Fehime had placed her plate on the table and was pulling the chair out to sit.

"Morning," she said.

"Morning," Dannaks returned firmly. His delivery of that one word worried her so much that she remained standing. Rafael was approaching. "Tell Meryem to give herself up."

"What do you mean?" she said, offended. "I don't know where she is. How can I–"

"I know."

She was stunned and blanched. That was enough for him.

"Tell her."

"I would if I could," she retorted angrily.

Rafael was almost upon them. Hülya and Yunus were also approaching.

Dannaks nodded, showing her that he didn't believe her. "Tell her," he said again quietly.

As he left he heard Rafael question her, but heard no reply. "You should complain," said Rafael, loudly so that Dannaks could hear him. He reddened, but didn't turn around.

"What was that all about?" asked Reupke, when Dannaks sat in his place.

"I'll tell you later."

Reupke raised his eyebrows. The Russian was watching them over the edge of her coffee cup.

"Hallo," said Katja. "Didn't you see me wave?"

Dannaks jumped up and she smiled.

"No, sorry," he said pulling out the chair next to him. Should he kiss her?

She smiled and sat.

"Morning," she said to the Russian who returned the greeting.

Katja placed her plate in front of her, turned her cup the right way up on its saucer and reached for the coffee pot. "You're up early."

Reupke leaned over to her and spoke quietly before Dannaks could answer. "I hate to be rude, but we were just about to leave. We want it to look as if we're still here. You know? As if were just going to collect some more breakfast."

Katja nodded. "How exciting. Is Dagmar here?"

One corner of Reupke's mouth went up. "She said she wanted to have a late breakfast."

He turned to Dannaks. "Be quick." He then picked up his plate as if he was going to get something more to eat and then marched off.

"I don't know when I'll be back," said Dannaks.

"Let's meet for lunch, then."

"Yes. Twelve thirty. Here."

She nodded. And he felt that in Reupke's absence she wanted some intimacy. But to kiss her now could be seen as a parting ritual.

"I'm, er, sorry if I may have disgraced myself last night," he said quietly.

"Don't be silly. You were sweet."

He loved her smile and smiled too, unable to hide some creeping sadness. Then he stood, picking up his empty glass of juice.

"Can you get me some too?"

The Russian was holding up her glass. He hesitated, trying to suppress his embarrassment.

"Orange juice?" he said.

"Please."

He glanced at Katja and she nodded her head ever so slightly.

Dannaks went to the restaurant with the two glasses, mindful not to look in Fehime's or the Hawaii shirt's direction.

In the restaurant he made a B-line past the tiled island of cheeses, sliced meats, tomatoes and cucumbers, for one of the kitchen doors. He just hoped it was the right one. In going? Outgoing?

He resisted the urge to look over his shoulder as he placed the empty glasses at the cereals. The sulking punk with dyed black hair with purple streaks was spooning yoghurt into a bowl. He thought to thank her for being an integral part of the serendipitous moment in his life: meeting Katja. But she spectacularly ignored him. The world was made up of insects and he was no exception.

The kitchen was all heat and steam, shooting flames, hard surfaces, sharp implements and brushed steel.

"Just go straight through," Reupke had said. Indeed at the far end of the large kitchen was a single corridor choked with boxes, trolleys, and all manner of things that hadn't found storage room. He looked no one in the eye, but someone said something in Turkish and although he didn't catch it, it sounded more an exclamation than a challenge.

Pushing open one of the double doors at the end of the corridor he found himself at the loading bay. Other than Reupke there was not a soul in sight.

"Come on," said Reupke, as if Dannaks had been dawdling.

They proceeded down the steps to ground level and followed the road round to the main gate. Dannaks wasn't sure he could keep up the cracking pace.

They smiled and nodded to gate security. The uniformed man was so astonished that he nodded back. Worry sent him into his concrete hut where he snatched up the phone.

On the other side of the road were some shops in front of which stood two taxis. That is all the two men saw. The blazing shop fronts, a kaleidoscope of colours, the shrivelled toothless man sitting on some steps, the dog lying on its side playing dead, the young man gesturing at his array of sunglasses, another grabbing a

T-shirt and holding it up for them to see, were registered, but treated like white noise.

Dannaks couldn't imagine the blood-soaked killer fleeing this way unnoticed.

A man jumped out of his taxi and looked at them excitedly. "Taxi?"

"Yes," said Dannaks unfolding the fax with the address on it.

The man was jubilant and the others returned to their business; one man adjusting the position of his display of sunglasses, the other folding the T-shirt.

"We want to go here," said Dannaks in his best Turkish.

The driver looked at the sheet. He was a small man. Although he looked to be in his forties he had a small body. Dannaks was a good head taller than him.

"You know this place?" Dannaks asked.

The other taxi driver had got out of his car and was watching them over the roof of his vehicle.

Reupke was patting his thigh, almost hopping from one foot to the other. He kept looking back at the hotel entrance.

The other driver spoke. He wanted to have a look at the address.

"Oh man," said Reupke.

The driver ignored the speaker and pointed to a word on the fax. Dannaks did his best to pronounce it. The driver nodded.

"Okay," he said.

09:26

The two detectives sat in the back. Dannaks was perturbed by the fact that there were no seat belts and he felt strangely vulnerable.

At first Reupke looked out of the back window a couple of times. Eventually he settled down.

"So," he began. "What was all that about with Fehime? You really can't leave her alone, can you?"

Dannaks raised his eyebrows wearily. "Actually I was working."

"In your state?"

This elicited a ghost of a smile. He was still fighting an encroaching dullness. The day was becoming too bright. The dust and exhaust fumes parched his throat; either the front doors had no

164

windows or they were wound down out of sight and this appeared to be the vehicle's a/c. The driver sat on a tasselled cushion and still barely peered over the steering wheel. Frantic Turkish music was playing on the radio and Fatima's eye set in deep blue glass spun and winked at them under the rear-view mirror.

Although the road wasn't particularly busy, there was little green and the trees and bushes were dusty. There was a lot of waste ground covered in bric-a-brac. The houses varied tremendously: from new, perhaps unfinished, to old and falling apart. Most were sand-coloured or whitewashed concrete blocks.

On one side he saw palms, dogs, chickens, donkeys, waif-like children, brisk young men, old men outside at tables in the shade of a café playing Mah-jong or dominoes drinking tea from small glasses, women hanging out washing, sweeping out a doorway, guest houses, shops screaming duty free, watch shops, market-like shops, barber shop, restaurants, a discotheque, stables and horses, on the other side, beach-side, were high walls, security, pristine gardens, immaculate hotels.

"It was just a hunch really," Dannaks began. "The Russian said that Fehime can't stand the smell of coconut." He waited for Reupke's confirmation. "Well, yesterday I walked her to her room. Remember? I told you. She had a plate with three cakes. One was coconut."

"Maybe she likes coconut again."

"I don't think so. Guests stay here on average for two weeks, three weeks tops. If she told a guest then this information is no older than that. It's recent."

"Maybe it was for someone else?"

"Who? She doesn't share her room."

"Well, maybe she's got used to the smell now. Anyway they hardly had any coconut in them. "

"Possible. But also, when I left her I was able to see into her room for a moment. The chair was up against the cupboard."

"So?"

"Someone could have climbed up to the top. You know, where we have put our bags. There's enough room."

"You think Meryem's there?"

"Like I said, it's possible."

"It's all a bit thin."

"There are two more points."

"Go on."

"When she came to open her door she dropped her keys and cursed loudly."

"You think it was a warning to someone inside?"

"It's possible."

"You really should look for another word, you know." Pause. "You said two points."

"Yep. When I confronted her just now she didn't react as I expected her to. Oh, she protested and became irritated, but I wasn't completely convinced. I can't really say why."

"It's you and this body language course again, isn't it?"

"I think it was more about what she didn't say."

"What did you say to her?"

"Indirectly I told her I knew she was hiding Meryem."

"What do you mean indirectly?"

"I told her to give Meryem a message. Nothing new. Just that she should give herself up."

Reupke was quiet for a while. "I can't believe she's in Fehime's room. I mean, the police searched everywhere. How could she avoid them?"

"I don't know. Maybe she's not there."

"Aren't you tempted to search the place?"

"Yes. But what shall I do? Storm in? And what if I'm wrong?"

"Why didn't you tell me this before?"

"Because I wasn't sure. The coconut thing gave me a push."

Reupke accepted this. "It doesn't hurt to rattle a cage, I suppose."

They'd arrived at a large roundabout. Turning right would take them into Side town centre, the harbour, the ruins, tourists and shops. The taxi turned left and headed into residential area. They soon left the press of buildings and drove past those with more space. Again there were contrasts of old and new.

Then they turned into an area of exclusively new buildings. This was something of an estate of what appeared to be detached holiday homes; yet, although it could be argued that the same architect had been at work, each building was different. The cars parked outside said that there was money here.

The taxi driver pulled over in front of a building and pointed to it. Before he could ask for the fare Dannaks said that they would like him to wait and that they'd pay him later. He wasn't happy with this arrangement. Dannaks gave up and told Reupke that the driver would wait, but that he wanted the money for this part of the journey. He was probably afraid that they were going to do a runner. The poor man was certainly no match for either of them. Reupke agreed saying that he should get his tip at the hotel. Both detectives were growing aware of the wasted time. Dannaks explained as he handed over the money and the man nodded.

The three men climbed out. The taxi driver leant against his car, but then jerked away as if burnt. He pulled out a crumpled packet of cigarettes.

The sun beat down upon them fiercely and Dannaks realised that he hadn't creamed his face, shoulders and arms.

There was nobody about. Who would be out in this heat? They walked towards the building, set back from the road by a pavement broken by young trees, offering meagre shade from the brutal sun.

Although a shoulder high whitewashed wall surrounded the building, they could see enough of it to appreciate the pleasing, if not hackneyed, architecture. It was a Mediterranean villa done in the Spanish style. The entire building was whitewashed; the roof was terracotta tiles and all the woodwork: the gate, the shutters, the balcony fence and an overhang support, were in dark, bronzed pine. All the windows were rendered opaque by mosquito mesh. Necessity clamped two eyesores on the building. They were a cylindrical metal water tank lying horizontally on a metal framework on the roof and a fan contained in a large metal box on the side of the house. A third eyesore of debatable necessity was a white satellite dish. Hardy plants in rectangular plots added green to the place.

At the chest high gate that was the only break in the two-metre wall they stopped. There was no bell. Reupke lifted the latch, but the gate was locked. A large jail-sized keyhole was situated under the latch. They scrutinised the house but could see no signs of life or recent occupation. Except for the sounds of birds all was quiet.

"Looks empty," said Dannaks.

"Yes, but maybe they're just out." Reupke looked beyond Dannaks to the houses opposite, then those on the left and right.

167

"Come on, we've come all this way." And he hoisted a foot onto a corner of the gate and heaved himself over.

Dannaks looked about and thought he saw movement at a window of the opposite house. "I think somebody's watching."

"We'll be out of here in a minute," Reupke said, shielding his temples and pressing his face to a window.

Dannaks placed both hands on the rim and lifting himself he tried to get his foot at the corner of the gate. But he couldn't reach and instead attempted to stamp his way up the wall. His sole dirtied the white paint.

Reupke glanced back. "Stop fooling about," he said, walking around the building.

Dannaks grunted.

Try as he might he couldn't get over the gate.

"I can't get over," he said, although he couldn't see Reupke.

There was no answer.

Dannaks looked back at the taxi driver. He was still in position, but had finished his cigarette.

Minutes ticked by.

"Olaf," he called.

Dannaks waited and was beginning to grow anxious when Reupke appeared.

"Didn't you hear me call?" asked Dannaks.

"No." He didn't stay near the house but he didn't approach the gate either. "I got a good look through the patio doors. It's an open plan job. If anybody is staying here now, they're damned tidy." He paused. "There's a swimming pool back there. You should see this place. Talk about how the other half live." He pondered. "Perhaps property is not so expensive out here." He waited a moment for Dannaks to speak. "Are you okay?"

"I could do with a drink."

"It's a bit early."

"I meant water."

Reupke ignored him. "There are some steps at the side. I think they lead up to the roof. Let me take a look."

Dannaks nodded.

"You do look rather pale. I'll be quick."

Dannaks about faced and leant his back against the gate.

The taxi driver was now hidden behind a broadsheet newspaper. He was still leaning against his car. Only his legs and fingers showed.

Since they'd been there not a single vehicle had passed by. Apart from the ubiquitous twitter of birds there was little sound.

Having voiced his thirst, like an admission, it became an obsession. He was gasping for some water. And he then felt weak. Attempting to climb the gate had sapped him. Dannaks knew he was having a relapse of some kind. He needed to sleep. The best he could do was slide down the gate to sit on his haunches.

After a while his legs began to ache. But he didn't have the energy to stand.

He heard a car coming to a stop and saw the front grill of the vehicle appear behind the taxi. Why hadn't he heard it approach?

The taxi driver folded his newspaper.

Intrigued he tried to get up, but his legs had seized.

Car doors opened and slammed shut

Dannaks used the ground and gate to help himself up. By the time he had straightened and begun brushing himself down they were almost upon him.

10:09

The fresh-faced young men were in the unmistakable navy blue uniforms and caps of the Turkish police.

They spoke to him in Turkish and Dannaks replied as best he could. He told them that he was a German policeman. They didn't believe him. Of course his ID card was meaningless so he hadn't brought it. As far as he knew Reupke's would be in his wallet in the safe too.

The taxi driver was pleading his innocence when Reupke appeared.

This sent the uniforms, neither of whom was over twenty-five, into overdrive. They became agitated and demanded that he get off the property. Reupke smiled and tried to calm them with palm down take-it-easy gestures. He climbed the gate and the second he was over they spun him round and slapped on a pair of handcuffs. Dannaks gave himself up willingly and allowed them to cuff his hands behind his back. They didn't have another set for the poor driver and after he'd surrendered his car keys he got a plastic strip commonly used to bundle wires rather than wrists.

The taxi driver stepped up a gear too and spoke so rapidly that Dannaks only caught the odd word.

On the way to the blue and white patrol car with the word 'Polis' on the doors and bonnet Dannaks saw someone move away from an upper floor window of the house opposite. There was something quite undignified about being handcuffed, but Dannaks wasn't particularly bothered. This was all a mistake that would soon get sorted. His only concern was that he would be back at the hotel in time for lunch with Katja.

He glanced up to the window again as his head was pushed into the back of the car. Without the use of his hands he tumbled onto the back seat and shuffled across just before the taxi driver was pushed in. Reupke was last in. It was such a squeeze that Dannaks decided to lean forward slightly.

One of the uniforms stood outside the car, the other returned to the house, climbed the gate and disappeared.

The one at the car looked in at them and then went to the taxi and locked up.

Eventually the uniforms climbed in.

When they set off, the three men in the back, incapacitated as they were, rocked from side to side, bumping into each other. Dannaks considered wedging his shoulders on the backrest with the others when he almost fell into the foot well. He thought of relating a slow motion tumble later, turning it into an Inspector Clouseau moment. He even considered a controlled roll onto the floor. Although he dismissed the idea, it humoured him and staved off his craving for water for a while.

He eased himself back and Reupke compensated by sitting half sideways onto the door. This created enough space for them to continually bump into each other and initially mutter apologies.

No matter where Dannaks held his clamped wrists: in the small of his back, at the top of his buttocks or at a hip, there was no comfort. He began to sweat.

The car slowed as they entered Side town centre, which was choked with cars and people. To their left was an antique theatre and ruins: a real tourist attraction. Then, to their right they passed an area of taxis and cars and mini-buses.

They turned into a side road and thankfully came to a stop.

The doors were opened and they stumbled out with the help of the uniforms.

Dannaks was soaked and clammy and felt like a common criminal. But he was too wretched to appreciate any sense of humiliation. Reupke on the other hand looked decidedly cheesed-off.

Side police station was a pip-squeak of a building, little more than a shoebox. It was obviously an outpost: a place to take a drunken tourist before being escorted back to his or her hotel. Dannaks wasn't sure it was big enough to offer accommodation for the night.

Some tourists stopped to let them enter the building and a boy spoke to his mother.

"Are *they* pickpockets, mummy?"

"I don't know, dear."

The uniforms spoke to the officer behind the desk and then they took their captives through to a spartan room that contained some wooden chairs and a table. The room was bereft of adornment. There were no shelves, pictures, flags, maps or cameras. A window had been boarded up.

This was their version of an *Untersuchungsraum* (examination room), in which property and personal effects were listed and bagged, and along with shoelaces, belts, ties and the like removed before being locked up, if indeed, they had a jail.

The cuffs were removed and they were told to sit. The detectives sat and rubbed their wrists whilst one of the men cut the taxi driver's bonds.

Dannaks asked for water and then rested his forehead on the table. His thirst and wretchedness had taken its toll. One of the uniforms left the room.

He returned with three plastic cups filled with water. Dannaks greedily drank his down in one go.

The taxi driver pulled out his box of cigarettes only to be told to put them away.

Nothing was said and the minutes ticked by.

Then a big man, in his forties and also in uniform, bustled into the room. He spoke to the other two, one of whom began relating the story so far. The big man, obviously the ranking officer, listened. His breathing was laboured even at rest. A thick brush of a moustache didn't camouflage the amount of nostril hair that bristled out like wire from his large knobbly nose. His skin shone like glazed pastry.

Dannaks tried to follow the young man's story. A neighbour had called in a burglary in progress and they'd driven to the address. They'd found the Turk at the getaway car disguised as a taxi, a man as a lookout at the gate and the younger third man actually on the premises.

Reupke turned to him and spoke quietly. "Tell them to phone Azure Skies. They should ask for Turgut."

Dannaks realised that they had been given no contact name from the police: no liaison officer had been allocated to them. They had been left to their own devices. But of course, this could have been done on purpose. After all, they were here to collect a body and nothing more.

When the young officer finished talking the big man asked his questions. Had they checked the authenticity of the taxi driver? They hadn't had time. Had the house been broken into? No. Was a bag of stolen property found? No. Had they spoken to the neighbour at the scene? No.

The big man was disappointed and Dannaks was about to speak when he thought their conversation had come to an end. But before he could the taxi driver started babbling. The fat officer hushed him and spoke to the detectives. He asked whether they needed a translator. Dannaks thought not and explained as best he could that they were German detectives and that they had come to collect the body of the recently murdered boy. The moment he stated their purpose the blood drained from the man's face. He heard Dannaks out and then stormed out of the room, curtly scolding the two uniforms on his way. The purpose of their presence had impressed him more than the fact that they were detectives. The two uniforms stood humbled in a corner and looked younger than ever.

Dannaks slumped back in his chair feeling that things could only get better. One of the uniforms asked him whether he would like another drink. He said yes.

"You could have had mine," said Reupke, when the uniform left. He hadn't touched his water. "It's probably not bottled."

Dannaks groaned. On top of everything a Delhi belly would be all that he needed. Ha, it could get worse.

The uniform returned with another plastic beaker of water and Dannaks felt obliged to at least sip it.

11:26

One of the young uniforms drove the detectives back to the hotel. The taxi driver made a bid for the trip, but the big huffing-puffing uniform said that there was no time for the roundabout route of driving out to his taxi first. The detectives were expected at the hotel. An officer had been waiting for them for an hour.

The detectives paid the taxi driver, giving him a good tip, which probably couldn't make up for the lost custom.

They were taken through front gate security and dropped at reception. Dannaks would have liked to go back to the room. He wasn't feeling as bad as he had at the station, but he wasn't fit either. He'd gone to the toilet at the station – a hole in the ceramic tiled floor – and hadn't experienced anything other than normal. He could not tell whether his stomach was acting up. It made some gurgling noises and during the drive he had stifled the sound of passing wind. The thought of a drive out to Manavgat, or wherever, to see the body did not appeal.

"It can only get better," said Reupke.

"That's what you think," muttered Dannaks. He'd drunk the water. "My stomach feels queasy."

"I know," said Reupke. "The silent ones are always smellier."

They trudged into the building. Some guests were at reception speaking in subdued tones, changing money, ordering a taxi, making a complaint or enquiry. Ercan was at his desk delivering his spiel to an attentive couple. Behind his routine he was all confidence. He was naturally shy, but like many retiring people he grew disproportionately in his field of expertise. A young family occupied a sofa and easy chair arrangement. A pram was parked at one side, a boy of about five or six was on the floor at the coffee table playing some board game with his seated parents. The bellboy was picking something from under his nails.

A man resembling their taxi driver came up to them. He had been sitting in the lobby bar with someone Dannaks took to be an undercover man.

"*Herr* Dannaks? *Herr* Re-up-key?'

He held out his hand and they shook it in turn.

"Roip-kah," said Reupke.

"Roi?"

"Olaf."

There was something beaten about him. He didn't appear sad or even melancholic. He just looked worn out. Here was a man in desperate need of a holiday. One could say he looked like Dannaks normally felt.

"*Sprechen Sie Englisch?*" he asked.

"A little," said Reupke.

"Some," said Dannaks. "I understand some Turkish too."

"Good, good," he said in English. "My name is Ismail. I am from what you call your *Mord—*" He cut himself off. Perhaps realising that dropping in the occasional German word – he was obviously going to say *Mordkommission* – that he could not properly pronounce was not a good idea. "Homicide." He regarded Dannaks. "Shall we sit? You do not look well."

"I could do with a drink." He caught the bellboy looking at him. The duration of their eye contact disturbed him. Was he still upset because he hadn't received a tip?

"Okeydokey."

Dannaks assumed that he meant yes.

"Are we going to see the body?" asked Reupke, before they could move off towards the lobby bar.

Ismail's expression became apologetic. "No. I am sorry."

"Why not?"

"I, er, know not. I was told yesterday that it – how do you say? – would not be possible."

Dannaks could see that Ismail knew this was weak but didn't or couldn't elaborate.

They walked to the bar in silence. Everyone was out in the sunshine. Ismail declined the offer of a drink and Reupke suggested Dannaks take a cola for his stomach.

They took their drinks to an easy chair arrangement, not unlike that of reception.

Ismail draped his jacket over one of the unoccupied seats. It was a tweed one that wasn't quite classy enough to have come from London's Oxford Savile Row, but was very British nonetheless. His chequered shirt, buttoned up to the limp collar looked inappropriately thick for the weather.

Ismail smiled at the detectives. He was obviously uncomfortable.

"So, you are not bringing us to the body, what have you come here for, if not to take us to the body?" asked Reupke.

174

Dannaks had already pigeonholed the visit as a courtesy call.

"To answer your questions."

Reupke looked at Dannaks.

"Which questions?"

"All of them." Before Reupke could continue Ismail raised his hand.

"But first you must tell me what you do this morning."

"We took a little trip," said Reupke.

"No problem. But you – how is it said? Shook off your tail. Why?"

"We were fed up," said Reupke.

"We wanted to see how easy it would be," Dannaks offered.

Ismail tilted his head to one side and slanted his thin mouth-line in disbelief.

"The tail is for your safety." He looked from one to the other. "There is a murderer on the loose."

Dannaks found it interesting that he hadn't said murderess. But perhaps he wasn't aware of the distinction in English. Or maybe it was he, Dannaks, who was wrong, and the distinction had fallen out of use.

The cola was cool and the carbon dioxide refreshing.

"If you wish I shall instruct them to follow you no more."

"Great," said Reupke, glancing at Dannaks who nodded his approval.

Ismail waited a moment before continuing. "I have heard you have been conducting questionings."

"Nothing official," said Reupke.

"Ah, but you must be careful. I believe Rafael has spoken to his lawyer."

Shit, thought Dannaks. If the Turkish police knew then it could be going up the ranks. Should any of this get back to Germany they could find themselves in deep water.

"I have another question." Reupke gestured for him to continue. "What were you looking for at the house?"

The big Side officer had obviously told him everything.

"We wanted to surprise an old friend," said Reupke.

Ismail nodded. Whether he believed them or not was another matter.

"The house is owned by a *Herr* Volker. Is he your friend? Or were you meeting someone else?"

"Volker," said Reupke, growing uneasy with impatience.

"Really?" Ismail had noticed his uneasiness.

"Yes."

"This has nothing to do with the murder?"

"No. Look, like my colleague, I am tired." He rubbed the back of his neck. "It was a big night last night. The trip and then that pair of rookies handcuffing us. Ah, it is okay. I do not want to get them in trouble, even if they were, er, overzealous. Technically we were trespassing."

Ismail sighed.

"Can you tell me about Volker?"

Dannaks could see Reupke's mind writhing. How much to give away? What he revealed could have consequences.

"He is a small time Hamburg politician," said Dannaks. Ismail's simple English gave him the confidence to speak. "Can I ask you something?" Ismail nodded. "Are you a leading officer in the investigation?"

Ismail shook his head. "I am just – how do they say it? A soldier–"

"Trouper," said Reupke.

"But you are on the investigating team?" said Dannaks.

"Yes. And I have been authorised to answer your questions."

"That is great," said Reupke.

"Are you closer to catching the killer or killers?" asked Dannaks.

Ismail's expression said that this was not a question he had expected. He took his time answering. "We have a number of leads." Clichés were the same the world over, thought Dannaks. "But no, we are not closer to catching the killer or killers."

"Do you think Meryem is the killer?" asked Dannaks, perking up.

"Are you asking me, er, personally, or the team?"

"How about both?" said Reupke.

"Everyone is a suspect."

If the situation had been otherwise Dannaks may have added the words "very good" to a slow clap.

"But personally, no, I do not think she did it."

"Why?" asked Reupke.

"Because of the violence and the shoe print."

"What shoe print?" Reupke was faster.

"There was a print in the blood of a size forty-seven shoe. You didn't see it?"

"Yes. But we could not tell the size."

"Oh."

"What size does Rafael take?" asked Dannaks.

"Forty-four."

"I have to ask," Reupke began. "I know it's a big shoe, even for a man, but could it belong to a woman?"

"She would be very big," said Dannaks.

Reupke glared at him momentarily. Ismail should be answering the questions. Dannaks returned a "sorry, point taken" nod.

"Mr. Dannaks is right. She would have to be very big. And we have come across no one that big. She would stand out."

"Of course." Reupke hadn't given up. "But it would have taken someone strong to beat Peter."

"Someone strong or with the advantage of surprise and a weapon. He was hit with a tyre iron before being stabbed."

"Do you mean crowbar?" asked Reupke.

"What is crowbar?"

Reupke produced a pen and lightly, so as not to tear it, drew a line with a curved two-pronged end on the thinly padded paper mat that he took from under his glass.

"No," said Ismail. Reupke drank down the remains of his water. "It was straight, like this." And he drew a straight line with two prongs at one end.

"Where did you find it?" asked Dannaks.

"In the room."

"Ismail," said Dannaks, pulling out his notepad, "why do you not walk us through it?"

"Walk?"

"Tell us what you – your team – think happened," said Reupke, taking out his notepad too.

"From the beginning," said Dannaks.

"We will not interrupt," said Reupke, glancing at his colleague.

Ismail went over a lot of ground that was familiar to the detectives, but as promised, they didn't interrupt him. As he proceeded Dannaks realised they had hit the jackpot. From the level of detail he appeared to be telling them everything. Dannaks also felt that Ismail was disillusioned with the slowness of the case.

The killing took place on Monday evening, ten days ago. That evening the animation team performed a few sketches, introduced the touring guests and wound up with the club dance and the appeal to wander into the disco. The touring guests comprised a local carpet outlet presenting their wares with a belly dancer interrupting as a side attraction. This was followed by a Fakir who walked on glass, pulled his organs in so that his stomach area was a cavity, and bent an iron rod using a point at the top of his chest and bottom of his neck against the force of two men from the audience. Finally a dance troupe of three women and three men accompanied by three musicians presented folk dances to traditional music.

During this show, which lasted about an hour and ten minutes the animation, team were free. Only Yunus, Cemil and Fabio, doing lighting, sound and playing dog's body respectively were present the entire time.

Habip had the day off and had left the hotel and didn't return until after the police had arrived. Meryem was meant to do the introductions, but Fehime did them for her as a favour. Meryem appeared in one of the initial sketches before going up to see Peter who also had the day off.

According to all concerned Meryem and Peter were becoming a couple.

She was supposed to be on stage with the rest of the sketch crew and the performers at the end of the show for the club dance. She didn't appear. They expected her to be at the disco. When she didn't appear there too, Rafael volunteered to go and get her.

The last anyone saw of her was when she picked up two bottles of water at the plaza bar to go to Peter.

What went on in the room is speculation. However, Peter was probably hit with the crowbar before being stabbed. The only prints on it were his and they were in his blood and centrally positioned.

The detectives listened intently, jotting notes for subsequent discussion.

Meryem's blood type was found on a partial palm print on the side of the bathroom doorframe.

The killer took the knife, but not the crowbar, which was left between a bed and a wall. This explained the brown tip of the unidentifiable object in the photograph.

Residue, the kind used as a lubricant for latex gloves, was found on the crowbar and Peter's body. Dannaks realised that this pointed to premeditation: murder rather than a spontaneous crime of passion.

Peter was stabbed in the upper torso. His hands and arms showed defence wounds. A main artery was hit so he would have bled to death within minutes. But the killer chose to leave nothing to chance and cut his throat. This last act and the initial bludgeoning had not been made public. All the media had was that Peter had been stabbed to death.

Rafael arrived between eleven fifteen and eleven thirty. He entered the room. Seeing Peter and realising he was dead he ran down to reception and the police were called. Before they arrived security posted a man in front of the door.

Other than some blood, Meryem's type, on a wall not far from the room, and smudges of Peter's blood on the path there were no clues outside. Ismail promised to show them the wall.

"We interviewed everybody," Ismail said, some tension dropping from his shoulders as he came to the end of his monologue. "Especially large men with forty-seven shoe." He paused. "Rafael has size forty-four. He was taken in and thoroughly interviewed." He paused again. "I think that is all I can tell you."

"Is there more?" Reupke asked. "I mean, what about trace? Hairs, fibres..."

"No."

"What about leads?"

"We have many."

Reupke waited and Ismail's expression gave him away.

"Anything you can tell us?" Dannaks added.

"I do not think so."

"I have more questions," said Reupke, flipping a page of his notepad, absently trying to decipher his scribble.

"Please," Ismail nodded.

"You said Peter's prints were the only ones on the crowbar. And you said that they were central. Like this?" He held his pen in the middle with two fingers and a thumb."

"Yes," said Ismail, "but it was a part hand print, of course."

"Of course."

"There were fingerprints but not enough for proper identification. It was said that they could all belong to the victim."

"So Peter was not holding it at one end," said Reupke.

Dannaks knew that he was implying that Peter had grasped the crowbar in a defensive rather than aggressive way.

"So we could say he was holding it to swing it."

Ismail nodded. "Yes, but how he was holding it first we cannot say."

"Could the crowbar have belonged to Peter?" asked Reupke. "For protection?"

"We have no evidence to suggest this."

"And none to say it was not the case."

"No."

They silently digested what had been said.

"What about the Peter's missing book?" Dannaks asked.

Ismail raised his eyebrows.

"We saw the clear patch on the photograph and we know he was writing a book," Dannaks explained.

"We have it not."

"Did Rafael say he saw it?"

"No."

"So someone was there before him. Or the killer took it. Or Meryem."

"You do not believe the killer and Meryem are the same person?"

"Do you?" asked Reupke.

The detectives waited, but it soon became obvious that Ismail wasn't going to answer.

"There were two bottles of water in the room," said Dannaks. "Did she bring those?"

"Possibly. Her prints are on them. The barman too."

"Carrying bottles of water to the room is hardly the action of someone who is about to kill."

Ismail smiled and nodded.

"What about the excrement on the walls of the plaza toilet?" asked Dannaks. Ismail clearly didn't understand the word excrement. "*Scheiße*? Shit?"

Ismail continued to smile, but this time he shook his head slightly. "You have learnt much for detectives who are not investigating." He regarded them momentarily. "We have nothing. These incidents started weeks before the killing. They may be unrelated." Ismail checked his watch. "I shall have to leave soon."

"What about other leads?" asked Reupke.

"I cannot say."

"We are police."

"Not Turkish police. And not investigating."

"Then there is no point going on," said Reupke, demonstratively snapping shut his notepad.

"What is your personal opinion about what happened?" asked Dannaks, comparatively calmly.

Ismail looked at him. Was he wondering what he was allowed to say?

"Do you think Meryem killed him?"

Ismail shook his head. "We have the training shoe print that does not belong to anyone we know. The killing was with much violence."

"And a crowbar is not a woman's weapon of choice," said Reupke. "The blows were delivered with terrific force."

"Passion?" said Ismail. "She did not scream or call for help if someone else killed him."

"You have not answered my question," Dannaks pointed out.

Ismail smiled resignedly. "No."

"No you have not answered my question or no she did not do it?"

"I do not think she is the killer. But this is my personal opinion and—"

"Let us say for a minute someone else killed Peter," Dannaks said. "How did the killer get into the hotel? And more importantly, how did he get away drenched in blood?"

"He could have sneaked in from the beach," said Ismail. "And that is also how he got away."

"He washed himself off in the sea. True?" said Dannaks.

"Maybe he used the bathroom," suggested Reupke. Of course, they had not seen any photographs of the bathroom.

Ismail was silent for a moment and when he spoke he spoke quietly as if he didn't want to say it. "No. I do not think so. There was no blood in the toilet."

"Your theory coincides with mine," said Dannaks triumphantly.

Ismail smiled, but didn't give anything away. He looked at his watch again.

"What about hotel cameras?"

"Nothing of use." He explained that they only covered the hotel entrances and hotel area of the beach. Other hotels also had cameras. Some weren't working. Also it was dark and anyone near the sea, beyond the loungers or between hotels would be merely a shadow if caught. Ismail again looked at his watch.

"What time is it?" said Dannaks rhetorically, because he then looked at his own watch. He was horrified to see that it was nearing twelve thirty.

"You wanted to show us where the blood was found outside," said Reupke.

"Yes," said Ismail, leaning forward. "Then we should go now."

The detectives closed and pocketed their notepads.

"I will meet you up there," said Dannaks. Then to Reupke: "I said I'd meet Katja at twelve thirty. I'll tell her I'm going to be late."

12:35

Dannaks hopped from one foot to the other with impatience. He'd arrived outside the restaurant spot on twelve-thirty. The doors had opened and the glut of people had swiftly disappeared. Now he stood to one side as people streamed in and out.

Katja was now only five minutes late, not enough to warrant an apology.

He wondered what he was missing: what Ismail was telling Reupke.

He checked his watch and saw that only fifteen seconds had past since he last looked.

Dannaks strolled away from the restaurant. He walked nonchalantly at first, but when he was close to the furthest table from the restaurant he stopped and looked about. Another glance at his watch told him it was twelve thirty-seven. He looked about again and then strode off. He kept looking as he negotiated the amphitheatre, but now he hoped he would not meet her.

He raced across the plaza and took the steps up to reception two at a time.

It was twelve forty-three when he reached their room. He was panting and there was a sheen of sweat on his skin. A drop formed at his temple and edged downward. He brushed it away and rapped on the door. There was no answer and he couldn't hear them. He stepped away and stood and listened. Then he wandered away from the building, deciding to go uphill.

"Dannaks." It was Reupke. He was standing behind a short wall. Ismail came into view.

When he reached them he saw that they were standing in a dip in the ground, not deep enough to be called a ditch. The dip was the end of the hill and the wall was the boundary of a ground floor terrace. Like their own, this too was the size of the balcony above it.

"We found blood on this wall," Ismail repeated for Dannaks's benefit. "And, er, sick, here." He pointed to an area nearest the wall.

"Was the flat door open or closed when Rafael arrived?" asked Dannaks.

"A little open."

"And he went in?"

"Yes. He said he knew the victim was dead. But he went in to find Meryem."

"Then you know that someone left – or entered – the room during the killing?"

"No," said Ismail.

"Why do you say that?" asked Reupke who looked annoyed.

Dannaks slipped into German. "Because it just occurred to me what was bugging me about the photos. There was blood on the a/c. The slats were closed."

"That means a door was open," said Reupke, also in German and brightening.

"Yes," said Dannaks, "but we found blood on the inside. Which means that the door was closed at some point during the killing." The clean patch showing where Peter's book had lain had distracted him from the subtlety of the closed a/c unit.

Ismail looked from one to the other. "I do not understand."

"We will show you," said Dannaks.

Ismail looked at his watch.

"Have you time?" asked Reupke.

"Yes."

They led Ismail back to their apartment and stood him in front of the a/c unit with the key in place and the front door ajar. The unit remained closed. Reupke shut the front door and the unit hummed and shuddered into life, the slats rotating open to emit cool air. Dannaks pointed out the brown the blood. Ismail fingered the smudge where Reupke had taken his swab.

"You know it is blood?" said Ismail. It was a question.

"Yes," said Dannaks.

"So," began Reupke. "As he said–" he tipped his head towards Dannaks – "someone entered or left during the killing."

"Was the struggle taken to the door?" asked Dannaks. "And that is how it got closed."

Ismail looked as if his thoughts had been rudely interrupted.

"No, there was not enough blood."

They stood in silence for a moment.

"Maybe you should have spoken to us earlier?" Reupke was still irritated.

But the Turkish officer didn't rise to the bait. He merely watched the a/c unit. "Someone will come and check this," he muttered.

The three of them stood silently.

"Now I must go," said Ismail suddenly.

"Shall we come with you?" asked Dannaks.

"I know the way."

As an afterthought he stopped and pulled out his wallet and gave Dannaks two visiting cards.

The two detectives reciprocated.

"Give him your handy number," said Dannaks. "He may need to contact us."

Reupke almost reluctantly wrote down his handy number on the back of his card.

Ismail must have felt obliged to do the same. He took his card back from Dannaks.

Dannaks walked him to the door.

When he was gone Dannaks said: "You were a bit hard on him."

"Well, I'm fed up with it. We haven't been told anything." He had opened the terrace doors and was looking outside.

"He was the first person to give us something and you chewed him out in the end."

"And what did he give us that we didn't already know?" he asked drilling Dannaks with his eyes.

"His personal theory." Reupke slanted his mouth to question its worth. "He may not have told us everything, but his theory is based on all he knows. All the evidence."

"Okay." The tension left Reupke s shoulders.

"And his theory coincides with mine—"

"Don't get carried away. It's all conjecture."

"It's all we've got."

Reupke showed his palms.

"I'd say somebody left when the killing started," said Dannaks. "And I'd go further and say that that someone was Meryem. Why she didn't go for help or call out, I don't know. The killer left and went down to the beach and washed himself off in the sea."

"I wonder whether anyone reported seeing a dripping wet giant."

Exacerbated Dannaks threw his arms in the air.

Reupke knew he'd gone a little too far. "I'm tired." He walked over to the bedside table with the telephone.

"Me too, but at least I'm trying."

"Okay." His hand was reaching for the phone. "When are you meeting Katja?"

Dannaks blanched. Shit. He'd forgotten all about her. "I, er, didn't see her." It had turned one.

Reupke raised his eyebrows. "I'm phoning Dagmar." Dannaks turned to leave. "You might want to take that shower before going."

Shit.

13:23

He had probably taken one of his quickest showers in history. Dannaks had almost fled the room towel in hand, hobbling out with his sandals not properly on, closing the top of his khaki shorts.

Reupke had stayed behind. Dagmar had had a late breakfast and wanted to meet at a quarter to two for lunch. This suited Reupke because he wanted a lie down.

Dannaks would have liked to question Reupke about what Ismail had said in his absence. But there had been no time.

Before he reached reception he put his watch ten minutes ahead. He was disgusted with himself for doing it, but could think of nothing better.

The standing billboard on the stage of the amphitheatre reminded him that it was Gala evening and that black and white was the dress code.

The restaurant was still quite busy, but the clientele had changed. There were very few children and of the families present most were waiting on one member to finish.

Katja was sitting alone at a table in the shade eating a creme caramel. She looked up just before he reached her.

Dannaks adopted a pained expression as he apologised.

"What happened?" she asked.

"The police arrived to talk to us. I waited here – well, over there–" he gestured behind himself to the main path leading to the restaurant "– until a quarter to–" he tapped his watch "– to tell you I would have to come later."

"I'm surprised. I was here at twelve thirty-seven." She tilted her head to look at his watch. "What time do you make it?"

When he told her she said that he was running ten minutes fast. Dannaks queried this with a waiter cleaning a neighbouring table. "Your right," he said, turning back the hands of his watch. "I'm running fast. I'm sorry." He was still standing at the table.

"Aren't you going to get something to eat?"

He felt awkward. "Er, yes."

When he returned she had finished eating and was drinking water. They were silent for a while. Then Katja said: "The restaurant opens at half past twelve. I'm surprised you didn't realise."

Dannaks thought to argue that they could have opened late. Instead he smiled awkwardly.

"I'm not a detective all the time."

"Off duty?"

His smile didn't improve.

She evidently noticed his awkwardness. "Still, I suppose it was good of you to come at all. And I was a tick late. I'll try to be more punctual next time."

"And I'll show more patience," he said, hoping that put an end to the subject.

"Did the police have anything to say?"

"Nothing we didn't already know."

She smiled. "I know you can't tell me anything."

"Sorry."

"What about your trip?"

"It all went rather wrong."

"Oh?" And he told her about going to the house and getting arrested and taken to Side police station. He even talked of the novelty of being handcuffed. But he omitted divulging the owner of the house.

They fell silent again and Dannaks took the opportunity to make inroads on his plate. He hadn't taken much; wary of how his stomach could react. But he now realised he was famished.

"I waited until that Russian woman said something before telling her that you weren't coming back."

Dannaks paused. "Sorry. I didn't ask."

"You're eating," she said.

Katja was like his mother, a pacifier, always taking the compromise rather than conflict route.

Katja grew animated. "A guy in a Hawaii shirt asked me where you had gone. He was pretty angry. I said I didn't know – which was true. I had trouble later. They asked me again at the plaza when I was getting ready for Nordic walking. They didn't believe me and almost stopped me going."

"But you went?" he asked, concerned.

"Yes."

"Did they bother you any more?"

"No. And if you say you're sorry, I'll hit you."

He laughed and she smiled. In that moment any vestiges of unease were swept away.

Dannaks put down his knife and fork. "I'm still hungry, I'm afraid."

"Go and get some more. I'll keep you company."

Dannaks returned with another plate of food and was pouring himself another glass of water when Reupke and Dagmar appeared, plates in hand.

"Mind if we join you?" asked Dagmar. She looked strangely ragged and yet attractive and glowing.

"Be our guests," said Katja.

"I need to show you something," Katja said to Dannaks.

"The photos?" Dagmar asked and Katja nodded.

Dannaks's expression questioned them. Reupke was in the know but inexplicably pretended to not know.

Katja answered. "Of the show."

"Oh," said Dannaks, feigning interest. "Are they, er, any good?"

Reupke concentrated on his food and kept his head down.

"Some of them," said Dagmar.

"The dancer," said Reupke without looking up.

"Olaf," exclaimed Dagmar thumping him on the arm.

Reupke smiled broadly.

"Some of them," repeated Dagmar to Dannaks. And she went on to describe a couple of photographs. Then the conversation dropped into an analysis and reliving of the highlights of show.

"What about tonight?" Dannaks asked, placing his knife and fork on his empty plate. "Have you all got something black and white to wear?" He'd only brought one white shirt and it was long-sleeved. He had intended flying back in it, carrying his tie in his pocket until they reached Hamburg. His neck had recovered, but the edge of the collar was no longer white and the thought of it rubbing his neck worried him. He hadn't expected the tie to make such a difference and he certainly should have removed it during the flight. Perhaps he could risk wearing the shirt on the return journey, but not tonight. Not in front of Katja.

The women nodded and Reupke did too.

"Buy something at the shop," Katja suggested.

Dagmar nodded her approval.

"Good idea," said Dannaks.

Katja asked whether he was going to have dessert. He had eaten two main courses. When he said no, she said she wanted to get back to her paperback. Dagmar asked her what she was reading and the girls talked about books and authors for a while.

Meanwhile Dannaks spoke to Reupke. "I'll need the key."

Reupke handed it to him. "I wanted to do the three o'clock gym, so I'll need to get my kit. Where will you be?"

"I don't know."

"I've got a place at the adult pool," said Katja. Dannaks wondered how she could listen to two conversations at once. "Would you like to laze around with me?"

"Yeah," said Dannaks. Then to Reupke: "I'll be in the shop, at the room or at the poolside."

"You left out the beach and reception," smiled Reupke.

"We might take a beach walk," said Katja, looking at Dannaks who nodded. "But we won't go until we've seen you."

Reupke nodded; his was mouth full.

"Okay?" Katja asked Dannaks reaching for a floppy bag hanging from the back of her chair.

Dannaks downed the remains of his water and nodded.

13:54

At the plaza they looked at the clutter in the window for a moment, Katja saying that she'd let him shop alone. He would have liked her help. Then they went into the photographer's and stood at one of the lecterns with the embedded touch screen.

Behind the desk at the end of the corridor of lecterns was the photographer's friend or apprentice. He looked bored and was cleaning some camera equipment.

Katja tapped her way through the menu and scrolled down the file index of passport-sized photographs. Dannaks realised that the photographer had had a field day. Each couple had been photographed performing each task at least once. He'd also captured the delight of some member of the audience. Habip and the girls were there too. And there were at least a half a dozen shots of Patricia in compromising positions on the chair. But all these were secondary to the ones of Dannaks himself. Most had caught him heavy-lidded as if he was drunk. Katja looked flushed with alcohol in some pictures. One shot stood out above all others. The camera angle used during the golf ball game made it look as if Katja was giving him a blowjob. His rapturous expression didn't help. "Oh God," he exclaimed.

"Don't say what it looks like," she said.

"They're all deplorable."

"These aren't bad," she said, gesturing to some posed shots of them on their thrones wearing their crowns. "I think I might buy one."

"I'll buy it."

"You—"

"I insist. I'll buy a copy for myself too."

They followed the menu and made their purchase using Dannaks's room number.

"How do we get the photos?" Dannaks asked the young man.

"You pick them up here, tomorrow."

Once outside Katja said: "You can't see where I am from here. See that towel with the tiger on? I'm over there, off to the left."

"I'll find you."

"Don't forget your trunks and towel."

He nodded.

"Around three. Give or take half an hour."

He smiled at the broad time margin. "Leaving nothing to chance then?"

"Don't forget to haggle."

She left and he turned to the clothes shop, but he didn't go in. Instead he checked Katja's progress before entering the photographer's again.

"Listen," he said to the youth. "Would it be possible to buy all the photographs?"

"Yes."

"No, I mean including the, er, source. The originals." The youth didn't understand. Damn digital. He couldn't say negatives. "I want them removed from the system."

The youth was horrified. "I don't know. Why?"

"It's what I want."

"I must ask."

"Okay. I'll come back later."

He left and wandered into the shop. The amount of stuff was so overwhelming that Dannaks didn't immediately see the only other person in the place: a man sitting on a carpet at the far end of the shop. They nodded to one another and then the man went back to drinking his tea from his liquor-sized glass. He had a number of papers on the floor and Dannaks assumed he was sorting bills or doing his accounts.

All manner of bric-a-brac covered every available surface and wall. This was a veritable Aladdin's cave. Between the clothing were souvenirs, games, water toys, postcards, miniature carpets, beads and jewellery. Compared to the stylised hotel shop where everything was laid out in small quantities this place was chock-a-block. It was the kind of place that exhausted the imagination of what might not be available. After a time his eyes became more

190

discerning. He could see something of order in the arrangements of clothing, both hanging and on shelves.

Telling his eyes to seek out clothing in black and white, he quickly reduced the choice.

He was fingering a white cotton shirt, wondering whether the embroidered pattern was too effeminate, when someone entered the shop.

"*Guten Tag*," said the man, who Dannaks recognised as one of the men he'd often seen sitting at a table with others in front of the shops. He was in his mid-thirties, dressed in black trousers and black open-necked shirt. In fact a sizeable portion of his chest was on display. A gold chain hung about his neck, but it was quite short and didn't dangle. Matching this were his gold bracelet and two rings on the little and ring finger of his left hand.

"Hallo," Dannaks said.

The newcomer spoke in Turkish to the older man on the carpet. Dannaks knew he had scolded him for not attending to the customer. The man on the carpet wasn't having any of it and retorted that Dannaks hadn't wanted any help and besides he was busy and not sitting outside in the sun. The newcomer flared and said something along the lines of: we'll speak later.

"Can I help you?" he asked.

"Maybe. Is this, er, a man's shirt?"

"Of course, of course. Look at the buttons."

"It's for tonight."

"Then you'd want black trousers. Or perhaps a black shirt?"

"Yes, but how much is this shirt?"

"Ah, let's worry about that at the end. I'll give you a good price."

"Yes, but–"

"Do you just want the shirt on its own?"

"No–"

"Then, let's put it all together and you will see. I will give you a good price."

Dannaks acquiesced. And thus he gave himself up to the slaughter. The white shirt was placed on a glass counter Dannaks had not noticed. Then came a suitable pair of black linen trousers. The man said that he had seen him with the beautiful blonde woman. Maybe he should buy a black shirt too. Then she could decide what would suit him best. Dannaks's hesitation was taken as consent. And then there were shoes. They had a good range of black socks. Dannaks said he'd heard they didn't last. Of course this was not true. Anyway, they were so cheap, said the man, that even if Dannaks only wore them twice he would be getting a bargain. And here, feel the thickness. That wasn't going to wear away quickly. The boxer shorts were next. And I see you looking at that sweatshirt. What about a T-shirt? A part of Dannaks was a willing customer in the frenzy of buying. He didn't normally buy clothes. So when he did make the effort, he tended to give in. Once one item was bought, the floodgates opened and he was open to further purchases. Half way through the killing, Dannaks said that he couldn't carry any more, but the man had an answer to this too. "Here, we have cases." At some point, when Dannaks was behind the small railed curtain pulling on a pair of jeans he was asked whether he would like a tea. He declined, mainly because he was growing quite hot in the heavy air of the shop. He had seen an appropriate gift for his nephew and once that was placed on the pile he had to find gifts for his niece and the rest of his family.

There was one small incident during the slaughter. Two boys ran into the shop. They were loud and rude and opened and unfolded what took their fancy. The old man got up and the boys ran off. "Your children know no respect," he muttered in German.

The younger man scolded him in Turkish and apologised to Dannaks who merely shrugged.

Eventually the killing was over. Even the man lost his enthusiasm and only half-heartedly, asked whether he would like to buy anything else. His purchases filled the small case he had chosen. The man went through the stuff tapping into his pocket calculator.

"Two hundred and fifty four euros and sixty seven cents. But I'll give it to you for two hundred and forty."

"No. That's way over what I want to pay."

"Look at this case. It is solid; made to last a hundred years."

"No, let's put something back."

"Wait, wait. What do you want to pay?"

Dannaks looked at him and then the pile of clothing.

"What is your price?" asked the man.

"I don't know."

"You have a full wardrobe here. Tell me your price?"

"Two hundred."

"Oh, please." He looked pained. "All this for two hundred. Please. I have to make a living. You should give me something."

"I–"

"Wait." And he tapped into his calculator again. "Okay. You are a good customer. You want to hear my best price? Just for you."

Dannaks nodded.

"But listen, don't tell anybody. Not even your girlfriend. Otherwise you will make me bankrupt."

"Okay." Dannaks was getting a little peeved. He was annoyed that he was allowing himself to be so easily duped.

The man lowered his voice, leaned forward and glanced at the door. "My best price?"

"Yes."

"Two hundred and thirty."

"No, no. Look I–"

"Tell me then. What do you want to pay?"

Dannaks wanted it to end.

"Two twenty."

"Oh," he exclaimed wounded. But he was hurrying because he could see that his customer was losing patience. "Okay. Final price. Two twenty five." And he slammed the flat of his hand on the top of the case.

"Okay," Dannaks sighed with relief. The man held out his hand and they shook on it.

Dannaks explained that he would have to go to get the money. He showed the man his room key and left.

15:06

He was horrified when he saw the time. The sound of one of the animation team over the amplifier alerted him. Music punctuated his speech, rising and lowering, as he delivered the afternoon programme.

Reupke hadn't turned up looking for the key. He must have changed his mind about going to sport.

Dannaks paused at the watch shop. His favourite watch enticed him and he was still in the grip of vestiges of his spending spree. But there was no time.

He walked swiftly through reception, nodding at Ercan, who was at his desk. The bellboy smiled and he gave him a quick smile back.

When he got to their room a cleaner's trolley was parked in front of the open door. Amongst the shower gel refills, toilet rolls, cleaning implements, was a clipboard and pen. He noticed this because there was also a ledger of sorts on the wall.

He went in.

"Merhaba," he said to the woman with her shiny face framed by a dark headscarf. She was wiping surfaces with a damp cloth.

He smiled and jabbed his finger at the cupboard. She said something he didn't catch. He opened the safe and took money from his wallet, folding it into his pocket. After hearing the safe close with a whirr, he stood and found his swimming trunks. He grabbed the nicely folded towel. Reupke's was clumsily folded. In the bathroom, he went to the toilet, put the trunks on under his underpants, squeezed some sun cream onto his hand and hurriedly creamed his legs, arms, shoulders, neck and face. Then he was out and rapidly descending the path.

The plaza was busy with people drinking coffee and eating cake. The crew was milling about.

At the shop he paid the man and they agreed to put the case filled with his purchases to one side for a later pick-up. Before this the man dropped in a gaudy necklace with large fruity stones looking like oversized wine-gums. He explained that it was a gift for his beautiful wife. Dannaks smiled, but he had mixed feelings. This was confirmation that he had been had. Oh, the necklace wasn't expensive. But the gesture said that the man had made a killing and this offering was to promote good will or alleviate any guilt.

Once outside, although it was coming up to three thirty, he didn't go directly to Katja. Instead he entered the photographer's. He'd seen the photographer sitting inside before going into the clothes shop.

"Hallo, I was here earlier and asked whether I could have the originals from yesterday's show. I'll pay."

The man was prepared, primed by his assistant who was arranging packets of memory cards in the cabinet behind the desk.

"I am sorry. It is not possible."

"Why?"

"I cannot do it."

"Look let's say three other people will want to buy them, then I'll give you three times the price for each photograph."

"Why do you want to do this?"

"Never mind. Can I buy them?"

"I don't understand."

"You don't have to understand. Can I buy them? Yes or no."

"You want them deleted?"

"Yes."

The man shook his head. "I cannot do it."

"Five times."

The man's eyes widened.

"Come on. Five times."

"In four weeks I'll give them to you for five times."

"No. It has to be now."

The man tutted. "I can't."

Dannaks sighed and threw his hands in the air. "Your loss." He knew that all he had accomplished was to arouse the man's suspicions.

"In three month's they will be gone," the man called after him.

Dannaks half-waved him away and found himself out in the daylight.

Music was playing; five adults, four women and a man were doing leisurely lengths in the pool. More than half the loungers were occupied; towels, bags, paperbacks and toys claimed the rest. He was angry but nobody paid him any attention. A glance was the best he got and he was pleased that there was nothing more. He wasn't in a good frame of mind and was struggling to lighten his attitude.

He found Katja lying on her back, her face behind her paperback. Two loungers away was the tiger towel, crumpled and abandoned. He realised that he'd never seen anyone with it. It was continually abandoned and yet it was never in the same place. Katja was so engrossed that she didn't dip her book until his unmoving shadow disturbed her.

"Hi," she said, lifting her sunglasses and squinting. "What time is it?"

"Half past. The shop took longer than I thought."

"You didn't get fleeced, did you?"

"No, but I put a significant hole in their stock."

She smiled.

"I even had to buy a suitcase."

She laughed. "Come on big spender, find yourself a lounger and park it next to me."

He was manoeuvring his lounger next to hers when Yunus asked them whether they wanted to take part in the poolside game.

"No," said Dannaks.

"What are you doing?" asked Katja.

"I don't care what it is," said Dannaks, arranging his towel. "I've had my dose of humiliation for this year."

"We've got a surfboard," said Yunus, "and you've got to balance on it from one side of the pool to the other."

"It sounds fun, but not today."

Yunus moved on without insisting. Mustering up enthusiasm was not his forté.

Dannaks sat down, pulled off his sandals, shorts and T-shirt. When he emerged out of his T-shirt he found Katja looking at him queerly. She smiled, put her book facedown on her lounger and said: "Come here." She reached over to his cheek and he thought she was going to kiss him. "You've got a streak of sun cream on your face." She rubbed it in and her touch filled him with ecstasy.

"I feel like a little boy," he said.

"All men are."

She unscrewed the top of a bottle of water at her side and drank deeply. He lay back and stretched, putting his hands behind his head. "You didn't bring anything to read?"

"I'm not a great reader. Go ahead. I'm happy." And he was. Even if the shopkeeper had made a killing he couldn't complain about the price. Certainly he would have paid double that in Hamburg. And did the photographs really matter? He realised too that he no longer felt wretched. His stomach was fine. He felt cleansed and vulnerable.

"I could get used to this," he said.

"You said that yesterday."

He nodded, but she didn't look over. "I don't want to keep disturbing you–" She looked over at him, the paperback poised in the air. "But did Olaf come by?"

"No. I haven't seen him."

"I'll shut up now."

He closed his eyes. Then he opened them at the sound of some commotion. He couldn't locate its source. Was it boys' screaming with delight or pain? The sound wasn't repeated and he assumed delight.

Dannaks put his arms down at his sides. He wondered about getting a drink. He sat up and looked around. An elderly woman sedately doing the breaststroke, her hair piled up on her head, looked at him. She looked away before he could. He expelled at blast of air and looked down at the meanderings of an ant moving in short straight lines as if joining some invisible dot-to-dot picture Dannaks couldn't see.

"I–" he began.

"Okay, come on," she said snapping her book shut.

"I didn't–"

"I've reached a good point to stop."

"I–" his expression became a plea. "I guess I'm not very good at this."

"At what? Relaxing?"

"Yes," he admitted. She'd seen it right away. He wasn't good at relaxing. Huh, that something like taking it easy required practise was a revelation.

"Let's go for a walk."

He didn't really want to go for a walk, but he couldn't think of anything better. They put on their sandals and strolled towards the shack.

The game was starting. A young man ran towards the surfboard Yunus held in the water. He balanced on it as it moved with his momentum across the pool. But he didn't get far.

They went past the loose queue of contestants. Groups of children were watching; others were playing tag. "No running," said some woman. "It's slippery and you'll crack your skull open."

The white tablecloth hanging over the tables laden with coffee and cake fluttered and caught their eyes. "Another reason for a walk," muttered Katja.

They went past the children's pool, their ears assailed by the cacophony. Toys floated at the edges, but mostly there were splashes and yelps coming from the slides. Mothers chatted. Fathers stood about with cameras looking somehow uncomfortable and lost. In the small round pool a father, oblivious to it all and beaming with pride, sat playing with the baby in his lap.

There was a slip of peace after the poolside before the sound of the aerobic session pulsed in their ears. The repetitive thock of tennis balls being hit to their left was eventually drowned by the continual rush of the sea. More kids were in the children's club playground.

At the beach they removed their sandals and walked on the sand.

"You're very quiet," said Katja. "Is everything okay?"

"Yeah, fine. Sorry. I guess I'm sad about going back tomorrow."

"Enjoy it while you can."

"Yes, I suppose so."

They passed no man's land and the embers of some party. He needed to learn to relax. Maybe Katja would teach him?

"You know it's funny. I feel as if I've only just arrived." Yet, their arrival, standing in the foyer with the Turkish police, the young translator and Goldfinger, seemed aeons ago.

They walked on.

At some point they stopped to look out at the sea, to fill their lungs and feast their eyes. And on impulse Dannaks held her hand. He felt a glow he hadn't felt in years and he wanted to open up to her. He wanted to tell her everything, so that she could see that he was lonely and pitiful, and that her love would solve all his problems in one fell swoop. But he couldn't. To do so would be to scare her off. So he chose silence.

Katja stooped and picked up a small shell, but it was broken and she dropped it. He began looking for shells, hoping to find one to please her. He found one and showed it to her. She took it and examined it. And he realised that they were no longer holding hands, but resolved to let her make the first move.

Many people were walking. An occasional hawker, with gossamer pastel scarves, beaded necklaces and bracelets or fruit tried to grab their interest.

"Shall we turn around?"

Dannaks nodded.

He felt content. The silence between them was easy: practised like a married couple. It wasn't as if they had nothing to say, more that words weren't necessary. Their connection was that strong and they knew each other well enough to make silence a bond.

Of course they hadn't left the mayhem, but the beach walk had delivered them. It had given them some sanctuary.

The music from the aerobics session had slowed and the participants were on mats doing floor exercises. The nearest tennis players were rubbing the backs of their necks with towels or drinking from bottles. A lot of the children had left the playground. In the short space of their walk things were noticeably winding down.

Dannaks didn't want the day to end. He wanted more time with Katja. He wanted more fun and he wanted to relax. So that when he got to the children's pool he found himself watching a man having a race with his son on the wide undulating slide. "That looks like fun," he said.

"I will if you will," said Katja.

Dannaks was dumbstruck.

"You went on stage for me yesterday. Let's do it."

Yes, damn it. Reupke was having fun. Why couldn't he have some too?

He couldn't put down the joy in her face and smiled. "Okay. You want a race?"

They slipped off their sandals, Katja placing her heavy-rimmed glasses on a table, and went up the wet fibreglass steps that resembled stone. There were half a dozen children at the top.

"Hey, Schimi," said one of the boys, over the sound of running water.

"Behave yourself or I'll have you in eights," called Dannaks.

The boy gave him a puzzled look and Dannaks clapped his wrists together to show that he meant handcuffs. He had used the police-speak to impress the boy.

"I'll go over there," said Katja.

"Are you racing?" asked the boy.

"Yes," said Katja.

"We'll race with you," said another boy.

Katja looked at Dannaks.

"Okay," he said, looking down the faded rainbow of the slide and the continuous flow of water that kept it wet. The slope seemed steeper up here.

"Me too," said a third boy.

"There's not enough room," said Dannaks. "Somebody could get hurt."

"Heiko," said a man with a camera at the poolside. "I can't wait all day."

"Are we going?" asked Katja, sitting at the edge.

Dannaks and the two boys took up position.

"Hands in the air," said one of the boys.

Dannaks looked at Katja who raised her hands.

"She counts," said Dannaks.

"On three," shouted Katja. "Onnnnne, twooooooo, three."

Dannaks launched himself with a shove and was in the water before he could properly look around.

"I won," said one of the boys.

"No way," said the other.

Dannaks looked for Katja and spotted her head bobbing some distance away. She would get out at the other side. He couldn't cross the path of the slide to get to her.

"Let's have another go," suggested one of the boys.

"That's enough for me," said Dannaks. The cold of the water was more exhilarating than the slide. The boys half waded and swam with him.

"What about the chute?" asked the boy. "It's better than that."

"It's like a slalom," said the other. "It goes dark in the middle too."

"No, I don't think so."

Dannaks walked up and down in the sun near his sandals until Katja arrived. Then they went back to their loungers and dried themselves. On the way Dannaks said that he was glad they did it.

As he was drying himself he saw that the tiger towel was gone.

Katja drank water from her bottle and Dannaks did too. Then they lay down.

After a moment Dannaks felt like having another drink. But the sun seemed to be sapping him of energy, rendering everything a gargantuan effort. Even the thought of sitting up drained him. He closed his eyes and within minutes he was fast asleep.

17:11

"What? Uh?" For a moment Dannaks didn't know where he was.

Startled, he jerked up, looking at her with wide-eyed urgency as if something terrible had happened.

Then pieces fell into place one at a time. It was daylight. Katja was crouched near him. She was touching his shoulder. She had said something. Shadows were longer. The breeze had an edge to it. Kids were still yelling. The music was gone.

"It's okay. You were snoring. I had to wake you."

"Huh. I was? Oh. Was I loud?" She shook her head. "I'm sorry."

"Why?" she smiled. "You obviously needed it."

She smiled and he couldn't help looking at her lips, wanting to lean over and kiss them. Instead he was compelled to wipe the dribble from his cheek. She went back and sat on her lounger and the moment was lost.

"What, er, time is it?" he asked unnecessarily for he was wearing his watch.

"About a quarter past five. I was thinking of packing up. It's getting chilly and I need a long bath before dinner."

The nap had split the day, as if the events before it belonged to another time. Were they at Herbst's place this very morning? Had they gone for a beach walk only an hour or so ago?

"You know," he began, "that's a damned good idea."

With that they gathered their stuff, agreed to meet, exchanged a peck of a kiss and parted.

Dannaks was already at the foot of the steps to reception when he remembered his booty. He turned and went back to the plaza. There, after nodding to the older shop assistant who was smoking and playing backgammon with another at a table outside the shop, he fetched his suitcase.

The case wasn't especially large and his plunder not especially heavy, so carrying it wasn't cumbersome. But he felt awkward, especially as he walked through reception. Luckily the bellboy was nowhere to be seen.

When he got to the room he noticed that the cleaner had forgotten her ledger. It was still resting on the wall. He would take it to reception when they went to dinner. With the key in one hand, the case in the other Dannaks unlocked the door and pushed it open. He half expected to find a note from Reupke lying under the door.

The room had been done: floors cleaned, beds made, curtains drawn and the towels this time twisted and curved to make up a heart shape. The smell of disinfectant assaulted his nostrils. He pushed the towel aside and swung his case on to his bed. Then he

201

pulled back the curtains and opened the terrace doors. The air rushed in because he'd left the front door open.

There was no indication that a police technician or whoever had checked the a/c.

As he walked to the front door his stomach began to tingle with excitement. He stopped. Then he opened the cupboard and took out a pair of cotton underpants. He went to the entrance and stared at the slate marble effect on the hard cover of the book. Could it be? He looked about. There was no one to be seen. Using his underpants to cover his fingers he picked it up and took it inside. He closed the door and carried the book to the largest available flat surface, which happened to be his case.

He exhaled through thinned lips. Still using his underpants he lifted the cover by the lowest corner and let the book fall open. He watched the beginning pages follow the cover, flipping over naturally. This was no ledger. There were no columns, just lines and lines of handwriting. The pages stopped turning, but rather than wait for the last to topple, he blew it on its way. Then he crouched and read.

After a few moments he stood. There was no doubt about it. This was Peter's book.

The book offered the pages with which it was most comfortable. He bent closer. The pages were slightly buckled in places. The book would have lain this way when the killing began. The clear patch on the photograph was too big for the book to have been closed. Had Meryem seen something here that had caused her to turn violent? Dannaks examined the paper and found a faint brown smear. There was a streak too. The pages had been wiped clean, but not quickly enough to stop the crinkling of the paper. Somebody would have picked it up, perhaps hastily wiping it. Whatever, it would have been carried closed.

He read the words, initially for some inflammatory remark that could have incited the Right. He didn't find any. But then the fact of the book itself was probably enough for that; the content itself wouldn't have significance. What he did spot was a name that gave the possible culprit for the theft, if not the murderer, away.

Dannaks wondered what to do. In front of him was an integral piece of evidence in a murder investigation. Of course he would hand it in. That was not the question. The question was when. Where was Reupke?

He used his underpants-clad fingers to carefully turn to the last page of writing. After skimming over the last paragraph he stood up. The book was two-thirds full: about forty pages of writing. He could read it and then hand it in. After all, it had been lying outside for a good few hours. He cursed as he thought of all the time he'd spent at the poolside. But then he knew such thoughts were counterproductive. He couldn't turn back the clock. He had to act. If he hurried he could still squeeze in a bath before dinner.

He went to the bathroom and rifled Reupke's toiletry bag. In the side pocket was an unopened packet of latex gloves. He felt sure Reupke wouldn't mind.

Back in the room he pulled up the chair to the suitcase. It was indeed the best place. He took out his notepad and pen and sat. Then he ripped open the plastic bag and pulled on the latex gloves. Touching the merest edge he closed the book and then opened it to the first page and began to read.

Dannaks sat in front of the book for a good hour. He took notes; flicked back a few pages a couple of times. Otherwise he read, sometimes skimming over what he considered irrelevant descriptive chunks.

When he'd finished he stood and his legs protested as if they'd seized up. There was agonising satisfaction when he rolled his shoulders and turned his neck. At the mini bar he tore off the gloves, took out a bottle of water and drank directly from it. All the while he was deep in thought.

What he'd read was partly mundane, but mostly a diatribe of notes that had flooded out from Peter's mind. The angle of the scrawl gave away the passionate points; the number of spelling mistakes too. Peter had started off in a structured way, but after a few pages he'd drawn horizontal lines and inserted notes that broke the chronology. The entries below the lines explained current events, coming from immediate memory, were necessarily more detailed and emotional, than those above, which were told like a story with a narrator's detachment. Thereafter this became a frequent occurrence. The effect made the whole incoherent: a cross between his memoirs and a diary. Only when Dannaks had finished – and it was an unfinished story – could he reorder the pieces in his mind.

He didn't need to refer to the dossier he had read. Originally compiled by REX, before Dannaks's arrival, and expanded upon by the *Verfassungsschutz* and *Zeugenschutz*, it dovetailed Peter's book. In fact the book added nothing new to his background, but it was interesting to get the personal viewpoint.

He was so deep in thought that Reupke's entry was an intrusion.

"Where'd the suitcase come from?" he asked. He looked dishevelled and tired.

"From the shop," said Dannaks.

Reupke raised the plastic bag in his hand. "I was there too. The idiot tried to sell me more." He appeared genuinely irritated. "But I just wanted a souvenir."

Dannaks wanted to ask what he had bought. His bag was bulky, but it didn't appear to contain clothing. Of course he really wanted to tell him about Peter's book. He waited for him to notice it.

"Is something wrong?" asked Dannaks.

"No," said Reupke, about to swivel round and go to the bathroom.

"It's what's on my case that's interesting," he called after him. Reupke went into the bathroom and closed the door.

Dannaks heard the flush and then the rush of a tap. The door opened and Reupke came out, rubbing his hands on a towel. "What is it?" An exacerbation still in his voice.

"Peter's book." He stopped rubbing his hands, looking at the book and then at Dannaks. "I thought it was something you bought. Have you read it?" he asked, moving closer, drying his hands and dropping the hand towel on his bed.

"Yes. I used these," said Dannaks, holding up Reupke's gloves. "I hope you don't mind."

Reupke saw the gloves but was too interested in the book to reply.

"This is how it lay when Peter was killed," he said.

"Yes."

Without looking up he continued. "Have you called Ismail?"

"Not yet."

"Where was it?"

"On the wall outside our door."

"There's a name here—"

"Rafael."

204

Reupke straightened and turned to Dannaks. He then looked at his watch. "You read it all?"

"Yes. I made some notes too."

"And?"

"There's no real clue to the killer. There are plenty of things that point to it not being Meryem. But it raises at lot of questions too."

"How many pages are there?"

"Forty-two and a bit."

"There's no way I'm going to get through that before dinner. And we can't photocopy it. Shit."

"You could photograph each page."

Reupke nodded.

"But if you ask me it's not really worth it. I can tell you what to read. And we ought to get it to Ismail before dinner."

"It's gone six thirty. When are you meeting Katja?"

"Same as yesterday. Seven at the plaza."

"Phone her up. Make it eight. I'll call Dagmar. This'll give us time to go through it, have showers or baths and still get it to Ismail before dinner."

Dannaks agreed and called Katja. She said no problem. Reupke encountered no trouble with Dagmar either.

Because there was only one chair Reupke sat on it in front of the book wearing the latex gloves. Dannaks sat near the pillow end of his bed and flipped open his notepad. He too could see the book, but upside down.

"As you can see, he starts it like a book. Tells you about his family and all. A typical boy being brought up in a typical no-name village. The turning point comes when he's fourteen and his mother is killed in a car accident. A drunk driver was involved. He was a cook, an Italian. Everything falls apart for him then. He hit puberty and his father the bottle. I'm not being sensational. That's a quote. Then he spirals down the standard route. You know, finding a new family, a sense of belonging."

Peter's recruitment into the right wing scene was textbook. Like all boys and youths he had been fascinated with soldiery and then attracted to the affiliation of peers. There was mention of a school friend's older brother's room being full of Nazi paraphernalia. He'd thought it: *Stark*. (A German word for both cool and strong.) As a directionless youth he could equally have gone punk. Peter mentioned a girl he was attracted to at one of the meetings and this, coupled with a foreigner involved in his mother's death, may have swung it for him. He joined. When he did get to meet the girl, he was disappointed.

He said that a lot of the neo-Nazis were lonely, odd or violent head cases. Many were simply dropouts. Being of above average intelligence he began climbing the ladder of importance. "He was never completely comfortable with the ideology," explained Dannaks, "and I guess he probably would have developed into a right wing extremist or radical."

"What's the difference?" asked Reupke.

Dannaks smiled. "Neo-Nazis glorify Hitler and his ideas. Right-wing extremists reject democracy and want dictatorship. Right wing radicals, on the other hand, accept democracy and want to use it to further their ideals."

"Volker Herbst?"

"Yes. He'll be comfortable admitting that some of his ideas are radical, but not extreme."

"Patriotic."

"Nationalistic," corrected Dannaks. Reupke's expression questioned him. "Patriots love their land without devaluing others. Nationalists put their country above others."

Reupke nodded.

"Don't worry. The Right interchange both words." He smiled. "They all have the same enemies too: *Ausländer*, homosexuals, gypsies, punks, etcetera."

Reupke looked at his watch. "We'd better get on."

"Yeah, turn the page. No, the next one. There. That's what made him want out."

One of the lads in the right wing scene had befriended him. He made a play for Peter, who was disgusted. He speculated later whether his friend was truly gay, for that is one of the things the Right abhor. But women were scarce and there was evidence to suggest that there was an unspoken tolerance of homosexuality. In any case Peter had been disgusted and in the heat of the moment he betrayed his friend. The boy was beaten so badly he was in a coma for two days before dying. Although Peter had not taken part in the killing he was racked with guilt. Disenchanted with the entire scene and a sense that his life was going down the drain – as he put it – he gave in to the officers investigating the murder. He pointed the finger at the killers and disappeared into the witness protection programme.

The name of the dead boy was Peter. In obvious homage to him he had chosen to take his name.

He also explained that he had started working in the high-class hotel because of a yearning for contact with Germans.

"Too bad we haven't got any dates," said Dannaks. "Look there. He says he's met Meryem and is planning to tell her about his tattoos."

"He'd have to do that before getting intimate," said Reupke.

"Yes. Turn the page and again. Sorry, another one. Where was it? Turn again. There look. *I told her I had been a neo-Nazi and was an Aussteiger* (one who gets out). *She said it was all right and said: I have a secret too. Then we made love.*" Dannaks looked at Reupke. "What do you think? It wasn't written recently. So she knew. She didn't kill him because of what he had been. She knew."

"Okay. I heard you." Reupke looked at his watch.

Dannaks found himself rereading the rest of the paragraph. *I know so little about her. She says she'll tell me about her dog-bone pendant one day. I know she was married and lived in Berlin. And she knows Hamburg too.*

"We're running out of time," said Reupke. "One of us should phone Ismail. It'll probably take him some time to get here."

"I'll call him."

"Tell him reception at a quarter to eight. Then you go for your shower and I'll read some more."

"There is more," said Dannaks. "Also, talking of Ismail, I think we should discuss what was said."

"Then make the call," said Reupke.

Dannaks found Ismail's card and picked up the phone. As he tapped in the numbers, before composing the English sentences, he thought about Reupke's attitude. He seemed agitated. Had something transpired this afternoon? If he had argued with Dagmar, he would hardly have phoned her just now.

Dannaks called Ismail on his handy number and although what the person said on the other end was Turkish and scrambled by background noise, Dannaks spoke loudly in English. Dannaks explained that he had found the book after coming back from the poolside. He was careful not to say at what time. Ismail was excited. He told him not to touch it. Dannaks replied: "Of course not. But I did bring it into the room. I thought it was the cleaner's room plan or something."

"I'll read on," said Reupke when Dannaks hung up. "You have your shower. Then we'll talk. When is Ismail going to be here?"

"Seven thirty."

"Less than an hour."

Dannaks went to the bathroom.

19:07

"I finished," said Reupke.

Dannaks was in his underwear. The terrace doors were closed and the a/c had kicked in. He felt cold.

"Good. We're running out of time," said Dannaks, pulling the terrace curtains together.

"Let's talk. You can meet Ismail on your own. I'll stay here and get ready for dinner."

"Okay." He wasn't sure whether there was some tactic behind Reupke's suggestion. He was leaving him to do the explaining to Ismail. There again, he did find the book.

"Let's finish this and then we can talk about what Ismail said."

Dannaks agreed. Instead of asking to get some clothes out of the case he went to the cupboard and pulled on his Las Vegas T-shirt.

"You know it's black and white tonight?"

"I know."

Reupke momentarily adopted a puzzled look. Then he looked down at the book. "What do you make of this?" He read aloud: "Meryem wants us to leave. She wants us to up and go without telling anybody. This is a part of her I don't understand. It's as if she's another woman. One minute she's soft, the next she's kind of hard and crazy."

"I think that if she suggested that they run away, then why kill him?"

"Who knows what was said?" said Reupke after a while.

"Meryem would know," Dannaks suggested.

"Ha, bloody, ha. Come on. You wanted to talk about what Ismail said."

"Yes," said Dannaks.

Their conversation was mostly repetition. But they did agree on one particular point. If the crowbar wasn't already in Peter's room, then premeditation was at play. The presence of glove lubricant supported this. Also a crowbar was not a woman's weapon of choice and certainly not someone as petite as Meryem. The only way she would have used such a weapon would be if it was the nearest thing to hand, like the classic fireplace poker.

Reupke said that he got the impression from Ismail that Rafael had been accused of entering the room and finishing Peter off. Peter had written: *Meryem is terribly reluctant to get involved. Rafael has been trying for more than a year.* So Rafael had a possible motive for killing Peter. Even if someone else – the person who left the shoe print – or Meryem had incapacitated Peter first, Rafael was still under suspicion. Yes, he was on stage for some of the time. But he still could have cut Peter's throat. He would certainly be taken in again, after the Turkish police had examined the book. If they, Dannaks and Reupke, wanted to talk to him, it would have to be this evening. However, of all the staff, Rafael was the most uncooperative.

One thing Reupke said that Dannaks didn't know was that Meryem had shared with Hülya. Maybe they should have interviewed her. Reupke said she rarely saw Meryem, because she was always with Peter. So again, the sudden revelation that he was an ex-neo-Nazi occurring last week seemed unlikely.

There was something else that intrigued Dannaks. He wasn't sure whether it was significant. Peter had said that Meryem wore a fine silver necklace with a silver dog's bone, which she refused to remove, even when they made love. He knew it meant a lot to her, but she wasn't ready to tell him. The act of making love meant that she had seen his tattoos.

The killer probably had the knife in his or her hand, but leaving the crowbar suggested that the killer left in haste. Arriving with it meant premeditation. The hasty departure was supported by the fact that the bathroom hadn't been used.

Dannaks asked what else Ismail had said in his absence.

The blood outside the room was Meryem's group.

Ismail had said that there were some things that didn't go in her favour. They couldn't say whether any of her clothes were missing, but she appeared to possess no jewellery. She could have taken it with her after the killing. Also her hotel records were incomplete. Something had gone awry. They had no contact address for next of kin. She said that her parents were moving house and that she would supply their new address. She was able to produce a passport, but no personal identification card.

They stopped talking shortly before half past seven. Reupke wanted his shower and Dannaks had to meet Ismail.

During the conversation Dannaks opened his case and Reupke had recommended that he dress completely in black. He didn't like the white shirt with the embroidery.

"It may be a mistake dressing up," said Reupke, when Dannaks was dressed.

"Why? What do you mean?"

"Up until now you've sent Katja all the right signals."

"Huh?"

"Well. I think the way you've been dressing has shown her that you are a man in desperate need of a woman."

"Ha, bloody, ha," he said echoing Reupke earlier.

"You'd better use this bag," said Reupke, when Dannaks scratched his head thinking about transporting the book.

Reupke pulled out what Dannaks recognised to be the stem of a hubble-bubble. Further attachments were taken from the plastic bag, but they were concealed in sticky-taped wads of tissue paper.

"Check tomorrow's pickup time again," said Reupke handing him the bag. "Just in case there's been a change of plan."

Dannaks nodded.

As an afterthought Reupke spoke just before he left. "There's one thing you can be sure of. We'll see the body tomorrow. There's no way I'm getting on that plane without checking inside the coffin and seeing it go in the hold."

19:30

Ismail was standing alone near the reception counter. Dannaks strode over to him and shook his hand.

"Are you sure this is his book?" asked Ismail, coming to the point and dismissing the awkwardness of not knowing how to greet one another.

"Yes," said Dannaks, handing him the plastic bag.

Ismail peered inside, but didn't reach in. Instead holding the bag open he tipped the book from side to side.

"Did it come in this bag?"

"No," said Dannaks, thinking that the answer was obvious. If the bag was evidence he wouldn't have been handling it so easily.

"Let us sit down. You can tell me how it came to be in your possession." This seemed to be another English phrase he'd picked up from television.

They went to the lobby bar and sat down near the entrance, well away from the crowd that was at the bar or occupying the arrangements nearest it.

They dispensed with drinks and Dannaks explained how he found the book outside their door. He admitted seeing it in the afternoon when the cleaner was present. Ismail took notes. The cleaner would be sought and questioned. Dannaks added an hour to the time he left the pool. He didn't want Ismail thinking he had had time to read the entire book.

"But you looked inside?"

"Yes," said Dannaks. "I was not sure what it was."

Ismail nodded and snapped his notepad shut. He was silent for a moment, pondering what Dannaks had said. Perhaps he was weighing up the truth? Then the rigidity left his shoulders.

"I am not happy," he said. "You have not been honest with me."

Dannaks wondered whether he had slipped up somewhere. Now his shoulders tightened.

"You did not tell me about Volker Herbst." Dannaks relaxed, but he hid it by leaning forward and looking grave.

"You mean what kind of politician he is?"

"Of course."

Dannaks had been playing for time, but it hadn't helped. He didn't have an answer. "We did not get the opportunity. And we knew you would find out. So why would we hide it?"

Ismail merely looked at him.

"It is no good. I thought we were being open with each other."

"We were. I mean are."

"I think not."

Dannaks was irritated that he did not have an answer. "Well, information is a two-way process. We have been given nothing."

Ismail stiffened. He was visibly taken back by the change in tone. "You are here as our guests to observe."

"We have had nothing to observe." Dannaks sighed. "Ismail, we have not even seen Peter's body."

Ismail relaxed. "What you say is true. But we have been very busy."

"Are you getting anywhere?"

The question was another shock. When he recovered the smile was slow and despondent. "Not really." Dannaks could see that he was disillusioned with the slowness of the case. He could also tell that Ismail was a talker. He just had to coax the information from him.

"What do you want to know about Herbst?" Dannaks asked.

"I think we know everything."

Dannaks waited a moment. "Was he there last week?"

Ismail hesitated. "No. But someone else was. Two men, I believe. They have gone now. We do not know when they left."

"But after the murder?"

"Yes."

"How do you know this?"

"A neighbour takes care of the place. He was the one who called the police when you were there." Ismail fingered the plastic bag. He was bringing the meeting to a close.

"I hope that helps," said Dannaks.

Ismail looked at the bag and nodded. Dannaks remained quiet. He felt that he was teetering on giving something more.

"Why do you think the killer left by the beach?" Ismail suddenly asked.

"Because he would have been covered in blood and there are too many shops on the road at the front of the hotel."

Ismail nodded slowly and looked at him for more.

Dannaks merely raised his eyebrows.

"You know I think he went that way too."

"Yes. You do not think it was Meryem."

Ismail shook his head. He stopped and said: "Many do."

"Many? Investigators?"

Ismail was surprised by the question. He nodded.

"But you do not?" Dannaks persisted.

"No."

Dannaks felt that the time was right. He leaned forward. "Why?"

"Because there is a photograph." He fell silent.

"A photograph of what?"

"A red man."

Now it was Dannaks's turn to be shocked. He stammered in German and then in English. "You – Wh – That is a surprise." Then he grew suspicious. "You mean a man covered in blood?"

"We do not know. It could be paint."

"Wh – Ismail, why do you not explain it to me?" To vanquish any further hesitation he added: "We are leaving tomorrow."

Ismail nodded and composed himself. "On the night of the killing there was a beach party. About twenty English girls and boys, from an inland guest house, built a fire–"

"On the beach between the hotels?" he asked, remembering the remains of the fire, but regretting interrupting him.

"Yes. Like hippies they played guitar and got drunk on raki. Maybe they smoked some stuff too. Then they painted themselves. I think they were playing Indians. About midnight a big man appeared. Some said he came from further up the beach. Some that he came from one of the hotels. He used coal to make his face black and then the white and blue paint." Dannaks's mind was racing. So he didn't wash himself off in the sea. He added white and blue to his red. "He danced a bit and then ran off."

"Along the beach?"

Ismail nodded.

"Some of the hotels have cameras. Did they catch anything?"

He shook his head. "I tell you already. But we think he leave between hotels further up. He is not seen further up the beach. So we check street between hotels. Only two people say they see painted man." Dannaks could imagine that in the tourist tumult the sight of a colourfully painted man would have drawn fleeting attention at most. "But it is nothing."

"And the photograph?"

"Yes. A boy took a photograph with his mobile phone and he is in the background. It is not a good photograph."

"Did anyone talk to him?"

"No. They did not get good look at him. It was dark. This is all we have. "

"But you have a good description?"

"No. It was dark, most of them were doped or drunk or both and the man was there for about two minutes. Maybe five minutes. We know he had dark hair and was white."

"Caucasian."

"Cor?"

"Western."

"Yes. They thought he was Turkish. He did not speak. He just smiled."

"What was he wearing?"

"A workman's one piece thing."

"A car mechanic's overall?"

"Yes, yes," said Ismail, clearly impressed by Dannaks's English.

"You said he joined in. What do you mean? Did he just paint himself and dance around?"

"No. He take beer too."

"Did you get the bottle?"

"It was a can. And no. He take it."

"And no one spoke to him?"

"I think they were afraid of him."

"Why?"

"He was a big man."

"Did anyone describe him?"

"Not good."

"What about footprints or shoe prints?"

"Impossible in sand."

"So you found these Brits and interviewed them?"

"Yes," he said and added proudly: "I did many of the interviews." He paused. "They have gone now."

"Any chance of seeing this picture?"

Ismail was silent for a while. "I should, er, say no. But–"

"Maybe we know him."

Ismail looked doubtful. "It is electronic."

"Then you can send it to us."

"Have you a mobile phone?"

"A handy? Er, no. But Olaf has. He gave you the number."

"If I can. I will send it to him." Ismail shifted in his seat. He wanted to leave. Perhaps he felt he had given too much away.

Dannaks was hungry for more, but he saw that it was past eight o'clock. He was surprised Reupke hadn't joined them. He would have at least had to pass through reception.

"Pick-up is at ten tomorrow?" Dannaks asked as they rose.

"Yes."

"See you tomorrow, then."

"Yes. See you tomorrow." Ismai̇ picked up the bag and they walked back to reception.

After parting, Dannaks went to the board of staff photographs. He found Meryem and saw the fine silver necklace. He hadn't noticed it before and only recognised the pendant as a dog-bone because he had been told.

20:07

He spotted the three of them immediately. They were sitting at a table near the bar and towards the shack.

Dannaks walked briskly over to them.

He saw a couple on loungers further away. They were looking directly at him. The words on the girl's black T-shirt gave him a clue. 'No trespassing' was boldly written in white barbed wire. Her companion was also dressed in black. Dannaks thought he was the boy she was with yesterday on stage. Her two female friends were nowhere to be seen. He gave them a small wave. She waved back. He was too far away to discern its sincerity. The boy simply stared at him, before turning to speak to her.

The chess players had adapted to the evening: two cocktails apiece stood next to the board.

At the table Dannaks recoiled from the joviality. He cringed at the sight of the cocktails on the table. Alcohol still didn't appeal. Katja offered her cheek for his kiss. He didn't sit and his greeting was awkward and rebuffed their animation.

"You caught a bit of sun today," she said.

"Get yourself one," said Reupke.

"They're delicious," said Katja. In front of her stood a small curvaceous vase containing a thick bright pink liquid. Protruding from the top of the glass were a miniature paper umbrella, a slice of pineapple, a plastic stirring stick with a disc sporting the hotel emblem and a striped straw. The other two had similar drinks with such paraphernalia. Their straws were equally indispensable for attempting to tackle these drinks without the aid of one could result in serious facial injury.

215

"I have to talk to you," he said to Reupke.

"Sounds serious," said Dagmar.

Reupke's expression hardened.

Dannaks stepped away and Reupke left the table.

"Why didn't you come to reception?" asked Dannaks.

"It was almost eight." Reupke didn't like having to justify his actions.

"But you passed through?"

"No. From our room I headed straight down. I came out behind the restaurant."

"Why?"

"I wanted to see how long it would take to get to the beach. Come on, Dannaks. The killer wouldn't have passed through reception."

"So you think the killer went to the beach too?"

"It's possible."

Dannaks shook his head.

Reupke gave him a puzzled, slightly weary, look.

"It's what I've always thought and now Ismail may have given me the proof." Reupke nodded interestedly. Dannaks told him of the beach party and the red man, backing up the story with Timi's picture. The last point caused him to hiccup over the fact that he wanted to get the boy's address. He spoke of the photograph Ismail had promised to send.

"My handy?" asked Reupke.

Dannaks nodded. "I don't have one."

"Next you're going to tell me you haven't got a PC." His expression was enough. "I don't believe it."

"I go to an Internet café."

Reupke shook his head in dismay. "When are you going to join the rest of civilisation?"

"There's something else. Herbst's place was occupied last week. They scarpered after the killing."

"You think this mechanic was staying there?"

"Maybe."

"But he looked Turkish?"

"Let's wait for the photograph."

"If it comes." Dannaks was irked by Reupke's negativity. Although the track record of the Turkish authorities since their arrival justified his attitude.

They returned to the table.

"Is it serious?" asked Katja quietly.

Dannaks shook his head.

"You look good," she said. Her compliment reached him and he smiled.

"You too." She was in white slacks and blouse. A white cardigan was draped over the armrest of her chair. Her hair was pinned up like a petrified shot of a field of straw caught in a whirlwind.

"Are you joining us, then?" asked Reupke, referring to the cocktails. He had chosen a white open-necked shirt and sharp black trousers.

"Later," he said, noticing that contrasting Reupke's loud in-your-face attitude Dagmar was quiet and distant. She was in a long black evening dress, which could have been refined and sexy, but because of her demeanour appeared melancholic and mournful.

"Well, I'm famished," said Katja. "Shall we go?"

Dannaks watched Dagmar smile and nod to Katja. She caught him looking and smiled at him too, but it was a coy, sad smile.

He looked at Reupke, who was finishing his drink, and realised that there was no connection between the two of them. They were two people sitting side by side.

They all left the table, Reupke leading the way, Dagmar walking beside him. Katja linked her arm through Dannaks's. Even though he found it difficult to walk – and wasn't accustomed to such intimacy – he was pleased.

"What's wrong with those two?" he whispered.

"I think they've had an argument," she said quietly.

The restaurant had spared no expense. Ice sculptures brought the presentation of the food to a new level. The cooks had excelled. An ice cream bomb and a chocolate fountain threw diets out of the window.

Despite this, dinner was a comparatively subdued affair. The boisterousness of the evening before was conspicuously absent. Dagmar's dark mood coupled with Reupke's overwhelming efforts at humour with cruel undercurrents perversely scythed any flow in conversation and relegated them to small talk. The disjunction was too obvious to ignore and excuses were sought.

For a while Katja and Dagmar found sanctuary in talk of the hotel wellness and cosmetic treatments. Dagmar voiced praise of the hammam and the massages.

"Time has passed so quickly," said Dannaks, sipping his glass of red wine. He had been unable to resist the bottle on the table.

"But it's still hard to believe we've only known each other for two days," said Katja, a teaspoon of creme caramel poised in her hand.

"All good things must come to an end," said Reupke.

Dagmar scowled.

Dannaks grew aware of an intangible dynamic that went something along the lines of: one couple's discord was the bonding of the other. For he felt a deep connection to Katja. There was easiness between them and he felt he could tell her anything and everything.

At one point Dannaks found himself alone at the table with Dagmar.

"Your friend is an arse," she said suddenly and in quite a matter of fact way.

Before he could react Katja and then Reupke returned.

He felt party to her demise and wondered whether she blamed him for apparently locking Reupke out of their room last night. He hadn't been asked to confirm his colleague's story.

Somehow the subject of whether the two detectives knew each other before this case came up.

"Yes," said Dannaks. "We worked for a short time on the Hangman case together."

"You joined us towards the end," said Reupke.

Dannaks nodded. "But we had no contact after that." He was strangely pleased to distance himself from his colleague. He almost felt Dagmar physically warm to him.

They talked about the unrest and rioting in Hamburg at the time of the Hangman's killings. This led them onto the rarity of serial killers in Hamburg.

"There was the *Heide* murderer," said Reupke.

"Why was he called the *Heide* murderer?" asked Dagmar. "The *Lüneburger Heide* is south of Hamburg."

"His first victim was killed there and the name stuck," said Reupke.

"His second and third murders occurred in Hamburg," said Dannaks.

Thomas H. was a graphic designer who lived in Hamburg. He was something of a sonny boy, much like the American serial killer Ted Bundy: with the same boyish trustworthy good looks, which he used to win over his victims. He felt driven to kill. During his trial he confessed. His Jekyll and Hyde personality got him in psychiatric therapy in the high-security prison Hamburg-Ochsenzoll.

"Didn't he have an affair with his psychologist or psychiatrist or something?" asked Katja.

"Yes," said Dannaks. "She helped him escape that time."

"Oh," exclaimed Katja. "I remember."

"He gave himself up pretty quickly," said Reupke.

"Then there was the acid murderer Lutz R."

"I don't know him," said Katja, brightening.

Dannaks smiled. He wanted to kiss her there and then. She was radiant. Her liveliness was a torch to the dark moods of Dagmar and Reupke. The unobtrusive fine blonde hairs of her cheeks softened her face.

"He got life in '96 for killing two women and disposing of their bodies in barrels of acid."

"They say he probably killed more," Reupke added.

A short silence ensued.

"When are you leaving tomorrow?" asked Katja.

"Pick-up is at ten," said Reupke.

Dannaks knew that the women weren't leaving until Monday.

Another silence grew.

"I'm looking forward to the show," said Dagmar, bravely displaying a semblance of nonchalance under the sudden attention of the others.

"No more than me," said Katja. Then to Dannaks: "We can just sit and watch."

Dannaks smiled and then he remembered her photograph. "Ah, I picked up the photos. I left yours in my room."

"Don't worry."

21:14

The plaza was shaping up into the usual mayhem. The bar was barely visible behind the choke of guests. There was a queue at

219

the cocktail end. Five barmen were frantically working and practically falling over one another in the confines of the bar. Two mixers were continually whirring.

The plaza itself was in semi-darkness. Small candles flickered in glasses on the tables. Brilliant spotlights lit up the amphitheatre and brightened the area further.

"Find a table," said Reupke. "Dagmar and I are going for a walk." He looked serious and Dagmar stricken.

An after dinner walk appealed to Dannaks. The restaurant had been relatively quiet and he recoiled from the crowd and loudness. What could be more romantic than a last evening beach walk with Katja? "We could go for a walk too," said Dannaks.

Katja touched his arm. "No," she said. "We'll find a place to sit."

"I didn't mean with them," he explained, when Dagmar and Reupke were out of earshot.

She hummed an acknowledgement, but he was not convinced she believed him.

"I thought we could go for a beach walk together," he said, following her to an empty table.

She didn't answer, but sat at the table.

He despondently plonked himself down in the chair next to her. When she held his hand he was electrified. He looked at her, but she was surveying the stage. So he gave her hand a little squeeze.

"Do you want a drink?"

She turned to him and then looked towards the bar.

"Let's wait for the queue to go down," she said and he knew despite the poor light she had noticed the softness in his eyes. He smile was sympathetic and he couldn't help himself. He leaned forward, ignoring her momentary surprise and kissed her on the lips. It wasn't a long or passionate kiss, more tentative and exploratory. Of course he had kissed her last night. But he didn't remember it. His feelings had been awash with alcohol rendering him unappreciative of emotional subtleties.

Dannaks sat back. Katja smiled. He noticed traces of surprise in her face. Yes, it wasn't like him to be so forward. At dinner he'd drunk only two glasses of wine. He felt happy. He marvelled at the feeling. For he knew that he had not felt happy, truly happy, in a long time. Oh, he'd not been sad. He had simply grown accustomed to being alone, tackling bouts of loneliness and melancholy as part of the course of life. He had been content. This happiness was warming, but it threatened his contentment and he was afraid the insecurity it brought on would show. Not only was happiness an unaccustomed feeling, intimacy and – dare he hope? – love, were unfamiliar territory and he had to tread warily.

The connection lingered for a moment, their eyes searching one another. A child crying distracted Katja. Dannaks saw the kid and an anxious mother hastening towards her. Then he saw Rafael bounding down the side steps of the stage.

"Just a minute," said Dannaks.

He got up and glanced at Katja before moving to cut off Rafael who appeared to be heading for the sound box at the top of the amphitheatre.

The congestion of people in chairs arranged to see the show hindered him cutting Rafael off. The noise level made shouting senseless and he found himself having to climb the amphitheatre.

The climb was surprisingly strenuous. Whereas Rafael leapt up the steps, Dannaks began pushing his hands on his thighs to straighten his legs. Yunus was at the top of the amphitheatre, beyond the last row, manning a spot.

Dannaks was sweating and had to catch his breath at the open door of the sound box.

Cemil saw him first. He was seated at the impressive tabletop panel of flickering lights, buttons and sliding levers of the soundboard and lighting. Rafael was standing beside him, leaning over, one hand on the soundboard, the other holding the backrest of Cemil's swivel chair. Rafael was speaking, but the voices behind Dannaks meant that he didn't catch what he was saying. Rafael noticed Cemil's distraction and turned. His face clouded.

"Could I speak to you?"

Although he nodded, Dannaks noticed his jaw clench.

"We're leaving tomorrow," he said loudly like an announcement.

"What is it?" he asked at the door.

"Somewhere quieter would be better."

"I haven't got the time."

Dannaks peered past him. "Cemil, would you mind leaving us for a moment?"

"Children's club starts in a couple of minutes."

"This won't take long. I promise."

Cemil reluctantly got up. They let him pass. Dannaks closed the door on when he was outside.

"So?" asked Rafael impatiently.

"Peter's book was left outside our room this afternoon."

"And?"

"I know you left it."

"Bullshit," he knee-jerked.

"It was open when the killing took place–"

"I don't see why you're telling me this–" He moved to leave, but Dannaks stepped into his path.

Dannaks slightly raised his voice. "Remnants of blood told us which page. Yours was the only name other than Meryem's on it."

"That doesn't mean anything."

"No?"

"No. Now let me go."

"Maybe you're right." This sudden change arrested Rafael and Dannaks took advantage of his hesitation. "But I think the Turkish police might come to the same conclusion."

"I–" He blanched. "I don't know what you're talking about."

Dannaks showed his palms. "I just came to warn you."

"Why?" he asked, but he was faltering. "Why would I take it?"

"Do you really want me to tell you?"

"Go on."

"I–" There was a knock on the door and Cemil shouted something.

Rafael called in Turkish that he should wait. He nodded to Dannaks.

"I think you saw your name in his book and took it."

"You still haven't said why I would take it."

"You fancied Meryem and were jealous of Peter. I think you thought you could – I don't know – maybe get closer to her."

He issued a short bitter laugh. "You're some detective, Schimi. If you hadn't noticed, my so-called rival was dead."

"True. But I still think you wanted to know what he had written. Maybe you were hoping to find something about Meryem."

"This really is bullshit."

"I just want to know whether you noticed anything else."

"I told the police everything. I don't need to tell you."

"They'll take you in again."

Dannaks could see Rafael teeter. He looked up to Heaven for mercy or guidance, or simply to stave off tears. Was he about to break down?

Cemil knocked on the door again and Rafael straightened. Staring at Dannaks with wide-eyes he said: "I have nothing to hide." He then pushed past him, tore open the door and was gone. Dannaks was rooted to the spot and Cemil stared at him as he brushed past. The soundman hit a button and using two fingers slid two small bricks up their calibrated slots. The jingle of the children's club was instant and deafening and annihilated conversation. The sound snapped Dannaks out of his trance-like state.

21:33

On the way back to Katja he toyed with the idea of queuing for cocktails. But then he wasn't sure what she would drink.

"Work?" she asked when he sat down beside her.

He nodded apologetically.

"The queue hasn't gone down," he said leaning towards her. On stage fifty or so children had formed a large circle and were chanting and mimicking some complicated dance routine that Hülya, Necla and Tanya were performing to the music. Bemused parents either wandered the stage taking sanctuary behind cameras of all shapes and sizes; others stood behind their children and rocked with the music; and still others tried to follow the routine, generally faring little better than their children.

"I'm fine," Katja called back.

So they sat silently in the overwhelming sound. Dannaks was relieved each time a tune came to an end, believing that it couldn't get any worse. Yet, each song was more maddening than its predecessor. Oh, he could see the delight in many of the guests' faces. But he regarded the sound as a form of torture. He was contemplating excusing himself when it came to a merciful end.

The stage was cleared and people began to settle. Habip appeared and began announcing the winners of various tournaments that had taken place during the week. Names were called out for archery and volleyball. Prizes of medallions, T-shirts and caps, which were awarded with certificates. Other accomplishments such as completed sailing or windsurfing courses were also acknowledged with certificates.

Dannaks saw them first and tapped Katja on the arm.

Dagmar and Reupke were approaching hand in hand.

"Thank god for that," said Katja, before they arrived.

"What? No drinks?" said Reupke.

Dannaks turned around. The cocktail queue had dwindled.

"What do you want?" asked Dannaks.

"A strawberry daiquiri," said Katja.

Reupke took Dagmar's order and the two detectives joined the queue.

Although he was tempted by the barrel, relatively neglected tonight, he decided to have a cocktail too. He scanned the list for something suitable.

As they waited Dannaks said quietly: "I spoke to Rafael."

"Yeah?" said Reupke, disinterestedly. "What did you say?"

"I told him I thought he left Peter's book."

Reupke nodded. "How did he react?"

"He was his usual aggressive self. But I think I shook him." Pause. "I'm sure he was on the brink of telling me something."

"So you warned him, then."

"Yes."

"I suppose it'll be interesting to see how he reacts."

The man and woman in front of them left with their hands full.

The lights went down and the 'ladies and gentlemen show time' tape started announcing that they were going to have a good time and to clap their hands. Dry ice came out in long spurts across the stage and the sound of the crowd diminished to a susurration.

Within three minutes they had their cocktails too. They weren't as decorative as the ones before dinner. No doubt all the decoration had been used. The glasses were merely adorned with a slice of fruit.

They reached their table as the curtains were pulled back and the first number started.

Dannaks was amazed at the slickness of the song and dance. The costumes were bright and wonderful. The singing was recorded, but the team mimed so well it looked as if they were singing. Dannaks was sure many of the children would not realise that it was taped.

The opening number came to an end and when the applause subsided Reupke proposed a toast. "To good times."

Nonetheless Dannaks wasn't sure of the appropriateness of his words, but the others didn't seem to mind and they had their glasses in their hands, straws at their mouths. A piece of ice must have lodged in his straw for he drew and nothing happened and then his mouth was suddenly full. By then it was too late. His drink was exceedingly cold and a sharp pain hit the back of his left eye. At that moment Katja leaned over to him and said: "Aren't the costumes spectacular?" But he couldn't speak. He put his glass down and pushed himself away from the table in case he couldn't swallow. "Are you okay?" There was too much to swallow and he couldn't hold it in his mouth. He swallowed painfully. He still couldn't speak and the others were now looking at him, concern etching their faces. The pain behind his left eye had moved into his sinuses. He placed his hand on the left side of his face. It felt as if the cavities of his cranium were filling with dry ice. The alcohol of the drink burnt his throat, but the ice turned it to menthol. A tear escaped his left eye. He tried to speak, but spluttered a hoarse apology instead.

The next number began on stage, quieter than the opening number.

"I'm okay," he eventually gasped. "That was damned cold."

"Yes," said Dagmar. "They don't hold back with the ice."

"I think my optic nerve froze."

"What are you drinking?" asked Katja.

"A whisky sour."

She pulled a face to show her distaste and he smiled. Few women were whisky drinkers.

"I'll have a taste," said Reupke. "Urgh. How can you drink that stuff? It's like petrol on ice."

"You didn't expect single malt, did you?"

Reupke turned back to the show.

"You haven't seen Lion King, have you?" Katja asked.

He shook his head, touching his cheek below his left eye with the back of his hand. It felt damp, but not wet.

"It's a good story."

They fell silent and enjoyed the show.

The entire crew appeared to have taken part, their numbers bolstered by about half a dozen children who had been given bit parts. Habip had majestically performed the role of Mufasa. Rafael had played Scar almost psychopathically. Fabio was Simba. Patricia had been an elegant dancing Nala. Dannaks thought Fehime miscast as a jabbering Zazu. Tanya and Hülya had played Pumba and Timon. Hartmut led Necla and Ercan as hyenas. At least two faces from the reception desk had played incidental animals.

When it was over, some forty minutes later, he agreed that it was a good story. Katja said that they had, of course, abridged it, but hadn't lost its essence.

"Very professional, I thought," said Reupke.

"The children were good too," said Dagmar.

Habip was on stage with the rest of the crew. They were posing with the children as a whole and then in clusters. Representatives from the front desk including Turgut marched onto the stage to reap some thanks. After this there followed a handful of cooks. Then Habip went into his rounding off spiel. Many at the amphitheatre were on their feet. There was the inevitable congestion at the cushion container. Parents contended with suddenly exhausted children pleading to be carried. It was five past eleven.

Then music split the air and the club dance began.

"Come on," said Dagmar, getting up. Katja followed suit. Dannaks was the last to rise. He copied Katja as best he could: the silliness was a shot of endorphins that filled him with elation.

After the dance they sat down. They had long finished their drinks and the bar was lined again. Cocktails were no longer on offer.

Dagmar and Reupke exchanged nods and then Reupke announced: "We're going to the disco."

"Do you fancy coming?" asked Dagmar.

Dannaks looked at Katja. Even he thought the evening was over too quickly. She shrugged and tipped her head to one side to say that she would go if he was going.

"Yeah. We'll come," he said.

"Great," said Dagmar.

The two women, wanting to powder their noses so to speak, said they would meet them in the discotheque.

Dannaks and Reupke made their way across the plaza, manoeuvring between the tables and chairs. Inside they found an unoccupied alcove and Dannaks waited whilst Reupke went to get himself and Dagmar a drink. Dannaks didn't know what Katja would like and said that he would wait. He was beginning to regret coming to the disco. Katja had said it wasn't really her thing and it certainly wasn't Dannaks's thing. Coloured lights stretched and shrank as they wandered the dark walls like fish. A stationary mirror ball sparkled expectantly. There was no bubbling DJ. He would probably appear later. The music merrily bounced through genres and decades without rhyme or reason.

He spotted 'No trespassing' in another alcove united with her girlfriends. Her boyfriend and two other lads were present.

Most of the crew were present. Although he couldn't see Rafael or Fehime.

Reupke returned with a beer and a Campari and orange. The music relegated talk to the absolute necessary and so they were silent. The girls arrived and Dannaks went to the bar and fetched a glass of water for Katja and a red wine for himself.

Three young women and a lanky youth were jiggling about on the dance floor. Dannaks thought them brave, drunk or both. Yet, in this situation, part of him wanted their freedom of expression. Normally he never found himself in this situation. He would even call it predicament. For he didn't like dancing. He always felt exceedingly self conscious: aware that he may not be dancing to the beat, that his legs were not as coordinated as he would like them to be, that he was dancing the same way for the last two or three completely different tunes, that he didn't know what to do with his arms, they were extraneous and in the way, dangling uselessly.

He'd only just sat down when Dagmar said: "Oh, this is my favourite. Let's all dance." She was effervescent, a completely changed person.

Reupke put down his beer and nodded.

Katja raised her eyebrows at Dannaks. He smiled awkwardly.

"He's still learning to let go," said Reupke.

"This is the perfect place to learn," said Dagmar, standing. "Nobody knows you. You can do what you want. Be who you want."

He smiled at her. He wanted to answer that he was being himself. Dancing was not him. And yet...

Dagmar held out her hand to him.

He acquiesced and wearily stood. Was it a reggae number? He inwardly groaned. Katja and Reupke were also up. He let Dagmar lead him by the hand onto the dance floor.

She turned to him and began gyrating. She lifted her arms in the air to push her fingers through her hair. Dannaks wondered whether she was drunk. Reupke appeared comfortable. He had shut everything out and was doing his own thing. Katja's dance wasn't as ostentatious as Dagmar's, but she too projected an element of ease. Dannaks shuffled as rhythmically as he could. The music was familiar but not reggae. Then he had it. It was a Michael Jackson number.

When it began to come to an end he looked to Katja for a mercy killing. There was no time. For between the songs there was no pause. They overlapped and now he was trapped in a Bob Marley number. He was surprised when Katja smiled at him. For he felt clammy and knew he was glistening with sweat. How could she smile?

Dagmar was dancing in front of a nonchalant Reupke.

Dannaks leaned towards Katja. "I can't dance."

"It doesn't matter. Just let go."

He closed his eyes and tried to move with the music. On opening his eyes he knew that he had been jerking rather than dancing. The girls' bodies flowed. They seemed to have allowed the music inside them. Reupke was making a good go of it. But he, Dannaks, couldn't find the pulse. His mimicry was blatant and embarrassing. Somehow he muddled through.

"I'm tired," said Katja, as the next number jauntily got into gear.

Dannaks didn't believe her, but was grateful for her insight. "Sorry," he said as they made their way from the dance floor.

"Don't be silly," she said.

At their drinks they watched Reupke and Dagmar.

"She's having a good time," said Katja.

Dannaks nodded.

"I'm glad," said Katja. "But he's going to dump her, isn't he?"

Dannaks was so shocked he initially couldn't speak. "I, er, don't know." Katja nodded knowingly. And he felt that she thought his allegiance was to Reupke rather than her. "Really. I don't know." He looked for acceptance in her face. "I don't really know him."

He wasn't sure whether he had convinced her. It was too late. Dagmar and Reupke were leaving the dance floor. Before they reached the table Katja leant over and touched his thigh. He felt as if she'd shot a thousand volts through him."Let's put you out of your misery and get you home."

"You're not that comfortable here, are you?"

She smiled but didn't answer. "I have to pay a visit first." Her hand left his thigh.

Katja stood and left. Dagmar and Reupke flopped into their seats and drank greedily. Reupke pushed out his bottom lip and blew air up his face. He looked like a little boy.

"It's a nice way to shed some kilos," said Dagmar.

"And not as gruelling as Fehime's sessions," Reupke gasped, finishing his beer and looking at Dagmar's drink. "I'm getting another. How about you?"

"I shouldn't."

"You're on holiday."

"If I got an euro for every time I've heard that I'd be a millionairess."

Reupke turned to Dannaks. "Another red wine?"

"We're thinking of going."

"One for the road?"

"Are you on commission here?"

Katja returned. She had refreshed her make-up. She remained standing and Dannaks got up.

"Here, you take the key," said Reupke, holding it out.

"It doesn't matter if you lock the door this time," said Dagmar, her eyes sparkling. Then she laughed.

Reupke smiled. "I'll be at the room around, er, eight tomorrow morning."

They kissed passionately and barely acknowledged Dannaks's and Katja's departure.

Outside the cold caught them unawares and they huddled together.

"I'll come and collect my photograph, if that's okay."

Dannaks was stunned. Surely he'd see her tomorrow? Of course he knew what this meant and grew excited and could barely contain himself. Then trepidation overcame him. It had been a long time, such a long time.

Friday
01:41

They had left the bathroom light on and the door ajar.

"I'm sorry," he said. "I'm really out of practice." As he had feared it was over all too quickly. If she was disappointed she was gracious enough not to show it. There again, in the half-light it was hard to tell what she thought.

"Don't worry about it," she said. "We can have another go later."

"Yes," he said thickly, suddenly feeling appallingly tired. It had been a long day. What with the visit to Herbst's place, getting handcuffed and taken in, meeting Ismail, then the pool slide, the shopping, reading Peter's book, dinner, the show, the eyeball freezing whisky sour, the disco and now this. Not to mention the fact that he hadn't slept well last night.

"Although I'm not sure how those two can spend an entire night in a single bed." She was referring to Dagmar and Reupke. Dannaks had pushed the beds together, but she insisted on only getting under his bed sheets. So he half lay on top of Reupke's made bed.

Dannaks was about to suggest that maybe Dagmar and Reupke didn't sleep. But this could highlight his lack of sexual prowess. "You look terrific with your hair down," he said.

"Thanks. But it's too hot to carry it like that."

They were quiet for a while. He felt himself drifting off.

"Did you lock Olaf out last night?"

He started. "No," he said, glad to tell someone and equally glad to show his true allegiance.

She shifted slightly. "Were you falling asleep?"

"No," he said, widening his eyes in an attempt to stave off the weariness. "And if I had locked him out, he could have got reception to open the door."

She nodded.

He knew she wanted to talk, but he felt so warm and cosy in her embrace. Sleep was seducing him. He enjoyed breathing the fragrance of her hair. The very femaleness of it was alien to him. And something stirred within him. But he knew it was too soon and let the moment pale. He squeezed her contentedly and she reciprocated. Snugness was the last thing he remembered.

"Dee." He woke with a start. "You were snoring."

"I was? I, er, must have dropped off." He struggled to stay awake. "Sorry."

"Why don't you sleep in Olaf's bed?"

"Aren't you comfortable?"

"Yes. But I'm not lying between two beds."

"I'm happy."

Silence consumed them.

"Actually I'm surprised you managed to get a room together. I would have thought you'd have to double up with someone from the animation team or so."

"This was the only free room. It was Peter's."

"Peter?" she stiffened. "You mean the boy who died?"

"Yes."

"He was killed here?"

"Yes." He could feel her mounting horror.

"In this room?"

"Well. Yes."

She brusquely sat up.

"Not in this bed," he said.

"But in this room."

He was wide-awake now.

"It's been cleaned."

"That's not the point." What then was the point? "I can't sleep here." He winced when she switched on the bedside light. "And I really don't see how you can." She got up.

"What are you doing?" He was sitting up now.

"I'm going." He couldn't take his eyes off her nakedness.

She ignored him and gathered up her clothes. Standing sideways to him she dipped into her bra, straightened and clipped it. He pushed the sheet off and found his underpants.

"I can make my own way."

He wasn't sure of her mood. "I'll walk you."

"You don't have to."

"I know."

He walked her back to her room. The only living soul they saw was the man behind the reception desk. At her door they kissed.

"Shall I come in?" he asked. He felt ready now.

"I think what you really need is sleep." She rubbed his shoulder as some form of consolation.

He got back to his room just before three. Although he felt dead beat he couldn't sleep. For a while he sought the scent of her in the bedding. Initially he sensed her, but the sensation rapidly dissipated, leaving him with the frustration of memory. Movement between his legs brought on an "Oh, don't be silly." He thought about her for a long while. Then his mind wandered. All that had transpired the last few days surfaced in a kaleidoscope of disconnected fragments. He fell asleep just after five.

07:19

The rap on the door was hard, but he sensed that it had begun earlier and softer. He looked at his watch as he wearily climbed out of bed. Maybe Dagmar had kicked Reupke out?

"I'm coming," he croaked, stepping into his underpants. Shuffling to the door he tried to rub some life into his face.

A harpoon sat between his eyes. The slightest movement caused it to shift giving him instant pain.

He had a hand over his face as he opened the door just enough to show his head. Disbelief dumbfounded him.

She seemed shocked by his appearance. "Hallo, *Herr* Dannaks."

"Er, Fehime, yes, good morning."

The cold air crept in from behind her and goose-bumped his skin.

"Morning," she returned. She was dressed for the day; zipped up in a hooded jacket sporting the hotel emblem.

Dannaks, bringing down his eyebrows in concern, and finding that it relieved the pain, held the expression. "What is it? What's wrong?"

"Can you come with me?"

"Er, I have to get dressed first." When she didn't answer he left the door ajar, gathered his clothes and tossed them on the bed. He took the opportunity to lower and raise his eyebrows. He even stopped to pinch the top of his nose. The pain could be caused by alcohol, but he felt it more sleep related. Of course it was probably a combination of mixed drinks and sleep deficit. "You want to tell me what this is about?" he called, sitting on the bed and pulling on a sock.

"You'll see when we get there." She was still outside, although the door had opened a little.

"You can come in if you want."

She didn't answer and remained outside.

"My, er, partner isn't here and I'll have to lock up. Can you tell me where we are going? I can leave him a note."

"My room."

He was dressed now. Tearing a sheet from his notepad he began to write. He asked her for her room number and wrote it in. At the door he tried to wedge the slip of paper above the lock, between the door and the frame, but it was too flimsy. "Find me a stone," he said.

She looked about, returning with a stone about the size of a walnut. He placed it on top of the note on the ground in front of the door.

"Okay," he said and they headed in the direction of her apartment. She looked grave.

Although early it was quite bright. Between the tall trees daylight glinted with an intermittent harshness akin to sunlight on a pool.

"Will this take long?" he asked.

"I don't know," she said stony-faced

What would Reupke think of this? He had goaded him a couple of times about seeking Fehime's favour.

They greeted an elderly couple. Early birds. Otherwise they saw no one.

Less than a minute after leaving Dannaks's apartment she was unlocking her door. She led the way. Her terrace curtains were pulled back. But her light was also on.

He closed her door and followed her into the main room. Before he entered he knew from the way she had half-turned to him that someone else was in the room. Then everything slowed to an excruciating level. Was it Rafael about to bludgeon him? A sense of prescience then took him. Every nuance: Fehime's critical look, the light at the terrace doors, his heavy gait as if walking in treacle, the smell of stale food and sweat, took on the guise of a premonition. He recalled a similar sensation in the alley, the shifting light, the sudden tension, just before he was attacked and beaten to within an inch of his life. For this moment carried the portent of an accident about to happen. The figure sat at the pillow-end of the furthest bed. Her legs were on the floor between the beds. Her knees were clamped together her hands clasped in her lap. He stopped just inside the room and she looked up with big swollen eyes.

"Hallo Meryem," he said quietly.

She merely looked at him and gave him nothing. All emotion had been beaten out of her.

Her appearance horrified him. Her eyes were burnt out coals, dead, even the defiance of a cornered animal was absent; the bags under them puffed like bloated gourds ready to add more water. One of her cheeks was red.

He glanced at Fehime.

"She came here this morning," she said quickly. "She's giving herself up. And she wants you to escort her."

"I thought you said there were two of them," said Meryem. She spoke in Turkish. Her voice was meek, almost a whisper. She was fragile, ready to shatter at the merest pressure. Dannaks caught the words: "two of them."

Fehime looked at her and answered, also in Turkish, caring but firmly like a nurse to her patient. "The other one wasn't there."

"He'll be here soon," Dannaks assured. The girls exchanged looks, obviously realising that he understood Turkish.

Meryem dropped her head. He wanted to get closer to her, in every way. But to move could ruin the delicate triangular balance in the room. An approach could seem threatening. He slowly and exaggeratedly looked at his watch. "It's just gone twenty past seven. He wanted to be at our room for eight." He assumed a more matter-of-fact tone. "To go to breakfast." Again he glanced at Fehime, but she said nothing. "Do you, er, mind if I sit down."

Meryem shrugged without lifting her head. She wasn't in turmoil, consumed by her own thoughts. She was simply wasted: a shell.

The room was identical to his, but whereas his was bereft of personal touches, overt attempts at making this one a home were evident. A patchwork of photographs was spreading on one wall. Party faces, funny faces, posed faces and distorted close-up faces intermingled coloured paper flyers advertising various shows. Dannaks saw the Lion King one. A medium-sized hubble-bubble stood on the bedside cabinet next to a plastic bottle of hand-cream standing on a thick paperback like a plinth. Hanging from the headboard was a beaded necklace with a Fatima's eye.

Dannaks stepped forward and Fehime pulled out the chair next to her. He ignored her and went between the beds, both of which were made, to sit almost opposite Meryem. Fehime sat in the chair. Meryem didn't remain still. She shifted herself to sit on her hands.

He could see that she was wearing the clothes she had worn that night. It was the standard crew outfit with the addition of the light blue club sweatshirt that zipped up at the front. Fehime was in the same sweatshirt, now unzipped. The similarity ended there, for whereas Fehime's was clean Meryem's had a brown stain on the shoulder and a smear on the right sleeve near the wrist. Although she had obviously washed herself, her clothes were stale and reeked

Her hair was clean, but uncombed. A patch had been roughly cut away high above her left ear. The end of a cut peeked out from a row of four household plasters. There was a receding lump under the cut. The skin around it was taut and still had a bluish hue. Because of the raised area the cut under the plasters was probably more of a gash.

At first he was glad she cast her terrible eyes downwards. He wasn't sure he could bear them at such proximity. The redness on her right cheek looked like some kind of rash.

Meryem was petite, certainly less robust than Fehime. Although wretched she looked healthy and agile and fit enough to climb up into the top cupboard. He glanced at the wardrobe unit and the top three doors. Maybe she didn't have to remove the extra bedding.

"I could do with a coffee," he ventured, looking over at Fehime.

"I've tea," she said, gesturing to the two cups and chromed coil with its plug under the mirror behind her. The television was absent. Dannaks saw the small heap of various teabag envelopes next to the hairbrush and litre bottle of water.

"I'd prefer coffee," he insisted apologetically. He turned to Meryem. "I'm sure Meryem would like one." But she appeared to have slumped into a catatonic state. He looked at Fehime again. "Could you get us some?"

"I don't know," she said, ignoring him and staring at Meryem.

Without lifting her head she glanced at Fehime swiftly and gave her an almost imperceptible nod.

Fehime didn't react immediately. Then she abruptly stood.

"Milk? Sugar?" she asked almost tetchily.

"No," said Dannaks, "to both."

"I'll be as quick as I can."

He wasn't sure for whose benefit she made her last statement, but seconds later she was gone.

Dannaks waited a moment then he pinched the bridge of his nose. "I'm sorry. It was gala night last night and they were serving these cocktails." She remained unmoved. "I guess you know about that. Anyway, a cocktail too many, I fear." In truth he'd only had one cocktail.

"I think I'll have a drink of water," he announced. Receiving no reaction he slowly rose. At the mirror he filled two cups. "Here," he said, lowering his hand to show her the cup. She was obliged to take it and lifted her right hand from under herself. She brought her left hand out too and held the cup at her knees. He sat down again.

Her hands were those of someone not unused to manual labour. A cleaner, perhaps. Then he noticed the ancient scars of small cuts on her fingers, wrists and forearms.

Dannaks sipped his water. "Your head looks bad. Is it still hurting?"

She shook her head slightly.

"If you don't want to talk, it's okay." No reaction. "Do you want to talk?" She shrugged and even this was an effort. "Tell me how you feel?"

He waited. Just as he was about to speak she lifted her cup to her lips. Repositioning her cup after a sip she said: "*Leer.*"

She had not only told him how she felt, she had told him that she spoke German.

"You feel empty?" He was having trouble keeping his voice level. There wasn't much time and every word had to be wrung out of her. "I can understand that."

"Can you?" Her voice was quiet and her tone full of disbelief, perhaps mockery.

The way she spoke German, her accent, told him that she was not someone born in Germany.

"Have you been hiding here all the time?" She stiffened at the question. He knew he was taking a terrific risk. There was no reason why she should talk to him. And in her state she could just clamp up.

"No," she said quickly.

"Where have you been?"

Her answer was a shrug.

"Okay," he said quietly. He imagined Fehime arriving at the restaurant. Nevertheless he drank some more water. The harpoon had disintegrated. Only splinters of pain clouded his thoughts. "Can you tell me why you hid?"

"Because I killed him," she hissed, suddenly looking at him. Her glare was short but hard like a challenge: you'd better believe me. She looked away before it could soften to: you believe me, don't you? Moments before she had appeared on the brink of collapse. Her face had been soft. In an instant she turned hard and cold. There was an ocean of anger or hate in her eyes. He was transfixed and aghast and could only return her stare.

Then she looked down again. Her elbows were still pressed tightly at her sides. He could feel her making herself as small as possible.

Time was running out. Fehime would be back soon.

Dannaks thought about the interview course he had attended. There had been a wealth of body language aspects.

He needed her eyes and he needed her hands. Of course, he'd successfully got her to take her hands from underneath herself, but now they held the cup.

He reached for the cup and she recoiled. "I was just going to take it, before it spills." She didn't look up, but took her hands from the cup. For a second it balanced on her knees unaided. It was a belligerent act. Dannaks grabbed it.

Placing the cup on the bedside cabinet he prayed that she wouldn't now sit on her hands.

"How tall are you?"

She shrugged. Her head was still down, but he could sense her perplexity.

"One sixty-five?" Minute movement of her ears betrayed the tightening of her jaw. "Peter was a big lad. You must have stood on the bed to hit him with the ashtray."

The stillness was awesome. Then she whispered.

"What?"

She raised her voice exaggeratedly and brought her head up. Her eyes met his. She pressed her hands together and wedged them between her thighs. "It was a crowbar," she croaked.

Dannaks nodded as he searched her face. The crowbar was not public knowledge. Of course in trying to trick her he may have lost any trust he had accrued. "I know," he admitted. "But I had to find out whether you were there." He smiled. "Where did you get the crowbar from?"

Her eyes widened momentarily. She had not been prepared for the question. "I, er, don't remember. I think I found it."

"Where?"

"I don't remember." She fidgeted now. The tension left her. Her legs moved as if she wanted to get up. Her feet shifted, pointing towards him and the way out between the beds. Her hands separated and moved down her thighs as if smoothing out creases in her club slacks. "I stabbed him." Dannaks nodded. "In a frenzy."

He hadn't asked her. She was volunteering the information.

"You must have been in a rage."

She nodded. "Yes, I suppose I was." Her hands held her thighs and she lifted her shoulders.

"Was it your knife?"

She floundered but quickly recovered. When she spoke she did so slowly. "Yes. Yes it was my knife." She blinked rapidly three or four times. Then she continued as slowly as before, but he thought in a higher pitch. "I always – It was a – I bought it. From the market." She touched her nose, noticed him watching her, and brought her hands back down to her lap where her fingers twitched. She wore no rings. "I know it's unusual for a girl to carry a knife, but you heard about the strange things happening here. One of the toilets was smeared with shit. And then – well, you know. I thought it prudent to protect myself." She widened her eyes. Dannaks thought there was some emotional delay here. The widening of her eyes was more appropriate to her talk of the strange happenings. Not now. "So, that's why I, er, decided to get – buy a knife. From the market."

"Where is it?"

This stopped her in her tracks. All movement came to a halt. Even her breathing appeared to have been arrested. Her eyes remained wide. She licked her dry lips and squeezed them together, as if smoothing lipstick, but now to spread the moisture. Dannaks noticed the sheen of perspiration on her forehead.

"I don't remember."

He nodded.

"I must have dropped it." Her right hand moved to her neck, then chin and then covered the rash on her cheek, her little finger trailing over her lips. "I did it," she said again.

Dannaks nodded as if he believed her. Her eyes remained fixed on his, but there was no longer any challenge in them and eventually she looked away.

On his body language course they had touched on NLP (Neuro-linguistic programming) and said something about the movement of the eyes when lying. If the person was right-handed and the eyes moved up and to the right when speaking then the person was being creative rather than recollective. That is the person was making something up or lying. Of course this premise rested on the person not having a tick or foible, or being a practised liar. Somebody in the course mentioned that a fly or something could distract the speaker and cause a diversion of his or her eyes. The tutor agreed but then added that a rehearsed lie would move from creativity to recall and therefore be remembered. The eyes then were not to be trusted as an indication of lying. Indeed, no one single trait could be relied upon. But there were indicators for telling whether a person was lying. They had to be looked for in clusters.

Only if he could have recorded all her actions and all that she said. He couldn't even take notes.

"Why?" he asked.

The door opened and shattered everything.

Dannaks cursed in his mind.

"Coffee," Fehime called bringing in three cups on a tray. The door slammed shut. She used the tray to shift stuff under the mirror. The silence hadn't gone unnoticed and she turned to them.

"Thanks," said Dannaks.

"I spilt some," she said looking alternately at each of them. "I'll, er, just get some toilet paper."

As she left the room, Dannaks turned to Meryem.

"Why, Meryem? Why?"

"Because he was a Nazi." The hardness returned to her eyes, but she couldn't hold it. Even her mouth-line, thinned with contempt, didn't last.

Fehime returned with a toilet roll. She tore pieces off and dabbed the tray, throwing the sodden pieces in the nearby bin. Then she picked up a cup, wiped its underside and handed it to Dannaks. He gestured to Meryem. "No milk, no sugar," said Fehime and he took the cup.

Fehime then handed Meryem a cup and sat in the chair.

The silence grew awkward.

"It's almost eight," said Fehime suddenly. "I'll phone your room."

Dannaks nodded and drank his coffee. Meryem merely held hers like the cup of water and stared into the brown liquid, transfixed.

At the far bedside cabinet behind him Dannaks heard Fehime tap in his room number. He watched Meryem. Behind his back Fehime could try to communicate with her.

Meryem didn't look up.

They waited. Dannaks thought Fehime should give up. Nobody was answering. After a good thirty seconds Fehime said: "He's not– Hallo. Yes. *Herr* Reupke. Yes."

Whilst she spoke Dannaks leaned forward. "Why are you lying?" he asked quietly.

She didn't look up or stiffen or give away any outward sign that she had heard him.

"No. He's here." Fehime was saying. "Can you come here? Dry? Yes. Now. You'll see when you get here. I know. As soon as you can." She gave him her room number and brief directions before hanging up. "He was in the shower."

"Didn't he get my note?"

"Yes. Obviously he didn't think it important." She returned to her chair and coffee.

Dannaks wondered why Reupke went to all the trouble of getting reception to open the door. That was the only way he could get in. Why hadn't he come here? "We should call the police."

"Not from here," said Fehime. "I have to pay for outside calls."

"Then we'll just have to wait."

Meryem had shut down and Dannaks was desperate for more information.

"Meryem," he began. "I'm not part of the investigation. Huh, back in Hamburg, I'm not even in the *Mordkommission*."

Something must have reached her for she lifted her cup of coffee to her lips.

"So," she said with icy precision. "I don't have to talk to you."

He wasn't sure whether it was a question or a statement. Either way he could only be honest. "No. You don't have to talk to me."

"I think she's had enough," said Fehime.

"That may be. But the Turkish police may not be as understanding." He sighed. "Do you want to tell me anything?"

She shook her head.

"Can I help you in any way?"

Again she shook her head.

He really felt like shaking her, knowing it wouldn't help. He wanted to ask her how she could have cut his throat at the end; that he knew they had made love and Peter had revealed his past days or weeks before his death. Her motive was flimsy. Why she was lying completely flummoxed him. He could think of no plausible reason. Yet, there was the remotest possibility that she was not lying. He had seen a deep-rooted hate in her. Or was it stress? A kind of petrified hysteria? If she had killed him, then all this was simply a domestic killing: a crime of passion.

Dannaks needed a key question to unlock her. He felt frustratingly near to the answer. But she was not only inexplicably holding back, she was lying. She had to be lying. All else was nonsense. But why? Why?

"Well" Dannaks began cheerily. "Whatever, Azure Skies is a nice place to come to for a holiday." He glanced at Fehime. "You lot certainly put in a hundred and fifty percent effort. I could never do it. Always showing a happy face and trying to motivate the punter."

Fehime nodded and smiled, clearly confused by his breezy tone.

"You're probably running on empty most of the time."

"Yes," said Fehime. "Pure adrenaline."

They were quiet for a moment.

"I guess sometimes someone burns out," he said solemnly.

"An aerobics teacher ran away two years ago," said Fehime.

"Oh?" If she suspected that he was steering the conversation towards possible consequences of burn out, such as someone breaking down or committing murder, she didn't let on. In truth he was not sure where he was going with the conversation.

"She was German and met some local boy. One day she just upped and left."

The rap on the door froze them. If it was Reupke then he had been quick. Fehime got up. As she reached the door out of their sight Dannaks spoke quietly and distinctly to Meryem.

"Meryem," he began, and she looked up. All that small talk, like preamble, appeared to have paid off. "What's your secret?"

Dannaks saw the flash of emotion he knew was termed a micro-expression. Lasting a split second it was normally missed and rarely consciously registered. Her eyes widened, her skin paled, her jaw dropped a mite and her lips parted. It was a look of shock and horror, maybe disbelief. Instantly her face dulled over, eyelids dropping, mouth closing and jaw-clenching causing her cheeks to twitch. And she was gone again and he was left with deadpan.

Fehime led Reupke into the room. Dannaks watched his eyes notice him before locking onto Meryem. "I need to go to the bathroom," said Meryem, standing suddenly.

She walked past Fehime and then Reupke. The latter questioned Dannaks with a look. But Dannaks was watching Meryem. There were brown spots on the back of her sweatshirt. When Fehime followed Meryem Dannaks stood. If there was any communication between the two girls, he missed it. He heard the bathroom door lock. Before Reupke moved to speak Dannaks silenced him with a gesture and went to the bathroom door to eavesdrop.

He could hear them hurriedly talking, but they were virtually whispering and he couldn't tell what they were saying. Reupke stood by limply.

The lock turned and Dannaks stepped away hastily. Half turning to Reupke he noticed the thin silver necklace with the silver bone pendant on the shelf under the mirror. He couldn't believe Fehime also possessed such an unusual object. It was possible, but he decided that Meryem had given it to her either as a gift or for safekeeping.

"Didn't you get my note?" he said quietly.

"Yes."

"Why didn't you come?"

Reupke answered him with an expression that said: "You don't really want me to answer that."

Piqued Dannaks was about to retort that not everyone was like him: chasing skirt. Instead he slanted his mouth and shook his head. "You got here quickly."

Reupke was surprised by the remark and replied just as soberly. "I, er, came this way yesterday, when you were talking to Ismail."

Fehime came out closing the door behind her. Dannaks tried vainly to read her face. The three of them waited. Then the toilet flushed.

"We're going to call Ismail from reception," Dannaks explained.

"Have you got his number?" Reupke asked.

"No."

"Then we'll have to stop on the way down."

They heard Meryem washing her hands at the bowl. Eventually the door opened and she stood in the doorway.

The girls exchanged looks and then Fehime said: "Shall we go?" She gestured for the detectives to lead.

Dannaks glanced at Reupke. "I'll bring up the rear."

His colleague obliged and manoeuvring between the girls he opened the door and went outside. Fehime followed him and then Meryem. Dannaks walked up behind her scrutinising the brown marks on her back. He closed the door.

They stood gathered at the door for a moment. Meryem looked about. Was it possible that she had been cooped up for the last eleven days or so? Fehime gestured for Reupke to lead the way and held Meryem's hand.

Other guests were underway, most of them heading down to breakfast via reception. There were very few coming the other way. If any of them recognised Meryem nothing was shown. Nevertheless Dannaks felt conspicuous and self conscious.

They stopped near their room and Dannaks threw Reupke the key. He went in and the three of them stood idly on the path.

Meryem seemed nervous. Fehime squeezed her hand, doing her best to project a calming influence.

Reupke locked up and rejoined the group.

Dannaks saw Meryem's shoulder blades flinch at the sound of hurried footsteps behind them. She turned, ashen-faced. And Dannaks turned too. Two boys were hurtling down towards them in some kind of race. They bounded down the steps and Dannaks felt sure one of them would fall. By now the party had stopped and the boys faltered but continued. They passed by and when they were a few paces ahead of Reupke one of them shouted "Schimi!"

and the other one laughed and stumbled but recovered. Then they were gone.

Reupke raised his eyebrows at Dannaks who simply returned a dull look.

08:27

Fehime and Meryem wandered over to the empty seating in the reception area. Reupke went to the reception counter. There were few people about and no one waiting to be attended. Dannaks couldn't decide and meandered in the space between the two girls and Reupke.

"I'd like you to call this number," said Reupke.

"You can make the call," said the man.

"It's the police," said Reupke.

"I don't think you have to bother," said Dannaks, nodding to the undercover man talking into his handy.

"Maybe," said Reupke. "Get me the manager."

The man behind the counter stiffened and flushed. Then he got up and went into a back room, returning a moment later with Turgut.

"Hallo Mr. Reupke, what–"

Reupke moved aside so that he could see the girls.

"Call this number please."

Turgut absently took the card without taking his eyes off the girls. Then he shook himself out of it, like a dog shaking off water, looked at Reupke and then the card. He snapped something at the other man, who took the card and began dialling.

"Thank you."

"Listen," said Dannaks to Turgut, "I don't know how long this is going to take, but we haven't had breakfast."

"Of course, of course."

Dannaks and Reupke went over and sat with the girls.

Over time more staff appeared. A plain-clothes man ran into the area, disrupting the tranquillity. Realising that there was no urgency he slowed and tried to stifle his heaving chest as he walked over to his companion. They conferred.

Then it seemed as if everyone observed from a distance.

Two cooks arrived with trays of tea, coffee, bread rolls, butter, cold meats, cheeses and jams. They placed them on the low table in front of them. The girls were in a two-seater sofa, with

Dannaks on another at one end and Reupke in an armchair at the other end.

Reupke tucked in. Dannaks ate too, but held back somewhat. Fehime nibbled on half a roll and Meryem ate and drank nothing.

Dannaks scrutinised her. There was so much to ask. Her clothes were crumpled. The wrinkles could have been through sleeping in them. But he thought they were more consistent with having been screwed up. It was hard to believe that she would have cleaned herself and continued to wear her soiled clothes. She must have worn something else and put them on now.

There was very little talk as they ate.

An ignorant or irreverent couple sat down with an arm full of ring binders from different tour operators containing day trips. They appeared unaware of the strange group.

Dannaks would have liked more time with Meryem. The questions were coming to him in a storm. But he knew he would get no answers.

"Have you packed?" he asked quietly.

Reupke shook his head.

Dannaks hadn't even showered.

09:03

Dannaks wondered what Ismail thought as he entered the building and set eyes upon the picnic scene. Of course Ismail was not alone. Two further plain-clothes men and six uniforms accompanied him. One of the plain clothes men, a podgy clean shaven man, with a head shaved even cleaner, pointed positions to the uniforms.

Dannaks and Reupke stood. The three detectives and two uniforms came straight to them, their eyes mainly on Meryem. Bullet-head, who reminded Dannaks of Mussolini, led the way. From a side door next to reception Tasköprü, the hotel manager, appeared. He intercepted the group, beaming, speaking and keeping pace with them, arriving a little ahead of them to extend his arm and hold out his palm, as if Meryem needed presenting. And as if he'd engineered the entire thing. Dannaks pondered how long he'd been waiting – no, hiding – in the back room. Fehime was standing too. Only Meryem sat, staring at the table, sometimes looking up disinterestedly.

The click and whirr alerted them to the hotel photographer who had evidently crept up on them from the plaza entrance. The circus was complete. Dannaks groaned.

Mussolini barked curtly, reprimanding the photographer and stopping the nonsense. The manager was given sort shift too. He was more or less ignored. But that didn't stop him from beaming.

The third detective produced a set of handcuffs and approached Meryem. She wearily got to her feet and held out her wrists. She glanced at Fehime. Dannaks spotted the connection in the exchange. Meryem appeared wasted, but Fehime looked distraught, perhaps more shaken than her friend.

As Meryem was escorted away by this detective and two uniforms Mussolini again spoke. Ismail translated, introducing his boss and stating that they needed to talk.

"Can I go?" asked Fehime, in Turkish. "I have a gym session to take."

Mussolini answered that she should wait. He then turned and spoke to Tasköprü. Dannaks gathered that he was asking for a room in which they would not be disturbed.

The four detectives ended up in Turgut's room. Extra chairs were brought in, filling up the area in front of the desk almost to the point of making a shoehorn necessary for them to get to their seats.

"This is cosy," Reupke mumbled.

And so began the interview: Mussolini asking questions, Ismail translating, both of them taking notes, with Dannaks testing the limits of his English and Reupke remaining quiet. Dannaks didn't admit to the extent of his conversation with Meryem. He did mention that he was left alone with her when Fehime fetched them coffee. But essentially he said that she was devastated and not talkative. When it came to the question whether he knew where Meryem had been hiding he said he didn't know. As to why he was fetched rather than his partner, he had to say that he was in the right place at the right time. Reupke explained his whereabouts. Dannaks couldn't find a reason why they had been called rather than the Turkish police.

The translating and note taking prolonged the interview and during a lull that could be taken as the end of the interview Reupke said that they were to be picked up at ten and they hadn't packed. A glance at his watch told Dannaks that pick-up was merely twenty minutes away.

Ismail translated and Mussolini stared at them blankly. Dannaks could almost hear him ticking off a mental list of questions.

"Yes, you can go," said Ismail when his superior answered. "I'll tell them you'll be late."

"Thanks," said Reupke, the first to rise.

Ismail and Dannaks got up too. Only Mussolini remained seated. Hands were shaken, goodbyes said and the German detectives left the room. Ismail closed the door on them.

Fehime was sitting where they had left her. The breakfast spread had been tidied away. Habip was standing talking to her. In addition to carrying his small rucksack a pair of training shoes dangled by their laces from his right hand.

"I'll meet you there," said Dannaks to Reupke, who knew he was going to Fehime and huffed as he turned away.

Habip looked at his watch as Dannaks approached. There were others in the reception area. Two uniforms conversed near the main entrance. A man from hotel security was talking to four undercover men near the plaza exit. Nobody seemed bothered with Fehime.

Habip held out his hand. "Goodbye *Herr* Dannaks. I've got to go."

"He's taking my ten o'clock class," she said despondently, as Dannaks sat in the chair next to her.

He didn't know what to say and simply nodded.

"They may not keep you long," he said. He waited a moment. "I told them I didn't know where Meryem was hiding."

She pouted.

Dannaks wasn't sure what she felt, but he had no time for subtlety. "What did you and Meryem talk about in the toilet?"

"Nothing."

"I'd like to know."

"It's not important."

Dannaks stared at her until she acquiesced.

"I suppose it doesn't matter. She thought you'd be carrying guns."

"Why?"

She shrugged.

"She was afraid of something, wasn't she?"

Again she shrugged.

"That's why she wanted us to escort her. The killer is still out there, isn't he?"

"I don't know."

"Fehime, I know you hid her. What did–"

"I didn't hide her. She came to me this morning."

Dannaks sighed. "Okay. Any ideas why she waited so long before giving herself up?"

"Not really." Dannaks gave her more time. "So she could get her head together, perhaps?"

He waited, but she had nothing more to say.

"Okay. Thanks for your help. I've got to pack." He leaned forward to get up.

She nodded and looked at him. He saw the uncertainty in her eyes.

On the brink of rising he said: "Just one more question." She closed her eyes on him and he waited for her to open them. "Do you believe she did it?"

"Why shouldn't I believe her?"

Dannaks smiled. Then he got up. She hadn't answered the question. She had evaded it.

"Goodbye Fehime," he reached down and shook her hand.

"You know," she began suddenly. "She said she's not destined to be happy."

"Why?" said Dannaks, taken aback by the unexpected burst of honesty.

"I don't know." The moment was fading fast. Fehime's presence was receding.

"She would have said more than that," he said, unable to hide his desperation.

Now it was her turn to be surprised. She was quiet for a while. Then she smiled bitterly at a memory or thought. "Not really."

"You remember something."

"She – It's not important."

"Please," he coaxed.

Fehime's shoulders sagged and she cast her eyes to the table. "She said history repeats itself."

"History repeats itself?"

Fehime stiffened.

"What did she mean?"

"I don't know." Hard eyes met his and he smiled bitterly. The moment was gone.

"Okay Fehime." He straightened. "Live well."

Her eyes had softened and were full of melancholy – *Hüzün* – as she nodded.

He left reception and went back to the room as fast as he could. He arrived a touch out of breath. Reupke was in the bathroom. Dannaks pulled out his bag and opened his case onto his bed. Then he began emptying the shelves.

Reupke came out of the bathroom carrying his zipped up toiletry bag. "Well, that's something. All nice and tidy." Dannaks stopped and looked at him. "It's solved just as we're about to leave."

Dannaks was shocked. "You don't believe that, do you?"

"It doesn't really matter, does it?" he said breezily.

"I think it does," he said techily.

Reupke silently packed his case. Dannaks went to the bathroom and brushed his teeth. There was no time for a shower. When he returned to the room with his toiletries Reupke spoke. "Did she tell you anything?"

"Who?"

"Meryem. Or Fehime, for that matter?"

Dannaks considered how to respond. "Meryem said enough for me to believe that she didn't do it."

"What did she say?"

"It's what she didn't say."

"Come on Dannaks, spit it out."

"She said she did it. But her entire body language said she was lying. And she refused to look at me."

"I can understand that."

Dannaks issued a short insincere laugh.

"That's it?" asked Reupke, after a while.

"More or less. Look, there wasn't enough blood spatter on her sweatshirt."

"If that's the one she was wearing."

True. But surely unlikely?

"Did you see the scars on her hands?"

"Yes."

"What do you make of them?"

"I have no idea. She was a cleaner before this."

"I thought it might be from carpet weaving."

"Maybe."

Dannaks came across a slip of paper in his trouser pocket. On it was the name Timothy Hoyer. He'd forgotten about the boy who'd drawn the red man: Timi. With the family name he should be able to get the boy's home address.

Reupke had discovered something too. He opened a soft paper handkerchief to reveal two orange blobs that looked like Plasticine.

"What's that?" asked Dannaks.

"Earplugs," said Reupke. "Dagmar gave them to me." He wrapped them up again and tossed them in the bin. "Your snoring is unbelievable." Dannaks continued packing. "Do you remember that first night when we hunted mosquitoes?"

"Yes."

"Well I woke you later on saying that I'd killed one. Do you remember?"

"Vaguely."

"There was no mosquito. I clapped to stop your snoring."

"Lucky you found Dagmar, then."

Reupke didn't answer.

"I'm ready when you are," said Dannaks.

09:55

Rather than wait for bellboy they shouldered their hand luggage and lugged their cases down to reception.

Katja was waiting for Dannaks when they arrived. Fehime was gone. The Turkish police and undercover men were also nowhere to be seen. There were two men leaning against the reception counter. One of the chess players was also there, talking to the woman behind it. The bellboy was skulking near the main entrance. Dannaks felt guilty for not calling him.

"You're cutting it fine," she said. She looked radiant: ready for a new day in the sunshine.

They pecked one another on the lips.

"Yeah, we were busy," said Dannaks.

Reupke went to reception and placed their key and the metal piece from the safe on the counter.

"I heard," said Katja. "You caught her then."

"She gave herself up." He retrieved an envelope from his bag. "Here's your photograph. Katja I–" He wanted to say something about last night but Turgut appeared.

"Ah, our V.I.P.s are leaving us," he said.

"Yes." Dannaks smiled awkwardly.

"Those men—" he gestured to the two at the counter – "are to take you to the airport." Until now the Turkish police, if they had turned up at all, hadn't excelled in punctuality. Now, when Dannaks would have appreciated a little extra time, they were waiting for them. "I hope you will speak favourably of your time at our hotel."

"Of course. Just a minute." He turned to Katja. "Kay, why don't you get to your Nordic walking? I know you want to and I'm no good at goodbyes."

She smiled. "It's not goodbye. I've got your number."

"I haven't got yours."

"I have to get to know you a bit better."

"Yes," he said, piqued. She glanced at Turgut and smiled broadly at Dannaks before turning on her training shoe heel and striding off. He wondered what she would do with the photograph. It was too big to pocket and she couldn't carry it and walk with those sticks. He wanted to call after her and say that he'd take the photograph, and give it to her when they met in Hamburg. But he knew he was being desperate. Whatever, although she had said it's not goodbye, the farewell galled him.

Reupke came over.

Dannaks returned his attention to Turgut. "Sorry. Yes, of course we'll recommend your hotel."

Turgut held up a pair of scissors. "May I?"

Dannaks didn't know what he wanted until Turgut moved to reach for his hand. Dannaks obliged and Turgut cut off his wristband.

"Like being demoted," said Reupke, holding up his wrist. "You know, having your stripes ripped off."

Turgut moved closer and lowered his voice. "It's over now, isn't it? We can get back to normal."

"Yes, I suppose so," said Reupke.

"But you could do me a big favour," said Dannaks.

"Please?"

Dannaks presented him with the piece of paper. "Can you get me this boy's home address? They were here two weeks ago." The manager regarded the piece of paper. Dannaks could see it went contrary to what had just been said. "It's just a precaution." Turgut nodded slowly and Dannaks pushed gently. "Now?"

"Yes. Yes, of course." He walked off.

"No Dagmar?" asked Dannaks.

"We said our goodbyes."

A blond boy with his mother entered the main entrance. Dannaks recognised him and raked his memory. What caught him was the boy's towel. Although it was slung over his shoulder he could make out the black and orange of the tiger. Then he remembered that he was the boy with the bloodied nose.

Turgut returned. Dannaks was surprised to see Ismail in tow. Turgut handed Dannaks a sheet of hotel paper. He had scrawled the boy's address on it. The boy lived in Spandau, Berlin. But it was Ismail who spoke.

"Good. You are still here."

Reupke raised his eyebrows.

Ismail's glance sent Turgut on his way.

"We are looking for Rafael," he continued. "Have you seen him?"

"No," said Reupke. Dannaks shook his head.

Ismail scrutinised them before relaxing his face and wishing them well.

"You will still send us that photograph?" said Dannaks.

"I do not see why."

"Please."

"We have the killer. She has confessed."

"Do you believe that?"

"Come on, Dannaks," said Reupke, "it's for them to sort out."

Dannaks remained steadfast without taking his eyes off Ismail.

"Do you?"

Ismail features relaxed. "I will send you the picture."

Dannaks smiled. "Thanks."

Ismail turned to the two at the counter and told them in Turkish that the German detectives were ready to leave. "Their German is not good and they don't speak English, but they know what to do."

"We are going to see the body," said Reupke.

"Of course," said Ismail.

Dannaks waved at the bellboy and pointed to their bags.

The detectives met the men at the entrance and the four of them went out together followed by the bellboy with their bags on a trolley. An unmarked car was parked in front of them. One of the men opened the boot and helped the bellboy arrange the bags and cases. The other climbed into the driver's seat.

"Out with a whimper," muttered Reupke, so that only Dannaks could hear him.

The sun was up. Everyone was on the other side of the hotel and there was a sense of leaving quietly by the backdoor.

Reupke climbed into the back of the car. Dannaks remained standing. He intercepted the bellboy before he could take his empty trolley back inside. He stuck out his right hand and the bellboy, taken aback, was forced to shake it. Dannaks produced a twenty-euro note in his left hand and gave it to him. The bellboy's eyes grew and then he smiled.

Dannaks turned and climbed into the back of the car. The bellboy was rooted to the spot. "*Danke, Danke.*"

10:37

At Antalya airport the driver, who had raced along the coast road as if his life – and no one else's – depended upon it, dropped his colleague and the two detectives off. Dannaks was pleased to alight and couldn't envisage how the man drove with lights and siren.

There was a press of about a hundred tourists at the entrance. It wasn't an orderly queue and the multitude seemed to simply converge on the door.

The Turkish detective, a lanky man, a good head taller than either of the German detectives, ignored the crowd and went to the entrance. Dannaks and Reupke followed hauling the cases along. Dannaks thought of Reupke's comment. They had arrived to the welcome bang of something of a fanfare. Now they were truly leaving with a whimper. Lanky spoke to someone inside. An airport security man then made space for the detectives to enter.

"Hey papa, that's unfair," said a small boy.

Inside Dannaks was surprised to see large scanning machines. This was the reason why most of the queue was outside the building. Strange that all the baggage should be checked at the entrance. Dannaks ignored the peeved looks.

They went in turn through the metal security doorframe. Collecting their bags on the other side they followed Lanky into the check-in hall. Here, queues of people, gathered about their luggage, extended from the counters. Lanky gestured for the detectives to wait. He then went to the front of the queue and spoke to the woman in attendance. She stopped tagging bags and picked up the telephone. After she'd made her call she spoke to him. Lanky then went to a neighbouring unattended counter and waved Dannaks and Reupke over. A flustered guest, near the front of the neighbouring line gave them accusatory looks. Dannaks smiled and the man turned to his wife.

An attendant arrived and sat down. The detectives passed him their tickets and passports.

"Excuse me." Dannaks turned. The flustered man's wife regarded him sternly. "Are you checking in for Hamburg?"

"Yes. But I think this is just for us."

She stared at him for a while, then, apparently at a loss as to what to say, she returned to report back to her husband.

Others in the same queue looked their way uncertainly or resentfully. To quell any doubt Lanky turned to them, spread his arms and shook his head.

The attendant returned their tickets and passports and pointed out the gate number on their boarding cards circling it with a pen.

Moving swiftly, now that they only carried their hand luggage, the detectives followed Lanky through passport control. Again they jumped queue. On the other side they met his partner, the one who had driven the car and an airport security man.

The detectives were led away from the mass of travellers into the bowels of the building, along empty corridors and seemingly unused areas. The security man spoke into his brick of a walkie-talkie. Any speech sounded like static to Dannaks. Eventually they stopped at a room. Two burly men in baggage attendant overalls with plastic identification cards swinging from their hips were waiting outside. One unlocked the door.

Lanky went in first. Strip lighting strobed the small windowless room. The driver and detectives entered as the lighting settled and buzzed evenly.

There were three things in the room. On the floor in one corner was a square cardboard box, which was opened and contained a polystyrene carton. It was labelled: "Fragile. Handle with care. Human remains." Propped up against this box was a large see-through plastic evidence bag containing Peter's stained clothes and personal effects.

Sitting centrally in the room was another open cardboard box. It carried the same labels. This one was rectangular and substantially larger and sat on a wooden air shipping tray. Inside this box was a fibreglass casket.

Reupke gestured for it to be opened. The Turkish detectives bent down and lifted the clasps. Dannaks pulled out his photograph of Peter. Reupke did the same. With the lid unclipped the detectives lifted it and moved it downwards so that the bottom end jutted out over the cardboard box. The black body bag inside was surrounded by ice.

Lanky unzipped the bag so that Peter's ghastly face could be seen. Some of his left shoulder and the top of the roughly sewn autopsy Y also showed. Dannaks compared the photograph with the face of the corpse. Peter's paleness made him look unreal. His face looked plastic. Hollywood would have made a better play at making him look human.

Reupke gestured for them to pull the zip further to expose his chest. The detectives then stared at the tattoo with its anaemic knife punctures.

Reupke looked to Dannaks for confirmation and then nodded to Lanky. The driver put the plastic evidence bag on top of the polystyrene carton and folded the cardboard flaps closed. He called and one of the baggage attendants came in with a roll of tape. He sealed the box.

Reupke and Dannaks helped Lanky fit and clip the casket closed. They too closed the box and held the flaps down for taping. The attendant took out a black marker pen and wrote HAM and their flight number on both boxes.

Lanky then led the detectives back to the waiting area. After pointing out their gate he left them alone. They dropped their bags and remained standing.

"Mission accomplished," said Reupke.

"Three days to look at a body for two minutes–"

"As we're about to leave."

They were quiet for a moment, watching the restless waiting mass and those milling about.

"Did they really think we wanted to look in the other box?" asked Dannaks, referring to the polystyrene carton containing Peter's extracted organs.

"We had the option."

"We've got an hour," said Dannaks. "Let's find some seats. Are you buying any duty free?"

Book Two

16:20

Their plane landed at Hamburg airport a little over three and a half hours later. During the flight Dannaks detailed his talk with Meryem. But Reupke was barely interested. He agreed that her confession was shaky, but his attitude was that it was out of their hands. The Turkish police would investigate. They had done what they had set out to accomplish.

Perhaps Reupke saw that Dannaks wasn't happy, because later he said: "You remember I said Dagmar and I had said our goodbyes, well that wasn't strictly true."

Dannaks waited.

"We had a serious chat this morning. I told her it was a great holiday romance, but all holidays come to an end." Dannaks had guessed as much, but even now had nothing to say. So that was why he was back before eight. She had kicked him out. Dannaks wondered whether the chat had occurred before or after sex. "You and Katja will probably go the same way."

"Maybe," said Dannaks, feeling his blood boil. But he'd do his damnedest to make sure it didn't go that way.

They were relatively quiet after this conversation. Both of them wrote notes for their reports.

Dannaks dozed off and Reupke woke him saying that he wished he hadn't thrown away the earplugs.

An airhostess, after asking them to identify themselves in the cabin, told them to stay on the plane after everyone had disembarked.

Just before landing Dannaks went to the toilet and banging his elbow only once managed to put on his tie.

The other passengers were as eager to leave the plane and get through customs as they had been at the check-in. Dannaks and Reupke sat tight and waited until only the crew remained on the plane. Eventually a hostess directed them to the tail exit.

It was a hot summer's day, but of course cooler than in Turkey. There were too many clouds in the sky and the breeze was biting. But the engines and tarmac upheld the warmth.

At the bottom of the steps were three airport security men and Leidner of *Zeugenschutz,* who had briefed them after Iceman's speech.

A police van and an unmarked car stood nearby.

"As soon as the body's loaded we can get on," shouted Leidner above the sound of nearby aircraft.

"Debriefing?" said Dannaks, loudly.

"Debriefing."

A baggage collector was grabbing the cases from a conveyor belt at the plane and roughly arranging them in the short chain of three trolley-like wagons. His partner was inside the hold loading the cases onto the conveyor belt. Four other attendants also in orange overalls and wearing large protective headphones loitered.

The detectives stood about idly, the sound of engines rendering conversation impossible. Dannaks watched his case loaded onto a trolley.

When the aircrew left, a team of cleaners entered the plane. A petrol truck arrived and was hooked up.

The last few cases were unceremoniously tossed onto the pile in the last wagon. The man got in the cab of the small vehicle that pulled the train and drove off. Then the four attendants methodically swung into action. Three joined the man in the hold and the fourth pushed some kind of gurney, a wheeled stretcher that could be raised and lowered to the end of the conveyor belt.

As the box came down, the square cardboard box following it, Leidner called out: "Is that it?"

"Are there others?" asked Dannaks.

Scotched Leidner looked up at the hold. "I don't know."

"That's it."

"Butenfeld?" asked Reupke.

Leidner nodded. Butenfeld was the street upon which the *Institute für Rechtsmedizin* (Department of Legal Medicine) resided. Part of the sprawling UKE (*Universitätsklinikum Hamburg-Eppendorf* – University Clinic) and responsible for, amongst other things, forensic pathology, the street name had become police shorthand.

They watched the box lifted off the air tray and onto the stretcher. Only when it was safely inside the van with the internal organs box did Leidner tell them that he'd meet them on the other side.

Leidner left with a security guard. Another climbed into the van. A third security guard took the two detectives to an airport vehicle and drove them to the main building.

Reupke and Dannaks didn't have to queue at customs and their cases were standing next to an empty carousel that had stopped running. They found Leidner was standing next to the escalator in the waiting area. There were no reporters or ranking officers. Dannaks suppressed the urge to tear off his tie. He felt dirty and sticky and in desperate need of a shower.

"You want me to take something?" Leidner asked, nodding to their bags. The detectives shook their heads. "So, how was your journey?" he then asked, leading them towards an exit.

"Uneventful," said Reupke.

"And the Turkish Riviera?"

Dannaks smiled.

Receiving no answer Leidner looked to each of them. "Don't tell me it was all work."

"No," said Reupke.

"Far from it," said Dannaks, feeling obliged to contribute, but immediately regretted his remark. "We only saw the body at the airport this morning."

"Save it for the debriefing."

17:35

The debriefing took place on the first floor of the *Polizeistern*, so called because the building resembled a star: a wheel with ten protruding wings like spokes on the wrong side.

On the way little was said. Dannaks marvelled at the greenness of the streets. By comparison Hamburg was lush. Trees lined the roads, hedges and bushes fronted houses. And there was colour amongst all this succulent greenness. The city was in bloom.

At this time of day on a Friday the building was all but deserted.

Leidner's boss *Hauptkommissar* Sturm, who'd also been at the briefing three days earlier, was waiting for them in his office. Three chairs stood in front of his desk, on which he'd cleared an area for a flask, sachets of sugar, small plastic containers of milk and some mugs. The sight of which dashed all hopes of getting out within the hour.

After offering coffee he asked: "How was the journey?"

Thankfully, he didn't linger on small talk. He too wanted to get into the weekend. Sturm suggested they go at it day by day.

Reupke and Dannaks pulled out their notepads and the reports they'd sketched on the plane.

Dannaks had to correct himself a couple of times. He called the victim Peter instead of his real name Matthias. After that he made an effort to refer to him simply as the victim.

They went through everything they knew: starting with the shit smearing and somebody seeing a waiter on the night of the murder, on to interviewing the animation crew and going to Herbst's place.

They said Rafael acted suspiciously, but put it down to having had a hard time with the Turkish police and they didn't believe he was the murderer.

When they spoke of the book Reupke pointed out that the Right could have got wind of it and were afraid of what he could say.

"I don't know," said Sturm. There was little white to his eyes and this coupled with his dark, heavy eyebrows gave him an intensely dangerous look. His jutting square jaw complementing his expanse of forehead did little to alleviate the impression of associating with an unpredictable caveman. But when he spoke his wit was as sharp as a scythe. "I won't rule it out. But the truth is the *Verfassungsschutz* said he'd done all the damage he could."

Reupke talked of the a/c and Dannaks was irked that he was given no credit.

Dannaks then told them of the red man and the theory that he was the killer. Ismail, also part of the investigation, favoured this theory.

When it came to Meryem Dannaks did most of the talking.

He explained how he'd questioned her idly to gauge her baseline behaviour under the circumstances. He agreed that stress had swamped the signals, but it had also made her careless. Rehearsed explanations came across as rehearsed and the unexpected threw her completely. Although she was burnt out, when he asked her about the knife she had delivered a plethora of information. In attempting to sound convincing liars tend to fabricate a little too much. They embellish their story with irrelevant or insignificant detail.

"That course certainly taught you a thing or two," said Sturm. "Go on."

Dannaks said that she couldn't explain what she did with the knife. She didn't mention slitting the victim's throat. And she didn't say why she hid. There was too much saying that she couldn't have done it.

He came across his four words he'd jotted from what Peter had said written about her: "Married – Berlin, knows Hamburg". But the information didn't seem relevant to the debriefing and he decided to leave it for his report.

"I don't think she did it," he concluded.

Sturm nodded acceptance and then looked at Reupke.

"I don't know," he said refusing to glance at Dannaks. "It's possible."

Sturm nodded again. He sat back, resting his elbows on the armrests of his swivel chair and bringing his fingertips together. He took a deep breath, dropped his hands and leaned forward.

"Like yourselves, I think we'll have to wait. Meryem confessed. We'll have to see what the Turks make of that." His posture and burdened eyes said he was far from finished. "We've been busy here too. And I think I'm safe in saying–" he glanced at Leidner – "that we have not one suspect. This end. I don't think the Right were actively after him. And we have no reason to believe that we have a leak here." In the pause he again held their silence with his heavy-browed stare. "Matthias's father has consented to a second autopsy. But I'm not expecting any surprises. I don't think there's any call to actively pursue the case."

"Shouldn't we look into Meryem's background?" asked Dannaks. Sturm was about to speak, but Dannaks repeated Fehime's statement about Meryem saying history repeats itself.

"I don't see any reason." Dannaks could see the words resources and manpower running around in his head. "The Turks have handled this so far. We'll let them get on with it."

And that was the end of it.

Dannaks accepted Leidner's offer of a lift when they left Sturm's office. Reupke said that his girlfriend would pick him up. The three of them went down to Leidner's car. Reupke fetched his bags and nodded to Dannaks over the car roof. "Keep in touch."

Dannaks doubted that Reupke still had his card with his private number written on the back.

19:48

Leidner dropped him off outside his door. Dannaks lugged his case up the stairs. As he pulled out his keys at his door he feared

261

his neighbour, old *Frau* Schumann, would open her flat door. He didn't want small talk and was pleased when he was inside his flat.

The silence emphasised his aloneness.

He left the case at the door and took his holdall to the sofa bed in his main room. His entire flat was no bigger than the room he'd shared with Reupke. On one side of the short corridor to the flat door was the kitchen, on the other the bathroom. His main room was his lounge, dining room and bedroom in one.

At the window he stared out at the low sun. The roads below were as busy as ever. There were still some boats on the Alster. His flat may be a cubbyhole but the view was breathtaking. He opened the window and the swish of traffic invaded the stillness.

Deflation filled him. He felt as if he'd never been away. Everything was so familiar and yet different. Of course nothing had changed in his absence. And he knew he saw it all anew through different eyes. In some small way he had changed. Whether temporarily or permanently he wasn't sure. But his surroundings were pushing the break in Side to memory, perhaps even dream-level.

He still felt dirty but decided that it was too late to shower.

In the kitchen he ran the tap and emptied the kettle. The contents of the fridge disappointed him. The frozen meals didn't entice either.

He flicked on the kettle after filling it. Then he looked at his watch. Katja would be sitting down to an aperitif now. Would she eat with Dagmar?

Something akin to a plan formed in his mind.

He switched on the television to compete with the traffic. A twinge of excitement took him when he opened his case on the small coffee table. But the feeling of being a kid discovering his goodies dissipated as soon as he'd laid everything out. He'd thought there was more, but nothing was missing. From his holdall he lifted out the cardboard tube. He extracted the bottle of whisky and regarded the label with relish before shelving it.

Dannaks made himself a green tea and after closing the window began unpacking.

By eight thirty he was finished. Changing his shirt for a sweatshirt, grabbing a jacket and his case, in which he'd stuffed his holdall, he left his flat. He went up to the loft and unlocked the padlock of his small caged storage area. There he left the case, placing it with all his other belongings for which there was no room in the flat.

Outside he turned away from the traffic and the lake and took a side road to the *Lange Reihe*. He ignored the street-life: pretty young things, raucous groups, couples, beautiful people in their prime sitting at the tables that spilled out onto the pavement from the various chic restaurants. Crossing the road he strode down another side road, bereft of activity.

Two minutes later he found himself in front of the *Narzisst's Eck* (Narcissist's corner).

Karl-Heinz greeted him as he entered. Frauke and Hagen had claimed their favourite spots. Dannaks nodded a greeting. He didn't so much have a favourite spot as a favourite area. Two lads sat near the door. An older couple were having an intense conversation in one of the corners. Otherwise the place was quiet.

This pub was not only off the main track; its thick glass closed it off to the outside world. It had nothing in common with the brash openness of the bars along the *Lange Reihe*. People who came here were regulars who sought refuge from the madding crowd. Inadvertent visitors would take a drink, but rarely return. Here no jukebox shattered the peace, no television flashed mute images and no voices rose above a murmur. Predominantly a man's pub, this was a place for serious drinking and the poison was whisky. Beers and wines were on offer but to see them was a novelty and usually labelled the uninitiated.

If he felt deflated in his flat he now bordered on depression. This was his beloved local, his stagnant refuge. And the moment he envisaged seeing it through Katja's eyes it became a mausoleum.

He ordered a whisky-cola. Karl-Heinz didn't balk at the very idea. He stocked cheap whiskies and knew Dannaks wanted a longer drink.

Dannaks knew better than to ask for a menu. Karl-Heinz would tell him to get himself to a restaurant. But occasionally, subject to Uta's whim, some simple fare could be had.

"Anything other than sandwiches tonight?" he asked.

Karl-Heinz, wiping a glass with a teacloth, gave him a scolding look, without so much as a falter in his motion.

Dannaks absorbed the look, returning a passive stare.

Karl-Heinz had a head of white hair that was wispy like candyfloss and carried a beard to match. His skin was weathered beaten copper. He could be Iceman's father. His demeanour was equally scathing, but in his caustic humour there was warmth that Iceman lacked.

"I'll see," he eventually said. He put the glass on a shelf and then went through the back door. He returned a moment later. The scolding look was now one of anger. "You're in luck, Dannaks. There's some lasagne."

"Sounds about right."

Karl-Heinz disappeared again.

Would Katja have finished eating and be sitting in the plaza waiting for the show?

Hagen was drinking his standard tipple. Yes, thought Dannaks, this was a place for regulars only. And these regulars were all lonely people looking for a semblance of company. These people could equally as well sit at home and drink. The semblance of company was founded in the fact that to approach any of them would be to encroach upon their privacy.

Dannaks was a regular.

Saturday
08:21

Sunlight peeking over the top of the curtains woke him. He felt groggy. The lasagne should have been a good line of defence against the bombardment of whisky he had sent his stomach. His head said that it had not sufficed. He struggled out of his sofa bed, noticing that he had forgone putting a sheet over the cushions. He went to the toilet and then to the kitchen. He flicked on the kettle and filled and drank a glass of water, refilled it and took it back to the sofa bed.

Deciding against pulling back the curtains he lay down.
09:16

The sound of *Frau* Schumann's door closing woke him. His bottle of duty free wasn't on the shelf. He located it on floor in the corner underneath the coffee table he'd shifted to open his sofa into a bed. Two whisky colas had been followed by two Balvenie Double woods, he'd finished the evening in his flat with a generous nightcap of his newly purchased Dalwhinnie Distiller's Edition.

After drinking some water he closed his eyes on the world.

He smiled as he thought of Katja. She'd be Nordic walking now. Inexplicably Karl-Heinz intruded, bringing him his lasagne. He had draped his dishcloth over his arm in a mockery of a waiter.

Dannaks smiled again, stretched, got up and pulled back the curtains. Daylight flooded his room and highlighted its mustiness. The road below was full. Two lanes each way, chock full of impatient drivers some switching lanes to jockey a few metres ahead.

Dannaks opened the window, allowing the urgency of modern day life to supplant the peace.

In the kitchen he flicked on the kettle again and spooned some instant coffee in a mug. He then went to the toilet.

Returning to the room with his coffee he turned his bed back into a sofa, his quilt and pillow concealed in a compartment under the cushions. The bottle of whisky was shelved. Shifting the coffee table back into the centre of the room his bedroom became a lounge again.

He sipped his coffee for a while. Then he got up, closed the window and turned on the radio. In the kitchen he poured milk over a bowl of cereal and took this to the lounge.

He looked at the clock. It was ten past ten. Katja would have finished Nordic walking.

He told himself that if he didn't stop thinking about her he'd go nuts.

With a sense of the day passing him by, he finished his cereal and coffee, flicked on the kettle for another coffee and climbed into the bath for a shower.

By ten thirty he was ready for the day. More than this he felt dynamic: ready to get things done.

Five minutes later he was outside, his canvas bag hanging from his right shoulder. He initially took the route he had last night. At the *Lange Reihe* he walked towards Hamburg's main station, but before reaching it he took a side road and strode into Patel's shop. The first thing that struck newcomers was the amount of stuff. Outside the building looked unimposing, inside it took on the dimensions of a warehouse. When one traversed the labyrinth of cram-packed shelving it was easy to miss Patel or any of his assistants if they stood still. Taking an inventory would be a nightmare and yet Patel could locate anything in his shop. And when it came to foodstuffs anything could be found here. Chinese and Asian script adorned some of the packages. Of those that were vacuum packed in clear plastic the absence of translation rendered the contents unknown. Fresh fruit and vegetables could be had here too.

If that wasn't enough four PCs were arranged in a corner. Patel's latest enterprise was running an Internet café.

He exchanged a few words with Patel at the till before a customer arrived. He asked for some time on a PC. Patel called one of his young men. Dannaks had the impression they were his sons or nephews or their friends. Most were boys. One such boy appeared and led Dannaks to the PCs and booted one up for him.

Dannaks sat before the machine. Time came in half hour slots and he aimed to pay for one slot. He logged into his free email account and found seven new mails. All of them were advertising. One was from the free mail account itself, urging him to become a paying member with skies-the-limit options. He marked them all and pressed delete.

He decided to use his last twenty-five minutes to check the watches on eBay.

With one exception Dannaks rarely spent his money on what he called luxuries. He had a passion for chronographs or, as he called them, timepieces. As far as he was concerned digital watches weren't timepieces. Battery driven watches weren't timepieces. Only automatic watches were timepieces. And to date he possessed eight of them. His financial pain threshold stopped him from buying more. As he scanned the pages something better occurred to him.

Peter had been investigated, but they knew precious little about Meryem. He had jotted in his notepad that Peter had written that she had been married and lived in Berlin, adding that she knew Hamburg too. He called up the available online telephone directories. Ideally he needed at least two-year-old information. There was no point calling up actual entries. But her ex-husband or family might still live in Berlin. Turkish divorce was not unheard of. He tapped in Turan and was disheartened by the fifty-one hits. He recalled reading in the British reporter's article that after Istanbul and Izmir the third largest Turkish city with 1.6 million Turkish people was Berlin. None had a first name of Meryem. But he hadn't expected her to be listed. And if her name had appeared he would have almost regarded it as coincidence. Most of the names were private, but half a dozen or so were companies. He changed the location from Berlin to Hamburg and received a list of thirteen names.

After dismissing the idea of printing the lists he then located the Turkish daily *Hürriyet*. His command of Turkish meant it took him a while to click through the pages to the small piece about Meryem's capture. Under the poor photograph of her with a number of proud looking officials was a simple paragraph of text. The gist of it was that the ex-Nazi's killer had been caught and had confessed. Dannaks sensed the ambivalence in the text and the picture. Both portrayed Meryem sympathetically.

He signed off.

At the front of the shop he nodded to Patel and picked up a basket. As always he went to the special offer bins first. These were filled with all manner of things about to go off or reach their sell-by date. Normally Dannaks purchased only wine and ready-made meals, frozen pizzas, cheese, soups and tins, but today he also bought some apples, tomatoes, a cucumber, a red paprika and a lettuce. This was going to be the new healthy him.

At the till he added three German dailies to his purchases.

On his way back to his flat, his shoulder aching with the weight of the bag, he passed two Muslim women wearing headscarves. St. Georg was a colourful area in Hamburg so the sight of them was not unusual. But they sent his thoughts back to the cleaners at Azure Skies. More specifically he remembered being told at the briefing by Sturm and Leidner after Iceman's talk that Meryem had started as a cleaner at the resort. Her German had been noted and she had taken the opportunity to help out at the children's club. She had done so well they decided to offer her a job.

He plodded up the stairs to his flat. The lower flats were actually offices. Only *Frau* Schumann and he lived in the building. Again she didn't appear when he reached their floor.

Whilst putting away his purchases in the kitchen he came across his collection of potatoes. He hadn't bought any because he knew he had a decent supply. His face dropped when he saw the state of them. Were they so old? The smaller ones were shrivelled and wrinkled, the substance of them gone into the thick roots that struck out like petrified spiky worms. He threw them in the bin.

There was a big one that he thought he could use. He broke off the roots that it too had sprouted.

He placed another cup of coffee on his table in the lounge and picked up his telephone. He tapped the number of his partner and friend from his days in Drugs. Uwe picked up on the fourth ring.

"Hallo vacationer. Listen, we're just off shopping. Can I call you back?"

"Sure." Dannaks hung up. He wasn't sure why he had called Uwe. He just wanted to chat. He wasn't sure he was ready to talk about Katja, but it could have been pried from him.

His coffee was too hot to drink, so he made another call. His father picked up after a long while.

"Hi Papa."

"Hallo son. Shall I get your mother?"

"You don't have to." He found it easier to talk to his mother. He and his father were never relaxed. The tension was minuscule, but present nonetheless. It was as if each of them needed to uphold a certain level of intelligence. And this resulted in a sense of challenge that made them wary and thus uneasy. Dannaks also suspected that he favoured his younger brother more. Maybe both his parents did, but his mother didn't show it. His brother, Jürgen, was married with two children.

"You're not cancelling, are you?"

"No." The family was coming together tomorrow for the afternoon. He suddenly didn't know what to say.

"What's happening?" His father could just as easily have said: "Why are you calling?"

"Nothing really. I just got back from Turkey."

"Oh, that's right." He seemed pleased that they had a topic. "You went to pick up that boy's body."

"Yes. But we ended up with quite a bit of free time."

"That's good."

The conversation was drying up. He should have asked for his mother.

"I'll tell you all about it tomorrow."

"Good. I'm looking forward to it. We both are."

"Me too."

"See you, then."

"Yes." Dannaks hung up. He sighed.

As he sipped his coffee he surveyed the room, trying to see it through Katja's eyes. Compact but orderly. There was no room to be untidy.

When he got up and put a CD in his player he saw the dust. He calculated that he last vacuumed about a month ago. But then he thought his potatoes were a week old. There was nothing for it. He would have to bite the bullet and borrow *Frau* Schumann's vacuum cleaner.

He sat down again and scoured the papers for anything on Meryem's capture. They all carried a paragraph or so on an inside page. Basically they reported the same thing. Meryem had been taken in. She had confessed to the killing. Matthias's body had returned to Germany. Only the *Bild* accompanied the text with a photograph. It was Meryem's club photograph.

"Right," he said suddenly and got up. Time to confront the old lady.

In the end he thought he got off relatively lightly. Despite declining offers of tea, coffee and even schnapps, he was in the old lady's flat for almost an hour. But he didn't mind. He had the time. In fact he wasn't sure how he was going to spend the evening. He hadn't checked the television, but sitting in front of the box with a bottle of red wine appeared to be taking shape.

She, of course, did most of the talking. He sat on her sofa, leaning forward and concentrating on paying attention to the barrage of words just in case there was a hidden question requiring a response. In the relatively short space of time she covered recent international events, her son's tour as a violinist and inevitably crime. When he mentioned just getting back from Side, she spoke about holidays with her long-departed husband before digressing into a short discourse on Turkish restaurants in Hamburg.

Her flat was three times the size of his one and he envied her space. Consolation was had in the fact that being on the other side of the building it didn't have the view.

He didn't possess a vacuum cleaner and didn't really have the room to store one. So he bought the refill bags and gave her the company she obviously sought.

15:03

He was quite chuffed with himself when he sat down with his cup of tea. After lunch he'd vacuumed his flat, wiped all the surfaces with a damp cloth, cleaned his bath, toilet and bowl and emptied his bins. For a while he was on a roll and contemplated tackling the windows. But by the time he had finished all his other chores he no longer had the energy.

Dannaks finished his tea and then went out for a long walk around the Alster. He considered this exercise even if it was more of a stroll than a walk.

He felt good. The world felt good. He bought a bottle of water from a vendor. It was an expense he felt he couldn't ordinarily afford, because he could bring his own water or wait till he was back in his flat. But this was his pat on the back. He sat on a bench and contentedly watched the world go by.

16:59

In his flat he set about making himself dinner. Today he was going to make the effort. This was the beginning of the new him. He cut up some of the tomatoes, the red paprika and half of the cucumber. He then tore off and washed leaves of the lettuce. He cut up an apple and added that too. His soup bowls were too small so it all went into a plastic bowl. When he searched for some salad dressing he discovered he didn't have any.

In the lounge he chomped through it all.

How was Katja spending her evening?

An hour later he was hungry again and he unpacked a pizza and threw it in the microwave. The oven would have been better, the base was always flaccid and rubbery when micro waved, but he didn't feel he had the time.

He'd finished his pizza and was filling his time reading the papers before the seven o'clock television news when the telephone interrupted him.

"Reupke," said the voice at the other end, above the background conversation.

"Hallo," Dannaks returned.

"Now how did I know you would be in on a Saturday night?"

"I was out yesterday." Dannaks imagined him in a pub or restaurant.

"Listen. This is, er, a little awkward. But my girlfriend–" Dannaks sensed that she was also listening "– doesn't believe I was faithful. She smelt perfume on my shirt. I told her you had a girlfriend out there. She doesn't believe me. Can you talk to her? I'll pass you over. Oh, and by the way Ismail sent the photo–"

"He did? Can you see the red man?"

"Yes. But he's in the background. A couple of grinning idiots take up most of the picture. Look I'll give you Steffi, you–"

"Where are you?"

"Dannaks we're having an evening out – What?" Dannaks heard the girlfriend in the background. Sound was then muffled. Reupke had put his hand over the phone. His girlfriend hadn't let him out of the pub or whatever to make his call. She wanted to hear every word. "Okay. We're in Paddy's, the Irish pub. Do you know it? Off *Mönckenbergstrasse.* "

"Yes. I'll be there in thirty minutes."

He was there in thirty-seven minutes. With the meeting as an excuse he successfully extricated himself from any extended conversation with *Frau* Schumann when he returned her vacuum cleaner. On the way he thought about the call. Saying that he knew he'd be in on a Saturday night had been an unnecessarily snide remark. They were never going to be buddies. Of course Reupke had been playing to his girlfriend. What had he told her? That Dannaks was stuffy? And now Dannaks was being called in to lie for him again. But he wanted to see the photograph and if this was the price, then so be it.

There were still shoppers milling about on Hamburg's main street. Many more would be in the neighbouring shopping arcades.

Paddy's was an insignificant corner pub tucked away on a desolate office block and flats area away from the hustle and bustle. The large gloss-green double doors could have been that of a serious establishment: solicitors, lawyers, some peace or conservation movement. The minute Dannaks pushed open one of the doors the sound of revelry dispelled any doubt.

The bar girl, carrying a tray of empties, nodded to him as he entered. Although the place was busy with very few seats or bar stools available it was not packed. From the entrance Paddy's was little more than a corridor. The bar started almost immediately and ran almost to the steps at the far end. Near the door and opposite the bar were round dark burgundy tables. A corridor perhaps two people wide separated the bar and these occupied tables. Bar stools encroached this space reducing places to single person width.

Beers and stouts were predominant but Dannaks was pleased to see a good selection of whiskies.

Reupke and Steffi were not here so he moved on to the far steps. On the way he noticed a door to the kitchens and another to the toilets. Between the kitchen door and the bar a band had squeezed in its gear. There was a full drum set, an accordion and fiddle.

He climbed the steps conspicuously loud.

At the top of the six steps the place opened out into a room. Here the space was uninhibited by the bar and opened out to the full width of the building to accommodate eight to ten tables, all of which were occupied.

Dannaks spotted them immediately. They were sitting at a table in the far corner.

Reupke stood and they shook hands.

"It's been a long time," said Reupke, facetiously. "This is Steffi."

Dannaks shook her hand. He slipped off his summer jacket and hung it over the back of his chair. Then he sat with them.

The waitress he'd nodded to when he entered was standing at his side. Although the other two had drinks he asked whether they wanted anything. They declined and he ordered a Bushmills sixteen-year-old three wood.

Of course he couldn't help but compare Steffi with Dagmar. She was disappointingly plain. She did not possess Dagmar's voluptuousness. Her thin lips lacked passion. Yet, the ends of her mouth-line peeked in a comfortable smile. And whereas Dagmar had a dark somewhat heavy brow, Steffi's was light and inquisitive.

"What did you do last night?" Reupke asked.

"I went down to my local."

Reupke nodded. "And Katja comes back Monday?" He wasn't wasting any time.

"Yes. Although I don't expect to hear from her until Tuesday."

"You met her out there?" Steffi asked. She appeared intrigued.

"Yes." Dannaks went on to explain almost bumping into the punk and then having seen Katja earlier at Nordic walking. During his story his whisky arrived with a glass of water.

His mind wandered as his story drew to a close. He'd learnt that liars tended to embellish their stories with too much detail. Had he given too much detail? He hadn't lied, but his story had been his pitch for Reupke. His motivation was to cover for his colleague, who carried the brunt of a lie. So he felt uncomfortable even though he had told the truth. And he wondered about Meryem. Could it be that she hadn't lied? Was it possible that she had helped kill Peter and was protecting an accomplice? Who could this accomplice be? For some reason Fehime sprung to mind. Then Rafael. Could it be?

"How romantic," said Steffi.

Dannaks smiled awkwardly and sipped his water.

"You shared a room," she said. "How did you cope with my Olaf's snoring?" She squeezed Reupke's forearm reassuringly.

"My snoring is silence compared to him," said Reupke.

Steffi laughed. "Now you know what it's like." Whereas Dagmar had come across as an intriguing mystery that would take time and effort to discover, Steffi was an open book: accessible and easy to talk to.

They were silent for a moment.

"So, why Dannaks?" she asked, giving him a beguiling smile. "Is your first name so bad?"

"No. It's to do with an incident in the past. It received a lot of publicity, but they couldn't print my name. So the papers referred to me as Götz D. I switched to using my surname and, er, just got used to it."

"See," she said to Reupke. "I told you I'd get his first name. You only had to ask."

He wasn't sure why he had told her. Katja didn't know his first name. Maybe he felt she was owed some honesty. Or perhaps he was falling under her spell. He could see why Reupke was with her. She was fun. Joy radiated from her and made her shine. This made her attractive.

He also realised that Reupke had targeted Dagmar for her looks. He hadn't cared one iota about her personality.

"I like him," said Steffi to Reupke. The statement told him that Reupke had given her a different impression.

Dannaks felt a rising confidence and said: "Any chance of seeing the photo?" Since arriving he'd been dying to see it.

"Yes, of course," said Reupke glancing at Steffi and taking out his handy. She sat back with her glass of white wine in her hand. "You'll be disappointed."

In Side Reupke was hard and independent. Here he wasn't so much subdued as happily subjugated. He was firmly under

273

Steffi's spell. And there was truly something bewitching about her openness.

Reupke brought up the picture and passed his handy over. Then he too sat back with his drink.

Dannaks scrutinised the picture.

Two big beaming faces loomed out of the darkness. They were squashed together vying for domination as if they were in a photo booth. Parts of their faces were so close that their features were blanched and over-exposed. One of the boys either had a peculiar nose or his proximity had distorted it. Their faces were painted and should he pass either of them in the street he would not recognise either of them. The interesting figure was beyond them, between the tops of their heads. It was the red man, although only a sliver of colour on a cheek showed. His head was turned away from the camera and only the back of his neck; his right ear and part of his right cheek were visible. His hair was dark and unkempt. Some of his torso was visible. He was wearing some kind of collared overall and his biceps looked substantial.

"Can you zoom in?"

Reupke leaned forward and held out his hand. "I've tried, but it just gets blurred." He tapped away and manoeuvred the figure into the centre of the frame. Then, with Dannaks watching, he zoomed in. The figure became indiscernible.

Dannaks sighed. If this was the killer then he wouldn't recognise him either. He sat back.

Reupke continued tapping. "There's something else." He turned the handy to Dannaks, who leaned forward again. "Ismail sent this text with it."

"*Here Foto. M confesses. Parens: M not M.*"

"Parens?" said Dannaks.

"He must mean parents."

"The parents are saying that Meryem is not Meryem?"

"That's how I read it."

Reupke pocketed his handy. "Did you catch the news last night?"

Dannaks shook his head.

"They showed a clip of Turkish television with Meryem being taken into custody. Then they showed her club photo. I guess the parents saw it."

Dannaks was silent for a moment. "You know," he began, "Meryem said a lot that only someone in the room at the time of the killing could know." Reupke nodded. "I still can't believe she did it, but..."

"But?"

"Maybe there were two of them and she's protecting someone." Rafael, Fehime, the red man, someone else? What did they know of Turgut's whereabouts on the night of the murder? But then Ismail and co. had interviewed everyone. They knew so little.

"This is a change. Out there you were convinced that she was innocent. Now you have your doubts."

Steffi leaned forward to take advantage of the lull.

"I think that's enough shop, boys."

Reupke nodded.

"One question," said Dannaks. He wasn't comfortable with his own ambivalence and wanted a push one way or the other.

Steffi shrugged acceptance.

"Do you think she did it?"

Reupke stared at him before eventually saying: "The truth?"

Dannaks nodded.

"I don't know. But she's guilty of something, that's for sure."

Had he ducked the question? Dannaks wasn't sure he had answered. And yet he himself was no longer sure. Could she have fooled Peter so completely? His book –

"Let the Turks deal with it," said Reupke. "On Monday–"

"One two," a voice boomed over loud speakers.

Reupke raised his voice. "You'll be back at work–"

"One two."

"– and you'll have enough to do. I–"

"Good evening, Hamburg. We're the Blarneys."

Despite being furthest from the loud speakers talking became impossible the minute the Blarneys launched into their first jig.

"I didn't know this was your thing," said Dannaks between numbers.

"It's not. I didn't know a band was playing tonight."

"I'd like it if it wasn't so loud," said Steffi.

"They think they're playing in a stadium," said Dannaks, who quite liked the music.

During the fifth number Steffi and Reupke silently communicated. When the waitress emerged from the crowd they asked for the bill. Dannaks decided to stay and ordered another Bushmills.

Sunday
10:36

He slept well.

He slept well and didn't wake up with a splitting hangover. Oh, he felt a little fuzzy at first, but when he was fully conscious he felt ready for the day, come what may.

He lay for a while recalling the events of the evening, conjuring up the photograph. After Steffi and Reupke had left he had moved into the corner to look into the room and the direction of the music. All chairs were taken and part of his table commandeered, but nobody seemed to mind him sitting in the corner. There again, he wasn't invited to participate. Everyone was a good ten to fifteen years his junior.

In the pub he had found a handmade flyer. He had turned it over and made a list from his notepad. He often resorted to lists on his cases. They were arbitrary in structure, because they were musings, questions, impressions and possible clues. His entries began with a question. *Not Meryem? History repeats. Married Berlin/knows Hamburg. Small cuts. Beelzebub/Red man. Shit smearing/sabotaged toilets. Bone Pendant? Is Meryem innocent? Yes? Why is she lying? To protect someone. She was witness to the killing.*

Dannaks left when the band packed up around midnight. The walk home seemed long. It had turned exceedingly chilly and his summer jacket was meagre defence.

In the flat he had made a green tea and caught the late news. There was nothing on Meryem or Peter.

Just after one he had climbed into bed.

This morning he felt convinced he had seen Peter's killer. The photograph was a spur, but what could he do? Why had Meryem lied? Surely doing so was an admission of some guilt?

He got up, performed his toilet, turned the bed back into a sofa, drank his coffee looking out over the Alster and then ate a bowl of cereal listening to the news on the radio. There was again nothing on the case, but he hadn't expected anything. He looked over yesterday's papers before placing them at his door to take down to the recycling bin on his way to the station. Then, as an afterthought, he picked up the Bild newspaper and found the picture of Meryem. He took the page to the lounge and cut out her picture with a pair of scissors. He regarded it for a moment. Then he carefully folded it and placed it in his wallet.

He decided that one corner of his room was becoming an unsightly clutter. So he began extracting superfluous items for the bin or his loft storage area. This took up most of the morning. Despite the memories the items brought, his mind was not really on the job. He knew he was doing this more for Katja than for himself. His motivation was irrelevant, he told himself. The fact was that he was being productive.

He left his flat at quarter past twelve.

At Lübecker Strasse he took the U1 up to Volksdorf. There he alighted and walked for about twenty minutes to his parents' house, arriving at five past one.

Retirement had turned his parents into full-time gardeners. They possessed a modest villa with a large – large enough to accommodate a pond – garden. The house itself was beginning to show signs of neglect. Dannaks had observed this decline in older people. Pride was a fickle thing. Repairs were subjective. So parts of the house, especially those out of the sight of visitors, fell into neglect or were just temporarily patched. It was all a matter of priority.

His parents had both worked: she in a bank and he in insurance. They had been shrewd with their money. Dannaks's younger brother, Jürgen, had followed his father's footsteps into insurance. Only Dannaks had danced out of the financial line by joining first the *Schupo* before moving on – under special circumstances – to the *Kripo*.

He had lunch with his parents in the winter garden. His father was also partial to red wine – good for the heart, son – and Dannaks had brought a bottle. There was always a strange politeness when he was alone with his parents. Talk was sober and laughter restrained.

He gave them an abridged version of his time in Side. His father exclaimed that such resorts were merely Germany transposed to a place with more sunshine. "Your mother and I did that ten day tour a few years ago." There was so much to see. His mother, as always the pacifier – even when there was no apparent conflict –

said that he had gone to pick up that poor boy's body and had not been on holiday.

The day was exceptional and his parents decided to set up the coffee and cake outside. So Dannaks helped them with the table and chairs and large umbrella that afforded some shade, then with transporting utensils and crockery.

Another thing that set him apart in the family was that Jürgen was married to Verena and had brought his parents two grandchildren: Adriana and Tobias.

So when they arrived later that day for coffee and cake his parents came alive. As if the liveliness of the children was infectious they became more animated.

Dannaks handed the kids their packages. Seven-year-old Adriana opened up her gossamer pink belly dancer outfit and nine-year-old Tobias unwrapped his Spiderman T-shirt. Both children thanked their uncle Götz and wanted to wear their presents immediately. Because they were outside Verena insisted that Adriana wore her outfit over her clothes. The little girl thought it unfair that her bigger brother didn't have to wear his new T-shirt over the one he was already wearing. Tobias charged off squirting imaginary webs from his wrists. Verena helped straighten her daughter's outfit and then the latter began gyrating. The women showed the little girl how to move her arms, wrists and fingers in a flowing motion. And the men looked on delightedly.

Adriana ventured off too when the adults' interest began to wane.

They touched upon his excursion to Turkey. And he held back from telling them of Katja. To do so would only have brought on unwarranted excitement and a flood of embarrassing questions. And since he couldn't really talk about the case, there was very little left to say.

Then Verena announced that Jürgen had been promoted to team leader. Congratulations were expressed, followed by questions about what his new role entailed.

Dannaks caught a glance from his father. In itself it was merely a fleeting contact of their eyes. Nothing was said and the moment between them was buried. However, behind it was bewilderment. For after all these years he'd only reached *Oberkommissar.* He'd not shot up the ladder. Why his own boss, Frank, was maybe ten years his junior. He'd tried to explain that the higher you rose up the ranks the more you became a pen-pusher, managing bodies, cases, resources and playing office politics whilst juggling statistics to make your department appear successful if not the best. This wasn't for him.

To change the subject from his promotion Jürgen asked after his father's best friend. Dannaks was not up to date and his mother told him that Jan had had a stroke. He was still in hospital and apparently there was no change in his condition. His father was appalled by the attitude of Jan's children. Naturally they were concerned, but behind all their concern sat the problem of what to do with him. Their mother was dead and Jan lived alone in the house in which they had grown up. He said Jan's children appeared more concerned – perhaps bothered – by the awkwardness of the situation. They all wanted him in a home and there were undercurrents of unspoken, and vehemently denied, inconvenience at having to take care of their father.

Dannaks's father didn't know whether there were homes for the elderly in Turkey. He thought that there would be very few. Dannaks agreed that there would be few and pointed out that aging childless people would be a target group, but nearly everyone had a relative somewhere. He said that contrasting German society, indeed the western capitalist society, Turkish society treated age with proportionally increasing respect. If parents and grandparents didn't live under the same roof as their children's families, they were often close by to give the appearance of an extended family. In Germany the elderly were often treated worse than children. At least with children their behaviour could be excused. There was no such tolerance with the aged. Shame was not as pronounced a part of the western world's makeup.

Dannaks again heard the old man in the Azure Skies shop. After effectively chasing off the two boys who'd stormed in, he had muttered: "Your children know no respect."

Suddenly Adriana yelped and came running over to the table, fat tears rolling down her cheeks.

"Tobias hurt me," she wailed, falling into Verena's arms.

"What happened?" asked Jürgen looking at her and then glancing to the end of the garden where his son meandered, head down, watching his feet.

"He hurt my finger," she said. She held her little finger up for their inspection. It did look a little red.

"Tobias," Jürgen called. "Come here."

The boy reluctantly approached. "I didn't do anything," he said, his expression hard with angry determination.

"Come here." His approach was dawdling.

Jürgen's anger rose as he waved the boy to hurry.

"I didn't do anything," he repeated, his forefinger and coming up to his mouth. And Dannaks saw Meryem in his mind's eye. Her right hand had moved to her neck, then her chin and then covered the rash on her cheek, her little finger trailing over her lips. "I did it," she had said. And she had lied.

The moment he was within reach Jürgen grabbed his arm and Tobias's eyes filled with water.

"You did that cola, didn't you?" said Jürgen. "I told you not to do it on your sister."

"I didn't do it hard," he blubbered, tears quivering in his eyes.

Adriana's tears had dried.

"I don't know that one," said Dannaks's mother, trying to defuse the situation.

"You don't want to know," said Jürgen.

A tear spilled from Tobias's left eye and ran down his cheek.

His grandmother made to protest, but Verena stopped her with a hand movement and a shake of the head.

"Try it on me," Dannaks piped in.

This arrested Tobias's tears. Bewildered he blinked them back.

Adriana now had an expression of delight.

Tobias looked at his father. "I don't want to," he said.

Perversely, Jürgen released him and said: "Your uncle Götz wants it." He glanced and Dannaks who nodded, wondering if the sacrifice was worth it. "Go on," he commanded.

Verena shook her head at her husband and he pretended to miss the gesture.

Tobias came round to Dannaks and hesitated. Another glance at his father spurred him on. "Hold out your hands like this." He held out his own hands, palms down, fingers spread.

Dannaks obliged.

"Which do you prefer, Coca Cola or Pepsi Cola?"

"Oh, I don't know. Coca Cola."

Starting by tapping Dannaks's far left little finger Tobias spoke the syllable aloud: "Co-ca Co-la *kommt aus der* Oooh Esss."

He grabbed Dannaks's remaining little finger and twisted it until he said: "Ah".

(Coca Cola comes from the U.S.A. The letter A in German is pronounced Ah.)

"I'm sorry," said Verena.

"That's okay," said Dannaks. "It didn't hurt." He massaged his little finger and made a silent oh with his mouth.

Tobias's expression was a confusion of pride and sympathy.

"It's something they learnt at school."

Monday
07:23

"*Moin, moin,* holidaymaker," said Reinhart, when he entered the office. The northern greeting was more hallo than morning.

"Morning," said Dannaks hanging up his jacket.

"You're in early." He was sitting at his desk in front of a file. A banana skin was in the waste paper bin. A vase of flowers sat on the windowsill and filled the room with their aroma. Dannaks wasn't sure what they were, but knew Reinhart would educate him sometime during the day. He was surprised there were any left that he didn't know. "How was it?"

"Tough," he smiled.

"I bet. The toughest thing was resisting all that food and drink. All-inclusive, wasn't it?"

Dannaks nodded. Although he was Reinhart's superior they had an easy working relationship.

Contrasting Dannaks's leisurely wear Reinhart was always semi-formal. He wore a collar and tie.

"You lucky old goat. Knowing you, you probably went over the top."

"Actually, in one way it was almost a waste of time." He sat down and looked over his desk. He was beginning to get that same feeling that he had when he first returned to his flat. As if he'd never been away.

"Oh?"

"The Turks didn't give us anything. Oh, we saw a few crime scene photos, but it was a token gesture."

"Getting Matthias's room was bizarre."

"It's all they had," said Dannaks, unlocking his desk. His service weapon in its clip holster was in the second drawer. "What's been happening here?" He took out his sheet of activities and a pencil.

"Not much. You only missed three days, remember?"

"Yeah." The break was already memory. But so much had happened, that work seemed aeons ago. He looked down his pencilled list of things to do. He'd been putting together a case together for *DIE*. The *Dezernat Interne Ermittlungen* was similar to the Complaints investigation Bureau of London's Metropolitan Police or Internal Affairs in various US States. DIE investigated not only corruption in the police force, but also all other authorities in the state of Hamburg. Reports had come to them of prostitution at a home for asylum seekers. None other than the social worker was suspected of pimping them. He had also been sifting through their files of left-wingers. An individual, but more likely a gang, was going about setting fire to expensive cars in affluent areas of the city. The target vehicles suggested left-wingers. A group of foreign students had been beaten because they had been mistaken for drug dealers. Although nobody had been badly hurt, the *Mordkommission* processing the case had asked REX for assistance. He had also been documenting the broken and swastika-smeared Jewish gravestones. Then they were still following the antics of a Turkish gang called the *Schwarzer Freitag* (Black Friday). Finally the department responsible for robbery had asked for information on a skinhead suspected of being a member of the so-called petrol station gang: a gang of four or five balaclava'd youths specialising in late night petrol station robberies.

"You look good for it," said Reinhart.

Dannaks glanced at him. Yes, he felt good. He noticed combing his hair at the bathroom mirror this morning that although he wasn't tanned he appeared to be glowing. After leaving his parents he had spent a quiet evening in front of the television. Perhaps it had been the fresh air, but he had felt tired and gone to bed early.

"I saw on the news that the girl was caught. So it's all as good as wrapped up too."

"I wouldn't be so sure."

Dannaks got up and poured himself a coffee from the coffee maker.

Reinhart watched him.

"I heard she confessed."

There was too much to say and yet he had nothing. How could he convey that she had been melancholic to the point of perhaps feeling that she deserved to be imprisoned? Where was the knife? There were too many holes. Then again, maybe he was wrong. Stress could have made her nervous and yet she told the truth. Stress could also swamp any signs of deception. There were so many loose ends. And what of Fehime's history repeating itself? Did it mean anything?

"Yes, she did," he said, returning to his desk and absently fiddling with one of his desk puzzles: a pair of intertwined chromed metal. He looked over his list. "What happened about the petrol station gang?"

08:00

The entire team gathered as usual for the early morning meeting in Frank's office.

Frank welcomed Dannaks back and waited for the quips from the others to die before continuing. He said that he didn't have much. Dannaks knew then that a routine week lay ahead of them.

What had Reupke said? "REX is a sleepy backwater." And Dannaks had mentally added where all the dead wood ended up. But Reupke had continued, trying to fathom why Dannaks worked there: "I guess the department appeals to your sense of righteousness." He knew, though, that Dannaks would dearly love to join the *Mordkommission*. Indeed part of his decision to join REX was to get some homicide work and contacts. The other part was to get out of Drugs.

Soko REX worked with OK *Organisierte Kriminalität* (Organised Crime), *Rauschgift Dezernat* (Drugs), the *Mordkommission* and *Zeugenschutz*. They liaised with social services and the *Verfassungsschutz*. And, of course, they were affiliated to LKA 7 (*Landeskriminalamt* – State office of criminal investigation. LKA 7 was responsible for *Staatsschutz* – State security). Their main duty was gathering information. This was their currency with other departments. Often one or other of the team would be seconded to support another department. There had also been occasions in the past when they had done a lot of footwork for the *Mordkommission*. A *Soko* set up to tackle a serial killer for instance invariably took at least one of them. The Hangman case, with Reupke as their liaisons officer, had occupied half the team. So Frank's team was a pool of bodies ready to jump in when the workload required. One advantage of this was an added variety to their work. The disadvantage was that they were often given the dirty or tedious jobs to do.

"We'll save you till last," Frank said to Dannaks.

They sat in something of a semicircle in front of Frank's desk. As usual Frank imparted any relevant news. The only thing of note was at the end of his speech. "EWO (*Einwohnermeldedatei* – resident registration dataset) is down. I'm not sure how long it's going to be out of service. As I understand it they combined a major upgrade with a disaster-recovery exercise. And I guess it was more disaster than recovery."

Wulff sat at one end and Frank looked at him to proceed. Wulff had wanted the Side assignment. Schuppenhauer and Reinhart hadn't been interested. Frank had chosen the ranking officer.

In turn members of the team talked about the progress on their assignments and what they were intending to do next. Frank listened occasionally asking questions or making suggestions.

Yes, they were a motley crew. Dannaks, as *Oberkommissar*, was the second in command. But Reinhart was the oldest in the room. Wulff and Schuppenhauer were oddballs in their own way. He'd not been able to work out what Frank had done or whom he had upset.

Then it was Dannaks's turn. Over the next ten minutes he précised his time in Turkey, drawing from the notes he'd made for the debriefing and his report. He ended by saying: "I could get used to these kinds of assignments."

"You'll have to wait in line," said Wulff.

"How long will your report take?" asked Frank.

"The morning," said Dannaks.

"What have you got from last week?"

Dannaks looked down his list and answered.

Frank then glanced at them all. "I'm done," he said. They all got up and left, Schuppenhauer and Wulff taking their chairs with them.

Dannaks stood and approached the desk. "Can I have a word?"

Frank gestured to the chair and Dannaks sat down again.

Although Frank wasn't half his age, he was quite a bit younger and his superior position was proof that Dannaks was getting older. There was a time when all his superiors were older than him.

"I'll come straight to the point," he began, leaning forward in his seat. "I'd like to find out more about Meryem."

"Why?"

"Because I don't think she did it."

"But you're not sure?"

"No," Dannaks conceded.

"Then why?"

"It's a gut feeling. There are too many things wrong."

Frank took a deep breath and met Dannaks's eye. "I'm sorry. It's a no go. Even if I said yes, it's not our case. And I don't just mean REX. I mean this country. The Turks will have to sort it. She's one of them. No. We haven't a case. Your secondment ends with your report this morning. I need you back on the team."

Dannaks was still, as if his silent insistence could change Frank's mind. Then he slumped before straightening and getting up.

He spent the rest of the morning writing his report and he found himself seeding it with the things that bothered him. He entered them as unnecessary remarks or embellishments. He wrote things such as: "in her poor German she said..." and "Matthias told her of his past and she said that she had a secret too."

Rather than conclude the assignment his report writing had the adverse effect of compelling him.

At midday he left for lunch. Instead of going over to the Wandelhalle at the main station for a slice of pizza he headed for Patel's. It was a brisk eight-minute walk. He was covered in a sheen of sweat when he arrived. After waiting impatiently for a customer to pay he paid for the cheese and tomato baguette he had picked up and bought some time on the computer.

"You should think about buying your own," said Patel, referring to a PC. Patel was a slight man who had grown an ineffectual moustache to compensate for his boyish body. He was an Indian version of Ismail, but not as downtrodden and with alert brown eyes. His hair, like his moustache, was impeccably cut. Then one false move with the scissors could destroy the latter. He always dressed smartly, but the quality of his clothes let him down. No matter what the weather he invariably wore a plain sleeveless pullover, like a waistcoat, upon a buttoned-up shirt with a tie. Even now in July he looked dressed for winter. Perhaps Hamburg's summers were his homeland's winters?

"Then you'd be out of business," Dannaks retorted. The truth was that he had two main reasons for not possessing one. "Does anybody use them other than me?"

"My staff," said Patel.

Dannaks laughed. As he walked away he suddenly stopped and turned to Patel. "How's your English?"

"Better than my German."

A remark along the lines of "that's not saying much" occurred to Dannaks, but because he might need his help he simply nodded.

One of Patel's boys appeared as Dannaks seated himself in front of a machine.

"Use this one," he said. "That one's down."

"Depressed, is it?" said Dannaks changing seats. The boy clearly didn't understand, but ignored the comment.

This was one of the two reasons why he didn't possess a PC. He had heard too many horror stories of them throwing wobblies. The second reason was that he was afraid he would become something of a junkie and the thing would devour his evenings.

Dannaks had contemplated using the PC at work. It was located in the storeroom next to the photocopier and was shared by the entire team. Unlike the *Polizeistern* where almost every desk carried a PC, out in the backwaters they had to share. Because he had been told that the case was closed and what he had in mind would take time he decided to do it privately. This, of course, separated him from the likes of Reinhart, Schuppenhauer and the rest of the nine-to-five officers. But then, Dannaks had no commitments or family. That, he hoped, would now change. But doing what he was now doing put him in his element. He enjoyed the chase. For wasn't this just another puzzle to be solved?

Dannaks started a new email with Ismail's card in front of him. He wrote in English: *"Hallo Ismail. Thank you for Foto. Sorry for bad English. I have questions. Is Meryem staying with her–"* Here he got up and found Patel. He explained the word he was looking for and returned to his text. *"– confession? Do you believe her? Have you found Rafael? Yo say parents say Meryem not Meryem. Is this correct? Give me her birthday and other info and I look here. Hope you understand. Dannaks."* After sending it he opened another new email. He took out the slip of paper Turgut had given him. Above the boy's hand written address was the Azure Skies letter head including an email address. Because he could write in German this message to Turgut took half the time. Yesterday he'd seen that many of the serious websites that offered searches for people required a date of birth. The more information one could supply increased the likelihood of finding the person. He had Meryem's name and her age, but little else. So he wrote to Turgut also asking for her date of birth and as many other details he could supply.

Dannaks spent the next half an hour scouring the people search websites. He came across all manner of locations. Many were disguised lonely-hearts sites; there were marriage agencies advertising Thai girls, sites to find old school friends, girlfriends, boyfriends, relatives. Some were free but didn't look serious enough, some appeared to be free and some wanted a fee immediately or upon locating the sought person.

The police did use such services, but everything obtained had to be verified and double-checked. Private firms weren't to be relied upon, but occasionally they came up with a name that they hadn't found. They had their own computer service, but it was inundated with requests and hampered by formality.

He chose five sites and entered Meryem's name, current age, that she was married and had lived in Berlin up until about two years ago, adding that she may have been in Hamburg during this Berlin time.

Dannaks hastened back to the office. There he picked up the threads of his work before the trip to Side.

17:30

He packed up for the day at the same time as Reinhart. This was rare. Reinhart was something of a clock-watcher and ended his working day punctually. Dannaks often stayed on. But today he wanted to get to Patel's. He didn't think any of the people search groups would have anything for him and he wasn't expecting a prompt reply from Ismail, but he did think that Turgut would have answered.

Patel called one of his boys before Dannaks could open his mouth. A youth appeared and led Dannaks to the row of PCs.

He logged into his email account and was pleased to see five new entries: one from Azure Skies, one from Ismail and three from person search sites with whom he'd registered. He opened Ismail's first.

"Hallo Dannaks. Why I give you information? You lie to me. You say you not know Peter's book. If you look inside your fingerprints must be on. We find no fingerprints. Also not yours. You look at book. We know. I have trouble. I cannot trust. Ismail."

Shit, he thought. Of course his prints weren't on the journal.

He opened Turgut's mail next. Here too he was disappointed. Turgut wrote that the hotel had been instructed not to give out any information related to the case.

"Scheiße," he said under his breath.

The three other mails were acknowledgements of his search request. One asked for more information and another wanted him to click on a link, which would take him to a selection of Asian girls who could make him very happy.

He opened Ismail's reply and read it again. Then he logged off and went back to Patel.

"I was only on for ten minutes," he said.

"Yes," said Patel. "You can pay after another twenty minutes next time."

Dannaks thanked him and walked briskly home. He had intended to pick up a half a chicken with chips from the grill-house, but he had no time.

In his flat he tore off his shoes and threw his jacket onto the sofa. He snatched the phone and tapped in numbers on Ismail's card. The tone was strange and after the tenth ring he began to whisper: come on, come on. There was a clatter and then the hiss of an open line. A small voice said hello.

"Ismail?" Dannaks said loudly. "It is Dannaks."

"Who? Oh. Dannaks. Yes."

"I am sorry." He waited but no acknowledgement came. "Yes. I looked at Peter's book. I was, er, interested. You understand?" Again silence met his question. "Ismail? Are you there?"

"Yes."

"You would look. If you found it, you would look."

"Yes," he conceded. "I would look."

"I am just helping. You want to catch the killer. I too."

"I cannot talk."

"Can we talk online?"

"No."

"Outside work?"

"Chatting is too dangerous."

"I did not mean – Okay. Of course. Have you a personal email?"

"Yes."

"Then write to me."

"Okay. Tonight at eight."

"Seven would be better." Patel's closed at eight.

"Seven. Okay. Goodbye."

"Yes. Bye."

He planned his evening as he hung up his jacket and straightened his shoes. The first job had to be eating. He inserted two slices of bread in his toaster and opened his packet of sliced cheese. His watch told him he had over an hour.

For a moment he thought of Katja. She could be in Hamburg now. She had promised to phone and although he had told Reupke and himself that he thought she would phone on Tuesday, he hoped that she would phone straight away. Perversely he was glad he wasn't going to be in the flat sitting next to the telephone.

At five to seven he was back at Patel's logging onto his email account. There were two new mails: one from Ismail and another from a person search site. He opened Ismail's message. Disappointingly all it said was: *"This is private address."* Dannaks found his previous message to Ismail and cut the text. He then hit the reply button. *"Thank you. Can you answer questions? Is Meryem staying with confession? Do you believe her? Have you found Rafael? You say parents say Meryem not Meryem. Is this correct? Give me her birthday and other info and I look here."* He hit the send button and sat back for a moment. Then he leaned forward and opened the person search site. They wanted to know his age. He shook his head in dismay. He deleted the entry and pressed the refresh emails icon. There were no new emails.

Dannaks fidgeted. He looked about. There were a few shoppers, but the size and layout of the place made it appear empty.

He hit the refresh button again and a new entry appeared. It was from Ismail.

"Meryem says is killer. Parents coming. Maybe Meryem not Meryem. Rafael here. We are talking. He is crying." He wrote DOB followed by Meryem's date of birth. *"Team finished. Case closing."*

Dannaks replied: *"You believe Meryem? What about red man? Why Rafael crying? Can case close?"*

After hitting send he again had to wait for a long five minutes for a reply.

"No. I not belive Meryem killer. Red man yes. But confession... So case closing. But not close. Less men. Rafael took book. He sad. He like Meryem. I must go now."

Dannaks read Ismail's message quickly and typed fast. *"I search Meryem here. Maybe past help us."*

Then he wasn't sure whether to wait for an acknowledgement or not. Using the emails and reference numbers the websites had given him he added Meryem's birthday to the search details.

Before signing off he checked for new emails.

Ismail had replied: *"OK."*

Back in his flat he poured himself a small whisky and pulled out his bumper IQ puzzle book. Whilst pondering puzzles he found himself staring absently at the telephone. Just after nine he switched on his television. He resisted another whisky and made himself a green tea instead.

Nobody rang.

Tuesday
07:32

The new day started harmlessly enough. He strolled into the station relatively early. Although he didn't understand the greeting from the uniform on duty behind the glass he didn't comment and after being buzzed through climbed the stairs to his second floor office. The building was a standard police station in that the public saw the uniforms that occupied the ground floor and if unfortunate a cell in the basement. Despite being a small team of five REX took up most of the first floor offices. The remaining room and the upper floors housed ranking uniforms.

The uniform had said: "Morning lover or morning fun lover." Dannaks hadn't caught it.

He knew why he was feeling good. Katja was going to call today. Of course there was a level of anxiety linked to her not calling, but he felt confident that he would hear from her.

Reinhart was sitting at his desk when Dannaks entered the office. He was wearing a yellow patterned tie on a blue shirt. Because he was eating his banana he was only able to nod and grunt a reply to Dannaks's: "Morning." Reinhart hastily chewed. It was obvious he wanted to say something. Dannaks was bemused as he hung up his jacket.

He was at the coffee maker fetching a mug when Reinhart, pulling a newspaper from his briefcase, spoke: "Have you seen the papers?"

"No."

"You'd better look at this." He had opened a copy of the Hamburg *Morgen Post*, affectionately called the *Mopo*, on his desk and was turning the pages.

Dannaks looked over his shoulder. Reinhart didn't point and at first nothing caught Dannaks's eye. He was about to speak when he suddenly sensed that a picture looked familiar. Horror widened his eyes as the photograph realised itself, as if coming into focus. He looked at the headline: "*Der Kommissar und das Mädchen*" (The detective and the girl.) He was both flattered and appalled. Because he'd been quiet for so long Reinhart turned awkwardly to

291

look at him. Dannaks didn't take his eyes off the text. He was reading. But he shook his head in dismay for Reinhart's benefit.

Dannaks read and his expression said he wanted absolute silence.

"I know I said yesterday," Reinhart began, and Dannaks, again without taking his eyes off the text, showed him he was concentrating and didn't want to be interrupted, "that I thought you'd go over the top, but–"

"Have you seen the other papers?" Dannaks snapped.

"No," said Reinhart, hurt by the tone.

He looked at the photograph again. The grain helped disguise his features. The text said he was one of the two officers sent to pick up Matthias's body. The gist of it was whether the taxpayers' money was well spent on such antics.

Of course the photograph only got the back of Katja's head. She was safe.

Dannaks now understood the uniforms remark.

Reinhart was recovering. "It looks as if she's giving you a blow–"

"I know," he barked. Then he took a deep breath and forced himself to stay calm. "Sorry, Reinhart," he said evenly. "I know what it looks like. I, er, I'm going to get the other papers."

Reinhart nodded.

Dannaks snatched his jacket and fled the room as Reinhart picked up his half eaten banana and looked at the page again.

As he strode over to the main station he remembered trying to buy the photographs. Had he drawn attention to them with his insistence? He should have offered more money.

At one of the newsagents he bought copies of the *Mopo, Bild Zeitung, Hamburger Abendblatt* and the *Hürriyet*.

Walking back across the car park he tried to rifle the *Bild Zeitung*, but being a broad sheet and with carrying the other papers, watching where he was going and fighting a breeze he hadn't noticed, he quickly gave up.

He barely looked at the uniform as he was buzzed through. He saw three of them in the back and couldn't help feeling they were talking about him. Hadn't they taken a sideways glance at him?

Reinhart spoke immediately he entered the office.

"Frank's here. He wants to see you." Dannaks didn't want to hear it. He had thrown the papers on his desk and was hanging up his jacket. "And, er, someone from our Press Office wants to talk to you."

"Okay," he said curtly, standing over his desk and opening the *Bild Zeitung*. Reinhart remained seated but craned his neck to see.

As Dannaks expected this paper had beefed up the story. They'd made it more sexual. Their title was "Casanova of Azure Skies." There was little text between the four photographs, but what was there was scathing enough. He'd always thought the paper inventive with its humour and had admired the word play. But to be on the receiving end of such humour showed him that it was crude and cruel. Like the *Mopo* this paper carried the blowjob photograph, albeit larger and in Technicolor. Although a black bar mercifully obscured his eyes his slack gormless expression of drunken abandon unmistakably said what state he had been in. They also had an official photo of their arrival with the Turkish police. His face was highlighted in a black circle. The third photograph was one they'd used before. It was the standard full frontal of Matthias. The smallest picture had been cut from television and was that of Meryem being taken in. A final fifth photograph was that of him and Katja posing with their crowns. The question under this photograph was: Who is this woman?

He was opening the *Abendblatt* when Frank appeared. He looked at both men before targeting Dannaks. "My office," he said and turned.

"I told him you wanted to see him," blurted Reinhart.

Worm, Dannaks thought, but muttered: "Morning, Frank" instead.

Frank ignored them both and left.

Dannaks glanced down at the paper. He couldn't look at Reinhart. Then he left too.

Frank was already sitting behind his desk when Dannaks knocked and entered.

"Close the door," he ordered. The team had an open door policy.

"Frank, I just wanted to see what I was up against," Dannaks said, by way of an excuse for not coming to him straight away. He saw the folded copy of the *Abendblatt* on the end of the desk.

"I'll come straight to the point," Frank began, his tone harder than normal. "Weske wants you at his office at nine." He gave Dannaks a moment to think about the gravity of being summoned by the *Kriminaloberrat*. Weske was the head of LKA 7. "You want to tell me anything about this?"

"I won't say it's harmless," said Dannaks, knowing that such a statement could be nothing other than provocative. Frank nodded his approval, but his expression remained cast in granite. "But–" he shouldn't have started with but – "the only taxpayers' money that was involved was the flight. We were the Turks' guests." Frank knew all this and his stare said he wanted more. "I suppose saying that I was off-duty, won't help."

"What do you think?"

"No," he said, unnecessarily.

Frank allowed him some silence. "I don't know how you could have got yourself in this situation. It's so out of character." It was true. Dannaks was a conscientious workhorse. Being single he was apt to work long unpaid hours. Every year he had to be forced to take his leave allocation. And then he didn't really know what to do with himself. His job might not be his vocation, but it was the centre of his life.

"I was drunk," he said quietly. Then he remembered Turgut. "The hotel gave us a bottle of red with our aperitifs. You know, before eating–"

"I know what an aperitif is."

To quell Frank's irritation, Dannaks added: "I just wanted to, er, emphasise that I drank on an empty stomach."

"Where was Reupke?"

"Watching."

"Is there any more of this to come?"

"I don't know what you mean, Frank."

Frank stared at him as if this kind of conversation called for less familiarity, but Dannaks couldn't break the routine and suddenly call him sir.

"I mean," said Frank, showing that he was containing himself. "The Press are going to dig deeper. Have you embarrassed us any more?"

Dannaks was about to shake his head, but decided to think first. When he spoke, he spoke firmly. "No. There's nothing else."

"This is all?"

"Yes."

Frank digested this and then visibly relaxed. "It's not good, Dannaks. But it's not me you've got to answer to. See me when you're back."

Dannaks nodded and left the room.

Reinhart glanced at him and then looked down at his paperwork. Dannaks had thought him a worm, but he was essentially a good chap. From the arrangement of the newspapers on his desk he knew that Reinhart had looked at them.

"Reupke phoned," he said without looking up.

"Okay. Thanks." The ease in his voice enticed his colleague to raise his head. Dannaks smiled at him as he folded the papers. "Anything else in them?"

"Aren't you going to read them?"

"On the way to the presidium."

"Weske?"

Dannaks nodded and took out Reupke's card from his desk drawer.

"No," said Reinhart as Dannaks pulled over their shared telephone. Dannaks stopped, his hand poised over the receiver. His perplexed expression and nod at the papers prompted Reinhart to elaborate. "There was nothing else in them." Dannaks reanimated himself with a nod.

Reupke picked up on the second ring. "*Mordkommission.* Reupke."

"Dannaks," he announced. "You're in early."

"Yeah. We're pretty busy." He paused. "You've seen the papers?"

"Yep."

"They want to talk to me."

"I've been summoned."

"Who by?"

"*Kriminaloberrat* Weske and the Press Office."

"I wouldn't worry about it. It was all harmless."

"You know the Press."

"Yes. But it's all trivial. It'll blow over."

"I hope so."

"There is one good thing that has come out of all this." Dannaks could for the life of him not think what good there could be. "Steffi doesn't need any more convincing that you had a girlfriend out there."

"Ha," Dannaks exclaimed, surprised by the bitterness in his voice. "Maybe we can have lunch together."

"Call me when you've been through the mangle."

8:28

Dannaks attended the eight o'clock meeting. As he anticipated it was over within ten minutes. The Monday morning one was generally the longest. EWO was still down.

He left the office at twenty past eight and took the U1 from the main station via *Jungfernstieg* arriving at *Alsterdorf* some seventeen minutes later.

During the journey he felt vulnerable as if the focus of the whole world were upon him. Every fleeting glance, every huddle of conversing people, certainly everyone carrying a newspaper recognised him and was talking about him. He could see it in their critical eyes.

He used the time to bury his head in the papers, scouring them for detail. The *Abendblatt* carried only the arrival photograph. They hadn't circled him but said that he was fourth from the right. The article didn't elaborate on anything he hadn't already read. Like the others it too said that there had been no one available for comment.

He walked round to the presidium and identified himself at the gate. He was heading towards the building when he saw Rüdiger Krohn walking away to one of the neighbouring buildings. They acknowledged one another with nods. Theirs was a thin allegiance born out of dislike and subsequent bonding via Krohn's son. Krohn looked old and haggard: a broken man.

Dannaks climbed the steps up to the building. He passed security set behind glass and used his card to properly enter the building. All the time he tried not to catch anybody's eye. Having worked in the building in the Drugs' squad the chance of meeting someone he knew was high.

He took the lift up to the fifth floor and identified himself again. He was told to wait and took one of the functional chairs in the hallway.

He prayed that he wouldn't see Iceman.

At five past nine Weske opened his door and popped his head out. "Dannaks?"

Dannaks got up. "Sir."

He entered, closed the door behind him and sat in one of the chairs facing the man's desk.

Weske looked like an emaciated long distance runner. His clothes hung from him. He may have been sinewy in his youth, but now he just looked ill. He was a humourless man. Even on the rare occasions when he joked there was an edge of bitterness in his voice. He seemed perpetually irritable.

In the silence Weske was either composing himself or sizing Dannaks up.

"Tell me Dannaks," he began, "do you like your job?"

Shit, he thought. Where was this going? "Er, yes. Yes I do, sir."

"You're proud to be in the service?"

He was being left no room to manoeuvre. "Yes, sir."

"How does this manifest itself?"

"Er, sorry. Sir. I, er, don't understand the question."

Weske eyes, slightly too big for his lids and also hinting at some illness, closed on him. He wanted Dannaks out of his sight.

"How do you show that you are proud of your job?"

To Dannaks it seemed like an impossible question to answer.

"By, er, doing a good job. Being of service, sir."

"By good job, you mean professional?"

"Yes..." He was getting an inkling of where this was going. "Sir."

Weske nodded.

"You were given a high public exposure assignment. Don't you think your behaviour unbecoming of an officer of the Hamburg police force?"

He wanted to say that he was off-duty, but knew that the answer would be that the nature of the assignment – a high public exposure assignment – meant that he was never off-duty.

"Yes, sir."

"Have you any excuses?"

He wanted to say that he had been drunk. Or that romance had enticed him. But it was all squirming. "No, sir, I don't."

"This'll go into your personal file."

He'd never be given a similar task.

"Not only did you behave improperly, your dress was inappropriate." Even now he was casually dressed in a thin sweatshirt, jeans and summer jacket. Weske wore a sober tie and white shirt. Yet, the reference to dress echoed Iceman's view and he wondered whether these were Iceman's words. The terrible thought of asking Weske whether Iceman had mentioned anything about being an ambassador flashed through his mind. But this was not the time for such insouciance.

"Can the Press do us any more damage?"

"I don't think so, sir."

Weske's eyes seemed to grow and come towards him as if they were telescopic.

"I read your report." He tapped a closed cardboard file on his desk. "It doesn't mention any of this. Rectify that."

Dannaks nodded.

"What's this about Herbst's place and getting taken in?"

"We needed to check it out, sir. Reupke – my, er, partner–"

"I know who he is."

"Yes, sir. He got permission from his chief to take a look."

"He got permission to offset expenses," said Weske.

"Yes, but he explained what we wanted to do."

"What?"

"Explained what we wanted to do, sir."

Weske leaned back in his big wire mesh chair. Dannaks knew that it was an expensive model suitable for people with back problems. He appeared to have finished reprimanding him. Dannaks remained silent as Weske steepled his fingertips and brought the index fingers of his connected hands to his nose. If his palms had been pressed together it would have looked as if he was praying. He tapped his index fingers against the line that separated his nostrils.

He was obviously weighing up whether to say something. He suddenly dropped his hands and leaned forward.

"Herbst knows that you went to his place, but we've not heard anything from him. He probably wants to keep it that way. The mayor knows and it won't take long for it to leak out. I just hope that you acted professionally."

"We did, sir." Did they?

"Close the door after you."

Dannaks was stunned by the abrupt dismissal.

The Press Office was located on the same floor next door to Iceman's office. This enabled the police president to react swiftly with the outside world.

Dannaks knew the mayor would be leaning on Iceman, but was he also receiving flak from the *BKA*?

Four people were waiting for him when he entered. Three were from the Press Office. They comprised a smart looking man and woman and a trainee poised to take notes. The fourth person in the room was Brenner, not in his police capacity, but as a representative of the BdK (*Bund Deutscher Kriminalbeamter* – Union of German detectives).

Brenner began by stating that he was present solely in the interests of his union member, Dannaks. After which, for the duration of the meeting he said next to nothing.

Whereas Weske had slapped the back of his hand, the Press Office was sympathetic and protective. They were concerned with projecting a professional image and they were also interested in damage limitation. Dannaks was advised not to speak to the media. All statements were to be made through them. They agreed that their statement would claim that he had been castigated. Taxpayers' money had only been used for the flight. If push came to shove they would say that a member of public had coaxed him on stage and against his better judgement he had embraced the generous hospitality of the hotel. They had given him a complimentary bottle of red wine.

They talked about the trip to Herbst's place and a standpoint was agreed. The officer in question had not trespassed. If pressed they could say that the other officer had entered the premises because he thought he heard voices in the garden. At no time did either of them enter the building.

Just after ten they were finished. Brenner concluded by saying that Dannaks should keep him posted. The union was there for him.

Dannaks asked to use the phone and tapped in Reupke's extension. Somebody else answered and said that he had been called out. It didn't matter because it was too early to go to lunch.

He left the building, amazed that he'd not bumped into any old colleagues. He certainly felt better than an hour or so ago.

Dannaks went to Frank first. He outlined what had been said. "Lucky," was Frank's one-word comment. Dannaks then said that he had to add a page or so to his report.

Reinhart picked up a sheet of paper when he entered the room.

"How did it go?"

"Better than I expected."

"I've been playing secretary whilst you've been away." He read from his sheet. "First you had a call from that Craig chap. You remember? That British freelancer."

"What did he want?"

"He wanted to know if he could help."

Dannaks nodded. He was a reporter they had interviewed during the Hangman case. He was a reporter nonetheless. He could even be working on someone else's behalf. Dannaks wouldn't phone him.

"Uwe Albrecht called." His friend deserved a return call, but Dannaks couldn't face it. He was probably just being inquisitive. "And someone called Katja–"

"Did she leave a number?"

"No."

"What did she say?" He could barely contain himself.

"She said she'd phone again."

"When?"

Reinhart gave him a peculiar look and adjusted his tie. "She didn't say."

Dannaks forced himself to act casually. "I mean here or at home."

"She didn't say."

"And your mother phoned."

Dannaks spent the rest of the morning explaining his stage appearance to the callers. He chose his words very carefully. At lunchtime he told Reinhart that he wanted to stay at his desk. He said that he felt guilty about losing another morning to his non-REX activities. Reinhart fetched him something from outside and he had lunch at his desk. They both knew that he didn't want to go outside.

The afternoon dragged because he couldn't concentrate on his work. He wanted it to consume him, but its tedium denied him such an easy escape.

Somehow he made it through the afternoon and left a few minutes after Reinhart at five past five.

The *Kripo* worked eight and a half hour days with half an hour for lunch. They were on flexitime with a core time of nine to three. Reinhart always worked a little more to accrue enough time for a day off in the month.

On the way home he stopped in at Patel's to check his emails. Two of the search sites reported being unsuccessful in finding Meryem Turan and were discontinuing their search. The third also had no success but claimed that being professional their searches were thorough and he could expect the results in a week. However, he could receive the results within twenty-four hours if he ticked the priority search box. This was one of the paying sites and the priority search would bump up the price to a nice round one hundred euros. He ignored the mail and logged off. Patel and he had agreed upon a running tab. He bought some provisions, carrying them in a cardboard carton.

At the *Dönermann* he ate *schaschlik* with two slices of bread, standing at a table near the front window, idly watching the pedestrians go by.

In his flat whilst putting away his purchases he came across the large old potato. He held it in his hand as if weighing its consistency. Yes, it was in a sorry state, but deep inside it could be fine. The thought of Katja discovering it tipped his decision and he dropped it in the bin.

He took a cup of tea into the lounge and contemplated calling Uwe, but because he wanted the line open for Katja, he decided to sit in silence. He sat on the sofa doing nothing for the best part of fifteen minutes. Then he got up and fetched his sudoku book.

He half-watched the seven o'clock news wondering when she'd call. There was nothing on the case and nothing on his misdemeanour. At ten to eight the phone rang and he jumped up. He stopped with his hand poised over the receiver so that he could compose himself.

"Dannaks," he answered.

There was a moment's pause and for a second he thought the caller was a prankster or from the Press. "Albrecht."

"Uwe."

"Any chance of an autograph, then?"

"*Verpiss Dich.*"

"Can I quote you on that?"

"I've had a rough time."

"I bet."

"Weske slapped my wrists."

"You should be grateful that's all."

"It's in my file."

"I wouldn't worry."

"Maybe. But these things have a habit of coming back on you. You don't need a good memory when it's on file."

"You want to talk about it?"

"Not now. I'm expecting a call. We could meet up for a drink."

"Annelore says you should come over for dinner. Saturday?"

"Yes, that'll be great." Maybe he could take Katja. Then maybe it was too soon and they should do something alone. "But can I get back to you on that?"

"Turning your nose up at a free meal has got to be a first. What happened to you out there?"

"A lot. But you'll have to wait. I'll call you tomorrow or Thursday. Is that okay?"

"Fine. We'll hear from you, then. We've never had a celebrity to dinner."

Dannaks held back the curse on his lips. "Bye Uwe."

He checked the television programme in one of the newspapers and located an acceptable film that started at eight-fifteen.

The phone rang just as he was becoming immersed in the film. It was almost nine o'clock. She'd certainly kept him on tenterhooks. He turned down the volume of the television and picked up the telephone announcing himself airily. It was Reupke. He didn't have much to say. He had been asked to deliver in writing his version of events. Luckily he had remembered to mention the complimentary bottle of red wine before dinner. Dannaks cut him short telling him that he was waiting for Katja to call.

He got back into the film, which was scheduled to finish at nine forty-five. At nine-forty the phone rang again. He snatched it up.

"Dannaks," he said firmly.

"Katja."

302

"Oh," he exclaimed, scrambling for the remote control and accidentally pressing the volume up rather than down. "Sorry," he said after he'd found the mute button. "Pressed the wrong button."

"Were you watching something?"

"Not really." But he did want to know who had done it.

"I can phone back."

"No really. It's fine."

"Let's start again. Hallo Dee."

"Hallo Kay."

"Sorry it's got a bit late. I called earlier, but both times it was engaged."

"Yeah. One was Reu – Olaf."

"How is he?"

"Fine."

"Well he shouldn't be. I think he was the worst thing that could have happened to Dagmar."

"How, er, is – was – she?"

"Not good company."

"How were your last days?" He didn't want to talk about the newspapers, although he knew there was no avoiding the subject.

"A little empty."

He was pleased. "I'm sorry."

"Don't be." She waited a beat. "What about the papers?"

"What about them? It's all trivial stuff." He explained that there was little to the accusation of wasting the taxpayers' money. Yes, he'd had his hands slapped. Even he found the phrase tiresome. He did his best to play the situation down. "I'm sure that's the end of it," he said. "They haven't got anything else and it'll all be forgotten in a day or two."

She was silent.

"Kay?"

"Yes. I'm still here. I hope you're right."

"Shall we meet? We could go for dinner."

"Yes. Okay." She didn't appear too sure.

"You don't sound that enthusiastic."

"Sorry. I was just wondering about the papers."

"What about them?"

"They haven't bothered me, yet. But–"

"They haven't bothered me either. Kay, it's not really a story, is it?"

"I suppose—"

"I know an excellent Italian in St. Georg."

"Okay. When?"

"Tomorrow?"

Wednesday
07:00

The alarm tore him out of a deep sleep. He thought that he had dreamed but he couldn't recall anything and felt disorientated.

He got up, flicked on the kettle, slipped two toasts in the toaster, and went to the toilet. By the time he had finished turning the bed back into a sofa the kettle had boiled and the toasts had popped up. He made himself an instant coffee and buttered and jammed his toast. He took a bite out of one of the toasts and left to take a shower. He was dressed when he returned to his cup of coffee. It was drinking temperature. Taking it with his plate of toast to his window he drank and ate whilst regarding the panorama. As always the tranquil expanse of water was ringed by the continual flow of vehicles.

Dannaks felt relatively relaxed and ready for the day. Yet, he couldn't shake off the hint of trepidation. He wasn't sure whether it was linked to what the papers might say or to his date with Katja this evening.

After his coffee he donned his jacket and shoes and left his flat. At the first opportunity he stepped into a kiosk and bought the day's editions of the same four papers he had yesterday. He was relieved to see that there was nothing on any of the front pages. Outside, halted at a crossing and waiting for the signal to walk, he opened the *Bild*. On the fourth page he discovered that the outrage had not abated. The signal changed and everyone crossed the road except him.

There was a photograph of him and Katja and the boys with their hands in the air on the slide. The text followed the same lines as yesterday, the indignation perhaps greater. The picture had come from the father of one of the boys. He'd obviously sold it. More damaging was the fact that he mentioned that Dannaks had been nicknamed Schimi out there. So the title to the piece was: Is this the face of the real Schimanski? The erstwhile television cop was sympathetic because of his heart, but he was a maverick nonetheless, bulldozing his way through the cases. He'd left the police force to continue in a spin-off series as something of a private detective. But Herbst's place was mentioned and there was a strong implication that it could be linked to Matthias's death. For the girl in custody, Meryem, seemed an unlikely killer. They thought that she was an accomplice, giving the killer or killers' access to the compound. Herbst was not available for comment.

Dannaks folded the paper and marched across the road when the lights allowed.

Entering the station he expected the uniform to call him Schimi and although he had no retort he had prepared his best withering glare. The uniform behind the perspex glanced at him. If he had wanted to make a remark Dannaks's incensed expression effectively gagged him.

Reinhart greeted him soberly. He still said "Moin, moin," but without his usual chirpiness. Dannaks spotted the copies of the *Mopo* and *Abendblatt* at the end of his desk.

"I've only looked at the *Bild*," said Dannaks, pouring a coffee into a mug. "What do those say?"

"Probably the same," said Reinhart. "With less pictures and brashness."

Dannaks picked out the Mopo from the pile he had placed on his desk.

"Mind if I look at the *Bild*?"

"No problem," he said nonchalantly. He wasn't sure of the derivation of his nonchalance. It was as if the papers were writing about someone else. Perhaps he felt untouchable. Perhaps he was numbed to the onslaught. Then perhaps meeting Katja tonight gave him mettle.

Reinhart noted his apparent indifference. "As they say in English: the shit has really hit the fan."

The *Mopo* had taken up the line on Herbst. They had a photograph of a holiday home in Side, claiming that Herbst's would be similar. There was the same speculation about Matthias's killers having used it as a base, the same question marks about Meryem's confession.

Next came the *Abendblatt*. Again Herbst was mentioned, but the wording was much more careful. Any speculation was left to the reader. Instead the tone leant more towards police corruption. They had dug up and chronologised a list of past stories. There was the famous one about Purchasing accepting gifts from companies vying for contracts for bulletproof vests and other equipment. The end of the article was a punch in the face. There was a quote from the mayor. She said ominously that disciplinary action was not out of the question.

"I don't like what the mayor says," he said, annoyed that Reinhart had not mentioned it.

"There's no getting round it," said Reinhart. "You haven't done yourself any favours making an enemy of Iceman."

Dannaks's face was afire as he folded away the *Abendblatt* and picked up the *Hürriyet*. He turned the pages of this latter paper, scouring the Turkish articles for key words in the titles and – when the title was obscure – the text. He found nothing.

Eventually he pushed the papers aside, but not out of his mind. He didn't really need to check his "to do" list, but he scanned it anyway. Then he picked out his file and began work.

The eight o'clock meeting was again short. The only reference to the papers was when Frank said that the less said about it the better.

At twenty past nine the phone rang. Reinhart picked it up.

"It's for you," he said proffering the receiver. As Dannaks reached over Reinhart gave him a queer look and said quietly: "Frank." Their boss wasn't known for laziness. His office was almost opposite theirs.

"Dannaks," he announced firmly as if he did not know who was on the other end.

"Can you come to my office?"

"Yes," he said, rather surprised. How could he say no?

"Bring your service weapon, keys and ID."

Dannaks blanched at the request. He knew what this meant. Hanging up he opened his drawer and took out his gun in its clip holster. Reinhart was watching him and he knew he was as pale as if he'd seen a ghost. He patted his trousers for his keys and then stood.

In Frank's office he didn't need to be told to close the door.

He sat down, his right hand holding his holstered weapon on his thigh. Frank looked as stricken as he, Dannaks, felt.

"I'm sorry Dannaks," he began, his eyebrows arched with pain. "They've given me no choice. It's what they want. I'm suspending you from duty until further notice, effective immediately."

He knew it was coming, but even with this anticipation, it was still a shock. He began to speak but issued a croak instead and had to start again. "It is all ridiculous, you know."

"Maybe," Frank conceded. "But I believe this comes from the top." The mayor was involved. "And even if it doesn't I don't think Wischnewski was impressed by your conduct." No, he'd not hit it off with Iceman from day one. Inappropriately dressed and – "I asked you yesterday whether there was anything more."

"Going to Herbst's place was in my report."

"I was talking about the photograph."

"I didn't know it was taken."

"I'm still finding it hard to get my head round it. You weren't drunk on the slide, were you?"

"No. I – Oh what's the use?"

Neither spoke for a moment.

"Because of the publicity DIE have been asked to look into it." Ha, he was to be investigated by the very people for whom he was putting a corruption case together.

"This has got to be a joke." But he knew it was not. "Has Reupke been suspended?"

"I don't think so."

Dannaks shook his head in disgust.

"You'll be on full pay until the results of the inquiry are out." Dannaks knew the procedure.

"Any idea when that might be?"

"Your guess is as good as mine. DIE are inundated. Certainly not this week. Phone me tomorrow. I'll see what I can find out."

He nodded and the tension left his shoulders.

Frank waited.

Then Dannaks straightened and stood over the desk. He placed his holstered Heckler and Koch P 2000 in front of Frank, dug out his keys, his Kripo brass tab and identity card and set them down too. He was surprised how much giving up the small collection hurt.

The silence was appalling.

When he was done Frank spoke. "It's no consolation, but I wouldn't have suspended you."

"Thanks," Dannaks muttered. There was nothing more to say and he left the room.

He tidied his desk, which was enough for Reinhart. "You want me to call the BdK?"

"No." He didn't want to talk to Brenner or anyone from the union. Escalation was the last thing he wanted.

09:37

Dannaks left the building with something akin to tunnel vision: he saw neither to the left nor to the right. Yet, he again felt acutely everyone looking at him. As if they had been audience to the ceremony of his expulsion he felt humiliated and had to ignore them to run this gauntlet.

As he walked the air liberated him. He relished the warmth of the sun and the caress of the breeze. Most of all no one really paid him any attention. Life went on. Regardless. The city tour bus was filling up with a Japanese party, the men with cameras like pendants, swinging from their bellies as they fussed over their flocks of bemused women and children. At the edge of the station building, the addicts were shuffling but going nowhere. A pair of uniforms sauntered into the station. Office types and holidaymakers alike hastened to the station. Those leaving spilled out bewildered, pointing or poring over maps or guides.

Dannaks felt as lost as those looking in their guidebooks. The day was suddenly completely open and he didn't know what to do. His mind was swamped in a maelstrom of thoughts. He needed to focus and get his head round his predicament or at least get his head cleared. Drink was tempting, but it wasn't an option, certainly not at this time of day. A long walk round the Alster seemed the best idea. He could sit on a bench and watch the boats or read. The papers were tucked under his arm.

He hesitated for a moment then briskly walked to the bus stop. Then before he could change his mind he stuffed the papers in the bin.

Almost unconsciously he found himself heading for Patel's. The man himself was not at the cash till, but the youth apparently knew Dannaks and called someone to take him to the computers.

Dannaks found only one new email. It was from Ismail, posted yesterday evening shortly before eight.

The email read: *"Parents see Meryem. Say Meryem not Meryem. Say passport is Meryem. She say she Meryem. We think she not Meryem. You find Meryem in Germany? I tell boss you look. He say good. We know child Meryem a cotton picker. Ismail."*

Had he expected Dannaks to reply straight away? Damn. He undoubtedly thought he was communicating with a home computer.

Dannaks reread the email. The parents said that she wasn't their daughter. But did Ismail mean that she had their daughter's passport? One thing seemed certain. She was not Meryem. And which Meryem was a cotton picker? Then he remembered the scarring on her hands.

He hit the reply button and wrote. *"Still looking for Meryem here. Slow."* He paused as an idea took hold. *"You tell boss to ask German police to look. Official. Ask for me."* He stopped again, wondering whether he should elaborate. To mention his suspension would mean explaining the lead up to it. *"I look at mail at seven tonight. Meeting at eight. Otherwise tomorrow. Dannaks."* He was about to press the send button when a question occurred to him. So he inserted the following in front of his name: *"Is Rafael free?"*

After sending the email he returned to his in-tray and located the person search email offering the priority search. He ticked the box and added the following: "This is police-related work. I will require an official receipt."

Then he searched the web for information on cotton picking in Turkey. He soon found himself side-tracked so that when he glanced at his watch he saw that he'd been online for almost an hour.

He now knew that child labour was a real problem in Turkey. Entire families travelled across the country, moving with the various harvesting seasons: picking cotton, digging sugar beets, reaping fruit and vegetables. Children as young as six worked alongside their parents. School was compulsory until fourteen, but many rural children attended only two months a year, when no crops were to be picked. By law under-fifteens were not allowed to work, but agriculture was exempt and rural children relatively neglected.

He also knew that cheap labour kept the textile prices low, but the Turkish cotton industry was facing fierce competition from China.

Before signing off he decided to check his emails. The priority search site had replied. *"Your standard search has been upgraded to a priority search. We will be happy to supply a receipt. Your standard search has yielded results. We have also given your priority search an urgent tag. This means you can expect full results tomorrow morning. Our policy is to supply partial results. For the full results we will require payment. You can do this after seeing the partial results or now by clicking on the* Pay Now *button."* He thought for a moment and then hit the "Pay Now" button.

11:01

His flat seemed cold and inhospitable by comparison. Emerging from Patel's into the brightness of the day had been like leaving a cave. But at least in the shop there had been activity. Here, despite his panoramic view there was a ghastly stillness. The day and life was outside. His flat was a capsule in which time had frozen. To stay was to reside in a state of suspended animation.

He switched on the electric kettle and made himself an instant coffee. In the lounge he picked up the telephone. Reupke picked up immediately.

"You've heard?" Dannaks asked after greetings.

"Yes. You were unlucky." In that instant he remembered calling Reupke lucky and him answering that there was no such thing as luck. And if there was, then you made it yourself. Those had been his words. Apparently there was such a thing as bad luck.

"What about you?" Dannaks could sense his guilt in the pauses.

"They want more details about our visit to Herbst's place. I've heard he's talking of break in and entry. Trespassing, at the very least." Reupke lowered his voice and he sounded as if he'd cupped his hand over the mouthpiece. "You wrote that when we were there we called out, didn't you?"

"I don't think so."

"But I did. You remember." He didn't remember. "There was no bell and we thought there might be someone out back. Remember?"

"I don't remember," Dannaks said irritably. "Don't you think I've got enough on my mind?" A sense of injustice, he didn't know existed, rose up like a bubble of bile to burst on the surface of his consciousness. Reupke had been the one to enter the grounds. He was also galled by the fact that Reupke had been the one with the fun-loving attitude. He himself had made more of an effort to treat the trip as a job.

"Yes," said Reupke, clearly shocked by his sudden anger. "I'm sorry." Dannaks remained silent, forcing Reupke to speak. "Look, there's, er, just one other thing. The Press may get hold of more photos. If, erm, there're any of me with, er, Dagmar... Maybe you could say that I was making up a foursome?"

"Yeah," agreed Dannaks, but the cadence in that one word expressed his disinterest.

"Thanks," he said. "I've got to go."

"Hmm."

Bye." And he hung up.

Dannaks's jaw was set as he returned the receiver to its cradle.

He slumped in his sofa and sipped his tea. He needed to shed his despondency, certainly before meeting Katja tonight.

He was piqued by the realisation that Ismail could mention that he, Dannaks, had suggested officially asking for him to help finding out about Meryem. He should have explicitly told him not to mention that it was his idea.

When he left his flat thirty minutes later, carrying a novel he'd been meaning to read for the last three months, he toyed with the idea of sending Ismail another message. Something turned his back on it all and he headed for the water.

His walk was not long. He stopped to eat at the first opportunity and took an outside table near the water's edge. A quarter of an hour later all the tables were taken for lunch. One end of his own table was given up to a pair of exhausted Australian backpackers. Dannaks couldn't help but hear their plans. It amused him that they were "doing" most of Western Europe in three weeks. Such was their concept of space.

When he came to pay up and leave most of the tables were again free. The backpackers had left for the station, having done Germany in two days. Better than nothing, Dannaks supposed. Apparently Belgium had been allocated an afternoon.

He stopped at a florist and chose a colourful bouquet of mixed flowers that bordered on gaudy. Buying flowers was totally out of character. Reinhart would be proud of him. Perhaps he'd slip it in some time. Frank, of course, would fall off his chair. His flat had never seen flowers, but their scent and colour could brighten the place up.

In his flat again at about four thirty he was more at ease with his situation. He greeted a woman from the offices below his flat. Most of the time the building appeared to be occupied solely by *Frau* Schumann and him. This was especially true at the weekends.

But during the week the other floors were busy. Normally he was at work at such times and rarely observed this activity. This woman's smile was a compliment and he felt happy. He swiped away the vicious thought that she may have read about him in one of the papers.

To his consternation he discovered that he did not possess a vase and he had to leave the flowers in the kitchen sink. The thought of presenting the flowers to Katja occurred to him again and again he thought of the awkwardness of carrying them to the Italian restaurant. Tackling *Frau* Schumann to borrow a vase reared its ugly head. Then he recalled packing a *Krug* and stowing it in the loft. But could he find it again?

Searching for the infernal item took up a good hour of his time, but he was successful. He cleaned it up and was chuffed with the way the flowers filled up the room with their colour and fragrance. Their scent was pleasant but slightly irritating. He was used to flowers because Reinhart invariably brought some to the office. But in the confines of his flat their intensity was magnified.

He spent his time pottering and putting finishing touches to his flat. He used the box from Patel's to loosen the clutter of his shelves, storing it too in his loft space.

At six he ate a toast with peanut butter to take the edge off his hunger. Then he spent some time searching for something suitable to wear.

He left the flat at ten to seven and was at Patel's for seven.

19:03

There were two emails waiting for him. Ismail had replied, but his message was disappointingly short. *"Boss say maybe German police look. Fehime free, no charges. Rafael free, but charge obstructing justice. Ismail."* Dannaks wrote asking him not to say that he, Dannaks, suggested an official request for assistance. The second email was from a person search site. They had found no one called Meryem Turan in Berlin. There was nothing about searching Hamburg, but he waived asking them to do so. Tomorrow he'd see what the urgent priority search would yield.

He was in the large newsagents at the main station at twenty to eight. They'd arranged to meet at ten to eight; the table was booked for eight o'clock. Although he said that they should meet on the ground floor, with time to spare he went upstairs to the foreign section. There he hunted for an English dictionary, but all he found were novels. Time ran out and he went back down. He spotted Katja at the women's magazines.

She wasn't browsing anything, merely staring at the racks.

Although dressed for the summer and in this respect no different from what she wore in Side she appeared different. He couldn't fathom why he saw her so. Her hair was up and she was wearing her glasses. Only her handbag was new to him. Was it simply a matter of context?

"Hallo Kay," he said, quietly because she had not registered his approach.

She swung round. Her smile was not instant and this alerted him.

"Dee," she smiled.

He leaned forward for a peck of a kiss. She looked down before looking at him.

"How are you?" she asked.

He remembered her beauty spot under her left eye being larger. And he felt as if he were seeing her afresh.

"Fine," he said. Then seeking levity and also wanting honesty – or was it sympathy? – he added: "I've been better."

Her smile slanted understandingly. "I can imagine."

"We'd better get going."

"Is it far?" she asked, as they left the shop. She seemed distracted, elsewhere.

"No. About ten minutes." Her absence unnerved him. He pushed on, nonetheless. "Actually I do have some news."

She nodded and glanced at him. Negotiating the other people entering and leaving the station hindered him from elaborating. When they were relatively alone he elaborated. "I had the day off today. Er. I've been suspended." He had intended telling her later, over dinner, but something inside him sought connection.

"What do you mean?" She seemed genuinely horrified.

"Relieved of duty."

"Oh Dee, that's terrible."

Her sympathy delighted him. "It's only temporary," he said loudly. Traffic was on the move. "It's the publicity." They paused at the pedestrian crossing. A man in a herringbone jacket waited alongside them. Dannaks waited until they were on the other side of the road before continuing. "The mayor wants an inquiry. So DIE –

have you heard of them?" She shook her heard and he explained. "It'll all blow over. I've done nothing wrong."

"Of course not." Her voice drifted and he knew he was losing her again.

Two fast walking fast talking youths overtook them.

For every shop on the Lange Reihe there was a pub or restaurant. The latter, with their outside tables, reduced the pavement area to single file.

"But that's enough about me. How are you? How were your last days in Side?"

"Oh, I'm fine," she began, distantly. Then she seemed to come to herself. "After you left, things eased up completely. Almost everyone had a newspaper. And all those undercover guys disappeared. But can you believe it? One of them approached me."

"Approached you?"

"Yes. He wanted to take me out."

Dannaks laughed uneasily. "What did you say?"

"What do you think?" Her annoyance wiped the smile off his face.

They walked in silence for a while. He regretted not taking her hand when they were outside the station for they walked separately.

He racked his mind for something to say. Now, in the real world, without the carefree holiday perspective and supportive backdrop of the resort, he realised they had to work for the relationship.

She broke the silence.

"Dee," she began slowly, as if she was still choosing her words. "This whole thing–" dread gripped him "– with the papers. It's – I–"

"You want to save this for the restaurant?"

Katja huffed and nodded. She looked troubled. He scrutinised her expression, hoping for a clue as to what she had been about to say.

"We're nearly there," he said.

The man in the herringbone jacket walked quickly past them. Dannaks was surprised that he had not overtaken them earlier. Their pace was quite leisurely. He was wearing trainers and looked light on his shoes. He turned abruptly and Katja and Dannaks faltered in their step. "Any chance of an interview?" he said quickly, a hand bringing up a camera. They were stunned and stopped in their tracks. Dannaks reached for the camera as it flashed. The man stepped back as Dannaks moved forward. Half-turned the reporter moved away from them.

"Get out of here," said Dannaks for want of something better to say.

The man was two car-lengths away when he turned and took a second shot of them.

Dannaks glanced at Katja. She was pale and stricken. He lurched forward and the man retreated. Dannaks knew that there was no way he was going to catch him, but he gave chase all the same.

He was out of breath when he returned to Katja. She was visibly shaken and hadn't moved from the spot.

"Are you okay?" he asked.

"Yes," she answered. "No. No, I'm not. I'm sorry Dee. I can't do this."

"What do you mean?" Then he tried to make light of it. "Come on. You'll feel better after a drink. We're here now. The restaurant's just there."

"No," she said, turning towards the road.

He was stumped.

She waved and he saw the taxi crawling in the line, a couple of cars away.

"If you leave you're giving up." That didn't come out right. "I mean you're letting the likes of him win. Don't let them get to you."

If she was listening she didn't show it. Her eyes were fixed on the taxi that was almost upon them.

"Kay," he said.

Only when the taxi stopped, there was no room to pull over, did she turn to him. He sought her eyes with an imploring expression. "I'm sorry Dee." She kissed him on the cheek and stepped onto the road. "I'll call." She climbed into the taxi and he watched her leave. She didn't look at him.

Now it was his turn to be stricken and rooted to the spot.

He couldn't believe what had just happened.

Dannaks wasn't sure how long he stood there absently watching the taxi disappear, but eventually he shook himself and went into the restaurant. The place was packed, with only one table for two reserved in the corner. The sight of the small tapered vase with an opening just large enough to accommodate the stem of the rose set his decision. He found Guido and apologised. The lady had taken ill, he said. Guido smiled and nodded that it was no problem. He had plates of food in his hand. They were so busy the waiters alone couldn't keep up. He served the table next to Dannaks who turned to leave. Out of the corner of his eye he saw Guido snatch up the reserved card from the table.

Dannaks stepped outside as a young couple went in. He knew where they would be sitting. The *Narzisst's Eck* beckoned, but he didn't want that. He was too angry.

He began walking towards his flat, oblivious to the revelry about him.

His thoughts had entered an endless loop examining what had transpired. Was she cooler towards him before the reporter accosted them? She had wanted to say something about the papers and he'd told her to save it for the restaurant. Damn. Well, it was all her doing. She was the one who had dragged him on stage. Then he scolded himself for he had been easily persuaded. Yes, he'd been a willing victim. He knew such thoughts were madness. They got him nowhere. But his mind relentlessly rotated them.

He wanted to carry on walking but found himself all too soon at the entrance to his building. With nothing better to do he wearily climbed the stairs. He didn't bother switching on the lights and ascended in the meagre light that came from the occasional window. At his flat door he couldn't see his lock for the key and punched on the hall lighting.

The moment he opened the door to his flat the aroma assaulted his nostrils. He closed the door, hung up his jacket, slipped off his shoes and strode into the lounge. The scent overpowered him. He was sweating in the plaza toilet cubicle of Azure Skies. A wry smile at once cynical and amusing grew as he saw himself scrambling for his coins; Reupke asking: "Need some help champ?" He opened a window and seized the beer Krug of flowers. "I told her it was a great holiday romance, but all holidays come to an end," Reupke had said. "You and Katja will probably go the same way." Anger bubbled under the surface of him, threatening to erupt like a volcano. He carried the flowers to the kitchen sink and grabbed them in a stranglehold with one hand, lifting them to drain their water, his other hand lifting the lid of his bin. He was about to dump them when he saw the large potato staring up at him. Contemplation held him poised in this position. Then he set the flowers down, back in the makeshift vase, and picked out the potato. After examining it he washed it under the hot water tap. Then he peeled and sliced it and fried it up with a sprinkling of chicken grill spices.

All the while he inexorably went over their short meeting and the incident with the photojournalist or reporter or whatever. "I can't do this," she had said. Can't do what? Go for a meal with him? Well, how about an aged potato back at my place? Relish a relic. And then he was back in Side, meeting her for the first time. The punk with the dyed black hair with purple streaks moving off. He had reminisced before, but now it all came flooding back. He remembered the pain of his frozen eyeball. He saw himself with Katja on the slide. And imagined or saw out of the corner of his mind's eye a father of one of the boys raising his camera. He actively shunned memories of the events on stage, blocking them when they arose, but he couldn't help seeing the poster. Party people wrapped up and oblivious to the sinking of their ship.

He returned the flowers to the coffee table and ate at the sofa with the television on. The oiliness of the food was used as an excuse to indulge in a tipple. After all, he wasn't going to work tomorrow. So a mid working week drink was allowed.

On the regional magazine at nine he caught a street interview with Herbst. He was on his way to his car with half a dozen reporters and photographers encroaching his space like flies, the former sticking microphones or hand-held dictation machines in his face, the latter clicking away like mad. Herbst was a blustering toad of a man with jowls that quivered as he walked. Strangely Dannaks felt some sympathy for the man and hostility towards the way the media was badgering him. "No comment, no comment," he kept saying. His driver, an imposing bullet head opened a car door for him, his mere presence halting the group a good step away from Herbst.

One question was shouted above all others and was heard clearly: "Why do you have a place in Turkey?"

Herbst turned to face them and the moment he spoke they hushed, but still jostled like jockeys in starting cages.

"Why shouldn't I have a place in Turkey? I don't hate the Turkish people. My politics are directed at their over-proportional presence in this country. That's all. They–"

As usual they didn't let him finish. They'd judged that the question had been answered and that it was time for another before he got it into his head to turn and leave. He took umbrage at the forerunner question that preceded the pack.

"Of course it's a coincidence that I have a place there. Many Germans have holiday homes in Side. It's a popular place. But I hope you're not insinuating that my place is in any way linked to the death of that boy." He never referred to Matthias by name.

The reporters may have expected him to continue and were caught on the wrong foot when Herbst turned to the open door. The babble of questions fell on his back and the stony face of his chauffeur. The programme switched back to the attractive studio presenter.

Dannaks stayed up until almost midnight watching television. He drank more *Highland Park* than he intended and was wobbly on his feet as he pulled the bed out of his sofa. Shuffling back from the bathroom he sat on the edge of his ill-made bed and could barely get his clothes off. The temptation to fall backwards onto the bed was great, but he persevered with undressing.

Thursday
09:37

He had a bad night. Thirst forced him to traipse to the kitchen twice. On one of these trips he took the Krug of flowers and left them at the draining board. Their fragrance irritated him. He opened a window despite the swish of traffic and cool air. A full bladder had sent him to the toilet. He closed the window. And sweat and the same recurring thoughts, hammering relentlessly at him had ensured that he remained uncomfortable, tossing and turning, almost pirouetting in bed.

Dannaks dragged his weary self to the kitchen. He flicked on the electric kettle and spooned two heaps of coffee granules in a mug. Then he dropped two slices of bread in the toaster. This morning routine did nothing to lift him out of feeling sorry for himself. He put his hopes in a long hot shower.

His hopes were dashed the moment he switched off the water and began drying himself. He didn't like the wretch that looked back at him in the mirror. A shave would have helped, but he couldn't face the incessant buzz. He opened his medicine cabinet and fetched two aspirin.

In the kitchen he topped up his mug of coffee with cold water so that he could drink it and down the aspirin straight away. After buttering his toast and spreading the jam he pressed the mug to his forehead in an effort to disperse the pain.

Thoughts of Katja were shunned. He was too exhausted to indulge in anything and certainly not misery.

Just over an hour later he was out on the street. The breeze was welcome and he breathed deeply. Of course he dreaded reading the papers. What would they say today? Was he still the Casanova of Azure Skies? The wry cynical smile twisted his mouth line again. Casanova. If only. Nothing could be further from the truth.

He went to the café that served breakfast and carried magazines and newspapers for their customers. There were only two other people in the place and Dannaks grabbed all three German dailies from the rack. He ordered the smallest breakfast and opened the papers.

The focus of media attention had shifted to Volker Herbst. They'd got all the mileage they could cut of Dannaks who was referred to as Götz D. Suffice to say the officer in question had been suspended pending an inquiry by DIE. The bulk of the articles concentrated on the right wing politician. He protested that the police had overstepped the mark; that they had infringed his civil rights. They should have quietly approached and questioned him. He hinted instead that what amounted to an attempted break-in was thwarted by a diligent neighbour. He was furious about the innuendoes that his place was linked to the recent death of that boy.

Herbst was in his element. Once again he was playing the persecution card. The last time he'd done this was during the election campaigns. He'd claimed that foreigners and leftists had attacked his stands. Conflicting versions of these scuffles were reported. Passers-by said that the right-wingers manning the stands had been provocative, if not downright aggressive. For all his spiel about being victimised his blatant fishing for sympathy was interpreted as whinging.

Dannaks returned the papers to the rack and picked up the *Hürriyet*. Until now he had bought it in vain. Today he found something relevant on an inside page.

He sensed from the wording that Meryem was being applauded for killing a racist in their midst. Although it was unclear why she had killed him there was speculation about molesting. This paper too mentioned Herbst's holiday home and ran a short exposé on his political leaning and background.

Dannaks paid up and left. He felt better, but still groggy and sluggish.

Contrasting the merciless brightness of day Patel's was a welcome hole. Not only cool by comparison but also dull: a place to hide. An index finger pointing in the general direction of the computers was given a nod by the owner. Dannaks was surprised to see someone at the machines. He was a longhaired bedraggled looking youth in shabby attire. Was what Dannaks wore any better? If he let his own hair grow he too would look like an archetypal nerd.

Dannaks greeted him and sat in front of a screen. By now he didn't need assistance booting up and logging on. Until recently he'd logged on every two or three months, the REX computer having covered his technological needs. Now it was a daily occurrence.

The nerd swivelled his chair so that his shoulder covered what he was typing. Dannaks looked over and noticed that he'd diminished the size of his windows, some of which were black with white text racing upwards, like the speeded up credits at the end of a movie.

There was nothing from Ismail, but the paying person search had results. They had found no Meryem Turan with the supplied date on birth in Berlin. They had found two other Meryem's in Berlin. One had died aged seventy-nine last year. The other aged thirty-eight had left three months ago and was living in Frankfurt. They had found one Meryem Turan with the correct date of birth who had lived in Hamburg just over two years ago. Details follow. But she was no longer registered in the city. Should they start another search? (For an additional fee.) They could try to follow her trail? Should they widen the net and search for other Meryem's in further cities?

Dannaks caught the nerd surreptitiously glancing at his screen. He collapsed his window to display the desktop.

He took out his notepad, clicked open his window after checking the nerd, and jotted the last known Hamburg address of the Meryem Turan. He thanked the site for their efforts and wrote that he would get back to them should the need arise.

As he closed the PC down Patel passed by. "*Oberkommissar* Dannaks signing off," he said. Patel nodded, but Dannaks was watching the nerd whose shoulders tightened. Dannaks stood and the nerd seemed to shrivel in size.

Outside he strode back to his flat. His mind was a hive of activity. He had two choices for the day: mope or do something. He resolved to do the latter. Before he reached his building he had almost planned the entire day.

Inside he began the day again. The kettle was switched on for another coffee whilst he shaved. After washing and drying his face he took his mug of coffee to the telephone. As he set it down to tap in the number he realised that he had drunk too much coffee and that he was quite sick of the taste of the stuff. He put down making it to being on autopilot.

Frank picked up immediately. "*Hamburg Polizei. Soko REX.* Neumann."

"Dannaks. Hallo Frank. You said I should call."

"Yes. I'm afraid I haven't got anything for you. Phone tomorrow."

"Oh. Okay. Er, same time?"

"Yes."

He hung up and took his coffee to the window where he sipped the top of it and almost scalded the tip of his tongue. Because he was itching to get on he took the mug to the kitchen and, unable to face wasting it, he placed it on the draining board.

Two minutes later he was on the street again.

Dannaks's mental map of the city was based on the U-Bahn (underground) system. If he possessed a car his map would likely be quite different. Meryem's last known address was a housing estate off *Trabrennbahn* on the U1.

He boarded the train at *Lohmühlenstrasse* and alighted 16 minutes later at *Trabrennbahn.* He went down the steps and stopped outside the entrance to take out his street map and get his bearings. In front of him was a car park for *Edeka,* one of the larger supermarket chains. Trade appeared to be good. Off to his right under the railway bridge were quiet housing-estate-looking four-storey blocks, but his map told him to turn left past the short row of shops and across the road.

Dannaks took off his jacket, threw it over his shoulder and strode off. Within two minutes he was in a labyrinth of bewilderingly similar four-storey blocks of yellow-brick flats. The numbering system was something to be desired too. Contrasting the activity near the station the area was deserted. There was no one to ask for help. So he was quite pleased with himself when he located the correct building and stood at the array of labelled bells. The name on the number he required was written in biro which was so faded with age that it was unreadable.

He pressed the bell and waited. And waited. There was no reason why the person who now occupied the flat should be in. But with merely an address he could not have telephoned. He pressed the bell a second time. There was a crackle and then a small voice said hello. A woman? A girl?

"Dannaks. *Kripo* Hamburg. Can I speak to you for a moment?"

There was a long silence save the crack and pop of static. He was about to speak when the buzzer for the door release sounded. Dannaks climbed the stairs to the second floor. Each floor accommodated two flats. Here only one carried a name label: M. Knaus. He went to the anonymous flat and pressed the bell, standing back so the person could spy him through the peephole. The darkening of the glass in the peephole told him he was being spied upon.

The door cracked open, but remained on a chain. The sound of a child crying in the background shattered the stillness of the hallway. A sliver of face – a cheek and eye – of a small timid looking woman in her early thirties appeared at the gap.

"Yes?"

"Dannaks. *Kripo* Hamburg," he said again. He prayed that she wouldn't insist on seeing identification.

Another child spoke above the crying one in what Dannaks took to be Polish.

"Yes?" she asked Dannaks again ignoring the child's words. The woman was very pale with fearful wide doe-like eyes.

"I'm trying to find out about the person who lived here before you. Can–"

"I don't know them."

"Well, er." Dannaks hadn't expected such a sudden response. Maybe she wasn't all that timid. He scrambled for his newspaper cutting. "Perhaps you could have a look at her. She–"

"The flat was empty when I came."

"Please," he unfolded the clipping and held it up to her. "Just have a look."

"No," she said, beginning to grow anxious. Was her anxiety for the crying child? "The flat was empty. No one was here." She edged back to close the door.

"Please, wait. When – when did you move here?"

"About two years ago."

"Okay. What about the caretaker? Can you tell me where I can find him?"

"Huber. House number one."

"Thank–" She closed the door on him and the sudden stillness swallowed his "– you."

11:15

Having unravelled the numbering system he found the block with ease.

"Wait," ordered the electronic voice after he pressed the bell labelled Huber.

Dannaks waited. Eventually he stepped away from the building into the sunshine. A large pedestrian area separated the lines of buildings. No doubt the distance conformed to that required for a possible road.

The main door opened and a small brittle-looking man with a severe expression came out. His hair was grey and he stooped slightly. He seemed engrossed by his clipboard and ignored the detective.

Dannaks walked up to him.

"Yes," he said, without looking up. He was making some markings on a sheet of paper.

"Dannaks. Kripo Hamburg. *Herr* Huber?"

This caught the man's attention. He looked up. "Yes." Would he ask for identification?

"I'd like to ask you a few questions."

"I've got to do my rounds."

Dannaks didn't know what he meant. "Can I walk with you?"

The man nodded.

Despite his age the man set a terrific pace. His slight stoop aerodynamically aided his rapid gait. Dannaks had missed the starting pistol and raced after him.

"I'd like to ask you about a woman who lived here about two and a half years ago," he said once he'd matched the stride of the spritely chap.

"Do you know how many people live here?" he asked. His weathered face was like clay: every wrinkle was a hairline scar. Speckles of stubble shone like stardust on his cheeks and covered his chin like sandpaper. His gruff voice and demeanour matched his outward roughness. "What makes you think I'll remember her?"

"Nothing. Let's say: it's a long shot." He took out his cutting, but Huber was unlocking the door of a block. Dannaks followed him into the building. Huber began inspecting the concrete floor and stairwell that was damp and in places wet. It sparkled with quartz in strange harmony with Huber's stubble. They heard the sound of someone moving about on the stairs leading down to the cellars.

"Here," said Dannaks, proffering the photograph.

Huber paused and irritably took the cutting. "This is that Nazi's killer," he said.

"Possibly." Would he link it to the photograph of him on stage?

"Of course I don't recognise her. They all look alike after a while, you know. Turks, poles, niggers–"

Dannaks cringed. "Her name's Meryem Turan." Huber gave back the cutting.

"Yes," he said, the word voiced distantly as he searched his memory. "Wait. I do remember." He began climbing the stairs and Dannaks was forced to follow. "I don't remember what she looked like, but she's the one who upped and left. Turan." Huber swept a finger along the windowsill at the top of the first flight. "Her type always brings trouble. We even had a murder in that block. They're all the same–"

"What do you mean her type?" he asked taking out his notepad and pen.

They were almost on the third floor. Huber gave the corners extra scrutiny.

"Women," he began. "Single mothers from the *Frauenhaus* (Battered women's home or refuge). I wouldn't have them. But it's

324

not up to me. I don't think housing management want them either. But they've no choice."

"Meryem was a single mother?"

Huber stopped to think and Dannaks scribbled *Frauenhaus*. Then Huber began climbing the last flight of stairs. "*Herr* Huber?" he prompted, making after him.

"Wait. I'm thinking," he said. On the top floor he turned to Dannaks. "No. As I recall she didn't have any children. I'm not sure, though."

"What do you mean you've got no choice?"

"The state claims some of the flats." He continued his inspection. "Ridiculous. These flats are top. If you ask me they don't deserve such a place. We're too generous."

"And she just left?"

"Yep. Although I suppose disappeared is a better word. I don't think she took anything with her."

"You mean she left everything."

"I thought you said that you were a detective. I said she didn't take anything with her. That's what it looked like." They began descending.

"How do you know?"

Huber let out an exacerbated breath. "Because I opened up for them."

"Who?"

Huber tutted. "Housing management and the police." On the ground floor, to spell it out, he stopped and turned to Dannaks. "She obviously hadn't been paying her rent." His eyes were hard. "I always thought her husband got her. They all get found out eventually." Then he headed for the cellar. "But it looks as if she got away. And look what she went and did."

Dannaks hesitated. "Did you ever see her husband?" he called after him.

"No."

"What happened to her belongings?" he asked, but Huber was gone.

Dannaks went down. "*Herr* Huber?"

He found Huber in something of a tiled utility room with a line of three washing machines and a drier. A woman in a headscarf was hunched over a sink rinsing a bucket.

"You're using too much water. Everything is soaked." Huber was saying. The woman acted as if she did not understand him and this infuriated him into berating her further. "And you're too slow. You should be half way through block nine now. You're this close–" he held the tips of his index finger and thumb about a centimetre apart – "look at me when I'm speaking to you." She petulantly dropped everything and turned insolent eyes and a pouting mouth to him. "You're this close to losing this job. And don't think I won't do it. I've got a queue of people wanting this work."

Huber noticed Dannaks and faltered. His tyrannising was over, but he didn't want it to look as if Dannaks's presence had anything to do with it. "Now get a move on." He left the room and Dannaks smiled sympathetically at the woman before giving chase. On the way up to the ground floor Dannaks heard the poisonous little man mutter: "Bloody foreigners. They've got no idea."

"*Herr* Huber. What happened to her belongings?"

"Who? What?" He had a hand on the door.

"Meryem Turan's belongings." Dannaks permitted himself a measure of exasperation. "What happened to them?"

"Oh. I don't know. I think the *Frauenhaus* got most of them."

"You said something about a murder."

"Look, I haven't got time to stand around chatting," he said. Dannaks thought to point out they had been far from stationary. "You can look up that kind of thing, can't you?" He glanced at his clipboard and pulled open the door. "Anyway, it happened about a year before your girl disappeared." He stepped outside, but Dannaks didn't follow him.

13:54

Leaving *Lohmühlenstrasse* he came upon an *Imbiss* (snack bar) and popped in. He bought himself half a flat loaf filled with pork and salad, which he wolfed down underway. By the time he entered his flat he had finished his meal and formed a fully planned strategy to find Meryem's husband. For until now he – no, they – had thought that Matthias had been the target of the killer. What if Meryem had been the intended victim? What if Matthias had simply got in the way or had been protecting her? This threw everything they knew out of the window. But it also explained a lot.

The red man could be the husband. With him on the loose it could even explain why Meryem had hid. But it didn't explain why she confessed.

The very idea excited him. It made him anxious to discover as much as he could about Meryem's husband. Then again, he had to caution himself. He had to keep an open mind. Matthias could still have been the intended victim. But like a bloodhound stumbling on a strong scent he was aroused and at the same time in danger of missing something because of the thrill of the chase.

He kicked off his shoes and hung up his jacket. He was about to flick on the kettle when he saw the mug of coffee on the draining board. Taking it into the lounge he placed it next to the telephone.

Reinhart picked up on the fourth ring. His off pat greeting sounded out of breath.

"What have you been doing?"

"I was coming back from the photocopier."

Dannaks thought to ask whether he'd been copying more plays. But he didn't want to get off on the wrong foot. Besides the likelihood of him doing personal stuff at this time of the day was slim. He wouldn't dare.

"Can you do me a favour?"

"That depends."

"Give me Hahn's number. He's from OK."

"I don't know."

"I can take the long route." He could phone the *Polizeistern* directly and ask for Hahn of *Organisierte Kriminalität* (organised crime).

"Just a minute." Dannaks heard him shuffling papers and then turning pages. "Hahn, Hahn," he said under his breath. "Ah, here he is." Reinhart read out the number.

"Thanks. Now, just one other thing. If anyone asks for me just say I'm out of the office." He knew better than to ask Reinhart to transfer his calls. His colleague couldn't aid a suspended officer. Of course posing as a detective without authorisation to Huber and the occupant of Meryem's flat had been a significant bending of the rules.

"That's it?"

"Yeah. Don't mention that I've been suspended. It's embarrassing, you know."

"There's no harm in that, I suppose."

"Thanks."

"Any idea when you'll be back?"

Frank obviously wasn't keeping the team up to speed. "No."

"Enjoy the free time."

He hung up.

A sip of his coffee caused him to wince. It was cold and bitter.

On the journey to Trabrennbahn he had been dull and preoccupied by his suspension and Katja's behaviour. Negative. The return journey had been completely taken up by thoughts of what he had learnt. Positive. He was also pleased that Huber had not recognised him. Maybe nobody could recognise him. His gormless expression and the black bar across his eyes undoubtedly helped disguise him.

There was no reason to be mean. He needed to be good to himself: to think positive. So he took the mug of coffee to the sink and tipped it away, chasing it down with a blast from the tap.

He waited for the kettle to boil, thinking about the wording of his next calls.

Dannaks then rang Hahn. Nobody picked up for ages and Dannaks began cursing.

"Kripo Hamburg. Hahn."

"Dannaks." He steeled himself against the anticipated flak.

"Hallo lover-boy."

"It's not what it looks like."

"That's what they all say."

Silence was Dannaks's reply.

"I heard you got suspended from duty."

Damn. "You heard right." It appeared as if he was going to get off without the barrage of jibes he had anticipated.

"So, to what do I owe this unexpected honour?"

"You told me about a raid some months ago where you had so many foreign prostitutes you had to take them to a *Frauenhaus*. Remember?" Many Asian women or women from behind the former Iron Curtain were enticed to the West with promises of working as a model, nanny or in a noble hotel. They were smuggled in and imprisoned in the sex trade.

OK was one of the largest departments in the police force. In the *Polizeistern* they occupied five of the eight wings of the third floor and were sub-sectioned into weapons offences, fencing stolen property, financial crime, operative measures including raids and prostitution offences. The latter related more to crime in the underworld than to prostitution. For prostitution was a legal profession in Germany.

"Yeah. What about it?"

"I need the name of the social worker you worked with."

"What for? What are you doing?"

"I can go the long way, but I thought you'd help."

"*Mann oh*, Dannaks. You've got nerve."

"Thanks," said Dannaks, before Hahn could say any more. "I'll call you back in fifteen minutes."

"Make it half an hour."

"Twenty minutes, then."

"*Mann oh*."

Dannaks hung up, amused by his "*Mann oh*" exclamations. Mostly children used the expression as a substitution for expletives. Translated it was roughly equivalent to "oh man," with the intonation on dejection.

He bided his time by changing the water in the *Krug* and generally pottering about.

Eventually he was standing over the telephone waiting for the last minute to pass.

Hahn picked up almost immediately. "I've got two names for you." He was talking quietly and Dannaks couldn't ask him to speak up. "*Frau* Gropp and *Frau* Mertens." Dannaks noted the numbers and thanked him.

He tapped in the first woman's number only to discover that she was out and wouldn't be back in the office until Monday. No, he couldn't have her handy number. So Dannaks called the second woman.

"Mertens."

"Dannaks. *Kripo* Hamburg."

"Do I know you?"

"No. I'm with REX, but I'm dealing with a case that involves a woman from one of your *Frauenhäuser*. Her name's Meryem Turan."

"Sorry. The name doesn't mean anything to me."

"But you do deal with *Frauenhaus* women?"

"Not only. But yes. You do know that Hamburg has six *Frauenhaüser*?"

"No, I didn't. Well, er, do you know how I can get–"

"Just a minute, I'll see if I can get a name for you."

"Thank you."

"Hold on."

Piped music began like a Möbius strip. It didn't matter what was played. By nature the tune became monotonous and then torturous.

Dannaks was writhing and didn't know how much more he could take when the woman came back on the line.

"Hallo? Are you still there?"

Did her question betray a ploy? "Just about."

She said that he required a *Frau* Poschmann and gave him her number, which he tapped in the moment they severed the call.

"Poschmann," said the woman.

"Dannaks. *Kripo* Hamburg."

"Yes?"

He explained that *Frau* Mertens had given him her number and that he was looking into Meryem Turan's past in connection with a murder.

"I know her. But I can't tell you anything. Certainly not over the phone."

"Actually, at the moment I'm interested in locating her husband. Can we meet?"

"Yes. But I'm not going to the trouble of meeting you if you're not who you say you are."

"Naturally. Phone the police and ask for Dannaks, *Soko* REX. But before you do, let me give you my private number. My colleagues don't know it, but I'm on a special out-of-office assignment."

She took his number and hung up.

He imagined Poschmann calling some number she had for the police and asking to be transferred to him. Reinhart would pick up and say that he was not in. But his imagination ran on optimistic time and she didn't call back until almost eight minutes later.

"Okay *Oberkommissar* Dannaks today's out, but we can meet tomorrow. I have a half hour slot at eleven. Do you know Steilshoop shopping arcade?"

"Not well." He knew Steilshoop, but not the arcade.

"There's a café there. Café Ines."

"I'll find it. How will I recognise you?"

"It's not a big place."

"Okay."

"Eleven o'clock tomorrow, then. *Tschüs.*"

"*Danke. Tschüs.*"

15:32

Dannaks spent the rest of the afternoon in. He contemplated going for a walk, but Huber had exhausted his exercise quota for the day. He thought about checking his emails again, being tempted to write to Ismail and tell him of his discovery, but he didn't really have anything concrete to say. Finally the *Narzisst's Eck* beckoned, but again he decided against it. Alcohol did not appeal. Memories of his drowsy state that very morning were still fresh.

Normally Thursday night was reserved for his Turkish class. But it was the summer break. Nonetheless he pulled out his textbook and did some of the exercises.

He cooked and ate at six.

Sometime during the evening he pulled out his map and found the Steilshoop shopping arcade. To his consternation there wasn't a nearby U-Bahn or S-Bahn station. The thought of a good couple of kilometres foot march along an ugly dual carriageway didn't fill him with enthusiasm. He couldn't justify the expense of a taxi and knew he'd have to find out about the buses.

At seven he watched the news followed by a local news magazine. There was nothing about him or Herbst.

He didn't hear from Katja either.

Friday
09:26

Dannaks slept neither badly nor well. He'd stayed away from alcohol, but his mind had restlessly ticked over. Succinctly put he was excited.

After his shave, shower and breakfast he called Frank.

"It's your daily call," he said.

"This time I have got something for you. You should call DIE. Ask for Möller." Dannaks knew him, assuming it was the same man. DIE operated a five-year rotation system. Because working in anti-corruption could corrupt the investigators they were only allowed a single term.

"Okay."

"You need the number?"

"No."

There was a pause.

"Oh and Dannaks, I get the impression they're going to dismiss it. So don't plan any trips."

Frank sounded busy and Dannaks decided to forgo telling him what he had been doing.

Möller was at his desk.

"You asked me to call."

"Yes. Dannaks. Just a minute." He heard him shuffling papers. "Ah yes, Dannaks. This really is a bagatelle offence. Even the word offence seems too strong here." He sighed. "Just more paperwork for us." He wasn't really saying anything, but Dannaks didn't like to interrupt him. "But we have to go through the motions, don't we?"

"Yes," he said quietly.

Möller seemed to brace himself and when he next spoke there was decisiveness in his voice. "Come in on Monday morning, will you? Say ten."

"Okay."

"You know where we are?"

"Johanniswall."

"Yeah. Number four."

"I'll be there. Have a good weekend."

"You too."

He put the phone down and uncannily it began ringing straight away.

"Dannaks," he said, snatching it up.

"Too busy to call?"

"Uwe," he exclaimed. "What do you mean?"

"You said you'd call by Thursday at the latest. Remember, the meal on Saturday? Or did you manage to find something better?"

"I – No. Sorry. I forgot. I was busy."

"You're at home, aren't you?"

"Yes. But – I'll tell you tomorrow."

"So you're coming?"

"Yes. Sorry."

"Tomorrow at eight – if you can fit us in."

"I'll be there."

10:53

Café Ines was a dreary place. The furniture was functional rather than fashionable. Their cheapness conferred them a premature weariness. The furnishings too were pared down to the essential. Altogether the feel was that of trucker's pit stop: a place for something hot and wet, a place to take a break, but not a place to linger.

The young waitress's smile brightened the drabness.

Dannaks ordered a coffee and a chicken sandwich.

His newspapers sat on the chair beside him. There had been nothing new. Certainly no picture of Katja and him with shocked looks. There was little satisfaction in the thought that the reporter who had stalked them had missed the boat. The damage had been done. Herbst had featured in the *Mopo*. There was a quote from some amateur footage taken at a right wing meeting shortly after news of Matthias's death in which he had commented: "You can see from his choice of refuge where his allegiances lay." Rich, considering the subsequent divulging of the location of his holiday home. Dannaks couldn't help feeling that in the eyes of the media he resembled a pantomime villain. He became ridiculous and although evil they had a hard time taking him seriously. Because of his politics Dannaks felt no sympathy for him.

He had ridden the U-Bahn to Barmbek where he got on the S-Bahn alighting at Rubenkamp to begin his brisk walk. Progress was slow and he realised that he was going to be late. Luckily he was near a bus stop when a bus arrived. The driver said that he stopped not far from Steilshoop shopping arcade and Dannaks hopped on and arrived early.

Most of the patrons were of course shoppers; their foot space limited by bulging plastic bags.

Frau Poschmann came in just after eleven. Dannaks knew it was her because she surveyed the customers rather than the seating. He nodded to her and as she came over he stood.

"Dannaks?" she asked.

He held out his hand for her limp handshake. "*Frau* Poschmann." She had a hard stare that would be a challenge to Iceman. And her demeanour didn't evoke empathy.

In her youth, before starting work, she would have been attractive. The burden of everyone else's problems had taken its toll and she had aged prematurely. Her features said that smiles were rare visitors to her face.

They sat. "Thanks for seeing me. What can I get you?"

"A tea and cake," she said, slipping her jacket and handbag over the back of her chair.

He gestured to the waitress who came over and took the order.

Poschmann clasped her hands in front of herself and stared at him. "Before we begin I'd like to see some eye-dee."

He blanched and then smiled. Smiling was a mistake and quashing it gave him a twisted expression. "I told you I was on assignment. If I get caught with my identity card my cover will be blown."

"You mean you're undercover?"

He nodded.

"You must think I was born yesterday," she said haughtily, leaning back and folding her arms. "I'm not telling you anything."

"Why don't you hear what I want first?"

They were silent as the waitress served her order.

Dannaks waited until they were alone.

"Have you read about the arrest of Meryem Turan? She confessed to murdering Matthias Kerner, the ex-neo-Nazi. Do you know what I'm talking about?"

She ate her cake without saying a word or giving him any clue as to whether she knew what he was talking about.

He sighed, but persevered. "I know that she came from one of your *Frauenhäuser*. This means she was running away from somebody. Probably her husband." Still no reaction. He pulled out his clipping of Meryem and slid it towards her plate. "This is her." She glanced at it but said nothing. "All I want to know is the whereabouts of her husband. That's all. You see, I don't think she killed Matthias." The rhythm of her mastication hiccupped. "I'm not interested in anything else. I just want to find him. If this girl means anything to you then you should help me." She'd almost finished her cake. "I'll get this information sooner or later."

She picked up her tea and he slumped back, defeated. He then picked up the remains of his sandwich and took a bite. She watched him over the rim of her cup. He returned her gaze impassively. It was as if they had started a children's game. The first to look away lost.

Poschmann looked down and returned her cup to its saucer. Still she remained silent. She popped the last bite of cake in her mouth and before she had finished chewing she wiped the edges of her lips with the paper serviette.

He finished his sandwich, resigned to the fact that she wasn't going to talk to him.

She put down her empty teacup and looked at her watch. On the phone she had said she had a half hour slot. He estimated that she still had a good quarter of an hour to kill. He couldn't see her sitting it out with him.

Brinkmanship was his last resort. He downed the rest of his coffee and stood. "I'm sorry to have bothered you."

"Sit down, *Herr* Dannaks," she said calmly.

He obeyed and silently waited for her to speak.

"You're looking for Erdogan or Erkan Turan. I can't remember. But I'm sure his first name began with E." Dannaks whipped out his notepad and pen. "He lived and worked at some health club – I can't remember the name – in the Lüneburger Heide. I think he was a tennis instructor. Maybe he's still there."

"Thanks." He decided he had nothing. "I spoke to Huber yesterday. He's the caret–"

"I know who he is. He's an arse."

"Oh?"

"He wanted to get some friend or relative one of those flats. He tried to take one of ours. We only had two. Both for young women with children. I don't know where he got his information but he told housing management that one of the women topped up her income with prostitution. They wouldn't have her. Luckily Meryem had a steady job and we were able to act quickly and get her in instead."

"Where did she work?"

She stared at him, obviously weighing up whether to tell him.

"Barbados," she said. "It's a *Gaststätte* (a restaurant/pub) in Billstedt. Now I think I've said enough."

He nodded and made to slide the clipping away from her. He changed his mind and tapped it. "One last thing. Is this Meryem?"

She peered at the photograph and he took his finger away.

"It says so, doesn't it?"

"Yes. But is it her. You remember what she looked like?"

"Yes. But it's very grainy." He thought the picture quite distinct.

"Do you think it's her?"

She picked it up and stared at it.

Then she slowly nodded. "Yes, that's her. That's Meryem."

12:55

Dannaks reversed his journey, taking the bus to the S-Bahn, changing to the U-Bahn to arrive at the main station and walk directly to Patel's. There he logged on and checked his emails. Other than advertising there was nothing. He put in the search words "Lüneburger Heide tennis" and almost fell off his chair when he saw the number of hits. Substituting "Health club" for "tennis" shortened his list. But he still spent an hour sifting through the websites for those that offered tennis lessons. He ended up with a list of a half a dozen possible locations with telephone numbers. He located the address of the *Gaststätte* Barbados in Billstedt with ease. Thank heaven for the Internet.

He cleared his debt with Patel and returned to his flat.

After making a cup of tea he began systematically calling the numbers on his list. He used the same story each time and in keeping with Murphy's Law the right place turned out to be the second to last on his list.

The receptionist gave her standard greeting and Dannaks announced himself only in name.

"How can I help?"

"I'm looking for a particular tennis instructor. A friend of mine met him two or three weeks ago in Side, Turkey and recommended him. He works for you, or at least worked for you about two years ago. He's Turkish and his surname is Turan. Does he still work for you?" This was where all the previous receptionists had said that they had at no time employed anyone by that name and he had asked whether they knew the name from one of their rival clubs in the area. Before they could extol the virtues of their own instructor he had apologised, saying that he had evidently got the wrong hotel, and hung up.

"Yes, he does."

"Great," said Dannaks, circling the name of the health club.

"He's teaching at the moment. When were you thinking of coming?"

"Next week probably. But tell me; was he away for a few days two weeks ago?"

"I don't think so. It must be someone else with the same name. It's fairly common."

"Oh I know. But could he have slipped over?"

"I suppose he could have. I'm not here all the time. Should I get him to call you back?"

"No. No. That's okay. Is he there tomorrow?

"Yes, from nine till two. But you can't–"

"You've been very helpful–"

She began speaking at the same time. "Don't you want to book?"

"Thank you very much."

"It's peak season."

"I'll get back to you. Goodbye."

"But–"

He hung up.

Dannaks sat still for a while, looking at the phone, sipping his tea.

He suddenly felt very hungry. It was four thirty: a silly time to eat. Rather than snack, because a snack wouldn't be enough, he decided to stave off his hunger by busying himself.

Half an hour later he was again in Patel's. There he checked the trains from the main station to *Dannenberg* in the *Lüneburger Heide*. A return would cost him forty euros with a journey time of two hours each way. Then there was the additional, but unknown, cost of a taxi from the station to the health club. Hiring a car doubled the cost but halved the duration of the journey.

His stomach gurgled as he signed off.

Dannaks walked round to a side street not far from the main station. The car hire office was a small single room with a long counter, behind a corded off area at the end of which was a queue here sign. Running the length of the wall opposite the counter were soft black leather bucket seats with chromed piped frames. Apart from the girl behind the counter the place was empty.

Twenty minutes later Dannaks had booked a car for nine o'clock tomorrow morning.

By now he was famished and wanted immediate gratification. This limited him to fast food. The trouble was that he believed fast food not only meant that it was served quickly, but also required eating quickly. This could mean painfully overeating or soon becoming hungry again. The thought of chicken and chips appealed and he went straight to the American Diner off the *Lange Reihe*. Diner was a misnomer, because the place was little bigger than a kiosk with a running counter and stools for about a dozen customers. Also the menu was relatively limited. Nonetheless they offered the best spit-roasted chicken in the area.

Dannaks initially bolted the food and felt rather sickish for it. He then slowed down and tried to indulge.

18:22

The meal sat like lead in his belly and instead of trudging back to his flat he went to the *Narzisst's Eck*. He felt he needed a digestive short to cut through the grease. He also felt he deserved a reward for his hard work.

Karl-Heinz greeted him with accustomed disdain.

Dannaks smiled and ordered a double Glenmorangie Port Finish.

Frauke was in her usual spot, but Hagen's place was empty. There was another loner whose weary face was becoming a regular feature.

Dannaks savoured his drink and left at ten to seven hoping to catch the seven o'clock news.

Karl-Heinz was surprised by his brief visit, but Dannaks didn't provide him with a reason. He would have liked to drink another one or four, but he was driving tomorrow and he wanted his wits about him.

In the flat he thought about calling Reupke to tell him what he had discovered, but because he might ask about Katja he decided against it.

Until now he had successfully avoided thinking about her. Sitting alone he had no choice but to confront his thoughts and memories. She could call, but he wasn't banking on it.

After the television news he phoned Uwe.

"You're not cancelling, are you?"

"No. But I want you to write this down."

"What?"

"Just do it?"

"Okay. Just a sec. Yeah. Okay. I'm ready."

"Tomorrow I'm meeting a tennis instructor called Turan at the *Sport and Wellness Hotel Sonnenblume* in the *Lüneburger Heide*."

"Sport and wellness? What's happening to you? Dannaks that is you, isn't it?"

"Yes. Just take note. Have you got that?" He repeated everything and Uwe read back to him what he had written.

"So why are you telling me this?"

"It'll take too long to explain."

Uwe allowed him time to possibly elaborate.

"I'll tell you tomorrow."

"You're not putting yourself in some kind of danger?"

"I'll tell you tomorrow."

"You're working, aren't you? Damn it, Dannaks. You're not normal."

"Maybe."

"This is not going to make you late, is it?"

"No. Don't worry. I'll be there."

Saturday
10:46

Dannaks took forty minutes to break free of the congested city. He hadn't considered this in his calculation and the drive took him an hour and a half. Still, quicker than the train. The initial traffic gave him time to get used to the car.

It was good to get out of the city. He enjoyed the drive especially on the country lanes. The sun brought out the colours of the countryside. Merely the panorama of land and sky was a pleasure.

On days like this you didn't need to fly south to the sun to relax.

The navigation system was a dream and took him straight to the hotel. He contemplated how many marriages this simple device had saved.

Throughout the journey a point niggled him. It was something that he had dismissed by telling himself that all leads should be followed.

The entrance to Sport and Wellness Hotel *Sonnenblume* was an arch tucked in a stretch of roadside woodland that he could easily have missed. A rutted track took him through a pine forest

339

before opening up onto asphalt and an expansive field of sunflowers that made him wish he had brought his camera.

At the end of the road was a large old villa annexed to which was a modern block. Although the modern part was stylish it could not compete with the character of the villa. A sign directed him left to the car park.

At least thirty vehicles were in the parking area, but it was far from full.

Over the last hour and a half he had planned his approach. Arriving unannounced he was taking a risk. If Turan was teaching without a break he would not be able to talk to him. But without identification he didn't want to make an appointment through reception.

He reckoned the chance of being recognised out here was relatively slim.

He removed the clipping and some cash from his wallet, pocketing it in his jeans and returned his wallet to his jacket. When he got out of his new VW Golf, leaving his jacket on the passenger seat, he heard the distant sound of tennis balls being hit. He followed his ears round the back of the old villa. A breeze picked up and the sound disappeared. He found himself before an undulating grassy area, broken by occasional bushes and lone trees, gently sloping to a lake. Half a dozen children were running about near the water's edge. Two rowing boats were on the water and a couple were sitting on a bench looking out. Immediately to his right behind the old building was a patio with about twenty thick wooden garden tables and chairs. Interspersed between them were large rectangular canvas canopies standing in paving stone blocks. Five tables were occupied with couples of various generations finishing late breakfasts or reading. To his left were planted bushes that made up something of a hedge. Above one of the shorter ones he spotted high wire mesh. A waitress was clearing the used crockery of a vacated table.

No one paid him any attention.

A feeling of rest and recreation pervaded. It reminded him of the easy late afternoon atmosphere at Azure Skies.

The wind dropped and the rounded cork-popping sound of tennis balls being hit confirmed his suspicion that the courts were on the other side of the wire mesh behind the bushes to his left.

He followed the path through a gap in the hedge and came upon a row of red grit tennis courts nearly all of which were in use. Turan was easy to spot for he appeared to be the only teacher with a shopping trolley full of brilliant yellow balls on his court. Everyone else was playing. His pupil was a gorgeous blonde in a tight pale blue top with two white stripes across the shoulders and down the short sleeves and a white pleated mini skirt that concealed very little leg.

Turan was a handsome fit-looking man with windswept blue-black hair and bluish stubble on his tanned face.

Dannaks made his way round the mesh to some benches next to a whitewashed concrete hut on a raised viewing area. He sat down and surveyed the scene, always returning to Turan and the blonde. He was convinced that this was his man for he was the only person with dark Turkish-looking features. He was also about the right age for Meryem.

Was he looking at Peter's murderer? He looked athletic enough. Maybe he did some kind of self-defence? He was undoubtedly attractive to women, but Dannaks felt something diabolical in his heavy eyebrows. Violence was undoubtedly part of his makeup. He'd beaten his wife into running away from him.

Dannaks felt conspicuous sitting alone watching their court. Turan no doubt thought he was admiring the girl, for Dannaks caught his eye as he picked up a ball with the head of his racket and the outside of his foot. Perhaps that's why at one point he stood behind the girl holding her waist with one hand, his other grasping the wrist of her racket-carrying hand to guide the swing of her stroke.

A member of staff was collecting odd glasses and Dannaks interrupted him.

"I'm not a guest here," he began, "but could I get a drink and pay in cash?"

"Of course, sir. What would you like?"

"A cola."

"Small, medium or large?"

"Medium."

"Light? Diet? We–"

"Standard.

"Thank you."

"Er, can you tell me whether that instructor is *Herr* Turan?"

"Yes. Yes it is sir."

"Thanks."

Dannaks had to wait another half an hour before the tennis lesson ended. By then he had long finished his cola.

The girl thanked Turan and said that she would see him in the bar at eight. The man followed her off the court stepping ahead to graciously open the mesh door for her. She smiled deliciously. His smile was smarmy. She glanced at Dannaks, her eyes hardening with malevolence. Turan's eyes glazed over with indifference as he closed the door and began kicking or hitting the balls dotted about the court towards the shopping trolley.

Dannaks waited until the girl was gone before walking down to the court.

"*Herr* Turan?" he called.

He looked up and nodded.

Dannaks opened the gate and walked towards him, but before he could introduce himself Turan said: "You could make yourself useful."

Dannaks walked to a far corner and began rolling the stray balls in the direction of the trolley.

"I've got another lesson in fifteen minutes. What can I do for you?"

"It's about your wife, Meryem."

"Ex-wife," Turan corrected. "What about her?"

"She's been involved in a murder."

This halted the tennis instructor.

"Who are you?"

"*Oberkommissar* Dannaks, *Kripo* Hamburg," he said, moving a hand towards his heart. "Sorry, I left my ID in my jacket. It's in the car. Shall I go and get it?"

"What murder?" Then his face opened up with realisation and Dannaks feared that he might be recognised. "You don't mean that Nazi in the *Hürriyet*?"

"Yes."

Turan relaxed. "I read about that." He then shook his head. "That's just somebody with the same name."

"What do you mean?"

"Meryem."

"That's not your wi – ex-wife?"

"No. She looks similar, but it's not her."

Dannaks pulled out the clipping from his back pocket.

"Are you sure?" he asked approaching Turan.

"I should know my own ex-wife," he said without looking at the clipping.

"Please," said Dannaks, proffering the rectangle of newspaper.

Turan sighed, took it and examined it. "No. That's not the Meryem I know."

They were silent for a moment as Dannaks shoved the clipping back in his pocket.

"Reception said you've been here all season."

Turan nodded. His perplexity turning to irritability.

"You didn't pop down to Turkey for a few days a couple of weeks ago?"

"What? No." Again his eyes grew with the realisation of what the question could mean. "You think I had something to do with that murder?"

"Did you?"

"Of course not. That's preposterous. I was here all the time. Teaching."

"We'll check up on that."

"You do that." He seemed flabbergasted. "I didn't even know that Nazi. Why should I kill him?"

"Maybe you were after Meryem – this one–" he touched his jeans pocket – "and he got in the way."

"Then why should I kill her? Whoever she is."

"You tell me."

"What? Get out of here. Even if that girl were my ex-wife, why should I kill her? We're divorced."

"But she ran away from you."

"Yes she did. Stupid bitch couldn't handle the occasional slap." He became pensive. "Back then I suppose I was angry enough to kill her. But I could have got her at the *Frauenhaus*. But now. What for? I'm happy."

"Perhaps you couldn't find her?"

"Oh come on. I knew exactly where she was." Yes, this was the point that had niggled Dannaks. Meryem had not changed her name. Did she no longer feel in danger? It was something he couldn't reconcile. And he was goaded by the thought that the trip was a product of blinkered thinking: a result of the all-consuming scent of the chase. His saving justification was that he was essentially investigating a murder and all, absolutely all, leads had to be followed. Horror then overcame Turan. "I think I will see that ID after all. You're a reporter, aren't you? Well, you got it wrong. That's not Meryem. Now, I'm not saying another word."

20:20

Turan didn't say another word and when he greeted his next pupil, another magnificent looking woman, who sat on a bench untying the thongs of her sandals to slip on her training shoes, Dannaks was forced to leave. He went to the patio and idly picked up a menu from an empty table. He balked at the lunchtime prices. Of course, what he had paid for his cola should have alerted him.

In his car he flipped open his notepad and made notes about the interview. His gut feeling told him that Turan was telling the truth. Dannaks had spotted no telltale self-comforting or stress-related gestures. If he wasn't telling the truth then either he was a damned cool customer or a damned good liar. Of course his whereabouts at the time of the murder would have to be checked. That meant more phone calls: first to the hotel itself to obtain the telephone numbers of guests who'd had lessons with him and then the guests themselves. This was the work of a team, perhaps utilising the local police and certainly not a man on his own without authorisation. Turan could have paid someone to carry out the murder. But if he was divorced then surely there was no motive. "What for? I'm happy," he had said. Yes, he didn't portray the heartbroken dumped man. He did seem to be happy. "I could have got her at the *Frauenhaus*." How could he have known of her whereabouts?

The most perplexing thing was that he said that the girl in the cutting wasn't Meryem. Poschmann had said the opposite.

Dannaks left and found a roadside café that offered basic fare.

The trip back was uneventful and when he hit the outskirts of Hamburg his progress inevitably became hampered. Indeed, the closer he got to the city the more sluggish became his progress. He pulled into a petrol station, tanked up and because there was no time to get back to his flat and grab a relatively decent wine he was forced to buy a bottle of plonk at an exorbitant price.

Miraculously Dannaks wasn't late for his meal with Uwe, his ex-colleague from Drugs, and his wife Annelore.

The meal with the couple hit all the right buttons. He'd forgotten how tiresome driving could be.

"You hired a car," exclaimed Uwe, filling their glasses with the red wine. They were sitting at the laden table. Annelore had put together numerous small dishes: marinated artichokes, cubes of sheep' cheese with pomegranate seeds, figs containing cashew nuts, olives with slices of garlic, humus, etc.

"Yes," said Dannaks, aware that Annelore wanted to make an announcement.

"We're eating Moroccan," she said. "Don't fill yourself. There's a main course to come."

"Impressive," said Dannaks.

Uwe made to reach for the bread but stopped when she picked up her glass. "Here's to you getting back to work."

"Thanks," he put the wine to his nose and then to his lips. He rolled it in his mouth for a moment and then swallowed. It was so awful that he smiled and smacked his lips loudly.

Uwe raised one eyebrow when he had tasted it. Dannaks saw Annelore caution her husband with a look. But he didn't need her allegiance. The wine was appalling and there were no excuses.

"I'm driving," he said. "So I'm only having the one glass."

They laughed.

"I'll use it for cooking," said Annelore.

"Or paint-stripping," Uwe muttered, getting up to fetch a bottle of their own wine.

Dannaks told them about the drive and interview with Turan. In doing so he had to tell them about uncovering Meryem's past.

"You're playing the white knight again," said Uwe. Uwe often called him a white knight. "And you've chosen one of the most hackneyed quests." Annelore and Dannaks waited for him to explain. "Rescuing a damsel in distress."

Describing his day's activities compelled him to backtrack. And then he went back to Side. He censored little of what he said because there was no case and he felt he could talk freely.

He played down Katja's role and this time, when Annelore curtailed any enquiry from Uwe, he was grateful for her allegiance.

At one point Annelore said: "So Meryem is not who she says she is. A nameless assassin. How intriguing. Just like a real crime story you see on television."

Over the main course of lamb with couscous, nuts, raisins and dates he divulged his suspicions. They had been so focused on Matthias that they hadn't considered that Meryem could be the intended victim.

Eventually he brought them up to his suspension and his interview with DIE on Monday.

"I'm sorry to say it," Uwe began, "but however it ends, you've kicked any chance of getting onto the *Mordkommission* into touch." This had contributed to his decision to move to REX. It brought him a little closer to joining. Of late, he wasn't so sure the job was for him.

Later, over desert, Uwe said: "I bet you were in the *Eck* last night."

"Guilty."

"I knew it. You haven't changed. I do worry about you." He waited a moment. "And you're in danger of becoming an alcoholic." There was some truth in the statement.

"But I haven't been there all week."

"Who are you kidding?"

"And I'm not drinking tonight."

"Boys, boys," said Annelore. "I thought *I* was married to Uwe. But you two bicker more like a married couple than we do."

Sunday
09:25

Dannaks parked the hire car in the allotted spot and dropped the keys in the slot at the office. At the main station a headline compelled him to buy the papers. Herbst's villa in Side had been ransacked and the walls smeared with graffiti by persons as yet unknown. The outer walls were covered in swastikas and words in Turkish, German and English along the lines of "No Nazis, Nazis out". The Turkish police were investigating. Again Herbst was not available for comment.

Asked three or four days hence what he, Dannaks, did today he would have trouble remembering. He had frittered away the time. There had been a walk, a change of bedding, some laundry, fresh water for the flowers, cleaning the bathroom, the completion of two Sudoku puzzles and a television evening.

Monday

He was at the DIE offices at five to ten. Actually he'd wandered the shops of Mönckebergstrasse for a quarter of an hour beforehand. Although their offices were located in a small road no more than fifty metres from the so-called *Einkaufsmeile* (shopping mile) the contrast in atmosphere couldn't have been greater. Blank-faced buildings with heavy doors and sober brass nameplates replaced the brash open window displays and shop fronts.

Möller met him in reception where he issued Dannaks with a visitor's badge. He was about Dannaks's age. A greater weariness sagged his shoulders and his features bespoke tedium. The two men had met once before, but their acquaintance had remained strictly formal.

"We have to conduct it here," said Möller, gesturing to an interrogation room similar to those in the police station. For some reason Dannaks had expected to sit in a lone hard chair set apart and facing a panel of three or so judges behind file-laden tables. Not so. Here, he was in a room with a tape recorder on a utilitarian metal table and four hardy chairs as if he were a common criminal about to undergo an interrogation. Möller must have noticed his shock as he followed him in. "Sorry," he said placing his files on one side of the table and so claiming his place. Dannaks was obliged to take the seat opposite. "This shouldn't take long," he began when they were seated. The top sheet of his open file appeared to be a list of questions. Dannaks noticed that his own report was underneath. No doubt Reupke's was there too.

After Dannaks declined the offer of tea or coffee Möller said: "I'll put you out of your misery straight away. We intend to clear you of any misconduct. But your actions, I think you'll agree, were ill judged. Our recommendation is going to be a caution with a return to full service."

Dannaks knew that he couldn't get off scot-free. The mayor had to be appeased.

"You heard about Herbst's place?" Möller asked.

Dannaks nodded. He had indeed worried that the wrecking of Herbst's place would have an influence on the outcome.

"I can't promise how the heads are going to react, but that's our recommendation."

"Thanks."

"I have some questions."

Möller essentially wanted to confirm his understanding of Dannaks's report. This took up some twenty minutes at the end of which Möller asked whether he had any questions.

"When do you think I can get back to work?"

Möller sat back and smiled. "You know as well as I do it's got to do the rounds. Everyone has to put his or her potato-stamp on it. I'd give it at least three working days."

"So I guess we're talking about this Friday or even Monday next week."

Möller nodded, his smile askew with sympathy. "Anything else?"

"No. Except thanks."

11:55

The journey from the main station eastwards to Billstedt on the U2 took just thirteen minutes. Once there, armed with his city map, it took him a further fifteen minutes to find the place.

This part of the city was similar to Steilshoop. Here too were ugly blocks of flats, worn-out shop signs, graffiti and the heat, the main roads, overwhelming buildings and exhaust fumes choked any of the green that was on offer.

Despite the positive result from Möller Dannaks felt dejected. He was in two minds about continuing delving into Meryem's past. His energy was ebbing. Thoughts of Katja were insistent and winning through by sheer attrition. So the current cheerless environment suited his emotional state.

Like all areas there were exceptions. Off the beaten track in a residential area, where some of the buildings were survivors from an all but disappeared village, he came upon the *Gaststätte* Barbados. From a distance at the end of the quiet road all the glass made it resemble a school classroom. Over the main entrance at the top of some wooden steps was the name, Barbados, bracketed by inward curving palm trees. Either side of the building was a track. This gave one the impression of a wooden trailer – it was a concrete structure – plonked in the middle of some waste ground. At each track was a sign. One had the simple silhouette of a car with a fat arrow, the other a motorbike rider over the same kind of fat arrow.

Inside, the wood panelling of the walls and ceiling maintained trailer impression. A bar counter ran most of one length of the room. Padded single-legged chromed stools with short backrests were fixed into the floor along the bar. Elsewhere, padded in the same salmon coloured vinyl, were immovable pairs of benches sandwiching Formica topped tables. At the far end of the bar was a large plastic palm tree. Colourful metal placards advertising various beverages, both alcoholic and non-alcoholic, adorned the walls and bestowed the place with a fifties nostalgia. A confederate flag was the centrepiece of one wall. This place was more of an American diner than the place he had visited yesterday.

Dannaks was the only person in the room. The choice was his and typically he chose a corner looking into the room, the bar and entrance.

Nearby stood a strange structure. Attached to a metal pole stem at regular intervals like shelves were circular discs the centres of which were the pole itself. Along the edge of the shoulder level disc were loops of metal supporting metal coat hangers. There were four of these structures in the room. He hung his jacket up.

At the table he looked over the glossy A3 card that offered all manner of food and drink. There were smaller shiny cards with the condiments and sauces.

Just as he was beginning to think he was completely alone in the building he heard noise. Behind the counter a door with a porthole window opened and he glimpsed the kitchen. He looked at the menu to recheck his order and when he looked up the woman was almost upon him.

She was a big woman and, because of her girth, she appeared dwarf-like with a dumpling of a body and a face to match. For her face was a blob of dough, with terribly pale features puffed out by the lumpiness. It could have been a jolly face, but it wasn't. Her eyes were relegated to bunkers' machine gun slits. A thin line of lipstick marked where her lips should be, sunken in the valley of her cheeks and chin. The side of her face and forehead were matt white with powder or was it flour? Her protruding cheeks and chin were not rosy but shiny as if brushed with glaze. Her hair was in the curls of a tight perm. Altogether she looked like a crabby battle-axe.

"Yes," she said curtly.

Dannaks refrained from expressing any wisecrack along the lines of friendly service with a smile.

"I'll, er, have the cheese and onion flan."

"Drink?"

"Coffee."

"Mug or all you can drink?"

"Oh. What's the difference?"

Irritably she tapped the menu in front of him with her pen, directing his eyes to a block of text and the steaming coffee pot icon. "Three euros more." Dannaks quickly worked out that he'd have to drink more than two cups to make it financially worthwhile.

"Mug," he said, adopting her laconic style.

"That it?"

"Yeah."

She waddled off to return a few minutes later with his coffee.

"I have a question," he said before she could leave. "Do you remember this girl?" He pointed to his clipping he had placed on the table.

She looked at him and snorted. Then she picked up the picture. If she was squinting, he couldn't tell.

"This is from the *Bild*," she said.

"Yes."

She looked at Dannaks again.

"I believe she used to work here," he said.

"Maybe."

"Her name's Meryem Turan. Does that ring any bells?"

"Aren't you the detective on that stage?"

Dannaks smiled wearily. "You're right on one count. I am a detective, but not that one. Yeah, I look like him, but I'm afraid I'm not that lucky."

"I thought he was sacked."

"Was he?" He looked her in where he thought her eyes should be. "Do you remember her? She may have left abruptly, over two years ago now."

She looked at the photograph again.

"I remember she just stopped coming." She handed him the photograph. "But whether that's her or not, I don't know. You could ask Britta."

"Britta?"

"She's doing your flan. I'll send her out."

"Thanks."

Before his flan was ready six bikers arrived. They were dressed like Hell's Angels: heavy boots, black leather, silver decoration, skulls and cross bones, eagles, lizards and snakes.

Thankfully they decided to occupy the other corner. They placed their helmets on one of the circular shelves.

Britta and the oversized dwarf appeared. The latter went to the newcomers armed with a pen and pad. The former approached Dannaks with a plate.

Britta was younger than the dwarf who would be in her forties, but she was equally formidable in her own way. How old she was, he couldn't but hazard a guess. She was attractive in a brutal manner. Her nose and thick lips were pierced and the rims of her ears from lobe all the way round to the top were studded with earrings. Her hair was unnaturally jet-black and her eyes an amazing pastel blue. Her black leather buttoned-up waistcoat not only bunched her breasts, it showed that her belly button was pierced too. As a young girl she would have been pretty, but life had toughened her.

"You want to ask me something?" she said, placing the plate with the flan before him.

"Yes." Her eye-catching tattoo put him in a quandary. On the one hand he wanted to look at the butterfly and on the other he didn't want to be caught staring at her breasts. The butterfly looked strangely elongated and was perhaps adorned. She didn't appear old enough to have sagging breasts. "Do you remember this girl?" He gave her the clipping. "Her name's Meryem Turan. She worked here two and a half years ago or so."

"Yeah. Meryem worked here. But I'm not sure that's her. It's a long time ago, you know. And we have a high staff turnaround here."

"So you don't recognise her?"

"We were only together a couple of weeks. I'd just started, you know. Then she just stopped coming." She handed back the photograph as the dwarf, who was as tall as this girl, appeared. There was cooking to be done. "I'd have to see her in the flesh to know."

He held up the clipping. "Have a closer look."

"She said she doesn't know," said the dwarf.

"Sorry," said Britta. "I guess if it says it's her, why shouldn't it be?"

Dannaks nodded and the women left.

More bikers arrived as he ate his flan. Two took bar stools and a loner went to a table.

The coffee was so strong he felt his heart pound. But the flan was good.

13.23

By the time he paid the dwarf and grabbed his jacket to leave it had grown quite loud with about twenty bikers in the place.

At the door he pocketed a business card.

As he clambered down the steps he heard a side door open. He decided to move to the pavement leading away from that side of the building. There he looked back and saw Britta leaning against the wall at the top of some steps lighting up.

He walked back to her. She watched him nonchalantly indulging her cigarette.

"Taking five?" he asked, looking up from the bottom of the steps.

"More like two," she said exhaling with evident relief.

"Did anything else occur to you after we spoke?" This often happened. Things would come to a witness after an interview.

"Not really. I'd have thought Katja would have helped you."

"Who?" he said shaken.

"Katja," she said, perplexed by his reaction and nodding back into the building. "The Dumpling. You know?"

"Oh," he managed. "Yes."

"She owns the place. Or her husband does."

"She said she didn't remember."

"We have a high staff turnaround here," she said, evidently no recalling that she had said the same inside. She drew on her cigarette.

Dannaks nodded but didn't leave.

"It's not important," she began distantly, "but..."

"Even the trivial stuff can be important."

"I did think it strange that she left when she did."

"What do you mean?"

"If you're going to leave you'd leave after pay day, wouldn't you?"

"She didn't phone in, then?"

"Nothing. From one day to the next she simply didn't turn up. I thought she'd found something better. That's not difficult. I mean something better than this. Landing it is the difficult part." She took another pull on her cigarette and exhaled.

"You didn't bother to check up on her?"

She made to speak but a coughing fit took her. Her breasts quivered, the butterfly fluttered, and he looked at his shoes.

"Like I said," she began in a dried-up voice. "I only just started. If anybody should have checked, it should have been the Dumpling." She pinched something from the tip of her tongue. "But they have this instant dismissal policy here, you know. Sounds posh, don't it? It means if you don't turn up for work and you haven't cleared it, then you're fired."

"You didn't think it strange that she didn't come in to claim the money she'd worked for?"

"It was strange. But no, I didn't think about it."

"So she was forgotten."

"Until the *Bull* – police turned up – oh, I don't know – maybe a year later looking for her." She had been about to say the *Bullen*. In Germany the police were called bulls rather than pigs. "By then I'd almost forgotten about her. Apparently she'd stopped paying her rent and they had to break in. We didn't know anything. It's as if she was abducted. You know aliens, X-File style."

"Anything else?"

"Not really. This place has a high staff turnaround, you know." He did. "I'm one of the longest standing ones. I should get a medal. You have to put up with a lot, you know. And I'm talking about the customers as well as the work." Dannaks watched her take a long drag on her cigarette. "The pretty ones don't last. It doesn't matter how well you cook, you've still got to bring it out to them."

A dark girl Dannaks had not seen opened the door and popped her head out. "Britta?" The sounds of cooking told him that this door opened directly onto the kitchen.

"Yeah."

"You're needed," she said, glancing coyly at Dannaks before disappearing.

Britta took a last drag, dropped the stub and ground it into the step with her shoe. "She's been here a week. I'll give her another." She opened the door and went in ignoring Dannaks's thanks.

He wasn't sure what she had meant by her last statement. Was the new girl going to get the sack? Or would she fold under the pressure? He was glad he didn't ask for he suspected he'd heard the answer a few times during their conversation. For some reason, perhaps because of the Americanism of the place, the phrase "go belly up" came to mind.

13:49

Dannaks went to Patel's when he got back to the centre.

"Don't you have a job to go to?" asked Patel.

"Not at the moment."

The shopkeeper was astounded, but Dannaks didn't elaborate.

In less than five minutes he checked his emails – there were none – and logged off. He took the opportunity to rummage through the special offers, but couldn't muster the enthusiasm to cook, so he bought a microwave meal that was two days away from its sell-by date.

Plodding back to his flat he knew that he had exhausted all his options. There was nowhere to go.

The Dumpling hadn't really looked at the photograph, but without authorisation he couldn't formally interview her. And Turan's alibi needed checking. But again, without authorisation he was powerless.

It was only Monday. A full week lay ahead of him and he couldn't think what to do with himself.

In the ground floor corridor of his building he unlocked his post box to discover two pieces of junk mail and a plain hand written envelope. He didn't recognise the handwriting and there was no sender's address. The postmark showed that it was posted in Hamburg on Saturday. It felt as if it contained a card. Rather than open it there he dropped it in his bag with the packet meal.

He grew excited as he climbed the stairs and pulled his keys out before he reached his floor. Not only was he eager to open the envelope he wanted to get inside before *Frau* Schumann could catch him.

In the kitchen he examined the envelope again. For his eagerness had given way to a sense of dread. He turned it over looking for further clues, but didn't find any. Then, with a utility knife, he sliced it open. Inside was indeed a card. It was plain white with a small teddy bear holding a handkerchief to an eye, the English word "Sorry" written in italics underneath.

He felt better as he opened the card to read the contents. The handwriting was what he would call bubbly: all loops and rounded letters. The letter K at the bottom jumped out at him. He

354

registered the small x after the letter too. But it was tiny and its size tightened his stomach. Then he read the message from the top. *"Dear D, I am sorry that I reacted so strangely on Wednesday. My only explanation is that I was emotional about meeting you. Yes, I do care about you. But I believe that we are different people. My gut feeling tells me that it cannot work between us. And I don't want to get involved only to be disappointed again. I'm not ready for that. It's nothing to do with you. I think you're a wonderful person. Try to understand. I am just not ready, yet. Sorry. Love, K x."*

Rereading the letter gave him nothing more. Except that he snagged on the word "yet" in the last sentence. He hung on to it. Did it mean later?

He put it back in the envelope and calmly flicked the kettle on for a tea. Carefully he put away his purchases.

He looked at the postmark again.

The kettle boiled and he made himself a mug of tea, which he took into the lounge.

The colourful flowers were looking a little sorry for themselves, but they had another day or two left in them. Dannaks put the mug down on the coffee table and opened a window. He took the *Krug* to the sink and lifted out the flowers, tipped away the water, opened the bin and dropped the dripping bouquet in. Then he washed the beer *Krug* with scalding water. He burnt his hands before he adjusted the temperature of the water. After drying his hands on a tea towel he snatched up the letter and took it into the lounge.

On the sofa he read the card again. If he was hoping to glean more substance he was disappointed. He realised that his initial reaction was shock. That was why he was so calm. Now anger began to bubble inside. How dare she talk about her gut feeling. How could she possibly know that it would end badly? If she wanted a pause, then he was willing to wait. She had given him no choice. He couldn't reply. Was he being judged on that single night in bed? He'd told her it had been a long time and that he was out of practice.

He sipped his tea.

She'd sent him a silly card with a bear on it. Sorry. He hoped that she was sorry. Ha, she didn't have the gumption to tell him to his face. He thought she was made of sterner stuff. Evidently not. Well, damn you, Kay.

He got up and put on one of his favourite Stones album's "Some girls", only to switch it off when "Miss you" immediately started playing. He exchanged the CD for "Tattoo you".

Her loss, he thought to himself.

And jerked his head to "Start me up."

15:33

The CD was finished and he was content with the silence.

He sat on the sofa with his third cup of tea looking about the room for inspiration. He had thought of looking at his notepad, to see what he could do tomorrow, but he'd had enough. His books of puzzles didn't inspire him. And he didn't have the energy for a walk. As a last resort he turned on the television and searched the channels, eventually settling on an old film he suspected he had seen.

He was suddenly very hungry but it wasn't the right time for a meal. He searched his kitchen and came across a tin of salted cashew nuts that he peeled open. In the lounge his whisky collection beckoned.

At four o'clock he could hold out no longer and poured himself a glass, saying to himself that he'd have one and then eat. He then convinced himself that a second glass wouldn't hurt and poured another.

Dannaks sat there staring into nothingness. He looked into his glass, tipping it this way and that to admire the slickness of the amber liquid. He rolled a swig in his mouth, savouring its taste, explosion of vapours and thinning viscosity. Then something happened that took him completely by surprise. He was so shocked he had no time to fight it. Curiosity told him not to fight it. It said let it take its course. It wanted out and needed to be out. Yes, he felt wretched, but oddly happy.

He didn't need to go to the mirror to know that his face was broken. Hot tears rolled unhindered down his cheeks. He blubbered. The sound was pathetic and his tenuous happiness dissipated. Immediately it did he felt sorry for himself. This was something he didn't want to feel. Yet, he welcomed the release. A tear met his lips and he tasted its salt. Crying seawater. And he saw the beach and heard the crash of the sea. He brushed away the tears, although there were still more within him. He tried to stave them off with an awkward smile. But he wasn't strong enough and the tears sprung anew. He cursed and brusquely swiped at them.

Steeling himself he picked up his glass and took a hefty gulp that almost had him spluttering. He sat back, tipping his head to look up at the ceiling. Then he closed his eyes and welcomed the sanctuary of exhaustion.

Length-wise his sofa comfortably seated two and could take three at a pinch, so to lie down he had to adopt something approximating a foetal position. Closing his eyes on the world he promptly fell asleep.

The ringing of his telephone ripped him back to misery. He jumped up, hitting his shin against the coffee table. So he was rubbing his leg as he scrambled for the receiver, which he then almost dropped.

"Yeah?" he said. He'd missed the caller's name.

"Dannaks?" It was a male voice.

"Yeah?"

"Are you okay?" It was Frank.

He stopped rubbing his knee and tried to massage his face awake. His cheeks felt strangely soft and puffy.

"You're not drunk, are you?"

"No. No. I'm fine." His assertion was met with silence. "Really. I was, er, asleep. Sorry. Frank."

"I've got some good news."

Dannaks pulled down his brow attentively. "Yes."

"The Turks have requested our assistance. More specifically they've asked for you to look into Meryem's background." He paused. "I don't have to tell you that the heads aren't overjoyed... I'm not particularly happy about it either. REX has suffered enough... Dannaks?"

"Yes. I'm still here."

"You can start tomorrow."

"Am I alone on this?"

"Essentially yes. But you can have support. Reupke was spoken to but he's snowed under and I got the impression he wasn't interested. You can have Reinhart part-time if you want."

"Yes. Great." Part-time wasn't great, but it was better than nothing.

"See you tomorrow, then?"

"Yes."

"And Dannaks..."

"Yes?"

"It's good to have you back."

"Dannaks," he said to the uniform on duty behind the Perspex. Of course they recognised one another, but nonetheless the man had to check his list before buzzing him through. Dannaks's expression nipped any remarks on recent events in the bud.

After Frank's call he had endeavoured to sober himself up. In the kitchen he had thoroughly washed the Krug and then filled it with cold water, which he forced himself to drink in one go. He didn't make it. About two thirds down he felt nauseous and had to take a break. Only if Frank had called an hour or so earlier, he thought, he wouldn't have been in this state. After drinking the remains of the water he felt too full to eat. So he went for a brisk early evening walk.

It was a torturous poignant walk. Lovers and friends were laughing and enjoying the remains of the day. The Alster was a pleasure to view in the softening light. Parts of it sparkled so intensely that he had to wince and look away. Everything said rejoice. But he was too fuddled to connect.

Outside his flat door, still feeling cloudy, but now quite hungry, *Frau* Schumann accosted him. Her door opened just as he was about to push his key in. The jingle of his keys must have alerted her. Unless she had a chair parked behind her door and she periodically got up to look through the peephole or watched for the hall light to go on, he had no explanation for her uncanny timing. In any case, there was certainly nothing wrong with the old woman's hearing.

"Oh, *Kommissar*, I'm glad I caught you." He had long given up telling her that he was an *Oberkommissar*. "Do you – Oh, you don't look well. Have you been eating properly?"

"Yes, I'm fine. I'm just tired."

"Oh, it's this weather. It takes it out of you." She didn't pause long enough for him to react. "Now. Do you remember me telling you about that leak in the washing machine?" There was a shared washroom in the cellar. She didn't wait for a reply. "Well, I told *Herr* Wolter about it and to date he's done nothing." *Herr* Wolter was the caretaker. "He promised to have a look last

Thursday. But I don't think he did. I really–"

"Maybe I should take a look?"

"Haven't you noticed? I really can't understand why he hasn't bothered. A bad leak could flood the cellar. Think of the damage, then."

"I'll take a look."

"You should talk to him. I get the impression he doesn't listen to me."

"I'll have a look. Maybe something's just come loose."

"Well, if you could that would be good. Although I don't see why you should do it. He should sort it out. It's his job, after all. But I thought you being a policeman and all you could talk to him."

Dannaks wanted to say: "Arrest him perhaps?" but he didn't want to prolong the conversation. It had gone on long enough and the theme hadn't changed.

"I want to use it on... now let me see... what day is it today? Monday. Yes, Wednesday," she said and he made a mental note not to do his laundry then.

"I'll look at it tomorrow. I, er, I'm sorry, but I'm expecting a phone call." He hadn't used that excuse in a long time.

Safely in his flat he had filled up the *Krug* with water and drank half.

He couldn't be bothered cooking properly and micro waved the packet meal he had bought. He had others, but they had some time before their sell-by date.

He ate in front of the television and finished the remains of the water in the *Krug*.

Despite his efforts at getting himself together he didn't feel good. This was probably because he had slept badly. He had lights-off by ten, but at about one he had to get up to relieve himself. Around three he woke up again. This time his mind began to tick over. A terrible thought occurred to him and his mind relentlessly began exploring the consequences. At about five he mercifully fell asleep. His alarm jolted him into sluggish consciousness at six thirty.

"*Moin, moin,*" said Reinhart, looking up from the file on his desk.

"Morning," Dannaks returned, as he slipped off his jacket to hang it up.

"Good to see you. But, er, if you don't mind me saying so, you don't look too good."

"Couldn't sleep."

Reinhart nodded. He tapped the file he was reading. "I've almost finished reading your report. So I'm up to date."

"You're not, I'm afraid," he said sitting at his desk and opening a drawer.

"Oh?"

Dannaks smiled, putting his "to do" sheet on his blotter.

"In your time off?" he asked, incredulously.

His smile remained but his eyes became weary. The expression said that he was tired, and he was tired of Reinhart asking such a question because he should know him by now.

Reinhart adjusted his tie.

Dannaks was taking out a pen when Frank knocked on the open door to announce his arrival. He then came in and Dannaks stood to shake his hand. Reinhart took his sitting down.

"Come and get your things," he said. "Give me five. Reinhart you come too. We could do a quick briefing." He looked at Dannaks. "If that's okay with you?" Dannaks nodded and Frank wheeled about and left.

"I'd better get a coffee, then," said Dannaks.

"I'm not going to get this finished in time."

Five minutes later they were sitting in Frank's office.

Dannaks's holstered Heckler and Koch P 2000, his keys, brass tab and identity card lay together on Frank's desk.

"So," said Frank, leaning back in his chair. "Where do you want to take this?" He was really asking what the case was going to cost in time and money.

"I'd like to put a new light on what's known so far," said Dannaks. Frank prompted him with raised eyebrows. "We've been asked to look into Meryem's past." Frank nodded. "Do you know why?"

Frank was irked by the question and Reinhart spoke. "Because she may not be who she says she is."

"Correct."

"Dannaks, what is all this?" asked Frank. "Cut the cryptic crap."

"Sorry, but you see, I don't believe she killed Matthias."

"She confessed," said Reinhart.

Frank nodded.

"Yes. She confessed. But there are too many inconsistencies. There's the brutality, the lack of motive – him being a neo-Nazi is flimsy – they were lovers according to Peter's – Matthias's journal–"

"We've read your report," said Frank.

"Then there's the kid's Beelzebub drawing and the handy photo."

"What photo?" This had not appeared in his report.

Dannaks explained. He concluded by saying: "That's the real reason the Turks want to find out who she is."

"Are you saying they think she's innocent?"

"Officially no. The confession has been accepted. But they're suspicious."

"How do you know?"

"Because I'm in contact with one of the investigating team."

"And he's told you that they don't believe her?"

"No. As far as I can gather the investigation has been wrapped up. But he and at least one of his superiors are suspicious and that's why they've asked for our help."

"So the Turks are no longer investigating, but we should?"

Dannaks nodded.

"They've got budgets too," said Reinhart.

Frank ignored him. "Does anyone else know this?"

"I doubt it," said Dannaks. "But there's more–"

"So we're tying up their loose ends."

"Courtesy."

"Okay. What were you going to say? About there being something more."

"I don't think Matthias was the intended victim."

"What?" As if spring-loaded Frank shot forward on his chair. Reinhart's jaw dropped in astonishment.

"I think Meryem – or whoever she is – was the target."

Frank's brow furrowed.

"It's just a gut feeling." Frank looked sceptical. "I met her. I admit that it's possible that Matthias was the target and she had a hand in his murder. But she didn't do it. Someone else was involved."

"So she had an accomplice?"

"Maybe. But I read Matthias's journal. I really can't believe that she wanted to kill him. Before it happened he wrote that she wanted to run away with him. There's–"

"Okay," said Frank. "Let's say she was the intended victim. What's the motive?"

"I don't know, yet. But it's in her past. I, er, did some investigating in my free time."

Frank shook his head in disbelief. "Go on."

Dannaks brought them up to date as briefly as possible.

"I'm impressed," said Frank. "When I spoke to you yesterday it sounded as if you'd spent your time sozzled and feeling sorry for yourself."

"But after all that," said Reinhart, "you still don't know who she is."

Dannaks smiled. "Meryem says she's Meryem. Her parents say she's not. Poschmann said it's her. Turan says it's not. And the Barbados staff didn't know. Take your pick."

"Why would she just up and leave?" asked Frank.

Dannaks shrugged.

"The same reason she hid after Matthias's murder," said Reinhart.

"And what was that?" asked Dannaks irritably.

"She was afraid."

"Afraid of the real killer," said Dannaks, his face brightening.

"With all those police about?" said Frank.

Dannaks nodded slowly.

"Let's cut this short," said Frank, glancing at his watch. "It's all speculation. So, square one, where do you want to take this?"

"The first port of call has to be *Personenfahnder* (Missing Persons)," said Dannaks. "They probably interviewed everyone I did. Maybe they've something more. At some point I'd like to contact Ismail. He's my contact over there. But that's when we've got something. Maybe he has something himself? Otherwise that's it."

"So we're talking a day or two?"

"Yes."

"Okay, do it," said Frank.

The two men rose. Dannaks reached for his belongings. "Stay behind a minute," said Frank. Reinhart left. "Sit down." He waited before continuing. "I suspect you got this Ismail chap to ask for you. It doesn't matter. I know for a fact that the upper echelons are not happy with you getting this job. It's only the Turkish insistence that wangled it for you. Suffice to say the Gods are not only watching; they're waiting. Waiting for you to slip up. And when and if you do, they'll bury you forever."

"Drama was never your style, Frank. I'm surprised."

"I'm just warning you."

"Thanks. But I've been here before."

10:14

"What do you want me to do?" asked Reinhart.

"I want you to interview one of the guests."

"Okay." He had a pen at the ready.

"Her first name is Katja." This was the terrible thought that had kept him awake. It had never occurred to him to suspect her, but she had dropped him pretty smartly. He had no illusions about his looks, but unlike Dagmar, it could be said that she picked him up. Of course, this was the stuff of films and novels, but...

The Turkish officers had interviewed the guests and groups could corroborate their whereabouts at the time of Matthias's death. But singles could easily have slipped away during the show. He could think of no motive, but that could lie in her past. After all, what did he really know about her?

"Surname?"

"I don't know. She returned to Hamburg last Monday."

"There may be more than one."

"She travelled alone and is about five years younger than me."

"It's that girl in the paper, isn't it?"

Dannaks hesitated. "Yes."

"You suspect her?"

"Why not? She readily befriended me–"

"Yes, I can see that's suspicious," Reinhart chuckled.

"And here she dropped me just as quickly," he said, instantly swiping the smile off his colleague's face.

"What do you want to know?" said Reinhart soberly. If asked whether he was chasing her for private reasons, Dannaks would not have been able to give an honest answer. He wasn't sure.

"Her whereabouts at the time of the murder."

"You didn't ask?"

"Yes, of course I did. I need an impartial assessment." As he recalled he hadn't asked. She had volunteered the information.

Reinhart nodded. "You don't think she'll tie this to you,

then?"

"Tell her it's routine and that we're questioning all the guests again. Say that maybe something got lost in translation, that sort of thing."

"That should keep me going," he said. "I've got REX stuff too. Any starting points?"

"Try Leidner at *Zeugenschutz* or Reupke, you know. They might have the guest list. Start with Leidner. And, er, ask for the entire list. We may need it."

If Reinhart suspected an ulterior motive then he was prudent enough to keep it to himself.

"Is EWO back on line?"

"Yes."

He made a note to check it for Meryem Turan. "I'm going to contact *Personenfahnder*. By the way, did anything come out of Matthias's second autopsy?"

The question caught Reinhart off guard. "Er, no. No, nothing."

Dannaks spent the next half an hour consulting his notepad and listing prompts for questions he had for *Personenfahnder*. He also pulled a new paper file and filled it with the notes he had made at home, the Barbados card and Timi's number on the Azure Skies note paper.

He waited for Reinhart to finish his call. Leidner had the list and had explained were to find it on file. Reinhart got up and left for the computer room. The team shared two terminals located down the corridor in a storage room next to the photocopier. They still referred to it as the computer room.

Dannaks went through central.

"Hamburg Police, *Personenfahnder*, Kraft."

"Dannaks, *Soko* REX."

"Hallo, colleague, what can I do for you?"

"I need everything you've got on a Meryem Turan."

Within the police departments non-sensitive information was exchanged without formality. "The case is about two and a half years old."

"Everything?"

"I've a list of questions."

"How long is this going to take?"

"Ten minutes?"

"Okay, I have a meeting in a half an hour." In Dannaks's book five minutes usually meant five minutes or less. Ten minutes could mean up to half an hour. Kraft apparently possessed a similar book. "Just let me pull up the file."

"Thanks."

"Turan, right?"

"Yes."

Dannaks waited.

"Okay, got it. Fire away."

"What's the status of the case?"

"Open, but inactive."

"What does that mean?"

"Yeah." Dannaks imagined he was smiling. "Okay, listen. She was over eighteen. So she was classed as an adult. To all intents and purposes adults can do what they want. For them we have three criteria, which we use to decide whether or not to open a file and investigate. The first is that the person has dropped out of his or her accustomed circle. The second is that their current whereabouts are unknown. And the third is that the person is in some danger. Because of her background we decided that she could be in some danger. You know about her background?"

"*Frauenhaus*?"

"Yes. Okay. We opened a case. I see here that her social worker disagreed."

"What do you mean?"

"She didn't think Meryem was in any danger." Dannaks took note.

"We looked into it anyway. In my experience battered women remain spooked for the rest of their lives. They often disappear. Or they get caught by their men folk and disappear. Either way they disappear. In this case the social worker turned out to be right. We had the missing woman's husband and he was happy to be rid of her. His relatives were indifferent too. Oh, it says they were divorced." Dannaks heard him mumbling as he read. "Yeah. That's about it. After we established that she wasn't in any immediate danger we more or less dropped it."

"So you didn't find out where she went."

"No." He sighed, reluctant to explain, but realised that he must. "Look we get over two thousand missing persons reports a year. Sometimes it's as many as two thousand five hundred. Two thirds are adults. We solve half of what we get within a week. Within a month our quota is eighty percent. But twenty percent take longer – if ever. They go to the BKA, who put it on Interpol."

"Where it stays open?"

"For up to thirty years."

"I understand. So her husband's alibi checked out?"

"Yep. Local police interviewed him and the hotel staff." Dannaks didn't bother saying that he could have sent somebody to harass her.

"Does it say anything in there about her picking cotton in her youth?"

"What?" He sighed again. "Look, we dig deep, but maybe not that deep. You think it has something to do with her disappearance?"

"I don't know. Is there anything there?"

Dannaks waited again.

"No."

"Okay. What about the date of her disappearance?"

"That's a tough one. We can't be one hundred percent sure. If you count the day she didn't turn up for work–"

"The Barbados in Billstedt?"

"Right." He gave Dannaks time to jot down the dates. "She worked on Friday and didn't turn upon the Monday. That's about the best we can do. The owner at Barbados said that she had booked a three-week holiday. But that wasn't due to start until a week later. The neighbours weren't very helpful. By the time we questioned them she'd been gone for more than a year." Dannaks knew that witness statements were notoriously unreliable, none more so than when nothing extraordinary had occurred. Routine played tricks on memory. "Some reported seeing her as late as six months after she didn't turn up for work. One neighbour said that she had gone on holiday, to Turkey, and that she hadn't seen her since. She seemed to know her well. Her statement coincides approximately with the time she didn't turn up for work."

"What was her name?"

"*Frau* Mohr." He wrote it down.

"What was the name of the caretaker you interviewed?"

"Huber."

"Okay." He circled *Frau* Mohr's name.

"And her social worker?"

"Poschmann."

"And she said that Meryem was in no danger?"

"That's right."

"But you checked anyway," he said absently. He was looking at his list.

"You might find something in the POLAS (*Polizei Auskunftssystem* – Police Information system) archives."

"I'll look," he said. "How could her hus– ex-husband have known about her whereabouts?"

"That's easy. She went to a *Frauenhaus*, right." Dannaks answered with a hum. "Well, they charge rent."

"You're joking."

"No."

"I never knew that. I thought the state supported them."

"It does. But only up to a point. And it's not enough. So these women – and let's face it some of them only have the clothes they're wearing – have to find a job sharpish. And that usually means registering locally. To receive social service money they have to register too."

"And once they're registered their whereabouts are known."

"Correct. Then it doesn't take much to find them." He paused to let Dannaks digest this information. "The *Frauenhaus* have a period of leniency of course. But it's a ploy to ensure a high turnaround." He smiled as he heard Britta's voice in his mind. "Not many stay more than a few weeks."

"What about next of kin?"

Reinhart came into the room.

"The parents were contacted," said Kraft. "Turan gave us their address in Turkey. The Turks came back saying her parents hadn't seen her and weren't bothered about seeing her."

"Why?"

"Because she had shamed them." He didn't need to explain. Her parents had rejected her because she was a divorced woman. The relationship to a daughter invariably depended upon the religious fervour of the family. The less zealous the more cherished.

"Okay. Who notified the police?"

"The housing management and a bank. Do you want the names and numbers of the contact persons?"

"Yes." Dannaks wrote down the details.

"Anything else?"

"Is there more?"

"Not really."

"Thanks for your help. I may come back to you."

"I was afraid you might say that."

Dannaks hung up. He looked down at his notes, considering whether to add anything. Then he looked at Reinhart questioningly.

The position of his tie said that they were nearing midday. Because Reinhart was right-handed and forever adjusting his tie without the aid of a mirror the knot tightened as the day progressed. His tie didn't noticeably lengthen, but it was nearly always askew to the left. Like a sundial Dannaks reckoned he could tell the time of day from the position of Reinhart's tie. Of course a visit to the toilet often returned him to zero hour.

"I've got a meeting with her at her workplace at two." He must have called her from the telephone in the computer room. Typically he wanted to keep his evening free. "She was a bit wary. Worried that I might be a reporter."

Dannaks knew that she worked for a shipping company. At the moment he didn't want to know any more. "Reinhart," he began. "I don't want her to know I'm involved. I'm not sure whether I said anything about REX; so don't mention it. And you don't know me. Be discreet."

His colleague nodded.

"You want this?" asked Dannaks pointing to the telephone.

"No."

Dannaks debated fetching a cup of coffee but then picked up the hand piece and entered the housing management number. "Dannaks, *Kripo* Hamburg," he said when a woman answered. He often omitted to mention REX. To do so invariably required a tedious explanation. He asked for *Herr* Walther and was told that he was out of house and expected back late in the afternoon, if at all. Could she take a message? Dannaks gave her his name and number.

He then tapped in the number of the bank employee. A woman answered.

"I'd like to speak to *Herr* Kloth," he said after he rattled off his introduction.

"Oh, he's not on this number any more. I'll transfer you."

Piped music began to test his patience. Thankfully it didn't last long.

"Dr. Kloth's office," said the woman's voice. So he was a

doctor, not a mister. "My name is Böll. How can I be of assistance?"

"Dannaks, *Kripo* Hamburg. I'd like to speak to Dr. Kloth."

"May I ask what it's in connection with?"

Dannaks explained.

"Oh, I think that would probably have gone to central."

This was turning into a real paper chase and he wished he had fetched a coffee after all.

"I'd like to speak to him, anyway."

"I'll see if he's available."

The piped music caused him to groan. Again it was mercifully short.

"I'll connect you now."

"Thank you," he said, but she had already severed the connection.

"Dr. Kloth."

Dannaks introduced himself and explained.

"*Oberkommissar* Dannaks, I'm not at liberty to give you any confidential information over the telephone."

"My questions are of a general nature and would save me a trip."

"Okay."

"Can you tell me whether you're still looking for her?"

"No. We resolved the situation."

"What do you mean?"

"We cut our financial losses and wrote her off. Are the police still looking for her?"

"How did you resolve the situation?"

He didn't answer straight away. Perhaps he was miffed that his question had been ignored. "Well, you didn't locate any next of kin, or if you did they weren't interested in the girl's stuff. So a social worker, responsible for some *Frauenhaus*, laid claim to the belongings. We came to an agreement and she purchased them at a premium. We split the remaining financial damage with housing management."

"Can you tell me the name of the social worker?"

"Surely you have that?"

"Was it a *Frau* Poschmann?"

"Yes."

"Thank you *Herr Doktor*, you've been very helpful."

"If you do find her, we'd be interested. Our losses were written off, but..."

"I'll do that."

17:37

After speaking to Dr. Kloth he had called Poschmann. Her name had come up too often. Unfortunately she was out and not due back for the rest of the day. He didn't bother leaving a message. He then logged on in the computer room and checked the POLAS archives for anything Kraft may have omitted telling him. He found the original missing person's appeal that had been posted and sent to every north German police station. He read it carefully, but didn't learn anything new.

He checked EWO too. But he didn't learn anything that he didn't already know.

Reinhart left and didn't return to the office.

Dannaks got hold of the number for *Frau* Mohr, the witness who appeared to have been best acquainted with Meryem. She still lived at the same address. He called her and she said naturally she remembered Meryem. He then asked her whether she had been following the case of the murdered boy in Turkey. More importantly, had she seen the picture of the girl who had been arrested in the connection with the killing? She said no. He hesitated before arranging to visit her at her flat.

He alighted at *Trabrennbahn*. A sense of déjà vu took him. But of course he'd been last Thursday.

Coming down the steps of the station he recognised a figure riding the upward travelling escalator.

"*Herr* Huber," he said, stopping and moving closer to escalator to allow people to pass.

The old man looked over angrily, as if outraged at having his thoughts interrupted.

"Dannaks," he said, to jog the old man's memory. "*Oberkommissar* Dannaks."

"Hallo," he said. His expression remained unchanged. Then he looked away in the direction he was travelling. Perhaps he didn't remember.

Huber was now going past Dannaks's position. Dannaks about-faced and climbed the steps. Huber noticed his change in direction, but chose to ignore him. Dannaks met him at the top of the escalator.

"Do you remember me?"

Huber nodded, moving out of the way of the stream of passengers heading towards the platform.

"I'd like to ask you something more about the girl who went missing. You remember, Meryem Turan."

"Yes," he snapped impatiently. "I don't want to miss my train."

"You won't."

"What do you want?"

"Do you have a master key for the post boxes?"

"Of course. Ever since Turan disappeared, bloody housing management said I have to watch for any build up of post."

"You opened Meryem Turan's box for the police."

"Yes." An approaching train distracted him.

"Do you remember what was in it?"

"Junk mail, letters from housing management and warnings from the bank."

"Anything personal?"

"Not that I remember." The train was stopping. "I thought you lot took all that stuff."

"We probably did." Dannaks had forgotten to ask Kraft about her post.

"This is my train," he said. Dannaks nodded and Huber stepped away. In afterthought he turned. "I told you her type bring trouble." Then he was striding towards the open doors of the train.

The doors closed and Dannaks watched him pass by.

He was preoccupied all the way to *Frau* Mohr's flat.

The old woman answered within a few seconds of him pressing her bell. The intercom crackled and he announced himself. She said: "All the way up." The door buzzed and he pushed it open. He climbed to the very top, passing Meryem's floor.

Like the Polish woman's below, the door was opened on its chain. A small face resembling an oversized albino bat squirming at the old lady's chin distracted him. "Stop it Oskar," she said, holding the thing lower.

He whipped out his identification card. "*Oberkommissar* Dannaks. We spoke on the phone *Frau* Mohr."

She squinted at his card and he held it closer.

Then she closed the door, took off the chain and reopened it.

"Come in."

She closed the door behind him, sliding the chain back in its slot.

He noticed the shoe rack and saw that she was in slippers.

"Shall I take off my shoes?"

"Oh no." She was a small woman, stocky and yet, frail. She had alert blue eyes and a pleasant face. Her hair was white. In her youth she would have been a real beauty. Considering the weather she was overdressed in a heavy skirt, thick stockings, buttoned-up white blouse and limp cardigan with a large brooch in the shape of a parrot. Her manner appeared easy and trusting and Dannaks liked her.

She noticed him looking at her dog. "This is Oskar," she said proudly. At the sound of his name he began yapping and fidgeting. It was no larger than a kitten, with a bat-like face, large pointed ears, snappy fangs and swollen orbs rather than eyes. Most appallingly it appeared hairless, as if newborn. And thus indeed it was *Frau* Mohr's cherished baby. Dannaks thought it an abomination. A real dog would bark. "I'm going to put him down. Don't be alarmed, he'll probably fuss, but he'll settle down after a while."

He braced himself as she set the thing down.

The thing yapped at him, but didn't approach. It moved uncertainly forward, ran round its owner's feet, came closer, ran back, looked up at him then to her, her to him, him to her, its tail whipping about and all the while running frenetically getting ever closer to him.

"Shall I take your jacket?"

"No. I'll keep it on if that's okay."

"We should sit down," she said, gesturing to a door standing ajar behind him.

He turned and entered the lounge.

Huber had been right. The flats were good.

Despite the wall-to-wall carpeting Mohr had put down thick rugs. The wall units and shelving were old-fashioned teak affairs. Visible wall space was reduced to strips between framed photographs and pictures. Ornaments and knickknacks covered every surface. There was only one recent picture of her holding a tiny baby. The others showed her at various stages in her life. There were many pictures of a boy becoming a young man, then with a

372

girl, and with the same girl and a baby between them. She had surrounded herself with memories.

She pointed to a chair and he sat.

"Can I offer you anything? A drink?"

"No thank you. I'll try not to keep you too long." Oskar quietly sniffed at his shoes and trouser leg.

"Oh please, stay a while. I don't get many visitors nowadays."

Frau Mohr sat on the ancient but hardwearing sofa with the patterned tasselled throw.

"You wanted to show me something?"

"Yes." He leaned forward and took out his clipping.

She too leaned forward and picked up her glasses from the coffee table before taking the clipping.

"Is this Meryem?"

"Oh dear, it's not a good photograph, is it?"

"No, I suppose not."

She made a humming sound as she concentrated on the picture. "If I didn't know any better I'd say it was her friend. Now what was her name?"

"Are you saying it's not Meryem?"

"Well, they did look similar. I always said they could be sisters... But this is all a couple of years ago now. She went on holiday around our nine-eleven."

"She probably wasn't here in 2001," said Dannaks, thinking that maybe she was senile.

She stared at him, her eyes magnified to the rims of her glasses. "Oh, I don't mean those planes and the world trade centre and whatnot. I'm talking about our very own nine-eleven."

"I'm sorry. I'm not following you. Your nine-eleven."

"The murder of course." Seeing his reaction she continued. "Our nine-eleven. I mean, not a lot of people can boast of a murder in their house. Actually, it was a double murder."

He was flabbergasted.

"Can you, er, tell me about it?"

"I can do better than that. I kept a scrapbook." She got up and the dog raced over to her.

"I think I might have that drink now, if I may?"

"Of course. What would you like?" She glanced at a wall and he followed her gaze to a photograph of a baby that was in fact an ornate clock. She saw him looking. "About this time I usually have a little plum wine with my tea."

"That'll do me fine."

"I'll get my scrapbook."

Whilst she was out of the room, Oskar traipsing after her, he remembered that Huber had mentioned Meryem disappearing a year after the murder. But of course he had meant that they had discovered her absence a year later. He didn't know when she had actually disappeared.

Poschmann too had talked of two flats allocated to them. That meant two women from the *Frauenhäuser*.

He remembered Fehime's shoulders sagging as she cast her eyes to the table. "She said history repeats itself."

Frau Mohr returned with a fat book, the thick pages buckled within the cardboard covers. She had it open and was searching for something. Oskar followed her. He looked at Dannaks, his tongue out, eyes excited. And Dannaks wondered whether he was reflecting his expression for he had to restrain himself from jumping up and snatching the scrapbook out of the old lady's hand.

"Ah, yes. Here we are. Shaziye was her name. A lovely girl. Quite shy."

"May I?" He leaned forward his arm outstretched.

She looked up as if just noticing him.

"Yes," she said snapping it shut. "Yes, of course." He took it from her and didn't hear her say that she would go and make some tea.

The cover was a watercolour depiction of some countryside-farming scene. Somebody – probably *Frau* Mohr – had ruined the picture by writing 'The murder' in black marker pen across the pastel sky.

The inside cover was blank and the first page had a cutting from a Monday edition of *The Bild*. The article had taken several columns and these had been cut to fit on the page. A single picture dominated the top half of the page. Taken outside the house, it showed a body being moved on a wheeled-stretcher into an ambulance. The headlines read 'Double murder'. Dannaks skimmed the text, locking onto keywords. For this was an initial report and information was skimpy. Nonetheless the journalist had padded out over many columns. The victims, Michael T. and Shaziye A., had been living together. Witnesses said they saw a stocky man fleeing at about the time of the killings. A man was helping police with their enquiries.

He turned the page and found more of the same from other papers.

Dannaks vaguely remembered reading about it.

Cuttings from subsequent days added more detail. The picture with the same stretcher being wheeled to the ambulance was enhanced with passport-like photographs of a girl who he knew to be Meryem but whose name was Shaziye A. embedded in the right hand corner, alongside which was her boyfriend Michael T. There were no eyewitnesses, but almost everyone in the house heard the screams. The victims had been beaten and strangled. Who had been beaten and who strangled was unclear. An unnamed witness said he'd seen a man leaving the scene covered in blood. Another had seen a man running down the paved area to a car.

Frau Mohr came into the room carrying a tray with a teapot, two cups on saucers with teaspoons, a sugar bowl with yet another teaspoon dug into the sugar, a tea plate of sugar encrusted biscuits and a small jug of milk.

Oskar trotted in after her and beat her to the sofa, hopping onto his place.

Dannaks rose to help her. He didn't remember asking for tea.

"Sit down," she ordered. "I may be old, but I'm not an invalid." He moved some magazines for her to set down the tray on the coffee table. "Thank you." Then she went over to a glass cabinet and fetched two small glasses and a purple-blue bottle. All the time he had the scrapbook open to the small passport photograph of Meryem.

He watched her pour out two glasses of plum wine. She handed him his glass.

"*Zum Wohl* (to your health)," she said and he reciprocated.

The liquid was pleasant but far too sweet for his palate. He was hungry, but the dainty biscuits looked terribly sweet. They weren't so much dusted as laden with sugar.

"What do you think?" she asked.

"Very nice."

"I mean my scrapbook."

"It's a Godsend." He held it over to her and tapped the photograph of Shaziye. "I know her as Meryem."

"Oh no, that's Shaziye."

"Have you a photograph of Sha– I mean Meryem?"

375

She seemed bewildered for a moment. "No."

He nodded and smiled.

Holding the top of the china teapot she poured two cups of tea. "Earl Grey," she said.

They sipped their drinks in silence.

"*Hauptkommissar*," she began. He was itching to get back to the scrapbook, which he had balanced on the thick armrest of his armchair, and didn't bother correcting her. A promotion was a welcome change from a demotion. "Are you telling me that Shaziye is still alive?"

"To be honest *Frau* Mohr, I'm not sure what I'm saying. But the girl in my clipping looks like her, don't you think?"

"Let me have another look."

"I don't suppose you know whether she had a twin?"

"Oh, I wouldn't know that." She was scrutinising his clipping and he moved the scrapbook on his lap. She rose and came to the side of his chair. Oskar followed, jumping up onto the armrest the other side of Dannaks, panting and looking with wide-eyed eagerness at the book and the humans as if expecting them at any moment to explain what was so interesting. Holding the clipping next to the passport photograph she said: "It must be her twin or a sister."

He nodded. She smelt of flowers.

"I mean Shaziye is dead. Her boyfriend too. And her husband is sitting in Santa Fu."

"I haven't got there yet."

She reached over and turned the page. Despite her age she still had something. He noticed the border where her makeup finished and her neck began, just below her ear.

He read that Shaziye had run away from her brutal husband, Mahmut A. He had tracked her down and killed her and Michael T. He had been apprehended two and a half hours after the killing on the A24 to Berlin.

Dannaks wasn't comfortable with *Frau* Mohr hovering one side of him, Oskar sitting on the armrest the other side. He turned the page and was relieved when she returned to the sofa and her tea. Oskar jumped down and resumed his place beside her.

She offered him the plate of biscuits and he took one, thinking it couldn't be sweeter than the plum wine. He was wrong. In fact there was so much sugar it soaked up the saliva in his mouth and he had to crunch it down. His tongue found caches of the stuff nestled between his gums and cheeks. These biscuits undoubtedly kept dentists in pocket.

Further details emerged over the next few days.

It appeared that things had been turned over in the flat: drawers emptied, cupboards opened, books, papers, etc., scattered. The police were quoted as saying that Mahmut A. had tried to make it look like a robbery.

Dannaks looked up at the sound of *Frau* Mohr returning her cup to her saucer. She smiled and he returned a short smile. "Sorry," he said.

"Please, take your time."

Mahmut A. had been returning to his Kreuzberg home. He denied having anything to do with the killings.

With the turning of each page the evidence against Mahmut A. mounted. An ordinary dinner fork became crucial in the case against him. And suddenly he confessed to killing her and her lover. She had shamed him and his family. An honour killing, then.

Michael T. was a former employee of Mahmut A. The latter worked in the family business. Shaziye had fled to a *Frauenhaus* in Hamburg. Michael T. had followed almost half a year later. There was speculation about the delay. Perhaps Michael T. didn't want to arouse suspicion.

The next report was a week later.

Shaziye was an import bride.

Then there were pages that were sellotaped down one side, because the articles covered both sides of the glossy paper. They were taken from *Der Spiegel* and *Stern*, who had done features on foreigners in Germany with a focus on the Turkish population.

"There's a lot here," Dannaks said. He had skipped swathes of text, but reached the last page.

"Oh, take your time," she said. She was sitting stiffly on the edge of the sofa, her teacup and saucer poised before her. Oskar was observing him with his big, uncomprehending eyes.

"Actually I was wondering whether you'd let me borrow it." She paled and he did too. "I'd like to read it tonight." She seemed terribly disappointed. "I – I'd give you a receipt." He felt as if he had truly let her down, as if he no longer enjoyed an elevated status and had dropped down into the pack. "If you'd rather not, then, er, maybe you could–"

377

"No, it's okay. Take it." But there was resignation in her voice. Had she wanted him to spend the entire evening with her? It was possible. Apart from Oskar, the panting bat-face, she probably had little company. "But I would like a receipt, if that's okay?"

"Of course," he said. "Have you a piece of paper?" He felt his notepad would be too insignificant.

She got up, went to a drawer and came to him with a pen and paper and a magazine to lean on. He tried to look into her eyes but she wouldn't let him have them.

To re-establish the connection, and perhaps compensate her with more of his time, Dannaks spent a good ten minutes on the receipt and tried to involve her in the wording. But the game rapidly dropped into tedium and he quickly came to an end. He knew he had been spurned.

20:14

On the train journey home he had resisted the temptation of reading the scrapbook. Except for some boisterous young bloods talking loudly in Turkish the train was quiet. They were larking, bubbling and falling over themselves. He found it interesting, that despite their German upbringing – he heard them speak perfect German at one point – they were culturally different nonetheless. Oh, youth made them loud and full of themselves. They didn't know how fleeting youth was and, even if they had thought about unemployment, they saw only an exciting and apparently endless future ahead of them. Age and responsibility would quieten them. Had they been German youths, they would have been aware of their loudness, aware of breaking some unspoken rule of reservation. This, in itself, would not necessarily have stopped them. But in public spaces most loud voices spoke a foreign language or German in a foreign accent.

In his flat he scoured the scrapbook, absorbing every detail and noting keywords on a sheet of paper.

Dannaks closed it a little over an hour later and sat staring at his notes. A proper drink was tempting. He had drunk tea with his peanut butter sandwiches. After all that sugar, he had needed something savoury.

He had learned little more and now had questions the scrapbook could not answer.

He needed to contact Reupke, who would have access to the murder files. Perhaps he had worked on the case. He wanted a

378

second opinion and no one else was qualified. More than anything else he wanted to share. He searched for and found the scrap of paper upon which Steffi had written their private telephone number.

She picked up. "Hallo?"

"Dannaks."

"Oh hi."

"Do you always greet people anonymously?" he asked. It was customary for caller and recipient/receiver to announce themselves by surname.

"It's safer." Did she mean she had something to fear? Or was it related to Reupke's line of work? He wasn't sure what she meant, but let it go. "How are you?"

"Fine."

"You were suspended?"

"Yes, but I'm back on the job. They didn't have anything on me."

"Have you met your girlfriend? What was her name?"

He really didn't want to engage in the chitchat and certainly not talk about Katja, but he had no choice. "Katja," he said. "She's fine. We're just taking a break until all the publicity blows over."

"I thought it had blown over. You're back at work–"

"There was the break-in at Herbst's place."

"Oh yes. So when are you seeing her again?"

"I don't know." He couldn't keep the irritation from his voice.

"Sorry," she said.

"No, I'm sorry."

"You've broken up, haven't you?"

He was stumped and couldn't answer.

"Dannaks? It's none of my business, but don't let it get you down." How well did she know him? "Appreciate it for what it was. At the time it was great, but it wasn't to be... That's life. You've got to move on. "

His face was on fire. He issued a meek: "We're just taking a break." Later he would wonder whether she could be that astute. Maybe Reupke had said something about it being a holiday romance and that it wouldn't last.

"I'm sure you didn't call to speak to me," she said. He was being let off the hook. "Take care."

"You too," he muttered. He heard her muffled voice under the covered mouthpiece. He felt sure she said more than "Dannaks for you" but he couldn't make it out. Had she told Reupke of Katja? And then was it a plea for him to be sympathetic?

He braced himself as the hand piece was given to Reupke.

"Dannaks," he began. "This is a surprise."

"Yes. It's important, though." He spoke hard and curtly, as if he was Reupke's superior. He explained that he was officially investigating Meryem and had just interviewed an old lady who had pointed him in the direction of a murder that occurred in the block in which Meryem had lived. Other than the date and place he didn't give Reupke any details.

"I need to look at the case file."

"No problem. Come by tomorrow. I'm sure I can find a few minutes for a colleague. We can look at it together."

"I think we'll need more than a few minutes."

"I can leave you with the file."

"I'd like you in on it."

"Dannaks, I really haven't the time. I've got this pub brawl from Saturday night–"

"I'd like to look at it now."

Reupke didn't say anything and Dannaks gave him some space before speaking into the silence. "It is important. I need you to see something."

Reupke sighed. "Don't you have a social life?"

In the background Dannaks heard Steffi reprimand him. He didn't hear what she said, but it was enough for Reupke to cover the mouthpiece and answer her. They had an abrupt terse conversation before Reupke came back on. "Okay. I'll meet you there in half an hour."

"Thanks–" But Reupke had already hung up.

21:09

The taxi dropped him off at the barrier a few metres in from the roadside. Dannaks wasn't comfortable with the expense of a taxi, but he wouldn't have made it in time otherwise.

He showed his ID card to the uniform on duty and walked on to the building. There were a few lights on. He passed by the security area and used his card to push through the turnstile.

The *Mordkommission* had their offices on the third floor and took up a complete wing.

Dannaks rode the lift and moved round the ends of the wings until he reached the right one. The area was only accessible to authorised personnel and Dannaks's card wouldn't get him through the door. He then realised that he didn't have Reupke's number. He'd have to return to the entrance and get the duty officer to call. For lack of a better idea he knocked and waited.

For a moment he heard nothing. Then Reupke opened the door. Seeing his expression Dannaks decided against smiling.

"Thanks for doing this," he said to Reupke's back. He had not waited for Dannaks to enter.

"I've pulled the file already." He waved to his right. It was a sort of dismissive wave, one that you'd use to shoo a fly. "Interview room one." He was going elsewhere. "I'm getting my coffee," he explained in a matter-of-fact way.

Dannaks went into the room alone, dismissing the fact that he had not been offered a drink.

The room contained a sturdy four-legged table and four chairs. Set high in the wall opposite the door was a frosted glass window. High in the right hand corner was a camera. There was nothing on the beige walls, not even a one-way mirror.

On the table was a paper folder, thick with what appeared to be loose papers.

Dannaks sat down, slipping his plastic bag onto the chair next to him.

When Reupke entered he realised he had forced him to sit opposite. "So, what's this all about?" He seemed happier with a cup in his hand. He sat and slid the file to himself and placed a hand on it, as if only a good explanation would remove his guard. Evidently he hadn't opened it.

"I'd like to see the photos of the dead girl."

Reupke waited a tick, then lifted his hand and shoved the file towards Dannaks. "Be my guest."

Dannaks ignored him and opened the file. He quickly skipped the introductory sheets, the investigating team, the references to computer files and physical evidence. Few papers were actually loose. They were thematically bunched with staples or paper clips. He saw the artists drawing of the flat and the two bodies in the lounge. He passed over pages of witness statements and came to one of two large envelopes, stapled to which was the standard pathologist's form filled out with the date and time, pathologist's name, his assistant and anyone else present at the autopsy. He put aside the one marked Michael Tidau and opened the other, noting the name of the lead detective, *Hauptkommissar* Hofmann. He slid the A4 autopsy photographs onto his palm and went through them on the table. Only when he'd seen them all did he go back and pick out a full facial.

Reupke sipped his coffee. He looked as if he was about to erupt.

Dannaks turned and pulled out the scrapbook from the plastic bag.

Reupke raised his eyebrows at the sight of it. Still he held his tongue.

Dannaks found the good portrait photograph of Shaziye and looked from the autopsy photograph to the newspaper cutting and back. He did this, looking from one to the other, until Reupke interrupted him.

"Dannaks," he said, placing his cup on the table to free his hand to deliver a blow or blows if necessary. "This is–"

Dannaks spun the scrapbook round to Reupke. "What's the name of the victim?"

"I'm in no mood for games."

"What's her name?"

Reupke looked at the cutting. "Shaziye A., but she looks..."

"Like Meryem."

Reupke nodded without taking his eyes off the picture.

"Now look at this." He passed him the full facial. Reupke stared at the photograph. "Tell me it's not the same girl." Dannaks knew the autopsy photograph showed a similar looking girl, but they were not the same. It was difficult to tell, because her eyes were closed, her face not only bereft of make-up, but also white with the pallor of death, lifeless. "Sisters, maybe," said Dannaks.

"Just be quiet a minute," said Reupke irritably. Dannaks watched him read the name on the envelope: Shaziye Aksoy. "I..."

Eventually Dannaks began to speak. "You could argue that it's an old photo and people change. But not that quickly."

Reupke ignored him and turned a covering page to check the names of the investigating detectives. Then he picked up the envelope marked Michael Tidau. "Let's see if he's the same."

Dannaks got up as Reupke rifled the photos for a suitable facial. By the time he found one Dannaks was peering over his shoulder. It was the sight of the preliminary photos, the ones showing the body how it had been received, that made him whistle.

The face looked as if it had been battered to a pulp. Without doubt the report would speak of multiple fractures to the cheek and jaw. The right eye had disappeared behind the eyelid which was ballooned and closed and resembled a walnut. Teeth were missing, lips swollen and split. Only his forehead appeared unscathed.

Reupke nodded in acknowledgement. "The killer really went at him."

They made the comparison in silence, both coming to the same conclusion. At least one victim had been correctly identified.

"His parents identified him," said Reupke, locating the appropriate form. "Death by asphyxiation," he added.

"Who identified her?" asked Dannaks.

Reupke went back to the file and found the right form. "Her GP. A Dr. Kilic." He turned awkwardly to look up at Dannaks with an expression that said he didn't like him hovering behind him.

Rather than return to his seat Dannaks took the one next to Reupke.

"That's Meryem, right?" he said pointing to the scrapbook.

His colleague nodded, but appeared elsewhere. "This is a serious error," he said. "I can't understand how it wasn't seen."

"Maybe it was – by someone – and they just thought the papers had made a mistake. It was an open and shut case. I mean, how many people actually saw the victim? They are similar too."

"This was a *Schlot* (factory chimney stack) Hofmann case. It would have been one of his last ones too. He went on sick leave not long afterwards and never came back. Lung cancer. It took him this year. January, I think." Dannaks was silent and Reupke turned back to the cover sheet. "Two-Packs Thiel worked with him. That's no surprise. They were the West team." He glanced at Dannaks. "I don't have to explain, do I?"

Dannaks huffed and shook his head. West was obviously their favoured brand of cigarette. Although Dannaks knew the teams comprised five persons he remained quiet.

"If you meet Thiel, don't let him hear you call him Two-Packs. He struggled to give up during his partner's absence. When *Schlot* died he stopped. As far as I know he's not had another since. He's an irritable bastard, though." Reupke picked up his cup and sipped. When he put it down he said: "You want one?"

"Tea, if you've got it."

Reupke regarded him as if he was surprised by the answer.

They got up and the younger man pointed to the book. "Is this yours?"

"No. It belongs to someone who lives in the murder building."

Leaving the room Reupke led him to a utility room that amongst other things contained kitchen surface and cupboards and a sink. Two kettles and two double filter-coffee makers were available. Reupke filled the kettle with enough water for a cup or so and confirmed that Dannaks had asked for tea. He opened an overhead cupboard to display the tea on offer. Dannaks chose green with lemon. After popping the tea bag into a mug they began to wait for the kettle to boil. "So how does it feel to be back on the job?"

"I never really left."

"I don't get you."

Dannaks explained his activities whilst out of work.

21:46

"Let me get this straight," began Reupke, when Dannaks finished. The kettle had boiled, the tea bag yo-yoed and disposed of and they were making their way back to the interrogation room. "You paid for a hire car and for an Internet search. Why—"

"And I just paid for a taxi."

Reupke was stunned but he managed to complete his question. "Why didn't you use EWO?"

"I was out of a job."

"But you could have got someone—"

"EWO was down, remember?"

"Yes. Yes, that's true." They were at the room, the case file spread over the table. "You know Dannaks, I can't help feeling that you need a hobby." This made a change from saying he needed a girlfriend. Then maybe Reupke had meant that, but under the circumstances couldn't say it.

"This is it," said Dannaks.

"You're a victim," Reupke smiled, shaking his head in disbelief. "You really are."

Dannaks wasn't sure exactly what he meant but assumed it was *Mordkommission*-speak for loser. Maybe he was a loser. If that was what it meant. For he'd been the conscientious one on their assignment. And it wasn't him who'd jumped the fence at Herbst's place. Yet, it was he who'd caught the flak in Hamburg, he who'd been suspended. And Reupke had been right about his relationship not making it beyond the holiday romance stage.

After re-seating themselves, Reupke sipping his coffee, Dannaks began to examine all the photographs. His tea was too hot to drink.

"So, what are we looking for, boss?" asked Reupke.

"I don't know. Anything."

"I find it better to go through COMVOR for an overview." *(Computergestützte Vorgangsbearbeitung* – The computer supported transaction processing was used as a general documentation tool. To say its implementation had teething problems would be an understatement. It took more than a decade to put together, springing all envisaged budgets. And when it was installed it was ripe for an immediate overhaul.)

"I prefer hard copy," said Dannaks. "You can spread everything out." And, as if to emphasise his last statement, he separated the file into piles. "Besides, I got my overview from the scrapbook." After he'd finished laying the papers out he said: "It all fits, though. Peter wrote that she had been married and lived in Berlin. He also said she knew Hamburg."

"So, who's the dead girl?"

"Meryem. The real Meryem. Shaziye's neighbour."

"This was her secret. Her name's Meryem but she's dead."

Dannaks ignored him. "I'd like to go through the killings and then Mahmut's background."

"Dannaks," he began, a mixture of weariness and amusement on his face. "We know that the girl the Turks have is probably Shaziye and not Meryem. How that happened, I don't know. But for me the sixty-four million dollar question is why this Mahmut guy said he killed his wife when it's not her. Have you an answer?"

"I've two."

Reupke didn't hide his astonishment.

"The first is that he thought it was her–"

"Oh come–"

"Yes, it is unlikely. But possible nonetheless."

Reupke shook his head but acquiesced. "Okay, let's go for poor eyesight."

"The second is a little harder to explain." He looked at Reupke for a moment. "It's shame. As I see it this was an honour killing–"

"He killed his wife's lover."

"Yes, but he was out to kill them both. She left first. Michael followed months later. Perhaps he wasn't really her lover at the beginning. Perhaps they had an affair. Otherwise they would have run away together. I don't know. I think Mahmut was out to kill them both. I don't know why, but he killed Meryem instead of Shaziye. He was caught pretty quickly. He probably decided to say he had killed Shaziye to save face. We know her GP identified her. That's a loose end."

"There seems to be a lot of those, if you ask me."

"There's only one. How could the identities be mistaken?"

"What about how did Mahmut find them? Where was Shaziye? I mean our Meryem. Where did she go? How did she get away?"

"She used Meryem's passport and ticket."

"She–"

"Look, the neighbour told me Meryem had booked a flight. If Shaziye took her passport identity then she almost certainly took her flight ticket. It was the perfect opportunity. The girls were friends. Both were from *Frauenhäuser*." Dannaks glanced at his watch. "Have a look at the scrapbook or COMVOR. I'd like to look through this lot."

Reupke sat back with the scrapbook propped up on his lap and against the edge of the table. He was through it within fifteen minutes and turned to the case file Dannaks was going through systematically.

Mahmut had entered the flat on a Sunday afternoon in June. How he gained access was unclear. Meryem – called Shaziye throughout the paperwork – could have opened the door. Dannaks couldn't imagine Shaziye or Michael voluntarily letting him in. He decided to refer to her as Meryem.

Nobody knew how long it took before the fight occurred. A blow to the jaw had incapacitated Meryem. Michael had stabbed Mahmut in the shoulder with a dinner fork. His blood and Michael's finger prints were found on the utensil, left at the scene. Puncture marks consistent with those of such a fork were found in Mahmut's shoulder.

Such an insignificant wound would not have hindered Mahmut. He was built like a body-builder. His jaw and crew cut made his head look square. His neck was almost equally as thick.

Michael was contrastingly slight, almost beanpole like. He had not stood a chance against the burly mechanic. Michael had worked at the same garage, Mahmut's father's business, but apparently he'd been something of a dog's body. He had helped with correspondence and communication with the German authorities, played driver, cleaned and polished the vehicles.

Mahmut had smashed Michael's face with his bare fists and finished him off by strangling him with such force that in addition to fracturing the hyoid bone, he had damaged the thyroid and cricoids' cartilages, the lining of the larynx, and badly bruised his neck muscles. The tip of boy's tongue, trapped between his teeth, had been bitten off.

After killing Michael he had returned to Meryem and snapped her neck with a sharp controlled twist of her head.

He then spent a few moments going through the flat. The investigating detectives speculated that he did this to make it look like a robbery gone wrong. Dannaks thought of a further reason. He was trying to find a clue to Shaziye's whereabouts.

Michael had been in some kind of overall at the time of his death and the bathroom photograph explained why. The photograph showed that the bathroom walls were being tiled. In a box on the floor Dannaks saw toothpaste and brushes, soaps, cosmetics and an electric shaver. Most important of all was a woman's hairbrush. It would have been the easiest thing to test for DNA and so prove that the dead girl was not the flat's occupant. But, of course, this had not been deemed necessary. She had already been identified. Albeit mistakenly.

What Dannaks had not confirmed was whether the victims, Meryem and Michael, were lovers and Shaziye was the neighbour. Shaziye and Michael had known one another, but maybe they had not had an affair. Then both victims had occupied the flat. He would have to ask *Frau* Mohr.

A neighbour, a Herr Zapf, had seen Mahmut on the stairs. This neighbour was so shocked at the sight of the man that he ran into his flat and locked the door. Zapf described Mahmut as looking crazed with blood on his face. Some children playing football on the paved area had seen him hastily get into a brown van. They remembered him because their ball had rolled his way and he had ignored their calls for him to kick it back.

At a service station on the A24 outside Berlin an off-duty police officer had seen him enter the toilets. His neck and T-shirt were flecked with blood and he was holding his shoulder. Dannaks surmised that he had cleaned up his face at some point. The officer called in and heard about the search for a thickset man driving a brown van. With the help of two garage assistants he apprehended and held the man until an alerted patrol arrived.

There was a photograph of the van; a Renault. A technician had noted that it was a repainted delivery van. Under the paint he could make out an unidentifiable logo and a word made up of the letters S-i-something-s-e-something-something. The information remained a spurious detail and because the case was solved it was not followed up.

Dannaks could tell by the way Reupke rummaged through the various piles that he had picked up the scent. Dannaks thought that the thrill of the chase may have taken longer for him to reach because solving murder was his bread and butter and therefore somewhat routine. And Dannaks still hadn't worked out whether Reupke was a Reinhart: a strictly nine-to-five man. Or like him, someone driven, someone with a passion for the job. Of course he was too much a sonny boy with a healthy personal life to be completely like him. Dannaks knew that he was an oddball. But he savoured his colleague's interest and felt a kinship for him.

"So," began Reupke, leaning back and stretching, then throwing himself forward with a reserve of energy, to pick up his coffee. "You think Peter just got in the way."

"I'd say so," said Dannaks. "And it fits in with what Fehime told me Meryem – Shaziye – said to her."

Reupke urged him on with a slight nod.

"She said M–"

"Let's call her Meryem out there. Just like Peter and Matthias."

Dannaks nodded and Reupke took the moment to finish his coffee.

"She said Meryem had once told her that history repeats itself or something like that."

"You didn't tell me."

"Didn't I? I thought I did."

They were quiet for a moment. Dannaks tried to remember telling Reupke of the statement.

"Of course," Reupke began despondently, "if this is true and Mahmut killed Meryem, the neighbour, rather than his wife, we've got a grievous miscarriage of justice." The consequences of his department having made a grave mistake were preoccupying him. Although it wasn't directly his fault, the mistake was a blow to the *Mordkommission*. And departments were very proud of their work. With any mistake the immediate consideration was *Schadenbegrenzen* (damage limitation). Added to this was the pressure on Dannaks not to show anything that could be interpreted as *Schadenfreude* (gloating).

This latter consideration compelled Dannaks to help with the former. "Have we?" He waited a beat before adding: "He still killed two people. There's proof enough here."

Mahmut was sitting in the *Justizvollzugsanstalt* (prison) Fühlsbüttel, better known as Santa Fu, on a life sentence of fifteen years.

"Yeah, well you never know with those lawyers, they could go for a mistrial."

"I hope you're joking," said Dannaks picking up his tea.

Reupke's expression said that he was not being funny.

"What about these green fibres?" Dannaks asked, holding up a *SpuSi* report. The technician stated that a lot of unidentified green fibres had been found strewn about the flat. His guess was mohair from an Angora pullover. But they had found no such item in the flat or with Mahmut. They had not been sent for analysis because of the lack of comparative material. As usual the state prosecution decided what was necessary to nail the perpetrator. And as always, there was a financial aspect to having evidence analysed. Technical analysis was therefore always prioritised and carried out when deemed necessary. The fibres had not been used in evidence and whether they were indeed mohair from an Angora pullover was anybody's guess.

"What about them?"

"Their source was never identified."

"Oh, come on Dannaks, you're acting like an amateur. Who knows how many people passed through that flat?"

"I was thinking that they could have come from a second killer."

Reupke was quiet. Obviously it was something he had not considered.

From his expression Dannaks knew that Reupke was simmering. Nevertheless, without disrupting the silence to search for the statement of the first officer at the scene, he pressed on. "And then there's the water in the corridor outside the flat." Drops and small puddles were found on the floor. By the time the technicians had arrived all but the largest puddle, no bigger than the palm of a hand, had shrivelled to a drop. Unlike the fibres it had been analysed and found to be ordinary water with traces of soap. "There's no explanation for it."

"Mahmut could have washed without drying himself before leaving."

"No. In Mahmut's confession he said he fled after the killing."

"He didn't admit to ransacking the flat, either."

Dannaks conceded with a slow nod.

There was no real proof that a second killer was involved. By all accounts Mahmut had been alone.

"Shall we pack up?" asked Reupke, although it wasn't really a question. Dannaks nodded. "What's your next move?"

"This has to go higher." He was tempted to add: "I'm afraid," but thought better of it. There was no way this could be hushed up. If heads had to roll, then so be it. "My brief was to investigate Meryem's past for the Turks. All this throws a completely new light on everything. Like you said they're going to want it wrapped up tightly. This kind of mistake is never pleasant. I'd like to show a photograph of the dead Meryem to some people. Her ex-husband, for one." He paused to pass Reupke a sheaf of papers. His colleague had taken the organisation of the file upon himself.

"I'll get you copies," he muttered.

"Thanks. I'd like to interview Mahmut too." He didn't give Reupke time to react. "But I know he's unlikely to see me." Criminals rarely had time for cops. More than anything else, it was considered bad form.

"Can you take the cups back?" said Reupke when the file was almost in one piece again. "I'll put this away."

Dannaks was washing the cups in the utility room when Reupke appeared. "You can leave that."

"I've done it now." Reupke seemed suddenly impatient to get home.

Dannaks hastily began drying one of the mugs with a tea towel and Reupke picked up the other one.

They were silent on the way to the lift. Yet, Dannaks struggled to think of something to say. Only when they got in and Reupke pressed E for the ground floor – he'd evidently parked in the visitor's car park rather than underground – did Reupke speak.

"No wonder the Meryem we know looked beaten. Being an import bride must be one of the worst fates a woman can suffer."

Dannaks wanted to comment that there were worst fates, but Reupke had said one of the worst fates. And of course it wouldn't do their strained relationship any good. "Yeah, I could tell you a few stories." He was too tired to do so and he knew Reupke didn't want to hear them.

Outside Reupke turned and they shook hands. "I go in the opposite direction," he said. "But I could give you a lift to the station."

"No, that's okay. I'll walk."

Wednesday
07:23

Dannaks was taking his jacket off when Reinhart entered with a sheaf of papers. He'd apparently been at the photocopier. No doubt running off another play. Dannaks's colleague was an amateur actor. This was the main reason for him being a strictly nine-to-five man. Although with Reinhart it was more like seven to four.

"You're early," said Reinhart, trying to hide his embarrassment.

"I couldn't sleep."

By the time he had arrived at his flat last night it was almost midnight. Although beat he was too excited to immediately go to bed and he felt he deserved a toddy. Vowing to only drink one glass of whisky he made it a hefty one. Standing at the window he had drunk it whilst viewing the dark panorama. He opened the window to let in the breeze and swish of the vehicles below.

At a quarter to one he was in bed with the light off. He slept almost immediately, but woke around three and fought to empty his mind. He wanted to be fresh at work. Close to five he fell asleep again only to wake at six fifteen or so, his mind active once again. He gave in and got up.

Seeing Reinhart he remembered Katja. He'd almost completely forgotten about his colleague interviewing her. In the light of what he now knew it was naturally rendered superfluous.

"How did the interview go?"

"Fine," said Reinhart, jamming the sheaf of papers in his briefcase and then sitting up. He began to peel his banana. "She seemed like a nice person." Reinhart saw that Dannaks wasn't fishing for approval. "She said she was at the show. Said that a family she sat next to could corroborate her presence there. That's it." Then, as was customary after an interview, he expressed his gut feeling. "I'd say she was telling the truth."

"I'd say so too," said Dannaks, using his notepad to make bullet points on a sheet of plain paper. He knew Reinhart was perplexed by his passing interest.

"Have you got something else for me?" he asked, biting off the top of his banana.

"Loads," said Dannaks. "But I have to talk to Frank first."

Frank arrived half an hour later. As usual he went into each office to greet everyone. Dannaks said he needed to talk and Frank asked for a quarter of an hour to get himself set up for the day.

Dannaks led the way into Frank's office. He was carrying his bullet point sheet and a plastic bag.

"Oh, you shouldn't have," Frank quipped on seeing the bag.

"I'm afraid I didn't," said Dannaks, taking the chair next to Reinhart.

Frank looked at the two men sitting opposite him, before focusing on Dannaks. Using his bullet point sheet Dannaks related all he had discovered.

When he finished Frank said: "Come on, then. Let's see this woman's scrapbook."

Dannaks lifted it out of the plastic bag and put it on the desk. Reinhart leaned forward as Frank turned the pages. Dannaks sat back relishing the pause.

"I vaguely remember this," said Frank.

"Me too," Reinhart added.

Frank leaned back and Reinhart gestured to the scrapbook that he had been viewing upside-down. Frank nodded and Reinhart picked it up and placed it on his lap. As he went through it Frank spoke. "I suppose you and Reupke are absolutely certain there's been a mix-up?" Dannaks nodded. "I'll speak to Weske. He'll want to meet. Who do we need in on this? Apart from the *Mordkommission*, of course."

"Yes, but who from the *Mordkommission*? I'd like Reupke as well." He refrained from asking for Two-Packs Thiel.

"We'll let them decide. But I'll mention him. Who else?"

"Sturm and – or – Leidner from *Zeugenschutz*. Reinhart." His colleague nodded absently. The scrapbook was absorbing.

"Somebody from the prosecution office?"

Dannaks watched Frank write a name and put it in brackets. Then he looked up from his list and Dannaks shrugged.

"Okay. I don't know when this is going to happen. What do you want to do?"

"Everything needs confirming. We've assumed that the neighbour was the victim. I'd like to get photographs of the dead girl to her ex-husband and her social worker."

Frank nodded: "Reinhart?"

"Sure," he said, looking up.

"I'd also like to interview Mahmut. He probably won't see me. But I'd like to try."

"Okay."

"And the GP who identified her needs to be talked to."

"He's in Berlin, isn't he?"

Dannaks nodded.

10:16

Frank popped his head into their office.

Dannaks and Reinhart looked up.

"Weske. The presidium. Eleven o'clock. We leave in five."

The two men nodded and tidied and locked their desks.

Dannaks had called Santa Fu requesting an interview with Mahmut. The prison official said he would ask and get back to him. If he accepted Dannaks could be talking to him tomorrow morning.

He had called Poschmann too, only to be told that she was out. This time he left his number and asked her to call him back.

Reinhart had occupied himself with REX work.

Frank returned. He was wearing one of the ties he kept in his office for just such occasions. Dannaks understood Frank, but he did not approve of such behaviour. Out here his boss dressed casually and was one of the troops. At the *Polizeistern* or at official meetings he put on a tie and sometimes donned a new shirt to become Frank the Leader.

They were at the door when the telephone rang. Frank nodded and Dannaks picked it up. "Kripo Hamburg. Dannaks." He waited but nobody spoke. "Hallo?" He wasn't sure whether he could hear breathing over the natural hiss of the line. "Hallo? Can you hear me?" He glanced at his colleagues. "I'm hanging up." He gave the caller a moment before putting the phone down. "Funny." When he was in uniform such calls were not unusual. But as a *Kripomann*, effectively removed from engaging with the public, such calls were rare.

The three men travelled by train. Frank didn't want to give up his parking space and joked that his car was in a side street so far away that it would be quicker for them to take the train.

Dannaks took the opportunity to broach the subject of travel expenses. He'd kept his train tickets and yesterday's taxi receipt too. He knew that all he had undertaken in his free time could not be authorised. And Frank said as much. Even last night's trip to the *Polizeistern* fell into this category. After all, he could have asked to make the trip during office hours.

When they alighted at Alsterdorf a light drizzle had begun. This was astounding because what they could see of the sky appeared cloudless. Dannaks folded over the top of the plastic bag with the scrapbook and wedged it under his armpit.

None of them carried an umbrella and when the drizzle became rain they increased their pace. The sky quickly became overcast and the rain became a downpour.

"The gardeners will be pleased," remarked Reinhart.

"I'm not a gardener," said Frank, setting the breathless pace.

They were soaked by the time they entered the building shortly before eleven. The three men took a lift to the third floor and went to the nearest toilet to dry themselves.

At two minutes to eleven they entered a conference room in the *Mordkommission* wing. At one end of the long desk, not unlike that of the conference room next to Iceman's office, papers and files, pens and in one case, spectacles, claimed seating places. Standing at the window were Weske, Sturm and a stranger. Near them stood another stranger and Reupke. Introductions accompanied the handshakes. The stranger positioned with Sturm and Weste was the head of the *Mordkommission*, Stapelfeld. The world-weary man with Reupke turned out to be Two-Packs Thiel. Hofmann, his partner, who'd led the Mahmut double murder, may have died of lung cancer but Two-Packs looked as if he was following his footsteps. His face was drawn and gaunt, his skin ashen. Dannaks thought that some of the corpses he may have seen could have looked more alive than him.

Weske was at the curved end – the head – of a long oval table. To his right sat Stapelfeld, Two-Packs and Reupke. Opposite them Sturm had seated himself. Frank took the place next to him and Dannaks and Reinhart took the neighbouring seats.

Weske leaned forward and picked up the pen on his pad of paper. "We've all got an idea what this is about, but I want everyone up to speed as soon as possible." He looked at Frank.

Frank nodded and looking directly at Weske said: "I think the best man for that is sitting next to me." Weske nodded slightly. Frank gave everyone a passing glance before settling on Dannaks.

Dannaks cleared his throat. Although he thought he might be called up to explain, he had not prepared. Naturally Frank was giving him the chance to redeem himself in the eyes of his superiors.

The crackling of the plastic bag embarrassed him as he pulled out the scrapbook and his paper file, including the bullet list he had used earlier.

He began by explaining the assignment he'd received yesterday. However, the moment he started to use names Weske interrupted him and asked him to briefly relate his earlier investigating. Dannaks hadn't intended to go into his private activities. Weske had probably got wind of them through Frank.

Dannaks tried to explain as casually as possible what he had done during his time off. The heads listened approvingly. He knew they would; it was his peers' eyes he avoided catching: for they would be both amazed and dulled. To his peers such work drew admiration and alienation. The latter was underpinned by the belief that Dannaks could only be arse licking. To them there was no other explanation. Only those that really knew him, Uwe, for instance, would know that nothing could be further from the truth. Dannaks wasn't interested in point winning. Nonetheless he did his best to play down his activities.

He concluded by talking of the victim mix-up. Two-Packs kept his head down.

"Shoddy work," said Weske, when Dannaks finished. For an instance he thought of joking that he'd done his best. But of course Weske was referring to the double homicide.

"I don't know," said Stapelfeld, in defence of his subordinate. He pointed to the scrapbook and Reupke leaned forward to take it from Dannaks. Meanwhile Stapelfeld opened the murder file.

The scrapbook, opened at the photograph of Shaziye, was pushed in front of Weske alongside the autopsy photograph of the murdered girl. Sturm, his heavy brow hard like granite and resembling a president in monument valley, leaned over to get a better look and Reinhart, furthest away, craned his neck before giving up.

Reupke slid some duplicate copies of the female victim to Dannaks who nodded his thanks.

"Very similar," said Stapelfeld. "I think you'll agree."

Weske nodded. "But not the same." He looked up. "Other than these crime photos have we a picture of this neighbour, Meryem?"

Frank said: "No."

Stapelfield piped up. "There was no reason to run any DNA checks. She'd been identified."

Weske raised his hand to silence him. "Let's get this all confirmed. And please, let's keep a lid on it. The Press don't need to know. When we know without doubt that the victim was the neighbour, I'll talk to the prosecution office. We can't afford any more mistakes. What about the other victim? Is he who he should be?"

"The boy's parents emigrated to Australia. They had to be contacted." Stapelfeld was spinning it out to emphasise the laborious machinations of the case. "They came back, identified him, and returned after his burial."

"Did they know the girl?"

Stapelfeld hesitated. It was a question he hadn't anticipated.

"No," said Two Packs.

Weske looked at Frank and Dannaks. "Speak to the Turks when you're sure the girl they've got is Shaziye."

"Shouldn't we dig deeper?" said Dannaks. "Sir."

"What do you mean?"

"If she was the intended victim, then the killer is still out there."

"Our task was to find out who she is. We've done that."

"Yes, but delivering a suspect has to be a matter of professional pride."

Weske couldn't help a wry smile.

"Give it a rest, Dannaks," said Stapelfeld.

Dannaks ignored him. "The killer could be in Turkey. Perhaps Mahmut hired him. Sir."

"Or not," said Weske.

"As you said, sir," said Stapelfeld. This was a true point-winning prelude. "Let's inform the Turks and let them take it from there."

"Sir, I believe the roots are here," said Dannaks agitatedly. "We've come this far. Why stop now?" As he asked the question the word budget popped into his mind.

"You've had your fifteen minutes, *Oberkommissar*," said Stapelfeld.

Frank made to speak, but a hand movement from Weske arrested him.

"Talk to the Turks. See what they have. As far as I know they've closed the case."

"We can't just stop. We must prove that she is innocent."

"Are you deaf? It's over." It was Two-Packs. "Get back in your kennel."

Dannaks flinched. The reference to kennel was to do with the name of their *Soko*. There was a popular television series about a police dog called *Kommissar* REX. "And you're–"

Frank grabbed his forearm and squeezed before he could continue.

"Arse-licking to boot," said Two-Packs. Obviously he felt he had nothing to lose.

Dannaks tore his arm free and jumped up.

"Stop this shit." Weske slapped his hand flat on the desk. The sound lingered in the ensuing silence.

At street level, amongst the uniforms, swearing was punctuation and as such relatively ineffectual background noise. Higher up the ranks it became less frequent. This made the use of even a relatively mild expletive quite effective.

Weske waited for the reverberations to completely subside. He stared Dannaks back into his seat. Then he looked at Frank. "I can see your man is passionate about this. And I do admire your diligence, *Oberkommissar*. Can we spare him?"

"We've been without him so long now; a few more days won't matter." Frank's humour was a relief to everyone except Two-Packs. Even Stapelfeld smiled, but it may have been for Weske's benefit.

"Okay Dannaks. You've got till the end of the week." That meant a further two working days. It wasn't enough, but Dannaks knew that he had no leeway. Weske then turned to Stapelfeld. "You get your house sorted. Put that GP who identified Shaziye under the magnifying glass."

12:36

Reinhart and Dannaks had lunch together in the ground floor canteen. Frank wanted to eat with an old colleague. Dannaks dropped calling Uwe because that would leave Reinhart alone. Reupke appeared a few minutes after them with Two-Packs and a third man. They chose a far table.

Reupke's allegiance had to be to the people with whom he worked.

"I'd say you successfully vindicated yourself back there," said Reinhart as they ate. "The people that matter appreciated your footwork."

Dannaks was silent. He didn't feel like talking. And he didn't feel vindicated. Two-Packs had soured any sense of personal victory.

"And you've got my admiration."

Dannaks smiled wearily. "Thanks Reinhart. But actually I feel kind of deflated." He suspected the feeling had deeper roots, something to do with Reupke perhaps, but by way of explanation he added: "Two days isn't much time."

"It's better than nothing. And I'm sure Frank will close an eye to anything I might do to help."

Dannaks nodded distantly. Maybe Reupke, like most of the others, thought he had engineered things to shine. But the footwork he'd undertaken in his free time was done because that was the kind of person he was. He wondered why it bothered him what Reupke thought.

They ate the rest of their meal in silence.

Frank entered with two ranking strangers as they left.

The rain had abated. There were no distinguishable clouds, but the sky was a light grey rather than blue.

During the train journey Dannaks asked Reinhart about his latest play. There existed an unspoken rule that gagged them from speaking about work in public. Reinhart and his wife were part of some theatre group. Like many of his plays this one was in English too.

At the office Dannaks checked with Schuppenhauer and Wulff whether there had been any calls. Their telephones were grouped and after five rings the call was flipped to the next office. Should the caller persist and the other office also empty the call would finally be transferred to Frank.

Somebody had called but had hung up without speaking.

In their office they filled out expense forms attaching their tickets. During this time a *Herr* Walther from housing management called. Dannaks thanked him for returning his call and kept the conversation short by saying that he no longer had any questions.

"Can you get a photograph of the dead girl to Turan?" said Dannaks. It wasn't really a question. "I can't see Frank authorising a trip to the Luneburger Heide. You can try, I suppose. You'll have to get the local police to show it to him. Then–"

The telephone interrupted him.

Reinhart picked up.

"Kripo Hamburg. Keller speaking... Hallo?" Dannaks and he exchanged glances. "Halloooo. I know you're there and I know you can hear me. This is not funny. I–" Reinhart took the handset from his ear and looked at the ear piece, as if he could see the caller. "They hung up on me."

They were silent for a long moment.

"Maybe you could go to the Barbados in Billstedt?" said Dannaks, handing him the business card from his file. "Get them to look at the photograph. Ask for Britta – " Reinhart noted the name "– and Katja." He looked up. "Another one. She's also known as the Dumpling."

"What?"

"Never mind." Then as an afterthought he said: "I can recommend the cheese and onion flan."

"My wife will have something for me at home."

"You're thinking of going today?"

"Why not?"

Dannaks shrugged.

Reinhart waited for more tasks.

"That should keep you going for now." He felt obliged to explain his intentions. "I'm waiting for a call from Santa Fu. If I don't hear from them within the hour I'll call. Then I want to get this scrapbook back to *Frau* Mohr." To claim the travel expense it was easier to make the trip during office hours.

Reinhart got up and left the room.

Dannaks left too and went to the toilet.

When he returned he heard the phone ringing whilst he was in the corridor. He dashed in and snatched it up.

"Kripo Hamburg. Dannaks." He swung the stand attached to the elbowed arm between their desks, upon which the telephone sat, his way and seated himself.

"*Justizvollzugsanstalt* Fühlsbüttel, here. My name's Pfohe. We spoke earlier about interviewing Mahmut Aksoy."

"Yes."

"I'm afraid the prisoner has declined."

"That's no surprise." He couldn't completely hide his disappointment.

After hanging up he crossed Mahmut's name off his list. He saw Poschmann's name again. The social worker had not returned his call.

He picked up the telephone to try to reach her but put it down when he saw Frank pass their open door.

"Frank?" he called.

He returned to the doorway.

"Santu Fu just called. The interview is a no go."

Frank entered the office and Dannaks glanced at his list.

"I'd, er, like to interview the Aksoy family. They're in Kreuzberg."

Frank raised his eyebrows. "I'm not sure I can justify the trip. What do you hope to learn? If he or his family have anything to do with this, they're hardly likely to co-operate, are they?"

"True. But I may get something. And in Spandau there's this kid who drew the red man. Remember?" Frank nodded but looked vague. "I'm convinced he saw the killer. He may know something. I could interview him too."

"Are we talking a day trip here?"

"It'll be a bit tight."

"So you want a hotel too?"

"If you can swing it. Otherwise I'll pay for it myself."

Frank chuckled. "You've really got the bit between your teeth."

Dannaks smiled.

"I'll do my best," Frank promised. "Have you phoned to see if they'll speak to you?"

"Not yet."

Reinhart returned.

"Do that first. Then I'll see what I can do."

The phone began ringing and Frank left.

Reinhart was seating himself, but the phone was on Dannaks's side of the table so he picked it up.

"Kripo Hamburg. Dannaks." Silence met his announcement. "Hallo."

"You," began a very small voice. Dannaks opened his mouth to speak, but the voice began again with a little more determination. "You must think I'm an idiot." The voice was breaking up with emotion. "I – I can't believe you'd do something like this. How could you?" Dannaks tried to speak but she continued. "You must think I was born yesterday." Her breathing grew heavy. "And you know what? You know what?"

"Kay," he said quietly, his eyes coming up to check on Reinhart. His colleague had his head down, but could be listening.

"Don't Kay me, Dannaks," she snapped. He didn't know what to say and eventually she continued. Her tone became reasonable. "Do you know what's tragic? I regretted breaking it off. I was beginning to think that maybe it could work." Her voice then took on a hard edge. "But this. Spying on me. Well–" She appeared lost for words. "Well, you can bloody well forget it." She slammed the phone down and Dannaks listened to the dead tone. After a long moment he replaced the receiver delicately onto its cradle.

She had chosen to call him at work to leave him no room to manoeuvre.

How could she have known he was behind Reinhart's interview? He had told his colleague to be discreet. But somewhere he had made a mistake.

"Reinhart," Dannaks began. "When you spoke to Katja yesterday, you didn't mention REX, did you?"

"No."

Dannaks nodded and thought long and hard. "Did you give her your card?"

"Well, yes." Handing over a business card at the end of an interview, in case the interviewee thought of anything pertinent, was standard procedure.

Dannaks shook his head sadly. Although REX wasn't mentioned on it, Katja could have put it together. "We've got the same phone number."

"Oh," said Reinhart. "Sorry." Dannaks looked away from his pained apologetic expression. He wasn't ready to accept his apology.

Dannaks looked down at his list, struggling to pick up the thread of what he was doing.

15:14

"*Kripo* Hamburg, Dannaks," he said. Then he explained that he had been involved in the Azure Skies murder and wanted to tie up some loose ends.

"I don't know," said Timi's mother.

Dannaks pressed on. "Your son drew a picture of a red man. I–"

"Oh, *Herr Kommissar*–" he refrained from correcting her for the demotion "– children have a vivid imagination. Timi draws blue men and–"

It never ceased to amaze him that many people could handle *Kommissar* and *Hauptkommissar*, but they had a blind spot for *Oberkommissar*.

"*Frau* Ruwolt, this is a murder investigation. I know that you didn't say anything to the Turkish police. And I can make this official and invite you to a Berlin station with solicitors and the entire rigmarole. Or we can do this comfortably."

"He's only four and a half for god's sake. What do you expect to get from him?"

"I'm not going to grill him. I just want to ask him a few questions."

"How long will this take?"

"Fifteen minutes – half an hour max."

He allowed her a moment's silence. "Okay. When?"

"I'll have to get back to you on that. Either tomorrow or Friday."

"He finishes Kindergarten at one, tomorrow. He'll be home from half past onwards. On Friday he's got a dental appointment at eight-thirty and he's not going to Kindergarten. I think we'll be back about nine-thirty."

"Thank you. I'll call you back."

He hung up and listened to the silence in the room. Reinhart had left for the day. He'd gone to Billstedt to interview Britta and the Dumpling.

Dannaks was still reeling from Katja's call and busied himself to keep his thoughts from spinning. After the call and talking to Reinhart he'd gone to the toilet to be alone. Then he went to the computer and wrote an email to Ismail, saying that he had important information and suggesting a Monday morning telephone conference. Half an hour later Ismail's reply agreeing to the conference was in his mailbox.

He now picked up the phone and called the Aksoy home. The number listed in the crime file was no longer in use and he had to go through directory enquiries.

An older man picked up and answered to the name of Aksoy.

"Yes," he said after Dannaks had introduced himself.

"I have some questions about your son." The man grunted in acknowledgement. "Could I come and talk to you about him?"

"Who?"

Had he not heard him? "Your son, Mahmut."

"He is in prison."

"I know. But I'd like to talk to you about him and Shaziye."

"She's dead."

This was becoming tedious. "I know. I'd like to talk to everyone who knew her: the immediate family and the workers in your garage."

"We don't want to talk."

Dannaks used the same bluff he had on Timi's mother. "*Herr* Aksoy, we can do this the hard way and bring you all in and interview you at the station."

The man was silent.

"Or we can keep this discreet and I'll visit you alone."

After a long moment the man said: "What is your name again?"

"*Oberkommissar* Dannaks. *Kriminal Polizei* Hamburg."

"Wait."

With an undignified clatter the man put the phone down. Dannaks could hear him far off talking to someone. He couldn't hear what was being said. Then the sound of footsteps grew. Dannaks braced himself as much for the clatter as the refusal.

"When?"

"Tomorrow or Friday. Can I get back to you?"

"Okay."

"Thanks I'll–" But the man had killed the connection.

Dannaks went to Frank's office and waited for him to finish a call.

"It's on," he said.

"Which one?"

"Both."

"Excellent. When do you want to go?"

"Tomorrow." He paused before posing his question. "I don't suppose there's any chance of a vehicle. This kid lives somewhere in Spandau."

Frank's expression was enough. Public transport it was. "Arrange it with Tanja. But you might want to check with Reupke first. I believe he's chasing that GP."

"Since I'm going anyway, I could talk to this GP."

"I don't think they'll like that."

"No. I suppose not." Departmental pride overrode the expense.

Dannaks turned on his heel and left. In the office he immediately called Reupke.

"I'm going on Friday," said Reupke, after Dannaks said that he was planning to travel tomorrow.

"Oh. When are you coming back?"

"Friday."

"Did you get a car?"

"Next you'll be asking me whether I'm travelling first class."

"We could travel back together, then."

"We could." Dannaks was beginning to think it was a bad idea. "But I haven't got an appointment. So I don't know when I'm returning." Dannaks was about to suggest that they forget the idea, when Reupke asked: "Which hotel are you staying at?"

"I don't know, yet."

"Phone me tonight."

Dannaks made a tea and put it on his desk. Then went to see the secretary.

REX was too small a group to have their own secretary, so they shared the station's *Schupo* chief's one. Frank wasn't happy with the arrangement because the woman gave her boss's work priority. For expedience he would have liked to take a lot of the formalities/bureaucracy into his own hands.

Dannaks climbed the stairs to the top floor. Irrespective of when you knocked on her door, you were always interrupting her.

Tanja was a compact woman with a hard reedy no-nonsense voice. In accordance with her demeanour her straw blonde hair was cut efficiently short.

They looked at the computer together. The timetable offered a train every half an hour on Thursday morning. Because he wasn't sure when he was interviewing they agreed that he should book the journey. She reminded him that hotel check-ins were traditionally between one and two. Then she gave him an account code for the booking and said she'd get back to him about the hotel.

At his desk he tentatively sipped his tea. Then he picked up the phone and called Timi Ruwolt's number. He spoke to *Frau* Ruwolt again and agreed to come between ten and eleven on Friday. He then called the Aksoys. The same old man picked up. They agreed upon a one o'clock meeting tomorrow afternoon. His third call was to *Frau* Mohr. She promptly answered and agreed to see him in an hour or so.

He then went to the computer room and was dismayed to see Wulff on one and a uniform on the other. Although the screens were allocated to REX, and the uniforms had their own, they could also use them. His colleague said he'd only be a moment and would tell him when the terminal was free.

He returned to his desk and looked down his list. He saw Poschmann's name yet again. He tapped in her number. The phone rang and rang, but he stubbornly held on, starting something of a list of questions for Timi and the Aksoys. Eventually a breathless man picked up.

"Yes," he gasped.

Dannaks introduced himself and said that he wanted to speak to *Frau* Poschmann.

"She's out."

"Do you know when she'll be back?"

"Just a minute." Muffled voices followed. He was talking to someone in the office. "Hallo?"

"I'm still here."

"She's on a long weekend. Back on Monday."

Wulff appeared at the door and signalled that the terminal was available. Dannaks nodded.

"Please leave a note on her desk. I think she has my number, but I'll give it to you anyway."

After hanging up he picked up his tea and rose to go to the computer room. The trill of the phone stopped him. Tanja summoned him to come and pick up his forms for Frank and him to sign. She had booked a three star hotel in Kreuzberg.

He sighed and went to the secretary's office. He collected the forms and took them to the utility room that was now empty, stopping on the way to pick up his mug of tea.

He made his bookings and after completing the forms in his office, dropping them with Frank and gesturing, because Frank was on the telephone, that he was leaving, he stood at his desk and picked up the plastic bag containing the scrapbook. Deciding to take one last look he opened it on his desk. He remained standing and turned the pages. He knew the contents practically by heart and he also knew that he should leave. Yet, he had an inkling he may have missed something. Part of him was reluctant to give it up.

He didn't spot anything new and a quarter of an hour later he left. He didn't cross the paved area to the main station. Instead he took a detour and walked to Patel's where he made three unusual purchases.

At *Frau* Mohr's door he was disturbed that he had to identify himself again. Oskar seemed genuinely pleased to see him. Even his stupid slavering enthusiasm seemed endearing.

Frau Mohr led him into the lounge. She had prepared tea. They assumed the places they had occupied yesterday.

He pulled the scrapbook out of one of the plastic bags he carried. "It was a great help. By way of a thank you I bought you something." He then handed her one of his purchases from his second plastic bag. The bottle-shaped brown paper wrapping gave the game away. But *Frau* Mohr appeared delighted as she read the plum wine label. "Oskar shouldn't go short," he then said taking out the smallest package.

Before opening it *Frau* Mohr waved it under Oskar's nose. He panted wide-eyed with insentient fervour. The old lady carefully removed the paper. The hard oatmeal bone was set on cardboard behind clear moulded plastic. "Oh what a treat. Look what the nice man has brought you." She again waved it under his nose. "He'll get this later." As she folded the wrapping, undoubtedly for reuse, she asked whether he would like some tea.

19:18

Dannaks ate a microwaved frozen pizza in front of the seven o'clock national news. There was nothing outstanding. Merely the usual round of political scandals, natural and man-made disasters, the sufferings of the disadvantaged. And yet, all these events were outstanding. They had made the national news. What had happened was that the news had become repetitive and bland. He was simply numbed, perhaps overwhelmed, by it all. Complacency tinged with an appreciation of his advantage was how the news left him.

He would have liked a glass of red wine with his pizza, but he didn't want to drink an entire bottle. He dismissed drinking half and leaving the rest till Friday evening. Whisky didn't appeal.

He'd spent almost an hour with *Frau* Mohr. He was pleased to hear that she had recognised him at her door, but wanted to keep up a good habit. She feared falling into the trap of believing she knew someone and letting her or him in. Dannaks agreed that it was a good habit.

As she poured the tea he took out a copy of the facial autopsy photograph of the dead girl.

"*Frau* Mohr," he began, "Please don't get upset. But I'd like to show you a picture. I'd like you to tell me if you recognise her."

She finished pouring the tea. "No milk, no sugar. Correct?"

"Correct," he said, wondering whether she had heard him.

She nodded, but didn't hand him his cup. "I'd better get my reading glasses." When she got up he realised that she had been steeling herself.

Returning to her seat, opening her case, donning her glasses, she looked over at him and solemnly reached for the photograph he held. He let her stare at it in silence. Oskar stood at one point to have a good sniff at it, but a delicate hand movement from her put him back in his place. "I thought you were going to show me something horrible." She didn't take her eyes off the photograph.

407

"Of course, this is horrible, isn't it?" She now looked at him, pointedly, over the rim of her glasses.

"Can you tell me who it is?"

"So she's dead as well."

He nodded. "But can you tell me who it is?"

She looked at him irritably. "Why, it's Meryem, of course."

"Sorry. But I needed you to identify her."

"She is dead?" She took off her glasses.

Dannaks nodded, taking back the photograph.

"How terrible."

He nodded.

"They were lovely girls."

He didn't nod. He would have liked to have told her that Shaziye was still alive.

"One last question *Frau* Mohr." He paused. "I'm a bit confused about whether Michael was with, er, Shaziye or Meryem. I mean, which girl lived alone?"

"Meryem had her own flat. She was here first. Then Shaziye came and later Michael appeared and moved in with her."

"Thank you. You've been very helpful."

After finishing his pizza he took his plate to the kitchen and made himself a green tea. In the lounge he picked up the phone. He mentally prepared himself for Steffi. Although he didn't have a response should she ask about Katja.

Reupke answered.

They quickly came to Reupke's arrangements with the GP. "Kilic finishes at one on Fridays. But you know how these practices are. There're always stragglers. I'll get the morning train, have lunch and be there just before one. With luck I may be out by two or so. Then I'll just get the next train back."

"I'll be in Spandau till about twelve at the latest. Where is his practice?"

"In Kreuzberg."

"I could come there. It seems safer than meeting at a station."

"Have you got a handy?"

"No."

Reupke's exhalation was a miniature hurricane on the line.

"Give me the address," said Dannaks. "I'll sit in the waiting room."

"Yes, you will." Reupke evidently wanted to keep this strictly a *Mordkommission* investigation. "And nobody knows about this."

Dannaks was irked, but agreed. "It's your interview."

After hanging up he went into his cubbyhole kitchen and washed the crockery and utensils.

Thoughts on Katja were beginning to overwhelm him. He sought sanctuary in a glass of whisky and a mid-week movie.

It was generally considered impolite to telephone after ten, emergencies and prearrangements proving the exceptions. Although the film had not finished at a quarter to ten he could resist no longer. As he tapped in her number he still didn't know what he was going to say. With the film as distraction, his finger on the mute button of the remote control, he let it ring and ring, but nobody picked up.

Thursday
08:22

Dannaks went into work before travelling to Berlin.

Reinhart told him about his trip to Barbados. Except for the positive identification of Meryem and being intimidated by both Britta and the Dumpling he had nothing new to impart. Dannaks asked whether Britta had spoken of a high turnaround. Reinhart said yes and wondered how he knew. The phone rang during his report and after listening and hanging up he told Dannaks that Turan had also positively identified his ex-wife as the victim.

At the station Dannaks bought some papers. The *Hürriyet* reported that Meryem had retracted her confession and changed her story and thus her plea. Apparently a big man had stormed in, attacked, and killed Peter. She had been injured but had managed to flee. Dannaks pictured her leaving the room dazed, collapsing and being sick round the corner.

He wondered what had made her change her story.

10:44

The train journey from Hamburg main station to Berlin main station took an hour and forty minutes. Once there he boarded the U-Bahn and within half an hour he alighted at Kochstrasse, near the famous Checkpoint Charlie, which had been reduced to little more than a traffic island with a white shed and a small symbolic wall of sandbags. After consulting his map he made his way to Hotel Floyd.

Although his one glass of whisky had been large he felt okay. The sun was shining a mite too brightly and the concrete and steel prickled his skin with their heat. Everywhere was vibrant with activity and colour. But no more than the Lange Reihe. For what the Bronx was to New York, Kreuzberg was to Berlin.

Hotel Floyd had seen better days. Oh, it fitted admirably with its surroundings. The building was nestled in amongst a blaze of shop fronts. It was taller than it was wide giving it a sandwiched-in appearance. Painted above the entrance in weathered green lettering on a flaking white background was the name of the hotel. The name appeared again in blue neon tubes leaning in italics affixed just under the gable. The lights were off and Dannaks imagined that in true American film noir tradition, the nearby rooms would hear the buzz. Maybe a letter even flickered.

Dannaks strode in. He found himself in something of a corridor like that of a house. Framed photographs adorned the walls. A few steps in, the wall to his right was broken by an archway revealing a room containing half a dozen small square tables covered in white table cloths decked with condiments and a plastic flower in realistic-looking dirt in a ceramic flower pot. Above the arch in black paint was the word: Animals. Dannaks smiled and took a closer look at the photographs in the corridor. One was of two men shaking hands. One of the men was on fire. Another picture in blue was of the three great pyramids in Cairo. A third showed the Berlin Wall with the band on stage, searchlights sweeping the night sky.

The corridor opened onto a room with a small mahogany hut with a counter that reminded him of a church pulpit. But the man behind the counter was neither solemn nor stern.

"*Guten Tag,*" he chimed.

Dannaks returned the greeting and said that he had a booking for one night. Behind the man he was surprised to see some thirty or so pigeonholes. He would not have thought the place could have so many rooms.

To the right of the reception hut was the entrance to what appeared to be the bar. Above this entrance were the words: "Dark side of the moon."

"Ah yes," he said. "I'm afraid your room's not ready."

"That's okay. Can I drop my bag here?"

"Of course. But I'm still going to have to get you to sign in."

Dannaks filled and signed the form.

"Would you be wanting dinner with us tonight?" The way he formulated the question caught Dannaks off guard. At first glance Dannaks would have put the man in his mid-thirties. He looked fit and young and his dark hair was neither thinning nor receding. But up close his skin betrayed him. He could actually be over fifty. Although he didn't wear an earring his right ear was pierced.

"Can I see the menu?"

The man slipped his hand under the counter and produced a sheet of paper. "That's this week," he said. "We sometimes have specials."

Judging from the place Dannaks interpreted specials to be repackaged leftovers. But then, a small hotel like this needed to survive. "Yes, I'll have dinner here. What about lunch?"

"Breakfast and dinner only, I'm afraid."

To the left of Dannaks was a desk upon which was a rack of leaflets of the what-to-see-in-Berlin kind and next to this was a keyboard and flat screen.

"Internet?"

"Yes."

Dannaks nodded approvingly. "Do you know where this is?" he asked, pointing to the address in his notepad.

"I don't know the place, but I know the street. It's not far from here." He then rattled off some instructions that incorporated traffic lights, a large department store, a chemist and finally an *Imbiss* (snack bar).

Dannaks left his overnight bag and found himself once again in brilliant sunshine, almost as if the hotel had been dingy. But then the reception was set in the middle of the hotel and didn't have access to natural light.

The old rocker's directions were perfect and ten minutes later Dannaks saw the Aksoy's *Kraftfahrzeug* Werkstatt from the *Imbiss*. He was early and because the *Imbiss* looked clean and there were other people eating he went in and ate a piece of pizza, washing it down with cola.

He was in a side road, off the beaten track. Most of the buildings looked like flats. They were plastered in graffiti. Layers of flyers and posters thickened lampposts and trees in a skin of paper.

They were searches for flats or lost pets, sales of everything from cars to furniture and then advertisements for underground concerts and local flea markets. Some of this was torn or peeled and tatters flapped in the breeze and especially the trees looked diseased. On a couple of corners were a grocer's and some kind of mini-market, not unlike Patel's. There weren't many people about, but characteristically those that were, were engaged in conversation. This underlined another difference between the German and Turkish peoples. The former had little time for standing around. Here the street offered the pulse of life.

An old woman pushing a shopping trolley laden with her worldly treasures shuffled past the window.

At two minutes to one Dannaks left the *Imbiss*.

Aksoy's *KFZ Werkstatt* (KFZ *Werkstatt* – *Kraftfahrzeug Werkstatt* motor vehicle garage) was like many Dannaks had seen. A gate closed off an alleyway whose length was defined by the depth of the buildings and little more than the width of a car. Beyond this was an open area that may at one time have been a courtyard. He spotted a patch of cobbles under the grime. The enclosed space was bordered on three sides by walls of buildings, the windows of which appeared a good four metres up. On the third side, opposite the alley, facing him was a wooden structure that could have been a barn or milking shed. Only the pair of garage doors gave the game away. Everywhere there were cars millimetres from one another. Not one looked roadworthy and the area resembled a dump: a place of disrepair more than repair. Apart from a single crooked aisle the courtyard was choked with them. In the wooden building were further vehicles. One was elevated to head height on some kind of forklift affair. The other was a large white VW van with the words Simseks *Lebensmittel* (foods) over a brazenly colourful fruit and vegetable arrangement. Three men in dark blue overalls were milling about, tools in hand.

Dannaks pictured the red man on the handy photograph. His overall had been dark, but could it have been blue?

To his left, cut into this building was a windowed standard sized door. The word "office" was painted on its front.

Because of the parked vehicles he couldn't quite make a B-line for it. However, before reached the door a Turkish lad in an overall appeared.

"Can I help you?"

"Yes. I have an appointment. *Oberkommissar* Dannaks."

"In here." He turned to the office door and opened it.

Inside there was a wooden counter and standing room only. The counter itself was littered with stacks of leaflets advertising Aksoy's and some other garages specialising in tyres and bodywork. Behind the counter was all the paraphernalia of a disorderly but working office. Upon the battered swivel chair was an orthopaedic cushion for someone with back problems. Apart from the two of them the room was empty.

There was a room beyond this one, the door to which was open. "Staff only" was written upon it.

The lad led Dannaks through.

This was a larger office, no tidier, but with a cheap desk and an incongruously large and expensive black leather chair. In it sat a tanned but weathered man with that typically squarish Turkish head. At that moment cigarette smoke obscured his face. He was stocky like Mahmut but with a potbelly appendage. This was undoubtedly Mahmut's father: *Herr* Aksoy.

The lad introduced Dannaks in Turkish and the smoke cleared to reveal a severe looking face. Aksoy was a man who had seen a lot. He was also a man with whom one did not mess. Yet, his eyes appeared weary. They were rheumy and this undermined their penetrating hardness. Dannaks could not decide whether this state was a temporary weariness or a sign of his age.

Although clean-shaven the white flecks of his stubble made him look as if he'd not shaved. His dyed black hair was slicked back, accentuating his receding hairline, the colour contrasting his bushy white eyebrows. He was dressed like a businessman in a jacket, shirt and tie, but his clothes lacked crispness and appeared as dreary as the office itself.

When he spoke it sounded as if he were gargling a mouthful of gravel. So he didn't so much speak as growl.

The lad obeyed the order and left to round up the team.

Dannaks surmised that the man still had an iron grip on his business.

He didn't make any movement to shake hands. Instead he took another long drag on his cigarette and waved Dannaks – as if sweeping crumbs off an invisible surface – in the direction of the worn sofa that lined the wall opposite the desk.

On the wall above the sofa were numerous framed certificates: awards for one of the best garages in the area. There was even an article by the *ADAC* (*Allgemeine Deutsche Automobile Club* – similar to Britain's Automobile Association). As far as Dannaks could tell everything was dated almost a decade ago.

Another wall was plastered with old and curling postcards.

Far more interesting were the group photographs of the mechanics adorning an adjacent wall.

After a moment three young Turks sauntered in. One was the lad who had fetched them.

On the old group photographs he counted at least ten overalls. These were obviously taken during the heydays of the garage.

Dannaks stood, dismayed. In the confines of this office his interview wasn't going to work.

"I'll stand," he said. "Why don't you all sit down?"

They glanced at Aksoy, who was grinding the stub of his cigarette in a bristling ashtray on his desk. Dannaks didn't see him nod permission, but he may have done so. He then noticed a folded copy of the *Hürriyet* lying at one end of the desk.

Dannaks looked at each of them but before he could begin Aksoy said: "Speak."

Unruffled by the command he said: "I'd like to know who worked here when Shaziye was around."

The two lads the third one had fetched shook their heads when he looked enquiringly at them.

"Can they go back to work?" growled Aksoy.

Dannaks ignored him. "How long have you been working here?" he asked one of the two.

"About a year."

"And you?"

"I started a couple of months before him."

"So you neither of you knew Shaziye?"

They shook their heads.

Dannaks nodded. "I guess you can go, then." They looked at Aksoy before leaving.

"Is this your entire workforce?"

Aksoy nodded.

"You've seen better days," he said gesturing towards the photographs.

414

The old man glared at him and Dannaks turned back to the remaining youth.

"What's your name?"

"Ayhan." Dannaks wrote the name in his notepad. The click of a lighter distracted him for a moment.

"Are you related to the Aksoy's?"

"No."

"Surname?"

The boy had a pleasant enough face. He looked intelligent, but he had a troubled brow and intensity in his eyes.

"Simsek."

"Like the van outside?"

Ayhan nodded.

"Any connection?"

"It's one of my father's," he said quietly

This implied that he possessed more than one van, maybe a fleet. If his father was that successful, why was Ayhan a mere car mechanic working in a failing backstreet garage?

"And you knew Shaziye?"

He nodded.

Then Aksoy exploded. "What is all this about? Why are you asking about that whore? She's dead."

Dannaks calmly turned to him. There was froth in the corners of the old man's mouth. His breathing had become laboured and he rattled and wheezed not unlike some of the wrecks he had probably received.

"*Herr* Aksoy, you know as well as I that she is not dead."

Nobody moved. Aksoy remained emotionless.

"But Mahmut killed her," said Ayhan eventually.

Dannaks reluctantly took his eyes off Aksoy, as if he was conceding defeat in some kind of staring match.

"No. He killed her neighbour."

Again a silence began to stretch before them.

Aksoy spoke, his words barely discernible through the churning gravel in his throat. "My son was honourable."

"There's no honour in killing, *Herr* Aksoy."

"What do you know, policeman? You know nothing of such things. You were brought up in a world of selfishness, greed, corruption, chaos. I open my door and I see obesity and anorexia. I see addiction and poverty. I see your youth without a future

415

roaming the streets with blades." Dannaks's attempt at speaking merely increased Aksoy's volume and the white froth gathering at the sides of his mouth. "I see a society out of kilter. A society that has paid a terrible spiritual price for what it calls freedom. Freedom to do what? To blindly consume. To sit behind closed doors surrounded by material things and view the world through a television screen. You have no values." Dannaks again tried to speak. "Your churches are empty and crumbling. But we – we have order. We have family, obedience, hierarchy, the mosque, the Koran, Allah."

"*Herr* Aksoy, we are talking murder. There–"

"No. We are talking honour. You have no idea of the shame that whore brought on us. You–"

"*Herr* Aksoy, save your words. I've heard them all before."

The old man took a last long pull on his cigarette before it too was ground into the overflowing ashtray.

When he spoke he spoke calmly with icy conviction. "If she should come through that door now I would tear her apart with my bare hands."

Dannaks knew that there was no point in continuing. Even Ayhan wouldn't tell him anything, certainly not in front of the old man.

"You know what your country needs?" His main tirade was over, but evidently Aksoy had more to say.

Dannaks gave him a disinterested look.

"A strong leader."

Dannaks hadn't expected this. He thought he would say something along religious lines. "We had one in the last century. The results were disastrous."

"He was the wrong–"

"Yes, yes," he said impatiently. "Let's not waste any more time." He strode over to the wall with the team photographs. Peering at each of them, he slowly spoke, hoping to keep Aksoy from rattling. "So." He had quickly whittled the choice down to two photographs. There was little difference between them and he chose the one he could view with ease.

Ayhan stood beside him. Dannaks didn't know whether Aksoy had ordered him to or not. He had his back to them.

"That's you at the end, right?"

Ayhan nodded.

There were about a dozen overalls in two loose rows in the picture. Two people weren't in this uniform. Aksoy, not in an overall, sat on a chair in the middle. The rest of the front row was kneeling in front of a standing back row. The picture resembled that of a football team. And if circumstance had been otherwise Dannaks would have asked: "Where's the ball?"

"That's Mahmut," he said, pointing to the man standing on the far left. Ayhan nodded. "And there's Michael." His was the only non-Turkish face. He was the second person not in an overall. "Who are the others?"

"Part-time workers," snarled Aksoy from his desk. "They have come and gone." This could be true. Apart from Aksoy, Mahmut and two others the rest of the photograph was made up of youths. Ayhan, himself, was little more than a boy.

"Who are these two?" Dannaks pointed to the two remaining men.

Ayhan hesitated.

"The older one was a good friend of the Aksoy's."

"Was?"

"He died last year."

Aksoy blew a gasket again. "This has gone far enough. We have nothing more to say to you."

Dannaks matched his aggression. "Do you want me to haul you all in? The sooner I'm done, the sooner I'm out of your hair."

"And this one." He pointed to the comparatively big man.

"That's, er, Volcan."

"And how did he fit in?"

"Er, he's *Herr* Aksoy's youngest son."

"Mahmut's brother," Dannaks said, more to himself, than to them. He needed a moment for this to sink in. "Where is he now?"

"He left," said Aksoy.

"That's not an answer."

Dannaks waited the silence out. During this time Ayhan stepped away.

"I don't know," said Aksoy. Dannaks didn't believe him. A father would know about his son, even if they had fallen out.

"Okay," he began, turning to look at Aksoy. "When did he leave?"

417

Aksoy shrugged. He appeared uncharacteristically lost for words.

"Then why did he leave?"

The old man stared at him blankly. Something grumbled in his chest. His mouth was clamped shut, but the grumbling increased, like the far off roll of thunder. Then he spluttered, the white at the corners of his mouth overflowing. He brought his shirtsleeve up to wipe away the spittle. The rumble forced his mouth open. Dannaks thought he was trying to gag himself with his forearm as the coughing fit began. He shook and quivered, his chest sounding like an old toolbox. He rasped as his eyes watered and Dannaks thought he was going to choke on all the grunge that bubbled inside.

As the fit subsided he reached down behind the desk and produced a dark bottle. Dannaks hoped it was water.

Aksoy took a swig and then cleared his throat, forcing the tar and mucus back down.

Dannaks glanced at Ayhan. He was sitting on the sofa fixated by a point on the desk.

The old man then lit another cigarette. Dannaks had not seen him finish the previous one. He knew better than to say that they were doing him no good.

"You know I'll find out," said Dannaks.

"Then work for your money, policeman."

He nodded and again looked at Ayhan. Then he decided on a last provocation. He tapped the newspaper. "You know very well that she's alive."

"And she'll rot in prison," barked Aksoy.

Dannaks smiled at the admission. "Maybe."

The staring game began again. This time Aksoy broke it off to tap some ash from his cigarette. "Finished?"

"Not quite," said Dannaks. "I asked to see everyone. I haven't seen your women."

Aksoy's expression bordered on explosive for a moment and Dannaks prepared words for a fight. Then, surprisingly, he turned to Ayhan and said: "Take him."

The youth – he was probably nearing the end of his twenties – got up. "Follow me."

13:39

418

They left the office the way they had entered and crossed the courtyard to a door Dannaks had failed to notice, at the top of some steps in the corner of the buildings to their left.

As they walked, Ayhan leading, Dannaks noticed the numerous patches on his overall. They were stitched on the tops of his sleeves and across his back at shoulder blade level. Although colourfully different they were all mechanic of the year awards for various years. As far as he could see either he'd stopped being the best a few years back or the award-giving had stopped.

"Is somebody else winning now?"

Ayhan turned at the walled steps that led down to another door to what must be the cellar. He looked puzzled until Dannaks gestured to his patches.

"We stopped entering."

He turned and pulled open the ground floor door and Dannaks found himself in relative darkness.

Ayhan flicked a switch and an overhead light flickered into life. The corridor was cold and neglected, the walls painted in a cheap fading yellow that returned the nicotine stench of Aksoy's office to Dannaks's nostrils.

"He should cut down on those cigarettes," said Dannaks. He knew it was a needless statement and merely wanted to get the young man talking.

"It's too late," said Ayhan without turning. "He's very sick."

The walked the rest of the bland corridor in silence.

As they waited for the lift Dannaks tried again.

"Business doesn't look good."

"No."

"Your father's custom probably keeps the garage running."

The remark went unacknowledged.

The lift arrived and they entered.

It was one of those central cage affairs with the flights of stairs spiralling around it. Ayhan pulled the concertinaed metal gate closed. Then he pushed the third floor button. The lift clunked and then jerked into motion. The uncertain movement and metallic squeals didn't instil confidence.

"I'm surprised nobody's asked why a detective should come all the way from Hamburg."

At first Ayhan didn't respond and Dannaks wondered whether he'd heard him.

"If you think she's alive then you probably have something to do with Mahmut."

The lift juddered to a stop with a disconcerting noise that sounded like the protest of bending metal. Ayhan pulled back the door.

Dannaks wasn't sure, but he felt Ayhan was troubled.

They stepped out and Ayhan slipped off his shoes. Dannaks followed suit lining his up with the others.

The apartment door was not locked and they padded into the carpeted hallway.

Ayhan called out above the sound of Turkish music to register their presence. Dannaks guessed that the music came from a radio somewhere. He heard movement. The music was killed, plunging the flat into silence.

Ayhan led him into the living room, which was empty and quite still.

"Wait here," he said.

Numerous overlapping rugs made the floor uneven and quite spongy in places. At one end of the room nearest the window were three settees arranged in a C-shape surrounding a low coffee table. On the wall directly above one settee hung a flat screen television. On the opposite one was a large Turkish flag. He spotted a hubble-bubble in a corner. Various other knickknacks littered the room and some shelving, but by far the most interesting place was the sideboard. Upon this stood a small array of framed photographs.

Dannaks went straight to them. He recognised a scrawny topless boy in shorts standing proudly in the sunshine as a younger Ayhan. He must have been about twelve. Then there was one of Aksoy and a woman Dannaks took to be his wife. Mahmut's face filled another. Then there was Volcan with a terribly young doe-eyed girl holding a baby. There were others Dannaks didn't recognise. A particularly distinguished looking gentleman with a bouffant of silver hair looking like a flamboyant film director or orchestra conductor stood out incongruously. Shaziye was not in any of the pictures.

He was still peering at the photographs when Ayhan led the four women into the room. They weren't veiled-up but their faces were framed in black headscarves, hair tucked out of sight. They wore their abaayas like cloaks and resembled nuns. And like nuns their faces were almost bereft of make-up. Only eyeliner highlighted their eyes.

Dannaks straightened. "Just admiring your photos."

He recognised one of the older women as Aksoy's wife. The girl with the baby was there too. Although the baby wasn't present.

Three of the women sat on the settee under the flag. The girl and finally Ayhan took the adjacent one, effectively leaving Dannaks to sit alone under the television.

When he was seated he took out his notepad and pen. He then proceeded to take their names and relationship. They wearily complied, spelling their names when necessary. The older woman was indeed Aksoy's wife. The other older woman was her sister. The doe-eyed girl was Volcan's wife. The fourth girl was a friend of the family.

Dannaks waited almost theatrically before starting.

"I'd like you to tell me all you can about Shaziye."

He waited, but nobody spoke. He then directed his attention to Aksoy's wife. She simply returned his gaze. She'd been taking lessons from her husband.

"You know that she's alive?" he said looking from one to the other.

The women remained unimpressed.

Then Aksoy's wife spoke. "And you know we will tell you nothing."

Dannaks sighed.

"Can you tell me where Volcan is?"

Only Aksoy's wife met his gaze. The others found points of interest upon which to meditate. The silence grew and Dannaks eventually flipped closed his notepad. Aksoy's wife looked at him dully. When he rose nobody moved. Even Aksoy's wife didn't look at him anymore. Only Ayhan seemed to be aware of his movement.

"I'll see myself out."

But Ayhan got up.

Dannaks left the room. Ayhan followed.

"I know the way," Dannaks said at the door.

"I have to work."

Outside the flat they put on their shoes. Dannaks heard the indiscernible babble of women's voices before Turkish music drowned them.

In the lift Ayhan spoke.

"Do you really think she'll get off?"

"I think there is a good chance."

"But she confessed."

"There is some evidence that says she didn't do it." That was as far as he could go.

Silence.

The lift reached the ground floor. Dannaks reached for the metal grip to pull back the door, but Ayhan held part of the frame.

"Are you returning to Hamburg today?"

"Tomorrow. I'm staying at Hotel Floyd." He picked out his card and handed it to him. Ayhan looked at it, before slipping it into a pocket of his overall. Then he released the door.

They left the building in silence. In the courtyard Dannaks headed for the road. When he got there he stopped and looked over his shoulder to catch Ayhan going into the office.

18:25

After leaving Aksoy's Dannaks had time to kill. He didn't fancy going straight back to the hotel to be holed up in his room until dinner, so he idly wandered the streets, browsing the stands outside the shops, occasionally going in.

His activity was background to his thoughts.

On the surface he had learnt precious little from the interview. But they had told him that they knew Shaziye was alive. They had made it obvious that they hated her. They were fiercely Turkish, proud and easily offended. Business appeared to have taken a turn for the worse with Mahmut's absence. Maybe Shaziye was to blame for this too? In Volcan Dannaks could even have seen a photograph of Matthias's killer. It was Ayhan who intrigued him. The young man was a long-standing employee and yet he seemed willing to cooperate.

Ayhan's father continued to use the garage. Maybe his business kept the place afloat. For despite appearances there was apparently enough work to employ at least three mechanics. It was strange that he should remain a customer even though Mahmut had used one of their company vans, albeit presumably no longer in service, to commit murder.

A rule of three was Dannaks's personal investigating tick. The technician's side-note mentioned the van. A similar van was being worked upon at Aksoy's. And one of the mechanics was the son of the owner of the vans. These three appearances of the name in the investigation warranted a closer look. Of course in a full-blown investigation with complete resources a rule of one was deemed enough.

Just after four Dannaks entered the hotel. He wanted to do a search for Simsek on the computer but a boy was playing a game. So Dannaks collected his key to his room. There was a lift that could take three persons – without baggage – at a pinch. He chose to climb the steep creaking stairs, once grabbing the wooden rail of the banister and immediately releasing it when it wobbled.

His room had the efficient space-utilisation of a ship's cabin, but not alas the Spartan cleanliness. The carpet was too thick and Dannaks almost felt as if he was walking on a mattress. He was reminded of Aksoy's living room. The wallpaper was patterned with thick pieces of what he took to be felt. The single bed lined one wall right up to an armchair nearest the sash window. Lining the other wall were a wardrobe and a chest of drawers upon which stood a portable television facing the chair. The space between the bed and furniture was the width of one person. Next to the wardrobe was a door with a full-length mirror, behind which was the shower cubicle. Age had speckled the mirror in the top right hand corner. All the furniture was cheap, hardboard and plywood, a style-less hotchpotch of *Sperrmull* (junk) that would be lucky to go for two figures at a flea market. There was no toilet.

The size of the room made Dannaks's own flat seem like a spacious penthouse. It also explained how the hotel could accommodate so many guests.

He pushed aside the net curtain that was in dire need of a clean. The view was that of a bewildering jigsaw of tiled roofs, chimneys and edges of buildings, black drainpipes and the occasional pokey window fogged with grime. He turned the stiff mussel-shaped catch and lifted the window to breathe life into the place. It stopped after about six centimetres. Stoppers had been screwed into the frame to prevent the window being lifted higher.

Dannaks peered down. Yes, he was high enough to break bones, if not kill himself. He mused that such a dingy room could indeed push an already depressed person to suicide.

He didn't bother unpacking. Instead he tossed his bag on the chair and took a shower to wash out the sweat and city grime.

Refreshed he took the lift down to dinner.

The computer was free but the screen was blank and a laminated card "Temporarily out of service" stood wedged between the keys of the keyboard.

In the front room labelled "Animals" he announced himself to the waiter, who took him to a small table in a corner. A couple in their early twenties sat at one table. They were speaking Italian. At another was an old lady reading a paperback. Finally a family of four sat with teetering constraint, as if they were in a five star restaurant.

Dannaks noticed that the wallpaper was the same textured stuff in his room. Dominating one wall was a whitewashed canvas upon which a brickwork pattern was painted. This was littered with colourfully scrawled graffiti which – after reading "we don't need no education" – Dannaks assumed were lyrics.

He chose the beef ragout with noodles and a half carafe of house red wine. The former was acceptable, the latter bearable. He was reminded of the cask at Azure Skies. And for some inexplicable reason he was taken back to the freezing eyeball incident. The pain of the incident took him back to that evening of cocktails with Dagmar, Reupke and Katja.

A burst of laughter from the Italian couple snatched him from melancholic thoughts of Katja, merely to immediately plunge him back in again, pushing him deeper. He floundered and sought refuge in the graffiti.

Because he thought Ayhan might turn up he had decided to stay in the hotel. He couldn't face sitting in his room. So, after putting the dinner bill on his room, he went to the back room bar: The Dark Side of the Moon.

20:57

The Dark Side of the Moon was half the size of the front restaurant. Wall lighting rendered it half as bright too. Here the walls sported large framed concert posters behind glass: Wembley 1974 and 1988 and Berlin "The Wall" 1990. A fireplace opposite the bar contained some dry logs that looked real, but were lit by orange tinted spotlights.

Apart from him and the barman, who doubled as the waiter who had just served him, the room was empty.

Barely audible music he recognised to be Pink Floyd's *Wish you were here* was playing.

The whisky selection was standard fare and Dannaks opted

to stick with the house red. He ordered another half carafe. This would come out of his pocket anyway. Maybe the higher echelons could get away with claiming after dinner drinks; he couldn't, unless he could prove it was directly necessary to work.

Before his carafe arrived he was called to the telephone. The guy at the reception hut lifted the off-the-hook telephone onto the counter and busied himself with some paperwork.

"Dannaks," he announced.

"Hallo. It is me, Ayhan." He paused as if Dannaks should be shocked. "I – I need to talk to you."

"Okay." He thought he was going to have to cancel his drink and head off into the unknown.

"I'll come to you."

"Good. I'll wait for you in the bar. Ask for me at reception."

"I'll be there in twenty minutes."

Dannaks returned to his table. The carafe and single glass awaited him. He poured out half a glass but didn't drink it. Instead he tilted his wrist to see his watch in the half-light.

Eighteen minutes later, towards the end of *Have a cigar,* Ayhan walked in.

Dannaks was still the only person in the bar and he had hardly touched his drink. He rose and gestured to the chair opposite. Ayhan pulled it out from the table and sat. Dannaks sat too. "Drink?"

Ayhan nodded. "A Pils."

Dannaks was about to get up when the guy from reception strode to the table. He took the order.

Ayhan surveyed the furnishings with distaste whilst his beer was pulled.

"I always thought this was a gay place," he said quietly.

If the aging rocker behind reception was in his fifties then he would have been a young man in the seventies when a pierced right ear was a signal for being gay. Nowadays both sides were pierced and it didn't matter.

"Well I'm not gay. And from what I've seen of the guests, they're not either."

"It's probably just the two guys that run it."

They waited until the beer was placed on the table and the man had left them alone.

Dannaks watched Ayhan take a first sip of his beer and

place his glass back on the table. He wasn't going to push him and sought preamble.

"Where you born here? Or did you come across with your parents?"

The lad didn't answer immediately and Dannaks wondered whether he had something else on his mind. It wasn't a difficult question.

"I, er–" his nostrils flared – "was born here."

Dannaks worked at keeping the conversation flowing: light and easy. "Have you any brothers or sisters?"

"A younger brother," he said automatically.

"You don't get on?"

Ayhan shook his head.

He'd touched a nerve. "And you chose not to go into your father's business?"

"No."

The boy sipped his beer, regarding it as if it were an elixir offering sanctuary.

"I've just returned from Turkey myself. I can't say I've seen the country, though. I was on one of those camps." He wasn't reaching the lad. "Have you been?"

Ayhan looked up and smiled. He seemed suddenly relaxed and wanted conversation.

Shattering the thematic overkill Supertramp's *Crime of the century* started.

"I went back once."

Dannaks hesitated. "It sounds as if you didn't like it."

"I didn't."

"Oh?"

"You don't know the people. You don't see them on their own terms. They are a racist lot. Here I am Turkish. Yes, I was born here and I probably think and speak like a German. But I will still always be a Turk. I cannot change my appearance. I speak Turkish, but over there I am not Turkish. I am not German, either. They call me *Deutschisch*, which means foreigner. I am one of many trapped between two cultures. Neither one nor the other."

Dannaks waited a long moment before gently saying: "You didn't come to see me to talk about that."

Ayhan shook his head and smiled bitterly. "No. I came to talk about Shaziye." But he fell silent again and Dannaks allowed him his silence.

He stared into his beer and began without looking up.

"If what you say is true and she gets out, then, er..." His voice had diminished to almost a whisper and Dannaks had to lean forward to listen above *Bloody well right*. "Er, he'll go after her?"

"Who?"

Ayhan lifted his eyes.

"Volcan?" he asked.

"Maybe. I don't know."

"Who else could it be?"

Ayhan spoke miserably. "Another relative. A friend. Someone he's paid."

"You mean someone Volcan has paid?"

"Volcan, Mahmut, the old man. It doesn't really matter."

"The Aksoys."

Ayhan nodded. Then he said: "The old man blames her for his illness."

A man entered the bar. He saw them in the corner and chose the corner diagonally opposite at the bar. He sat on a stool and waited to be served. Dannaks realised that he was from the family of four. The waiter entered and he asked for a cognac.

"Where is Volcan? Is he in Turkey? Side?" There was no reason to talk quietly. The man could not possibly hear them and the waiter had left. But Dannaks did so.

"I really don't know."

"But he's been gone since before the killing of the ex-neo-Nazi?" To name Matthias and personify him could have an alienating effect. Ayhan was unlikely to have neo-Nazi sympathies.

Ayhan nodded.

They sipped their drinks in silence.

"Why are they so desperate to get her?"

The young man was truly surprised by the question.

"She ran away. And then it was discovered she was having an affair with Michael."

"Was she having an affair with him whilst she was here?"

"I don't know. I don't think so."

"Why not?"

"Because she left and then he did. They didn't leave together."

"How much time passed?"

"A few months."

Dannaks nodded.

Again they dropped into silence and drank.

"Okay Ayhan. Why are you telling me this?"

"Because Michael was my friend. We were at school together. I got him the job at Aksoy's."

"I mean why didn't you go to the police with it before?"

"Because I don't know whether it is Volcan."

"If Michael was your friend why do you go on working for Aksoy?"

"The old man is all right. He's hard but fair. His sons are the real brutes."

He sipped his beer and Dannaks sipped some wine.

"Michael's dead and Mahmut's in prison for killing him. So why are you interested in helping Shaziye?"

"Because I feel sorry for her. Her nightmare should have ended when she ran away."

"What happened to make her run away?" Dannaks had read that Mahmut had beaten her, but he wanted to hear it firsthand.

"You know that she was a purchased bride?"

"Yes. I read that her parents sold her for a so-called better life here." The waiter entered. "But why don't you tell it from the beginning? Over another beer." Ayhan nodded and Dannaks caught the waiter's attention and pointed to Ayhan's glass and mouthed: "Another one".

Two young men came in. They took the third corner diagonally opposite the entrance. The edge of the bar and the entrance were situated in the last corner of the room. They sat alongside one another looking into the room. Both were dressed in tight-fitting black sleeveless tops and sprayed-on black jeans. They wore silver-studded black leather dog collars and a similar but broader one on their right wrists. Their shoes were expensive patent black leather. Their attire highlighted the contours of their lithe bodies. They were lean with the taller one bordering on lanky. Their hair, dyed Chinese black, was also synchronised: short back and sides with a longer tuft combed slightly forward to hinder the sight of the right eye. They habitually flicked this tuft absently with either their fingers or a tipped back shake of the head.

For some reason Dannaks found them sinisterly reminiscent of the SS. There was something dark and eerie about their twinning appearance that harked back to Nazi times. He could not pinpoint the source of this feeling. Twins? Black leather? And they would have indignantly, no vehemently, reacted against the idea. For they inhabited the other end of the political spectrum. Perhaps there was a hint of Cabaret about them?

"I told you Michael and I were school friends," Ayhan calmly began. "After leaving I started at Aksoy's. I'd been working there on and off for a while. Saturdays mainly. Michael was unemployed and I told Abdurrahim–"

"Who?"

"*Herr* Aksoy. I said that although Michael wasn't good with his hands he was a good talker and good with numbers. I said he could attract more German customers. Aksoy said that he'd give him a try."

Ayhan's beer arrived. The waiter topped up Dannaks's wine glass with the carafe. Then he left them to take the orders from the newcomers.

"Michael had the front office job and dealt with the German customers. Business boomed. And Aksoy's became one of the best garages in Berlin. The *ADAC* did one of those uncover tests. You know, they have a car with some things wrong with it. They need to get it through *TUV* (*Technischer Überwachungsverein* - MOT) and see if the garage spots the things that are wrong. Aksoy's spotted all ten. If nothing else, Mahmut and Volcan are excellent mechanics.

"This is all before Shaziye arrived. When she came things started to go downhill. Mahmut brought her back with him as his wife after a summer trip to Turkey. She was little more than a girl and he was in his early thirties. I think she was about fourteen. And she didn't speak a word of German." The waiter returned a while later with pink drinks for the twins that Dannaks took to be strawberry daiquiris. The freezing eyeball incident vied for his attention and he fought to concentrate on Ayhan's words. "Of course, she was initially kept in the house. I don't really know why, but after about a year or so we saw her and she began to clean the offices. I think Mahmut had decided to work her to death and there were enough women in the apartment. I think she infuriated Mahmut and he hated her."

"Why?"

"She hadn't become pregnant and despite her background her aloofness put her above him. The funny thing is, the more he brutalised her, the more he fitted the caveman role and the higher she rose. If you see what I mean." He took a sip of his beer. "He began to call her She-Devil. And she was. I never saw her cry, although I suppose she did. Over the years she learnt a smattering of German. Especially from Michael, I suppose. I still don't think they had an affair. The garage was too busy. And if she wasn't there, she was in the apartment. She–"

Three disruptively loud young men burst in. Noticing the sedate atmosphere they subdued themselves. By the time they were seated at a wall table they were quiet.

"Until he married her Mahmut was good to work with. Over time he started to get crazy. He'd have violent outbursts in front of customers, which didn't help the business. Then Volcan married and they had a boy within a year. This tipped Mahmut over the edge. He'd always hit her, but now he beat her so badly that we didn't see her for weeks. And then she ran away. Nobody knew how she did it or where she went. I think now that Michael may have helped her."

"What time period are we talking about here? I mean, how long were they married?"

"About eight years." He took the opportunity to drink some beer.

"And all this time she was never pregnant?"

"No. I think she went for lots of tests."

"Do you know which hospital or clinic?"

"No."

The waiter came in and took the orders of the three newcomers. Dannaks noticed then that the two lads in black were kissing. The family man had gone. Dannaks realised that he and Ayhan probably looked like a middle-aged man with his gigolo.

"Okay. What happened after Shaziye left?" He hoped that Ayhan had not seen the kissing.

"Mahmut was furious, of course. And then rumours kind of began. Like I said, her German was very basic. So Michael came under suspicion. He took Mahmut's chiding for a few months then he too left. Or rather disappeared. This was a catalyst. Mahmut went wild and was away for days on end. He tried to pick up Michael's trail thinking it would lead him to Shaziye. He was right. I don't know whether Shaziye and Michael planned to get together. I don't know whether he contacted her or her him. It doesn't matter."

Ayhan paused to collect his thoughts. He finished his beer, but Dannaks didn't ask whether he wanted another. He didn't want the interruption, but made a mental note to look out for the waiter.

"When Michael left the German custom went with him. He was a great front man. Mahmut was preoccupied and Volcan was never as good as him. Mahmut was always the brighter one. The business declined. The old man became ill. Then Mahmut found them. And you know what happened."

Again Dannaks wanted some timescale. "How long had Shaziye been missing?"

"About three years." Her German had undoubtedly improved in leaps and bounds during her time in the *Frauenhaus* and then in Hamburg.

The waiter brought a tray of three drinks for the newcomers.

"Another beer," said Dannaks when he was nearby. He then turned to Ayhan. "You did want another, didn't you?"

Ayhan shrugged.

They were silent for a while. Dannaks noticed that a George Michael number was playing. "But Mahmut didn't kill Shaziye."

"No. But I thought he had. I didn't know. I only realised three weeks ago when I went into the back office and heard the tail end of a phone conversation. Aksoy said She-Devil and then I knew she was alive." He looked guiltily at Dannaks, as if he'd in some way let him down. "Then I saw her on television. When they caught her."

"Do you think Aksoy was talking to Volcan?"

"I don't know. I only caught the tail end." He gave Dannaks a moment. "Maybe."

"Tell me about Volcan. Has he been in trouble with the police?"

Ayhan considered for a while. "I think he's been taken in a few times."

"What for?"

"Fighting, drunk and disorderly. Nothing really criminal."

"Do you think he's capable of murder?"

"He's as hot headed as his brother."

Dannaks nodded. "Do you think you can get me a photograph of him?"

Ayhan blanched at the question. Dannaks looked away to

the waiter approaching with the glass of beer. Ayhan registered his distraction and remained silent.

After the waiter had delivered the drink and left he said: "I don't know. But you're leaving tomorrow."

"You could post it."

Ayhan nodded slowly and Dannaks raised his wine glass. "*Prost* (cheers)."

The younger man was obliged to raise his own glass and drink.

"Eight years is a long time," Dannaks began. "I know that the pressure to produce children must have been tremendous, not only for Shaziye, but also for Mahmut. Why didn't he take another wife? He could have divorced her in Turkey and remarried."

Ayhan's eyes looked glazed in the half-light and Dannaks wondered whether he was tipsy. "Because I think the problem wasn't with her, but with him. They sent her for tests to see if something was wrong with her. He never went." Dannaks knew that this would be down to pride. "I remember hearing that at twenty he had mumps. Do you know what I'm saying?"

Dannaks nodded. Catching the disease so late in life could make you sterile.

"So if he'd divorced her and remarried," said Dannaks, "then everyone would have known that there was something wrong with him."

"Yes." He took a hefty gulp of beer. The twins were tongue wrestling again.

They were quiet for a while. When Ayhan spoke he sounded far off. "This was his real shame. I think it made him full of hate—"

"Which he directed at her?"

Ayhan nodded and took another large swallow of beer. Dannaks sensed his urge to flee. He'd obviously seen the twins.

"You were Michael's friend, but he never told you about him and Shaziye?"

"No. And that's why I think they got close after she left."

"But Michael didn't confide in you when he left?"

He shook his head and seemed to sink into himself, as if realising that his dead friend had not been that close to him. "I think," he began slowly, voicing his thoughts without composing his words. "He didn't want me to know in case I got into trouble."

"Like Shaziye he left and never contacted you."

Ayhan gave a horrified expression. "No," he said, his voice belittled by dejection.

Friday
08:19

After Ayhan's departure Dannaks had remained to finish his wine. He too had felt uncomfortable and left the bar ten minutes later.

In his room he didn't immediately made preparations for bed. Instead he tried to clear his fogging head and make notes in his notepad. Again these were sparse-word bullet points.

At the top of the new page he wrote Ayhan and underlined the name making it a title. Under it he wrote: "Volcan – police record." His next bullet point was: "Born here. *Back* to Turkey." Ayhan had said he had been born in Germany. His German was perfect. But when he spoke about visiting Turkey he said back. If he was born here, why would he talk about returning? Then, why would he lie about his birthplace? Was it a trick he adopted to avoid awkward questions or simply to fit in? And what had been the purpose of coming this evening? Finally he wrote: "Simsek" before placing a large question mark behind the title word.

When his head did hit the pillow he fell asleep almost immediately.

He was awoken at some ungodly hour by a burst of laughter in the corridor, followed by loud male voices; then a door closing and muffled voices receding to silence.

A terrible thirst and an even worse headache kept him awake. He lay still, perversely denying both and urging his exhaustion to return him to the sanctuary of sleep.

He was almost asleep when the rhythmic squeal of bedsprings began. No matter how hard he tried he couldn't block out the sound. And when it stopped he listened intently. And when it resumed he felt even lonelier. He even began to feel sorry for himself: alone in a seedy room in an unfamiliar city. Long after the night activity was over he found himself fighting off all thoughts of Katja and so remained awake for a considerable time.

He lost his battle against his thirst and headache just after eight. Hoping that they were strongly linked, he got to his feet and unsteadily made his way to the sink next to the shower. There he took his toothbrush out of the plastic cup, filled the cup with water and drank it down in one go. He filled it again and drank half. His thirst didn't disappear. But the thought of drinking more was nauseous. However, as if a sigh had gone through his entire body, his headache eased. Its buzz shrivelled to localise itself at a point between his eyes.

He returned to the room, filling the cup first. There he placed the cup next to the television, pulled apart the curtains, opened the window, amused by the inability to jump and sat on the edge of the bed, his elbows on his knees, head in his hands.

He needed a few minutes to get over feeling sorry for himself.

"Come on, man," he said out loud, as some form of kick-start.

He picked up the telephone and dialled an outside line.

"Kripo Hamburg. Keller speaking."

"Dannaks," he croaked. "Morning Reinhart."

"Morning. Did whisky give you that deep voice?"

"Red wine."

"What's happening?"

"A lot. But I'm using the hotel phone, so it'll have to wait. I was wondering whether you could do me a favour." Reinhart issued a short hum, that was neither a yes nor a no, but simply a prompt. "Could you check the Berlin hospitals and clinics for records of Shaziye Aksoy? We're talking up to ten years ago."

"That's a tall one. And I'm not supposed to be working on this."

He knew Reinhart would do it. His colleague not only liked to moan, he liked to milk some acknowledgement of the favour.

"If you can't, you can't."

"I didn't say that."

"Then I've another one for you."

Reinhart's grunt was an 'oh-no' rather than a no.

"Mahmut has a younger brother, Volcan. He has a record here. Brawling, drunk and disorderly, that sort of thing. See if they've got a picture."

"That it?"

The name Simsek flashed through his mind. "You want some more?"

"No. Believe it or not some of us have got work to do."

Dannaks ignored the swipe.

"I'll see you on Monday, then. Have a good weekend."

"Yeah. You too. And a good journey back."

Except for the sounds of the day entering the open window the room was still. For a short while during the conversation he had forgotten his headache, now it returned with a vengeance with something akin to indignation at being ignored.

He downed the rest of the water, hastily pulled on the clothes he'd worn yesterday and went out to the toilet at the end of the corridor. As luck would have it, it was unoccupied. Whilst inside, however, the door handle was tried on two separate occasions during the quarter of an hour he sat there. He flushed, strode back to his room, pleased not to be identified as the culprit who'd commandeered the toilet for so long and, despite the open window, left it with a horrid stench.

In his room he stripped off and showered. The shower made him feel better. After it he dressed in fresh clothes from his overnight bag.

He grabbed his city guide and left

Reception was empty and most importantly the out of service card was no longer wedged in the keyboard of the PC. He pushed the mouse and the screen lit up.

A search with the keywords: "Berlin, Simsek" yielded over 140,000 hits, so he added the word: "*Lebensmittel*". This brought the number down to just under seven hundred. The first entry, a fruit and vegetable import website, was what he wanted. He recognised the same fruit and vegetable arrangement from the side of the van at the Aksoys. He looked over all the pages, but the "About us" page was by far the most interesting. There was a picture of Simsek and a young man. They were father and son. The son wasn't Ayhan. Dannaks was intrigued that Ayhan had not joined his father's business? Working for the Aksoys appeared to be a dead end. He suspected that the boy not only didn't get on with his younger brother he didn't get on with his father either. What was his relationship to his mother? Dannaks clicked on "contact us" and found the company's address. He jotted it down in his notepad and then looked it up on the online map. It wasn't far from the station Reinickendorf. He then checked the underground and discovered that this station was a mere nine minute journey from Kochstrasse. It was too good an opportunity to miss. He typed in "Reinickendorf – Spandau". Depending on the time he had one or two line changes to make and the journey time ranged from thirty to fifty minutes.

Whilst waiting for his Ummagumma breakfast, he opened up his map, put a cross on the road in which Simsek's company resided and did the same for the Ruwolt's in Spandau. Undoubtedly the easiest way would be to call a taxi. But he wouldn't be able to justify it as an expense.

He decided against phoning the Simsek's company. The man could well have appointments. Simply turning up and requiring just a few minutes and having travelled all the way from Hamburg carried weight that couldn't easily be deflected.

There were other guests in the room: a young couple he did not recognise, the man with his family, a single man, an older man and a youth. The twins weren't present and he had the impression that they weren't guests and merely frequented the bar.

Even if this hotel was a place for gays, it was on the fringe of the scene. The owners were too old and the place too small and quaint to be the wild techno-hub.

At a quarter past ten he was packed and standing with his overnight bag in front of the reception hut. The family man and his wife were in front of him. Their children were sitting on the sofa playing I-spy.

Dannaks hadn't banked on anyone else checking out and the couple were querying some item on their bill. Luckily his appointment with the Ruwolts was between eleven and twelve. Nevertheless he began to grow impatient.

At breakfast the guy who had manned the reception had played waiter. He now saw that yesterday's waiter was now working behind the reception desk.

The family left and he moved up to check out.

"Did you make any calls this morning?"

"Yes, I did." He looked up and then went back to the keyboard and screen tucked down almost under the counter. There was a ghost of a smile on the man's face. Doubtless with the advent of handies billed telephone calls had all but disappeared as a money making source.

When he saw the bill and the exorbitant price for the short call to Reinhart he had to question it. "I wasn't on the phone for that long."

"No. But there's a connection charge and a minimum duration."

Dannaks shook his head disgustedly.

Although the man didn't look up to witness his displeasure, he instinctively knew of it. "The terms are on the card next to the phone in your room."

Only when Dannaks signed and paid did he look up.

10:14

The nine minute train journey covered the greatest distance in the shortest time. But the walk to Kochstrasse, the waiting for the train and the walk from Reinickendorf to the gates of Simsek's company were not as efficient.

When he stopped at the pillbox by the iron gates he knew he had a window of less than half an hour. The security man checked his ID and then made a call.

After hanging up he pointed out the office buildings next to the aircraft hangar style warehouse.

Dannaks nodded and crossed the forecourt. This was relatively deserted except for the half dozen white delivery vans sporting the Simsek name and logo. There were enough parking spaces to cater for three times that number. Vehicles were undoubtedly underway. A sign pointed out the way to a visitors' and staff car park.

Two vans peeked out of the warehouse having been backed-in undoubtedly to be loaded. The whine of fork lift trucks and jovially booming voices testified to activity in the depths of the building.

Stacks of wooden pallets lined the walls of the single-storey office building.

Entering the relative darkness of the building, Dannaks found himself in a short corridor. To his left was a window behind which he saw three desks covered in the paraphernalia of a working office. The walls were hidden behind cupboards and shelving.

The sole occupant of the room was a woman in her forties. She got up from her desk when she saw Dannaks at the window.

"Good morning," she said.

Dannaks dropped his bag and pulled out his ID.

"*Kripo* Hamburg." He gave her a moment. People always needed a moment. Perhaps to let them go through all that they may have done wrong. "I'd like to talk to *Herr* Simsek."

"I'm sorry, he's not in today."

"Not at all?" Not that this mattered. He only had a slim

window of time.

"No. He generally takes Friday off."

Dannaks nodded slowly and the woman waited. Before her impatience showed he said: "Does he live in Berlin?"

This took her aback. "Er, yes, but I–"

"It's a police matter. Please."

"Well, I er, I'll have to call him first."

"Okay."

He caught a scolding glance before she returned to her desk. She picked up her telephone and pressed a button. Dannaks couldn't hear what she was saying and checked his watch. When he looked up she had replaced the receiver and was writing on a pad.

She slid open the moveable half of the window and handed him a piece of paper. He smiled when he saw that Simsek had a Spandau address.

11:22

It took him a good three quarters of an hour to get across the city and out to Spandau. And the trip was hot and sticky.

On the journey he pulled out his map and found and marked Simsek's road in Spandau. It was on the river Havel. Unfortunately the location was not close to the Ruwolt's or a train station.

He hadn't made an appointment or said that he would see Simsek today, but it was still too good an opportunity to miss.

The Ruwolts lived in a semi-detached house on a quiet tree-lined 30 kilometre per hour side road striped with speed bumps. Many children would be at school but there was evidence of street activity. Coloured chalk drawings and demarcations were testimony. A tricycle lay on its side at the edge of a front garden path. In another front garden a wooden structure like a tree house without the tree had been put together on stilts to resemble both a house and a ship. A skull and crossbones flag hung lifelessly from a wooden post.

Many of the ground floor front windows sported the same blue "neighbourhood watch" shield. And the closed sense of community made him feel like an intruder.

From the bus stop to their house wasn't far, but lugging his bag, his jacket sandwiched between the handles, in the breezeless midday warmth had given him a sheen of sweat. Even his headache, buzzing distantly in the wings, seemed poised to take centre stage.

A neighbour was tending her front garden. She looked up sternly as he lifted the latch of the Ruwolts gate. She was small and in her fifties with a bright but wrinkled face. Her green rubber gloves and dirt-caked garden trowel made her look like a crouching gnome.

"*Guten Tag*," he smiled, thinking that all she needed was a pointed red hat.

She returned the greeting, but didn't smile and resumed her digging.

Dannaks rang the front door bell above which the small brass nameplate confirmed that he was at the right place.

The chimes were a short tune that he knew would get on his nerves by the third visit.

Through the frosted glass panel of the door he saw someone approach. The woman opened the door just enough to keep a shoulder behind it.

"*Oberkommissar* Dannaks," he smiled, fumbling with his jacket for his ID. "We spoke on the phone."

He held it up to her. She looked at it but didn't take it and he knew that he could as well have held up a library pass.

"Yes," she said. Her smile was awkward but she opened the door. Further in the house, at the entrance to a room, stood another woman watching them but continually distracted by activity in the room.

He would have been a little surprised if she'd seen him alone and he had half expected her husband to be present.

"*Frau* Ruwolt?" He pocketed his card and held out his hand.

"Yes," she said again, extending her hand limply to allow it to be shaken.

She was a poker-faced woman with thin lips. Her make-up was immaculate and the nails of her slender fingers painted. Her eyes, large and blue, softened the harshness of her features. Her hair was strawberry blonde that appeared natural, although it didn't move and was rock perfect with hairspray.

He judged her to be in her early thirties.

Opening the door wider she ushered him in. He made his own way towards the other woman whilst *Frau* Ruwolt closed the door.

The other woman moved further into the room, which was a long lounge diner affair ending in glass door looking out onto a short patio and fenced garden. The room was as spick and span as a showroom. Other than a small cluster of toys under the table there was no evidence of a child in the house. There was no clutter. Even the small selection of magazines on the coffee table, sitting upon the white thick pile rug, was orderly. Like the parquet floor the surfaces were clean and everything had its place and appeared to be in its place: a vase with realistic looking flowers, an antique brass cannon on wheels that the kid was not allowed to touch, a photograph Dannaks couldn't identify, carefully chosen unobtrusive pictures hanging on the walls.

Dannaks was dismayed to see that Timi was playing under the pine dining table with another little boy. But he was pleased to see that he was playing with toy cars. Timi was the one with the big blue eyes.

"This is *Frau* Schmidt from next door." Then to the woman: "*Oberkommissar* Dannaks." She made no attempt to approach or acknowledge him; she appeared too busy appraising him.

He shifted his bag with his wedged jacket into his left hand, stepped forward, and boldly thrust out his hand.

Shaken, she glanced at *Frau* Ruwolt before taking his hand.

She had dark hair, a comparatively soft complexion and looked to be nudging forty.

He then realised that she was eyeing his bag.

"I got here last night," he said. "I had to check out of the hotel."

Then she turned to the children and he was relieved when she spoke. "Roland, come on, we've got to go."

"In a minute."

"No, now."

"You can come back after lunch," *Frau* Ruwolt consoled.

The women exchanged nods. Dannaks was left alone in the room for a moment as *Frau* Ruwolt saw them out and Timi, seeing that he was alone with a stranger, ran after them.

"Please, sit down," said *Frau* Ruwolt returning with Timi in tow.

"Thanks." Dannaks went to the dining table, pulled out a chair, placed his bag at his feet and sat. He made an effort to catch the boy's eye with a smile, but Timi was moving his toy car through the air like a plane behind the safety of his mother's leg.

"Would you like something to drink?"

"Anything cold."

"Apple juice? Water? Orange–"

"Water will be fine."

She went to the fridge and Timi, engrossed in his car, suddenly found himself again alone with a stranger.

Dannaks smiled and the boy faltered. Then he fled, but not to his mother. Instead he went to the lounge area and disappeared behind the sofa.

Frau Ruwolt returned with a glass of sparkling water and nothing for herself.

"It's hot," he said, taking the glass.

"The city is always stifling in this weather." She took an adjacent chair at the table. Initially he hadn't found her attractive. Close up he realised that there was something beguiling about her. He decided it was in her wondrous eyes. "It's usually cooler out here. But not today."

Small talk appeared exhausted and, after placing his glass on a coaster, that was a small version of a colourful twenties poster advertising Vogue, Dannaks came to the point.

He knew he had misjudged time and distance and that if he was going to rely on the buses to get back to Kreuzberg, there was a chance he wouldn't get to Dr. Kilic's to meet Reupke before one.

"I'd like to ask Timi about the red man he saw."

"Timi," she called.

His head popped up from behind the sofa.

"This gentleman would like to ask you about the red man."

The boy frowned, but didn't look at Dannaks.

"What red man?"

"Come here please."

As he came round he looked at Dannaks who gave him a reassuring smile. He ignored him and went to his mother. She hoisted him onto her lap and he repeated: "What red man, mama?"

"Beelzebub," said Dannaks.

The boy hadn't expected the reply from that direction and seemed startled. Then his big eyes widened – if that were possible – as he evidently remembered.

He fidgeted. Then he began hopping up and down gleefully as if he were riding a horse. "Beelzebub. Beelzebub. Beelzebub. B–"

"Stop it, Timi," she said firmly, grabbing his hips to hold him in place.

He frowned again and stretching an arm on the table lay his head on it. He looked at Dannaks who gave him a sympathetic look; then he brought up his other hand holding the toy car to move it on the table.

"Not on the table," said *Frau* Ruwolt.

The boy again looked at Dannaks. This time they connected, because Dannaks conveyed that if it was up to him he would let Timi play on the tabletop.

Dannaks glanced at *Frau* Ruwolt hoping she'd missed the connection. Then he went down to his bag, unzipped a side pocket and took out the folded map. He then shifted his jacket and zipped open the main area. He fished about till his fingers found the plastic bag, which, mindful of his dirty clothes, he carefully pulled out.

"I have something for you, Timi. But you have to answer my questions, first."

The boy sat up and made to reach for the plastic bag Dannaks had placed on the table. His mother stopped him.

Wanting to maintain their fragile friendship Dannaks decided to reach into the plastic bag and pull out the cardboard box. He set it down on the table for the boy to see whilst he folded the plastic bag. One long side and top of the box were clear plastic. Inside stood a blue and white police car. This was the third unusual purchase, along with the plum wine and dog bone, he had made at Patel's two days earlier.

"Do you remember drawing the red man?"

Timi nodded, finding it hard to take his eyes off the car.

"Good." He waited a beat. "Do you remember seeing him?"

The boy didn't answer and Dannaks wondered whether he'd made a mistake showing him the prize.

"Timi," said *Frau* Ruwolt, "answer the man."

"Are you a policeman?" he asked.

Dannaks nodded.

"Where's your uniform?"

"I'm not that kind of policeman. I'm a detective."

"Can I see your gun?"

Frau Ruwolt made to intervene, but Dannaks gestured that it was okay.

"I'm afraid I haven't got it with me."

"Why not?"

"I didn't think there was any danger coming here."

Timi seemed satisfied.

"Now answer the policeman's question."

He looked puzzled.

"Do you remember the red man?"

Although his attention was drifting back to the prize he nodded.

"Do you remember anything about him?"

The boy shrugged. General questions were hopeless. He needed to be specific.

"Was he as big as me?"

Timi looked at him, his bottom lip sticking out. Then he shrugged.

Dannaks hid his disappointment and prepared his next question. But *Frau* Ruwolt spoke. "It was dark *Herr Hau—Oberkommissar.*"

Her intervention annoyed him, but he hid this too.

"I know. But this is important." He turned to the boy again, whose eyes were transfixed by the police car. "Just a couple more questions, Timi." He paused, suppressing his growing sense that he was not goingto get anything from the boy. "Why did you make him red?" Timi shrugged. Dannaks didn't want to lead the boy by putting words into his mouth, but he needed answers. "Was he angry or wearing paint?

"He was angry because he had ouch and blood."

"Did you see his ouch?"

He shook his head.

"But he had blood on his face?"

Timi nodded.

"Do you remember what he was wearing?"

The boy was quiet and Dannaks prepared himself for a shrug. "Like Mama's lilac thing."

"Mama's?"

"I have a purple jump suit. That's what he means."

"I don't suppose you could get it for me?"

She looked at him suspecting that it was a ploy to get her out of the room so that he could question Timi alone. Then she lifted her son off her lap and stood. "Timi you can stay here with the nice man or you can come with me."

The boy eyed Dannaks and then returned to the car. "Stay."

Dannaks suppressed his smile. A surreptitious glance at his

watch told him he could still make it to Simsek's before going to Dr. Kilic's.

When she was gone Dannaks unfolded the small map on the table. The words "Azure Skies hotel resort" were written above the word legend, under which circled numbers in ascending order were translated. Number one was main entrance, number two reception, etc. Open it measured no more than half an A4 sheet. "Timi, can you look at this with me? It's like a treasure map. See these coloured blocks; they're the buildings. Here look, number seven, amphitheatre. Do you remember from the holiday? Here's the restaurant." The boy's interest was waning.

Frau Ruwolt reappeared with a purple jumpsuit and saw what he was doing. "You can't expect him–"

"Please," said Dannaks. "You were playing hide and seek. Do you remember?" The boy frowned. "Then you saw the red man. Beelzebub."

The boy brightened and was about to launch into a litany when he looked over at his mother.

"Do you remember where you saw him?" Dannaks began fingering the map. "Here, near the tennis courts?" The boy looked blankly. "Near the restaurant? No. How about up here?"

"You haven't children, have you?"

Dannaks looked at *Frau* Ruwolt. "No. But I thought he might remember."

"Like I said on the phone, he's only four and a half."

"Did he say anything to you? You know, where he was?" She shook her head. "And you didn't ask him to take you to where he had seen the man?" She made the same gesture. "So you didn't know where he was?"

She saw the implication and stiffened. "He was playing with the older children. He knew not to go too far. I think they were near the restaurant. Did you speak to the other children?"

"Is that the jumpsuit?" When she nodded Dannaks turned to Timi. "One last question and then you can have the car." Impatience took the boy and he hopped from one foot to the other. "Was the man wearing something like what your Mama's holding?" He nodded without looking and made a grab for the box. Dannaks was faster. "Please look, Timi," he pleaded as softly as he could. The boy looked at his mother and then Dannaks and nodded. "Did it have anything on it? You know, a badge or some writing." Timi shrugged. Dannaks released the box and the boy tore at it.

"Timi," said *Frau* Ruwolt. Then to Dannaks: "I'm sorry."

Dannaks shrugged. "That's okay."

"I can't believe he was wearing something like this. It must have been some kind of overall."

He looked at her seriously. "Remember that came from you."

"What? Why should I remember?" Horror took her. "You don't mean I –Timi – will have to testify?"

He smiled. "I doubt that very much."

She appeared relieved. By now the box was in shreds and Timi was examining the police car.

"Not on the table," she said to the boy. Turning to Dannaks she said: "It was nice of you to bring him something. I'm sorry your trip was a waste."

"I was here anyway." He checked his watch and decided not to ask about a possible bus route to Simsek's place. "Well, I won't keep you any longer. I'm actually running a bit late. Could I call a taxi?"

12:13

As soon as the taxi left all was still.

The road upon which the Simsek's lived was not a main road and was equally as quiet as that of the Ruwolt's. There the similarity ended. The houses here were individual in both style and setting. They were set back from the road. All front gardens shut out the road with impenetrable hedges or high walls. The rejection wasn't simply for the road. It was for the neighbours and then the rest of the world. The Simsek's house only resembled the others in size. They were all big places, but not necessarily residences. Many appeared to be small businesses or factories.

Dannaks pressed the incongruously modern bell at the intercom panel in the pillar: the base of an arch that bridged two wrought-iron gates. Looking up to his left he spotted the security camera trained on the bell.

There was no discernible wording on the arch, but the unevenness said that words had been removed.

An electronic voice belonging to a woman said: "Hallo."

Dannaks introduced himself and the woman said that Simsek was expecting him. A moment later the double gates juddered and eased open.

445

Dannaks checked his watch again as he slipped through the gates that continued to leisurely open. He strode round the circular gravel drive that resembled a traffic roundabout, in the centre of which was an island of shrubbery and an ancient grey tree that he realised carried walnuts.

Beyond the old red-brick house the drive opened up in front of a double garage. A basketball hoop was attached high up on the nearest side. Other than this the place educed an impersonal characterless atmosphere. Maybe it had been a pub or belonged to a rowing club at some time.

The two-storey house was clean and yet weary. The panelled cherry wood door was not only imposing in size, it shone with lacquer. A gold knocker in the shape of a jaguar – like the leaping one on the car of the same name – hung ornamentally. To the right of the door a discreet bell was embedded in the stone of the house. Before he could press it a voice said: "Please show your ID to the camera." Dannaks located the camera, again trained on the area of the bell, high up to his left. He dropped his bag, dug out his ID and showed it to the camera. Before he had pocketed it the door opened.

The woman who stood before him looked like a buxom cleaner. Her clothes weren't worn or old and she wasn't wearing an apron, but her one gloved hand held the glove of her other. They were of yellow rubber: the kind used to wash dishes.

"Herr Simsek is round the back." Her accent was thick. Russian? "You can go that way." She waved to Dannaks's right and then closed the door.

Shaking his head he lifted his bag and followed the paved path that hugged the contours of the house.

The two storey house was big, perhaps six-bedrooms, but it was in need of renovation. Perhaps it was listed, but the mod-cons stuck out like barnacles on an old ship.

For a moment he was out of sight between the house and bushes. Then the garden opened up before him. The size of the garden was hard to gauge. It could be merely twice that of his parents'. Beyond the expanse of green, uneven with brown patches and tufts, were trees and bushes, hiding a possible wall and effectively camouflaging the boundaries of the garden.

In keeping with the rest of the house, the place bespoke of money and lack of it. Like the luxury cars in the new garage he imagined the inside of the house to be expensively decorated. The at-first-glance modest appearance of the house was a sham.

The terrace at the back of the house extended too far and hinted at a former use. Perhaps it was the floor of some demolished structure or an area for chairs and tables. Two wooden loungers and a small matching wooden table were arranged under a large umbrella.

There was no-one in sight.

Dannaks stood for a moment, contemplating returning to the front of the house when he though he heard voices beyond the trees.

He spotted a track between the foliage and came upon a grassy patch on the banks of the river. A further two loungers and a table had been dragged here. Although there was plenty of shade, the furniture had been placed in the sun.

Despite their casual attire, they were in shorts and T-shirts, Dannaks recognised the man and the youth from the website. *Frau* Simsek wasn't there. Indeed, she had not featured on the website.

Although they had seen him and the youth had stood up, the man continued his monologue. Dannaks caught the tail end of what Simsek was saying to his son.

"So, you still ask even though it's already yours. It gives them a false sense of connection and perhaps power over you."

Simsek looked like a healthier and leaner version of Aksoy. But Dannaks couldn't pinpoint the resemblance. And then his son didn't resemble Ayhan. There again, Dannaks didn't have much in common with his brother, Jürgen.

Simsek then looked at Dannaks and the boy made to leave.

"You're a long way from home, detective." The man hadn't greeted him, offered his hand or so much as moved.

Dannaks wasn't meeting the man. He'd been granted the privileged of an audience.

"Please stay," Dannaks said to the boy, who glanced at his father uncertainly.

Simsek ignored his son. "How can I help?" There was to be no introduction, offer of a seat or refreshment. A pitcher of iced water and beakers stood on the small table.

Dannaks, suffering in the heat, became curt. He had little time for pleasantries anyway. "I won't waste your time, Herr

Simsek." The man didn't grace him with a response. You let Aksoy's carry out the maintenance on your company vehicles."

"Yes." His ease betrayed wariness. "Sometimes, my private ones too."

"Sometimes?"

He gave a wry smile. "The more exclusive ones insist upon using their approved garages."

Dannaks nodded.

"But surely you are not here to confirm where I take my car for repairs?"

"No. I just wanted to establish the connection. I assume you sold the one to the Aksoy's that Mahmut – Aksoy's son–"

"I know who he is."

"That he used in–"

"That double-murder." His impatience bordered on exacerbation. "Yes. What is your question, detective?"

"I'm looking into the murder of Matthias–"

"The Nazi in Turkey."

"Yes, but more importantly the girl involved."

"And?" he prompted, almost bored.

"Well, this is a routine enquiry. You'll understand that I–"

"Stop right there, detective–"

"Herr Aksoy, this'll go a lot quicker if you'd stop interrupting me."

"It'll go a lot quicker if you came to the point."

For a moment they silently stared at each other. But it was the boy, still standing who rocked uneasily.

"I understand completely." Simsek shook his head. "You want to know where I or my son were at the time of–"

Now it was Dannaks's turn to interrupt. "We could start there."

"No. We end there. Check it all with my secretary. Look around. You're supposed to be the detective." He pronounced the last word affectedly. "Even if I had anything to do with what you're suggesting, do you think I'd jeopardise all this and do it myself?"

"Good point. But that doesn't–"

"Why should I have anything to do with this?"

"I said it was routine."

"You're at the wrong address. Goodbye, detective."

Dannaks didn't move and felt there was more to say. In fact he felt he had missed something vital.

"Could I call a taxi?"

"Ask my housekeeper."

12:54

Dannaks spotted the underground station Haselhorst that confirmed his whereabouts and his worst suspicion.

The taxi driver was one of those archetypical celluloid New York cabbies: chatty and flitting from one end of a spectrum of information to another. His tried and tested ploy was to blind with his barrage of encyclopaedic knowledge. As soon as Dannaks had climbed in the man had established that he wasn't from Berlin. After stating his destination the man said: "Business or pleasure?"

"What?"

"Business or pleasure? You're not from around here."

"Business."

"Where are you from?"

As soon as Dannaks answered Hamburg his spiel began. He launched into what he knew of the city; how he had visited some decade earlier, dropping place names and filling them out with anecdotal "did you know" trivia.

Dannaks played along, interjecting that he should enter one of those television quiz shows as a contestant. Indeed his entertaining streetwise delivery meant he could compere such a show. All the while he took surreptitious glances at his watch. The driver had two rear-view mirrors, of which one was angled at the back seat. On more than one occasion their eyes met.

The train station told Dannaks that they were further north than they should be. He remembered the name when he'd looked at the map for the best route. In the next lull, which was a pause for breath, he immediately spoke: "Do you remember I said I was here on business?"

"Of course. I–"

"Well, as a police officer I don't like to be late for my appointments." Dannaks waited for his eyes in the mirror and caught the micro expression of horror. "So let's cut the city tour, shall we?"

Predictably the man had everything off pat. "This is the quickest route. Yes, I'll admit it's not direct, but this way we have the least number of traffic lights, and there's always congestion along Heerstrasse and Spandauer Damm has road works."

"Just get me there. Concentrate on that and give your mouth a rest."

The silence was instant. And Dannaks actually missed the jolly banter. But he allowed himself an imperceptible nod when the driver took the next available right.

Eventually they pulled over to double-park on a busy shopping street. The driver switched off the meter and looked balefully in the mirror.

Dannaks pulled out his wallet. "I'd like a receipt. Your tip is in the fare."

The driver's jaw tightened as he wrote out the receipt.

Dannaks handed over the money and checked the receipt before folding it into his wallet. He wasn't sure he could use it, but it was worth a try.

He climbed out, pulling his bag after him.

The insignificant front door, which could have given access to flats, stood between a chemist and an optician's. It was one twenty and the practice would not be admitting patients. He found Dr. Kilic on the panel to the left of the door and pressed the button. He didn't hear anything, but didn't expect to. The street was busy with cars and shoppers and the bell would have buzzed somewhere in the building. He waited and waited. Then he pressed the button again, longer this time. He couldn't believe that they would have packed up and left already. The last appointment would have been at twelve or twelve thirty. And the appointments were rarely held. A patient with a twelve thirty appointment would be lucky to be seen before one. He was ringing a third time and contemplating trying other buttons just to get in the building when the door opened and an old man stepped out. Dannaks stepped aside and tried to hold the door and his bag out of the way.

"Thank you, young man," he croaked, stepping shakily out.

It had been a long time since he'd been called a young man and he smiled.

Inside he let the door close on its elbowed hinge and made his way down the corridor. There were stairs and a lift to his right. The doors to the lift were closed, but when he pressed the button they juddered aside immediately. He looked in and saw only numbered floors: no indication which floor he required. He proceeded to the two doors at the end of the corridor. One faced him and one was to his right. Neither of the name shields was that of Dr. Kilic. He sighed and returned to the stairs to climb to the first floor. Again he came upon two doors. The one facing him had a framed sheet of paper behind glass. Dr. med. Recep Kilic *Facharzt für Allgemeinmedizin* (specialist for general medicine).

He rang the bell and heard it buzz harshly. Then he thought he heard voices and movement, so he waited. After a while he buzzed and followed it up by knocking on the door. Then he heard the unmistakeable sound of a woman's heels approaching.

The door cracked open.

"Dr. Kilic's practice is closed for the weekend. I'm sorry, you'll have to make an appointment for next week or go to a *Notarzt* (doctor on emergency call)."

She was about to close the door.

"Dannaks. *Kripo* Hamburg. I believe my colleague is there. *Oberkommissar* Reupke?"

"Oh yes." Then she opened the door. Behind her was the reception counter behind which stood another woman. Both women were middle-aged with their hair pulled back and tied in efficient buns. There was a no-nonsense, low-tolerance air about them. "He's in with the doctor now."

"Could I come in and wait?"

"Of course."

"Let's see some identity," said the woman behind the counter.

"Yes," said the one at the door quickly, kicking herself for the oversight.

He obliged and although he was already inside the woman moved to the side to close the door behind him. She then directed him to a chair near the doctor's door. There were four chairs in the space with an equal number of doors. One was marked private, one WC and the third "*Untersuchungsraum* 1" (Examination room 1). Perhaps there was an "*Untersuchungsraum* 2" somewhere. This then was a waiting area when you'd done your time in the waiting room. It broke up the duration and gave a semblance of progress.

The women were busy with paperwork behind the counter and all but ignored him. After about ten minutes the one who had opened the door to him said: "There are some magazines in the waiting room, if you want something to read."

"Thanks," he said, not sure he wanted to read, but finding himself getting up anyway. He went into the waiting room. On the low table in the centre of the room the magazines had been arranged in thematic columns, lying on top of one another, but juxtaposed to reveal their titles. Stacked as they were, they resembled the layout of a game of Patience. The thought amused him as he glanced at the empty chairs that lined the room.

He picked out an old Spiegel with a cover he didn't recognise and went back to his seat.

After scanning the contents he settled upon an article about a recent police suicide. He had just started reading when the doctor's door opened and voices broke the silence.

Dannaks recognised Reupke's back in the doorway. He obscured the speaker. They were shaking hands and Reupke was now thanking him for his help and wishing him a good weekend. Then he turned and Dannaks glimpsed Kilic.

Reupke nodded to Dannaks who was rising. The doctor was closing his door on them. For an instant Kilic's and Dannaks's eyes locked. Then the door was closed.

"You made it then," said Reupke, extending his hand.

"Yes," said Dannaks, as they shook hands. But he was raking his mind. He felt he had seen Kilic somewhere before. "What did he say?"

Reupke was perplexed. He glanced at the two women, who had paused during Kilic's appearance, but were now back to filing and sorting things away. "I'll tell you later."

Dannaks had asked the question to stall for time. He nodded. Still he couldn't place the man. He held up the magazine. "I have to put this back."

In the waiting room he took care to place it in the correct column. As he did so some glossy gossip magazine caught his attention. The splashed headline screamed exclusive and intimate photographs of some celebrity.

Dannaks froze as it hit him.

"Are you okay?" Reupke was standing at the entrance to the room.

Dannaks straightened. "What did he say?"

"Are you all right?"

"Did he admit to knowing the Aksoy's intimately?"

"What? No. He said he was her doctor and had identified her to the best of his knowledge, but he could have been mistaken. You want—"

But Dannaks was on the move and brushed past Reupke heading straight for Kilic's office.

He knocked twice and opened the door without waiting for an answer. One of the women may have said something but he didn't hear her.

Kilic looked up from his desk.

"Dr. Kilic my name's Dannaks, *Kripo* Hamburg. Why didn't you tell my colleague that you are a personal friend of the Aksoys?"

Kilic opened his mouth to speak, but one of the women, now directly behind Dannaks spoke first. "I don't care who you are. You can't just burst in on the doctor like this."

Dannaks ignored her. He didn't even turn around.

He stared at the man and the more he did the more he thought that he merely resembled the flamboyant grey haired man in the photograph in Aksoy's apartment. This man appeared thinner, more ashen. Even his bouffant had thinned too. He remained steadfast, but should the man protest that he didn't know them, Dannaks knew he had nothing but an apology.

Again the man made to speak and Dannaks decided on a last ditch bluff. "I saw your photograph at the Aksoys."

In the prolonged moment Kilic's expression remained granite, but Dannaks felt him going through a myriad of emotions from indignation and anger before settling in resignation. When the doctor looked away Dannaks knew he had won.

He pushed on. "You identified the victim as Shaziye to support Mahmut's claim. To help him save face. Who told you to say it was her?" Kilic's eyes remained downcast and Dannaks raised his voice. "Come on doctor. The old man Aksoy? Volcan?" Kilic remained motionless. "Who?" He shouted and Kilic visibly jumped.

"Aksoy," he said quietly.

"Which one?" Dannaks hissed.

"Abdurrahim." The old man.

"You know there'll be consequences." Then Kilic looked up. He appeared sad and broken. Dannaks shook his head disappointedly. He turned and almost bumped into the assistant who'd opened the door to him. Reupke stood a step or two behind her. "Let's go," Dannaks said to him.

There was a sense of devastation as the detectives left the practice. Neither spoke until they hit the street. Reupke broke the silence.

"What the hell was that?"

"I was doing my job." He still had some venom left. He was as surprised as Reupke at his aggression and wasn't really sure where it had come from, but suspected a mixture of frustration with the case and uneasiness with his colleague.

"Who do you think you are?" asked Reupke. Dannaks waited. "You can't come bursting into my interview. You should have spoken to me first."

"When? When he'd gone home? On our way home? And besides, as I see it, your interview was over. And you'd got nothing."

"He's warned now."

"Even you know that's not going to make any difference." Kilic could admit to making an error. A slick lawyer could probably get him off unscathed. Talk of how often he'd actually seen the patient, the pallor of death at the identification making him unsure, the similarity in the appearance of the girls and so forth.

Negotiating pedestrians and crossing busy roads made the silence between them acceptable but no less awkward. Each was consumed by his own thoughts and anger toward the other.

Dannaks thought that Reupke was still peeved because of the *Mordkommission* error he had uncovered. No department enjoyed the interference of another, especially when it entailed pointing out a mistake and then instead of keeping a lid on it and correcting it internally and quietly, allowing it to be exposed to those in authority. It was equivalent to uncovering a wound and going on to prod it with the tip of a knife.

They travelled the underground to the main station. Silence prevailed.

After they checked the timetable and noting that they had a half hour they agreed to find a place to sit. Only when they were seated with drinks and packet sandwiches did they properly converse.

"Was it worth it?" asked Reupke, sipping his orange juice after swallowing his first bite of sandwich.

Dannaks nodded as if he wasn't ready to talk. He took a large bite out of his own triangular sandwich.

Reupke waited for him to finish chewing. "You got something, then?"

"I have a suspicion."

"Let's hear it."

The hint of weariness in Reupke's toned irked Dannaks. "Forget it."

"What's this now? God, I'm sick of your one-man crusader bit. And watch out, you've got some diligence showing there." He brushed the side of his mouth with a finger.

Mimicking his motion Dannaks knocked a piece of grated cheese from his cheek. The reference to Weske's compliment admiring his diligence scotched him. So he couldn't thank Reupke for pointing out the cheese on his face.

"You can be so damned childish."

Dannaks smirked. "You too."

Reupke was surprised by the reply. He shook his head, but then he too smirked.

It occurred to them how ludicrous they were acting. Dannaks laughed and Reupke leaned back and did so too.

"You know what Steffi would say?" said Reupke. Dannaks looked at him questioningly. "She'd say we're like a married couple."

"Shut up or I'll hit you with my handbag," he said nodding to his holdall on the floor next to them.

"I'll hit you back." Reupke carried a thin attaché case.

"Mine's bigger."

"Stop boasting."

They settled down quickly for the banter was uneasy. For the next few moments they ate and drank. Again it was Reupke who spoke first.

"What did you find out?"

Dannaks waited a tick before calmly saying: "I think I got a suspect."

Reupke spluttered on his mouthful of sandwich and Dannaks grasped the opportunity to eat some of his own sandwich.

"Let me start with what happened today. It's not much, but perhaps another piece in the puzzle." He then explained interviewing Timi and establishing that the red man wore some kind of overall.

By the time he had finished talking about Timi it was time to make their way to the train. It took them a while to find seats that weren't reserved. All the foursome seats with tables were taken and they were left to sit side-by-side travelling backwards with respect to the direction of the train. The carriage became quite full with only the odd seat taken up by a bag.

Once they were underway Dannaks quietly began without prompting. He told Reupke of Aksoy's garage and the state of the business, of the apartment and Ayhan and the women, Ayhan's visit and finally Simsek. Reupke listened asking few questions.

"It's obvious you think this Volcan, Mahmut's brother, is our killer," said Reupke when Dannaks announced that he was done.

"He's certainly the best lead so far. He left when the garage desperately needs him. With Mahmut gone he would have been the ideal candidate for leadership. Instead he disappears for weeks on end. And it all fits. Think about it. The crowbar, the overall. I–"

"You don't believe he'd be stupid enough to wear his garage overall, do you?"

"No. And if he did he would have removed any labels."

"Like, er, one advertising Aksoy's garage."

"Yes." Dannaks ignored the attempt at humour. "But maybe the Aksoy's have another garage out there."

"That's a lot of maybes." Reupke had said this before.

"It's something."

"Yes, it's conjecture." Reupke must have sensed his irritation. "But I agree. It is a lead worth following. To be honest the best that's going to come of this is you handing it to Ismail or someone over there. We're out now. You know that." Dannaks nodded despondently. "In a novel or a film you'd be able to chase this up. But we're not in a novel or a film and ours is certainly not a Hollywood budget."

Dannaks knew he was right. He'd run out of time. "I suppose I could get myself suspended again."

Reupke chuckled. And Dannaks smiled bitterly.

They fell into an easy silence.

"By the way, Steffi's going to ask me." Reupke waited a beat. "Have you heard anything from Katja?"

"No," he lied.

16:55

456

The detectives were silent for the majority of the time on the train. Towards the end of the journey Dannaks had found himself dozing.

He had read the paper Reupke had purchased that morning. Reupke had offered it to him with the words: "Check out page six." On it Dannaks found a small piece on Herbst. The right wing politician had flown to Turkey yesterday to look at his place in Side. The culprits who had vandalised his property were still at large. There was no reference to the fact that the Hamburg police had inadvertently brought his ownership to light.

At Hamburg's main station Reupke changed to the underground and Dannaks walked out.

The late afternoon light had put a slump in the atmosphere. There was a sense of exhaustion not unlike the end of a day lying at Azure Skies poolside. The summer's day had been exhilarating and now it was time to wind down. Everything ran more sluggishly. The traffic was slow with dull-eyed drivers; the pedestrians trudged or hung around. Last vestiges of energy were being called upon.

Dannaks felt weary too. Travelling sapped. He also felt deflated. He had got a result in Berlin, but on Monday he'd have to pass it on to Ismail. Then he'd be plodding again. He pushed himself to think of ways he could continue investigating. Short of taking vacation, which he couldn't see being authorised, there was nothing he could do. Even Ismail going the official route seemed hopeless. What could he say? After all, they had someone in custody for the murder.

He went into Patel's to check his emails only to be told that the system was down. Because he was carrying his holdall he didn't feel up to burdening himself further with groceries. So he left.

As he returned to his flat thoughts of Katja returned. "Do you know what's tragic? I regretted breaking it off. I was beginning to think that maybe it could work." He wondered whether she had tried to call him at home. This was one of the rare occasions when he wished he had an answer-phone. His reasoning for not having one was that if the call was important the caller would phone again. It was not unreasonable that Katja contact him. After all, she had already sent him a card apologising for her behaviour after that reporter caught them. But then that hysterical call. Maybe she was too capricious for him and he was better off without her.

Saturday and Sunday

The weekend passed in a desultory way. On Friday he vegetated in front of the television. Saturday was spent more industriously. He shopped and did his laundry and even managed to fix the leak in the washing machine. On Sunday he visited his parents for afternoon coffee and cake and an update on his father's friend's old people's home saga.

He noticed a small change in the attitude of his father. Since the publicity the relationship between them had improved. The media furore hadn't directly brought them together, like a father rushing to protect his son. Instead his father appeared to respect or appreciate him more. It wasn't strictly a case of fallibility, for his father had never regarded him as a cold machine. And it wasn't quite sympathy. The stage antics, in fact being with a woman, seemed to have made Dannaks more human in his father's eyes.

All weekend he toyed with the idea of phoning Katja, arguing that she could have tried to contact him whilst he was away. But then she could of course catch him at work. So he held back.

Monday
09:03

Frank asked Dannaks to stay behind after the morning meeting.

"I'll come straight out with it," said Frank. "You've had a damned good run playing freelancer, but after this ten o'clock call, it's back to regular duties."

"I know, Frank."

"I know you know. I also know you. And that's why I'm saying it out loud. I don't want to discover you using REX time on this."

"You won't," Dannaks smiled.

Frank returned the smile before adopting his stern expression. "You know what I'm saying. And Dannaks on a personal level I'd prefer you to drop it too." He showed his palms before Dannaks could protest. "I can't dictate what you do in your free time, but for your own health you need to get away from this." Dannaks heard echoes of Reupke in his sentiments.

"The truth is Frank there's not a lot I can do, short of travelling to Berlin every weekend and staking out the Aksoys."

"I wouldn't put that past you."

458

Dannaks chuckled wearily.

"I'll sit in on this ten o'clock call," Frank said.

With that the conversation was over and Dannaks returned to his desk. As he sat in his chair Reinhart regarded him as if expecting him to explain the one-to-one talk. A quick glance told him that nothing was coming.

"*Frau* Poschmann just phoned."

"Did she leave a message?" said Dannaks, without waiting for an answer and pulling the arm of the telephone stand towards himself. She was now the only person who claimed Meryem was Meryem.

"No."

He rifled the papers in his file and found her number. She didn't pick up immediately and he was worried that he'd missed her once again. When she came on and he introduced himself she said: "Are you still undercover?"

"What? Er, no. No." Without pausing for breath, in an attempt to sweep away his stammering tracks, he added: "I need to interview you."

"Oh? Well, I'm very busy at the m–"

"Today."

"Out of the question. I haven't time the entire week."

"Do you want me to make this official?" He was bluffing. Frank had said in no uncertain terms that the case was over.

"You can forget that tone, *Herr Oberkommissar*," she said, a hard timbre to her voice. "I'm acquainted with my rights and your powers."

Dannaks was unruffled. "It's important and it'd be better if we met informally."

"Is this about Meryem again?"

"Yes." He waited a beat for dramatic effect. "And Shaziye."

Dannaks could sense her shock in the sudden silence.

"*Frau* Poschmann?"

"Yes. Yes. Okay. Do you remember where we met last time?"

"Cafe Ines. Steilshoop."

"Six o'clock."

"I'll be there."

She hung up before he'd removed the hand piece from his ear.

He wasn't overly keen about returning to Steilshoop and the only reason he could imagine a woman of her pretensions frequenting such a cafe was that she had a client or clients nearby.

Reinhart stared at him. What he had heard was enough for him to know that Dannaks was pursuing the case outside working hours.

"Keep it to yourself," he said.

Reinhart gave him a wry smile.

Dannaks's colleague had started checking out the Berlin hospitals and clinics on Friday but had not found any record of Shaziye Aksoy. He said that he would continue his enquiries on the side. This was another thing Dannaks had so far kept from Frank. It was also something for which he felt exceedingly guilty. For he hadn't told Reinhart that after talking to the Turkish police the case would be over. But then Reinhart would have guessed the content of his after-meeting chat with Frank.

He checked his watch and then his notes.

"I'm just going up to see Tanya for a couple of minutes."

Although the secretary's door was wide-open Dannaks knocked as he stepped in.

"Morning," he said.

"Morning, *Oberkommissar*," she said, glancing at him from the open drawer of the gunmetal filing cabinet. She went back to finger-walking the paper files. "How was Berlin?"

"Fine. But I wanted to talk to you about Hotel Floyd."

She stopped working and turned to him, concern sharpening the lines of her pixie face. "Oh? Was something wrong?"

"Why did you choose it?"

"I didn't really. It was recommended by a colleague in Berlin."

"Colleague?"

"A friend of mine. A secretary too. With the Berlin force."

"How well do you know her?" He knew she could be talking about a male secretary, but he wanted her to say it.

"We met at a seminar. Look, what is all this about?"

"The place is renowned for being gay."

A slow smile formed on her face only to be suppressed with exaggerated seriousness. "I didn't know. Was it okay?"

"Yes. But you know the publicity I've had recently. This wasn't going to help me, was it?" The papers would have had a field day. They would have labelled him as insatiable. He'd already been called Casanova. This would have thrown fuel on a dying fire.

Her expression became one of genuine concern. "I didn't know, honestly. And my colleague didn't either. I didn't tell her about your troubles. And it's not national news. I'm sure she didn't know about that." She pondered a moment and her features softened as something dawned on her. "All I said was that you were single, middle-aged and lived alone." They were silent for a moment. "I'll speak to her."

Dannaks nodded. "Do that." Then he turned on his heel and left.

10:00

The telephone gave an unaccustomed tone rendered all the more strange by being set to loudspeaker. There was a clatter and a breath of silence.

Dannaks leaned forward and spoke slowly and clearly in English.

"Hallo. This is *Oberkommissar* Dannaks."

"It is Ismail." His voice sounded strange. "How are you?"

"I am very good. I am here with *Kriminalrat* Frank Neumann and *Kommissar* Reinhart Keller. Are you with others or are you lonely?" He glanced at Reinhart as he said the last sentence. Reinhart was present not only because he had been involved in the case or that this was also his office, but because his English was probably the best in the room. Dannaks knew his last sentence had been awkward, perhaps grammatically wrong, but Reinhart didn't react.

"No. I am not alone." He introduced himself and five others present. They were of varying ranks and departments. There was at least one lawyer.

Dannaks cringed at the banality and the pause after each statement, which was going to be a hiccup in any flow in the conversation. He realised too that speaking English over the telephone was not going to be easy. The medium left one blind to the nuances of expression that were vital to gauging comprehension.

"Well." There was a silence and Dannaks scrambled to fill it. But Ismail continued. "You have something to tell us?"

"Yes." For a moment he couldn't think how to begin and glanced at his notes. "First of all we believe – er, we know that Meryem is not Meryem. Her name is Shaziye Aksoy."

"Shaziye Aksoy," Ismail echoed.

Again neither party spoke and the line popped and crackled.

"Meryem's parents must be told their daughter is dead," said Dannaks.

The silence swallowed his words.

"Maybe Shaziye will talk," said Dannaks for want of something to say.

"She has. She rescinded her confession."

"Sorry. I do not understand." Dannaks didn't know the meaning of the word rescind. He wondered whether Ismail was using it to impress others in the room. Reinhart mouthed that it meant retract, but it was too late.

"She says she did not kill Peter. She says it was a man she did not know."

"Why has she said this now?" He knew she had gone back on her confession. He didn't think it was due to the stress of interrogation, despite thoughts of Rafael.

"The same reason she tried to commit suicide."

"*Was!*" he exclaimed in German, correcting himself with a lame: "What?" Embarrassed by his outburst he smiled awkwardly at Frank and Reinhart.

He was mistaken to have thought only he had news. Ismail was showing that he could be dramatic too. Dannaks wondered whom he was trying to impress. "Please say to us what happened."

"She was hanging from her bed sheets. She was unconscious, but caught in time."

Dannaks needed a moment to compose his next question.

"But you still have not said the reason." Static filled the gaping silence. "The reason why she has now confessed," he added.

"Then you have not visited our prisons." He detected smugness in Ismail's voice. "They are not – How shall I put it? Welcoming places."

"I see. Did she say what the man – the man who killed Peter – looked like?"

"She said he was big."

Dannaks waited for more, but nothing came. "Is that all?"

"Yes."

"Did she say she knew him?"

"No... Why?"

"I, er, do not know. Maybe she knows him."

"You think they kill him together?"

"No. I don't know." Frank tapped his watch. "But, er, I have a name of who it might be." Again he wasn't sure how to proceed. "His name is Volcan Aksoy. He is her husband's brother." He realised that he hadn't said that she was married. "Er, she was married. We do not know where the brother is, but he could be over there. We think this brother, er, of her husband, tried to kill her." He knew he was making a mess of it. "We have a fax in English to send to you." Reinhart had summarised the murder case in English. "We also have a photograph of Volcan on file. He has a criminal history."

"A moment please." They could hear Ismail talking to others in the room.

"We have to wind up soon," said Frank.

Dannaks nodded.

Reinhart, an amused expression on his face, shook his head. He spoke quietly. "Two foreigners trying to communicate in a language that is foreign to both of them."

"This is news," Ismail began. "But she has been charged with murder. The new evidence could change that to complicity."

"Comp–"

Reinhart interrupted him with a hasty whisper. "They did it together."

"No," said Dannaks to the telephone. "I think Volcan was trying to kill her."

The subsequent silence irked him.

"Have you Volcan's DNA?"

So the killer had left something. "No. All his crimes were, er,–"

"Misdemeanours," said Reinhart, loudly.

Frank looked at his watch but saw that the silence was necessary. Ismail came back on.

"I do not know whether the case can be reopened."

"But–"

Frank raised his hand and shook his head.

"This may bring new evidence to the case. I am sure we can look into it. Thank you. I look forward to receiving the fax and the photograph."

"Can you give a fax number please?"

11:24

There was so much more Dannaks wanted to say. He would have liked to hear about Fehime and Rafael. Had anything new come to light? And what of the shit smearing in the toilet? These things were not on his list, but they were loose ends that bothered him.

After they'd closed down the conference Frank simply said: "That's it. Back to work."

Reinhart faxed his sheet and Dannaks sent the photograph of Volcan.

Dannaks spent the rest of the day picking up the threads of his REX work.

18:00

He left the office at five.

Again he arrived at Café Ines before Poschmann. He ordered a small pot of tea and although he was famished he said that he would wait for his companion before ordering. The taste of the tea was diabolical. As strong as coffee it tasted at if it had been brewing over the weekend. He normally took his tea black, but tipped two of the small plastic containers of long-life milk in.

Apart from an old man in a far corner and a dubious looking couple at the window near the entrance the place was empty. The old man chatted with the staff, which for most of the time simply ignored him. The couple wore black imitation leather adorned with silver chains. Apart from kohl about their eyes, they wore no make-up and looked thin and pale and in dire need of a good meal. By the way they slouched and the redness about their eyes and noses Dannaks guessed them to be addicts. They were sharing a cola.

Whilst he waited he scanned the menu and then his notes.

Poschmann entered at twenty past six, looking like a schoolmarm about to impart punishment. She didn't apologise when Dannaks stood and shook her hand. Incongruously, her scowl tightened her skin to banish her weariness and made her rather attractive.

"Hard day?" he asked when they were seated.

464

She stared at him indignantly as if he'd asked her the colour of her knickers. After a moment a minuscule amount of tension flew from her expression.

"Aren't they all?"

The waitress, pleased with something to do and yet with an expression that said she'd put in her full day, came to the table.

Poschmann didn't consult the menu and ordered an apple juice and a salad. Dannaks had decided to choose the same, believing that she would know the house best. But he wasn't a salad fan and knew it wouldn't satisfy him. He chose the giant *Currywurst* (a large sausage with sauce and curry powder) and chips instead. The cuisine level of the establishment often influenced his choice of food. His reasoning was that something so simple could not be done badly. On occasion he'd been proven wrong.

"I couldn't do your job," he said.

Her smile was askew. "I'd have thought your job was similar."

"Not really. I think the problems you face are sometimes insoluble. I've got clear guidelines."

"Which you follow to the letter?"

It was his turn to give a slanted smile. "Most of the time. But I think you find it hard to switch off. You take a lot of it home."

"And you don't?"

He gave a short laugh. "Me? Personally. I suppose you're right. I do take it home. But a lot of my colleagues don't."

A flicker of warmth swept across her face, but it was fleeting. Then the hardness receded and weariness came to the fore.

The waitress arrived with the glass of apple juice. Dannaks noticed one of the junkies looking their way. Was he contemplating doing a runner?

Poschmann took a sip when the waitress was gone. Dannaks didn't touch his tea. She put down her glass and looked at him enquiringly.

He nodded and took out his newspaper cutting. "Do you remember me showing you this the last time we met?" He unfolded it and held the edges open on the table.

"Of course." She barely looked at it and stared at him dully. He let it go and one side lifted and folded over.

"You said that the girl in the picture was Meryem."

She nodded.

"Please take another look."

"I don't need to." The hardness in her voice matched the returning hardness in her face.

They were both very still, as if movement could be regarded as a sign of weakness.

His long exhalation through his nose was almost a sigh. Then he abruptly leaned forward and spoke urgently. "You said it was Meryem, although she looks more like Shaziye."

"Well, they were very similar," she retorted.

He smiled. "So you knew them both?"

"I, er..." She cast her eyes downwards.

Dannaks proceeded gently. "We know that Shaziye's husband killed Meryem and Michael. He was after Shaziye. I can understand why he'd lie and say he killed Shaziye. There's even an explanation why her G.P. would lie. But there is only one explanation why you would lie." She looked up. Her gaze was blank. "You helped her. You gave her somewhere to stay after the killing, before she could use Meryem's ticket. You may even have helped her find Meryem's ticket and passport."

Her expression remained unchanged. "I don't know what you're talking about."

"If I have to, I could take you in. I could charge you with making a false statement and obstructing justice."

She remained unimpressed.

Dannaks knew the route was a cul-de-sac. He leaned back and she took a sip from her glass. Then he leaned forward again and was about to continue but changed his mind and topped up his cup of tea. "I should have chosen something bottled," he muttered. "I hope the *Currywurst* is better."

Astonishment raised her eyebrows.

He smiled. But she sank back into her trench.

"I can understand you helping her. Knowing her position, maybe I would too."

She shook her head in disbelief. "You have no idea." There was resignation in her voice.

"I think I do," said Dannaks. "My work brings me into contact with the Turkish population. I know about import brides."

"Oh, you know," she said with mocking disbelief. "You know that girls of thirteen or fourteen are sold and married off to men two, three or four times their age. You know about their intentional disintegration when they're here. How many of them are isolated and forbidden to speak German. How they're held prisoner, to produce children, to baby-sit, to do every conceivable household chore from dawn to dusk – twenty-four-seven. Not to mention the violence some of them are subjected to. Violent husbands, violent in-laws. And don't get me onto talking about the patriarchal tendencies in our society or the lack of condemnation for masculine violence. Ha, you know."

"Yes I do," he said calmly. He could have coloured in the gaps in her picture. He could have completed it by saying that many Turkish men resident in Germany went to Turkey in search of a bride. For various reasons there were families willing to sell their daughters at tender ages. The most obvious reason was money. Then there was the presumed better life for their daughter. And generally the parents wanted to avoid problems by marrying their daughters early, before they could lose their virginity.

Germany criminalised forced marriage in 2005. But it was a law difficult to apply and especially ineffectual when the marriage took place outside the country.

Noticing the approaching waitress they leaned back. Poschmann shifted her glass. Dannaks picked up the cutting.

Although both the junkies were almost lolling on the table they were watching them.

Poschmann's salad was in a shallow ceramic bowl and looked quite colourful with strips of red and yellow paprika, cherry tomatoes, slices of cucumber, grated carrot and cubes of cheese on a bed of lettuce. His oval plate was covered by a mountain of chips and a curved piece of rubber piping sprinkled with curry powder and poking over the edges of the plate. The meals looked as if they represented either end of the healthy eating spectrum.

"I don't think I can eat all this," he said, picking up the salt. "*Guten Appetit.*"

"Likewise," Poschmann muttered.

For a moment they ate in silence.

"That was quite an emotional speech," he said.

She didn't react.

"It convinces me that you take it home with you."

She wasn't going to speak.

"I'll be honest with you." This brought her eyes up from her salad. They dropped down again almost immediately. "We probably couldn't do very much about your false identification." Like Kilic a good lawyer could get her off. Both worked under pressure and came into contact with a multitude of people. And his newspaper cutting was hardly high definition.

"I know," she said. She probably did know. Her work often brought her into contact with the police.

They fell silent again.

"*Frau* Poschmann, I'm trying to help Shaziye. She's sitting in a Turkish prison awaiting trial for murder or at best complicity. I need to know what happened here." He didn't mention that there was a good chance that she could get off.

"*Herr* Dannaks, I don't know what happened."

"I think you do." He was still eating chips, trying to make an inroad on his plate so that he would have the space to manoeuvre his sausage and cut it in half. He began pushing them aside, but they kept tumbling into the space. So he paused and gulped some of the despicable tea.

He pondered telling her about Shaziye's attempted suicide, but dismissed the idea.

"Did you visit the two girls at all?"

"You mean after they left the *Frauenhaus*?"

"Yes."

"I had very little contact with them."

"But some."

"Yes. I visited them twice as far as I remember."

"They were good friends?"

"Yes."

"So Shaziye could have had a key to Meryem's flat?"

She was silent for a moment, happy to chew a little longer. Dannaks waited. "I don't know. Maybe."

"Good neighbours check on each others apartments. They water the plants, perhaps collect the post."

"Yes."

"You're not going to speculate with me, are you?"

Her answer was a disinterested smile.

Dannaks cut his sausage in half and then cut a piece off.

"Is there nothing you can tell me that might help Shaziye?"

She shook her head.

Dannaks nodded contemplatively. He chewed a mouthful of sausage, which was a welcome break from the chips.

The waitress appeared again. "Everything okay?"

"Fine," they muttered.

The girl dully surveyed the table and then looked at them both, undoubtedly pigeon-holing them as a married couple that no longer had anything to say to one another. There was nothing more she could do for her tip, so she smiled and returned to the counter.

"You're on file as having helped with the disposal of Shaziye's belongings and the stuff in the flat. What happened to it all?"

She looked at him wearily. "Michael's parents donated many of his things to charity. The furniture went to the State and the *Frauenhäuser.*" She stopped and Dannaks knew there was more.

"And the rest?"

She expelled something of a sigh through her nose. "We got in contact with her parents and they asked for money."

"You have an address?"

"Yes," she said reluctantly. "They settled using the blood money."

"Were they gypsies?"

"No, but they travelled the country for the best part of the year harvesting crops."

"Cotton picking?"

"That as well."

"Didn't the children go to school?"

She raised her eyebrows to emphasise his naivety.

"They lived in abject poverty: literally from hand to mouth. I think they lived in a tent. Having no proper home, means you're landless and that is about as low as you can get over there."

They were quiet for a moment.

"I'd like their name and address."

"It'll be on file."

"Please."

She acquiesced with a nod.

Poschmann finished her meal before him. He felt awkward eating in front of her and thought about stopping. For the taste of chips and sausage had lost their novelty. But he took a devil may care attitude and laboured on. Although he'd claimed that there was too much to eat, he finished it all. In the meantime she finished her juice.

Then she pulled a leather ring-binder diary from her bag. She tore out a blank sheet and then flipped the address book pages. She then copied out an address.

She pushed the page over to him and returned her book to her bag.

Their surname was Özer and the address was in Göre. Dannaks was surprised that she carried such information privately. But then, maybe he shouldn't be surprised.

"It's in central Anatolia," she said.

He thanked her.

As soon as he put his fork and knife down, she waved the waitress over. "I'd like to pay," she said to the girl.

"Together or separate?"

"Separate," Poschmann said quickly. Dannaks didn't protest and merely drank his tea. Yes, she had given him the address, but it was something he could probably have dug up. She was not going to help him help Shaziye and so he certainly wasn't going to buy her dinner.

The endearing hardness returned to her features as she dug in her handbag for her purse. She paid the girl who then looked at Dannaks. "I'm not finished." He gestured towards his tea.

The waitress took their plates and Poschmann's empty glass. The latter ignored Dannaks as she made ready to leave. Only when she stood did she look at him. "Goodbye, *Herr Oberkommissar*."

"Goodbye, *Frau* Poschmann."

Dannaks didn't touch his tea and after a good five minutes he too paid up and left. The addicts were still sitting near the door. He would never know whether they would pay or not.

The bus arrived and Dannaks was the only one to enter at the front and pay the driver. Everyone else boarded in the middle. The transport system worked on trust and the occasional unannounced inspection by ticket controllers who roamed the network in groups. After seven in the evening one was required to show bus tickets and passes to the driver. Here in Steilshoop, like in Billstedt and other problem areas, he had noticed that the drivers dispensed with this practice. Dannaks had never worked out whether the reason was kindness or fear.

The rest of the week

On Tuesday his last act with respect to the case was to place his notepad, although it still contained unused pages, in the paper file. He put Poschmann's sheet in too. Then he placed the file in a drawer of his desk. Reinhart observed him.

"You know how it is," he began. "In a film or a novel you'd be able to take this to a satisfactory conclusion. Unfortunately this is the real world."

His colleague's words uncannily echoing Reupke's did nothing to alleviate his frustration. If anything Reinhart had merely poked a wound.

Weske phoned on Wednesday morning.

"*Oberkommissar*, I want to thank you personally for the good work."

"Thank you, sir."

"Good. Well that was all. I'll let you get on."

"Sir. If I may?"

"Go on."

"A real thank you would be to strike that suspension from my file."

The short silence was ominous.

"Consider it done."

"Thank you, sir."

On Thursday afternoon Reinhart announced that he had located the Berlin fertility clinic Shaziye had attended.

"Well done," said Dannaks. "Her medical records could confirm her identity and place her in the flat with Michael. I'm sure there's some genetic material in the stored evidence. But for now there's no point. Maybe she's admitted who she is."

"I'm surprised we haven't heard anything from Ismail."

Book Three

August

Around the middle of the new month they received an email from Ismail.

"*Hallo Dannaks. Thank you for your work. I tell you now what happens. Meryem is Shaziye. She say killer is Volcan. We know Volcan was here, but we not find him. Just me and a partner looking for him. And partner only part time.*" Dannaks was reminded of Reinhart and himself. "*Trial against Shaziye start in second week September. Confession against her. Proof she was in room. Then hiding. Too much against her. Prosecution say have strong case.*" Dannaks toyed with the idea of going out there. He hadn't taken any holiday. "*We know another was in the room. We need Volcan's DNA. If we find Volcan before trial, then maybe she gets out.*"

Dannaks wrote back almost immediately. "*Hallo Ismail. Thank you for email. Sad to hear that Shaziye goes on trial. Hope you find Volcan quickly. I have a question. Did you find out about damage to toilets?*"

The reply came the following day. "*Toilet damage and other by fired employee. Hotel suing.*"

Later in that same week Dannaks received a call. The person said their surname but Dannaks still didn't know who was talking.

"Sorry, can you give me your name again?"

"Simsek. Ayhan Simsek."

"Oh, Ayhan, hallo." In the pause he grabbed some scrap paper and wrote his name. "And, er, what can I do for you?"

"I wanted to tell you that Volcan knows that you – I mean the Turkish police – are after him."

"Okay," he said, wondering where this was leading.

"I thought that, er, maybe I could help."

"Help? What do you mean?"

"I thought I could assist in the search."

"Well, that's very kind of you, but I think that's a question for the Turkish police, don't you?" Dannaks cringed at his own patronising ending. Silence. "Ayhan?"

"Yes. Yes, you are right. I wasn't thinking. I just thought maybe you could contact them."

"No, I'm afraid not. It's nothing to do with me. I'm off that case."

"Oh."

"Have you got anything that might help the Turkish police find him?"

"No."

A new silence began to open between them.

"Is there anything else?"

"No. Well, yes. Do you know when the trial is?"

"The last I heard was that it's to be in about four weeks. Why?"

"Nothing."

"Ayhan. Please."

"If she gets out, he'll be waiting."

"I suppose you're right."

"Okay, *Herr* Dannaks. I just thought I'd call."

"Yes, thank you."

After hanging up Dannaks wondered about the call. Of course he was right about Volcan waiting for Shaziye. But he couldn't see her getting out without evidence from Volcan. Ismail had said that the prosecution thought they had a strong case. They would undoubtedly go for complicity.

At the earliest opportunity he looked up Simsek's website and noted the telephone number.

A secretary picked up and answered that she would see if Simsek was available. Piped music cut off any protest. To his surprise Simsek came on the line.

"I remember you, detective," Simsek said, after Dannaks had introduced himself. His sudden silence was a prompt.

"I'll come straight to the point." Dannaks could almost hear the man thinking that this would make a change. "Something has always puzzled me." He waited a beat. "Mahmut indirectly linked you to the double-murder when he used one of your vehicles, yet you continue to use Aksoy's. Why is that?"

There was much that Dannaks could read into the silence that ensued. But when Simsek spoke the only answer was surprise.

"The incompetence of the German police service never ceases to amaze me." Dannaks took the met remark on a firmly clamped jaw. His mouth dropped open after Simsek next spoke, but he had the presence of mind not to issue a sound. "Abdurrahim Aksoy is my brother."

After what seemed an age, but he knew was really only a matter of seconds Dannaks said: "I see. Yes, we must have missed that. Thank you for your time Herr Simsek."

The brothers could plausibly have different surnames. Dannaks knew that in Turkey when a woman marries she generally adopts the surname of her husband. However, when a man marries he has the option of changing his surname to whatever he likes.

This vital piece of information shed a new and sinister light on Ayhan's motivation. Dannaks was not sure what to make of the boy.

In the final week of August Ismail sent another mail. The trial had been postponed. It was now set for the middle of October.

In that same week an article appeared in *Focus*. From the credits at the end of the page it was obvious that the content was a rehash of what had appeared in the Turkish press. The value of the piece was to bring it all together. Opening with the murder it drew suspicion on the case against Meryem. Even physically it seemed unlikely that she could have single-handedly over-powered the victim. Before speculating that she had in some way helped kill him, the article sidestepped to reveal that she was an import bride named Shaziye. There was a paragraph on her time in Berlin that underscored her captivity and slavery. A sidebar spouted some statistics. "Every year in Germany approximately 45,000 women with their children seek refuge in *Frauenhäuser*. In 2009 more than 850 women with 650 children sought shelter in Hamburg's *Frauenhäuser*. Although foreigners make up only 10% of the population they make up 50% of abused women. In Hamburg these figures are 14% and 42% respectively." After eight years of martyrdom she escaped to a *Frauenhaus* in Hamburg. Almost half a page was then devoted to the double murder. The issue of how Shaziye escaped or how she assumed Meryem's identity and travelled to Turkey was not directly addressed. Even the question of mistaken identity was skipped over with a sentence to the effect of ongoing investigations. "This petite frail girl saw no sanctuary other than prison and so she confessed to killing Matthias. Her suicide attempt in prison was not a last desperate cry for help. It was a serious attempt at ending her suffering. This act and the international interest had drawn the support of the IHD *Insan Haklari Dernegi* (Turkish human rights association), *Terre des Femmes* (Domain of women), Amnesty International and various women's rights groups. The latter mainly highlighting the plight of import brides and battered women in general.

September
Wednesday
12:27

In the first week of September he found himself at the *Polizeistern* for a presentation. He called Reupke before the event and they arranged to meet for lunch.

They met at the canteen entrance and exchanged perfunctory pleasantries. After collecting their food and arranging it on their trays on the table Reupke spoke.

"So what's new?" he asked before popping a spaghetti-laden fork into his mouth.

"I heard from Ismail last week."

Reupke pushed his mouthful into a cheek. "Have they caught Volcan?"

Dannaks shook his head. His own mouth was full.

As he wound spaghetti on his fork pivoted on his spoon Reupke said: "He was in contact with Stapelfeld over the double-murder. I think Ismail got short shrift from him." Dannaks shook his head in disgust, but chose to eat rather than speak. "I know he talked to Berlin too. Trying to get more on Volcan." He ate. When his mouth was almost empty he added: "I'm surprised they haven't caught him."

"They got the shit smearer. You remember, the shit on the toilet walls, the toilets full of sodden toilet rolls–"

"Yes. Yes." His expression was pained. "I am eating."

"It was a disgruntled ex-employee."

They tucked into their meals for a while.

"Have you heard anything from Kay?"

Dannaks was grateful for his full mouth. It gave him time to think up a response.

"The last I heard," Reupke continued, "was that you were taking a sort of break. Until all that media interest cooled down."

He had of course thought about her on and off, but the frequency of such thoughts had dropped to once every few days.

"No." It had crossed his mind to lie. To save face he chose a half-lie. "We're still in the cooling period."

His colleague pondered this for a couple of mouthfuls.

475

Then he suddenly said: "Why not call her and suggest going for a meal? You know: a foursome."

Now it was Dannaks's turn to ponder. "I'm not so sure that'd be a good idea."

"Oh?"

He took a moment before answering. "I think she felt for Dagmar. So I'm not so sure she'd want to see you."

Reupke blanched, but barely broke his eating stride.

Dannaks noticed the hardening of his jaw and his mastication seemed to grow more mechanical. "It's finished between you, isn't it?"

Dannaks nodded. He couldn't be bothered spinning it out.

Thursday two weeks later
10:03

"Hamburg *Polizei*, *Soko* REX, Dannaks speaking." Reinhart was not in the room.

"Hallo Dannaks. It is Ismail. How are you?"

"I am good." He glanced at the door, praying for Reinhart's return.

"I have news."

"Yes."

"We capture Aksoy."

"You have Volcan?" he asked, annoyed by the uncontrolled high pitch in his voice.

"Yes."

Reinhart came into the room and Dannaks pressed a button on the phone. "I switch to loudspeaker. Okay?" Reinhart gave him a puzzled look and Dannaks whispered: "Ismail. They've got Volcan." Reinhart nodded and sat quietly.

"Who is in the room, please?"

"My colleague Reinhart. His English is very good. Please inform us what happened?"

"Okeydokey. With a photograph and a name we find out that he rented a holiday villa not far from Side. Then we had – how do you say? A trail. Yes. We check all his relatives here. And then we suspect a cousin. Then we follow the trail. We find Volcan in Istanbul and a special unit of armed police get him in his flat."

Dannaks would have liked more details. "Can you prove he is the killer?"

"Yes. His ear is the same as on the beach photograph."

"His ear?"

"Yes. We have a one hundred percent agreement."

Dannaks knew that like fingerprints the contours of the ear were unique. But he thought the photograph and angle would bring an element of distortion into its shape. Also light and shadow would reduce the sharpness of the image for a comparison. Even with enhancement he couldn't believe the quality could be brought up to courtroom standard. "Anything else?"

"Yes. We have his DNA and it matches what we found in the room."

"At the time of the killing?"

"Yes." There was excitement in Ismail's voice. "What we have was left at the time."

Ismail's silence said that he wasn't going to elaborate.

"What happens now?"

"The prosecution must review. And a new defence must be built. There will be — what do you say? — a hearing. Shaziye should go free, but she will be needed as a witness."

"Tell me when this, er, hearing is. Maybe I can come."

"Yes. Good. I will try to find information. Thank you for your help."

"Yes."

"Goodbye."

"Yes. Goodbye."

"Well done," said Reinhart, when Dannaks cut the line. "Your English was fine."

"Thanks."

"You don't look too happy."

Dannaks smiled. "No. But I should be, shouldn't I? They've got him. It's as good as over."

"You're probably feeling deflated because it didn't end spectacularly."

Dannaks laughed. "You mean like in a film or book where I would have been in on the chase; maybe single-handedly capturing Volcan?" Yes, with the capture there was a sense of denouement. That he was not involved was something that often transpired. That was the irksome side of his work. A case could be begun, but frustratingly not seen through to a satisfying conclusion. Other departments got involved and one became a cog at best.

Last week of September

Ismail sent an email on Tuesday afternoon to say that the hearing was scheduled for the second week in October.

In that same week Dannaks threw the last remaining pair of socks he had purchased in Side in the bin. Every one of them had developed holes after three or four washes.

He also decided to take two weeks' holiday and cleared it with Frank.

Something of a reprise appeared in the papers. Herbst was selling his Side holiday home. Luckily no reference was made to any police complicity in the chain of events that forced this sale.

He emailed Turgut and discovered that they had rooms available at Azure Skies. It was now the end of the season. Turgut added that he would not be able to book directly. He would have to use an approved tour operator. During his lunch break Dannaks went to a travel agency and was appalled to find that there were virtually no available flights from Hamburg. "It's the school holidays," the girl said. "But we should be able to find one seat. I'll get back to you."

When Reinhart raised his eyebrows at the fact that he was going to Azure Skies as a holidaymaker Dannaks enigmatically explained. "I need to buy some new socks."

October
Saturday
16:28

The girl at the travel agency found a single seat for him, unfortunately from Hannover.

Even though he'd done the same trip in July this one seemed to take much longer. This wasn't necessarily due to the additional trip to Hannover airport. Perhaps it was the lack of company.

There was no welcoming committee at the airport. He had arranged to meet Ismail on Sunday afternoon. Once through customs a hotel representative guided him and other newcomers to the hotel bus. She ticked them off the list as they boarded the bus, having given up their cases for the driver to stow underneath. Dannaks waited on the bus with the other families for the rest of the guests to get through the airport. Apart from him and two groups of women, one a couple the other a threesome, families took up the bus. The noise level bordered on unbearable.

Last time he had been whisked through the airport, only to be hampered by posing for photographs. The cavalcade of vehicles had then cruised to the hotel. This hotel bus hurtled down the roads. Despite its size it overtook private vehicles. The only challenge appeared to be taxis.

Without a constricting jacket and tie he didn't feel as uncomfortable as the last time.

The familiarity of the hotel facade gave him a sense of returning home. But when he entered the reception area to check-in the only person he recognised was the waistcoat behind the counter. Either he didn't remember him or was too stressed by the sudden arrival of so many guests. Two other members of staff were with him. They appeared just as overwhelmed.

A girl, moving about the reception area, handing out welcoming drinks, forms and pens looked vaguely familiar, but Dannaks couldn't place her.

Patience was an alien word to the multitude of children and they ran about the area or insisted on exploring, barely heeding the pleas from parents not to stray too far and to come back soon. Others complained about being hungry. Still others wanted to go to the toilet. One child was appalled that a promised swim was being put off till tomorrow. A small boy and a two-year-old in a pushchair were unceasingly giving one another a high-five and low-five. The younger child squealing with delight with every slap of their hands. The older boy amused by his younger sibling's delight. Their father was either embarrassed or irritated, but their mother stopped him interfering. "Oh, leave them. At least they're occupied."

Dannaks was bemused, but weary of the hullabaloo. He tried to beat everyone else completing his sheet.

"What a journey," said one mother to another. "We're from Hamburg. I told my husband we're booking next year immediately we get back."

As he waited to hand in his filled-out form he spotted the bellboy standing near the entrance, possessively holding on to his trolley. They exchanged nods and smiles.

"*Oberkommissar.*" Dannaks was startled. Turgut was standing behind him. They pumped hands.

"This time it's just Dannaks. I'm on holiday."

"Welcome. Welcome." Then he reached for Dannaks's form. "Let me."

Turgut left and reappeared behind the counter.

"I'd like a safe," said Dannaks. Turgut nodded, shuffling papers and tapping keys on the computer keyboard. He placed a small pile of paraphernalia: fliers, key, safe cartridge and lastly stickers with his room number written in thick marker pen, on the counter in front of Dannaks. "Put these on your baggage."

Dannaks moved to leave.

"Wait." Turgut held up a strip of plastic. "Left or right?"

Dannaks smiled and held out his right wrist. Turgut clipped home the tag and snipped off the extraneous piece. He then gave him directions to his room.

Dannaks went outside to his case and placed a room sticker on it. Carrying only his hand luggage he went off in search of his room. He would have liked to chat with Turgut but the glut of new guest had whittled conversation to necessities.

This time Dannaks was housed nearer the beach and not up in the hillside forest. His room was not far from where Katja had stayed. But his was not on the ground floor and he had to climb some steps.

Once inside he threw his bag on the bed and opened the balcony doors.

He wasn't sure whether Turgut had a hand in the choice of rooms, but his balcony faced the beach. There was a row of buildings in front of him, but between them he could see the sea. The air and the vast azure sky had a cleansing effect on his mind. Actually he found the breeze quite chilly, but it was rendered bearable by its brevity and intermittency.

His single room was naturally something of a cell. The layout was similar to his twin with Reupke, but the main room was smaller. Even the balcony was half size, although two chairs could be squeezed onto it. On the surface next to the portable television were a bowl of fruit and a half-sized bottle of red wine.

Using the stress of travel and reception mayhem as an excuse he opened the bottle and poured himself a glass.

He was on the balcony sipping the wine, trying to convince himself that it wasn't too tarty, when there was a knock on the door.

He opened the door to the bellboy. Dannaks stood aside to allow him in with the case he had purchased last time he was here.

Then he fetched his wallet from his jacket he'd tossed on the bed. He was disappointed to see that he possessed a two-euro coin and some cents. He thought one euro for bringing the case a suitable tip. Then he thought, what the heck? He was on holiday and maybe some people didn't give him a tip or weren't in their rooms when he came by. So he smiled and gave the lad the two-euro coin.

The bellboy brightened and his eyes softened into something akin to a plea. Dannaks was puzzled and embarrassed and made a fuss of returning his wallet to the inside pocket of his jacket. The lad seemed to loiter for a moment and Dannaks did his best to ignore him. Then he left.

He returned to the balcony with his glass of wine and stayed until the chilliness became uncomfortable. Then he returned to the room and unpacked.

19:38

After unpacking he lay on the bed, flipped through his notepad to refresh his memory of staff names, and finished the bottle of wine. The alcohol made him feel light-headed and happy. It also made him feel exceedingly tired and he began to snooze.

He awoke with a start. But didn't know why.

His travel clock told him that he was too late for his aperitif before seven o'clock dinner. But then the wine had sufficed.

In the mirror he was appalled by his dishevelled state. His hair was a storm and his clothes looked as if he'd slept in them. Which, of course, he had.

He groomed himself hastily, throwing a sweatshirt over his shoulders and tying the sleeves loosely at his chest. Then he made his way to the restaurant.

His route took him past the pools and across the plaza. A few people were sitting at or near the bar having drinks. He saw the cask and smirked as if spotting an old friend.

Rounding the amphitheatre he came upon the outside eating area. The tables were sparsely occupied. Most of the guests had opted to eat inside. He too was uncertain. The chilly breeze was unpleasant and although he'd perversely held back from pulling on his sweatshirt he knew that he would have to soon.

He was still undecided where to eat when he entered the building and picked up a plate.

The spreads and displays had been ravaged but there was ample left. Although quite a few people were milling about there were no queues. Similar to that first time in the restaurant with Reupke he quickly found his plate full. Again it was a case of: oh, the chicken looks good and that fish too, some chips to go with it, the roast beef looks tender, the golden cooked sliced carrots appealed, a segment of Hawaii pizza would hit the button, and he couldn't go wrong with a little fresh salad.

He was about to search for a place to sit when he spotted Fehime talking to a guest. Something told him that she must have seen him and been held up by the guest. This didn't deter him from walking up to them. The guest was talking to her about sport and a knee injury. She glanced at Dannaks but carried on talking. Fehime had already expressionlessly nodded to him. She appeared vaguely interested in what the woman was saying and eventually advised taking it easy, not bending too deeply when squatting, but to continue exercising. If the pain persisted more than two weeks she should see a doctor. The woman nodded and apparently wanted to say more, but another quick and yet more thorough inspection of Dannaks curtailed her and she departed.

"Back again?" She held out her hand and attempted a smile.

Dannaks nodded. "Don't worry. This time as a guest."

"Oh."

"Well, actually I'm hoping I might see Shaziye – I mean Meryem."

"I know her name. We've all been following the case." A lad also wearing an animation team outfit appeared. "I'll see you there," she said to him and he nodded to her and Dannaks and moved on.

"A new team member?"

"Rafael's replacement."

"He's left?"

She nodded sadly. Before he could react she gestured to his plate. "Your dinner's getting cold."

"Where are you sitting?"

"I'm not. I've finished." Again before he could speak she said: "*Guten Appetit.*"

"Thanks."

And she was gone.

20:45

Although the table he found inside the restaurant was partially occupied, he didn't establish any connection with the guests. Talk of the food and weather led nowhere. Many of the

482

families were finishing up when he sat down. The children had long finished and grown fidgety and restless. Some were allowed to leave, others stayed put, playing with toys, experimenting with teas or other beverages. One child returned to the table with a vegetable soup hot chocolate concoction.

By eight thirty there were few guests left. And just before nine the waiters began collecting condiments and stripping the tables of their tablecloths.

The plaza was teeming with people. Getting a drink from the bar looked impossible. He joined the short queue for the cask.

Children and parents were on stage, standing in a huge circle that surrounded Necla and Hülya. The two girls led the dance routine to the bouncing jolly music.

The sheer multitude of guests made him feel that he should recognise someone. And he saw similarities with the guests he had known. He identified a group of young girls that reminded him of "Off limits" and her friends. He tried to recall the words of her other T-shirts and only came up with "Out of Bounds". He spotted candidates for the three witches. There were no takers for the chess players. But there was a woman, unfortunately with a man, who carried herself like Dagmar. There was nobody like Katja.

With two glasses of wine in hand he sought somewhere to sit. His search ended at the amphitheatre near the box of cushions. He felt both conspicuous and content sitting alone away from the throng and the lights.

The children's disco – as it was called – ended just after nine and the relative silence was welcome.

From nine twenty onwards the amphitheatre filled up in earnest. The congested flow of people collecting cushions near Dannaks was uncomfortable. It was like sitting on the floor in a busy train station.

Although billed for nine-thirty the show didn't start until almost nine-fifty. Similar to that first evening long ago the team presented the public with a series of sketches. Dannaks recognised one or two, but wasn't sure it was the same show.

After the applause Habip led the club dance, which Dannaks sat out. Then they were verbally ushered to the Silver Star discotheque, but by then, indeed during the club dance, people were returning their cushions and leaving in throngs.

Dannaks felt tired, but due to his early evening kip, not sleepy. So after returning his cushion he made his way to the disco. Fabio and Tanya were outside the door enticing people to join them. Despite the departing hordes there was an intermittent stream of people entering the disco. And Dannaks was only able to issue a quick greeting. He hadn't expected them to recognise him, but the two crewmembers returned the greeting and welcomed him back. Of course, Fehime would have spread the word.

People entered and headed for the bar or the tables that lined the walls and alcoves the central dance floor remained barren. This gap in the heart of the place gave a sense of cavernous space that made it appear empty.

Guests accosted the huddle of crewmembers, raising their voices above the thud of music. Dannaks had his turn too. But conversation was strictly limited to small talk. He found himself a seat at the end of an occupied table, hoping that perhaps a crewmember would join him. Here, against the walls, with heads almost touching, talk was just possible. But nobody took the vacant seat next to him and those already at the table were in a scrum or leaning back contemplatively.

Dannaks finished his wine and left.

Outside, the plaza was almost deserted. Three shopkeepers in jackets and pullovers and a man he vaguely recognised, but couldn't place, were sitting at a table near the shops. At the bar two male guests were conversing loudly. The barman looked more than bored; he looked peeved.

As he passed by, Dannaks gave him a sympathetic smile. The barman nodded without changing his expression.

Sunday
10:00

That first morning he was up before eight and at breakfast by half past. Only lunch could feasibly be taken outside. Mornings and evenings were simply too chilly.

He had arranged to meet Ismail after lunch between half past one and two in the reception bar.

After eating he wandered past the plaza. The shops were closed. In reception he checked the board of events for the day. Then he went to the staff photographs. Shaziye as Meryem was no longer on display.

He then went back to his room and changed his clothes. He put on his tracksuit and new training shoes. He waited until ten to ten before returning to the plaza to join the Nordic walking group.

At five to ten the call for the start of the day began. Somebody, perhaps Habip, read off the day's events over the loudspeaker system.

Many of the newcomers were sitting at the tables waiting to be shown the amenities and layout of the club. The tour was scheduled for ten. Families were especially interested in hearing about the children's club.

Dannaks joined the group standing at the table with Fabio. He was pairing sticks and handing them out. There were seven women and three men. There were also four older couples. They appeared sprightly and raring to go. Of the apparent singles it was hard to tell who was with whom. Like Dannaks, a bespectacled man, who had a skin problem, appeared to be alone. The two other men were conferring as if they knew one another.

It was only when they set off that groups formed. The real singles adjusted their pace to stay just behind or in front of one another. Whereas there was no such juxtaposition with couples or threesomes. Acquainted guests strode together. One man had his sights set and moved noticeably to get near a couple of women. Again, there were more women than men in the group.

They passed Captain Fruit's children's club. The thud-thud of music from Fehime and the gymnastics thumped the early morning drowsiness.

At the beach they stopped to have their sticks inspected and go through some warm-up and stretching exercises. Fabio got them to stand facing him and the sea in a loose arc. As they did so one of the single women spoke to Dannaks.

"Your stick is a bit short," she said in a husky voice.

Dannaks raised an eyebrow and the woman laughed. Those who had caught the remark smiled or chuckled.

His left hand stick was shorter than his right hand one. The lower half had not been screwed tight enough and had slid into the upper half.

After this small incident he couldn't help noticing her.

She was not unattractive. Her face was small and round. She was a blue-eyed blonde. Her wispy hair was far blonder than Katja's, almost golden and had it been thicker and longer she could have been Rapunzel. But when she spoke or opened her mouth into a smile Dannaks sensed something vulgar. The looseness of her jaw hinted at dislocation. She had nice teeth, but she bared them too often. When she articulated or laughed she showed too much gum, like a chimpanzee. Her joy was simultaneously infectious and peculiar. For all this she exuded sexuality.

After exercising and overcoming any self-consciousness Fabio led them in the same direction that he had when Dannaks had taken part. So they crossed the no-man's area and passed the remnants of the beach fire. It looked as if it had been used again since. When they entered the neighbouring hotel's area Dannaks noticed the man behind the beach bar. He was the same barman he'd seen months ago. And he was the same man he'd seen last night sitting with the hotel shopkeepers in the plaza. He was a good-looking bronzed beefcake of a man with a thick wedge of a moustache and unruly hair.

The pace stretched the group into a straggle of twos and threes which gathered at intervals for light exercise. Fabio varied the pace and moved up and down the group. His irrepressible enthusiasm spurred the most out of everyone. They were all relieved when he said that it was time to turn around and head back.

They dropped off their sticks at the shack and went their separate ways. Dannaks returned to his room and changed. He was tempted to take a shower, but decided that the end of the day just before dinner was the best time. He poured a glass of water from the bottle in the fridge and went out onto the balcony. There was a knock at the door just as he was about to leave. It was the cleaner. She became flustered and, by way of explanation, Dannaks placed his towel card in his novel, grabbed his sun cream, sunglasses and Azure Skies baseball cap, repeating the word "okay" as he did.

He swapped his towel card for a towel at the shack and then found a lounger as far as possible from the children's pool. The first few rows at the adult pool were taken and his lounger was off the paved area and on the grass. He made himself comfortable, convincing himself that the sun wasn't strong enough to warrant sun cream. He opened his paperback and read a few pages. The trickle of sweat at his temple told him it was time for protection. But rather than put on sun cream he pulled on his T-shirt and strolled over to the bar where he ordered a cola. He kept his place in the shade at the bar and watched the pool game that was underway. Guests were taking turns trying to get across the pool standing on a surfboard.

Finishing his drink, he wandered over to the photograph kiosk. There, as nonchalantly as possible, he searched through the photographs only to discover that they only went back three months. Ones of Katja and him were gone. He dismissed the idea of asking whether they took back-ups. Maybe it was better for it all to be consigned to memory.

He avoided pausing at the neighbouring shop but browsed the window of the end shop. He saw the watch that had caught his eye. Typically there was no price tag.

"I wouldn't bother with them," Off-Limits had said. "They won't last longer than the socks." And his socks had indeed not lasted.

The shopkeeper was inside at the glass counter fiddling with an array of small boxes. He looked up and Dannaks snapped his eyes back to the display. He kept the man in the periphery of his vision before casually wandering off.

He returned to his lounger and seeing that he had forty-five minutes until lunch he methodically applied the sun cream. As he lay back armed once more with his paperback, he thought that a swim would have been a good idea. There were quite a few people in the water. Some older children were larking. A father was playing ball with a boy and girl. But mostly there were older women leisurely doing the breaststroke, up and down, mindful of their bound-up hair. An older man did the front crawl, stopping for long pauses at each end of the pool.

The real pandemonium at the pool with the slides could be heard, but it was out of sight.

Dannaks lay back. No sooner had he started to read than a cloud obscured the sun and the breeze goose-bumped his skin. He estimated the speed of the cloud and checked the sky behind it. Deciding to wait it out he went back to his book.

He read a paragraph and looked up as two boys carrying water cannons raced past him. He was afraid that they were going to open fire. The brightly coloured canisters were like imitation scuba divers tanks and looked as if they could hold a substantial amount of water.

To his dismay Dannaks reconfirmed that he wasn't very good at lolling about.

The sun once again banished all shadows to the underworld.

And he made a concerted effort to get into the story of the novel.

Somehow he made it through the forty-five minutes to lunch.

At lunch he didn't connect with anybody and he was finished within half an hour. Despite the swiftness of his break he managed to overeat and felt uncomfortable when he left. People were continually arriving. Most were childless adults or elderly people. Families had been loosely queuing at the door at opening time. And Dannaks had arrived just as the doors opened and had to compete with the multitude that swarmed in. He made a note to take lunch later.

He couldn't face returning to his lounger and it was too early to wait for Ismail in reception. So he wandered down to the beach. At the children's club he tried the door. It was locked. He slipped off his sandals at the edge of the sand and walked in the opposite direction to the Nordic walking route. The food stretched his stomach and although he knew he should he didn't feel like walking. So he sat on a lone lounger and looked out at the sea. There were few people about. Evidence of their presence was everywhere, especially in the hotel beach towels that reserved loungers, given identity by a beach bag, small rucksack, books, children's toys or an item of clothing.

There was nobody at the Sunshine coconut bar.

He followed the windsurfers and catamarans and wondered how often his eyes were subjected to such distance. When he started thinking of his beach walks with Katja he decided it was time to leave.

At his lounger he pulled off his T-shirt – this one sported a skyline of silhouetted skyscrapers, the lighted windows of which spelt New York. He settled down to his paperback again. A quarter of an hour later he paused and placed it face down, but open, on his lap. He closed his eyes to enjoy the sun and its warm caress. The noise ensured that he didn't fall asleep in earnest, but he dozed, dipping in and out of consciousness. An occasional voice annoyed him but the lap of the pool water and the breeze gently rattling the foliage swallowed all other sounds.

13:10

Although Ismail wasn't due – at the earliest – for another twenty minutes Dannaks sluggishly gathered himself together. He

488

felt exhausted. There was no denying that lying around was draining.

He went back to his room for his notepad and then on the way to reception he went to the toilet. The sight of the condom machine brought on a slanted smile. Then he shook his head when the scent took him back to sitting in the cubicle with his head in his hands after winning Mr. Azure Skies.

The reception area was relatively deserted. No one manned the golf desk or the guest relations' desk. A girl Dannaks didn't recognise was behind reception speaking on the telephone.

There was a scattering of people in the bar, but Dannaks remained in the reception area. He checked the board again before going over to the shelf of ring binders. He pulled one out, placed it on the desk and flicked through the pages. The tour operator was unknown to him and he put it back after a moment. He then chose a folder of a tour operator he knew.

Inside he found very similar tours, even the photographs appeared to have come from the same source. He turned the pages before returning to the map on the first page. He was still bent over the desk scrutinising the map when he became aware of someone standing next to him.

Before he could completely turn, the affected English gave Ismail away. "You should see my country."

Dannaks shook his hand.

"Hallo Ismail. It is good to see you."

"Yes. And me to you too." Ismail's return precipitated a moment of confusion. He nodded to the folder. "Turkey has much to offer."

"Maybe I will go." He wanted to say that merely a morning of nothing to do after Nordic walking had been almost an ordeal, but the necessary English words failed him. Ismail had sensed that he wanted to say more and there was another silence. "The bar?"

Ismail nodded.

They collected cold drinks from the bar and chose a table near the wall. There was nobody in the vicinity. A youth was sitting hunched over a laptop, no doubt surfing the net. A couple with a pram had camped at another table and three men propped up the bar.

Dannaks pulled his notepad from his shorts when they were settled.

"I have questions," he said. He had formulated them with Reinhart's help.

"Please," Ismail smiled, placing his sparkling water back on the table. They now both leaned forward, almost conspiratorially. He was about to start when Ismail spoke. "I will try."

"Yes." Were there things he still could not tell him? Although the first question was written out for him, he contemplated it for a moment. "Can you tell me how you caught Volcan?"

Ismail swelled with something akin to pride and couldn't suppress his grin. He leaned back slightly. "I will tell you in confidence. Understand?" Dannaks nodded. "Then it is easy. We had a – how do you call it? Ah, a nation-wide search. We had his name and a photograph from your Berlin police. The police in Istanbul got a call. A, er, tip-off? You know?" Dannaks nodded. "He was caught in his apartment. Easy. But it was a long time before we got tip-off. We have long time checking relatives."

Dannaks was quiet for a moment. It was a pause he would allow after all Ismail's answers. There were two reasons for doing this. The first was to give Ismail time to add anything he may have forgotten and the second was to consider whether he had an on-the-fly follow-up question. He read his next question: "You say you can tie him to the crime. Can you tell me how?"

Again Ismail glowed with pride.

"When we had him he denied everything. Of course. But one of our experts explained to him the – er – special – no. The human ear is like a fingerprint. No two are the same. You know this, of course." Dannaks nodded. "We have the photograph of him from the beach. We make it bigger and sharpen it. And his ear matches on five points." Dannaks knew that the human ear was unique, but doubted that five reference points were enough.

"I am surprised that you got detail. The photograph and angle must have made it difficult."

"Yes, yes, it was not enough. But we have his DNA in the room."

"What have you got?"

Ismail looked at him. He gestured that he wanted a moment and picked up his drink. Dannaks knew that he was especially proud of what he was about to say. The build-up to it annoyed him but he stifled showing it by picking up his own glass and trying to appear relaxed.

Ismail replaced his glass and leaned forward and Dannaks hastily did likewise.

"One of our sharp-eyed–" he waited a tick to make sure Dannaks knew what the term meant – "technicians – you know, crime scene men, found saliva on a wall. The, er, outside edges had dried, but enough was there." Long-windedly Ismail explained that the technician took a swab. His lab also measured the rate of evaporation under similar temperature conditions and came to the conclusion that its deposition fell in a time frame of half an hour either side of the killing. They had already tested Shaziye and Rafael. That and the shoe-print pointed to another person being in the room.

Ismail surmised that during the fight Peter had struck Volcan causing him to issue the gob of saliva.

Dannaks, recalling all the blood in the scene of the crime photographs, complimented the sharp-eyed technician. He then asked, now that Volcan was in custody, whether Shaziye had explained what really had happened.

Shaziye now said that she thought she had seen Volcan a few days before the attack. Although she had not been sure it was him, it was enough for her to want to get away. She had asked Peter to go with her. Dannaks recalled Peter's journal entry.

On the evening of the killing Shaziye said that she had just under an hour of free time. Peter and she had agreed to spend the time together. With her rucksack on her back she had carried two bottles of water to his room. Peter's door was unlocked and she'd walked in. He had been in the bathroom. Because her hands were full she had not been able to close the door properly. At this point Ismail said that he too had always found it strange that Shaziye would carry two bottles of water to Peter's place if she had intended to kill him. Volcan had followed her and closed the door. By the time she looked up he was upon her. Hitting her with something heavy, most likely the crowbar, she didn't have time to scream let alone react. She lost consciousness for a few moments. When she came to the men were struggling. She was dazed and frightened. Everything was unreal. She didn't know what was happening. Blood obscured the vision in one of her eyes. She staggered out of the room, using the walls and then the main door for support. She must have closed the door behind her. Outside she reeled about and vaguely remembers wanting to get to Fehime's place. So rather than go down to reception she had gone uphill. She didn't get very far and found herself toppling to one side. Then she was sick and huddled against the wall before passing out again. When she regained consciousness she had no idea how much time had passed. She reckons that it must have been after Volcan had left and before or after Rafael had looked for her. Fehime wasn't in when she got to her place and she hid in a corner.

Dannaks interrupted Ismail to confirm that Volcan would have had to pass Fehime's to avoid reception and get down to the beach. Shaziye had indeed been lucky.

Shaziye said that she then wandered about, hiding here and there, cleaning her wound in the pool when nobody was about, always avoiding the police. But they had not believed her. They said that Fehime had admitted taking her in. It was a lie and she knew it, because she stuck to her wandering about story. Only when they agreed, in writing, not to take action against Fehime did she continue.

Shaziye's hiding place had not been good. She had sat in a shadowed corner of Fehime's building. Passing in and out of consciousness she had woken when Fehime returned to her room. But she had been too weak to call out. After Fehime had gone in she found that she had trouble getting up. Again she was unsure how much time passed, but Fehime was still up when she knocked.

Her friend had taken her in. Of course she wanted her to go to hospital, but Shaziye was afraid that Volcan was still about. Fehime said that the police were everywhere. Ismail said that they had taken her statement in reception. They had held everyone in the discotheque; all others still up had been gathered in reception.

After patching her head Shaziye had slept. Early in the morning the police knocked on all apartment doors. Shaziye hid in the upper cupboard until they were gone. Fehime identified herself and explained that she had already given a statement. It was probably at this moment that Fehime had crossed the line to truly help her friend. For Shaziye said that Fehime had always wanted her to give herself up, not least to get medical attention. Shaziye was afraid and undecided. And then she felt empty and didn't care. Nevertheless the girls established a kind of routine until she decided what to do. Perhaps she hoped to hear of Volcan's capture.

Dannaks asked about Volcan. Where had he gone?

Ismail said that he had rented a holiday villa outside Side. It came with a car. So after disguising himself at the beach fire with charcoal and ash and paint he had gone back to the street where he had parked it and simply returned to the villa. At this point Ismail said that they had checked to no avail all the hardware stores and garages in the area for the origins of the crowbar.

Volcan left the area. Maybe he went back to Germany. Maybe he went straight to Istanbul. He was waiting to see what happened to Shaziye. Dannaks knew that at least from the time of his visit to the Aksoys in Berlin he had been wary of returning.

They were quiet for a moment. Their drinks were long finished. And Dannaks had no more questions in his notepad.

"Drink?"

Ismail shook his head and glanced at his watch.

"Tell me about Rafael. He is not here. Do you know?"

"It is sad," Ismail began. "I think he is broken." He paused. "He disturbed the crime scene, so we were not, er, nice to him."

"You mean he took Peter's journal."

Ismail nodded.

"Do you know where he hid it?"

"In what they call here the radio shack."

Dannaks nodded.

"What about Shaziye? Her case is on Thursday. She should get out."

"Yes. I think so."

"Even with Volcan in prison she could still be in danger."

"Yes. Maybe. But she has many friends. Maybe they hide her."

"I know about the publicity."

"Yes. She is famous."

"Will she get protection? A new identity?" After all the deceit the very thought of a new identity was laughable. Unfortunately it was a bizarre thought he couldn't convey in English.

"I do not know."

"She has received threats."

"Yes." Ismail seemed at a loss as to what to say. Dannaks had the feeling he knew of the danger, but had no power to help her.

"She will come here," said Dannaks.

Ismail nodded uncertainly.

"I don't mean for her to work." Dannaks remembered seeing the bone pendant in Fehime's room. "To see her friends. To say goodbye. I don't know."

"Yes. Maybe after a day or two. But Ankara is not close."

Again Ismail fell silent. Dannaks knew he wanted to leave.

"Thank you Ismail."

"I thank you too, *Oberkommissar* Dannaks."

They both stood.

"Will you contact me on Thursday when you know something?"

"Of course."

Turning towards reception they left the bar. They stopped again near the entrance to shake hands and say goodbye.

Ismail nodded in the direction of the tour files. "See the country."

"I will."

Monday to Thursday

Because the course of each day was similar: breakfast, Nordic walking, lounging, lunch, walking and/or dozing, preparing for dinner, taking an aperitif, dinner, drinking, watching the show, bed, he lost track of the days. Time merged, memory floated and any incidents required effort to establish the day and sometimes the order of their occurrence.

Lounging remained an ordeal. And a fragment of the past returned to plague him.

"I guess I'm not very good at this."

"At what?" asked Katja. "Relaxing?"

"Yes."

He persevered with relaxing and by midweek had finished his paperback.

He also took to taking a swim before lunch. He even ventured into the sea.

Despite using strong sun cream he grew red, but not sore.

Another thing that contrasted his last visit was the lack of mosquitoes. He didn't need the dubious no-name repellent he had bought at Patel's. Oh, he had found the brand that Katja had lent him, but he had balked at the price.

He grew quite friendly with some of the Nordic walking participants. The bespectacled man with the skin problem, Thomas, was a decent chap. But with women his lack confidence was pronounced and he became embarrassing in his efforts to attract their attention. Dannaks could be shocking in some of the things he said, but Thomas could clearly give him lessons in the art of faux pas.

Vulgar mouth, Noreen, flirted and enjoyed the attention, but clearly had her sights set higher than Dannaks. He had written her off when he'd seen how much she smoked. Her nicotine-stained fingers could have been mistaken for henna.

Nevertheless, although there was no obligation, some of the group would meet for an aperitif before dinner and then spend the evening together.

Most of the crew remembered him and willingly exchanged pleasantries. Nothing significant was ever said.

He bumped into Turgut and exchanged a few moments with him at the plaza bar. He wasn't offered the hotel's better wine. Turgut had said that the incident was well and truly in the past. The cancellations had abated and eventually stopped and it was business as usual. Some people had heard of the murder but didn't realise that it was this hotel. Those in the know would casually touch on it, hungry for something firsthand, but it was well and truly a curiosity of the past.

On Wednesday he booked a three-day trip starting next Tuesday. He couldn't persuade any of the walking group to join him. Three days was a financial overhead that none of them was willing to accept. They couldn't understand why he wanted to be away for so long. A one-day trip was the most they were willing to do. He couldn't explain. Part of the reason lay in the fact that he couldn't face another week on the lounger. But there was another reason.

It rained on Thursday afternoon and the evening show took place in the lobby bar. Dannaks had been on tenterhooks since lunch. He expected to hear from Ismail at midday or in the early afternoon. Shaziye's hearing had been scheduled for ten that morning. Almost hourly he went to reception. At first he asked whether any messages had been left for him. Then he wandered about the area or casually fetched a drink from the bar, all the time making his presence known to the staff. And he returned to his room more often than necessary to see if a message or fax had been delivered.

At the show in the crowded lobby bar Thomas remarked on his distance. Dannaks shrugged it off saying that he was tired.

Friday

After Nordic walking he went to reception and receiving the standard reply he went back to his room, located Ismail's card, sat on the edge of his bed and phoned him. Nobody picked up for a long time. Then someone came on, but it wasn't Ismail. Dannaks asked for him and the man said something that he didn't catch. Dannaks spoke but whoever had picked up had gone.

Someone picked up and spoke in Turkish.

"Ismail?" More Turkish words. "Hallo. Ismail? It is me. Dannaks."

There was a pause. "Dannaks hallo. How are you?"

"Good." Silence. "You have not phoned me."

"No. You have phoned me."

"Yes. I know. But you wanted to tell me about Shaziye. Yesterday."

"Yes? Oh yes. But I think you know."

"No, I do not know." He regretted the tinge of anger in his voice.

"Ah. The hearing was moved to Monday."

"Oh. Why?"

"I cannot explain in English. A – how do they call it? A technicality."

"I understand." He wanted to say that he thought that justice systems were probably the same the world over. They were lumbering, burgeoning beasts choked by laws and rules, each and every one of which was further burdened with a myriad of exceptions.

"Monday."

"I will be away from Tuesday until, er, Thursday evening. I am on a trip."

"Good."

Dannaks was no longer so sure it was good.

As if he could read his thoughts Ismail added: "You are on holiday. Enjoy."

True, but he would like to see Shaziye. To ask her a few questions and tie up the loose ends that still bothered him.

"Where are you going?"

"Er, it is called the Cappadocia tour."

"That is a long way for three days. You will be travelling a lot." Perhaps he registered the scepticism in his voice for he then said: "But it is an interesting tour."

"There is something to see each day." At the back of his mind he had chosen the trip for another reason. It was a half-hearted undertaking that he wasn't sure he would carry through and so he kept quiet. Also he didn't want to give Ismail an excuse to question his motives. He was on holiday and he was going on a trip to see something of the country. That was all Ismail needed to know.

"Then have a good time. I shall contact you next, er, Thursday."

"Promise?"

Dannaks felt Ismail smile in the sound of his breath on the line. He couldn't tell whether it was good-natured or weary. "I promise. Maybe I come."

Saturday

The day followed the blueprint for all the days on this kind of holiday. But after lunch an incident transpired that got Dannaks thinking.

He was making his way across the amphitheatre when a young man pushing a pram with a towel draped over the front approached him. The glow on his face was one of pride and Dannaks couldn't help a smile as they neared one another. The smile was returned and they exchanged nods.

The baby in the pram stirred when a woman called out. She too was crossing the amphitheatre, but down near the stage. By now Dannaks had passed the pram-pushing man. He extrapolated the middle-aged woman's direction and realised that her call had halted a man outside the clothes shop. He was the good-looking hunk from the neighbouring hotel's beach bar. The Hunk looked around, his face blanched with what appeared to be embarrassment. For some reason he didn't notice Dannaks.

Dannaks kept an eye on them as he went to the plaza bar. When she got to him, they exchanged words, and he seemed mortified. She opened her handbag and he quickly looked around. Dannaks snapped his gaze to the bar. "A bottle of non-sparkling water, please," he said to the barman. He furtively glanced in the direction of the woman and the Hunk.

She was writing something on a slip of paper. He took it and without looking quickly stuffed it in his trouser pocket. All the while he was torn between giving her his attention and looking around. She was smiling. Such a youthful coy smile was somehow unsettling on a middle-aged woman. It didn't fit with her persona and was more suited to the person she would have been twenty years ago. The Hunk nodded and went into the shop.

It was a small incident. Almost insignificant. But it got Dannaks thinking. And he was glad after all these days of letting himself go to have something to think about.

Sunday

Today an incident occurred that threw him out of kilter. And it wasn't the fact that Habip took the Nordic walking in Fabio's place, because it was his day off.

By now Dannaks was a seasoned walker and happy to help some new arrivals. Two of the older couples had departed.

As usual after walking he went back to his room to get his belongings for the lounger. He quite looked forward to the rest after the exertion.

He'd been in his room for merely a couple of minutes when there was a knock on the door.

He opened it and the bellboy was standing there, empty-handed and with an awkward smile on his face.

Before walking, whilst gathering his sticks, Dannaks had noticed and nodded to him at the plaza bar. He had surmised that it was the lad's day off because he had never seen him out of uniform and outside the context of the reception area. In fact Dannaks had never seen him anywhere other than the accommodation buildings and reception. Indeed he looked lost without his trolley.

"Yes?" he asked.

The lad's eyes softened and he reached out. The plea returned to his eyes and confused and arrested Dannaks's reaction to recoil as the lad held his left hand. His right hand was still on the door handle. Dannaks watched as the lad lifted his hand and put it to his cheek, tipping his head as if resting on a beloved pillow.

Dannaks was frozen to the spot and simply looked on. The bellboy looked up and must have seen the horror in Dannak's eyes for he too froze. He had been moving his head slightly to stroke his cheek on the back of Dannaks's hand.

Events leading up to this moment flashed across his mind. There he was sitting on top of Reupke in the room re-enacting the crime. And then he was giving the generous twenty-euro tip when they left. But more than these two incidents there were the numerous smiles. Smiles that bore no such connection for Dannaks, but in retrospect could have been interpreted so.

"No," Dannaks said, shaking his head and delicately extracting his hand. The hurt was unfathomable and drew a "sorry" from Dannaks. The bellboy wheeled round and fled: the rejected lover. Dannaks remained at the door, too stunned to move.

The sound of a cleaner's trolley snapped him out of his trance. He slowly closed the door and went and sat down on the bed. He desperately needed a Dulwinnie or any kind of schnapps for that matter. But there was nothing of the sort to hand. Indeed there was no alcohol in the room.

For most of the rest of the day his thoughts were preoccupied by the incident. Even if the bellboy knew of Katja last time, he could believe that Dannaks was bisexual.

That evening, before, during and after dinner he drank a little too much and was louder than his usual self.

Monday
03:21

At first he tried to ignore his pressing bladder. He hadn't quenched his parched throat with the bottle of water on his bedside cabinet. Strange. He had drunk until he felt nauseous. And when he stopped drinking it was as if the water had merely run over his throat without absorption. Like baked ground that hadn't seen water for an age his cracked throat rejected the water. But maybe his thirst and need for relief hadn't been the only things to wake him. His sleep was restless and plagued by disturbing sexually charged dreams. And although it wasn't warm he had sweated and the sheets stuck to him, making turning awkward.

He got up and sluggishly went to the toilet. Afterwards he returned to the room and opened the balcony door. The cold air embraced him and he gasped. More than its embrace he wanted it to invade the room, to purge the stickiness. In bare feet he defiantly stepped onto the icy tiles of the balcony. His bleariness was shoved to the wings as he breathed in the night air and listened to the sea.

Within seconds he became uncomfortable and he was about to return to the room when he saw something flash between the buildings. He should have ignored it but he was curious. So he moved to the parapet and looked to where the person would appear should they take a straight path. Sure enough, seconds later he had a short but good view of the man. It was one of the waiters.

His mind ticked over as he returned to his room and closed the door. He remembered a witness claiming to see a waiter about the time of the murder. The sighting just now, as far as he knew was deep in the guest area – although the animation team were accommodated in no particular area – and served only to confirm his theory. His mind worked relentlessly.

He climbed into bed and realised that he was shivering.

11:24

The fax under his door when he returned from walking was from Ismail. All it said was that she was free. In itself it was of course good news and Ismail had certainly kept his promise, probably sending the fax as soon as he knew, but it wasn't enough for Dannaks. He wanted to know more. And more than anything else he wanted to know when she might be coming to Side. After all, his tour started tomorrow. Naturally there was a good chance that Ismail did not know, but Dannaks decided to phone him nonetheless.

As it rang he recalled the Hotel Floyd's receptionist's glee when he admitted to using their phone. He would have to check the Azure Skies prices for national calls.

Ismail picked up after four rings and Dannaks thanked him for the fax.

"It is good news. Is it not?"

"Yes. Very." Without a conjunction Dannaks could only pause. "Do you know when she will come here?"

"No," said Ismail. Then as if he could hear the disappointment in the ensuing silence he continued. "She is to be a witness for the prosecution." Becoming a witness for the state was to be expected. "She will stay in Ankara. There are formalities."

"I am leaving tomorrow."

"I do not think she will leave Ankara before Thursday. Go

on holiday. Enjoy" The silence betrayed Dannaks's indecisiveness. "There are many who want to interview her. She has many friends—"

"And enemies?"

This stumped Ismail and he hesitated. "Maybe. But you must not worry."

"I only worry that I might miss her."

"I think you should go."

Dannaks was silent.

"Will you go?"

"Yes. I think I will."

"If I can find out when she is coming I shall tell you."

"Do—"

"We are the police," he said, anticipating Dannaks's question. "I can find you."

Nevertheless Dannaks gave him the tour operator's name and the name of the tour.

"Okeydokey," said Ismail. He was winding the conversation down to sign off.

"I have one more thing," said Dannaks. He waited a moment for a response before realising that Ismail's silence was the acknowledgement. "I, er, do not know how to say this." Again he paused. "But you know that there is, er – that the male staff, some of them, have sex with the women guests? Sex for money?" Silence met his question. "Ismail?"

"Yes. I am here."

"You know this?" The practice explained the glut of single women compared to, say, those at the neighbouring hotel. It explained the sighting of the waiter in the early hours after the killing. It also explained the hostile attitude of the three witches. So much police presence had undoubtedly closed down the hanky-panky. And last night he had wondered about Katja and Dagmar. Had they known about the hotel before booking? Had they booked the hotel because of its name?

"I see you have not stopped investigating. To answer your question. Yes. We knew. But it is a thing that was, er, not relevant to the investigation." He stopped and Dannaks sensed that he had more to say. "I think it is also something you must keep to yourself."

Dannaks couldn't help a twisted smile. "I understand."

"Now you should go on holiday."

"I leave tomorrow."

Tuesday
07:00

Before seven he was at reception with his hand luggage packed for the coming three-day tour.

Mercifully the bellboy was nowhere to be seen.

The mini-bus coach arrived just after seven and Dannaks and a young couple were greeted by their guide: a man called Cem. Apart from the driver, the mini-bus was empty and they had the pick of the twelve seats.

Dannaks sat next to the window with his bag on his lap.

When they set off, Cem sitting up front with the driver, he turned to them and said that they would be picking up other guests from neighbouring hotels.

The gateman open the gate for them and they edged out onto the street. During the short wait, the bus angled upon the road with the curve of the hotel entrance, Dannaks could see the same two taxi drivers one of whom had taken them to Herbst's place. As usual the wares of the shops arranged on covered tables extended out onto the pavement. At this time in the morning there were no tourists about. That's why he noticed the young lad browsing the tables. He looked Turkish but his attire placed him in the tourist category. Of course an affluent Turk was not out of the question. Whatever, Dannaks watched the lad as they pulled out onto the road. There was something about him that had drawn his attention.

The driver changed gear clumsily and the lad looked up. For an instant his and Dannaks's eyes met. And then they were moving away. Dannaks turned in his seat to look back. The lad had turned away.

Dannaks panicked. "Stop the bus," he shouted.

Cem snapped his head round and began good-naturedly. "Have you forgotten–" But he didn't finish. Dannaks's expression stopped him.

"I need to get off."

"Are you ill?"

They were getting further away, but the driver was now distracted too, glancing at Cem for instruction.

"Let me get off."

502

Cem ordered the driver to stop and he pulled over suddenly to the blare of a horn from behind.

The young couple gave Dannaks worried, if not angry, looks. But he didn't have time to bother with what they thought; he was out of his seat and reaching for the door. "Are you coming on the tour?"

Dannaks pulled open the sliding door and hesitated, looking at Cem. He wasn't sure of his answer. Then he said yes, reasoning that he could buy some time to finally decide. "I'm leaving my bag."

"Then we'll pick up the others and pick you up last. At the Azure Skies entrance. Okay?"

"Yes," said Dannaks climbing out.

As he slid the door closed Cem shouted: "In half an hour."

Dannaks nodded and the minibus lurched out onto the road almost knocking a girl off her moped.

Dannaks hastened back to the shop where he had seen Ayhan. Why was he here? Of course it was a free world and he could be on holiday. But why now? And why was he near Azure Skies. He certainly wasn't staying at the hotel. Dannaks would have seen him.

The distance covered by the minibus was more than he thought. He was almost jogging back. The uneven pavement, broken by side streets, cracked by the rain and heat, hindered his progress.

He went past two mopeds, a white VW van and a pristine looking Ford Focus.

His thoughts sent him back to that evening in Hotel Floyd's dark bar. What had he said? Michael had been his friend and he felt sorry for Shaziye. "Her nightmare should have ended when she ran away." Despite this alarm bells had rung in his mind when he saw him. Was he over-reacting? Could Ayhan's presence be innocent? The boy was no Mahmut, in build or – apparently – in attitude.

The entrance to Azure Skies came into view. The two taxi drivers were still standing idly. The younger one was concentrating on his handy. But he couldn't see Ayhan.

"Hey," said the older taxi driver, evidently recognising Dannaks.

"Hallo," Dannaks said, nodding, and continuing rapidly. "Did you see the man here?"

The old man was perplexed. The younger one looked up disinterestedly.

Dannaks gave them a split second and then charged into the shop. The place resembled Patel's: a labyrinth. A woman in a headscarf looked up. Something was said. A young lad appeared. He wasn't Ayhan.

Dannaks darted about the shop. There were too many things in the shop, too many places to hide: nooks and crannies.

The lad spoke to the woman. He had trouble keeping up with Dannaks and tried to stop him. "Can I help you?" he asked in German.

Dannaks stopped. "Did a lad about your age come in here?"

It wasn't the reply he had expected and he stammered. "Er, no, I don't know." He turned to the woman and she answered that Dannaks was their first customer.

"But you saw the boy outside?" he asked the woman. She raised her eyebrows and the lad translated. She nodded. Dannaks felt triumphant. He was beginning to think he had imagined seeing Ayhan.

He spun round, left the shop, and looked up and down the road. The taxi drivers had gone back to hanging around. Surely they must have seen the boy.

He didn't have time to question them and went into the next shop. This one was at first glance as much a labyrinth as the one he had just left. The goods here were orientated less to tourist tack and more to foodstuffs, toothpastes, batteries of water bottles, toilet rolls and all manner of baby things from disposable nappies to one piece flannel suits. Of course there was some rhyme and reason to the layout of the goods on the shelves and in the freezers, but unrelated things cluttered the in-between spaces: batteries hung between the cereal packets, plastic dolls in boxes were hooked next to the teas and coffees. The overall effect was that essentials could be found, but anything out of the ordinary would have to be asked for or stumbled upon.

A dark-haired girl looked up from the cash till and small conveyor belt. In fact the till, counter and belt were scaled-down versions of the real thing. They were almost toy-like.

"Have you seen a young lad?" he asked. She clearly had not understood his question and he repeated it slowly. She looked at him blankly. He tried out his Turkish and she waved diagonally across the shop.

Dannaks was away. Of course the shop was made up of high shelving that reached beyond head height and he couldn't take a bee-line to the far corner. So he moved across the top of the shop, frantically looking down the aisles.

There was a chance he could miss someone at the other end of the aisle if they moved past as he did. He used light and shadow and any reflective surface. And he continually turned to look back at the girl at the toy-town checkout.

The shop appeared empty. But then, in the last aisle, he came upon a mother and child – a boy or a girl, he couldn't tell. He about-turned and made his way back to the entrance. Naturally, Ayhan could be crouched at the end of an aisle. But he could also be long gone.

Dannaks gave the girl at the till a shrug and went out to the taxi drivers.

He shook hands with the one who had taken them to Herbst's place and, to the man's relief, said that he did not want to hire a taxi. He said that he had seen the lad, but had not paid him any attention. He couldn't say whether he had entered a shop or left the area. The other driver had seen nothing.

Dannaks thanked them and walked away. He wasn't sure how long he had, but he didn't cross the road to the entrance of the hotel resort. Instead he went along the road and stood at the window to a jeweller's. From here he could view the shops without being seen.

The jeweller's shop was closed, but Dannaks was taken by some fine watches. He spotted the one that had taken his fancy in Azure Skies. All the while he watched the taxi drivers and the front of the shops.

Time passed.

The woman and child came out of the shop. She was laden with three bulging plastic bags that looked as if they could not take the weight. The child skipped alongside her, a lollipop in his or her mouth. They headed away from him.

If Ayhan was inside one of the shops then his patience was a display of remarkable fortitude.

A minibus halted at the Azure Skies entrance. He wasn't sure of the markings and took a second to realise it was his minibus.

Confirmation came when Cem jumped out.

Dannaks checked the traffic and crossed the road. He waved, but Cem had not seen him and disappeared round the front of the bus, no doubt to talk to the gateman or get a view of the building's entrance.

By the time he reached the minibus Cem had returned. "Ah, there you are," he said and he walked round to the side door with him. "Did you get what you wanted?"

"Er, yes."

"Good."

Cem pulled the door open and Dannaks climbed in. All but one of the seats was taken. His bag was gone too. As if he could read his mind, just before he slid the door closed, Cem said that his bag was in the back.

"Good morning," he said and the group responded with the same greeting.

All the window seats were taken and Dannaks had no option but to take the middle one at the very back. He peered out of the side and rear windows as he took his place. Nothing had changed.

Before they set off Cem turned to them and spoke over the idling engine. He said that they were now complete and welcomed them to the tour. They were running a little late, but he was sure that their driver, Galip, would make up the time. He added that every tour was individual and no two were the same. That was the beauty of a small group. Their first stop would be at the lake Beysehir Gölü, 150 kilometres from Side. He then handed out itinerary sheets and a clipboard with a form to sign that effectively waived all rights and accepted the company conditions.

Then they were off. Once they were away from the coast, the tourist belt, the vastness of the country made itself felt. They passed a couple of modern roadside mosques. For the first thirty kilometres or so the road was wide and they made good progress. Then it became narrower, with more curves and road works. The landscape was dry and hostile. Civilization became more makeshift: farm dwellings more ramshackle. The occasional concentrations of buildings were one-horse towns with one of everything: one cafe, one barbershop, one garage, one mini-market, etc. But there were bigger towns too. Here old and new stood almost side-by-side. There were sixties looking six to eight storey tower blocks with jutting concrete balconies and hanging washing like strings of parade flags.

They slowed to join a queue passing a car accident. Metal was crumpled like paper. But nobody appeared to have been hurt. In fact the small crowd looked bored as they waited. Dannaks had expected anger and gesticulating. Maybe there had been. It also made him wonder why he had not seen more road accidents. For everyone drove as if they owned the road.

The sound of the a/c and the motion of the minibus quickly lulled everyone into silence and their own thoughts. The only advantage to his position in the bus was that there was no seat in front of him and he could stretch out his legs. But he couldn't lean like those at the window. And every bump in the road seemed directly channelled to his bum.

Dannaks scanned the itinerary sheet.

The three-day tour had two overnight stops.

Day 1 (Tuesday): Drive to Konya. First stop at Beysehir Gölü. Then in Konya they would have lunch and visit a couple of mosques, a Koran school, a museum and bazaar. The evening meal would be taken in the hotel in which they would stay.

Day 2 (Wednesday): On the way to Göreme they would visit at least one caravanserai. The best part of the day would be spent in Göreme visiting the various cave dwellings. After lunch they would drive deeper into Cappadocia.

Day 3 (Thursday): A morning of sightseeing before making the return trip to Side, making refreshment stops on the way and taking in a leather factory, a jewellery outlet and a carpet-maker's factory.

Wednesday offered the only opportunity to satisfy his curiosity. The two-hour lunch break was a window he thought gave him enough time to make his private excursion feasible.

19:58

They spent the night in a hotel in Konya that had somehow attained a 3-star rating. Dannaks was surprised it had made the star scale. Someone said that the star-system was not the European standard. Everything was utilitarian and cheap. No particular style other than bland was projected. Décor was tacky. The framed pictures of Turkish landscapes appeared to have been cut from magazines. This was a place for backpackers and people seeking refuge for a night. It was not a place for a lengthy stay.

In the restaurant the group was given a string of tables pushed together to take up one length of the room. The patterned table cloths were sun bleached plastic. Menus were not handed out, as a set meal had been prepared. Cem explained that being an important religious city alcohol was not available. Dannaks wondered whether other restaurants were the same.

Cem and Galip made sure they were settled before departing to eat elsewhere.

The day's events and collective experiences broke the ice. However, conversation was sporadic and confined to small groups. Everyone was polite but restrained. "Weren't those blue green tiles magnificent?" said one woman of a mosque they had seen. "I thought the bazaar was great."

Vegetarians had made themselves known and received an altogether healthier-looking meal to the meat dish the others received. Nobody was sure of the origins of the meat and this produced a guessing game that inevitably descended into the absurd with suggestions of goat and dog.

Cem and Galip returned towards the end of their meal. Cem announced that just for them a special treat was in store. It wasn't on the programme, but a belly dancer would perform. Their plates were cleared and the tables were shifted to make space in the middle of the room.

Dannaks found himself alone with the elderly couple, next to the middle-aged foursome.

Sudden taped music, crackling and popping with age, blared out. The sound was a torturous barrage of noise, each instrument playing a tune that didn't seem to fit with the other. The belly dancer, who was more belly than dancer, appeared and began shaking and gyrating. If she had actually had a prime she was now well past it. Her bright, lurid outfit, although skimpy, looked as if it had been adjusted in places to stop her spilling out. Someone remarked that people of Arab descent liked their women a little portly to which one middle-aged woman said that she was in with a chance then.

A waiter stood near the bar and kitchen entrance and clapped with the rhythm and the guests felt obliged to follow suit.

Cem, sitting with Galip at another table, pushed a note between the dancer's ample hip and the elasticised hem of her flowing silken trousers. The waiter did the same. He chose to slip his money under a tasselled bra strap.

The family of four made a sudden and hasty retreat. The young couple took up a private do-not-disturb smooching position. Of their group this left a captive audience of the elderly couple, two middle-aged couples and Dannaks. There were about half a dozen other diners.

Egged on by his wife one of the middle-aged men opened his wallet. The dancer wobbled and jerked her exposed flesh in his direction. She tipped forward to offer him a good eyeful of her corpulent breasts and Dannaks wondered whether he was at the Reeperbahn. The man daintily slipped his folded note near a breast and the other middle-aged man passed a comment that reddened his friend and precipitated a burst of laughter.

The woman moved away and Dannaks felt her eyes fall upon him. She now chose to use areas between the tables that accommodated guests who'd not contributed.

Dannaks was pleased to find that he had a five-euro note for coins were out. Despite the clapping the dancer was aware of every movement of the guests and was nearing him before he had put his wallet away. She could tell he was on his own and gave him big eyes and a bright red smile that was meant to be sexy, but instead was brimming with delight and greed. He could see that her make-up had been heavily slapped on with almost clown-like application. Inwardly he recoiled as he too was presented with her quivering breasts. She slowed her movement, although momentum kept her breasts quivering. She nodded and grinned and he slipped his note under a strap. Then she took his hand. And although he shook his head she insistently held on to him. So he got to his feet and self-consciously pushed his arms and legs out in all directions trying to mimic her movements. His clamminess transformed into beads of sweat. At the earliest opportunity he sat down and she writhed away.

The elderly woman leaned forward and said that she thought the dancer was rubbish. Dannaks nodded in agreement and said that he thought she wouldn't go away until she got enough money. The woman looked at him peculiarly and then she turned to her husband. They both stood and said goodnight.

Dannaks sat alone until the assault of music came to an abrupt and merciful end and the dancer hastened away like a rejected lover. Then he got up and went over to Cem and Galip's table to make his request.

Wednesday
13:26

At nine-thirty, after a hearty breakfast, they found themselves again in the minibus and underway. Seating was taken as established. Dannaks had no choice but to accept his lot and retake his middle seat at the back and brace himself against the unevenness of the road and an additional blending of his breakfast.

Göreme was a fascinating place. Dwellings and churches were carved out of the stone. Elsewhere there were natural mushrooms and phallic structures also in stone.

"Are you sure you want to do this?" asked Cem, when they were alighting the minibus at the restaurant. "You will miss a very good meal."

They remained at the minibus whilst the rest of the guests went into the restaurant.

Galip had again wandered away to have a cigarette. He smoked at every stop.

Dannaks was tempted to drop the idea and eat, but he had come this far and he knew he would regret not taking the opportunity. "It is something I have to do."

"Okay. You won't have much time. Galip knows that he has to be here before three thirty."

Dannaks nodded. He believed he had enough time.

Cem called to Galip, who took a last drag on his cigarette before dropping it into the dirt and grinding it underfoot.

Galip got behind the wheel and Dannaks went round and climbed up to take Cem's place.

As soon as the engine started and the brake was off Galip switched on the radio. Once they were out of sight of the restaurant he wound down his window and picked up a soft cigarette packet from the dashboard. He carried another packet in his shirt pocket. "Okay?"

He waved the packet in front of Dannaks as he precariously took a corner and had to quickly change gear, the packet squashed against the gear stick.

"Okay," said Dannaks. There was enough room for two on the long seat next to the driver and Dannaks had chosen to leave some space between them.

Galip lit up. He was a man of few words, especially in Cem's presence. But he had picked up enough German to get by.

"Company says: no smoking in the bus," he said.

Dannaks didn't know how to respond. Was he meant to throw scorn on such a rule? Or admire Galip and bond with him for breaking it?

After all, the man was giving up his lunch break.

Nevşehir was some fifteen kilometres from Göreme, which they covered in twenty-five minutes. The address Dannaks had was in Göre just south of Nevşehir. He estimated that they would need at least an additional ten to fifteen minutes. Cem and Galip had said that it wasn't a proper address and that they'd have to ask someone in Göre for directions. Cem had asked him whether they were expecting him and Dannaks had to admit that he didn't know them and was arriving unannounced. There was a good chance that nobody would be at home. But for fifty euros Galip was willing to make the trip.

Leaving Nevşehir they drove for a few minutes and almost missed the small collection of houses gathered at the strip of road. Galip turned off to the right and the tarmac gave itself up to the dust and unevenness of a track. The vehicle rocked from side to side and Dannaks was glad he was not sitting in the back.

Although there was nobody about Galip pulled over sharply and jumped out without saying a word. He marched to the front door of the nearest house. In Germany the group of architecturally similar-looking dwellings would be called an estate. But here were so few buildings – a dozen or so – that it appeared as if the money had run out. Stretching away from them was wasteland; perhaps waiting for an influx of money to continue building. There were no shops or businesses, just residences.

Such a house did not fit with Dannaks's image of the Özers' abject poverty. They would not have received enough money from the sale of their daughter to afford such a place.

The afternoon stillness in the gasping heat was broken by boys' voices. But no one was to be seen.

Dannaks watched Galip and contemplated getting out. The door to the house was open, but whomever Galip was talking to was obscured by shadow.

He checked his watch. It had taken them forty minutes to get this far. And even then he still hadn't arrived. Allowing for the return trip left him with about half an hour or a maximum of forty minutes.

Galip returned to the minibus. Dannaks looked over at him, but he didn't say anything. He shoved the vehicle into gear and drove on down past the line of houses to the end of what appeared to be a cul de sac. But there was a track to the left that cut through the trees and bushes and was just wide enough for a single vehicle. Galip had no choice but to drop into first gear. The rocking of the minibus brought it dangerously close to the harsh foliage.

Out of his side window Dannaks caught glimpses between the trees and bushes of boys playing football on a dusty wasteland. Some looked over in his direction.

For a moment he wondered why they weren't in school, but then he realised that maybe school had finished for the day.

The track opened up onto an area of what at first glance looked like farm buildings. These wooden constructions may at one time have been farm buildings, but the extra windows and limp faded curtains said that these were places of habitation. And certainly the surrounding area did not look like tended ground.

Brutal rusting evidence of bygone farming banned to the limits of the cleared area protruded from engulfing hardy foliage.

An old sturdy-looking flat-back truck stood neglected and dusty in the forecourt area. Although it wasn't gutted it looked as if it hadn't moved in the last decade. The large tarpaulin on the back had collected dust, like trapped pools left by the tide of time, in its aged folds.

"That one," said Galip after he brought the minibus to a halt and ratcheted the brake. Dannaks followed his nod to the far building. Like the others it was a worn brittle wooden affair.

Dannaks climbed out and glanced back at Galip who'd also left the vehicle but was now lighting up. Before he reached the front door it opened. He half-expected a bare-chested hulk or a scrawny hard-bitten woman carrying a scattergun to appear. For there was a hillbilly feel to the pathetic cluster of isolated buildings. Instead there stood a middle-aged woman in a shabby floral dress over brown slacks. Despite the warmth she wore a shapeless pullover, limp with age, over her dress. A headscarf knotted under the chin framed her weary face.

"*Merhaba*," said Dannaks. She returned the greeting, but suspiciously. Dannaks was aware that neighbours had come to their doors.

She remained steadfast in her doorway and he came to a stop a few steps away from her. Her arms were folded and she spoke curtly.

His weak Turkish had no chance with her accent.

He gave her a feeble smile and called to Galip, who looked up from his musings and had to be called a second time.

"I'm sorry you are going to have to translate," said Dannaks when he arrived. Galip nodded unenthusiastically.

"Tell her I'm a German police officer—" Galip's eyes widened at this "— and that I have been involved in her daughter's case."

"What daughter?" asked Galip.

"Please. I haven't time to explain."

Galip translated and the woman listened impassively. When he finished they gave her a moment but she said nothing.

"Ask her whether she is Shaziye's mother."

Again she didn't respond after Galip had translated.

Dannaks noticed that like Shaziye her hands and wrists were cut.

Galip looked at Dannaks. "Ask her again."

A woman behind them called over and Dannaks saw that occupants had left their buildings and were watching. Even the boys he'd seen playing football were approaching.

Galip repeated his question and the woman nodded.

One of the boys shouted something, but Dannaks didn't turn around. Shaziye's mother looked past him and answered the boy shortly.

Galip said quietly: "He wanted to know whether we were the Press."

Shaziye's mother looked at them critically and spoke. Dannaks caught that she wanted to know what they wanted.

He had never really explained to himself why he wanted to see the family. Perhaps he simply wanted to meet people that would sell their own daughter. He had hoped that he'd be asked in for an open friendly chat. Instead he was sweating in the dry heat under the suspicious eyes of the entire neighbourhood. "Ask her whether I can speak to her husband."

He heard the boys' voices behind him receding. They'd lost interest in the visitors and were probably going back to their game.

Galip spoke and without flinching or betraying any emotion she answered him.

"She says her husband is dead."

"Oh." Dannaks exaggerated his sympathetic expression. Although he could see it fell on stony ground, he asked Galip to express his condolences. The piece of information was interesting if only to legitimize his next question.

"Ask her whether Shaziye can come back." Maybe her father alone had been the driving force behind the sale.

Galip looked at Dannaks as if he had misheard him. This time Dannaks remained stony-faced.

Shaziye's mother seemed outraged by the question and her jaw remained clamped shut with anger.

"Tell her, her daughter has been through a lot. It is time she found peace."

But Galip spoke to Dannaks. "Is this that girl who killed the Nazi in Side?"

"I'll tell you later. We haven't the time now. Please ask her."

Galip obeyed and the woman opened her mouth to react; then she changed her mind.

"Ask her if I could use the toilet."

Galip relayed her negative answer.

A woman, apparently alone, was not going to let two strangers, especially men, into her home.

Dannaks grew angry. "Ask her whether the money they received for their daughter brought them happiness."

This time Galip looked at Dannaks with a shocked expression.

Dannaks nodded firmly.

Galip was about to speak when three topless boys moved past them and her and entered the house.

"Wait," said Dannaks quickly. "Ask her if I could use the toilet now."

As Galip spoke, Dannaks put on a pained smile, as if he was desperate to relieve himself.

The woman sized him up and then nodded.

She spoke into the house, telling the boys not to touch something she was preparing for the evening meal.

She then stepped back off the threshold and Dannaks moved forward. He glanced at Galip, but nothing passed between them.

Inside the house she positioned herself at the corner to the entrances of a living room and the kitchen and pointed. Nodding his thanks he had no choice but to follow her finger to the door at the end of the corridor.

The toilet was the standard hole in the ground with the ceramic surround and footpads. The only other thing in the cubicle of a room was a short hose attached to a tap in the wall. Of course he wasn't alone. There were flies everywhere. He didn't really need to go but he went through the motions, using the hose at the end.

When he opened the door Shaziye's mother was gone. To his left a stairwell gave access to the upper floor from where he heard the creaking of someone moving about. Half way down the corridor he heard her voice. At the lounge entrance he saw her talking to two of the boys. They were still stripped to the waist and were slouching on a battered lumpy sofa. They leaned back with plastic beakers in their hands and attitude on their faces.

Nearest to them was a workbench that had been planed down to function as a dining table. The sofa split the room and was angled to the large old television, as deep as it was wide. Beyond the sofa was a circle of schoolroom chairs and in one corner a mountain of coiled wicker. Stacked shallow baskets rose in precarious pillars. What he could see of the floor was littered with strips of wicker. The window was covered by a large white sheet that lifted with the breeze like a sail.

There were few windows to keep the place cool, but at the cost of being perpetually dull. He noted the numerous candles strategically positioned about the room. The incessant buzz said that there was no shortage of flies here too.

Dannaks's presence drew the boys' attention and Shaziye's mother turned to him.

She had a pleasant face and Dannaks could see Shaziye in her. But her eyes were fatigued. She looked worn out. The bags under them and her sagging cheeks bespoke years of hardship.

He gestured that he would like a drink. Her expression scolded him, but he continued to project a pleasant demeanour. She turned and spoke to the boys and they reluctantly got up.

The third boy was nowhere to be seen and Dannaks surmised that he was upstairs.

He stood aside to let the boys traipse belligerently past, handing their beakers to Shaziye's mother. As they left the house she called after them. But instead of them peeking back Galip's head dipped into view. He held an arm out of sight and Dannaks assumed he held a cigarette. She spoke and Dannaks gathered that she was offering him refreshment.

Then she shouted into the house and the boy upstairs hollered back.

"Okay?" said Dannaks, pointing to the sofa.

Again her expression conveyed her displeasure. She nodded curtly.

She entered the kitchen and he walked into the living-dining room scrutinising every surface and object. There were no photographs. Other than a mere handful of books leaning pitifully against each other on a windowsill there was little of indulgence. Despite being bereft of anything ornamental the room appeared cluttered. An ancient armchair and cushioned footrest spoke of privilege. Maybe this was her seat now that her husband was gone. There again, maybe it was still his seat: for his presence could be felt everywhere. On the floor at the end of the table was a gutted car engine. Pistons and pieces of shaped metal, rings of rubber, a gasket, cotters, spanners, wrenches and pliers lay as if arranged about the immovable lump of metal. Gloves, black with grime rested upon the engine as if laying claim to it. If the armchair wasn't reserved for her husband, then this heap was surely kept in homage of him. Somehow Dannaks couldn't believe that the boy had anything to do with it.

He sat on the sofa and she re-entered the room. It looked as if she'd simply refilled the two plastic beakers the boys had given her. Galip followed her in. She handed Dannaks a beaker and Galip hesitated. He knew better than to sit in the armchair. She spoke and Galip moved round her to sit next to Dannaks. For a moment she stood disapprovingly before them. Then she sighed, turned and grabbed a chair from the dining table.

"Ask her if her daughter can return," said Dannaks quietly.

Galip didn't say anything and Dannaks wondered whether he had heard him. When Shaziye's mother sat down he spoke.

Sitting had relaxed something in her.

She shook her head sadly.

Dannaks was intrigued. The sadness contradicted her answer.

"Ask her why," he said evenly.

As if the question was impertinent her reply was such a torrent of words that Galip had to eventually hold up his hand to allow him to translate.

"She has brought too much shame on the family."

"She said more than that," said Dannaks.

"I didn't understand it all."

"Just tell me what she said," said Dannaks irritably.

Galip tried to match his irritation. "She was dead to us before, er, Mahmut, killed her. Does that make sense to you?"

There was challenge in his question. "Yes, it does. Go on."

Defeated, Galip thought for a moment then he spoke to Shaziye's mother, perhaps to confirm something. As he did Dannaks looked past him. He had noticed something silver dangling from the wooden knob of a chipped plywood wall unit.

As if entranced he didn't hear what Galip said and it was only when Galip said his name that he snapped out of it.

"What?" he said.

"Did you hear what I said?"

"No. Sorry. Say it again."

Galip didn't mask his annoyance. "Shaziye died for them when she left her husband."

Dannaks shook his head and saw that the woman had been waiting for his reaction. But he was still elsewhere. Nonetheless his reaction launched her into a tirade. Galip nodded in agreement throughout, again impatiently seeking a pause in which he could translate.

The moment she hesitated Galip spoke.

"She stayed with *her* husband. And she tried to tell Shaziye that sometimes a woman deserves a beating." Dannaks observed her as Galip spoke. "Otherwise they tend to have mad thoughts." Despite the speech he was unconvinced. He believed that her words were her dead husband's or perhaps her own mother's words.

"Whose idea was it to sell her?"

Galip was horrified. "I cannot ask her that."

"Then tell her that I think she wanted Shaziye to go to Germany for a better life."

She grew pensive as Galip spoke.

Dannaks was composing his next question when she began to talk easily. There was no emotion in her voice, not even resignation. This was fact, nothing more and nothing less.

"Of course it was for a better life for her. Their eldest had done well. And they could not pass up the chance."

She said that the old truck outside was their home for many years. They travelled the country as pickers and lived under the tarpaulin. Her husband also earned money fixing machines. He was a mechanical genius. But he couldn't abide being bossed and was quick of temper. So he never held down a job. So they remained landless and poor, living from hand to mouth.

"We must leave soon," added Galip.

Dannaks ignored him. "Tell her that Shaziye still wears her bone pendant." This is what had distracted him. The same small bone pendant that Shaziye had left at Fehime's was hanging from the cupboard knob.

He looked over at it as Galip spoke. And she looked over too. Her face hardened and she stiffened. She spoke tersely and stood.

"It belongs to her youngest. He doesn't wear it any more. He is ashamed of her too." Yet, Dannaks found it interesting that it remained in the house.

She wanted them to leave.

"Her youngest and Shaziye were close, weren't they?" he said as he stood. Galip stood too and Dannaks looked at him. "Ask her."

She didn't react to the words and Dannaks knew that she was not going to say anything more. But it didn't matter. He could imagine that Shaziye had been a second mother to her younger brother.

The woman stood her ground as they walked by. Dannaks tried a last shot. "What happened to her eldest?" Galip shook his head. Even he'd had enough of the questioning.

Dannaks heard someone descend the stairs at the end of the corridor. It was of course the third boy. He was still stripped to the waist. But that was all he could discern for the corridor was relatively dull and he'd moved away from the light of the stairwell. But there was a premonition that stopped Dannaks in his tracks. Galip, in front of him and almost at the front door, turned around.

Shaziye's mother not anticipating his standstill came too close and backed away into the room. She spoke but he didn't catch what she said. He was watching the boy.

When he was almost upon him, his features sharpening in the light from the entrance and kitchen window Dannaks knew what he was seeing. He was topless, just like the boy in the photograph in Aksoys' flat.

Urgency took him and he talked rapidly. "Ask her whether her eldest was a boy."

"What? I think–"

"Ask her," he barked.

Galip was shocked but obliged.

Dannaks watched her eyes and knew the answer before she spoke.

Her son was next to Dannaks, turning to leave the house. Dannaks grabbed his arm and stared at him. He yelped and then cursed. But Dannaks had seen enough. He was sure. He let the boy go. But instead of fleeing the boy remained and spoke to his mother, saying something about getting help. "Ayhan is the name of your eldest, isn't it?"

She looked at him blankly.

The boy spoke and tight-lipped she shook her head at him.

Dannaks looked to Galip, who appeared confused.

"He said that, er, she should say that he wasn't for sale."

Dannaks blanched. "You sold Ayhan?"

"You, er, want me to translate?"

"Don't bother. Just get me to a phone."

He looked at the woman and then walked past Galip. Outside he strode towards the minibus and Galip hastened after him.

"We should be getting back," Galip said as he climbed in behind the wheel.

"Drive. Get me to a phone."

Galip started up and manoeuvred the vehicle out of the area and onto the path.

Neither men spoke as they rocked down the track.

Dannaks's thoughts were tumbling. Ayhan was Shaziye's eldest brother. This explained his presence outside Azure Skies. He was honour bound to finish Volcan's job, himself trying to finish Mahmut's job. What a mess. He would have liked to know why the

519

Özers had sold their son. Daughters were often sold, but sons were prized and he'd never heard of a boy being sold.

"There's a phone at the restaurant in Göreme," said Galip when they were on the open road.

"Too far."

Galip's brow creased.

"Do you know anywhere in Nevşehir?" said Dannaks.

15:12

On the way to Nevşehir Galip attempted to glean information about Shaziye by expressing his knowledge of the case. But Dannaks cut him short promising to reveal all later. For now he needed to get to a telephone and then back to Side as fast as possible. Galip said that the tour ended tomorrow and they'd have him back in Side by evening. Dannaks said that he needed to get back now. Tomorrow could be too late.

He had opened his wallet and picked out Ismail's card. He also took out a fifty and twenty euro note. When they stopped outside a main road café Dannaks gave him the fifty but held onto the twenty. "This if you come in and tell them I need to use the telephone." Galip looked at his watch. He was critically late, but nodded. Dannaks gave him the twenty and they jumped out. "I need my bag from the back," he said.

After extracting his bag from the rear of the minibus they went into the café. Typically the clientele was all male. The place was about half full. The atmosphere was that of a Turkish *Teestube* in Hamburg. Here the tables were also taken by one to four men. Most sat and conversed, but some were playing dominoes or *Tavla* (a Turkish variation of backgammon). Some were smoking cigarettes; others were using hubble-bubbles. The walls were a distasteful yellow, but the stench was bearable. Hanging from one wall on a hinged bracket was a large television. A football match was in progress but the sound had been turned down to barely audible.

Galip talked to the owner who had risen from one of the tables and gone behind the counter at the end of the room. Behind him stood shelves of hubble-bubbles. Small labels, Dannaks assumed claimed ownership, were stuck along these shelves. A magnificent ornate samovar was in proud operation.

He felt as if everyone was watching him. The owner pointed to the telephone on the wall above a table at the end of the counter.

An old man with a grizzly protruding chin occupied the table. He wore a lumberjack-patterned cotton shirt buttoned up to the neck and a grey jacket. A glass of tea or alcohol stood on the table in front of him.

"You have to pay him," said Galip. Then he said goodbye and they shook hands.

And Dannaks was left alone, knowing no-one, in a town in central Anatolia.

He pointed to the telephone and the old man grinned a toothless grin. Dannaks said thanks as he got up and moved to the chair on the other side of the table. Dannaks pushed the chair in and picked up the phone. Holding up Ismail's card he tapped in the numbers. He knew he was probably being watched and looked at the wall and the cheap plastic telephone.

Apart from the occasional rush of bubbles and murmur the place was relatively quiet.

The phone rang and rang and Dannaks began to curse under his breath with every ring. But he hung on. He reckoned he rang for about two minutes before anyone picked up. The person at the other end was uncannily calm.

"Ismail."

The voice said that he was not Ismail.

Dannaks dropped into English. "I need Ismail. Important. Understand? Very important."

"No, Ismail."

Dannaks felt like screaming and he probably raised his voice a few octaves.

"Ismail call me."

The man said something and put the phone down. Dannaks waited. He glanced about. Only the old man noted his observation. "Come on, Ismail," he whispered, tight-lipped.

After what seemed an age someone picked up.

"Can I help you?" said the new voice in English.

"I need to speak to Ismail."

"He is not here."

Again Dannaks felt his blood boil. "I know. But this is, er, important." He wished he could think of a better word.

"Then I find out where he is. He can call you."

"Yes, but quickly."

"Yes, yes," said the man, "important, important."

"Sch–" he began, but stopped the expletive just in time.

"What?" asked the voice. Dannaks counted in his head until he felt he had control over himself.

"I give you my number."

There was no number on the phone and he groaned at this new hurdle.

"No," said the voice. "I see it here."

Dannaks gave a sigh of relief.

Before he could think of how to emphasise the importance of the call the man hung up. Dannaks had no choice but to hang up too.

He looked at the phone for a moment before turning to the bar and opening his wallet. He had some small change, but his smallest note was ten euro. He had no idea what the call should cost. It certainly wasn't local. So he handed over the note. The owner smiled delightedly and Dannaks using mime and his broken Turkish tried to explain that he had to wait. The owner nodded and spoke to the old man. Then the owner pointed to the chair under the phone and Dannaks sat down.

Five minutes later the owner came round the bar with a glass of tea balancing on a small saucer. He placed it in front of Dannaks who nodded his thanks.

He looked at his watch. He'd been waiting merely fifteen minutes, but it seemed like an hour. The tea was scalding and so terribly sweet that he was reminded of hot jelly babies. No wonder the old boy opposite him had no or very few teeth. And he didn't want to contemplate what the inside of the samovar looked like.

A young man suddenly appeared at his side. Dannaks looked up and to his alarm the man gestured to the telephone. He had no choice but to get up and move out of the way. The man leaned against the counter as he made his call. He spoke rapidly but quietly with his hand cupped over the mouthpiece. Dannaks didn't move away or sit elsewhere. He didn't want the man settling into a long conversation. At one point he looked pleadingly at the owner, who had simply stared back vacantly.

Naturally a *Teestube* was not a place of haste. It was a place of refuge for the men. The home was the realm of women in Turkish society. If they were having non-familial female visitors then the men, especially the eligible ones, had to make themselves scarce.

The young man hung up and Dannaks retook his seat, wondering whether Ismail had tried to reach him whilst the phone was engaged.

Aksoy had said that Ayhan was a mechanical wizard. He'd probably inherited his flair from his father.

Dannaks sipped his warm jelly babies and looked at his watch. Half an hour had passed. The wait was excruciating and the frustration decimated his thoughts. Using questions he had tried to shepherd them into coherence. Was Ayhan a danger? Of course. Why else would he be there? Was that the reason why he had phoned recently? He had wanted to know when Shaziye was getting out. And had he spent that evening with him in Hotel Floyd to gain his confidence? Yet, was he a killer? Dannaks knew he couldn't afford the risk. A life was always too high a price to pay. And what could have possessed the Özers to sell their eldest son, invariably the pride of a family?

A change in the rhythm of television picture attracted his eye. A word bar ran across the bottom of the picture and reporters and cameramen jostled in the strobed light as a woman in a headscarf left an official looking building. He recognised the woman to be a very tired looking Shaziye. The bags under her eyes and her drawn features made her look as if she hadn't slept in months. It made her resemble her mother. By the time he had the presence of mind to ask for the volume to be turned up the report had moved on to something else.

He looked up at the telephone to check that the man had returned the handset properly to its cradle. When his gaze returned to the table he caught the old man staring at him. Dannaks gave him a lopsided smile and the man nodded knowingly. He looked about the room. Everyone was involved in conversation or a game, scouring a newspaper or sitting with their thoughts. Despite the dispersion Dannaks knew that all the men knew one another.

The phone trilled and he jumped up almost knocking the set off the wall with his shoulder. Grabbing the handset he said hallo. For a microsecond he thought the call could cruelly be for someone else.

"Dannaks?"

"Yes. Yes. Ismail listen. Shaziye is in danger. Her brother is in Side."

"Her brother?"

"Yes. He—"

"But he is a schoolboy."

"No. She has an elder brother."

"An elder—"

Dannaks cut off his parroting. "Ismail please listen. I think he will try to kill her. He—"

"Yes. Dannaks, calm down. I think she still in Ankara."

This winded him.

"Dannaks, I think it okay." Ismail continued to fill the silence. "Do not worry, my friend. Continue your holiday. I will check."

"Is she in Ankara?"

"I think."

"You do not know?"

Dannaks sensed his exacerbation in the silence.

"Relax. I shall take care."

"You must check."

"I will check."

"I need to get back."

"No. Enjoy your holiday."

"I – Can you check and call me?"

"Yes. Are you in a hotel?"

"Yes – No. No. I am in a café. I got out of the tour."

"Got out? You mean left?"

"Yes."

"Oh, Dannaks. What are you doing? Trust me. I will take care."

"Can you help me get back?"

"I – I do not think that will be possible."

"No. But I must ask."

"Try to get back on your tour. Maybe not too late."

"No. I shall come back. Somehow I will call you. Give me your handy – mobile – number again."

15:53

For Dannaks a frustrating game of charades began. He spoke first to the owner, but it was the old man who guessed what he wanted. The owner went into a back room and returned with a map. He unfolded it on the counter. Using single Turkish words and tracing his finger from Nevşehir to Side he conveyed that he wanted to travel to Side. The old man spoke loudly and a few men rose to look at the map and Dannaks repeated his request. They spoke of a *Dolmuş* (a shared minibus taxi). Such a vehicle would make stops and Dannaks wanted to travel directly. And he wanted to leave now.

Some of the men shook their heads and wandered back to their tables. One man made what sounded like an offer and the others laughed, but Dannaks pounced on him and asked him to explain. The owner obliged the man by producing a pencil and paper. The man then wrote: "450 klms = 450 €". Dannaks smiled at his cheekiness. He held out his palm for the pencil, crossed out the right-hand 450 and replaced it with 150. The man laughed and shook his head. He then traced his finger along the route and held up all the fingers and thumb of one hand and pointed to the clock. Dannaks understood that such a journey would take five hours and nodded furiously that he understood. Then the man traced his finger back from Side and held up his other hand. It was a ten-hour round trip. Dannaks nodded despondently, although he heard the man murmur something about visiting a relative. The man then took the pencil and altered the 150 into 300. Dannaks crossed it out and wrote 200. The man smiled and wrote 250. Dannaks then nodded and held out his hand. But the man began pointing and holding his hand like a gun. Eventually Dannaks realised that the man wanted him to pay for one tank of petrol.

They shook hands and Dannaks had a good look at his face. For until now he had not really looked at him.

He was a poorer version of the Hunk from the beach bar of the hotel neighbouring Azure Skies. A Romeo nonetheless, this man was rougher, less groomed, and stockier. Dannaks saw him as more of a Chunk than a Hunk.

Dannaks picked up his bag to emphasise the urgency of the journey.

Chunk smiled and gestured for him to put it down. He then pointed to the clock and repeated what Dannaks understood to be a quarter of an hour. Dannaks sighed and nodded and the man left.

Whilst he was gone Dannaks took the opportunity to go to the toilet. Once again he was confronted by the hole in the ground, but this time his need was earnest. No matter how well he washed his hands under the tap they still felt dirty. He washed and sniffed, washed and sniffed and his imagination destroyed his sense of smell.

When he returned to the room little had changed. He went to his seat and started checking the time at what turned out to be two to three minute intervals. His mind began to spin too. He was at the Chunk's mercy. Would he return in a dilapidated truck? Or maybe the man was planning on doing the trip on a moped.

Realising he was hungry, he mimed putting food in his mouth and said: "Food please."

The owner nodded and left. He returned a moment later with a sticky sweet pastry and a glass of water. Dannaks offered to pay but the man shook his head and smiled. Although he cringed at the taste he wolfed the thing down. He was thirsty but decided to leave the water.

Every time the door opened he was given false hope. Ten minutes had passed. The pastry was but a few flakes on the plate. Had Chunk meant half an hour?

Then the door opened and there he stood. Dannaks picked up his bag and darted over to him, thwarting any possibility of him entering for a parting coffee or whatever.

Outside Dannaks was pleased to see a beige Mercedes. This was the standard colour of Hamburg's taxis and Dannaks wondered whether it had once been a taxi. He knew that the Greeks were fond of taking old German Mercedes.

He threw his bag on the back seat and climbed in. They didn't get off to a flying start. Chunk stopped at the first petrol station and tanked up, holding out his hand to Dannaks when he was ready to pay.

Before he started the engine to get underway Dannaks gestured and asked him whether he had a handy. The man took one out of the top pocket of his shirt. Dannaks simply nodded and held up his hand to explain that he didn't need it now.

When they properly set off little of the day was left. Within ten minutes of leaving the petrol station it was pitch black.

Language was indeed a barrier. Chunk attempted to find common ground. Establishing their names took some time. Chunk was Yavuz. Establishing that he was a plumber ate up a few more kilometres. Dannaks took up the challenge of explaining his job, eventually using Colombo as a name. This led to stuttering talk of film. But the intervening silences grew and they soon fell silent.

The run to Konya was relatively straight. Great stretches of road were unlit and the parched wilderness was infrequently interrupted by anything visible or of interest. The monotony and darkness could have sent him into a slumber. But Dannaks remained awake if not drowsy. He didn't know Yavuz. And he didn't know how fatigue would present itself. How much sleep had the man had?

Yavuz drove fast but not recklessly. Dannaks would not have minded some recklessness. But it was dark and the narrower roads were quite treacherous. He would have liked a little more speed on the straight wide roads. Of all the Turkish drivers in the country he had to get the cautious one. Of course they couldn't afford to have an accident. And he dreaded the thought of some other incident blocking their way.

Dannaks pointed to himself and the steering wheel and mimed driving. Yavuz smiled and went into trying to explain that nobody, not even his wife, drove this car. Dannaks thought that he said that his wife had another car, but he was not sure.

He then managed to communicate that if he got him to the hotel in Side before ten he'd give him 280 euros.

19:35

"Ismail?"

"Yes. Hallo Dannaks. Wait please."

He pressed Yavuz's small hardy close to his ear. The heating was on and the sound of the engine hampered his comprehension. He waited, straining to hear anything other than the periodic static.

"Hallo Dannaks?"

"I am here."

"She is flying here. She arrives at Ankara at eight of the clock."

Heavy static followed by a woman's voice way in the distance – a crossed-line – interrupted him.

"Ismail. Please say again. Say again. Bad, er, line."

"I have men meeting her. It is good. Where are you?"

"We are through Konya."

"You tell me. Where is Ayhan staying?"

"I do not know. But Ismail..." Again static furiously scratched the line. "I think he wait at Azure Skies. Understand?"

"Say again." The line was suddenly clear, as if Ismail was sitting next to him.

"I think he wait at Azure Skies. Understand?"

"Understand. Do not worry. I get her. Okeydokey?"

"Yeah, okeydokey."

"Goodbye."

"Bye."

Dannaks had a bad feeling when he hung up. He didn't like it. Ismail himself wasn't meeting her at the airport.

He checked his watch. She would be landing within half an hour. Was she travelling alone? As a prosecution witness she could be accompanied. But Ismail had said that protection had not been deemed necessary. After all, she wasn't a witness against some gangland boss. What about the media? Maybe reporters were with her?

Would she go straight to Azure Skies? Would they put her up? Did she have somewhere else to stay?

In spite of all these variables and possibilities that could thwart Ayhan getting to her Dannaks didn't feel reassured. Far from it. He felt a terrible knot of dread in his stomach.

21:28

About thirty minutes away from Side Dannaks borrowed Yavuz's phone again. This time, disconcertingly, Ismail didn't answer. Dannaks hung up and redialled. Again nobody picked up.

At the Azure Skies barrier Dannaks paid Yavuz the balance adding a ten-euro tip. He grabbed his bag, showed gate security his wristband and hastened to reception. His legs were stiff and wouldn't move as fast as he wanted.

Parked in front of the entrance was a marked police car.

Inside he saw a uniformed officer leaning against the reception counter idly talking to the young female staff member.

"Ismail?" said Dannaks, startling the man.

He glanced at the corridor to the offices behind reception before shrugging. Dannaks veered to the corridor and the man came towards him. Taking a guess Dannaks knocked quickly and opened the door to the office in which he and Reupke had first looked at the meagre number of crime scene photographs all those months ago. There was no name on the door but Dannaks assumed it to be Turgut's office.

The uniform was upon him as he looked into the room.

Ismail, Turgut and a large woman, he had never seen before, were sitting in front of the desk.

"Ismail–" Dannaks began, only to be cut off by the uniform.

Ismail nodded and calmed the man and gestured Dannaks to come in.

Dannaks caught a dirty look from the uniform as he closed the door on him. He dropped his bag but didn't move into the room.

"Where is she?"

The large woman cast her eyes downwards. Ismail's paleness said everything.

"What happened?"

"She is gone," said Ismail, resignedly.

Dannaks could barely contain himself. "What do you mean?"

"I think Ayhan has taken her."

"What?" he stammered. "Where? How–"

"Maybe you tell him," said Ismail to the woman.

She looked at Dannaks and spoke in German. "I brought her here. She's under contract. I–"

"You're a reporter?"

She had a pleasant, quite youthful, but very white face. Her eyes were large and owl-like. And this owl had the look of a predator: a sharp-witted predator. However, her head was dwarfed by her body, which had gone to seed.

"Heike Hausmann, *Bild Zeitung*." Her eyes narrowed. "Aren't you the–"

"I may be," he said curtly, giving her his most contemptuous look. "But I think you ought to know that Shaziye is in grave danger."

She blanched, no doubt seeing her exclusive rights or whatever she'd secured turning to dust. Her breathing grew slightly laboured.

"Now tell me – in detail – what happened."

"I was checking in when a boy appeared and started talking to her. I went over and he said that he was taking her to her family. Her mother wanted her back, he said. I wasn't sure about that, but I knew where she lived and said it was too far. He said she'd travelled to a place just outside Side. When I said I wasn't letting her go anywhere, he said that I could come too." Dannaks noted the glint in her eye. She had no doubt smelt more meat for her story. "It seemed okay with Shaziye."

"How did she look?"

"What do you mean?"

Dannaks didn't mask his exasperation. "Did she look happy? Sad?"

"She looked as she always has done: completely wasted."

"We have lost her," said Ismail, unable to follow the conversation and believing it had finished.

"When was this?"

"Well, I–" She glanced at her watch. Maybe an hour ago. Forty minutes."

"And when did he get here?" Dannaks nodded to Ismail.

"Twenty minutes ago."

Dannaks winced.

"What's he going to do?" Hausmann asked.

Dannaks stared at the woman. "He's probably going to kill her."

"But her mother–"

"Her mother is not here. I met her today in Göre. She doesn't want her back."

"Why did Shaziye go with him?"

"Because he's her brother."

"An honour... But why would she go with him if she knows what he's going to do?"

"Because as you so eloquently put it: she's completely wasted."

She shook her head. "I'll never understand these people," she said quietly, almost to herself.

Dannaks despaired too. "And this is the safe house you chose?"

She bristled. "She insisted on coming here. She said she had belongings to collect and wanted to speak to some people. I agreed for one night only."

Ismail spoke again. "I sent local police to her home in Göre."

Dannaks regarded him sympathetically. He couldn't follow the German and was out of sync with the conversation. This also explained Turgut's presence. Although he would have thought that Hausmann's English would have been good. "He has not gone there." He pressed the palms to the side of his head as if he was having a migraine. He was trying to think where Ayhan could have taken her. But he had nothing. Shaziye could already be dead by now.

Heike Hausmann was dwelling "I thought she'd be safe here. After what had happened the security here should be top."

The image of the Hunk sitting at a table flashed through his mind. So much for security.

"Just, just be quiet for a minute." He addressed his next question to Turgut. "What was Ayhan doing here? How did he get in?"

"He bought a day card." Turgut smiled sickly. "Staff noticed him because he spent the day in the lobby bar drinking water and reading the paper. Most people use the facilities. He–"

"Did he have to sign anything?"

"Yes."

"And give an address and phone number?"

"Yes. But we–" he nodded to Ismail "– have already checked. They are both false."

Dannaks cursed. "Where would he go? Where would he go?" He wasn't talking so much as thinking aloud. Where would Ayhan take her? Somewhere remote. And not too far. Somewhere he would know. Somewhere, perhaps, in common with Volcan.

"Turgut translate – please." He didn't have time to speak to Ismail in English. Turgut could translate directly into Turkish. "Ask him where Volcan stayed when he was here?"

"Volc–"

"Never mind. Just ask. Please."

Ismail listened. Brightening at the thought. He spoke rapidly to Turgut and taking out his handy he stood.

Dannaks's expression implored Turgut, for apparently Ismail wasn't going to answer him.

"He says he doesn't have the address, but he can get it."

Ismail was leaving the room.

Dannaks looked at Turgut and pointed to his bag. "Get this to my room, please." He didn't wait for Turgut to reply and followed Ismail out.

Ismail interrupted his call to summon the uniform who was again talking to the girl behind the reception desk. Dannaks strode with them to the exit. The uniform overtook them and went to the driver's side of the marked car. "Let me come." Ismail still had his ear to the phone. He gave Dannaks a stern look. "I know him." Ismail nodded.

Hausmann appeared at the car. She was out of breath. "I would like to come," she said in English.

Ismail said no before Dannaks.

Dannaks listened to Ismail as they mounted the road in front of Azure Skies and turned right towards Side. He obviously had an address and was now instructing the person at the other end of the line to scramble some armed units and an ambulance. He also said that a helicopter should be put on stand-by. When he asked for the local units to be notified, Dannaks realised that the main units were stationed in Manavgat and would take more than a quarter of an hour to arrive. Ismail told them to stay away from the building and to wait for him.

Ismail spoke to the driver who immediately switched on the car's siren and flashing lights. Dannaks felt himself being pushed back into his seat as the car accelerated. Vehicles in front of them began pulling over.

Dannaks wanted to speak, but waited until Ismail had tapped in the address on the navigation system. Ismail then pulled out his service weapon and checked the clip. He mumbled something to the driver.

Dannaks leaned forward. "We may not be too late," he said loudly. It was a statement and not the question he had intended. Ismail twisted in his seat to look at him. "Ayhan is not like Volcan." Ismail's expression was puzzled and Dannaks wished he could express himself better in English. There again, he should improve his Turkish. Three months learning the language wasn't enough. "He is not a killer."

Ismail nodded.

"My friend you must stay in the car. Leave this to us."

"I may be able to talk to him," said Dannaks. "I, er, do not know how his Turkish is."

"First you stay in the car."

Dannaks reluctantly nodded, slumping back in his seat.

At the main Side roundabout the navigation system instructed them to go straight on.

Tourist nightlife to their right glowed beckoningly.

Shortly afterwards they turned left: inland.

Dannaks leaned forward again. "I have a question." It was what he had wanted to ask earlier. "Why did you not get Shaziye at the airport?"

Ismail's voice had a hard edge of irritation as he spoke. He suspected that the reporter had bribed the airport staff to allow them to bypass the media welcoming committee the other side of customs. His officers had been inadvertently bypassed too. Anticipating Dannaks's next question he added that his officers should have intercepted Shaziye at the plane, but he suspected they wanted to be in the limelight and take her in front of the cameras. In good time they and the airport staff would be questioned.

A kilometre from their destination, as shown on the navigation system, Ismail ordered the siren and flashing lights off.

22:04

They left the main road taking turns right and left in a residential area. Unlike Volker Herbst's place these houses were more spaced out and done in quite individual styles. Some, with their ample quality wood and whitewashed walls, would not have been out of place in a Western set near the Mexican border. Others had gone classical with granite and marble that looked genuine enough. They were pretentious Romanesque or Georgian buildings with convex facades and mock Deep South pillars like Tara from the film *Gone with the Wind*. Here was money. Yet, these weren't sprawling ten bedroom or more buildings. They were slightly larger family homes with maybe four to six bedrooms.

"Volcan lived out here," Dannaks exclaimed.

Ismail half-turned around. "The place is owned by somebody called Simsek. They bought it last year."

Now Dannaks was certain that they were at the right place.

Headlights appeared behind them and Dannaks looked out of the back window. Another marked car was behind them. They had followed suit and had their siren and emergency lights off.

Fifty metres from their destination Ismail ordered the driver to halt. They got out and Ismail again told Dannaks to stay in the car.

Dannaks watched Ismail give instructions to the driver and the two uniforms from the other car. All three checked their handguns. The two new uniforms were the boys who had arrested Reupke and him outside Herbst's place. The big experienced sergeant was not with them. One of these lads left the group and returned to his car. When he rejoined them he was carrying a pump-action rifle.

Uneasiness caused Dannaks to shuffle in his seat.

Ismail looked over at him before he trotted away with the group.

Then they were gone.

Dannaks wound down the window. Apart from the sounds of insects he heard nothing. Yet the tension was palpable. He expected shouts and then a gunshot or more to tear through the silence.

He checked his watch and was surprised to see that his hands were damp with sweat. He touched his forehead. That was wet too.

A strange and almost irrelevant thought occurred to him. "I bet the Simseks are missing a crow-bar."

Minutes passed and the relative silence continued.

Dannaks was growing sticky with sweat. The air was still and the open window didn't help. So he got out and closed the door. He didn't move away from the car and stared into the darkness where Ismail had led his men.

Why was it so quiet?

He checked his watch again. Five minutes had passed.

It wasn't warm and evaporation cooled him. He rubbed his hands together and began pacing.

Being set back from the road by open drives, the occupants of the houses probably had no idea that police cars were parked on the road. With such wealth Dannaks had expected more security: high walls, fences, visible alarm systems, CCTV, perhaps security guards. But they were quite exposed. There were no streetlamps, but the houses had their own entrance lights, either as spots embedded in the ground and marking the edge of the drive like a runway, or a pair of lampposts or lanterns attached to a wall at the roadside entrance.

He checked his watch again. A further three minutes had passed. They had been gone almost ten minutes. Surely ample time to establish Ayhan's whereabouts?

"Come on," he whispered under his breath.

More minutes passed.

He heard the footsteps long before he saw the running person. They grew from barely discernible to urgent. Out of the darkness the figure emerged. Dannaks began to walk towards him.

The uniform slowed. Dannaks thought it was Ismail's driver. He gestured for Dannaks to approach and Dannaks began jogging.

534

"Come, come," said the uniform out of breath. It was the driver.

They both jogged down the road, taking a corner to their right. Dannaks would have liked to have questioned the man to in some way prepare. He didn't know what to expect.

The man led him past the corner house and entered the drive of the next house. The man didn't slow his pace as they neared the house, a comparatively humbler building. This was similar to Herbst's place: stylish but compact.

In the drive stood a metallic blue-green Ford Focus. As they passed it Dannaks spotted a pristine shovel in the foot well of the back seats. The maker's etiquette was still tagged to the handle.

Instead of entering the house the driver led him down a path. They passed the terrace and rounded an illuminated kidney-shaped swimming pool towards a wooden out-house. The lights were on and the door wide open. One of the other uniforms stood in the doorway. He was the one with the pump-action rifle and he was pointing it into the building.

He moved aside to allow Dannaks in.

His companion was to his left inside the room, his arm extended and his handgun pointing in the same direction. Ismail was over to the right. He too had his weapon drawn, but held it at his hip, his aim more casual than that of the uniforms.

In front of them, at the other end of the L-shaped room, sat what Dannaks at first sight thought was a skinhead tied to a chair. He quickly realised that it was Shaziye. Her legs were bound to those of the wooden chair and her arms were pulled back. No doubt her hands were tied behind her back. Her head was bare: her hair had been cropped back to a felt covering. Dannaks hardly recognised her. There was no emotion in her face. Her eyes looked sleepy. They were not wide, but dull. The bags under them bespoke untold stress and sleepless nights. Her cheeks were sunken as if the life had been drained from them. He couldn't see her mouth. It was sealed behind a torn piece of brown packing tape. Her posture was not taut with fear. She was slumped. But Heike Hausmann was right. She looked completely wasted: a wreck.

Ayhan was standing behind her. He was her opposite: a picture of physical health. His eyes were wild. His body stiff, muscles tense. His bloody left hand held her left shoulder. Her left shoulder was stained. His right hand held a large carving knife at her naked throat. The blade glinted painfully in the strip lighting that over-exposed the scene.

To their left, giving the rectangular room its L-shape, was the wooden cubicle of a sauna. To their right were four standing metal lockers. A slatted bench separated them from the police. In the corner beyond Ismail was a cold-water plunge. The floor was tiled with terracotta coloured tiles. Black plastic bin liners had been cut open and taped, using the same tape that covered Shaziye's mouth, to the wooden walls. One covered the frosted glass of the window behind Ismail, another the inside of the open door next to the uniform to Dannaks's left. Ayhan had prepared the room for the killing.

Not covering the floor was a mistake. Forensics could pick up miniscule traces of blood at least from the grout.

Ismail glanced at Dannaks. He didn't need to say anything.

"Ayhan," Dannaks began. Of the two of them before him, the lad appeared the more upset. Tears quivered in his eyes and blurred his vision. "It's me Dannaks. Don't do it." His words had the adverse effect of Ayhan adding pressure to the blade upon Shaziye's skin.

Dannaks dared to take a further step into the room.

Ayhan stiffened.

"It's enough," said Dannaks. He was poised to take another step.

"Stop," said Ayhan.

"Ayhan, don't do it. This must end."

"It's my duty." His voice was weak and broken as if he was about to cry.

"No. You have a choice. Choose life. Not this. Not this."

"I can't."

"Yes you can." He racked his mind for more to say. "You kill her and you're dead too. Look either side of me."

"You don't understand. How can I live if I don't kill her?"

"You can." He had no other words. "You must forgive."

He began shaking his head and Dannaks knew he was bracing himself to draw the knife across her throat.

"Ayhan, she's been through enough. Don't do it."

The youth's face became manic. A hideous smile twisted his expression. "It is her destiny," he said. "Ask her."

"She can't answer me," he said, knowing that the distraction of removing the tape would give Ismail the moment to take him out.

Intuitively the lad seemed to know that such an action would be his last.

"You're dead the minute you move," said Dannaks.

Ismail cleared his throat quietly. He wanted Dannaks's attention. Naturally he couldn't follow the German and as far as he could see Dannaks's presence had not improved the situation.

"It is my duty."

Dannaks knew there was still a chance. Ayhan was talking.

"Your duty to whom?"

"To my family. She has–"

"What family? Duty to whom? Özer? Simsek? Aksoy? Who?"

"My–" he croaked and began again. "My honour."

"Your honour? And just who are you, Ayhan? Özer or Simsek? This has nothing to do with duty or honour. No one has been shamed. And you know it. This is some perverse sense of loyalty to Aksoy. You're not a hothead like Mahmut or Volcan. You know better. You're more German than Turkish. Face it. Come on, she's your sister." Dannaks needed more words. "This is wrong. Killing can never be the way to live. Drop the knife."

Ayhan's eyes implored him. The plea in them said: help me.

"Choose life."

Then surprisingly Ayhan slowly took the knife away from her throat.

"Drop it," said Dannaks. For this was the pivotal moment in which the police could open fire. Ayhan released his grip and the knife clattered to the floor shattering the tension. Ismail and the uniform with the handgun were upon him as he stepped back. Ismail deftly swept the knife away with a foot as he grabbed Ayhan.

"Do not hurt him," said Dannaks in English.

Ismail looked at him angrily, but said nothing. The uniform was cuffing Ayhan's hands behind his back. Dannaks saw that the uniform next to him was paralysed in position, his rifle still aimed at the boy's head. Dannaks slowly moved his hand to the barrel and lowered the weapon.

The uniform looked at him sickly. He was visibly shaken.

Ismail was then untying Shaziye. Dannaks could see no wound at her bloodied shoulder. The material of her top was not torn.

Then the place began filling up. From behind him two ambulance men pushed forward. Dannaks backed out to allow the uniforms to bring Ayhan out. Outside were six men in matt-black body armour, carrying machine pistols; two held sharpshooter rifles with large night-sights.

Their leader moved forward to talk to Ismail who accompanied Shaziye with one of the ambulance men. Shaziye was rubbing her wrists. She looked at Dannaks. "Let him go," she said. He stared back at her. Nothing exchanged between them.

Dannaks then looked back into the building. The handcuffs had been undone and dangled from his right hand. The second ambulance man was tending to his left hand.

Ismail stopped to talk to the leader. Then they both issued instructions.

Dannaks followed everyone out onto the road, where more uniforms and vehicles were waiting. Some of the residents of neighbouring houses were at their windows, open front doors or even in front of their driveways.

Ismail came up to him and shook his hand. "Well done, my friend."

Dannaks smiled.

Then, almost confidentially he leaned forward and said: "I do not know what you said. But you took a risk moving to him."

"Yes," he said. He wanted to explain that he wanted to get Ayhan talking and saw no alternative other than threat.

The leader of the armed unit interrupted them.

Dannaks had no opportunity to properly talk to Ismail before the young uniforms from Side took him back to the hotel.

Thursday (Gala night)
07:46

Dannaks didn't sleep well. In fact he was not sure he slept at all. He felt exhausted, but was too restless and rose and went to breakfast.

Clouds covered the entire sky and the intermittent breeze was chilling.

In the restaurant he kept himself to himself nodding to Yunus and Tanya from a distance.

His interest was only aroused when Heike Hausmann

entered the restaurant just after eight. Dannaks picked up his empty juice glass and walked over to her as if he was on the way to the pressed orange juice. She was at the hot plate behind which the cook was frying eggs and omelettes to order.

"Good morning," he said.

"Oh, good morning."

"You heard about last night?" he asked.

"Yes." Then with something akin to justification she added: "He didn't kill her."

"No." He paused and in the pause he knew that she knew that his next question or statement was the reason for his approach. "When will she be here?"

"When the police release her," she said haughtily. She signalled for the cook to fold her mixed vegetable omelette.

He seethed, but held himself in check. She could not know that he had effectively saved Shaziye's life. He waited a moment considering how to proceed.

"And she'll come to you?"

"Yes," she said triumphantly. She proffered her plate to the cook who obediently scooped up the omelette and flipped it onto her plate.

"Then find me when she does."

She froze, her plate still poised in the air.

"Why should I?"

She turned to him and gave him her best cold stare.

"Because if you don't I'll have you for obstructing justice."

"What?" she blustered and again she was instantly out of breath.

"You bribed the airport staff at Antalya and put Shaziye's life at unnecessary risk."

"You're bluffing."

"Am I?"

She opened her mouth to protest but no words came.

"When are you expecting her?" he asked.

She hesitated. "I don't know. Between ten and eleven." That put paid to Nordic walking. But he was glad for the self-justification. He didn't feel up to it. In any case the group didn't expect to see him until tonight or tomorrow at the earliest.

"I'll be in reception or at the plaza." Despite being overcast he wanted to wait outside, but could only go there after the walkers

539

had gone.

She nodded and he turned away placing his drink on the nearest surface as he left.

He had crossed the amphitheatre and was at the plaza when he spotted Fehime coming from the direction of the reception. He changed course and intercepted her.

They exchanged morning greetings and he stood firm to indicate that he wanted to talk to her.

"I think Shaziye is coming today."

Fehime simply stared at him.

"She'll want to collect her belongings. You know, the bone pendant, for instance."

Her face broke and words suddenly gushed forth. "We kept her stuff for her. It would have walked otherwise. We had to say it was Hülya's. You understand, don't you?" Dannaks knew that she was implying that the police were light-fingered.

"It's okay," he reassured. "I just wanted to tell you to fetch me when she arrives."

Her face betrayed her sense of foolishness.

08:27

In reception he was pleased to see that Mr. and Mrs. Azure Skies had been yesterday's show. Thankfully he had missed it. But tonight was gala night and Lion King was again being presented.

The bellboy was there but he looked away.

Dannaks's breakfast sat heavily in his stomach. He suddenly felt exceedingly tired and didn't fancy falling asleep in the reception seating area. So he went to the desk and said that if anyone came asking for him he'd be in his room.

He set the alarm of his bedside travel clock to nine forty-five and slumped down on the bed. He didn't fall asleep immediately, but when he did it seemed as if he'd only just closed his eyes when there was a knock on the door. He got up and called out that he was coming. A glance at the clock told him that it was nine-thirty. By the time he got to the door the cleaner had moved her trolley to the neighbouring. She turned and said something. He nodded and scratched his head, widening his eyes after a yawn.

He closed the door and went to the bathroom sink and doused his face in cold water.

Picking up his sweatshirt he returned to reception taking a roundabout route to avoid the plaza. In the lobby bar he ordered a coffee and found a table with a discarded newspaper. It was a few days old, but it helped to pass the time.

At ten past ten he went to the plaza, which was all but deserted. Some guests clad in sweatshirts and cardigans lay on the loungers at the poolside. Children read, played cards, board games or computer-games on loungers next to their parents. One hardy old woman wearing a tight bathing cap was in the pool doing lengths in leisurely breaststrokes that hardly produced a ripple.

Cemil and someone Dannaks didn't recognise – probably Rafael's replacement – were at the radio shack. But the breeze and general apathy had subdued their enthusiasm. The music was sedate rather than blaring.

Dannaks found himself in front of his favourite watch. Conflicting thoughts again competed within his mind. One ran along the lines of the watch lasting no longer than the socks he had bought here. Against this was the argument that if he haggled the price down he had nothing to lose.

Thankfully the shop wasn't open.

Reflected in the glass he recognised Heike Hausmann's form. He turned to see her walking with Fehime, Shaziye and a uniformed policeman. Dannaks cut off their path.

"We were just coming for you," said Hausmann. None of them had looked about. They had come from the beach area and were making their way to reception.

"Sure," said Dannaks, seeing through the lie and instantly ignoring her. He acknowledged the uniform he didn't recognise, before turning to Shaziye. "How are you?"

She shut her eyes for a moment. He wasn't sure whether she was closing her eyes on him or his question.

Her blood-stained top was gone. She was wearing a blue/green hospital issue top.

"We're going to my room to get her stuff," said Fehime.

"Aren't you supposed to be taking gym?"

"Habip's doing it for me."

"I'd like to tag along." If anybody his question was directed at Shaziye. She merely shrugged. "Good."

They went through reception in silence. When they began the gentle climb towards Fehime's room Dannaks manoeuvred his position to walk alongside Shaziye, forcing Hausmann up front with Fehime. The uniform dropped behind them. They proceeded unhurriedly, not least because of Hausmann's huffing and puffing.

Shaziye spoke without prompting.

"I remember you now." Yet, her face adopted a puzzled expression. "You were there when I gave myself up."

"Yes." Aside from last night this was a girl he'd only met once and yet because of the amount of time and energy he'd spent on her he felt as if he knew her. But she hardly knew or recognised him.

"I'm sorry," she said in a barely audible voice. "I know I should be grateful to you for saving my life."

"But you're not sure, are you?"

She shook her head.

"I, er, have followed your case."

"The whole world has," she said bitterly.

He nodded.

"But you're the one who helped me in Germany." She glanced at him and he caught her eyes.

"Yes."

"Then I should again be grateful."

They were silent for a few steps.

"Maybe I could ask you a few questions?" He sensed Hausmann's attention. "What are you going to do?"

She shrugged.

"She will be protected," said the uniform in passable German.

Dannaks turned as they walked. He had all but forgotten about him and couldn't hide his surprise.

"She'll be given a new identity," he said and Dannaks almost missed his footing on the next step.

"How many times can a person start over?" she asked miserably.

Dannaks couldn't think of anything to say. So Ayhan's attack had been persuasive.

"What's going to happen to Ayhan?" he asked the uniform.

"He will be deported." Dannaks frowned at him. "She has dropped all charges."

Then they were at Fehime's place.

Fehime opened the door and they all crowded in. "There's not enough room for everybody in here," she said.

"I need to talk to Shaziye," said Dannaks.

Fehime looked at Shaziye, who said quietly: "I owe him."

Hausmann said: "I'm not leaving her out of my sight." And the uniform volunteered to wait outside.

Fehime opened first the terrace and then the cupboard doors. She pulled out a soft case from behind the hanging clothes and opened it on one bed. Hausmann sat on the other.

"Why don't you ask your questions?" said Shaziye fingering the contents of the case.

Dannaks wasn't happy about the reporter's presence, but he had no choice. He then saw the fluffy light-green pullover in the case. He stepped over and touched it. It was Angora mohair.

"Michael gave it to me as a birthday present," she almost whispered.

Hausmann watched him as he picked up a stray fibre from the denim next to the pullover.

"You were in Meryem's flat when Mahmut came."

"Yes," she said. "Michael was doing our bathroom." Dannaks remembered the half-completed tiling. "I was having a bath in Meryem's place."

Hausmann casually placed a dictation machine next to her and switched it on. Dannaks took the opportunity to pocket the fibre.

"We were good friends," Shaziye continued.

Fehime was sifting through jewellery she had tipped out onto the bed next to the case. Shaziye picked out the bone pendant and put it on.

"I know," said Dannaks.

She was quiet.

"Peter wrote that you wanted to run away. Is it because you saw Volcan?"

She didn't answer immediately. "No. Well, maybe I did. At the time I thought I saw Mahmut. But I knew it couldn't be him. But it scared me."

He let the silence grow.

"Poschmann gave you somewhere to stay afterwards, didn't she?" He didn't care about Hausmann getting the name. Shaziye didn't answer. But her non-denial was all the confirmation he needed.

If he was going to drop names then he might as well go the whole hog. "Why did you come here? The Simseks have a villa not

543

far from here."

"I didn't know."

"Do you know why your parents sold Ayhan?"

She shook her head. "He was four years old. I was a baby." She told Fehime that she could keep a particular item of jewellery. "I didn't know about him until I went to Germany."

"But you would have asked."

He waited.

She smiled to herself.

"What's going to happen to him?" she asked.

"I would have thought that's up to you."

"Then nothing," she said, glancing at Hausmann. And he not only knew that she was dropping all charges, she'd also effectively gagged Hausmann, with something along the lines of mention Ayhan and the deal is off.

Her question was whether Dannaks was going to do anything.

"Nothing then," he agreed.

A slight nod was her acknowledgement.

She straightened. "I've got all I want."

"Then let's go," said Hausmann, grabbing her dictating machine.

"Have you more questions?"

"Too many," said Dannaks.

She gave him a moment, but he just smiled.

11:16

Dannaks carried her case. At reception Hausmann checked out. And Dannaks moved away as Shaziye and Fehime talked and hugged and said their goodbyes.

Shaziye shook his hand and thanked him before leaving with Hausmann and the uniform.

Dannaks returned to the plaza. He felt terribly empty and somehow deserving of a treat so he went into the shop and haggling supremely bought the watch.

In his room he admired his purchase and then remembered the Angora fibre. He had to turn out his pocket to find it. He was going to put it in his wallet when he remembered the hotel envelopes. He fetched one from the writing set in the drawer and dropped the fibre in sealing it and then putting it in the safe.

Dannaks wasn't sure whether he'd ever bother about trying

to get a comparison done. Such analysis was unnecessary and probably too expensive. But he couldn't go against his inherent compulsion to tie up loose ends.

Saturday
05:23

Pickup for the 06:00 flight to Hannover was at the ungodly hour of 03:10.

Dannaks laboriously queued to have his bags checked, queued to check-in, queued to have his passport stamped and when he was finally through he sought a seat near the flight gate.

On Thursday he excused himself from his friends and went to bed before the gala show began. He was tired and he couldn't face watching Lion King. It could provoke too many memories.

He went Nordic walking on Friday morning for a last time and idled the rest of the day away. The sun was up and after some lounging around he started packing before dinner.

After dinner he drank and joked at the plaza bar. He even went into the disco with Thomas for an hour to dance with Noreen and her friends. One of these friends, who he had never really noticed, gave him the eye, but his frame of mind wasn't right and he left.

He was sitting squashed up between others when he saw Ayhan enter the area accompanied by two men from airport security. His escort found him a place to sit at the Berlin flight-gate.

Dannaks gave up his seat and walked over. The security men watched him, but didn't intervene.

"Hallo Ayhan," he said.

The boy looked up. He hadn't seen Dannaks emerge out of the crowd.

"Hallo," he returned disinterestedly, dropping his eyes to the floor again.

"How's your hand?" His left hand was bandaged.

"I'll live." He reddened as he realised what he had said.

Dannaks thought better than to agree.

"How did it happen?"

"I cut myself." He ran his straight-fingered hand like a knife over his bandaged palm.

Dannaks thought for a moment. "To work yourself up into a rage?"

"Something like that."

Boarding for the Hamburg flight was announced.

"Can I ask you a question?"

Ayhan nodded.

"Why did your parents sell you?"

At first he didn't answer and Dannaks thought that he was not going to answer. "The Simseks came over to Turkey with their little boy. They came to where my family were picking. Their little boy contracted meningitis and died suddenly. Apparently I looked like him and they bought me. It's as simple as that."

At that moment Dannaks realised that the Simseks were the real villains. But to go after them would inevitably harm Ayhan.

He didn't move and eventually Ayhan looked up.

"And then they had a son of their own," he said. Ayhan was as much a victim as Shaziye. With the birth of their second son the Simseks had all but rejected Ayhan. That was why he had ended up at Aksoys.

Ayhan stared at him blankly. And Dannaks knew this dead-eyed look. He'd seen it many times in the lad's sister. *Hüzün*.

December

Friday

19:47

Dannaks left Patel's and turned up his collar against the cold. All the emails had been advertising.

Ismail had sent him an email at the beginning of November, thanking him for his help and then expressing his regrets at not seeing him before he returned to Hamburg.

Like a phantom Dannaks hastened past the bars and restaurants teeming with youthful tropical life: wearing smiles and exuberant colours and attitudes that shunned the cold and grey.

The plastic carrier bag containing the travel brochures rustled in the breeze. After hearing about his holiday Reinhart and Frank had agreed that Dannaks didn't know how to relax. To which he had replied that he was not too old to learn.

He checked his Turkish watch before entering the *Narzisst's Eck*. It was still working.

Afterword

My youngest brother asked me the title of the book I was working on. He thought I said dog shit. This is, perhaps, in keeping with his knowledge of my "kitchen sink" trilogy *Nails*, *Bottle* and *Reifen*. When I repeated the title he exclaimed that it was barely pronounceable and that I should have a catchy title that everyone would remember. As you can see, author pride won out and for better or for worse I have stubbornly stuck to my guns.

Acknowledgements

I would like to extend a special thanks to Bernie Morris for her encouragement and editorial skills, Holger Vehren of the *Polizeipressestelle* Hamburg for his tireless patience, Arzu and Anis Gasmi for their advice on matters Turkish, Micha Kraus for his extensive knowledge of Side, my two daughters Mariana and Kiara for subjecting me to such holiday camps and finally my wife, Ulrike, for allowing me the time to write.

www.ingramcontent.com/pod-product-compliance
Lightning Source LLC
Chambersburg PA
CBHW030236030726
47493CB00022B/55